James Mitchell was born in South Shields in 1926 and was educated at South Shields Grammar School and Saint Edmund Hall, Oxford. After a brief spell at local repertory theatres he took up writing as a career. He now lives in London.

James Mitchell is well known as the creator of *Callan* and *When The Boat Comes In*, both extremely successful television series, and he is also the author of several acclaimed thrillers, most recently *KGB Kill*.

A Woman to be Loved

James Mitchell

KNIGHT

First published in 1990
by Sinclair-Stevenson Ltd

First published in paperback in 1991
by HEADLINE BOOK PUBLISHING PLC

This edition published 1999 by
Knight an imprint of Brockhampton Press

10 9 8 7 6 5 4 3 2 1

ISBN 184186 0239

Printed and bound in Great Britain by
Mackays of Chatham PLC, Chatham, Kent

Brockhampton Press
20 Bloomsbury Street
London
WC1B 3QA

For Delia
In loving memory

1

THIS TIME IT was winter. That had its advantages: the mud frozen hard and the skies clear, with diamond stars, so that it was easier to see to drive, but there were disadvantages, too. The ambulance didn't like the ice, and jolted far too often, and the frozen mud formed into ridges that jolted the wheels, augmented the pain of the men behind her, the men she must not look round to see: the maimed, the blinded, the ones with missing limbs. Even looking at the horses was better than that, the horses that strayed across the road that led from the Advanced Dressing Station to the Field Hospital: the pitted, battered road that jolted the ambulance and made the wounded scream, that night in December, 1917.

It was dark and her headlights had gone, which meant she couldn't see the ruts and ridges all that well, but of course it didn't last. It never did. Fritz began sending up star shells, and the whole battered landscape lit up like Piccadilly in peacetime, and at once the horses were clearly visible. The poor, patient horses, that pulled the waggons and gun limbers and water carts, stubborn as peasants, patient as saints – until the iron fell out of the sky, tearing, destroying. She swerved past them, the poor, wounded creatures, the maimed, the blinded, the ones with missing limbs.

Frantically she swerved round them, between them, as they dragged themselves from the bombardment, but there were more of them, and more, until – dear Jesus she couldn't help it – she hit one head on and it turned its blood-soaked head towards her, opened its mouth, but it was she who screamed.

The scream took the housemaid, Hawkins, by surprise, as it always did. She'd been doing all right going up the stairs with the mahogany tray – two cups, two saucers, tea, milk, hot water – but the scream got to her and her hand shook, and hot water darkened the whiteness of the tray's embroidered cloth. Still, better water than tea, or milk. She plodded upwards and onwards, feeling no malice. She *liked* Miss Jane. A good sort of a girl, well, – more a woman really – even if she did give herself the horrors dreaming about a war that had ended nearly eight years ago. Just like her own Uncle Albert. . . . And just like Uncle Albert, she was nice when the horrors let her be. Not like the Old Cow, her ma. Lady Whitcomb. More like that feller in the film, Ben Hur, the one that put the whip round the galley slaves, than a well-born lady. Her husband, Sir Guy, he was all right, but not Lady Whitcomb. Lady Whitcomb was a slave-driving bitch. . . .

Get on with it, girl, she admonished herself. Give them their morning tea, then sweep out the drawing room, polish the furniture, and then, seeing as it's Thursday, polish all the brass. And there was plenty of brass to polish an' all, after all that time they'd spent in India. Lady Whitcomb must have been in her element in India, she thought, bashing them blackies. . . . Resolutely she banished all emotion from her face and tapped on the master-bedroom door, but it was the mistress who answered. . . .

Jane Whitcomb lay on her back and examined the ceiling. It was a high ceiling with plasterwork at once delicate, unobtrusive and elegant, a ceiling she liked, but it gave her no pleasure, not that morning. *She had had the dream again*, she knew she had, in fact if she tried to, she could remember every detail of it, right up to the very last horse, the one that had made her scream, but she wasn't going to try. Having dreams – or even nightmares – in your sleep, that was just bad luck, a thing that happened, but to do it all again consciously, knowing you were doing it, that really was madness.

She wondered how loudly she'd screamed. Her instinct told her that it was a good one, one of her best in fact, and certainly loud enough to wake Mummy. She'd have to pay for that of course. Mummy was not in favour of girls who screamed, or had nightmares. Come to that Mummy wasn't all that keen on girls who lived to be thirty-two years old, and had failed to acquire so much as one single, solitary husband. Really, Jane thought, from Mummy's point of view she had been a most unsatisfactory daughter. And perhaps from anybody else's point of view too. . . . The thought was a dreadful one, but it had to be faced, and, very tentatively, refuted. After all, her father liked her, and so did Aunt Pen. John had adored her. . . . But then her father was ailing, and so was Aunt Pen. And John, there was no denying the fact, was dead. She looked back again at the ceiling. White meant purity of course, but she'd read somewhere that for the Chinese it was the mourning colour, the colour of death. – *The blood had gleamed so red in the snow.*

But before the idea could develop there was a tap at the door and she called 'Come in' at once. Anybody would be welcome, even Mummy. But it was Peggy Hawkins with tea, and chocolate biscuits, the ones she liked.

'Beg pardon, Miss Jane,' the housemaid said, 'but your mother would like to see you in her bedroom, as soon as convenient.'

So mother was not avoided, merely postponed.

'Very well,' Jane said.

Hawkins hesitated, but in the end valour overcame discretion.

'I shouldn't hang about, Miss Jane,' she said. 'Not this morning I shouldn't. If you take my meaning.'

Then she bobbed a curtsey and was gone, and Jane Whitcomb looked at her tea and biscuits and knew that if she so much as touched them she'd vomit, and got out of bed instead.

Her mother said, 'You woke your father.'

Jane looked round the enormous bedroom, vast enough to contain a brass double bed, two wardrobes, two chests of drawers, a dressing table and a washstand, and still look half empty.

'Where is Daddy?' she asked.

'In his dressing room, where else?' her mother said. 'Recovering. You woke him with all that screaming.'

'I didn't mean to.'

'You know his heart is weak.'

Jane said, 'I do when I'm awake.'

– 3 –

Instantly her mother flushed. As always, Jane thought, it was a colour impossible to describe in words. Somewhere between magenta and vermilion was about as near as she could get to it. Her mother was in many ways a splendid woman to look at: tall, regular-featured, of good carriage, but when she took on that colour she was quite hideous. It was the colour, Jane thought, of East End sprees. Gin and stout, and charwomen on the loose.

'You must learn to control yourself,' her mother said.

'You mean I must learn to control my nightmares?'

'A little will power,' said her mother. 'Perhaps a more restricted diet.'

'I'm over-eating then?'

Her mother shrugged. 'Too many chocolate biscuits cannot be good for you. . . . And all this entertainment.'

'What entertainment, Mummy?'

'You know very well, Jane dear.' That 'dear' was a warning that she well recognised.

'All that theatre. . . . All that cinema,' her mother said. 'It cannot be good for you, not in the nervous state that you're in these days. I fear that we must cut it out.'

'I go to the cinema once a week and the theatre once a month.'

'Too much,' her mother said. 'Far, far too much.'

Really, Jane thought, one would think the cinema was whisky and I was Mummy's vermilion-magenta colour.

'We must cut it out, dear. All it needs is a little determination. In a few months you'll be thanking me.'

Not even whisky: gin.

'Yes indeed,' said Mummy. 'That's what we must do. Cut out all those rich bikkies that upset your poor tummy, and all those vile entertainments that bring on the dreams. . . . There? . . . What do you say?'

What could she say? She'd been tried, found guilty and sentenced, and there was no appeal: not to Mummy. Not to Daddy either, not since his heart attack.

'What can I say?' Jane said.

'What indeed? I'm glad you see things sensibly.'

Mummy was winning and knew it. Already the colour had left her cheeks; her face was rich creamy-milk now, with just a hint of pink rose in the cheeks.

'Kiss me, child.'

Apathetically Jane kissed her. Apathy, she thought, must be the only solace known to whores. Perhaps her mother thought it too, because her next set of questions were the ones she'd been summoned to hear.

'What will you do today, Jane dear?'

Jane began to shrug, then controlled the impulse. Mummy didn't like movements that drew attention to the female body, not even the female body encased in a flannel nightgown and robe.

'Go shopping – if you need any.'

'None, I thank you.'

Mummy still remembered the Indian days, when there were servants to do the shopping, the days when ladies – and their daughters – shopped only for pleasure.

'In that case,' Jane said, 'I think I shall take Foch for a walk in Kensington Gardens.'

'Foch,' Lady Whitcomb said. 'Such an odd name for a Sealyham.'

'Monsieur Foch is a very remarkable Frenchman,' said Jane, 'and my Foch is a very remarkable dog. And he's not a Sealyham. He's a Scotch terrier.'

'Whatever he is,' her mother said, 'I think he excites you too much.'

This was bluff of course. Foch was the one creature alive that she would die for, and if Mummy wanted to remove him then Mummy would have to kill her dear daughter first, and Mummy knew it. Even so it was not *all* bluff: if Mummy couldn't harm Foch she could most certainly complain about him. On and on and on she could complain. Jane supposed that she was being offered a contract: stop screaming and I won't complain. It was a contract she desperately wanted to make, but couldn't possibly honour.

'I won't let Foch excite me,' she said.

'I'm delighted to hear it,' said Mummy. 'A little will power, that's all it needs. – As in so many things. . . . Have you seen that doctor of yours lately?'

'No, Mummy.'

'Why not?'

'You told me not to.'

'Indeed?' said Lady Whitcomb. 'Why did I do that?'

'You said that he excited me too much,' said Jane. Like Foch, she added, but only to herself.

'Perhaps I was –'

Wrong? thought Jane. Let me have pencil and paper quickly so that I may note the day when Mummy said she was wrong.

' – a little hasty,' Mummy said. 'Perhaps after all you should call on him. Tell him I said so. Tell him I think you should have a tonic.'

'Yes, Mummy.'

She willed herself to seem submissive: as if to see Lockhart again were a chore, and not a delight.

'Do it today,' Lady Whitcomb said. 'At once, in fact. Your father has a weak heart. Your screams can only make it weaker.'

She glared at her daughter then, making no effort to hide the hatred in her eyes. 'I've no doubt you are about to tell me that you don't mean to scream,' she said, 'but that doesn't make the least difference to the harm you do to your father. Cut along.'

When she got back to her room Peggy Hawkins was there, come back for her tea tray, munching the last of her chocolate biscuits with a fascinating intensity: inflicting pleasure on herself as carefully as Mummy inflicted pain on others. She made no effort to hide what she was doing as Jane walked in on her, and indeed how could she? The two women looked at each other, Hawkins's ecstatic look fading, to be replaced by wariness. Jane taller, fairer, and far too thin, even by the standards of 1926.

It's really up to me to speak, Jane thought. But what am I to say? The best she could manage was, 'Do they – do *we* – feed you enough?'

'Yes, miss,' Hawkins said. She didn't seem to be lying.

'You just like these particular biscuits, is that it?'

'I've never tasted anything like them, miss,' said Hawkins.

'Then I'm obliged to you for helping me to finish them,' said Jane.

Hawkins, who had scoffed the lot, accepted this without a blink.

'That's all right, miss,' she said.

Then the two women smiled, before Hawkins went off to polish the brass.

Jane dressed carefully: nothing too gaudy, nothing that Mummy might veto on the grounds of frivolity, but nothing too slipshod either: Mummy could not *bear* untidiness, and neither could her daughter. The grey two-piece, she thought. Long-waisted, *of course*, but with a hemline low enough to satisfy even Mummy's exacting standards, though Hawkins would have thought it dull in the extreme. (Hawkins on her night off, Jane was sure, would wear skirts that showed her knees, would consider it eccentric not to.) But the grey two-piece did have pretty rose-pink buttons, and a rose-pink band round the waist and hem. Not bad, really not too bad, not when one was thin enough to be a professional mannequin. (And wasn't *that* an idea to try out on Mummy?)

She sat at the mirror and looked at her hair. The hair was good. Blonde, of course, which was not ideal, but thick and lustrous, and fashionably shingled. Blue eyes. Mary Pickford-heroine eyes, when what she really wanted was eyes that smouldered darkly. Theda Bara eyes; the eyes of the femme fatale. Still, blue was what she'd got, and now they'd acquired an interest of their own, the blueness intensified by the dark shadows beneath them. And anyway, who was there to notice? . . . Mouth too wide, and a rounded chin that should have been more determined than it was, and there you had her: Jane Victoria Whitcomb; born 1893, debutante 1912, ambulance driver 1916–1918, neurasthenic idler and unmarried widow thereafter.

She went to her bedroom door and peeped out. Cook was just disappearing into Mummy's room. With the whole day's menus to discuss, that would take care of half an hour at least. She went downstairs, to where Foch sat waiting at the foot as he always did: Foch who was compact yet burly, shaggy yet neat, cantankerous and yet adorable even so. She could take him into the breakfast room and eat before Mummy launched another day's offensive; she only wanted toast and coffee after all, and a chance to be alone, but she didn't get it. Her father was there, which was surprising. He never ate breakfast, wasn't eating now, just tea and a Turkish cigarette, a diet even worse than hers. He looked up at her.

'Hello little daughter,' he said in Hindi. 'You have come for hasri?'

'Hello, burra sahib,' she said in the same language. 'If my father says I may join him.' It was what her ayah had always said.

He smiled at her, a tentative, even apologetic smile, and looked around the breakfast room.

'Not much like the old days,' he said.

The old days meant her ayah, and servants in turbans, punkahs and a screaming mynah bird and the sun outside, waiting fierce as a tiger. It meant three brothers too, and now only one of them survived.

'Not much,' she said. 'It was always so noisy, then.'

Not just the mynah bird, but Guy and David laughing – or fighting – and baby Francis yelling to be fed.

'They were never quiet chaps – your brothers.'

'They were fun,' said Jane, and her father smiled again, but this time the smile meant only remembered pleasure.

'I agree with you,' he said. 'And it's only fair, wouldn't you say? After all, they didn't have much time.'

Second Lieutenant Guy Whitcomb, Leicester Regiment, missing believed killed at Ypres, 1916. Second Lieutenant David Robert Whitcomb, Royal Flying Corps, shot down over Arras, 1917. Both had been twenty-three when they died.

'All those years ago,' her father said, 'and your mother and I still miss the laughter.'

She poured tea for herself, buttered some toast, then added marmalade. Not that she wanted it, but to face Lockhart she'd need all her strength.

'And so do I, Papa,' she said. 'Honestly. Sometimes I think the war killed even that.' And then, before her courage could fail her she added, 'I can't help screaming, Papa. I mean I don't do it deliberately.'

'Of course not,' he said. 'Who could possibly – ' He dropped off the words, then said again, 'Of course not.'

Jane said carefully, 'What I meant was I'm sorry if my screaming makes you unwell.'

'It doesn't,' he said. 'It's my weak heart that makes me unwell. That and my memories. . . . Guy won a scholarship to Merton, do you remember? David couldn't even wait to try for one. No time, Papa, he said. And he was right, you know. He had no time at all before he was killed. Dear me, how morbid I am this morning. What are you going to do today?'

'Take Foch for a walk.'

'Lucky Foch.'

The dog heard his name and thumped his stubby tail on the floor. Sir Guy was one of the few people he could tolerate.

'And then?'

'See Dr Lockhart.'

'I'm delighted to hear it,' her father said. 'Sooner or later the good doctor will get rid of these dreadful dreams of yours. I'm convinced of it.'

She knew then why he'd joined her for breakfast. For her to go back to Lockhart was his idea, and somehow he'd persuaded Mummy to go along with it. It couldn't have done that poor heart of his any good. She rose.

'If you'll excuse me, I'd better telephone for an appointment,' she said.

2

Dr Lockhart. James Adrian Belmont Lockhart. J.A.B. Lockhart. Inevitably and forever known as Jabber. Tall and gangling, even in his fifties, his suit neat but his hair as usual looking as if he'd just dried it. Doctor of Medicine, specialist in mental disorders, patient, unyielding, demanding Lockhart, her friend for life. Whatever sanity she had left, Lockhart had preserved for her, and she knew it. She grasped the hand he offered all too eagerly.

'I thought you'd sacked me,' he said.

'You don't sack your hope of salvation,' she said.

'Sit down,' said Lockhart, 'and oblige me by not talking rubbish.'

She sat and looked about her, at his consulting room in Harley Street. It hadn't changed – not once, in all the years she'd been there. Pale green lincrusta wallpaper on the upper wall, dark green dado beneath it. Whitewashed ceiling mottled by tobacco smoke – (he and most of his patients smoked too much) – a college oar on one wall, with names lettered on the blade. (J.A.B. Lockhart had rowed number five.) No pictures, no photographs, no books except text books. A room with no memory of the past or vision of the future, because it had to be like that. Lockhart's business was with the shell-shocked, the ones driven mad by the unbelievable fury of the war the newspapers called Great; the ones whose only chance was to live from day to day.

'Can you tell me why it's been so long?' Lockhart asked.

'I'd rather not,' said Jane, 'but I can tell you why my mother hates me.'

'Why?'

'Because both my elder brothers died in the war, and I didn't. And I'm a girl. Or I was then.'

Lockhart pounced on the last sentence.

'And what are you now?' he asked her.

'An old maid.'

'That isn't strictly true, is it?'

He was the only one she'd told about John. She'd told him because unless she could share the secret with someone there was simply no point to her life at all and, as he was a doctor, she felt that she could tell him without fear of betrayal, as if he were a kind of priest. But to be reminded of John at that moment seemed in itself a kind of betrayal.

'You don't fight fair, do you?' she asked.

'I don't fight at all if I can help it,' Lockhart said.

'What are you doing now then?'

'Listening to you.'

She flushed. It was six o'clock, and she was his last appointment of the day, an appointment squeezed in because of the short notice she'd given him. All day he must have sat behind that mahogany desk with its cigarette box, ash trays and petrol lighter, and listened to people like her – young men for the most part – telling him about their terrors. But John – John didn't belong with all that.

'Why do you bother?' she asked.

'Because I care about you,' he said. 'It's not just that you're ill, and I'm trying to make you better. That's only part of it. It's *why* you're ill.'

'And why am I ill?'

'Because you began by doing a good thing and went on to do a better thing,' said Lockhart. 'You began by helping your country and ended by helping mankind, and so mankind owes you a debt. And I am that part of mankind which might – just might – be in a position to pay it.'

She surprised herself then, if not him, by bursting into tears. It was the first time she had cried for a long, long time.

Lockhart watched her carefully, yet with detachment, as if trying to decide what good her weeping would do for her. At last her fumbling hands found her handbag, came out with a delicate scrap of linen and lace.

'I doubt if that will do much good,' Lockhart said, and opened a drawer in his desk, then reached inside to hand her a vast square of anonymous cotton that at once absorbed her tears – though even as she wept she'd noticed a neat pile of handkerchiefs in the drawer. Those who came to see Lockhart it seemed did a lot of crying, young men or not.

'I'm sorry,' she said.

'Are you? Sorry that you cried?'

She thought about it. It was always best to think when Lockhart asked you a question.

'No,' she said. 'Not sorry. Surprised. It's been a long time since anyone said something nice to me so seriously.'

'Seriously?'

'"How pretty you look",' she quoted. '"That's a nice dress". . . . "You're looking better today" – which is usually a lie. But nothing about what I *do*. – What I did, I mean.'

'It's all in the past then, is it?'

'You know it is.'

He nodded, which meant that he'd heard her: not necessarily that he'd agreed, then pushed the cigarette box to her.

'No thank you.' Tobacco smoke might make her eyes water again, and there'd been quite enough of that. He lit one himself, and dragged smoke down deep.

'About your not being an old maid,' he said. 'How can you be? You're neither old nor a maid. You will be old eventually – time will take care of that – but maidenhood, that's over. Finished. Do you regret the fact?'

'No,' she said. No hesitations: none.

'And why do you not?'

'Because I gave – it, to a man who loved me. We were to be married.'

'But you're not married, are you?'

'You know I'm not.'

'Why aren't you married?'

'Because he . . . John . . . was killed.'

'And you weren't.'

'And I wasn't.'

'But before he died – you gave him the most precious gift you had to offer.'

'My virtue?. . . I gave him rather more than that. I gave him what he gave me.'

Lockhart nodded again. He was still listening.

'I gave him all my love and had all his. But we had no time to share it.' Before he could speak she hurried on. 'I know that happened to thousands of women. Millions. I know we've just got to get on with our lives. All that. God knows I've heard it said often enough. . . . But there's one thing I haven't told you about John.'

'Then tell me – if you want to.'

'For years I couldn't bear to think about it,' she said. 'But you know all the rest so you may as well know this. John was shot dead by a sniper at twenty to four on the afternoon of 10th November, 1918. The day before the Armistice. If he'd survived for nineteen hours twenty minutes more – the war would have been over. He would still be alive.'

'You can't possibly know that,' Lockhart said.

'Of course I can.'

'Don't be silly.' Lockhart ground the stub of his cigarette into the ash tray. 'What about car crashes and sailing accidents and runaway horses? What about the Spanish 'flu that killed even more people than the war?'

'I survived even that,' said Jane.

'Only the dead know whether you're to be envied or not,' Lockhart said.

Suddenly she realised that he was trying very hard not to yawn.

'You're tired,' she said.

He shrugged. 'It goes with the job. . . . If he'd lived, what would you have done?'

'Done?' It wasn't easy to answer; not in terms of 'doing'. 'Been his wife, had his children, looked after him – and them.'

'That would have kept you busy?'

She smiled then. Only a man could be naive enough to ask such a question.

'Oh yes,' she said.

'And instead of that, you're idle?'

'I don't want to be,' she said. 'Honestly I don't.'

Once more the nod, acknowledging, rather than accepting.

'Who said you could come back to me?'

'My mother,' said Jane. 'But I think my father said it to her. He's awfully sweet, my father – only he had a heart attack after the Spanish 'flu, and he hasn't been much good for anything since.'

'Did your mother say why you should come to see me?'

'She said you could prescribe a tonic – '

'For God's sake,' he said, 'I'm a specialist in nervous disorders.' Then he broke off and grinned.

'Why not?' he said. 'A tonic could be just what you need. – Maybe I do, too.'

He went to a cupboard and came back with a decanter and two glasses, poured out two measures of honey-gold wine.

'Amontillado sherry,' he said. 'Medium dry.' He passed one to her.

'Should I?' she said.

'Doctor's orders.' He raised his glass. 'Good health.'

'Good health,' she said, and sipped. The wine glowed sweetly on her tongue. 'Tonic is right,' she said.

'Every night before dinner,' he said. 'Tell your mother I said so.' He yawned, hugely. 'I'm supposed to be going to the ballet tonight,' he said. 'I hope the music's loud enough to keep me awake.'

'What's the ballet?'

'*Le Coq d'Or.*'

'You'll stay awake,' she said.

'You've seen it then?'

'I was going to,' said Jane, 'but Mummy thinks the theatre excites me too much.'

'Go anyway,' he said. 'Just forget to tell her.'

'Is that your professional advice?'

'No,' he said. 'I just want you to see the ballet.' He reached for another cigarette. 'You're coming back to see me next week?'

'I expect so,' she said. 'Mummy doesn't mind my drinking – if it's sherry.'

'Then it's time I made you one of my speeches.'

'Very well,' she said.

The lighter flared, and he squinted at her through a grey-blue haze. 'I may act like God,' said Lockhart, 'because that's the only way we'll get anywhere. But remember I'm human, Jane. I make mistakes, just like everybody else.'

'I'll just have to risk that,' she said. 'And anyway – I bet you God doesn't smoke.'

– 14 –

He laughed so hard that he choked and she had to pound his back.

'God wouldn't need that either,' she said.

Maybe it was the sherry that decided her against taking a bus. From Harley Street to Aunt Pen's in Mount Street by underground was difficult, and in any case the darkness made her nervous. A bus would have been more feasible but tedious, and a taxi just happened to be passing as she left Lockhart's rooms. . . . The real complication was the money. Daughters of good family, even ageing daughters like herself, simply weren't given enough. A tiny allowance had to take care of such things as coffees and face powder, as well as transport, and there was never enough, despite the fact that Aunt Pen bunged her the occasional fiver, or even tenner. Money just seemed to disappear. For Jane a stocking prematurely laddered was like a budget crisis, indeed *was* a budget crisis, – but fortunately Mummy had sent her shopping a couple of days ago and forgotten to reclaim her change. Not theft, she told herself. Spoils of war, and hailed her taxi.

London traffic since the war had increased enormously. Mummy called it impossible, but then Mummy's idea of comfortable motion was a tonga or a phaeton – or even an elephant, Jane thought. Certainly not a motor car, unless it was both big and expensive. A Rolls-Royce perhaps, or a Hispano-Suiza. . . . From inside the cab she looked at the Austin Sevens and little Morrises shooting by, and the occasional Rileys and Jowetts nosing among the buses. One of them would be fine to own, perfect even, she thought. And there'd be no problem in driving it. If you could drive a wartime ambulance you could drive anything, even a London bus. A little Morris would be as easy as pie. . . . But that would be pie in the sky if you like. Mummy had even vetoed a bicycle (so unladylike) and a horse (the *feed* bills, child).

The taxi arrived at Mount Street, and the figure on the meter meant she'd have to walk home, unless Aunt Pen sent her home in the Daimler. But even if she forgot, the warm spring night was fine and she would have Foch for company, so she smiled at the cabbie as she paid him off and went to lift the knocker of Aunt Pen's front door.

Mummy hated Aunt Pen's house – not because it was ugly, it

was in fact, rather beautiful in its own spare, clean-lined Georgian way – but because it was rich, as everything about Aunt Pen was rich, including her butler, Marchmont, now opening the door: tall and stout and stately as a bishop. A parlourmaid just wasn't the same. Not that they always had parlourmaids. Parlourmaids were difficult, according to Mummy, and had aspirations inappropriate to their calling. Parlourmaids were apt to speak their minds and leave. On a bad day the best you could hope for would be Hawkins in a clean apron. On a really bad day it would be Mummy.

Aunt Pen was Daddy's sister, a small, pretty woman with a dry and delicate wit who had married into trade in the reign of Edward VII. It had been, as Mummy never tired of saying, a quite shattering thing to do, but yet she'd done it, marched up the aisle of the Anglican Cathedral in Delhi as if, so she told Jane later, the massed ranks of her disapproving family were ranged between her and Walter. Walter Nettles. I mean what a name! And a box-wallah, a commercial traveller sort of fellow who travelled around all over India taking orders for machinery, with all his worldly goods corded up in a stout, termite-proof box: hence his nickname.

But Penelope Whitcomb had adored him from the time she first danced with him, adored him – and yet studied him critically too, and what she saw was a man stubborn and determined, with a gift for commerce, and family connections with an up-and-coming light-engineering firm. So she'd fluttered her fingers at the lancer subaltern and ICS administrator who'd seemed to be making all the running, and shoved her way to the altar, become Mrs Nettles, and never regretted it, not for a minute, except that she'd never had children. . . . What she had got was a house in Mayfair and a butler and a Daimler, and a much-loved niece who was all she had to worry about, now that her Walter had gone.

Marchmont led her into the drawing room, where her Aunt Pen's empty seat was flanked by Foch on one side, and her aunt's own dog, an Airedale called Rob, on the other. The two existed together in a state of armed neutrality, but would always combine against an interloper. When she came in, Rob yawned, but Foch was up at once, looking reproachful, and indeed she had been gone for a long time.

'I shall tell Mrs Nettles you are here, miss,' said Marchmont.

Jane looked about her. Always there were flowers, whatever the season, and that evening the room glowed with roses. There were the kind of chairs and settees that promised sleep without dreams, let alone nightmares, and a Persian carpet that must have made even her rich Uncle Walter think twice before he bought it.

She sat down and Foch, after peering at her through the thickets of his eyebrows, sat down too. There were Indian treasures about her: good, old ivory and brass, a few small Moghul pictures, some photographs in silver frames: Aunt Pen, and Mr Nettles (it was a long time before he could be called Uncle Walter), Mummy and Papa, Guy and David and herself, and baby Francis in the ayah's arms. Ootacamund, that must have been. 1905 or 1906. Snooty Ooty. The magic land. . . .

One went there because of the heat on the plains in summer time, the heat that really was what all the clichés said it was: heat that struck you like a blow; burned the strength out of you; drove you crazy – sometimes literally. Heat like hell, searing and relentless. Heat that was in effect an invincible army, her father used to say. One could either surrender – or take to the hills.

And such hills, the hills of Ootacamund, five thousand feet above the scorching plain. Hills where water flowed, and grass was green, and the roses bloomed on and on and on, and the climate was like a perfect English summer's day, each day and every day. Guy and David used to practise cricket, she remembered, and she being a girl and youngest of the three was condemned to being forever a fielder, whoever batted or bowled, until one day the syce told Papa – up in Ooty for a weekend visit, – that she, Jane, could outride her brothers. He'd demanded to be shown, and she'd proved it, and from there on she'd ridden her pony. It had been the servants' children who took her place at point or third man or deep square leg.

She had loved that pony. It had been a bay filly called Rani, kindly yet courageous, and she could close her eyes and see it as clearly as she could close her eyes and see Foch. And when she did close her eyes to see Rani, all the rest came back, too: the roses and the curry smells, the kites and the brown arms of her ayah. Twenty years ago and more, and all she had to do was close her eyes and remember. Just like the war. . . .

3

HER AUNT CAME in, small and bustling, always determined to be on time, and never succeeding.

'Jane, dearest,' she said. 'Forgive me. I had to practise.'

What was it this time, Jane wondered. The piano? The ukulele? The Charleston?

'Quite all right, Aunt,' she said.

'But you looked so serious,' her aunt said.

'I was just – remembering,' said Jane.

Her aunt said warily, 'Do you think that's a good idea?'

'Ootacamund,' said Jane, and at once her aunt relaxed. 'All those years ago.'

'Really Jane,' her Aunt Pen said, 'it wasn't all that many years ago. How could it be? You're just a girl. I mean look at you.'

'I'm thirty-two,' said Jane.

'Yes, but do you think you should say so?' her Aunt Pen said. 'Especially when you look like you do. . . . I hope you don't make a habit of telling people your age.'

'I told my doctor.'

'He'd know anyway,' said her Aunt Pen. 'Doctors always find out your age first thing. It's all part of the power they seek. . . . How was he?'

'Kind,' said Jane. 'He's always kind.'

Her aunt would have none of that. 'Was he any *use*?' she said.

Jane said, 'He can't help me. Nobody can. I've got to help him, it seems.'

'Well at least Guy's made sure you can go to see him. Maybe you can help each other. . . . I phoned your mother.'

'What about?'

'Dinner,' said her aunt. 'I thought you might have it with me.'

'Oh goody. – Is it permitted?'

'Well of course it is,' her aunt said. 'I wish you wouldn't talk like that.' And then, with one of those oblique exercises in logic Sir Guy called Penelope's knight's moves, she asked, 'Why did you bring Foch here? I mean he's perfectly welcome. – Just ignore what Rob says. But why?'

Jane said carefully, 'Mummy thinks that Foch excites me too much.'

'Oh dear,' said her aunt, and then, another knight's move, 'she adored Guy and David.'

And there it was. Thirty seconds, maybe even less, to reach a conclusion she'd spent all morning on.

'She adores your brother Francis too,' Aunt Pen said. To anyone but Pen it would have been a statement of fact, but Pen knew it was a warning.

They dined in the first-floor dining room, Marchmont and a footman in attendance even though there were only the two of them and the table reduced, and Jane watched delighted as champagne was opened and poured.

'How dashing,' she said.

'Your mother said you were in need of a tonic.'

'I had one at Dr Lockhart's.'

'Another one won't hurt you,' said her aunt.

They talked of India. It was strange, Jane thought. Both of them were homesick for it, and neither had the least intention of going back there. Of course with her, money was the obstacle, as always, but not to Aunt Pen. And yet, Jane knew, Aunt Pen would never go back. The homesickness was for an era, a state of mind, even more than for a physical place. For Jane it was the memory of a little girl her ayah said was beautiful, yet a little girl who could outride her brothers. Watching her take Rani over the jumps had frightened her ayah, frightened her so much that she'd taken her to a holy man, a saddhu, to find out whether she should continue to risk her neck – and her beauty. The saddhu was adamant. He'd spoken in Hindi, but she'd understood, and remembered, every word.

'She must go on,' he'd said. 'Great things await this child.'

'But will she be safe?' The ayah had no wish for greatness.

The saddhu smiled then.. For the ayah it had been a smile of pity at such weakness, but for Jane it was more like complicity.

'To the leopardess you do not speak of safety,' he said. 'To be safe is the ambition of the deer.'

Jane pushed away determinedly what was left of her île flottante. Really, Aunt Pen's cook would make a gourmet out of even that saddhu.

'I wasn't much of a leopardess, was I?' she asked.

'You saved a lot of leopards,' her aunt said.

Jane said, 'Some were leopards of course. Even tigers. But there were deer too, and sheep, and monkeys. . . . All sorts and conditions of men. All they had in common was that they'd been hurt.'

She looked at her champagne glass.

'I'm beginning to talk nonsense,' she said.

'On the contrary,' her aunt said. 'You're beginning to talk sense. Fill Miss Whitcomb's glass, Marchmont, and mine,' she added as an afterthought, 'then later we'll take coffee in the drawing room. *Strong* coffee.'

Like many people who'd grown up in India, Mrs Nettles assumed that servants always knew everything about one's business. Even so she dismissed them before she asked her question.

'Did you ever see a painting called "The Judgement of Paris"?' she asked.

'I don't know,' said Jane. 'I don't often remember pictures.'

'You'd remember this one. It's frightfully rude. Three girls with no clothes on being stared at by a chappie in a sheepskin. He's supposed to be deciding which is the prettiest. I must say he seems to be taking his time about it.' She smiled then at Jane, and Jane remembered how incredibly beautiful her aunt had once been, not because of perfection of feature so much as that she was so alive.

'That was me or I or whatever it is,' said Aunt Pen.

'Standing about with no clothes on being stared at?'

'No, silly,' her aunt said. 'Doing the staring.'

'Oh the suitors,' said Jane.

'The suitors. Exactly.' Aunt Pen stared rather mistily into

the distance as if inspecting them. Clothed or unclothed? Jane wondered.

'Darling Jeremy,' said Aunt Pen. 'Beautiful Jeremy. He looked wonderful in full-dress uniform – and three thousand a year of his own. . . . And Richard. Clever *clever* Richard. Handsome devil. Scholar of Winchester, scholar of King's, double first. Bound to be a collector at least. Burra Sahib of Burra Sahibs. . . .'

'And Uncle Walter?'

'Not the most obvious winner of a beauty prize? No doubt you're right, though I never looked at him in that way. He was exciting, you see.'

'Exciting?'

Jane had drunk too much to hide her surprise, but then her aunt had drunk too much to be offended.

'Certainly exciting,' she said. 'He didn't shoot tigers or go pig-sticking like Jeremy, or make decrees and things like Richard. – He did more. He risked all his money, every penny he had, on deal after deal. And he shared it all with me. Every time. Exciting wasn't the word.'

'And he never went wrong?'

'Not after I met him,' her aunt said. 'Not until the very end, till the day he said to me, "It's only a bit of a cold. I'll be fine tomorrow."' Her voice took on Mancunian overtones in loving mimicry, then became her own again.

'They were the last words he ever spoke to me,' she said. 'Five hours later he was dead. The doctor told me he'd never known a case of Spanish 'flu so quick. But that was Walter. Always in a hurry. . . .' She shuddered. 'I've been lucky in love, wouldn't you say?'

'Extremely,' said Jane.

'There wasn't much luck the night he died on me. . . . People say that what you've never had you never miss. What do you think?'

'It's obviously true enough in logic,' said Jane. 'But it's a pretty negative attitude, isn't it? Cowardly even.'

'There speaks the leopardess,' said Aunt Pen.

Over coffee, hot and plentiful and very strong, her aunt said: 'I want to ask you something.'

'Very well.'

'I'm damn lonely,' her aunt said. 'If Walter were here he'd say bloody lonely, but then if Walter were here it wouldn't be true. Where was I?'

'Being lonely.'

'Well I am,' said her aunt, 'and I don't suppose your life's one giddy whirl of pleasure, so what I was thinking was why don't you come and live with me for a while? Be my companion?. . . Not that I'd call you that. Companions always sound to me like faded little women in sensible shoes and cotton next the skin. Still it would be nice to have you here.'

'It would be lovely,' said Jane. 'But I can't.'

'Why not?' Aunt Pen asked. 'Guy could have no objection.'

'Mummy could – '

'Honoria,' Aunt Pen said. 'Of course.'

' – But it isn't her, either,' said Jane. 'It's me or I or whatever it is.'

'What about you?'

'Sometimes I'm not entirely sane,' said her niece. 'Or you could put it another way. Sometimes I'm as mad as a hatter. – Dreaming and screaming all night long. That's not the way for a companion to behave.'

'I could put up with it.'

'But I couldn't,' said Jane. 'I mean I couldn't put up with you putting up with me.' She repeated the phrase in her head. *It seemed* all right, but, 'I think I'd better have some more coffee,' she said.

'There must be something I can do for you,' said her aunt.

'There's one thing.'

'Tell me.'

'You could let me have some money from time to time. I mean you do already and I'm grateful – but if it could be more regular. Ten bob a week say – or even a pound.'

'Well of course,' said her aunt, and then: 'But don't you have any money?'

'Mummy thinks I don't need it.'

'She *can't* think that,' said Aunt Pen.

'She says she never did, when she was a girl in India.'

Aunt Pen said, 'India was different.'

'Well of course it was,' said Jane. 'In India Mummy never took a bus.'

'Thirty bob a week do you?' her aunt asked.

'That's far too much,' said Jane. 'All I want is bus fares and cinema tickets and the odd pair of stockings.'

'Squander the rest then.' Her aunt searched in her bag, handed over two folded bank notes.

'You know Walter and I had a sort of ambition for you,' she said. 'Or maybe it was for us. One day we were going to spoil you rotten. I don't think he'd consider thirty bob a week was going too far.'

Foch and Jane went home in the Daimler, of which Foch approved, particularly its upholstery. For Jane its principal attraction was watching the chauffeur drive. On balance she thought that she herself was just a little bit better, but not after Dr Lockhart's amontillado and Aunt Pen's Krug.

Her mother said, 'Really your sister keeps most inconsiderate hours.'

Sir Guy looked at the bracket clock on the mantelshelf. It said ten seventeen and was always right.

'Hardly the middle of the night, my dear,' he said.

'When she *knew* that we would be anxious about Jane – '

'Well Jane's here now to tell us about it.'

'Do you mean about Dr Lockhart?' Jane asked.

'What else could your father mean?'

'Nothing Mummy.'

'Then get on with it,' Mummy said. 'We're your parents. You're our child. Does it not occur to you that we may be concerned?'

'Dr Lockhart considers that I've lost too much weight,' said Jane.

'It hardly needs a three-guinea consultation fee to tell us that.'

'He also considers that his fees should be paid by the War Department, if only I would fill in the necessary forms. He considers that what has happened to me is in the nature of a war wound.'

'Rubbish,' her mother said. 'You are quite unmarked.'

Unblemished, Mummy? Is that the word you seek?

Aloud she said, 'When my ambulance was strafed he considers that there may have been actual damage – physical damage – '

'It was nothing worse than a motoring accident,' her mother

said. 'You told me yourself – you carried on with your – job.'

'He considers that there may have been brain damage,' said Jane.

'Then he'll get no more three guineas from me. You may be nervous – that I do not deny – and you certainly dream too much, which is probably due to your diet – but you are not insane.'

'Oh hush, Honoria,' Jane's father said. 'Of course she's not insane. No one's suggesting that she is. But she served like a man in the war, and she's paying the price that some men are paying.' He raised his voice to drown out her interruption.

'Chaps I see at the club,' he said. 'Their sons – perhaps their nephews. Beddoes's boy, and Sinclair's. That young cousin of Brett-Lewis. All the same as Jane, except that some of them are a dashed sight worse.' He turned to his daughter. 'I don't say you're lucky, my dear, but you're luckier than some. . . . Shell shock they call it, don't they?'

'Yes, Papa. And it's true what you say. There are lots who are far far worse than me.'

For a moment Lady Whitcomb seemed outraged that her daughter should have a minor and therefore inferior version of any affliction that could affect the officer class, particularly one inspired by patriotism, but this was going too far even for her.

'You shouldn't have it at all,' she said.

Not for the first time Jane marvelled that this grotesque clown had once been the mother who loved her.

'If that dreadful man Nettles hadn't bought you an ambulance – ' her mother said. She made it sound like a superior kind of pram.

'Uncle Walter didn't buy me an ambulance,' said Jane. 'He paid for one. It was his contribution to the war effort.'

'He made you drive it.'

Jane said patiently, 'He didn't *make* me. I volunteered and was accepted. And Uncle Walter suggested it would be nice for the family if I drove *his* ambulance.'

Of course it hadn't been quite like that, not really. The odds were she wouldn't have gone to France at all if Uncle Walter hadn't paid. But that was none of Mummy's business.

'You should have asked permission,' her mother said.

All the old arguments were to be trotted out, it seemed.

'You and Papa were in India,' said Jane, 'and Aunt Pen said it was all right.'

'You are not Penelope's daughter,' her mother said, 'which makes it far from all right.'

'I was over twenty-one,' said Jane, 'and the war was going badly. By driving an ambulance I was able to release one more man for the fighting. Somebody had to do it, Mummy. It just happened to be me because I could drive.'

'That ghastly Nettles taught you, I suppose,' said Lady Whitcomb, then surprised her husband and daughter, and very possibly herself, by bursting into tears. The two of us in one day, Jane thought, and went to put her arms round Mummy because Papa was looking at her in a way that said, 'Don't ask me, – not any more,' – but Mummy didn't want to be comforted.

They were living in Kalpur, in an Indian state of middling size, and a population two thirds Hindu, one third Muslim. Papa was there as native adviser or resident to the maharajah, because the usual resident was being operated on for appendicitis. Kalpur was fine. They had a big bungalow, masses of servants and a vast maidan nearby where Rani could really go. And there was an elephant to take them on picnics and a Jersey cow that followed the elephant so that they could have fresh milk.

She and Guy and David liked Kalpur, but Mummy found it boring and Papa found it dreadful. The trouble was the maharajah. Officially he was a Hindu, but his real religion was cricket. Quite early in his career he had watched the great Ranjitsinhji bat, and had known, from then on, what his purpose in life was. (Ranjitsinhji had made one hundred and twenty-three not out against a British Army eleven, and both facts had their significance, Papa thought. The one two three struck some deep numerological chord, and to see the British Army thrashed by a princely Hindu held a more immediate significance.) The maharajah instantly caused a cricket pitch to be constructed at vast expense, as well as nets for practice, and a coach was hired from Bombay, a halfcaste who divided his time between cricket and the rajah's Scotch, and one who, drunk or sober, understood the maharajah's cricketing needs as poor Papa never had.

The trouble was that the maharajah played cricket so that he might appear triumphant. He didn't much care whether his side won, but it was vital, even inevitable, that he personally must triumph: a century in every game, and five wickets for fifty runs, or less. To this end the halfcaste, whose name was Hamish Buchanan, spent his working day rehearsing not only the maharajah's team mates, but the opposition also. (Opposing teams were invariably either the maharajah's subjects, or hired by him for money.)

Buchanan acted as a kind of ballet master or choreographer, drilling his white-flannelled corps de ballet in the mis-hits, dropped catches and fumbling on the boundary that would yet again allow the maharajah to raise his bat as a hundred was scored, or lead in the fielding side to a standing ovation (the spectators also were the maharajah's subjects).

At first the maharajah had been dubious of the potentialities of a cricketer called Hamish Buchanan. The Scots were not among the great names of cricket. But once Buchanan had demonstrated his talents as a régisseur all doubts were resolved, and cricket dominated the life of the state for at least five days of the week. The permanent resident approved thoroughly. Cricket was expensive, but not nearly as expensive as chorus girls or race horses or trips to Deauville and Monte Carlo. Moreover the maharajah would agree to anything, even sign anything, if one asked him just before it was his turn to bat. And so, as the resident knew his business, the state of Kalpur prospered and was happy, except for the inevitable gloom occasioned by the advent of the rains, and even that wasn't so bad when Buchanan rigged up an indoor practice pitch in the great hall of the palace, and the maharajah doubled his salary.

The trouble for Papa was caused by the fact that he too was a cricketer. The permanent resident had left careful notes of course, before he took the train for Delhi and the operation that King Edward VII had made so popular. The trouble was that Papa didn't get them − or at least not all of them. They had been censored. The permanent resident suspected Hamish Buchanan when they discussed it later, but Papa blamed the maharajah himself. Whoever it was, poor Papa had acted as he did out of an ignorance that amounted to innocence.

For Papa played cricket rather well. He was a goodish medium-paced bowler and a useful enough batsman at say six or seven, who had played for his college and had come close to a blue. It had seemed to Papa a good idea that he should turn out for a game at the first possible opportunity. Unfortunately, the maharajah refused to have Papa in his, the maharajah's eleven. His memory of his princely hero putting the Raj to rout was as fresh and green as ever. And so Papa turned out for the visiting eleven, the only man among the twenty-two – twenty-four if one counted the umpires, or several hundred if one added in the spectators – who did not know that he was foredoomed to lose.

The maharajah won the toss and elected to bat: the very coin he spun had been made to Hamish Buchanan's specifications. Even so, Papa bowled the maharajah first ball. The umpire called 'No ball', of course, even if it was a little late. In fact both umpires called 'No ball'. Hamish Buchanan had schooled them well. In the course of that innings Papa clean bowled the maharajah six times, and was no-balled every time. And yet Papa took six wickets for seventy-one runs. The maharajah was eighty-nine not out.

When it was his team's turn to bat, Papa scored seventeen runs in his first over, which was bowled by Hamish Buchanan. In his second over, when he faced the maharajah, he was given out lbw first ball, which he had touched with neither bat nor pad, nor any part of his anatomy. Papa left the pitch with an urgent need for a very large whisky and soda, followed by violent exercise. (The maharajah went on to take all ten wickets for seventeen runs.)

He took his stengah into his wife's sitting room, which was an unusual thing to do. His usual drink there was Earl Grey tea. His wife he discovered closeted with his daughter. They appeared to be grappling with French irregular verbs. Papa demanded an explanation, then looked at his whisky and soda, only to discover he'd just finished it, and yelled for another.

'Really Guy,' his wife began.

'An emergency,' said Papa. 'An absolute emergency, I assure you. His Highness has behaved in a way I had thought impossible for one human being to behave to another, always supposing he *is* human.'

He moved, rather stiffly, to a chair, and found he was still wearing cricket pads. He began to unbuckle them.

'That still doesn't explain the future perfect of "venir",' he said.

'It's young Guy,' said his wife.

'Oh Lord,' said their father. 'What's he up to now?'

'He's taken to speaking in Latin,' said their mother.

The bearer brought in whisky, soda and a glass on a tray, and Papa swopped them for his cricket pads.

'I thought only the Pope spoke in Latin,' he said.

'I hope he speaks it better than Guy. Ave mater dum est pabulum, indeed.'

'I *think* that means Hallo Mother, when is lunch?' said Jane.

'More or less,' said her father. 'Except it's more like when's fodder. Is David doing it too?'

'He says he prefers speaking in Greek,' their mother said.

'Quite right too. He's got a good chance of a scholarship to Rugby.'

'No doubt,' said her mother. 'But there isn't one single person in the place who can understand him – except you. So this young lady and I' – she stroked Jane's hair affectionately, 'decided to bone up on our French. At least we can talk to each other. – But why on earth aren't you playing cricket?'

'I've made the most extraordinary discovery,' said Papa. 'The bloody man cheats. At *cricket*.'

'Guy!' Her mother's voice was sharp enough, but there was the hint of a giggle in it.

'I apologise unreservedly,' said Papa, 'to both of you. But it's true.'

'Well of course it's true,' said Jane.

'And how do you know, miss?' her father asked.

'Everybody knows.'

'And who told you?'

'Ayah,' said Jane. 'She told me the first day we got here.'

'And did she tell you why he cheats?'

'Because he has to win.'

'Has to?' Papa said. 'What do you mean, has to?'

Really men can be awfully stupid, she thought. Even very clever men like Papa.

She said patiently, 'He's the maharajah, Papa.'

'Great God Almighty,' Papa said, but before Mummy could call him to order he began to laugh.

'All those players, all that crowd,' he said. 'And I was the only one who didn't know that in Kalpur cricket matches are preordained.' He bowed gravely to his daughter. 'Thank you for enlightening me. . . . Would you like to come for a ride, – or is the verb venir still unmastered?'

'Both of us have thought for quite long enough,' Mummy said. 'Jane's worked hard. She deserves a ride.'

So they'd changed while the syces brought the horses round, and for once ayah hadn't tweaked the elastic that held her solar topee in place. When the elastic snapped back it was very painful, but one mustn't cry, mustn't even call out. Her brother Guy had made that rule, and he was quite right. Her syce put her up and she settled at once, Rani ready to go, and yet responsive to her touch. They set off past the orange and lemon trees that encircled the bungalow with their nicely blended fragrance, on past the mangoes to the road that led to the palace, where the gardens ran wild because the gardeners spent all their time and skill on the cricket pitch, then turned off past the paddy fields where the kites screamed and soared high above them, and into the jungle. There was a path of sorts, worn down by the feet of villagers taking a shortcut from their village to their fields, a path that twisted and wriggled its way through undergrowth green as a bottle, unyielding and impenetrable except for the path. Dark, too. Not black but dark, like the inside of a church, because the trees grew dense and high and arched like a roof, and the creepers too grew dark with a green that was close to black; only the flowers held the glow of life, strong, vivid splodges of white and yellow and red; and all around them huge butterflies fluttered, birds sang or shouted or screamed, monkeys chattered and scolded and screamed back at the birds. And it would all have been jolly frightening, of course it would, except that Papa was with her, and with Papa beside her there was no need to be afraid of anything, because Papa was collector of Mussoorie District as well as acting resident of Kalpur.

Suddenly Papa reined in his horse, motioned her to stop, and pointed with his riding crop. Jane watched in silence as a herd of wild pigs crossed the path, a big boar in the lead, then a line of half-grown piglets with mamma pig following on behind nudging the others into a pack like the whipper-in of a hunt. Papa waited till the path was cleared, the sound of their progress through the forest faded, then he turned back to her.

'The Maharajah of Kalpur's Second Eleven,' he said, and winked, and Jane laughed aloud. Then afterwards they had a most wonderful gallop across the maidan and it didn't matter in the least that David and Guy were still spouting their silly old Latin and Greek, because now she could fight back with the future perfect tense of 'venir'.

Later over tea in the schoolroom David told them that he'd read somewhere that an American called Wright had flown off the ground in something called an aeroplane.

'Just the sort of stupid thing an American would do,' said Guy.

'That is xenophobic,' David said. 'I think flying's a good idea. One day I shall do it myself.'

'Like Icarus?' Jane asked. Not long before, Mummy had started her on Greek mythology.

'Certainly not,' David said. 'Icarus flew too high and was killed.'

Jane ignored the rebuke: she was happy. Despite that odd word 'xen-' something, they were at least speaking English.

4

I T HAD BEEN, she thought, one of the happiest days of her life
before John. It had stayed clear in her mind because Papa
had asked her to copy out the notes he'd made on it for his
autobiography: *Indian Days and Indian Ways. A Sahib Remembers.*
A book that would be for ever unwritten, she thought, but then
Papa didn't enjoy writing: he enjoyed remembering. . . . She
stretched out in the bed. A sliver of moonlight penetrated the
curtain, caught and held the eye like a magic sword, but she
made no move to pull the curtains together. If moonlight chose
to keep her awake, then thank you moon, because the only
alternative to wakefulness was sleep, and sleep, as the bard so
aptly put it, meant perchance to dream, except that there
wouldn't be any perchance about it, and it wouldn't be a dream
either. It would be the same bloody nightmare.

And of course it was. But this time she didn't wake up screaming. This time the nightmare went on and on. Which was absolutely right and proper, because this time the nightmare was the
retreat to the Channel ports, the 'backs to the wall' retreat of
1918, and that really had gone on and on, and the only way not
to see the wounded, malformed soldiers limping along beside
her was to stare straight ahead through the windscreen where
the night bombardment of our guns flickered like the light of a
cinema projector, flashing ever brighter so that she might see
the wounded horses.

But if she screamed aloud no one told her, or maybe, she
thought, the sound of the guns drowned out her screams. And

then she thought: now I really am going crazy. Now I'm treating nightmare and reality as if they were the same thing, and that could only be one more step down the wrong road. Now, she thought, I really have become useless. 'Surplus to requirement' the army called it. And so she was: beyond even Lockhart's skill and compassion. Now then was the time to die. It was obvious. Mummy detested her and Papa did his best but his heart was too weak, and if she were out of the way there were others to take her place with Jabber, more receptive patients, and probably more deserving, too. And even if Aunt Pen loved her, she didn't want to be saddled with a lunatic.

The trouble was how to do it. There was drowning, and the Thames wasn't far, but Papa had taught her to swim in the big tank at Kalpur, and Jane knew without doubt that she couldn't possibly find herself in deep water and not swim. Moreover she was a strong swimmer, and would almost certainly be rescued, probably with maximum humiliation: hair awry, wet clothes clinging, but not prettily. . . . She could, she thought, have shot herself had a gun been available, but it wasn't. Papa had given his away many years ago. Knives meant disfigurement like her nightmares and the only pills in the house were for Mummy's dyspepsia; Jabber had seen to that. Sleeping tablets were issued only on application, and never more than two at a time, and to save them up would amount to a kind of betrayal. Besides, who would take pills to bring on dreams like hers? Killing one's self was almost as difficult as keeping one's self sane, she thought.

And then she remembered Foch. It was wicked, it was downright sinful, that she had ever forgotten him. If she, Jane, died, Mummy would give him away. And maybe that would be a good thing, but only maybe. Mummy wouldn't worry about whether he went to a good home or not. She'd be too busy hating her dear daughter for the harm she'd done to the name of Whitcomb.

Then her obstinate honesty took over. And why not? she asked herself. Her suicide might solve her own problems, but it compounded everybody else's. She'd just have to go on living, she thought, then giggled in self-mockery. Goodness how decent I am. How brave. And all because a Scotch terrier needs me as much as I need him.

She went down to breakfast warily. Now that Hawkins was whacking into her chocolate bikkies she could at least manage some toast. Her father had already gone to his study to fiddle happily with notes and invitation cards and fading snapshots.

Her mother said, 'We have had a postcard. From Francis.'

'Oh yes?' said Jane.

'I had hoped for a little more enthusiasm,' her mother said. 'He is your brother after all. And he's away all term.'

'I hope he's well,' said Jane.

'You may judge for yourself,' said her mother. 'He has permission to come up to London – he and a friend. They are attending a meeting here, so naturally they will stay the night in London.'

Jane buttered her toast, and added marmalade. If she were to have a social life she must keep up her strength.

'What sort of meeting?'

'Political,' her mother said. 'Your father disapproves of it. – Naturally he would.'

'Why naturally?'

'Young men always adopt a political stance their elders disapprove of,' said her mother. 'Your father should be aware of that. In his younger days he twice voted Liberal. . . . I think perhaps we should have some cheese. Young men *need* a cheese course. Can I trust you to buy me some?'

'Of course, Mummy.'

'Then do so.'

'On account?' Jane asked. 'Or shall I pay cash?'

On account meant Harrods, which was far too expensive for undergraduate cheese. Reluctantly Mummy reached for her purse. . . .

Jane walked down the steps of Number 17, Offley Villas, and drew on her gloves. It was ridiculous to cover up her hands on a warm day, but Mummy had told her – and it was true – that no real lady ever went out without gloves, and so, 'Gloves will be worn.' But Jane rarely went out without Foch either, and there he was, briskly trotting beside her, the bushy eyebrows and enquiring eyes giving him the air of a cantankerous scholar. There was a look of self-satisfaction in his strut that day, she thought, and looked down at him.

'You needn't go giving yourself airs just because you saved

me from suicide,' she said. 'Jabber Lockhart helped you after all.'

Foch snorted, and strutted on.

Old Mrs Blyth-Tarkington, from Number 23, noticed the exchange and approved. A dog needed conversation like everybody else.

As Jane came up to her she said, 'They understand, you know, Miss Whitcomb.'

'Yes,' said Jane. 'I rather think they do.'

All the same, on the way to the High Street all she talked about was cheese, and on the way back, on the detour through Kensington Gardens, she didn't talk at all. Foch was too busy bossing every other small dog in sight to listen.

Instead she thought about Francis. She had never – the thought had to be faced – been close to Francis, as she had been to David and Guy. But then the reason was obvious enough. Lady Whitcomb's first three children had arrived at yearly intervals. She'd had to wait nine more years before Francis was born.

It must have been a struggle, she thought. The big three – so they must have seemed – always together, playing together, laughing together and, even though one was a girl, being siblings together, because they all looked alike. They really did. Tallish, fairish, loose-jointed, and all of them, all three, blessed with a marvellous co-ordination of eye and hand which made them good sportsmen, games players, equestrians. Laughing and effortless, that was the Whitcomb style, so David used to say. But he'd been quite young when he'd said it. David had never been anything other than quite young.

And then there was Francis. At first it had seemed to Jane that he wasn't a Whitcomb at all, for Francis was dark, rather short, and by no means slender. Not frightfully good at games, either, nor at laughing, and without the conventional good looks (what David had called 'the rather obvious prettiness') of the other three. Instead he'd been given a face to portray his moods: anger, gloom, despair, and occasionally a happiness close to ecstasy. But always he was beautiful. Not pretty. Beautiful. For one breathtaking moment Jane had decided that he wasn't a Whitcomb at all, and then she realised that of course he was. He looked very much as her mother must have looked at the time she met Papa.

He'd done well, no question of it. Head of his class year after year at school, then a Cambridge scholarship and a first in Part One last year, and almost certainly a first in Part Two in – when was it? – two or three weeks' time? The political meeting must be important. Francis had never been one to neglect his studies: they were too important to him. All he had, in a way, perhaps because they were all he wanted.

Pure conjecture, she told herself. You know nothing about Brother Francis – but that was because she'd hardly ever seen him. He'd always been in the nursery, or away at school, or Cambridge, or she'd been at Aunt Pen's or at the war. Even so, she ought to know at least *something* about her own brother, if only he'd let her. But all she had to go on was that he was going to a political meeting of which Papa would not approve.

Anarchists? she wondered. But anarchists were out of date. They belonged to before the war – wild-looking Slavs with beards and bombs. Bolsheviks, she decided. Still Russian, but with a passion for pamphlets and points of order before the actual trigger-pulling. Francis would approve of that. He believed in justice from on high every bit as much as Papa had done.

Firmly Jane separated Foch from the fox-terrier, the spaniel, the poodle and the pug that he was trying to form into a Soviet.

'It would never work,' she told him. 'Not in England. And even if it did the borzois would take over.'

Foch snorted.

'You intellectuals,' she said. 'You always think you can stay in control when the violence starts – but you never can.' Then she thought of Lenin. 'Well hardly ever.'

This time Foch said nothing. He knows he's lost, thought Jane, which is more than Francis ever did – or me, or Guy or David come to that. Poor Papa.

When she got back she rang the bell instead of using her key, because of the cheese. Hawkins answered, which surprised Jane. The parlourmaid – (Charlton was it? Railton? Lawson?) her notice given, still had a week to go.

'Good Lord, Hawkins,' Jane said. 'Has she run away?'

'No miss,' said Hawkins. 'She's serving tea. Proper tea. . . . Mr Francis came down early.'

'Oh I see,' said Jane. 'Did he bring his friend?'

'Not arf,' said Hawkins.

'What on earth do you mean?'

'You just wait and see, miss,' Hawkins said. 'I don't want to spoil it for you.'

Her eye flicked shut then open, fast as a lizard's, but Jane received the message. She had been warned. Slow and easy, she told herself. We can't have you screaming, not when there's company here. She opened the drawing-room door and went in, walking as the deportment school had taught her, and Foch trudged by her side, wary as John Knox at the court of Queen Mary, and there they were: Mummy and Papa and Francis and his friend: a large and muscular friend, a year or two older than Francis, with that look peculiar to Cambridge (according to Papa) of the man who had absorbed all the knowledge it was decent for one man to have, and now felt it to be his duty to pass it on to others. (Daddy had gone to Merton College, Oxford.)

'Ah,' her mother said. 'Jane. How late you are child.' Nevertheless there was relief in her voice. 'Come and meet Mr Pardoe.'

Pardoe stood up. There was an awful lot of him, thought Jane.

'Mr Pardoe – my daughter Jane,' Mummy said, and Pardoe's hand engulfed hers.

'I'm delighted to meet you,' he said.

'You're an undergraduate friend of Francis?' she asked.

'Pardoe took a first,' her brother said. 'Next year he'll be a PhD.'

He sounded petulant, as if he were being forced to state a fact that everyone should know, and Pardoe nodded in agreement, though without answer.

'I also played rugger for my college and got a half blue in boxing,' Pardoe said. 'I'm a naturally aggressive person.'

For perhaps the thousandth time Jane found herself wishing that Guy and David were there to share what looked like being a pretty good tea party.

'How fascinating,' she said.

'Not fascinating, precisely.' Pardoe's correction was kind, but firm. 'But I think one might call it interesting.'

'Oh indeed,' said Jane. '*Indeed*. And is your kind of aggression restricted to punching other very large men?'

'That and manhandling them on the rugby field. But both these aggressive acts are circumscribed by a set of strictly administered rules. The aggression is controlled.'

Jane took a cucumber sandwich from a plate the parlourmaid, Thomson? Withers? offered to her.

'And do you feel that all young males should take part in acts of controlled aggression? Francis, for example?'

Pardoe said, 'Francis is not a physically aggressive person. As his sister surely you must be aware of that?'

'I've always found him forceful enough in discussion.'

'A Marx rather than a Trotsky. Quite so.'

Jane leaned over to straighten Foch's eyebrows and whispered, 'You didn't tell me you'd invited friends to tea,' then Lady Whitcomb poured out a cup of Earl Grey, and passed it to her daughter.

'You approve of the current state of affairs in Russia?' she asked.

'Naturally,' said Pardoe. 'It's nice to see a country run by a set of logical principles for a change.'

'And long overdue,' Francis said.

'But it's moving now. On the march. You'll see,' said Pardoe. 'Russia's only the beginning.'

'You see it coming here?' Jane asked.

'You live in Kensington, just as Francis and I live in Cambridge,' Pardoe said.

As if he were very kindly explaining some difficult concept hitherto beyond my grasp, thought Jane.

'But you mustn't confuse Kensington, or Cambridge, with the United Kingdon – or Great Britain as I prefer to call it.'

'I never do,' said Jane.

Again Francis gave her that resentful look, but not Pardoe, who was in full cry.

'Great Britain is the Rhondda Valley and Glasgow and Tyneside,' he said. 'The tragedy of our present – and the hope of our future.'

Jane sipped at her tea. It was to be a sermon after all. She assumed the expression of polite awareness appropriate to Sundays and Morning Prayer, and was told all about the proletariat, the regrettable absence of a peasantry in what Pardoe preferred to call Great Britain, and the rôle of the intellectual in fostering proletarian aspirations.

When Pardoe paused at last for breath, Lady Whitcomb asked, 'Why do you prefer to call our country Great Britain rather than the United Kingdom?'

It was the first time that Jane could see the tiniest dent in Pardoe's armour of utter certainty, but then Mummy's action hadn't been controlled. She had asked the wrong question, used an alien set of rules, like Ludendorff attacking at random, probing for weak spots, in early 1918, rather than advancing on an entire front.

Francis said, 'Really Mummy, after what you've just been told, isn't it obvious?'

Sir Guy said, 'No' – just that one word and no more, but for a moment Francis became a small boy again. Pardoe sensed it too, and hurried in at once.

'You must forgive us, Sir Guy,' he said. 'Certain facts have figured so long in our discussions that we rather take them to be self-evident to everyone.' He turned to Lady Whitcomb, and shrugged on once more his kindly manner, as if it were an academic gown.

'We prefer Great Britain because it is a reality,' he said. 'The United Kingdom is no more than a concept.'

'You're a republican,' said Lady Whitcomb. 'I see.'

She made republican sound as if it were an affliction – like diabetes, Jane thought. Unfortunate, but containable, if one obtained the proper treatment in time.

'A believer,' Pardoe corrected her, 'a very *humble* believer, in the dictatorship of the proletariat.'

This, thought Jane, was the moment when Papa should explode, and perhaps even have a heart attack too, and she saw at once that her mother was aware of it without precisely understanding why – but the doorbell rang instead, and the parlourmaid went off to answer it.

'Who on earth can that be?' Lady Whitcomb asked.

Francis shrugged, Jane guessed that it might be the vicar because it nearly always was, but it was Pardoe who spoke aloud.

'Oh good Lord,' he said, and turned to Francis. 'I say I'm most frightfully sorry, but I rather think I asked her to meet us here – and clean forgot to tell you.'

Foch heard the unfamiliar note of apology in Pardoe's voice and stood up and glowered at him. He's got the eyebrows for it, thought Jane, and the kind of utter certainty that only the Scots possess and not even Cambridge can vanquish, but then the parlourmaid – *Moreton*, that was it – ushered in the visitor, and all thought of the Foch-Pardoe conflict was forgotten.

For what Moreton ushered in was the pantomime fairy, the one in the tutu who waves her magic wand at the Demon King and intones:

Your wicked plans be sure I'll thwart
And see your schemings come to naught –

while the innocent babes sleep on in the wood. . . . Or else it was the Sugar Plum Fairy herself, Jane thought, exactly as Tchaikovsky had first thought of her. An ice-maiden perhaps, though one, she thought after a second look, who would thaw, even melt, in the right atmosphere.

'Miss Georgina Payne,' Moreton said.

Hair of gold that positively gleamed. Could it be real? – And did it matter? Eyes of *such* a blue, and they were real enough, and a little rosebud mouth and slender figure that no one would ever call thin.

'Georgie!' Pardoe called, and moved towards her, then her mother and father rose, and last of all Francis. Foch ventured one tentative yap, then tried to pretend it had never happened. Georgina Payne was not the type to be snarled at.

'Pardoe,' she said. 'You're impossible. Why didn't you warn me I'd be interrupting a tea party?' Then she turned and smiled at her host and hostess: the sort of smile, thought Jane, that really merited the adjective 'dazzling'. Even her mother smiled back. Her father was positively grinning. She wore a blue blouse and a white skirt that showed her knees and Mummy smiled.

Pardoe said, 'I rather think that I owe you an apology, Sir Guy.'

Her father said, 'Not at all,' but Pardoe had recovered.

'Oh yes,' he said. 'In society as it is at present constituted, I owe you an apology.'

'Rules,' said Jane helpfully. 'Control.'

'Precisely,' Pardoe said. 'Miss Payne is to accompany us to our meeting – '

'Are you?' said Jane. It seemed incredible.

'Oh yes,' Georgina Payne said. 'There's to be music. I've been hired to play it.'

'Engaged,' said Francis.

'I beg your pardon?'

The blue eyes could have melted an iceberg, thought Jane, but her brother was concerned only with definition.

'Hired has rather a bourgeois connotation,' he said.

'Are you – ?' Sir Guy fumbled to find words not offensive. 'Leftist in your views?'

'Where I live,' said Georgina Payne, 'which is sort of Chelsea, one does meet rather a lot of them. It's – interesting.'

'And what sort of music do they play?'

'Experimental of course,' said Miss Payne. 'They're mostly Central Europeans no one has ever heard of. There's one called Béla Bartók whom I rather like, but the comrades never seem to be able to make up their minds about him. – Whether he's bourgeois or not.'

'And do you like playing that kind of music?'

'It keeps me up to scratch,' said Miss Payne, 'but the cinema's better.'

'The cinema?' said Lady Whitcomb.

'The Alhambra, Fulham, actually,' said Miss Payne. 'I play the piano there. It's lots of fun.'

'Indeed?' said Lady Whitcomb.

'Well I enjoy it,' said Miss Payne. 'A bit repetitive of course – lots of Tchaikovsky for the love scenes – and for the battles too, sometimes. "1812" you know.' She turned to Francis. 'Not your kind of Russian at all, I should think. . . . Then there's Suppé's "Light Cavalry", and "William Tell" and "In a Persian Market". And ragtime too of course, if there's a party. What I mean is you don't have to concentrate. Not like Béla Bartók.'

'And yet you play Béla – er – Bartók,' said Lady Whitcomb.

'Well of course,' said Miss Payne.

'May one ask why?'

'Because they pay me.' To Georgina Payne this was a silly question, but perhaps, thought Jane, she already suspected, and rightly, that Mummy was a talented amateur. 'They're not *madly* generous, but then I don't suppose they've got very much money, and every little helps as the old lady said, and I haven't finished paying for this skirt yet.'

Francis said, 'We ought to be going.'

'No no,' said Sir Guy. 'Don't rush away.'

Mummy continued to cross-examine.

'Don't you ever get bored, playing in a cinema?'

'Honestly, it's practically automatic, after a while, like breathing,' said Miss Payne. 'You hardly notice you're doing it.'

'But – ragtime,' said Mummy. 'I mean you must have been classically trained.'

'Just round the corner,' said Miss Payne. 'The Royal College of Music.'

'Then how – '

'Just after I took my diploma I went to hear Pachmann,' said Miss Payne. 'Three years ago it must have been. Did you go?'

'I don't think I – '

'He played Chopin *of course*,' Miss Payne said, while Jane marvelled that anyone, least of all a girl, could interrupt Mummy twice and get away with it. 'But even he must have been feeling good that day – the way he played. The "Revolutionary Study", and the Waltz in D flat, and the Fantaisie Impromptu in C sharp minor. They were like nothing I'd ever heard before – or since for that matter. But in the bus on the way home – I lived in Battersea in those days – I found myself thinking I couldn't even get close to Pachmann if he had rheumatism in both hands – never mind when he plays like that. So I gave up starving in a garret and went to work at the pictures instead.'

'Did you?' Jane asked. 'Starve in a garret, I mean?'

The wink she gave Jane flicked on and off so quickly that it might never have happened, like Hawkins's.

'Well where I lived was pretty much of a garret,' said Miss Payne, 'but I didn't actually starve. I adore my food.'

Foch got up from Jane's side and went to sit beside Georgina Payne, a rare mark of approval. Jane rather wished she could do the same. Being next to Miss Payne was like being bombarded with life instead of death.

'What do your parents think of your profession?' Mummy asked.

'They don't,' said Miss Payne. 'They divorced quite soon after I was born. Mummy married a penniless viscount and went to live in Kenya, – in the Happy Valley. I must say it sounds rather fun to be penniless there.'

'And your father?'

'He was killed quite early on, at a place called Le Cateau,' Miss Payne said. 'He was a regular.'

'I lost two sons,' said Lady Whitcomb.

Sir Guy said, 'We very nearly lost a daughter too.'

Miss Payne turned to Jane, astounded.

'You don't mean you were in it?' she said.

'Well – yes,' said Jane.

'Were you a nurse?' Miss Payne asked. 'Or was it a concert party? Oh God I'd have given *anything* to play in a concert party near the Front.'

'Nothing so glamorous,' said Jane. 'I drove an ambulance.'

'You *didn't*!' Miss Payne's voice now took on a sort of schoolgirl's squeak, and she looked at her as a third-former might look at a hockey captain. 'My dear how romantic.'

'Hardly that,' said Jane.

'And gallant.' Georgina Payne had no time for interruptions that clashed with her preoccupations. 'Driving those poor boys, through shot and shell – '

'For heaven's sake don't let's discuss the war,' Francis said.

'Don't discuss anything,' said his father. 'It is quite obviously time you left us.'

Pardoe charged in at once, spraying out oil over a potential tempest. 'What Francis means,' he said, 'is that there is simply no point in discussing such a vast and unnecessary slaughter.'

'Unnecessary?' said Jane.

'Certainly,' said Pardoe. 'This was a war to enrich the bourgeois – and it did. It also was intended to subjugate the masses by the intimidation of slaughter, and that too it achieved.'

'So that all those millions died for nothing?' said Jane.

'I think you're being just a little too pessimistic,' Pardoe said. 'It seems to me that without that ludicrous war the 1917 revolution could not possibly have succeeded.'

'So that in effect my brothers died to help the Bolsheviks murder their Czar?'

'I detect,' Pardoe said roguishly, 'the merest soupçon of irony. But in general terms the answer to your question is yes. And you are not alone in your loss, you know. I myself was deprived of a brother-in-law – and a cousin.'

– 42 –

'How ghastly for you,' said Miss Payne, 'but we really should be off now.'

She rose to her feet and the two men followed. Foch thumped his tail on the carpet in applause. Foch, thought Jane, is a superb judge of character.

Sir Guy too rose, and shook Miss Payne's hand.

'A pleasure to meet you,' he said. 'I mean it.' He turned to his son. 'Dinner will be at seven fifteen,' he said. 'Precisely.'

Georgina Payne crossed the room to take Jane's hand, and Foch came with her. 'So wonderful to meet you,' she said. 'I do hope I'll see you again.'

'I hope so too,' said Jane, knowing it was impossible, because seeing her again meant friendship, and no one wants a lunatic for a friend.

After they had gone and Moreton had cleared away, Mummy asked, 'Why did the old lady say that every little helps?'

Her father looked at Jane and then away.

'I've no idea,' he said. 'Some sort of idiom that the young people use, I suppose.'

'She did in fact talk rather wildly,' said Lady Whitcomb, 'but she was not without sense – though scarcely a suitable companion for Jane.'

Well at least we're agreed on that, thought Jane, as Mummy got to her feet.

'I shall lie down for a while,' she said. 'Visitors for tea and then dinner too. Just like old times. Quite ghastly.'

She left them then, and her father said, 'Oh dear,' and took out his cigarette case. 'Your mother often enjoyed old times,' he said when his cigarette was lit, 'but often one entertained dreadful people then, as now, and she has always found that to be an ordeal.'

'She finds Mr Pardoe dreadful?'

'I should think anyone would,' said her father. 'Don't you?'

'Decidedly,' said Jane.

'Then for once you agree with your mother. Did you like Miss Payne?'

'Very much,' said Jane. 'But Mummy was right about her, too. We wouldn't suit.'

Her father began to laugh, then choked on his cigarette smoke.

'Your jokes are often quite witty,' he said, 'but they seem designed to wound everyone: yourself most of all.'

'I think we should finish with Mr Pardoe first,' said Jane.

'You're running away.'

'From you, Papa, yes – but not from Mr Pardoe.'

'Very well. Then tell me about Mr Pardoe.'

'I find him awful, of course – '

'A sort of clown?'

'More like an enormously intelligent buffoon – if that's possible.'

'It obviously is,' said her father, 'since Mr Pardoe exists.'

'What makes him grotesque,' said Jane, 'is that he has no sense of humour. None whatsoever. It's as if he'd had it removed like an appendix. And yet, he's clever. And not just clever. He really wants the world to be a better place.'

'He wants rather more than that,' said her father. 'He wants to force the world to be better according to the one set of rules that he knows will work. To me he's a very dangerous man.'

'Francis thinks he's wonderful,' said Jane.

'That is Francis's privilege, after all,' said her father. 'You and I know he isn't.'

Foch snorted. He knew it too.

'Francis is in love with the idea of perfection,' her father continued. 'Nothing wrong with that, so long as you realise that's all perfection can be – an idea. Francis's problem is that he thinks his kind of perfection is achievable.'

'The Russian kind?'

'Russo-German, surely?' her father said. 'Lenin may or may not be doing the achieving, but it was Marx – Engels too of course – who had the perfect ideas.'

The phone rang, monotonous, repetitive. This is going to be a bad one, thought Jane.

'I hate that thing,' her father said. 'Back in India a bearer used to bring you a chit. That usually meant a chap had something to tell you, – because it was too damn hot to start writing chits unless you had to – especially in the monsoon season.'

Moreton came in. 'It's Mr Pardoe for Lady Whitcomb,' she said.

'Not possible,' said Sir Guy. 'She's resting.'

'Shall I go?' Jane asked.

'No,' Sir Guy said. 'He's bored you enough for one day.'

– 44 –

He moved stiffly off into the hall, where the telephone lay neatly centred between two draughts.

How old he looks, and how ill, thought Jane.

Foch came over to her, then slumped down heavily. Across his black back, one golden hair gleamed. Jack picked it up and looked at it: the root was gold too, and Jane found that she was glad. Foch sighed.

'Yes,' said Jane, 'I realise that you're in love again, but it won't do, Foch. She's much too wonderful for the likes of us.'

Her father came back in as she spoke, but he obviously hadn't heard a word. He was too busy being furious.

'That bloody man,' he said. ' – I'm sorry my dear, but what else can I call him? That *bloody* man has decided to cut dinner.'

'He told you so?'

'He did indeed. Then he handed the instrument to Francis, who also told me so.'

'But Papa – why be angry? Surely the loss of Pardoe is something to open the Bollinger for?'

'In an ideal world of course,' said Sir Guy. 'But in this one – in *ours* – there are forms and rituals and social obligations. And dinner parties are very much a part of all that.'

'But if something came up – ' said Jane.

'That's just the point,' her father said. 'Nothing came up. He told me so himself.'

'He didn't invent an excuse?'

' "I'm going to tell you the truth" he told me,' Sir Guy said, mimicking savagely. ' "Always the best thing in the long run – believe me, Sir Guy." As if I'd been a liar all my life. – "The truth is," he said, "what with the flow of ideas at the meeting and the extraordinary music Miss Payne played, I find myself in an exalted state." '

'Papa, he *can't* have said that.'

'I quote him word for word,' said Sir Guy. 'Then he added, "That being the case I am simply not in the mood for dinner tonight. Indeed the very thought of food is unendurable. I'm sorry but I shan't be able to be with you – and I rather fancy that Francis feels the same." '

'What did you say?' said Jane.

'I said I wanted to speak to Francis, and when your brother came to the instrument I told him that Pardoe could do what he liked, but no son of mine would disappoint his mother by such ungentlemanly behaviour. . . . Francis at least will dine with us.'

Sir Guy got to his feet and smiled. 'You know – losing my rag like that did me good. What's that stuff they talk about nowadays? – adrenalin, that's it. It must be sloshing about inside me like beer in a barrel.' Then the smile died. 'Better tell your mother, I suppose.'

'I'll go if you like,' Jane said, hating the thought.

'You're a good girl as well as a clever one,' said her father. 'And I have to decline your second kind offer – but I must. We'll have things to talk about.'

He walked out then, and Jane considered the things that she might do. Read? Play the piano? Knit? Sew? Mummy always preferred her to choose the last two. Music and literature were far too exciting. What she really wanted to do was lament the fact that Pardoe had cut dinner. Pompous, boring and opinionated Pardoe certainly was, but he had one undeniable attraction: he was a stranger, and she didn't see nearly enough of them. It would have to be Francis after all, and all that cheese. . . .

Only it wasn't. Suddenly and magically it wasn't. As she sat in the drawing room flicking over the pages of the *Illustrated London News*, Moreton came back in and handed her a note.

My dear, [she read]
    I told you that writing a chit was a serious business, and so you must consider this a serious invitation. Your mother and I have decided, since she would like to spend a cosy evening en famille with Francis and I would not, that I shall dine out.
    If you would like to accompany me I should be charmed to have you as my dinner guest at the Hyde Park Hotel. If not, Francis awaits you and I dine alone. The choice is yours. I shall be leaving here at precisely 7.30.
        Papa.
    PS I find that chits are not only serious, but useful also. By sending you this, I do not have to go downstairs again, then up.

Jane looked at the parlourmaid.

'Tell Sir Guy I'll be ready at seven thirty precisely,' she said, and she was. Papa hated to be kept waiting.

5

S HE WORE HER blue dress because, if it was not exactly
the most dashing, it was certainly the least demure, of her
three evening dresses. With it went the pearls Mummy had
given her, and the ruby brooch from Aunt Pen. It would have
been nice to wear her engagement ring too, the dear little diamond John had given her – all and more than he could afford
– but that was locked and hidden away for ever, even from
Papa.

The Hyde Park Hotel was marvellous, and Papa was a marvellous host. He even ordered Bollinger because, as he told her,
under the present circumstances she was right, and a total
absence of Pardoe was a definite cause for celebration. There
were sole bonne femme and lamb cutlets Reform too, and she
managed to eat quite a bit of both, while Papa sipped his
burgundy and remembered once again the maharajah who
cheated at cricket; but Jane no more objected to its repetition
than a four-year-old Jane had objected to the repetition of
Goldilocks and the Three Bears, a ritual at once beloved and
familiar.

Now and again she looked about her at the elegant room,
skilful waiters, diners as elegant as the room itself, and she was
glad that she had worn the blue, and the pearls that really were
rather decent, and the positively opulent ruby.

Her father said, 'I should have done this more often.'

She smiled. 'I thought I owed it all to Pardoe.'

'The skeleton at the feast?' Sir Guy said. 'The rather substantial skeleton?'

'Too too solid flesh,' said Jane. 'I'm glad he's not here. I'm having a lovely time.'

'I too,' her father said. 'I love you very much, you know – '

'Please don't make me cry, Papa.'

' – But I find that I'm unable to help you.' Sir Guy went on as if she had not spoken.

'Jabber Lockhart does that. At least he tries to.'

'I do nothing.'

'There's nothing you can do, Papa.'

'I might – restrain your mother. But my heart isn't up to it.' He signalled to their waiter and asked for coffee.

'She doesn't mean it, you know. – Or did I say that before?'

'It's because of Guy and David, you said. Because they died and I didn't.'

'That's putting it very crudely.'

'I suppose it is,' Jane said, but didn't recant. Papa expected to be argued with. It was her right, and Francis's, as it had been David's and Guy's.

'I couldn't help being born a female, Papa.'

'It's my good fortune that you were,' her father said, 'but your mother – she misses them quite dreadfully. She was very proud of them, you know. – And of you.'

'We were sort of a set, like toy soldiers,' said Jane. 'Only two of them got broken.' She paused, then said, 'Now *that* is putting it much too crudely, and I apologise.'

'Accepted,' said her father, then, 'Forgive me – but I must ask you this. Has it ever occurred to you that that ghastly war took its toll of her too? She isn't the woman who taught you the future perfect of "venir". I doubt if she ever will be again.'

It never had occurred to her and she admitted it. But it was true enough.

'Does Lockhart – make any progress?' her father asked.

'He's helped me to know my illness for what it is, and to live with it. I suppose that is a kind of progress.'

'And just what *is* your illness?'

'The price,' said Jane. 'The bill if you like – for all the things I saw and did, and thought were going to leave me untouched. I was wrong.'

– 48 –

'There was a proverb I read somewhere,' said her father. 'Spanish, was it? "Take what you want, says God, and pay for it." Would that be it?'

'That's exactly it,' Jane said, and added sugar to her coffee. 'And anyway you know it's quite wrong of you to say you do nothing for me. You put up with me.'

'Please don't make me cry, either,' her father said. 'Not in a public dining room.'

'But it's true,' said Jane. 'You never tell me to pull myself together, as if I were lying all over the floor in separate bits.'

'Your mother does that, I take it?' Sir Guy said.

'Only because she's changed,' said his daughter.

Then the band came on, piano and banjo, drums and saxophone and violin, and Sir Guy said, 'I hope they won't play Pardoe's music.'

'Béla Bartók,' said Jane and giggled.

'At the very least,' said Sir Guy.

But the band played the waltz from *Floradora*, and some bits from *Chu Chin Chow*, and Sir Guy decided that that was worth celebrating too, and ordered port for them both. After it arrived the band moved on to more contemporary tunes: ragtime and one-steps and the newly arrived Charleston. Bobbed and shingled women, short skirts flying, jogged and jittered in their partners' arms while Sir Guy looked on smiling, for all the world, thought Jane, like an anthropologist who had discovered a new and fascinating, though perhaps rather naughty, tribe.

'Do you do that?' he asked her.

'This is all since my time,' she said.

'Pooh, nonsense,' said her father. 'One of these days we'll take a few lessons and amaze them all.' Then he swallowed more port and grinned at her.

'I'd have liked that,' he said.

They sat on and watched and marvelled, at the women who smoked, and the women who drank cocktails all the way through dinner, and the women who powdered their noses while still sitting at the table. Papa was enchanted, and it was she who had to remind him when it was time to go home. And even then, Mummy had gone to sleep, and so had Francis, so that she was able to kiss Papa goodnight and go upstairs without a row, take off her least demure dress and put on her oh so sensible nightgown. What were all those smokers and cocktail swiggers and nose-powderers wearing now, she wondered. Silken pyjamas? Nothing at all?. . . She'd be thinking of John in a minute and that would never do. This was still the best day she'd had since he died.

And then of course the nightmares came. This shouldn't have surprised her and in fact it didn't, except that this time a new fear was added: the fear that she might see Bridget O'Dowd. All the usual elements were there: the groaning wounded she knew were behind her, the shattered heavy artillery lit up by the star shells, the maimed and screaming horses, just as the dream always was – but the fear that one of them might be Bridget, this was new. For Bridget had been John's horse – or rather the horse that John had inherited.

Originally she had belonged to a captain in the King's Royal Irish Hussars, who had left her in charge of a trooper called O'Dowd while he, the captain, had gone off to reconnoitre outside Mons in October, 1914. He'd told O'Dowd to wait, but never came back, and the commander of B Company of John's Battalion found O'Dowd and his officer's horse and his own, hours later, all three of them hungry and dejected. O'Dowd had wanted very much to rejoin his squadron, but couldn't abandon his officer's horse. The company commander, Captain Heron, had gravely assured O'Dowd that he would take on the responsibility, and O'Dowd trotted off, leaving Heron the proud possessor of a promising three-year-old bay mare, known as Bridget. Heron added the O'Dowd in memory of his benefactor, and rode her till he was shot dead, early in March, 1915.

The mare was promptly inherited by the next commander of B Company, Captain Trevor, who lost a leg at second Ypres a year later. There was another, and yet another, before John took over the company in 1918, the last of Bridget's riders: two killed, one wounded, one missing believed killed. Or to put it another way: two DSOs, three MCs, two mentions in dispatches. For weeks John had practised riding before his promotion. Until that time he had never sat on a horse in his life, a donkey on the sands of Whitley Bay the height of his equestrianism. He'd taken a few hard falls too, the poor darling, but she'd taught him herself, he had naturally good hands, and he'd never once fallen off Bridget, not until that terrible day at La Basseé: the 10th November, 1918.

And now here she was lying wide awake and sweating at four in the morning, remembering that she'd had the horse dream again, and that this time she'd have seen poor Bridget if she hadn't wakened up in time. It didn't make sense, she thought, and it was no good saying that dreams and nightmares never did make sense, because hers always had a crazy logic of their own. But not Bridget. Bridget made no sense at all, because Bridget had never been wounded, not even a scratch. True, Bridget had never been in a trench during a mortar bombardment, or charged a German machine gun, but she'd lived right through the war. And when she'd left, Jane remembered, she was believed to be pregnant, which is more than I was. . . . Her last owner, Lieutenant Gurney, had mourned, and honestly, for John, but he'd coveted Bridget O'Dowd. Nor could Jane blame him. John had felt the same uneasy mixture of shame and delight.

I should read, she thought, but she knew it was no good. Her memories were stronger than words on pages, and anyway, they were all she had. Thirty-two years old, and only memories left for whatever years she still had to endure. . . . Sweat it out, the Tommies used to say. Once you've signed on you have to sweat it out. Well she was doing her share of that, lying all still in the dark, because if you moved and got comfortable you might fall asleep, and if you did *that* the bogeyman would get you. .

But of course she did sleep. Champagne and port and exhaustion acted more effectively than tablets, but this time there was no sign of Bridget. This time it was a mule detachment behind the Australian line at Pozières, and German HE had landed smack in the middle of them, butchering, eviscerating. . . .

She was being shaken, and the dream faded, like a scene in a film, as her body rocked to the hands that shook her. Mummy come to tell her to pull herself together, she thought, but she opened her eyes even so. Even Mummy was better than the things her memories insisted she see. But it was Francis.

'I say,' he said. 'You were making rather a row.'

She lay back on the pillow and looked at him. Silk dressing gown, morocco slippers, and the most elegant pyjamas.

'How dashing you look,' she said.

'Never mind me,' said Francis. 'You were yelling your head off.'

'I was having a nightmare,' said Jane. 'I quite often do.'

'So Mummy told me.'

And why not? thought Jane. It wasn't supposed to be a secret. How could it be, when every servant knew? All the same, she wished that she had told Francis first.

Her brother took out a cigarette case from his pocket, and held it out to her. 'Want a gasper?' he asked. 'Or is it unladylike?'

'Yes to both,' she said, and took one. He lit up for them. She had smoked all through the war, like everyone she knew, but Mummy didn't approve. Francis watched her drag the smoke down into her lungs.

'You really needed that,' he said.

'I really did.'

'A lot of people at Cambridge say they're bad for you.'

'They're better than nightmares,' said his sister, and he looked at her with a kind of comprehending alertness that reminded her of David.

'You're seeing a doctor?'

'A man called Lockhart,' she said.

'J.A.B. Lockhart? The one they call Jabber?'

'That's right.'

She dragged smoke in, then blew it out again luxuriously. There could be no doubt that smoking was bad for you. It was so jolly soothing. . . .

'He's supposed to be the best,' said Francis. 'Lockhart, I mean. But isn't he the one who – doesn't he specialise in – '

'If you're asking me if he's the loony doctor the answer is yes,' said Jane. 'But with my particular kind it's known as shell shock.'

'Sorry,' said Francis. 'I didn't mean to imply that you're disturbed. Not for a moment.'

'But I am, love,' she said. 'Tremendously disturbed. That's why I have nightmares and scream.'

'And it's all because of the war?'

'I'm afraid so.'

'Please, Jane,' he said. 'Don't be ironic. I'd no idea – '

She looked around for an ash tray, and settled at last on the soap dish. 'I didn't mean to be ironic,' she said. 'It's just difficult for me to talk about it, that's all.'

'You must have thought Pardoe and I pretty beastly to discuss the war as we did. I'm sorry about that.'

'You said what you believed.'

'Certainly,' he said. 'But we must have seemed very insensitive. Though we weren't, you know. Not really. Just ignorant of the circumstances.'

'That's all right then,' she said. 'Did you have a nice dinner with Mummy?'

'Of course not,' he said, and she smiled. 'Mummy had bought about a stone of cheese.'

'And didn't you like it?'

'I can't stand the stuff.'

Cheese omelettes, thought Jane. Cheese soufflés. Cheese croquettes. Day after day after day.

'I say –' Francis said. 'My friend Pardoe. He was jolly impressed by you.'

'He doesn't know I'm a loony.'

'It wouldn't make any difference if he did,' said Francis. 'Not to Pardoe.' Then he realised his own words and flushed. 'And anyway you're *not*,' he said.

'I think,' she said gravely, 'we'd better leave all that sort of thing to Lockhart.'

'Yes, of course,' he said. 'It's just that Pardoe thinks – I don't want to embarrass you –'

'As if you could,' said Jane. 'Please tell me what Pardoe thinks.'

'He thinks you have great potential.'

'Does he indeed?' said Jane. 'I should have thought Miss Payne was more his style.'

'I don't mean that,' said Francis. 'At least not just that.'

He was concentrating now, weighing up the words he must use, and the beauty was back in his face, a beauty that neither she nor Guy nor David had possessed, and she realised once more that when he was beautiful he looked very like their mother.

'It's all to do with the way the world must go,' he said. 'The world of the future – and how we're going to achieve it. Of course in the end the people will rule –'

'The dictatorship of the proletariat,' said Jane.

'That's the technical expression for it,' said Francis, 'though in itself it's a kind of paradox – because if the people rule, the world must be *more* democratic, rather than *less*, so that by definition it will not be a dictatorship as we now understand it. But of course this will take time. The people must learn to govern.'

'And you must teach them?'

'Not just me. Us.'

'You and I and Pardoe?'

'Don't tease,' he said. 'You know what I mean. All the intelligentsia.'

Wit had no chance against Francis's singlemindedness. To use it was about as effective as throwing stones at a tank.

'Do I belong to the intelligentsia?'

'Pardoe thinks so. Pardoe thinks you've got a Beta-plus mind at least – once you've been trained to use it.'

'Never mind what Pardoe thinks. What does Francis think?'

'I think you're very clever indeed,' said Francis. 'But – '

'Go on.'

'I should have to be rude.'

'Go on all the same,' she said.

'I also think you're lazy. That's why you make jokes all the time, instead of making yourself useful. I also think you're not ready for the Party.'

'Party?' Her bewilderment was quite genuine.

'The *Communist* Party,' said Francis.

'Because I'm lazy?'

'Partly that.'

'What else?' He made no answer.

'Francis, I have to know,' she said, and it was true. She *must* know.

He said, 'You look back all the time. You never look ahead.'

'Look back where?'

'That war,' he said. 'That stupid war. It almost destroyed you and I'm sorry for that, honestly I am. But it's over now. Finished. And you won't let it go. Not even in your dreams.'

She said angrily, 'If you knew what my dreams were like – ' but he interrupted her.

'They're *your* dreams,' he said. 'Part of the you that exists now. You won't look forward – only back. The dreams won't change because you won't, and I don't think you ever will.'

'I thought we decided to leave all that to Lockhart,' she said, but even to say it was to admit defeat.

'You did ask me.'

'So I did,' she said. 'You'd better finish it.'

'You're no use to the Party so long as you cling to this stupid nostalgia,' he said. 'It's as if you'd had a love affair and it's finished and you won't let go.'

Somehow, by some strength of will she did not know she possessed, she neither jumped nor yelled. She had forgotten how perceptive her brother could be. If she gave herself away now he would know that what he'd used as a mere figure of speech had been the literal truth.

'Then you and Pardoe don't agree about me,' she said.

'He thinks you can change for the better and I don't,' her brother said. 'That's the only difference.'

'But then he doesn't know I'm a loony,' she said again. With Francis it was always best to be sure.

'You're not a loony,' he said. 'But he doesn't know Lockhart is treating you – not from me.'

Then Hawkins came in with the morning tea, and Francis saw the chocolate biscuits and ate one there and then, and Hawkins left in a huff.

'A bit of a tartar, isn't she?' Francis said.

'You just ate her biscuit,' said Jane.

'*Her* biscuit?'

'I always leave them for her.'

'Oh my God,' said Francis. 'Do you mean to say she doesn't get enough food?'

'That's what I thought,' said Jane. 'But she says she does. She just likes chocolate biscuits.'

'You don't think I should apologise to her?'

'She wouldn't understand why,' she said, 'and you haven't time to teach her, not if you're going back to Cambridge tomorrow.'

'Not tomorrow,' said Francis. 'Pardoe and I are going to a party tomorrow. Fancy dress.'

'Incidentally where *is* Pardoe?' Jane asked.

'Staying with a cousin in Knightsbridge.'

'I mean in the general scheme of things,' said Jane. 'His station in life. All that.'

'He's an economist. At Trinity,' said Francis. 'A junior fellow. Eventually he'll be a senior fellow.'

'Is that what you want to do?'

'It's what I must do,' Francis said, then added: 'Though not necessarily at Trinity.' He stood up. The conference it seemed was over.

'I say,' he said. . . . Not quite over.

'Pardoe really likes you,' he continued.

'Like Georgina Payne.'

'They all like Georgina Payne. But he really does like you. . . . He's something of a ladies' man. I just thought I'd better mention it.'

'I'm obliged to you,' said Jane.

'Not at all,' her brother said, and left her, passing Foch on his way in. Jane swung her legs off the bed, stretched, then looked down at Foch.

'What on earth was all that about?' she said. 'Pardoe likes me indeed. . . . And what about Miss Payne? "*They* all like her," he said. Not we. They. . . . I don't quite like the sound of that.'

But Foch was searching the carpet for chocolate-biscuit crumbs, and was too busy to answer.

6

HER MOTHER SAID, 'I understand that Francis came to your room this morning.'

It was eleven o'clock, and the two women were taking coffee together in the drawing room.

'Who told you that?' Jane asked.

'He did. I do not accuse him of impropriety – or you. I merely question the wisdom of protracted visits. Servants have the oddest notions of what is improper. Particularly housemaids. I have often noticed it.'

'Why did he tell you?'

'He thinks you're bored.'

Jane thought, well of course I am, you appalling old person. But that was not the way. Patience, tact and, above all, persistence.

'Why does he think that?' she asked.

'He is at Cambridge. He has his studies, his friends, clubs, meetings, sports. A life crammed with excitement. Yours by comparison *must* seem a little dull.'

How can you say so? thought Jane. Only two days ago I bought two pounds of cheese.

Aloud she said, 'Perhaps a little.'

'Francis is attending a fancy-dress ball tonight,' said her mother.

'So he tells me.'

'It occurred to us that you might attend it too, – as his partner. He has little opportunity to meet nice girls here when he spends half his life at Cambridge. There is, of course, the question of a costume.'

'Costume, Mummy?'

'It's a fancy-dress ball it seems. They almost all are these days, Francis says.'

'I'm to go then?'

'Have I not said so?'

'What does Papa say?'

'I broke it to him over breakfast. He could see no objection.'

'And the costume?'

'I thought the sari,' her mother said. 'With the choli of course, and those vulgar jewels, and those rather ghastly ruby ear-rings Nettles gave me one Christmas. You will not of course expose your midriff.'

Nor dance the Charleston, thought Jane, because I don't know how. And just to be on the safe side she thought it might be a good idea to find out if her father really wanted her to go.

It seemed he did. He even put aside his work (a viceroy's ball programme in New Delhi in 1918, with photographs of his party at dinner) to tell her so. 'And you're to wear the sari, I hear. Do you know how to do it?'

'Oh yes,' said Jane. 'Ayah taught me years ago when we used to dress up – Guy and David and I.'

'David was usually a Moghul emperor, I remember,' her father said. 'What was Guy?'

'Sir Arthur Wellesley defeating the Mahrattas.'

'And you?'

'Spoils of war,' said Jane. 'I don't think Sir Arthur Wellesley ever took spoils of war of that particular sort – but then Guy and David hadn't the faintest idea what they were. Nor did I – except I thought it rather boring. So I got hold of a helmet and spear – became a warrior queen instead.'

'That's much more like you,' said her father. 'And what will you be tonight?'

Her voice took on the demure sing-song intonation of a former acquaintance of theirs, a Mrs Lal, whose husband was a judge.

'I shall be examining with great curiosity the antics of these British people who are all the time finding it necessary to dance.'

Her father snorted with laughter, then asked, 'But won't you be dancing yourself?'

'Impossible to do so,' she said, 'lacking knowledge of correct procedure.' His laughter died, and she added in her own voice, 'I shan't wish to, you know. Not this new stuff. But I might risk a waltz if the sari can stand the strain.'

'We should have taken you about more once we got back from India,' he said. 'But I was ill – and after the boys your mother was distraught. But all the same we should have *tried*.'

'It's perfectly all right, Papa,' she said. 'Honestly.'

She lied of course, but she couldn't bear to hear him apologise.

Hawkins had ironed the sari while Mummy watched her, nervous of burn marks. But there were none. It was an old, and very beautiful garment, a gift to Mummy from the cricketing maharajah. Mummy had bitterly resented the insinuation that she might, under any circumstances, dress as a native, which was of course why the maharajah had given it to her, but for once Papa had been firm, and vetoed Mummy's immediate reaction, which was to cut it up for cushion covers. It was, he said, a work of art, and sacrosanct. It was certainly very beautiful; a great spreading sheet of wine-red silk, heavily embroidered in gold thread. The choli, the little jacket, was of white, with red and gold embroidery, and up in her bedroom after dinner Jane began the ritual that she and her ayah had performed so many times: long petticoat underneath with tapes tied tight, then the sari wrapped around, tucking it in as she went. Then she drew it over her shoulder, and fastened it with one of the 'terrible jewels', a ruby brooch set in heavy gold. There were bangles too, and a gold and ruby necklace, and Uncle Walter's terrible ear-rings which weren't terrible at all. They came from Cartier. Gold sandals with red drawn threadwork, and the dressing-up ritual was complete, and she remembered how it was to be nine years old again, to know the kites were screaming high over the garden, and the tame mynah bird was talking Hindi in Mummy's dressing room; that the smells were of jasmine and curry from the kitchen, and ayah's heavy perfume. And down in the schoolroom David and Guy were already duelling, scimitar against sword.

Then she looked in the mirror, and it was a woman who looked back, not an all-too-pert and precocious little girl. She looked at Foch, who seemed totally unimpressed by her Oriental splendour.

'You're just jealous,' she said. 'All the same I think Francis is right.'

Foch snorted.

'No honestly,' she said. 'I *do* live too much in the past. But I don't know how to get out.'

Carefully she used a little rouge to mark a beauty spot on her brow.

'I think you underestimate Francis,' she told Foch. 'Just because he can't laugh doesn't mean he can't think.'

Foch put out his tongue.

When she had done she went downstairs, back to Papa's study where he was once again rummaging happily among the material for his memoirs: this time a polo match on the Rawalpindi maidan; some kind of Indian Lancer regiment, it seemed, playing against the ICS. Papa had scored twice in the third chukka. Soon he would show her the photographs, but first she must be inspected. Straight and tall, shoulders back, her governess had told her. Girls can't be soldiers, a pert, precocious Jane had argued. Girls can still look smart, her governess had said, so straight and tall and shoulders back it was.

Her father walked round her as though she were a statue in a gallery. 'You look wonderful,' he said, and she started to giggle, then realised he meant it.

'Too tall,' she said. 'Too thin. Decked out like a Christmas tree.'

'Nonsense,' her father said. 'Jewellery suit you. Gold suits you. And riches.'

'They suit every girl.'

'Not as they suit you. Believe me. For some women wealth is a protective armour. Without it they're doomed. For you it's no more than a setting. You look wonderful.'

He said it that second time as if he were summing up the deliberations of a highly qualified committee. 'Let me show you.'

He rummaged among the fading sepia photographs he kept stored in shoe boxes, and came out with an envelope. Something special, thought Jane, as he opened it. There aren't many he protects so carefully. Not any more. . . . Her father laid a fading piece of cardboard down in front of her. A photograph was fixed to it, the photograph of a woman. The photographer had arranged some potted palms behind her, and she was standing on a tigerskin that had seen better days, but she was quite devastatingly beautiful. She wore a long skirted dress of forty years ago, and carried a parasol, striking a pose with it as a musical-comedy chorus girl might have done, and her figure showed up to perfection, even inside the enveloping folds of Victorian skirts. But her face had a beauty beyond fashion or custom. Jet black hair that flowed straight down, dark, unwavering eyes, straight nose, sweet mouth – one could tick off the list, Jane thought, and everyone would say Goodness! How pretty she must have been. But she wasn't pretty in the least. She was beautiful, just as Francis was beautiful.

'On her wrist there is a bracelet that a maharajah gave her. Round her neck is a necklace given her by a major in the Coldstream who was heir to a shipping fortune. The two together were insured for a hundred thousand pounds – forty-three years ago. Did you even notice them?'

'I didn't even know they were there till you told me. Who was she?'

'Her name was Posy Sanderson. – Ridiculous sort of a name. But with her a name didn't matter. She was an – Anglo-Indian we call them nowadays. Then we used to say Eurasian, if it wasn't "that bloody chi-chi".'

Carefully he replaced the photograph in the envelope, and put it back in the shoe box.

'What happened to her?'

'She died,' her father said. 'In childbirth. Poor darling girl. She lit up every room she entered. . . . The child died too.' He closed the shoe box.

'Better let your mother take a look at you,' he said.

Mummy was busy inspecting Francis, who had chosen to appear as a fox hunter: red coat, white breeches, top boots that gleamed. Mummy approved, as well she might, thought Jane. Any mother would approve such dark good looks, such elegant tailoring. . . . Then she checked Jane's midriff, was pleased to declare it adequately covered, and told them to enjoy themselves – though no later than twelve thirty. Jane must be home by one.

Moreton had found them a cab and they chugged off towards Knightsbridge. Two nights in a row, thought Jane. How fast I am becoming.

Francis said, 'The sari looks well on you.'

'Thank you,' she said. 'And you my dear – you're the young MFH to the life. Where *did* you hire that outfit?'

'I didn't,' said Francis. 'A chum of mine lent it to me.'

'A Cambridge chum?'

'Of course.' Francis sounded susprised that she could think that there were other kinds.

'He must be frightfully rich.'

'He is,' said Francis. 'He's at King's.'

She gathered that the two facts were connected.

'Is he a Communist?'

'Good Lord no,' Francis said. 'He's far too stupid.'

The taxi chugged on into the Brompton Road, then nosed its way past a crescent and a mews and finally settled at a house in a square.

'Somebody else who's frightfully rich,' said Jane.

Francis fumbled with half crowns and sixpences, and finally settled on a florin.

'Same chap,' he said.

'The one at King's?'

He helped her out and she rearranged her sari.

'Only rich chap I know. Only *really* rich chap. The house is his parents'.'

'Oughtn't I to know his name?' Jane asked. 'After all he *is* my host.'

'You're making jokes again,' said Francis. 'Being ironic – I've warned you about that. His name is Poynter. Richard Poynter. His father's in shipping.'

'His father owns the sort of ship that used to take us to India. – Francis Whitcomb – your chum's a capitalist.'

'You're hopeless,' her brother said. 'I knew you would be.'

They went inside.

It was a big, old house, built, she supposed, at the time of George III. There was a curving and very beautiful staircase, used, so it seemed, for sitting out; what was usually the dining room was a super room and bar, and at the back a marquee had been erected where a band was playing all over again the music of the night before: 'Varsity Rag' and 'The Charleston' and 'Get Out And Get Under'. Everybody present seemed to be drinking champagne, she thought, including the servants, but then she realised that they were for the most part merely carrying it and were comparatively sober. Meekly she accompanied Francis to hand over her coat to a maidservant, accept a numbered ticket in return and then, reminding herself that she was a Warrior Queen, prepared to join the party.

It wasn't as difficult as she'd feared. Francis, concerned, she told herself, not to embarrass her by undue attention, promptly went off and left her on her own. That gave her an excuse to wander, with that graceful carriage the sari seems to impose, and look at the people and think about Papa. She stared at Falstaffs and Nell Gwyns, Richard the Lionhearts and Madame Pompadours, but what she really saw was Posy Sanderson in a soubrette's pose, with a face so beautiful as to be scarcely real. Could it be, could it really be, that she had once had an elder brother – or sister – who had died at birth? And why had Papa waited so long to tell her? And if it were so, did it matter that it had happened? And did Mummy know? She wished that John were there to hear her questions, because there was no one else to turn to. But then it was just because there was no one else that Papa had shown her the photograph.

She wandered into the marquee to watch the dancing: a French sailor with a gypsy girl, a Felix-the-Cat with a Little Bo Peep, a gollywog with a Queen of Hearts. Then the band played a waltz and a Beefeater asked her to dance; she decided to risk it – like riding a bicycle, she told herself. Once you know the knack you never lose it, just one two three one two three. Watch-for-your-toes two three. For the Beefeater was nervous, and just a little drunk, but his place was taken by a Little Jack Horner who talked to her all the time in Urdu, and was enchanted when she replied in the same tongue. . . . Then there were a centurion, a sultan and a bull fighter, and then what she could only think of as a Cornet of Horse. That was what he had to be: a cavalryman of Wellington's time, all gold and scarlet and elegant frogging, overall trousers strapped under the foot. So young and dashing and pretty. But the band had grown tired of waltzes. It was 'I Want To See My Baby Do The Charleston' – and out of the question.

'I'm afraid not,' she said.

'Oh I say,' said the Cornet of Horse. 'I'm not that bad.'

'Of course you're not,' said Jane. 'It's just that I've had no supper.'

'Then I'll take you in,' the Cornet of Horse said, and offered his arm.

He had no difficulty at all in obtaining champagne for her, or lobster mayonnaise, though the crowd at the buffet had seemed to her impenetrable.

'You *are* adroit,' she said.

He flushed. 'Not really. I live here you see.'

'You're Richard Poynter?'

'We haven't met, have we? I feel sure I would have remembered.'

'No,' she said. 'We haven't. But I'm not a gatecrasher, you know.'

'I wouldn't mind,' Poynter said. 'Honestly.'

'Well I don't eat and drink so very much – '

'I didn't mean *that*.'

'But I *am* Francis Whitcomb's sister.'

'Oh good Lord,' said her Cornet of Horse. 'I say – would you mind if I got myself a glass of champers – '

'Get two,' she said. 'I'd rather like another myself. It's awfully good.'

'It's Bollinger,' said her Cornet of Horse.

'I bet you it won't work,' she said. But he was already gone.

And of course it didn't work, because after just two sips brother Francis appeared, and with him was Pardoe. But at least the awful moment was postponed, because before Pardoe could ask her to dance a woman dressed as Titania came up to him and said she simply must have a word with him about collectivisation. But then beastly Francis took her Cornet of Horse away, saying *they* must have a word about the Trinity May Ball. She sipped champagne and tried not to be jealous, until a tall man in evening dress appeared, the only person there not pretending to be someone else.

'May I join you?' he said. 'My name's Poynter.'

'Ah,' she said. 'The Colonel of Horse.'

He looked puzzled for a moment, then smiled.

'Actually I was in the Rifle Brigade, but I see what you mean. Young Richard's costume. He looks good in it, wouldn't you say?'

'If this were the Duchess of Richmond's ball before Waterloo he'd be just right.'

'I'm glad you like him, Miss Whitcomb.'

'He's – likeable,' she said. 'But how did you know my name?'

'I asked. Urdu-speaking maharanis are rather a rarity you know.'

'My friend Little Jack Horner?'

'He says you're very fluent.'

'So is he.'

The elder Poynter smiled. 'I'll tell him you said so. He's collector of the Bhopal District. Due back soon.'

'My father was in the ICS too.'

'So I'm told,' said Poynter. 'But not your brother?'

'Too young,' said Jane. 'He takes his tripos next month. And anyway he's an academic, not an administrator.'

'Is he, indeed? Not like Richard. Richard is not an intellectual,' Poynter said. 'In fact it'll take him all his time to take a pass degree, even with a following wind. But it doesn't matter.'

'Doesn't it?'

'Not in the least,' Poynter said. 'In a year or two he'll stop playing the fool at Cambridge and be what you called him – a Cornet of Horse.'

'I'm sure he'll do it delightfully.'

'He'll be a good officer,' said Poynter. 'Not over-burdened with brains, but good-hearted and conscientious.'

'May I wish him luck?'

'You certainly may,' Poynter said, then looked across the room, and rose. 'You must excuse me,' he said. 'I see young Millie Chetwynd over there. Richard's mother rather approves of her. Pretty little thing, isn't she?'

He bowed and went over to a dark girl dressed as Britannia, and not at all happy about it.

More heavy hints, thought Jane, though tactfully delivered. But there was no time to brood about it. The word about collectivisation had been spoken: Pardoe was upon her.

He approved of the sari. *Thoroughly* approved. Her wearing it went some way – some small and humble way – towards reparation due to a people who had endured almost two centuries of ruthless exploitation. Jane tried in vain to assure him that the inhabitants of the subcontinent had endured exploitation for rather longer than that; tried also to explain that no one was more adept at exploiting an Indian than another Indian. He didn't listen, perhaps didn't even hear: but then he wasn't made to listen. He was made to teach.

And teach he did, about majority rights and minority rights, self-determination and economic self-fulfilment, and Jane listened because although some of it was boring and some mere jargon, quite a lot of it was interesting and some even made sense. The fact did not surprise her. Pardoe was, as she had told her father, a very clever man. But she drew the line at being told about collectivisation. That was like being given another girl's box of chocs.

'But you can't mean you're jealous of Marigold,' Pardoe said.

'I might be,' said Jane, 'if I knew who she was.'

'Marigold Ledbitter. The girl dressed as Titania.'

'No,' said Jane. 'I'm not jealous of her.'

Pardoe seemed disappointed.

'She has a good mind,' he said, 'and is doing quite well at the London School of Economics, but she does have a tendency to put on weight, poor girl' – a tendency that Jane had already noted. 'Whereas you – ' He hesitated.

'Whereas I?' she prompted.

' – Are quite divinely slim,' he said and looked at her, – roguishly the only word. As if he expected me to roll over on my back with all four paws in the air, she thought. An impossible idea. Foch would never speak to her again.

'I think we should dance now,' Pardoe said.

The band was playing 'Love Will Find A Way' from 'The Maid Of The Mountains', so that she could not, like Mrs Lal, plead that she lacked knowledge of the correct procedure. Meekly she preceded him to the marquee, and his arms came about her.

He danced well, which surprised her. There was no hint of the rugger field or the boxing ring in the way his feet moved, his hands held. A little too inexorable perhaps in his decision on what line to take, but then Pardoe had been born inexorable. . . . For a few bars they danced in silence. He was assessing her, Jane decided; awarding her marks out of ten for responsiveness, awareness of rhythm, technical ability. To her own fury she discovered that she was exerting herself to dance her very best.

At last he said, 'Did your brother leave?'

'I think not,' said Jane. 'He went off with his friend Poynter.'

'Our genial host,' said Pardoe. 'You have met the father?'

'Briefly.'

'An almost perfect example of the genus capitalist. A man worth millions who thinks of no one but himself.'

'He thinks of his son.'

'A useless creature. Not even a capitalist. A parasite.'

'I think he's destined for the cavalry,' said Jane.

'And an obsolete parasite at that,' said Pardoe.

Jane, who had seen the effects of machine-gun fire at first hand, could only agree, but not aloud. With Pardoe one must never concede too much.

The waltz ended, and the drummer became busy with cow bells and cymbals, side drums, and what looked like a wash-board.

'Cacophony will supervene once more,' said Pardoe. 'Let us talk.'

He took her arm and led her gently, politely, inexorably, back to the supper room. 'I shall get you some lemonade,' Pardoe said.

'Champagne,' said Jane.

'How many glasses have you had already?'

'One,' said Jane, and was furious with herself once more; this time because she lied.

'One more cannot harm you,' Pardoe said. 'There is a saying among the more convivial men of my college: "A bird never flew on one wing." There is a certain merit in it – particularly when applied to a bird of paradise.' He went to the bar.

Oh dear God, thought Jane. This can't be happening. And yet he was clever, he was strong – and he was a stranger. Talking with him was like a match of really hard tennis: exhilarating yet slightly frantic.

He came back with the Bollinger – like a disease bringing its own antidote, she thought, but that wasn't *quite* right. The antidote didn't work.

'Your brother Francis feels the need of a close emotional attachment to another male,' said Pardoe. 'Now please do not misunderstand me. There is nothing wrong with that.' He waited, but she made no answer.

'Nothing *intrinsically* wrong,' he said, 'though I could wish that he had attached himself to someone more politically aware.

– 67 –

However, that is not the point of my thesis. My needs are not his, and why should they be?'

'Why indeed?' asked Jane, dreading what was to come.

'My emotional needs are, and always have been, heterosexual,' said Pardoe. 'For as long as I can remember. Even at Oundle. Need I say more?'

'Well yes,' said Jane. 'I think perhaps you should.'

Pardoe consented to do so. 'You have a good mind – I think I mentioned the fact to Francis – ' he said.

'He was kind enough to tell me what you said.'

'I wanted it to be known. A good mind, as I say, and a refreshing willingness to learn. To take instruction. I also find you enormously attractive physically.'

'Is this by any chance a proposal?' Jane asked.

'Not of marriage,' said Pardoe. 'Situated as I am at the moment – a mere junior fellow – marriage is out of the question. What I *am* proposing is something more of a liaison, a coming together of kindred spirits, with no binding commitment on either side. I think I can say without flattering myself unduly that I'm not without experience in these matters. I can promise you fulfilment, both mental and physical.'

He looked away and his manner grew wary. Jane followed his gaze, to see that Titania was hovering.

'This is not the place to press you for a decision,' said Pardoe, 'though of course I shall be in touch quite soon. I shouldn't have any more champagne tonight. The thought of you tipsy is a profanation.'

Then he moved away, quickly and smoothly for a man of his size, with Titania stumbling after. Titania *was* tipsy. His women probably always were, thought Jane, and then: *His women.* What on earth is the matter with me? It was time to find Francis and go home.

But she could not find Francis. There were only three places to look: the supper room, the marquee and the stairs – but he was in none of them. She took another glass of champagne despite Pardoe's instructions, and sat in the darkest, quietest corner she could find. 'Horsey Keep Your Tail Up' was not the ideal music for self-analysis, but she would have to make do. Pardoe, she was sure, would insist on that.

The trouble was – or part of the trouble was – that she was

thirty-two, and it had been seven years since a man had embraced her with passion, and she desperately needed that embrace. Not just the sex part – with John that had always been something of a gamble – but the feel of a man holding her, the certain knowledge that a man needed her. She had to have these things. After all she *was* thirty-two now. John would never ever be thirty-two. John was dead and buried and twenty-seven when he died and she missed him but she couldn't have him, ever again.

Whereas she could have Pardoe, and that was the horrifying thing. Pardoe could be had. Moreover she was prepared to bet that Pardoe would be a good lover. Loads better than poor darling John, because Pardoe had told her he was good and he wouldn't lie. He probably had a diploma in it or something, and when they did it she'd get to like it so much she'd put up with everything, even his prose style. . . . And there would be other advantages. New people for example. The only one she'd seen so far was Titania, who would hate her, but there would be others, from LSE and elsewhere – she might even go there herself – and have jolly chats about the means of production, distribution and exchange. Because soon she'd be on her own, she knew that now. Papa would never have shown her that photograph unless he was sure he was dying.

And she couldn't be on her own with Mummy. Couldn't possibly. Any more than she could be Aunt Pen's toady. The only other offer she'd had was Pardoe, and even that one might be withdrawn if he found out she was a loony – and besides, he might start explaining to her that she was like that because of the war that should never have been. . . . She beckoned to a waiter to bring more champagne, because for some reason she felt disinclined to walk to the buffet, even doubted her ability to do so. She gulped at it when it arrived, and wondered what the time was. . . . If Pardoe ever tells me that I'm a loony because I fought in the wrong war I'll kill him, she thought. It was a splendid idea and seemed to solve lots of problems. Then the band played that tune from the show she'd gone to with John on his leave in 1917. When they got to the bit about

And when I tell them – and I'm certainly going to tell them,
That you're the man whose wife some day I'll be,

They'll never believe me – they'll never believe me
That from this great big world you've chosen me

she began to cry, very quietly.

When Francis came up to her at last he seemed angry.

'Where on earth have you been?' he said. 'I've looked everywhere.'

'That,' said Jane, 'is a lie.'

He looked at her more closely.

'Good Lord,' he said, 'you're as tight as a tick.'

'And you,' she said, 'are as queer as a coot.'

She didn't shout, but her voice was a carrying one, and Francis looked about him, warily.

'Don't worry,' said Jane. 'I want it to be our secret. Just get me home.'

'How much have you had?'

'Five glasses of champagne,' she said. 'Not a lot for you varsity chaps – but too much for an innocent maiden. . . . You ask Pardoe.'

'Why bring Pardoe into it?' Francis asked.

'Because it's always bloody Pardoe,' said his sister. And then – 'What's his first name? Has he got one?'

'Of course he's got one,' said Francis. 'It's Cuthbert.'

'Cuthbert Pardoe.' Jane tested the name, and found it satisfactory. 'Cuthbert Pardoe. Cuthbert Pardoe and Francis Whitcomb. . . . Ruggery and buggery.'

'You're very rude,' said her brother.

'You were pimping for him,' said Jane, and fumbled in her handbag, found her cloakroom ticket. 'Go and get my coat.'

'What will you do?'

'Get up. Walk out. . . . Like a lady.'

'Do you think you can?' he asked her.

'I must,' she said. 'For both our sakes.'

Being biddable, he left her, and somehow she made her body do what she ordered it to do. An interesting exercise, she thought. One she had last performed eight years ago, when she had climbed out of her ambulance after the shell blast struck and helped unload the wounded, instead of lying still as any sane person would have done, and waiting for the next shell to land. Leaving a party wasn't nearly so difficult.

Francis found her waiting for him in the hall, and put her coat around her and took her arm, and together they walked out and nobody noticed, out into a London night already cold enough to make her feel it, and with a walk to the taxi long enough to help just a little. When the taxi came, she fell asleep – and snored, so Francis told her later. But she didn't dream.

Sleeping was a mistake, but then Francis hadn't had much experience of handling drunks – not like his big sister, Jane thought, one-time expert in bullying, coaxing, cajoling helpless young officers back to their billets. Francis had never done it before, admittedly, but when it came to holding up his sister with one hand and paying off a taxi with the other he was hopeless. No sense of improvisation at all. She told him so.

It was Hawkins who saved them, back from her night out, and with a skirt even further above her knees than Jane had thought possible.

'Are you all right, miss?' she said, and then, when Jane smiled at her, chuckled: 'No, you're not, are you?'

'Is it any of your business?' Francis asked – hacking away at our only lifeline, thought Jane, *and* he eats her biscuits.

'Please be quiet,' she said, and then to Hawkins: 'I have to go inside.'

'Yes miss,' said Hawkins.

'Only I don't think I can. Not just yet. I need a good sleep.'

She moved towards the doorstep, ready to sit, and Francis just stood there, but Hawkins blocked her off.

'Not now miss,' she said. 'There'll be a copper along in a minute.'

'Perhaps he can help,' said Jane.

'He'd wake the house,' Hawkins said.

'We can't have that,' said Jane, and then, 'Are you sure there's a copper?'

'Yes miss,' said Hawkins. 'He's keen on me.'

'I'm glad,' said Jane. 'You deserve a nice copper.'

She breathed in and out slowly, three long, deep breaths.

'You can get me up the stairs if my brother helps you?'

'Yes, miss.' She seemed quite sure.

'Open the door then, Francis,' said Jane. 'Put the prisoner back in her cell.'

They did it, too. Chaplinesque, the highbrow critics would call it: all that teetering and tottering and clinging to banisters, silent anguish from Francis when she stood on his instep, but at last they got her to her bedroom and Francis left without a word, but Hawkins put her to bed, folded her sari, left her and came back with aspirin and soda water, then forced her to watch as she shut each jewel in its case.

'Thank you Peggy Hawkins,' said Jane, and Hawkins turned the light off and tiptoed upstairs to the attic, cautious not to wake cook.

Jane slept. She didn't dream, but slept, on and on, so that when she woke her tea was cold and Francis, once more gorgeously dressing gowned, was eating her last remaining biscuit.

Jane thought: I should feel awful but I don't. Aspirins and soda-water. Peggy Hawkins, bless you. . . . She sipped her tea.

'Good morning,' she said.

Her brother said, 'I'm surprised you can still speak.'

'So am I,' said Jane.

'You couldn't much last night. Not at the end anyway.'

'There didn't seem much left to say.'

'No,' her brother said. 'I think you covered most of it. Ruggery and buggery.'

'Did I say that? I'm sorry.'

'Don't be. The chaps at college say I never make a joke. I shall borrow that one.'

'It's yours,' she said. 'With my compliments.'

'Who told you?' Francis asked. 'About me, I mean.'

'Pardoe,' she said. 'He saw nothing wrong with the way you make love – but he deplored your choice of partners.'

'He would,' said Francis. 'But he doesn't realise – '

'How lovely Richard Poynter is? But I do. I danced with him.' She sipped more cold tea. At the moment it tasted infinitely better than Bollinger. 'But Cuthbert wasn't the only one who told me.'

'Who else?'

'Richard's father. He came over specially to talk to me – give me a message, you might say.'

'What message?'

'You and the Cornet of Horse – Young Richard. His father forbids the banns, I'm afraid. Young Richard's earmarked for

Millie Chetwynd. He told me so very nicely – but I didn't enjoy it much.'

'He had no business to tell you at all.'

'Let's assume he thought I had a bit of commonsense,' said Jane. 'Let's further assume he's right. Who better to tell? Papa? Your college? The police? He's warning you off, Francis. What you do is your business I suppose – up to a point – '

'What point?'

'Upsetting Papa.'

She settled back among the pillows. Really a night without dreams was something she thought she'd never have again.

'We could be discreet,' Francis said. 'Damn it, we *have* been discreet.'

'Not enough,' said Jane. 'His father knows. And Papa is in no shape to take on Richard's father. And anyway – Richard's leaving Cambridge.'

'His father told you that?'

'He's going into the army.'

'No,' said Francis. 'Not the army. Nothing so vulgar. Richard's going into the Household Cavalry. The Life Guards.'

'How pretty he'll look,' said Jane. 'All that scarlet and horse-hair and burnished steel. You can go and watch him outside Buckingham Palace, and worship – from afar.'

'That sounds very like a command.'

'How can I command you?' said Jane. 'All I can do is tell you a pretty obvious truth. You're no match for Richard's father. None of us are.'

'Pardoe's right,' her brother said. 'You do have a good brain.'

'Why don't you call him Cuthbert?' she asked.

'Why do you make jokes as soon as you make sense?'

'But it wasn't a joke,' said Jane. 'At least I don't *think* it was. . . . Why don't you?'

'Because I don't want to.'

'Nor do I.'

'You said I was pimping for him.'

'Weren't you?'

'He likes you,' Francis said. 'Whether you like him or not is your affair.'

'I don't.'

'Do you want me to tell him so?'

She thought about that. Tipsy she might be able to tolerate him, but then he didn't want her to be tipsy, and she didn't either.

'Yes,' she said.

He rose. 'That's it then, I take it? We have a bargain. I keep your secret and you keep mine.'

'That's it,' she said.

He left her and she settled down to drowse and brood. Pardoe was out. O-U-T, but somebody else would have to be in and pretty damn quickly. Steps would have to be taken. . . . Taking steps was a phrase that Jabber used: she began to think of what she would tell him.

I used to think my whole life was predestined, she would tell him. But now I find I have a choice. I can either have nightmares or go to parties and get drunk on champagne.

Her eyes closed: she went back to sleep.

7

'So I HAVE a choice, do I?' said Jabber.

'Not you,' said Jane. 'Me.'

'Oh yes,' said Lockhart. 'It's your choice, I can see that – but it looks as if I'm the one who'll have to make it. – Or maybe condone it.'

'Not condone,' said Jane. 'At least I don't *think* so. I mean I quite like champagne – adore it as a matter of fact – but I can't go on shovelling the stuff down all day and every day. I mean apart from anything else I couldn't afford it.'

'And you'd spend far too much time falling down,' said Lockhart. 'Perhaps in the street.'

'Mummy would hate that,' said Jane, and then more fairmindedly: 'So would I.'

'Better if we just get rid of those dreams,' Lockhart said.

'We?'

'Neither of us can do it on our own,' he said.

'But do you think we *can* do it – between us I mean?'

'Yes,' he said.

He had never before been so uncompromising.

'We'd better get on with it then,' said Jane.

'I have a colleague with me at the moment,' Lockhart said. 'Dr Barker. He's from Sydney in Australia. He's doing pretty much the same kind of thing that I'm doing, and just for now we're exchanging ideas. One of these days we hope to do a paper together.'

'And will I be in it?'

'A starring rôle,' he said. 'Dr Barker's here now. Would you mind awfully if he joined us for a chat? I appreciate that it's a lot to ask.'

'If it's in the interests of medical science I can hardly refuse,' said Jane, 'but I may get a little tongue-tied with a strange man in the room.'

'He's a doctor,' Lockhart said.

'He's a man,' said Jane.

'Ah,' Lockhart said. 'You're thinking of your love affair. I doubt if it will be relevant to our discussion.'

Now and again Jane felt a sudden, urgent need to slap her friend Jabber and this was one of the times, but even so it would be unfair, she thought. Punishing him for something he couldn't help – like not being a woman.

Lockhart rose. 'I'll go and get him,' he said. 'Help yourself to a cigarette.'

She took one at once. The war was coming back to her.

Lockhart returned with a tall, balding man in a blue suit, stiff collar, and what looked like a college or old-school tie. In his forties, just beginning to run to fat, but shrewd and alert-looking. A little browner than most, she thought, but very much the Harley Street type.

'Jane this is Dr Barker,' Lockhart said. 'Miss Jane Whitcomb – Ross Barker.'

She rose and offered her hand.

'Miss Whitcomb, it's very good of you to agree to see me,' he said. 'I want you to know that I appreciate it.'

And there it all was, in the voice. The tall, lean young men in the villages behind Pozières in the uniform coats that were cut like Norfolk jackets: gamblers who spoke an English all their own, and were homesick for outlandish places with names like Parramatta and Gundagai, Rottnest Island and Broken Hill. John had told her once that they were the most foul-mouthed troops he'd ever met: worse than the Liverpudlians even. But she remembered only how strong and handsome they seemed, until the shells burst among them . . . then they'd looked as dreadful as everybody else.

Barker said, 'From what I hear you had quite a war, Miss Whitcomb.'

Not that he'd heard it: he'd read it in her file. But a lot of men didn't like the idea of it all being written down, and maybe this young woman didn't either. She shrugged. The words refused to come easily, but it didn't matter. He was used to that.

'Miss Whitcomb went to France in 1916,' Lockhart said. 'She served through right till the end.'

'You drove an ambulance?' Barker asked.

'I did.' The words seemed wrenched out of her.

'Ever drive any of our boys? Australians?'

For some reason that got her started.

'I drove everybody,' she said. 'Australians, Canadians, New Zealanders, French, British, Portuguese. . . . Even Germans.'

'Did you find that difficult?' he asked. 'Helping Germans?'

'They didn't look like Germans.'

'What did they look like?'

'Men in pain,' she said.

He nodded, as Lockhart might have done: her words accepted, but no opinion offered.

'They also looked broken for the most part,' she added, 'and nasty. Disgusting.'

'And yet you helped them?'

'It was what I was there for,' she said.

He reached for a cigarette, a tired old trick that meant only that he wanted time to look at her, think about her. What he saw was a typical upper-class lady Pom: right sort of clothes, right down to the shoes and gloves, right accent, right way of sitting. Under weight, certainly, but then a lot of women were these days – and tired almost to the point of exhaustion, but too many nightclubs could be the cause of that. But he'd known that would be false judgement on this one, even without a look in Lockhart's file. This girl was what the blokes used to call a stoush-merchant: a fighter. You might break her, but she wouldn't bend.

'Tell me about the dreams,' he said, and she told him. It came haltingly at first, but he knew how to listen, how to coax, and out it all came at last: the wounded men that she must not see, and the wounded horses who were all too visible, until at last she got to Bridget O'Dowd, not yet seen, but somehow lurking, the most dangerous threat to her hard-won control.

'This horse – Bridget – belonged to a friend of yours?' he asked.

'Yes.'

'What happened to him?'

'He died,' she said. 'Like so many others.'

'And was the horse hurt?'

'Not a scratch,' she said. 'She was a very handsome horse.'

And you would know, Ross Barker thought. You're one who would know all about horses, and maybe all about your dead friend, too. But that's no business of mine.

Aloud he said, 'Thank you for your time and patience, Miss Whitcomb. I have no more questions.'

She shook hands with him then, and pulled on her gloves as if she were leaving a tea party, and walked with Lockhart to the door. When he came back the Australian seemed hardly to have moved, so intent was his concentration.

'Well?' Lockhart asked.

'That's a very determined lady,' Barker said.

'She's going to fight it out to the end,' said Lockhart. 'One way or the other she's going to finish it.'

'No question,' Barker said. 'When did her friend die?'

'Tenth November,' Lockhart said. '1918.'

Barker whistled: 'Couldn't be worse,' he said. 'And yet she's still fighting.'

'It's what she knows,' Lockhart said. 'What she's good at.'

'Too right,' said Barker.

'What sort of chance would you give her?'

Barker took his time about it. 'I wonder what the Freudians would make of it?' he said. 'All those horses.'

'I should think that's pretty obvious,' said Lockhart.

'Yes, but the most important horse is a *mare*,' Barker said. 'You know it's interesting. Not just the mare but the whole thing – all that imagery. Because that's all there is. The whole case is just one vast image. When she doesn't dream – she looks balanced enough, wouldn't you say?'

'Lonely,' said Lockhart. 'Frustrated. Lacking employment. Unfulfilled. But essentially sane and – ' He hesitated.

'Go on.'

'Sad,' said Lockhart. 'Heartrendingly sad. She was made the sort of woman who needs the right sort of man, the sort of man who needs her, and for a time she had him and then he was just – smashed down. Carted off. She's a woman to be loved if ever there was one.'

'We're talking about seven years ago,' Barker said. 'There are plenty of young blokes about these days.'

'For her seven years ago is still last week,' Lockhart said. 'If I could make it *feel* like seven years – she'd be cured.'

'I agree,' said Barker.

'So what's your prognosis?'

Barker snorted. 'Prognosis? After one little chat?'

'Look into your crystal ball then.'

Barker said, 'You're very taken with this lady, aren't you?'

'Yes,' said Lockhart. 'I am. Not because I desire her, at least I hope not, although if I were younger I think I would. But it isn't that. She's one of the ones to whom we owe a debt, Ross, and I can't rest till it's paid.'

'Always supposing you can pay it.'

'For God's sake,' said Lockhart. 'Tell me what you think.'

'I think she'll make it,' Barker said. 'In fact I think there's a part of her that's already made up its mind she'll make it. What do you think?'

'The same as you,' said Lockhart. 'But it isn't just what I think – it's what I want. And that terrifies me.'

She went home to find that she'd received a postcard, which meant that probably everybody in the house had read it from Peggy Hawkins upwards. Certainly her mother would have read it. Her mother read every communication she received, however much it had been stuck down or sealed. For her own good, was how Mummy put it, but where the good lay in knowing in advance what her daughter would tell her anyway Jane could never quite work out.

The reading of the postcard annoyed her. She accepted it from Mummy's disdainful fingers (it seemed a foolish way to put it, but somehow they *were* disdainful) and knew that it must be something good and it was, it was something gorgeous, and that was what annoyed her so much. She should have got the good news first. Be careful, she told herself. Be very careful. For this was an invitation to a reunion of ambulance drivers, and this time she knew she could cope with it. But Mummy didn't approve of even one ambulance driver, let alone a whole gaggle of them.

'You'll decline of course,' Mummy said.

'No,' said Jane. 'I don't think I will.'

Mummy flinched then, surprise and outrage blended. As if I'd jabbed her with a pointed stick, thought Jane.

'You'll become excited,' said Mummy. 'That is never good for you. We know that to our cost.'

Jane thought of the parties of three and four years before, the cinemas and theatres and restaurants when all was going well, with a nice young man hovering, then something would set her off: something trivial or even silly: a scrap of a tune, the sound of a man's laughter, even a smoke ring lazily rising – then off she'd go, leaving confusion and consternation behind her, and for her the tears and hasty exits and hours locked in the 'Ladies' while she cried and cried. But that had been before she'd begun to dream of horses, when she didn't know what was wrong. Now she did know, and all she did was scream out loud in the darkness.

'It might be fun,' she said.

'Fun?'

Really Mummy used the word as if it could mean only orgies. But there wouldn't be any men there, only poor old Fred, who, John had explained to her, was a lesbian, but not really all that good at it by the look of her.

'Fun,' Jane said firmly. 'You're always saying that I never see enough people, and these are my friends.'

'Odd friends,' her mother said. 'Odd *women*.' And then she added: 'Rude mechanicals, your brother called them.'

'David used to call them that because he was jealous. We could repair an engine and he couldn't.'

'It sounds most unwomanly,' said her mother. 'Couldn't you have got some man to do it for you?'

'Better to do it yourself,' said Jane. 'Then you know it's done right.'

Her mother ignored this, perhaps didn't hear it.

'David did write to me about all that,' she said. 'I remember now. But are you saying that he met you and your friends?'

'Certainly,' said Jane.

'But where?'

'Behind Wipers,' said Jane. '1917. The offensive had just finished and we were resting. David's squadron was quite nearby and he flew over.'

'Wipers?'

'The Battle of Ypres,' said Jane. 'The Tommies called it Wipers. I didn't think there was so much mud in the whole wide world.'

'And David flew to you?'

The question touched her for once. It was the way Mummy used the word 'flew'. It was to Mummy that the frightened child should fly. And David had been frightened, as well as brave.

'Oh yes,' she said. 'He landed in the field where we parked the ambulances. It was a good landing, good enough for him to be pleased – which didn't happen all that often with David, you remember what a perfectionist he was? – anyway he got out of the plane and he was smiling, and so of course all my friends fell in love with him.'

'He was a very attractive young man,' her mother said. 'So was Guy. So in fact is Francis.'

Better not go into that, thought Jane.

'Francis has left us?'

'For Cambridge,' her mother said. 'He has neglected his work for long enough, he tells me.'

'With Mr Pardoe?'

'I assume so. Your father has decided that we shan't receive him.'

Banished into outer darkness and a good thing too, Jane thought.

Aloud she said, 'His first name is Cuthbert.'

'Do stick to the point,' said her mother, but all the same she was pleased.

'The point is I'm going to this reunion,' said Jane. 'Unless you and Papa object.'

Mummy's pleasure vanished. 'Papa can see no harm in it,' she said. 'He rarely can when you seek some form of self-indulgence.'

'But you can?'

'I have already stated my fears of what harm excitement can induce in you.'

The next fence was a swine, but she had to take it.

'You let me go to the ball,' she said.

'You had Francis to look after you.'

'Does he say that I behaved badly?'

'No,' said her mother. 'He seems to feel that you behaved well enough. But you had his support after all.' Jane waited.

'Oh go if you must,' said her mother. 'But don't come crying to me if it all ends in tears.'

Jane could think of no answer that was neither cringing nor effusive, and the ringing of the telephone bell absolved her of the need to try, until Moreton came in.

'It's for you, Miss Jane,' she said.

Her mother could scarcely credit it. Who, she wondered, could feel the need to speak to her daughter on the instrument? When Moreton told her that it was Mrs Nettles, Lady Whitcomb's annoyance intensified. Mrs Nettles was *her* sister-in-law. She should have asked for Lady Whitcomb first. Moreton's only response was a silence so strongly indicating patient resignation that in the end Lady Whitcomb said no more, and Jane went into the hall and, standing between the two draughts, picked up the telephone.

'Yes, Aunt Pen?' she said.

'What a time you've been,' said her aunt. 'Are you in disgrace because I called you to the instrument?'

'It's more or less my permanent state,' said Jane, then added: 'Are you all right?' Telephone voices were often strange, but Aunt Pen's had sounded quite weird.

'I want to see you,' her aunt said. 'Can you come? Now?'

'Of course,' said Jane.

'It's urgent, Jane. Don't say you'll come if she won't let you.'

'I'll come,' said Jane.

'That's my lovely,' said Aunt Pen. 'When I say now – better make it teatime. There's a man I must see. And Jane darling, I'll need to know how your father is. Have you seen him today?'

'Not yet.'

'Do it, will you? Then come over to Mount Street. In a *taxi*, darling. Aunt Pen will pay.'

'You already have,' said Jane. 'I've got an allowance from you, remember? Thirty bob a week.'

'Goodness how generous I am,' said Aunt Pen, and then: 'Replace the instrument, my lovely. I must go.'

Jane hung up and returned to the drawing room. Foch had appeared and sat with his back to her mother. It was one of the days when he and Lady Whitcomb did not speak.

'Aunt Pen wants to see me,' said Jane.

'Has she a particular reason?'

'There's something wrong,' said Jane. 'I know there is. But she wouldn't say that. Not on the telephone.'

'Is she ill?'

'I think perhaps she is.'

'And did she ask for me?'

'No, Mummy,' said Jane. No one ever asked for Mummy any more, not even Francis.

'No,' her mother said. 'Of course not.' Her fists clenched. 'You'd better be off, hadn't you? To visit the sick and attend your reunions and talk with your nerve specialist. . . . You fade away, don't you, Jane dear? You're so good at it. . . . Like the Cheshire Cat.'

'Why should I do that, Mummy?'

'To leave me alone with your father,' her mother said. 'Darby and Joan. He on his floor and I on mine. I doubt if we exchange fifty words a day.' Her right hand unclenched. It held her handkerchief. 'Go away child,' her mother said, and Jane left at once. She had no wish to watch her mother cry for the second time. Foch felt the same: he came too.

In her bedroom she took out her writing case and fountain pen and replied to her invitation. Harriet had written it. Harriet Ryland she'd been then. Now she was Harriet Watson. Dr Harriet Watson. Nice for her: a husband and a profession. She looked down at Foch.

'I honestly believe that you're the only one here who doesn't know what Harriet wrote,' she said. 'Unless you heard Mummy read it out to Papa.' Foch looked hurt.

Dear Harriet, [Jane wrote]
     Your reunion seems a super idea. Do count me in. It will be marvellous to see the old crowd again. . . .

Will it? she wondered. Or will it be disastrous? But whatever it will be I shall have to go through with it. Then Hawkins came in with clean hand towels.

'I'm sorry, miss,' she said. 'I didn't know you were up here.'

'I'm just going out,' said Jane, 'but I'm glad I saw you. I haven't had a chance to say thank you for helping me up to bed.'

'A pleasure, miss,' Hawkins said.

'Hardly that,' said Jane, and smiled at her. Hawkins smiled back.

'It was a pleasure keeping you out of harm's way, miss,' she said.

'You've done it before I take it?' said Jane. 'Helped the helpless I mean?'

'My dad always gets a bit cheerful if he's had a good win on the horses,' Hawkins said.

'I wasn't exactly cheerful,' said Jane. 'In fact how or why I got like that I simply don't know. I wish I did.'

'You wasn't used to it,' said Hawkins. 'I could tell. And anyway it gets very hot in them dances. Weakens your resistance.'

'I'll bear that in mind,' said Jane, then opened her handbag, took out Aunt Pen's pound note and offered it to Hawkins.

'You don't have to miss,' said Hawkins.

'But I want to,' said Jane. 'I only wish I could make it more. But I can't. Please take it.'

Hawkins took it, and stowed it in the pocket of her apron.

'Thank you miss,' she said. 'It's rotten being hard up, isn't it?'

Then she left Jane to apply a little powder, very cautiously, then go along the corridor to her father's study. He was looking at more photographs, a haphazard pile tipped out at random on the desk. He passed one to her.

'Shikar,' he said. 'Bengal. 1911.'

Two men in pith helmets, armed with rifles that looked as if they could stop tanks. In the background an elephant, kneeling at ease, its mahout asleep in its shade, and in the foreground two dead tigers.

'Billy Smith-Hatton and me,' her father said. 'We were at school together then he came out to work in Lucknow. Legal chappy. Mad on shooting.' He took the photograph back. 'We measured the tigers. Can't think why. It was just something one did. His was a touch bigger than mine. Just as well, really. He'd have sulked for days.'

'Good afternoon, Papa,' said Jane. 'How are you today?'

Sir Guy chuckled. 'Teaching me my manners?' he asked.

'No, of course not,' she said. 'Just wondering how you are.'

'Because I said you could go to your reunion? Not that I would, if I were you. Boring affairs for the most part. I haven't attended one in years.'

'I'll risk that,' said Jane.

'I thought you would,' said her father, and then: 'Don't take any notice of what I've just said. It occurs to me that your reunions are probably the equivalent of what this pile of old junk is to me – ' He gestured at the fading photographs. 'The joy of my life. You go. With my blessing.'

'Papa,' she said, 'have you seen your doctor recently?'

He chuckled again. 'You sounded just like your aunt, then. One of her famous knight's moves in logic, remember? Let me see if I can work out how you got there.'

He groped for his cigarettes, found them, and offered one to her, and she lit them both with his little silver lighter.

'I support you in your struggle for independence, even though it means upsetting your mother,' he said at last. 'This leads you to suspect that I have given up worrying about my health, and the only possible reason for that is that I am a hopeless case. Therefore you ask me whether or not I've seen my doctor. Well?'

She looked at him steadily. It was what he wanted: needed even.

'Pretty good,' she said. 'Flawless, in fact.'

'The answer is that I do allow Mahaffy to call from time to time,' said her father. 'He's an amusing fellow, but it serves no purpose other than sociability. Where are you off to?' The subject it seemed was closed.

'To take tea with Aunt Pen,' she said.

'The incomparable logician. A delightful woman, my sister. Hidden talents, too. Do you know she was once Ladies' Croquet Champion of Uttar Pradesh? I've got a photograph here somewhere – '

He reached for a shoe box, then his hand drew back.

'But why bother,' he said, 'when you can visit the original? Give her my love.'

'Of course, Papa.'

Carefully she stubbed out the cigarette, then kissed him on the cheek.

8

As she walked towards the taxi rank on the High Street, Jane found that she was thinking of Vinney. It must have been Aunt Pen's call, she thought, that and Mummy dredging up memories of *A Midsummer Night's Dream*. Because the rude mechanicals had been Vinney's favourite Shakespearean characters. 'Because they're so endearingly stupid,' she'd explained to Jane. 'So characteristically male.'

Vinney – Miss Vincent on state occasions – had been most uncharacteristically female. She had been her governess, chosen by Aunt Pen, paid for by Uncle Walter, to be governess to Jane, tutor to Guy and David, when they were home from school and needed tutoring. Vinney was one of those rare and gifted beings who could teach anything: quadratic equations, leg-break bowling, anything. It was she who had first persuaded Jane to explore the engine of Uncle Walter's car – to the fury of the chauffeur, until she'd co-opted him as a teacher, too. He'd turned out to be quite a good one.

'The male sex,' Vinney told Jane, 'has its uses.' Always 'the male sex'; never 'men'. For Miss Vincent was a suffragette, committed, resolute, dauntless.

Guy and David had thought this exquisitely funny, though they never laughed in front of her. Few people dared. But for Guy and David there had been more to it than that. Grotesque as the suffragettes had seemed to them, they loved Miss Vincent. For Jane there had never been cause for laughter in Vinney: only love. Vinney did not *look* lovable. She was too big, too competent, and much, much too forthright. She was a former scholar of Somerville College, Oxford, who had missed a first, and therefore a fellowship, by a whisker, and was all too ready to tell people so. But she knew how to teach, and how to offer love – and how to accept it in return.

She had courage, too, Jane remembered, and a wit all her own. In 1912, long after she had left Jane, she had trained a group of young women in the art of artillery so well that they had loaded and fired a cannon captured in the Crimean War, and scored a direct hit on the local Liberal club where Lloyd George was due to speak the next day. No one had been hurt (the cannon was fired at dawn) but the meeting had had to be abandoned. She had even written to Jane to tell her all about it, quite certain that Jane would never betray her, and anxious to reassure her that the male sex were not having things all their own way, not even in Tunbridge Wells.

I have in many ways been lucky, thought Jane. John, of course, always John first, but Guy and David also, and Mummy as she was, and Papa always. And Aunt Pen and Vinney, so disgracefully forgotten, and Lockhart who would not let her give way. . . . Very lucky she had been. But how many of them were alive now? How many would there be in twelve months' time?

She shook her head angrily, and Foch at the end of his lead, sensing the movement, looked up at her.

'And there's you, of course,' she said. 'I hadn't forgotten you, honestly.'

Foch snorted. He knew precisely how unforgettable he was, and preened himself all the way in the cab to Aunt Pen's. When she paid it off she had exactly ninepence ha'penny left.

Tea was good. It always was at Aunt Pen's: cucumber sandwiches and éclairs and Battenburg cake, and all the biscuits that she and Foch and Rob liked most. Jane ate all that she could – Aunt Pen's cook was an artist of extreme sensitivity – and Foch and Rob ate all that they could scrounge. But Aunt Pen ate hardly anything at all, which was strange: her appetite had always impressed her nephews and niece. But this time she nibbled at one biscuit and watched her tea grow cold as Marchmont hovered and Jane told as much as she could of the Poynter ball.

'You must have looked divine,' said Aunt Pen. 'Saris are so lovely.'

But she said the words as if she were reading them, thought Jane. Reading but not quite understanding.

Champagne, said Jane, and 'Love Will Find A Way' and an odd young don called Pardoe. Aunt Pen smiled and nodded, but unconvincingly, as if Jane were delivering a highbrow lecture miles above her head, but she was too polite to say so. And then at last Marchmont left.

Aunt Pen said at once, 'Did you speak to your father?'

'Yes of course,' said Jane.

'And how is he?' Jane hesitated. 'Please tell me,' her aunt said. 'I must know.'

Jane said, 'He believes that he is dying.'

'Snap,' said Aunt Pen.

Jane had been ready for that, or something like it, and yet even so was horrified. For her to have bad dreams was one thing: but for Aunt Pen, glowing and gorgeous in her elegant and resolutely out-of-date tea gown to announce her own death: it wasn't possible.

'But surely – ' she began.

'You think I may be imagining things?'

'Of course not. But – '

'Listen, my lovely. If someone tells you you're going to die, you don't just take their word for it. You ask another expert, and another and another – and hope you'll finish up with one who thinks you might live after all.

'Well now I've tried five. You remember I said I had to see a man this afternoon? He was the fifth one. He left half an hour before you got here – and he's as big a hanging judge as the rest of them. He was very sorry, he said. But he still took my ten guineas.'

'But what's wrong?' Jane asked.

'Cancer,' said her aunt. 'Of the *most* unflattering kind. Breasts and things. I'd be no price at all in the Judgement of Paris Stakes now.'

'But can't they operate?'

'If I let them,' said her aunt. 'But I won't.'

'Darling, why not?'

'He did give me the odds on that. A one-in-seven chance of success he said. Radium and dressings and all the time being sick and then dying anyway. . . . And even if I lived I'd hate

– 88 –

myself. My body, I mean. Or what was left of it. I know you young things are all for the boyish look – but I can't see any of you going that far.'

Jane got up then, went to where her aunt lay on a sofa, and embraced her. 'I love you,' she said. 'I always have. Since first I knew you. Uncle Walter, too. I loved you both. And so did Guy. And David.'

'The nicest thing about India,' said Aunt Pen. 'If it hadn't kept your father and Honoria there, we'd never have had you to love.'

'And now you're leaving me?'

'Like David? Like young Guy, you mean?'

'They had no chance,' said Jane. 'But even one in seven. I mean he could be wrong – '

'No,' said her aunt. 'The cancer's been kind to me so far. Dormant, Judge Jeffries called it. But soon it won't be.'

'What then?'

Her aunt shrugged. 'Narcotics,' she said. 'Stronger and stronger. Judge Jeffries does *not* approve.'

'Then how will you manage?'

'There's a man in Geneva who is more than willing to oblige me. . . . I shall be an addict, darling. What would your mother say?'

Jane's arms tightened round her and she rocked her aunt like a child. But Aunt Pen didn't cry. Not then. Not ever. Not for herself.

'Tell me about Guy,' she said.

'He's started doing what *he* wants,' said Jane.

'Defying Honoria, you mean. So that's how you know he's dying? What a macabre family we are. . . . Did he tell you he was dying?'

'He wasn't quite so forthright as you.'

Her aunt smiled. 'He was always the nicest man,' she said.

'We were talking about you,' Jane said. 'He told me you won a croquet championship somewhere. United Provinces, was it?'

'Yes,' her aunt said. 'And it's perfectly true. I did win it. Thanks to your father.'

'What did he do?'

'He showed me how to cheat,' said her aunt.

'The nicest man,' Jane mocked.

'Well so he was,' said her aunt. 'He knew I was dying to win. Dying. . . . What a stupid thing to say. . . . Has he got long?'

'He didn't tell me,' said Jane. 'If he had he wouldn't have dropped as much as a hint.'

'Poor Honoria,' her aunt said, and then: 'Posy Sanderson. Did he by any chance mention that name?'

'He showed me her photograph,' said Jane.

'Oh my poor sweet Guy,' said Aunt Pen, and that time, for her brother, she did weep.

Another of her famous knight's moves, thought Jane. Because Papa showed me the photograph, she knows he hasn't long to go. . . . Any more than she has. . . . How cosy Mummy and I will be together.

'It's all arranged, – going to Geneva, I mean,' Aunt Pen said. 'Or it will be quite soon.'

'You've spoken to your lawyer?'

'Not yet,' said her aunt. 'Though I'll have to of course.'

'Then – forgive me, aunt – but who's arranged it?'

'Why Marchmont,' said Aunt Pen. 'Butlers always arrange everything. He's going to marry Sophie.'

'Your maid?'

'The very same. One doesn't have to have one's hair done to be a dope fiend. He and the rest of them are going to buy a hotel in Hove. . . . I do hope Marchmont remains faithful, with all those housemaids in his power. So often butlers turn out to be positive pashas.'

'Do they indeed?'

'Sexual adventure has a great deal to do with opportunity. Haven't you noticed that?'

She has every right to an answer, Jane thought, and spoke at once.

'Opportunity is important,' she said. 'At least I found it so – but in my experience, my very limited experience, once the need is felt, the opportunity can be made.'

'Thank you for telling me, my lovely,' said her aunt. 'Somehow it was important to know.'

Jane said firmly, 'Talking of the male sex, I found myself thinking about Vinney today.'

Her aunt turned in Jane's arms to face her. 'What about her?'

she said, then began to laugh. 'Oh, darling, if you could see yourself. The picture of consternation. But there's no need to look so troubled. She isn't dead.'

'Where is she then?'

'In Delhi. Running a school for orphans. It was an ambition she had. . . . In almost anybody else one might have called it a vision. But Vinney didn't see visions. Only wrongs that must be set to rights. She came to see me, and told me exactly how much I must give her to help get the orphanage started. She was very nice about it.'

'She didn't come to see me,' said Jane.

'You haven't got any money,' her aunt said, and then – 'Don't let it distress you. Please don't. Vinney has no time to spare. Not even for love. So she opted for compassion instead. That means she sees only the very rich or the very poor. The middle classes are out.'

'I would have helped her,' said Jane.

'She doesn't need help. She needs money. And anyway – '

'Well?'

'She's fond of you. A lot of people are. But she can't afford to be near people she's fond of. They'd just get in the way.'

'Of the orphans?' Her aunt nodded. 'Girl orphans?'

'Whenever possible,' said her aunt. 'You don't approve?'

'Of course I do,' said Jane. 'In India an orphan girl needs every chance she can get. I hope you gave her a lot of money.'

'Yes,' her aunt said. 'I did. And speaking of money – how is your allowance holding out?'

'It isn't,' said Jane. 'I had to tip our housemaid a quid.'

'Rather a lot for a housemaid.'

'She did rather a lot for me.'

Her aunt nodded. 'Sounds like a story.'

'Oh it is,' said Jane, 'but – '

'But what?'

'Aren't you feeling tired?'

'No,' her aunt said. 'I don't think I shall ever feel tired again – until the pain comes. But let's get rid of this money nonsense first. How much have you got left?'

'Ninepence ha'penny,' said Jane.

Her aunt chuckled. 'You won't get fat on that. Unless – '

'Yes, aunt?'

'You could do me a favour,' her aunt said. 'Make yourself some money too.'

'Of course,' said Jane. 'What?'

'You could come here and stay with me. Until the pain comes I mean and I have to go away. I know I asked you once before –'

'And you were ill then, weren't you? But you didn't tell me.'

'I was still waiting to see Judge Jeffries,' said her aunt. 'But now we both know – what do you say?'

'I'd be glad to,' said Jane. 'That is – if Papa doesn't need me at home.'

'Let me talk to him on the instrument,' said Aunt Pen. 'I'm sure he won't mind sharing.'

'No. I'll do that,' said Jane. 'But I think I ought to tell Mummy first.'

'But you will telephone, won't you?' said Aunt Pen. 'And stay the night?'

'I haven't got any things,' said Jane.

'I have,' said her aunt. 'I'll set Sophie to find some that aren't too impossibly old.'

While she did so, Jane went to the telephone, which was in a sort of cloakroom in the hall, and enviably free from draughts. Aunt Pen, she told her mother, was not well, and had requested her company for the night. Her mother declared that the scheme was unthinkable and Jane said she must stay or else Aunt Pen would be left on her own.

'On her own?' her mother cried. 'The woman has seventeen servants.'

A slight exaggeration, thought Jane, but even so Mummy had a point.

'And what is wrong with her anyway?' her mother asked.

Jane lied without hesitation. A combination of Mummy and the instrument were not the means by which to break Aunt Pen's news to her father.

'That's why Aunt Pen wants me to stay,' she said. 'So that she can tell me about it.'

'It must be a most extraordinarily complicated affliction,' said her mother, 'if it's going to take all night to describe the symptoms.'

On the contrary, thought Jane, it's most fiendishly simple.

'Aunt Pen hasn't said so,' she said aloud, 'but I think she's a little nervous.'

'Then perhaps you had better stay with her,' said her mother, and went on to ruin the effect by adding, 'she always was a bit of a cry-baby.'

Jane said, 'Is Papa there?'

'Papa is extremely busy,' Mummy said. 'Upstairs. With his photographs.'

'Tell him I'll give him a full report tomorrow.'

'Very well.'

'Shall I give Aunt Pen your love?'

'Naturally,' her mother said, and hung up.

That evening they talked again of Vinney, and in particular of a day that Jane had forgotten, though not Aunt Pen.

'It was the summer that Walter rented that place in West Sussex,' she said. 'At one time he'd thought of buying it, but in the end I talked him out of it. West Sussex is too far from London, never mind Paris. – Marchmont was furious, I remember.'

'What on earth did it have to do with Marchmont?'

Aunt Pen glanced, rather furtively Jane thought, at the drawing-room door. It was shut. 'All good butlers are feudal at heart,' she said. 'And how can you be feudal without an estate? Walter had to raise his salary to make him stay on. Anyway it was a quite heavenly summer. 1907 would it be? 1908? You and I went to Paris in May, I remember. Vinney was furious because she'd spent so much time on teaching you to speak French properly, and she knew once we were away together we'd talk nothing but English.'

'I do remember,' said Jane. 'You bought me a blue velvet dress. . . . Didn't you have it made?'

'Of course,' said her aunt. 'It was very becoming.'

'It was for my fourteenth birthday,' Jane said. 'I adored that dress. . . . I wore it to the opera, didn't I?'

'*The Pearl Fishers*,' said her aunt. 'De Peszke was not in form. He made my teeth ache. . . . But we were talking about Vinney.'

'In West Sussex. The house was called Five Oaks, wasn't it?'

'You do remember. And there was a piece of grass miles from anywhere. Not the lawn – that was immaculate. This was just a great lump behind some cedars that somebody had decided would do for tennis courts and then hadn't bothered.'

'And then Guy and David decided it would do for cricket. For practice anyway. They used to bribe the second gardener's children to field for them. And then one day the fielders didn't turn up.'

'It was a Sunday,' said Jane, 'and the under-gardener was a Baptist.'

'You and Walter and I went for a walk and found them,' said Aunt Pen. 'And of course they had us fielding in no time at all.'

'They shouldn't have been practising and we shouldn't have been playing,' said Jane. 'It was a Sunday.'

'Guy and David had more than their fair share of chums,' said Aunt Pen. 'Like their sister. . . . It was just their bad luck that we had Walter with us.'

'He wanted to bat?' Jane asked.

'He *did* bat,' said Aunt Pen. 'It was part of the bargain he made – and Walter was very good at bargains. He had to be, being a box-wallah. Anyway he batted and Guy and David bowled, and they couldn't get him out, and being Walter he couldn't pretend to make a mistake and put himself out on purpose. No Yorkshireman could. So there he stuck and he wouldn't give way and neither would the boys – and then Vinney came looking for us.'

'She wanted to take me to Evensong because I'd missed Morning Prayers,' said Jane.

'Only she stopped to bowl at Walter instead,' said Aunt Pen. 'She got him in her second over.'

'It must have been a leg-break,' said Jane. 'She was awfully good at leg-breaks. Anyway I missed Evensong.'

'It's funny,' said Aunt Pen. 'Odd funny I mean. We were all so happy that afternoon but I can't remember any of us smiling – Vinney least of all. Not even when she bowled Walter. I suppose it's because cricket's sort of our second religion.'

Jane thought of the maharajah of Balpur and her father's rage.

'Oh it's much more important than that,' she said. 'One might miss Evensong, but one couldn't miss the Eton and Harrow match – not without a decent excuse.'

'You're a clever girl, my lovely, and Vinney would be proud of you,' said her aunt, 'but we *were* happy, weren't we?'

'I was,' said Jane, 'and I'm pretty sure that David and Guy were too, but that was because we were young and healthy, and quite adequately clever, and Aunt Pen and Uncle Walter were always there when they were wanted.'

'It was our – privilege, I suppose is the word I want,' said Aunt Pen. 'Or perhaps our good fortune. We were here, and Guy and Honoria weren't. Not their fault. We tried not to – '

'Take their place?' said Jane. 'You never did. You always had a special place of your own. So often – children like us – sent home to escape the heat – were just farmed out, housed on sufferance. Their lives were misery. Ours were magic, and we blessed you both for it when we remembered – which wasn't nearly often enough.'

Her aunt looked up at the clock on the mantelshelf.

'I hope it's nearly dinnertime,' she said. 'I'm rather hungry.'

After dinner they talked more of childhood, and Vinney's ability to insert knowledge into even the most reluctant head.

'And you never regretted not going to school?' her aunt asked. 'After all, your brothers – '

'They had no choice,' said Jane. 'One could almost say it was their fate – their karma if you like. But it was also what they wanted.'

'Did they?'

'Of course they did,' said Jane. 'It was what they were good at. Greek, Latin, cricket, football. Whatever they touched. . . . The shining ones.'

'The ones the gods loved,' said her aunt. 'Is that why they died so young?'

'Not too young to have known happiness,' said Jane. 'Every kind of happiness – like seeing their sister's governess clean bowl their uncle by marriage.'

'If they'd lived – ' her aunt began.

'If they'd lived they'd be here now, with you, just as I am.'

'And Honoria wouldn't hate either of us,' said Aunt Pen. 'Would you help me up, darling? Reliving one's life is quite exhausting.'

9

JANE WALKED UPSTAIRS with her aunt, and handed her over to Sophie. In her own room a small fire burned, despite the early summer, and on her bed were the night clothes Sophie had chosen: clothes her aunt must have long outlived: a negligée of quite outrageous frivolity, and a silk nightgown that Mummy would have condemned out of hand. Lucky Uncle Walter. She undressed and put on both, then sat in front of the fire and smoked a cigarette from the box on the bedside table.

It had been a happy evening, she did not doubt that, and yet it had been an evening devoted to death. None of the dead were perfect – how could they be? They were mortal or they would not have died – but there had been goodness in them, all three, a goodness that transcended their silly game, and yet somehow the game had captured the essence of all three of them, as it had of Papa when he raged about the maharajah.

They had been good people, but now they were gone, just as Papa would soon be gone, and Aunt Pen too, and she, Jane Whitcomb, still hadn't the faintest idea what she would do: what her mind would allow her to do, except that, like Aunt Pen, she would never cry out of pity for herself. Once she did that she really would go mad. . . . There had been a piece of prose that Vinney had been fond of: that she had made Jane learn by heart, and now it came back to her: 'O eloquent, just and mighty Death! whom none could advise thou hast persuaded: what none hath dared, thou hast done; and whom all the world hath flattered, thou only hast cast out of the world and despised. . . .'

She could hear Vinney's voice quite clearly. 'Sir Walter Raleigh wrote that, child. It's from his *History of the World*. He wrote it when he was imprisoned in the Tower, and had no hope of coming out. Not then. What courage he had. What style!'

'What praise for a member of the male sex,' Jane had teased.

'Male sex be damned,' Vinney had said. 'This was a *man*! There aren't too many of them, but he was one. You can jolly well learn it off by heart to remind yourself of that fact.'

So death was just, as well as mighty, Sir Walter claimed. That would take some thinking about. Had he been just to the soldiers in the war? That he'd been mighty was beyond dispute. . . . She woke up with a start. A coal in the fire had popped, and the smoke from her dying cigarette rose up like incense. It was time to go to bed. If she were going to have nightmares she might as well have them in comfort.

The mattress was firm, unlike the feather thing at home, and yet relaxing. Once, only once, she and John had shared a bed like that, when they went to Paris, and a room at the Ritz had absorbed their entire supply of spare cash. But it had been worth every penny: a night to remember. John had loved her quite beautifully. Maybe that was because the war was farther away. You couldn't even hear it except for the odd times when the Huns had used that incredible gun of theirs, the one called Big Bertha, to shell the city. Never more than a few rounds – even German technology wasn't up to a sustained bombardment – and it had been fun to watch the righteous indignation of civilians when they discovered that they too could be shelled. So John had laughed, and laughing had relaxed, and relaxing, loved her. The feel of his body had been wonderful, and hers enfolding his, until at last there had been neither his body nor her body, but theirs conjoined in one. And it had all been so wonderful she had yelled out loud.

Come come, she admonished herself. This won't do. You are guilty of what that incredible Girl Guide mistress used to call impure thoughts. (What Vinney had called them, apart from a bloody nuisance, she couldn't remember. They were just one more on the unending list of crimes the male sex would have to answer for on Judgement Day.) But she had called out aloud. She couldn't remember it, but John had told her so, looking smug. What on earth could I have shouted, she wondered. Howzat?

Another coal popped as the fire died. . . . Sometimes a nervous sentry, alone and vulnerable on the firestep, would imagine something moving, out in the angry dark, and loose off a shot without thinking. She'd heard it herself at a forward dressing station. . . . And then, John said, a sergeant or platoon commander would come running, swearing his questions to show how brave he was. And sometimes it would be nothing except a boy's need for his mother, or a man's for a wife deep breathing in a warm bed, and life, not death to look forward to. But sometimes it might be a raid, and the soldiers would come running from the sand-bagged shelters they called dug-outs, clattering along the duckboards to push back the Huns. Verey lights and machine guns and rifle fire, Stokes mortars and grenades. Or maybe Fritz got closer still and into the trenches, and then it would be rifle butts, bayonets, revolvers. John despised the British Army issue revolver for officers. It never hit what you aimed at. He'd bought a German Luger automatic from an Australian, instead. At least with that you had a chance. – Until 10th November, 1918. . . . The fire glimmered then died, like star shells falling.

And then it was daylight, and a bright and beautiful sun, and a much smarter maid than Hawkins, or even Moreton, brought her tea and biscuits, and Foch, who had spent the night in a kennel in the garden with Rob, ambled in and demanded his share.

'Good morning,' said Jane. 'I hope you slept well.'

Foch's tail twitched. Well enough, it seemed.

'I had a quite remarkable night,' said Jane. 'To begin with I am absolutely certain that I didn't scream, and I think you will agree with me that that in itself is remarkable.'

Foch waited for another biscuit, realised that he wasn't going to get one, and settled down to listen.

'And then I have no recollection of dreaming,' Jane said. 'I've no doubt I *did* dream, one of those sweaty fathoms-deep affairs Jabber talks about, but I don't *remember* it. And that's got to be a good thing, surely?'

Foch yawned.

'All very well for you,' said Jane. 'I expect all you ever dream about is rabbits, and the next Madame Foch – if I may so express it?'

Foch yawned again.

'I'm boring you, aren't I?' said Jane. 'You always get my problems. I know Mrs Blythe-Tarkington said I should talk to you – indeed she told us both, but dash it all Foch, there are limits.' Then almost shyly she added, 'What I mean is people might think that one or other of us was going crazy.'

She got up and stretched, and Foch, a diehard Presbyterian, averted his eyes.

'Breakfast first,' she said. 'Something nourishing for a change. And then we must go and see Papa. – Mummy too, of course.'

But it was Papa they saw. After a breakfast of devilled bones and kedgeree and toast and marmalade, it was late in the morning when Jane got back to Kensington. Papa was upstairs with his photographs, but Mummy was not at home. It was a second Thursday, Jane remembered, and every second Thursday Mummy took lunch with her old chum Miss Gwatkin, who speculated on the morals of the curate, who had, so it was said, been seen to one-step.

'Have a good evening?' her father asked.

'Yes,' said Jane. 'I did as a matter of fact.'

'You sound surprised.'

'I am surprised. . . . Aunt Pen isn't well, Papa. In fact she's very ill.'

'I thought she might be,' her father said. 'Pen's always been furtive about bad news. What's wrong with her?'

'Cancer.'

Her father nodded, then very deliberately began to put away the photographs that lay on the desk before him, and took a cigarette.

'Help yourself,' he said, and Jane lit up for them both with his little silver lighter.

'She'll have seen the best men?'

'Yes, Papa.'

'Of course. With her money she'd be a fool not to. Will they operate?'

'She won't let them.'

'I see,' her father said.

'Do you?'

'Oh I think so. If she won't let them operate she thinks there's no chance. And my sister was never a fool.'

'She wants me to stay with her for a while, and I think I should. It isn't as if I'd be far away – '

'Of course,' her father said, and then: 'I want to see her.'

'She wants that too.'

'And your mother?' Jane was silent. 'She ought to see your mother,' her father said. 'For your sake.'

'Because Aunt Pen had me with her as a child and Mummy didn't?'

'It's a debt,' said her father. 'Pen will want to pay it. Tell me about her.'

And Jane told him, almost everything, because now that Papa was dying he was strong again.

'Drugging herself like that,' he said. 'Do you think that what she's doing is right?'

Jane thought of Penelope Nettles: witty and graceful and charming: most feminine of ladies.

'Oh yes,' she said.

Her father grunted. 'You'll have a hard time persuading your mother,' he said.

'Mummy would have chosen the operation?'

'Certainly she would,' said her father. 'She is not to be despised for that.'

'Of course not,' said Jane. 'She's to be admired. Perhaps feared.'

'Did you tell your aunt about me?'

'She asked,' said Jane, 'and I told her. And she wept.'

'It'll give us something to think about,' said her father. 'Wondering which of us will die first. An extra pinch of chilli in the curry.'

'You're not being very kind, Papa.'

He looked up at her then, and his face looked puzzled.

'No I suppose I wasn't,' he said at last, 'but dying makes one selfish I'm afraid. You'll have to allow for that.'

Carefully he shuffled together the photographs before him and returned them to their shoe box.

'Better start packing up,' he said. 'You know dying's rather like one's last school hols. I mean when one has finished sixth form and one doesn't know whether the university will accept one or not. All the same – everything must be left tidy.' He put the box back with its fellows. 'Not that there'll be a devil of a lot to leave.'

'Don't worry, Papa.'

'I'll try not to, because I'm a lazy feller. Always was. All the same I *shall* worry – because you're my daughter and I love you. Maybe Pen will help you.'

'She's done enough already,' said Jane.

'I wonder if she thinks so?'

'Papa you mustn't ask her. Promise me.'

He looked into her face, troubled, sad, and yet somehow the face of a much younger Jane.

'Promise, Papa.'

'Oh very well,' he said. 'You have my word I won't ask.' Then he rose to his feet. 'Do you wish to titivate at all before lunch?'

'Just a bit.'

'Then I shall go down to the cellar,' he said, and snorted. 'Cellar indeed. A cupboard with delusions of grandeur.'

He came up with Bollinger, and the toast was 'Confusion to Cuthbert', but nothing more was said of Pardoe, to Jane's relief. The food was good: far beyond the average, as, Jane remembered, it usually was on second Thursdays, when cook's decisions were her own. Papa ate heartily, almost greedily, and Jane did her best to match his enthusiasm. After lunch they went back to his study, and there Moreton brought up coffee, and they sat and smoked and gossiped and remembered. Especially Papa remembered ayah.

'She loved you, you know,' he said. 'You're lucky. So many people have loved you.'

You don't even know about the one who loved me best, she thought, and I can't bring myself to tell you, even now, and it may be my last chance.

'She took you to a saddhu,' Papa was saying. 'Got herself all excited, I remember. Came and told me all about it. Great things awaited you, the saddhu said. Called you a leopardess.' He smiled. 'Naturally we thought it was all mumbo-jumbo. You were pretty and clever and by God you could ride. But great things – '

'Maybe he meant the war,' she said.

'It was great enough, God knows,' her father agreed. 'But your part in it was not. Honourable and courageous, certainly. But modest, rather than great.'

'Then the saddhu was wrong.'

'I used to think so,' said her father. 'But now I'm not so sure. Great things. God knows you're clever enough – and capable. Far and away the most practical of the four. You get it from your mother.' This time her face showed dismay. He said gently, 'We're agreed, are we not, that the war hit her hard?'

'Yes, Papa. And you.'

'But you forget – I told you I was a lazy feller. Your mother is never lazy.' He smothered a yawn. 'There you see. . . . I'm drowsy now, and all I did was eat lunch.' He spoke in Hindi: 'Forgive me, little daughter, but I must rest.'

In Hindi she replied, 'I wish my father a refreshing sleep.'

She was almost asleep herself when her mother returned, yawning over the *Illustrated London News*, while Foch fumed and fretted, impatient for exercise.

'Miss Gwatkin is well, and enquired after you most kindly,' her mother said.

Gravely Jane replied, 'I hope you conveyed my best wishes to her.'

'Of course,' said her mother. 'You gave mine to your aunt, I assume.' Without hypocrisy, how could civilised communication survive? 'You have news of your aunt?'

'I'm afraid,' said Jane, 'that she's dying.'

'Impossible,' said Lady Whitcomb, then: 'No of course it's not impossible. – It's just that if anyone seemed to me to be indestructible it was Penelope Nettles. You had better tell me all you know.'

Jane told her, and when she had done her mother said, 'So she is determined to avoid pain, come what may?'

'Whether she avoids it or accepts it,' Jane said, 'she is convinced the end will be death, and so she has chosen to avoid it.'

'You don't find her decision cowardly?'

'How can I judge unless I feel her pain?'

Her mother said, 'That is a very shrewd answer, and a charitable one. All the same, one cannot help thinking that your aunt may in a sense have opted for suicide – a most unchristian decision.'

Jane said nothing.

'Even so I shall pray for her,' Lady Whitcomb said. 'You have informed your papa?' Jane nodded. 'Tactfully, I trust?'

'I did my best.'

'And he?'

'He's resting now,' said Jane, 'but we ate a good lunch. We drank champagne.'

'Indeed?'

'It was to celebrate the absence of Mr Pardoe.'

'There is a whimsical streak in your father which he appears to have passed on to you,' said Lady Whitcomb. 'Genes do they call them? I can never remember.'

'He wants to see Aunt Pen,' said Jane.

'And I am also to have that privilege?'

'Of course.'

Baulked of one source of combat, Lady Whitcomb at once found another. 'And you are determined to go on staying with her?'

'So long as I'm needed.'

'You are needed here,' her mother said.

'Papa says not.'

'After you made him tipsy with champagne, no doubt. . . . I am of course powerless to prevent this act, selfish though it is, and I can only hope that you will have no cause to regret it.'

She had packed a case to take over to Aunt Pen's, but Jackson, Aunt Pen's chauffeur, would take care of that. She could walk in Kensington Gardens with Foch, and think. And what she had to think about was Sir Walter Raleigh: 'whom none could advise, thou hast persuaded'. Very well. One could accept that. Death couldn't help being persuasive. Death was machine guns against fuzzy-wuzzys. He just mowed everybody down. After all he was *Death*. He held all the cards. No wonder he was persuasive.

And Death was mighty, all right. She'd already thought about that and it was true. She'd seen for herself. Seen what he did. Yes indeed Death was mighty. She'd carried enough of his samples in her ambulance to know just how true that was. But *just*? That was the one that had to be worked out, chewed over, the way Foch when a puppy had chewed at the corner of a rug Mummy had detested, which was why she still had Foch.

Raleigh had died on the scaffold. She remembered that now. He'd died the way Vinney had said he'd lived, like a man – even though the executioner had been nervous, taken two swipes, threatened the dignity of a brave man's death. But Raleigh's manhood had withstood even that. It was a standard too high for all but a tiny few. Aunt Pen, for instance. Maybe Mummy was right, and her aunt was embarking on a form of slow suicide. But even so, God might forgive her – let her win on a technicality so to speak. If she understood Raleigh correctly, Death certainly would, because Death came to everyone in time. It was in that fact that Death was just. He spared no one. Whether one died in agony, or in one's sleep all unaware, was no concern of his. . . .

Foch was confronting a Great Dane, rather as the poet had confronted what was left of Ozymandias. Foch had no thought of combat; Jane doubted whether he realised that he and the Great Dane belonged to the same species. 'Round that colossal wreck,' he seemed to be thinking. But the Great Dane might not see it that way. Jane hastened to intervene, and arrived at the same time as the Great Dane's companion. It was Dr Barker.

'Miss Whitcomb,' he said. 'Gooday. Is that your dog?'

'Yes,' she said. 'But he isn't quite so foolhardy as he may have seemed.'

'Brave little Belgium defying the Hun? But Horatio here isn't a Hun. The Danes were neutral.'

'Wise Danes. . . . What brings you here, Doctor?'

'The need for exercise. He belongs to my landlady and takes me out for a run occasionally. And you?'

'I can't think unless I walk. Foch is my excuse for thinking.'

'And how are you? Forgive me. As a consultation I realise that this is a little impromptu, but I have to go back to Australia shortly, and I should like to know – '

'I am better than I was,' she told him, 'but I could wish that others were the same.'

'You've had bad news?'

'Bad enough. Soon it will be worse.'

'You'll hold on.'

'You sound so certain.'

'How could you bear to undo all Jabber's good work?'

'You can always tell a psychoanalyst,' she said. 'They're the ones who never fight fair.' Then she whistled for Foch, but the wretched animal had decided to stand directly underneath the Great Dane as if sheltering from the rain. For some reason he found this amusing, and didn't want to come.

'That dog means a lot to you?' Dr Barker said.

'He means everything. . . . No. Not quite. There are still a few bipeds left I quite like – but Foch is – special.'

'Don't like him any less than you do,' said Dr Barker. 'But try to love the bipeds more.'

The Great Dane moved off then, exposing Foch to the summer sun. He disliked it, and joined her in the shade.

'You're ready to go?' Jane asked him, and he snorted assent. She turned to the doctor. 'It's a pity you're leaving us,' she said. 'You'd have enjoyed a chat with Foch. He's a psychoanalyst too. Perhaps rather more intuitive than most.'

They moved on, and after a while she looked down at the sturdy, small black shape beside her.

'There's no need to snigger,' she said. 'I was rude to the poor man. There was no *reason* to be rude. It's because he was right, of course. – Except he said "like" when he meant "love". But how can one measure out love? A quarter pound here, a half pound there, when you need a ton.'

10

I T WAS NEVER dull at Aunt Pen's, partly because Aunt Pen refused – had always refused – to consider dullness as a way of life, and partly because she decided that now, this very day, was the time to do what she and Uncle Walter had always promised themselves, and spoil her niece. Any protest on Jane's part was met with the charge that she was refusing to comfort the last hours of a dying woman. . . . Being spoiled it had to be.

Being spoiled meant dresses by Chanel and Molyneux, and hats from little shops in Mayfair, and hand-made gloves, and all one's stockings made of silk. Because time was short, it also meant flying in a specially hired plane from Croydon to Paris for fittings at Chanel's, and a room at the Ritz for an overnight stop. It meant boxes and stalls for the plays and operas they both liked, and the Russian ballet, where the Bakst sets sent them out to do even more shopping. It meant Cartier and Boucheron and a Riley two-seater.

But it meant more than that. It meant being involved with someone in a way that brought back the memories but not the pain: Guy and David and Vinney and Papa – and Mummy as she once had been, and even John. Aunt Pen dying brought back even the dead, and made their memory sweet. The money helped – of course it did – and she revelled in it, but no money could buy the love that Aunt Pen lavished on her, the knight's move logic, and the feeling that in spite of all the scarves and brooches and shoes, she had to stay and be spoiled, not only because Aunt Pen needed her and her love, but because she,

Jane Whitcomb, needed the need. It was there inside her, a great well of giving, and now once more she had found a taker that she loved. And again it would not be for long.

One accepted that, as one accepted the onset of her aunt's pain, variable still; as one accepted Papa's visit, and even Mummy's. Papa had been clever about that, and chosen a Second Thursday, which meant that there were three for lunch, and four for tea. They had every single dish Pen remembered Papa enjoying, and Bollinger because Jane had told Aunt Pen just enough about Mr Pardoe, and Château Leoville Barton because it was Papa's favourite claret. It was a noisy, happy lunch, and much of the talk was in Hindi. When it ended Papa declined port, and asked for brandy instead. His new doctor, he said, thought highly of brandy as a stimulant in cases like his.

'What a wonderful doctor,' said Aunt Pen. 'My dear you *must* stay with him.'

'Of course,' said Papa. 'Till the end.'

And the two of them smiled at each other like conspirators.

When the brandy came Papa cupped the goblet, sniffed and said 'Aah!' then raised the glass.

'You have a little wine left,' he said. 'I think I should propose a toast.'

'To your doctor?' asked Jane.

'To your brother,' her father said. 'He was good enough to telephone me this morning. He took a first, it seems. His college has offered him a junior fellowship. . . . To Francis.'

'Francis,' Aunt Pen and Jane echoed, and sipped, as Papa added: 'However there *is* news of a doctor. Cuthbert Pardoe has taken a PhD and is now *Dr* Pardoe. Shall we drink to that?'

'Certainly not,' said Aunt Pen.

'I quite agree,' said Jane.

'But we must talk, you and I,' Aunt Pen told Papa, and then to Jane: 'And in private too. . . . Boring stuff. Walter's study will be the best place. Your father can smoke a cigar there. We'll try not to be too long, my lovely.'

She sat in the drawing room between Foch and Rob, and read the *Morning Post* and listened to them sleep. And then her mother arrived, shown in by Marchmont. Mummy was not best pleased to be received by her daughter.

'Miss Gwatkin is well and sends you her best wishes,' she said.

'I have no doubt you gave her mine,' said Jane.

Really she thought, it's like chanting the responses in church. Rob and Foch rose, lay in a pool of sunshine by the window, and went back to sleep.

'You have become very fine,' her mother said.

Jane looked down at herself. Today's dress was of peacock blue silk, and designed by Erté. With it she wore a sapphire brooch from Asprey. It had not been her idea: knowing her mother was coming, she had suggested something in grey and with much longer skirts. But her aunt had been firm.

'Your father and I have to look at you too. So let's see something worth looking at.'

'A gift from Aunt Pen,' said Jane.

'I had not supposed you had purchased it out of your pin money. In fact I would have been happier if you had not purchased it at all.'

.'You find it revealing?'

'I find it vulgar.'

Before she could stop herself, Jane laughed.

'I have amused you?' her mother asked.

Nothing for it, but to soldier on regardless.

'Really Mummy,' said Jane, 'you could call this dress a lot of things: revealing, immodest, shameless, lascivious. . . . But not vulgar. It's by Erté. He has enormous talent.'

Disconcertingly her mother considered the statement on its merits, as she sometimes did.

'You are quite right,' she said. 'Your dress is superbly designed, exquisitely made, and quite indecent.'

'That's better,' said Jane.

'You have also become pert,' said her mother. 'Penelope Nettles's company is not good for you. And please do not remind me that she's dying. That is no excuse.'

'It's the only one she has,' said Jane.

Her mother ignored it. 'Are you – what is the expression – on the catch for some man?'

'Really Mummy,' said Jane. 'I'm thirty-two years old.'

'But you are quite healthy – apart from your nerves. . . . Well?'

'Not *some* man,' said Jane, 'in the sense of any particular man. But one appropriately qualified might be worth considering.'

Her mother snorted. She sounded not unlike Foch, Jane thought, though both of them would be appalled if I were to say so.

'Your nerves then are better, I take it?'

'For the moment.'

'Cured by kindness?'

'I am not in the least sure I *am* cured,' said Jane.

'You will be,' said her mother. 'Once you become rich, and the kind of young man you so aptly describe as appropriate makes his appearance, your nervous problems will vanish – though mine may not.'

So there it was, and it had to be faced now, this minute, before fear and rage and grief took over.

'I'd no idea that I was to become rich,' she said.

'Don't be naive, child,' said her mother. 'Walter Nettles was unpolished, plebeian even, but he had an enormous talent for making money. Penelope has no children. Where do you suppose her money will go?'

'To Papa, of course.'

'That would be foolish. – And your aunt, despite a great deal of evidence to the contrary, is not a fool. Why cause two sets of death duties to be paid in such rapid succession?'

Here was realism indeed: Papa reduced to no more than additional death duties on his sister's estate.

'It is far more likely,' said her mother, 'that she will leave the bulk of her possessions to her brother's children.'

'To Francis and myself in fact?'

'To the best of my knowledge you are the only ones,' her mother said, and Jane thought of Posy Sanderson as her mother continued: 'Your brother, of course, being the male, will no doubt receive the larger share, but even the smaller part should prove enough to attract an "appropriate" man.'

'You are on the warpath today,' said Jane.

'I called it pertness,' said her mother. 'Insolence might be more appropriate. But if you are hinting that I am displeased, I can only agree with you.'

'You haven't fallen out with Miss Gwatkin?'

'Certainly not,' said her mother. 'One does not – fall out –

with so trusted and valued a friend. Nevertheless it's true that I feel the need – '

She paused, and Jane, remembering the last Owen Nares matinée that she and Aunt Pen had attended, tried to be helpful.

'To be bitchy?'

'Is that how it sounds to you?'

'I'm afraid so, Mummy.'

'Oh dear,' said her mother, and Jane thought how unfair it all was. Just as the fight got interesting, her mother turned human on her.

'Want to tell me about it?' she asked.

'That, I'm afraid, is impossible.'

Definitely Posy Sanderson, thought Jane, and proceeded to move to cheerful matters. 'Papa told us the good news about Francis,' she said. 'A first *and* a fellowship. Jolly good.'

'Your brother is outstanding academically,' her mother said. 'The master of his college told me so himself. But he lacks stability.'

'Stability, Mummy?'

'Emotionally he is still immature. Friends like Pardoe and that Georgina whoever-she-is. He must settle down. Establish himself.' Then once more she became human. 'I worry about him, Jane. He needs help. Don't you think?'

Horror upon horror.

'Really Mummy,' said Jane, 'I see so little of him – but to me he always seems so successful.'

'You're not listening,' said her mother. 'I told you myself he was successful in his work. It's his life that's so – inadequate. You could help him in that. I'm sure you could. . . . If you wanted to.'

It was then that Aunt Pen and Papa came back, and Jane tried not to appear relieved. Rob went at once to Aunt Pen, and Foch, ever the gentleman, settled down by Jane, who watched as her mother and her aunt exchanged kisses and felicitations, and made not the slightest effort to conceal their dislike for each other.

' – such awful news,' her mother was saying. 'Is there no possibility of a mistake?'

'None,' said her aunt. 'How well you're looking, Honoria.'

'One of us must stay well,' her mother said. 'Though it was kind of you to take Jane off my hands, ill as you are.'

Her father said, 'Jane has been making herself useful, Pen tells me.'

'Really?' said her mother, as if such a thing were impossible; on a par with 'Jane has been piloting an airship,' or 'Jane has just finished repainting the Sistine Chapel.'

'I hope your lunch was as good as ours,' said Sir Guy.

'It was adequate,' said his wife. 'Sustaining even – but not a subject for discussion.'

'Ours was,' said Jane. 'We drank a toast – to Francis.'

Lady Whitcomb turned to her sister-in-law.

'You have heard of Francis's success?'

'Indeed,' said Aunt Pen. 'And I've asked Guy to convey my warmest congratulations.'

Lady Whitcomb thawed perceptibly. 'I shall do so myself,' she said. 'I am visiting him quite shortly.'

'You too, Guy?' Aunt Pen asked.

'Not to Cambridge,' he said. 'That might be going too far.'

Once again brother and sister smiled like conspirators, then Marchmont brought in tea, and the footman brought in cucumber sandwiches, and the sort of cakes that Rob and Foch liked, and the talk became social: why Lawrence of Arabia had found it necessary to join the ranks in the Royal Air Force; would the League of Nations work; why miners had to go on strike all the time. There was no more chance of anything more personal until Sir Guy declared that it was time to go, and Jane kissed her mother because she wanted to kiss her father, too. When she came back she found that Aunt Pen, for the first time, looked very ill and in pain. She went to her at once, but her aunt pushed her away.

'It's nothing,' she said. 'At least I'm told it's nothing. It doesn't feel like nothing.'

'They stayed too long.'

'Oh no,' said Aunt Pen. 'These things have to be endured, and one mustn't rush them. Besides – your father and I had a great deal to talk about. You and your mother too, I daresay.'

'We talked about Francis. Mummy's worried about him.'

'Despite his academic triumphs?'

'It's his private life – '

Aunt Pen said, 'I've no doubt it is, but I'm sorry, my lovely, I

– 111 –

have literally no time to spare for Francis, and very little for your mother. Did you talk of nothing else?'

'My nerves,' said Jane, 'my frivolous way of life and my indecent clothes.'

'Goodness,' said her aunt. 'You did get a broadside.'

'I *think* we talked about Posy Sanderson too,' said Jane. 'If we did that would explain all the shot and shell. – Would you like to lie down?'

'Indeed it would,' said her aunt. 'Explain it, I mean. And I most certainly would not like to lie down.'

'If you're in pain – '

'I am *not* in pain,' said her aunt. 'The stuff that ten-guinea extortionist allows me still works. For the moment. . . . We addicts have our methods. Is Honoria unhappy?'

'Desperately,' said Jane.

He aunt nodded.

'You know the only man I ever slept with was your Uncle Walter. I had offers of course, some of them rather good ones – but somehow Walter became a habit – an addiction.' She shook her head suddenly. 'Addiction. . . . How inept of me. And so unkind. What I meant to say was I didn't ever feel the *need* for another man. He was really rather good at all that Judgement of Paris stuff. Am I shocking you?'

'No,' said Jane.

'Quite right,' said her aunt. 'It's far too late to be shocked. But what I'm saying is that Walter was so good he must have practised somewhere. I mean it's not something you're born with, like perfect pitch. *Someone* must have taught him those tricks of his.'

'Does it bother you?'

'No,' said Aunt Pen. 'It never did – because all that happened before we married. Never after. Don't ask me how I know – but I do know. Your mother's are a somewhat different set of circumstances. You must try to be nice to her.'

'She has Miss Gwatkin to do that.'

'Stir her up,' said Aunt Pen. 'Don't let her brood. You'll be able to do that.'

'I doubt it,' said Jane. 'But I'll try.'

'Of course you will,' Aunt Pen said, and then: 'Your father says I spoil you.'

Not a knight's move, thought Jane; not this time. More of a dive for cover.

'Is he angry?'

'On the contrary,' her aunt said. 'He thinks you look younger, more rested, and much, much prettier. In fact he wants me to spoil you some more.'

'You couldn't possibly.'

Her aunt took a deep breath. 'He wants me to buy you a horse,' said Aunt Pen, 'or rather arrange for you to rent one from those stables by Rotten Row.'

'I couldn't,' said Jane. 'You mustn't ask me.'

'I'm not *asking*,' said her aunt. 'Your father's asking. Why not accept? You were always such a good rider, for as long as I've known you.'

'If Papa asked you – then he must also have told you why I can't.'

'He said you dream of horses.'

'The horses I saw in the war,' said Jane. 'The ones that were hurt.'

'You haven't had those nightmares here.'

'That's true,' said Jane. 'But how do you know?'

'I would have seen it in your face,' said Aunt Pen, 'and perhaps I would have heard you, too.'

'I do yell a lot, that's true,' said Jane.

'But not here. Here your sleeps are dreamless. Rather boring, really.'

'Why does Papa want me to do this?'

'He thinks – he's thought very hard about this and he really does think – that it may help you.'

'Help me? How?'

'By showing you that a horse is just what you've always known it to be. A rather pleasant form of exercise with just enough danger to make it more exciting. To you, I hasten to add. Not to me.'

'The horses in my nightmares aren't like that.'

'The horses in your nightmares are all dead,' said her aunt. 'If the Huns didn't kill them then the army farrier would. It was his *job*, my lovely. Horses aren't allowed to suffer: not like their riders.'

'Why didn't Papa suggest this to me himself?'

'Because he couldn't,' said Aunt Pen. 'He thought – rightly or wrongly – that there were parts of your life during the war that he would never know about: that you would never tell. And I believe he's right. – So he asked me to do it, because two women can share secrets – or even conjectures – that a father and daughter would run a mile from. And he asked me to hire a horse for you on his behalf and I said No, I'd do that, because if there's any spoiling to be done, I'm the one who'll do it.'

'But I haven't any kit.'

It was a feeble objection, and they both knew it.

'Leave it to the Spoiler,' said Aunt Pen. 'Well?'

'Papa really wants me to do this?'

'He wants you to get well,' Aunt Pen said.

'Suppose he's wrong?'

'Can you become worse than you were when you first came to me? If you think that's possible, I'll tell Guy it's off. Of course I will.'

Perhaps she should talk to Jabber first, Jane thought, but with Jabber one discussed dreams, not horses.

'All right, I'll do it,' she said. 'Thank you, Aunt Pen.'

Aunt Pen said, 'By the look on your face you'd think I was offering you a dose of castor oil, but you're wrong, my lovely. You'll see. Now come and give me a kiss and we'll talk about what riding clothes you'll need – and then you can help me off to bed. I've had quite enough excitement for one day.'

She chose jodhpurs and a jacket of Lovat tweed, but there were also the right kinds of shirt and stock, a bowler hat, and the boots from Lobb. There were measurements and fittings and delays, but not nearly enough of them. Soon, far too soon, she was ready to go. Her aunt looked at her and smiled.

'You'll do,' she said. 'Will Jackson drive you?'

'No,' said Jane. 'I'll drive myself in the Riley.'

'Splendid,' said her aunt.

'Not at all,' said Jane. 'It's just that if you and Papa are determined I shall make a fool of myself, I don't want Jackson there to see it.'

But she didn't make a fool of herself. Not at all. All she did was park the Riley in the mews and take a look at the hacks for hire. Not exactly an exciting collection, but one of them, a bay gelding called Taff, looked as if he might have a little life in him. She used the mounting block and settled in the saddle, and Taff shuffled in an experimental sort of way to find out if Jane knew her business. Both of them discovered that she did, and after that it was just a matter of walking sedately across to the Row, and trotting when she must and cantering when she dared. Rather boring, really, compared with her childhood gallops on Rani. All the same she thought that Taff might be a goer, if only she could find some place where they could gallop enough to find out.

When she got back to Mount Street her aunt went to her at once, Sophie hurtled down to her, even Marchmont looked agitated. A bath, Sophie said. A bath was essential. And perhaps a preparation to guard against stiffness. As if she'd been riding in the National or something. But she took the bath and avoided the embrocation, and came down in a Chanel top and skirt that even Vinney would have approved, she thought. Liberated woman written all over it.

'How divine you look,' said her aunt. 'All Lysistrata and things. How did it go?'

'I rode a horse called Taff,' said Jane. 'Trotted a bit and cantered a bit. It was no more difficult than it ever was. I'm sorry I fussed so.'

'You think your father was right?'

Jane said gently: 'There isn't any point in thinking, darling. I'll just have to wait till bedtime to find out.' Then before Aunt Pen could worry about it, she asked, 'And just so that I don't spend half the night looking up the wrong reference books, tell me, please – who was Lysistrata? I feel I should know, but I've forgotten.'

'How upset poor Vinney would be if she found out. Lysistrata was that rather gorgeous Athenian lady who led a sex strike in Athens.'

'Gorgeous? Because she led a sex strike?'

'Gorgeous because it was to stop a war,' said her aunt.

'Is that how you see me? As a sex strike?'

'Not in that dress,' said her aunt. 'It's just that you look so – well – so in command of yourself.'

It was nice to have one's theories confirmed.

11

F OCH SAID, 'YOU realise that this is a significant breakthrough?'
Strange, thought Jane. This is the first time Foch has
actually *spoken* to me, and yet his voice does not surprise me. A
deep voice, rather precise, rather irascible, with educated-
Edinburgh overtones, like that surgeon in the advanced dressing
station at Arras. Major Buchanan. That was the one.

'I rather thought that might be so,' said Jane.

'Oh decidedly,' said Foch. 'Everything has changed now,
d'you see.'

Jane was lying on her side looking directly at Foch, who sat
on a gilt and velvet chair by her bed. Sophie or Mancroft, perhaps
even Aunt Pen, would have argued that he had no business to
be there, but they were unaware that Foch was not just her dog:
he was also one of her analysts.

'You're referring to my having ridden a horse?'

'Was there anything else of significance?' Foch asked.

'Not to my knowledge,' said Jane. 'Not if you include my
reaction to the outing.'

'Naturally I do.'

Really he was very like Major Buchanan, thought Jane. Bad
temper and all.

'You're not jealous, by any chance? – That I spent time with
another animal?'

'Of course not,' said Foch. 'My concern is for you. Have you
observed the time?'

She looked at the bedside clock. 'Seven forty-three,' she said.

'In the *morning*,' said Foch. 'You retired at eleven. Now tell me about your dreams.'

'I had none,' she said, then, remembering Jabber Lockhart's opinion on the subject: 'None that I can recall, anyway.'

'What you can't recall need not concern us,' said Foch. 'I've aye disagreed with Lockhart about that. But that horse and the absence of remembered dreams – that to my mind is a breakthrough.'

'Go on,' said Jane.

'It's my considered opinion that we were both afraid of regression when you got on that horse, but Sir Guy was correct in his conjecture. You slept well.'

'For one night.'

'The first of many,' Foch said. 'I am not saying that you will never dream again or undergo stress again – that would be absurd. But in the future it will be containable.'

'Are you saying I'm cured?'

'Insofar as you were ever ill – aye, I am,' said Foch.

It was the 'aye' that did it. Far too Harry Lauder for Major Buchanan, or Foch either, come to that.

She said aloud, 'This is ridiculous. I'm making this up, and I know I'm doing it.' Then she sat up in the bed and looked about her, and of course Foch wasn't on the chair. He was on the rug by the fire.

Jabber's going to love this one, she thought, and then – well yes. Maybe he is going to love it. Because I'm loving it. I mean I wasn't really asleep, just dozing and thinking, and I always talk to Foch when I'm trying to think. And what I was thinking was – *I didn't have that nightmare*. So maybe I am better. Maybe I'm even normal – whatever that may be. Then Foch opened his eyes and they looked at each other.

'Good morning,' she said. 'I'm sorry I gave you a voice like Major Buchanan. You deserved something much more grand.' Foch went back to sleep.

The next morning, early, she rode Taff again, and in the deserted tan bark she let him lengthen his stride and gallop. That night she dreamed not at all, nor did she talk with Foch. The next day she galloped once more, and that night she did dream. She was driving the ambulance, but it was nowhere near the Front. It was out in the foothills near Darjeeling, where she had not been since her childhood, and yet there she was, driving an ambulance, which she knew to be empty, because where would she pick up wounded soldiers in West Bengal, in a summer of wild flowers and birdsong and tea gardens, with the ramparts of the Himalayas to guard them?. . . A warm and lazy summer. And then suddenly there *was* a soldier, and it was John, it had to be John, riding Bridget O'Dowd. He cantered across to her in the way she had taught him, and gracious how young he was; so young. . . . She pulled up and got out, and John dismounted, and they got into the back of the ambulance and made love that was like magic, and how could she begin to tell Lockhart about *that*?

But there were other things that she had to tell, and not just to Jabber. Her aunt first of all. Aunt Pen had to know that the nightmares so it seemed were gone. And of course she celebrated the fact by giving her niece a present: a little Cartier leopard of rubies set in gold.

'Souvenir,' said Aunt Pen.

'But you couldn't possibly have known,' said Jane.

'If not for that, then something else,' her aunt said. 'But I rather think I did know all the same. And by the way it's a leopardess, not a leopard. That's another thing I just know.'

'It's the most wonderful gift I ever had,' said Jane. 'But you've given me so much already – '

'It's the only thing I'm really good at – giving prezzies,' said her aunt. 'But I rather think that this will be the last one – for a while anyway.'

'It's getting worse?'

'It,' said aunt, 'is getting unbearable. It's Switzerland next week, my lovely.'

'I'll come with you,' said Jane. 'I must.'

'No,' said her aunt. 'That's the only thing you could do to me that I couldn't bear. Now go and tell Guy your good news.'

But when she phoned that afternoon it was to be told by Lady Whitcomb that her father was resting, and not to be disturbed, and then she enquired after her daughter's health. She received the news that Jane was better and Aunt Pen worse without comment, but promised to inform her father. Jane said that she would telephone again later, on her return: for this was the day of the reunion party.

What to wear was the first problem. It would have been a problem in Offley Villas where she had practically nothing that was pretty, and was certainly a problem in Mount Street, where she had nothing that wasn't. Expensive, too. She didn't want to arrive like some opulent show-off. . . . Then she remembered them: Harriet, the doctor, Louise, daughter of a baronet who farmed about half of Wales, and Sarah the actress who had grown to be famous – what they called a star. She and Aunt Pen had seen her just a couple of weeks ago. Smart clothes wouldn't be a problem for that lot: they'd be the only kind of clothes they had. And Freda, she thought. Would she be there? Lesbian Freda, known as Fred. When John had told her what lesbians got up to, she'd thought he was teasing her, but it was true, it seemed. No wonder Fred was always so miserable, but she was a marvellous driver.

12

HARRIET'S HOUSE WAS in Hampstead, not far from Well Walk, so she went in the Riley. Jackson and the Daimler really would be going too far. It was a nice house, set off the road by a garden, and there were already two cars there, and one of them a Rolls-Royce with a chauffeur who was reading the *Daily Mail*. Jackson would have been furious. She went to the door and a maid answered, and behind her stood Harriet with a cocktail shaker in her hand, darting at Jane to kiss her before the maid had asked her name.

'Darling, what fun,' she said. 'And how intrepid of you to drive all this way. Do come in. The others are all here.'

Jane went into a drawing room that seemed packed with women drinking gin, although in fact there were only three of them, and two were dazzlingly pretty. Being smart hadn't just been a good idea, it had been an essential idea. Sarah of course she knew about, she'd seen: tall and fair and elegant, and with that air of belonging to a different world that some theatrical people never lose. But Louise. . . . Had Louise always had those looks? Jane could remember her only with tousled hair, bedraggled clothes, a smudge of oil on her cheek. And now here she was: dark, intense, *glowing* with beauty, and in such a dress. . . . And between them Fred, a little thinner than she had been, and wearing a mannish sort of suit not all that different from the uniform she'd once worn. Hair cut short, but in a masculine way, not even an Eton crop. Collar and tie, too. And a monocle. Jane rather liked the monocle. She went over to them, and more kisses, and a glass brought by Harriet.

'It's a cocktail,' Harriet said. 'Mostly gin and different kinds of vermouth. At this time of day I couldn't think of anything else.'

Fred offered her a cigarette. Fred had always had cigarettes to offer, Jane remembered.

'Now I'm quite sure you know who these good people were, but do you know who they *are*?' Harriet asked.

Jane sipped her drink. My God it hit like hammers.

'Harriet and Sarah and Louise and Fred,' she said. 'And you're Harriet Ryland as was, and now you're Harriet Watson. Dr Harriet Watson. I remember you were half way through your course when you came out to France.'

'I qualified in '21,' Harriet Watson said. 'Married Neil in '23. He's a doctor too. Dr Watson. . . . It isn't a joke we encourage.'

'I should think not,' said Jane, and turned to the actress.

'You're still Sarah Unwin,' she said. 'That I do know because I saw it on a programme two weeks ago.'

'Ah,' said Fred. 'But she's also Sarah Beddoes and she used to be Sarah Timms.'

'I can't help it if I rather enjoy getting married,' said Sarah. 'Was it "Faint Hearts" you saw?' Jane nodded. 'And did you like it?'

'I liked you,' said Jane. Sarah laughed.

'The perfect critic,' she said. 'Darling, you look marvellous. Doesn't she, Louise?'

The dark woman smiled. 'Putting us to shame as usual,' she said.

'How can you say so and you so grand,' said Sarah. 'You know who she is, don't you?'

'I'm afraid not,' said Jane, and Fred hooted.

'What a comedown,' she said. 'Jane Whitcomb you are in the presence of Louise, Countess of Hexham.'

'Oh check it, Fred,' said the countess. 'How are you, Jane?'

'Well enough now,' said Jane. 'I hadn't been for quite a while.'

'So that's how you managed to keep out of the papers,' Sarah said.

'What on earth do you mean?'

'My dear, we all expected something really dashing from you,' said Louise. 'Driving racing cars at least.'

'And how about you Fred?' Jane asked.

'I run a publishing firm,' said Fred. 'Nothing grand. Mostly technical stuff and school text books.'

'She makes a fortune,' said Harriet.

'Not yet, ducky.' Fred screwed her monocle into her eye and looked stern. 'But I will.'

Like snakes and ladders, thought Jane. They all landed on ladders. I'm the only one who got a snake. But that's over now. Finished. . . . Harriet came round once more with the cocktail shaker, and drew her to one side.

'How splendid you look,' she said. 'You outshine even the nobility.'

'Borrowed plumes,' said Jane. 'Well – not borrowed exactly, but undeserved, which is worse.'

'Did I hear you say you'd been unwell?'

'You did,' said Jane, 'but I've decided to give it up.'

Harriet looked at her. 'I see,' she said. 'At least I think I do.'

'Of course you do,' said Jane. 'You're a doctor.'

'Come and see me at my surgery,' Harriet said. 'That is – if you want to talk about it. Or anything else for that matter.' Then Sarah came towards them to talk about the time the Ford's big end went at Abbeville, and they drank more cocktails.

It was that sort of party: reminiscence and alcohol, whatever-became-of and do-you-remember? There was a lot of laughter, and after the gin took effect rather a lot of tears, too, especially from Sarah, who wept even more, Jane noticed, when she remembered her eight-thirty curtain, and Harriet produced sandwiches and coffee, strong and black as anything they had drunk in France seven years before. Jane drank coffee, too. She had no desire to telephone Jackson to come and drive her home. Aunt Pen would be sure to hear of it, and Aunt Pen must not be caused to worry.

When it was time to go they all kissed each other exuberantly and vowed to meet next year. And no doubt they would, thought Jane, though she doubted whether they'd ever think of each other again until the next time. Reunions were a bore really. Once she had thought that these women would be a part of her life for ever; supporting players in the romantic comedy that would star John and herself. And now she couldn't wait to get back to Mount Street to see how Aunt Pen was. But as she drove off in the Riley she knew it wasn't absolutely true. She would go to see Harriet again.

As soon as she walked into the house she knew that something was wrong. Aunt Pen wasn't in the drawing room but almost at once Marchmont appeared; stolid and competent as always, the way a good butler should be, but there was something else struggling to break through, something that didn't belong. Concern.

'Mrs Nettles is in her bedroom, miss,' Marchmont said. 'She asked for you to go to her as soon as you returned.' Jane raced for the stairs.

Her aunt was lying on the top of the bed. Jane, an expert now, could see at once that the pain was there, but that she'd taken enough of whatever it was to dull its edge.

'Darling,' said Aunt Pen. 'Did you have a lovely party?'

'Lots of gin,' said Jane, 'and too much remembering. But you didn't want to see me at once just for that.'

'No, my lovely,' Aunt Pen said. 'I didn't.'

There could only be one other reason.

'My father?' she asked.

Aunt Pen nodded. 'It was just after you left,' she said. 'We tried to find your invitation card so that we could call you, but – '

'I had it in my bag,' Jane said. 'Tell me about Papa.'

'I'm awfully sorry,' said Aunt Pen. 'There's no way I can make this easy for you. Your father is dead. Very suddenly it seems. He quite literally sat down and died.'

'Poor Papa,' said Jane. 'No more champagne on Second Thursdays.' Then she covered her face with her hands and wept, and Aunt Pen struggled from her bed to embrace her, and they comforted each other until it was time to go.

Jane had mislaid her door key and was obliged to knock – not a good omen – and the door was opened by Hawkins, which was even worse.

'Moreton?' Jane asked.

'Gave notice and left, miss,' Hawkins said. 'Last week. We haven't got another one yet.'

Jane looked about her: at the curtains drawn against the day-

– 123 –

light, the dark, unfriendly rooms. Who can blame her? she thought. Then she turned back to Hawkins. 'You won't do that, will you Hawkins?' she asked. 'We'll need you more than ever now.'

'Do me best, miss,' Hawkins said.

It was hardly an oath written in blood, but it would have to do. 'Where's my mother?'

'Upstairs, miss,' Hawkins said. 'The doctor's still with her.'

Jane went up at once.

It was Dr Somerville: white-haired, aged, and unmistakably Irish, but Protestant Irish, Church of Ireland in fact, which made him socially acceptable. He had had very little sympathy with her nightmares, Jane remembered, and had unhesitatingly blamed them on a faulty diet on the grounds that all young women ate the wrong food. His eyes took in the smartness of Jane's clothes, but he made no comment until Jane had gone forward to embrace her mother. Both women remained dry-eyed, which seemed to displease him.

'This is a sad business,' he said.

Jane could think of no adequate reply, and turned instead to the bed where her father lay, in pyjamas, hands folded over the sheet that covered him to his chest, eyes closed, the age-wrinkles already smoothed out by death. She knelt on the floor beside him.

'Dear Papa,' she said to herself, 'I hope you can hear me wherever you are. I'm most awfully sorry I wasn't here when it happened, but truly I didn't know, how could I? And you must realise that now. I loved you Papa, and I admired you, and now for the rest of my life I shall miss you.' Then she joined her hands. 'Dear God,' she prayed, 'have mercy on the soul of my father. He was human and by no means perfect, but he did his best for everyone who needed him. You know that that is true, dear God. Look what he did for me.' Then she rose to her feet.

'Perhaps you shouldn't stay too long,' said Dr Somerville. 'The sight of death is upsetting for young women.'

The old fool obstinately refused to remember, or maybe it was acknowledge, what she had done in the war, thought Jane. Maybe at his age the thought of what she had done was monstrous, as if the war had been the Crimea, and she one of Miss Nightingale's delicately nurtured young ladies.

Surprisingly her mother said, 'Jane has rather more backbone than that.' And then to Jane she added: 'You have finished your prayers for the moment?'

'Yes, Mummy.'

'Then we can go downstairs. Dr Somerville has signed the death certificate, and your brother has been sent for. There is no more that any of us can do until he arrives.'

Dr Somerville, having been told he wasn't needed, lost no time in going. As the drawing room door closed behind him, Lady Whitcomb said, 'He has become useless now, don't you agree?'

'I don't think he could have saved Papa,' said Jane.

'No one could have saved him. Naturally we called in a second opinion, and he too was quite sure. . . . What I meant was that we no longer need Dr Somerville.'

'You intend to change doctors?'

'Yes.'

'Who will you go to?'

'I have made no decison. First your brother must be consulted. After all he is head of the family now.'

And Mummy was quite serious, thought Jane, or at least had persuaded herself she was. The king is dead. Long live the king. But it was the queen who reigned. Determinedly she wrenched her mind away from these somewhat insulting conjectures. Now was simply not the time.

'You have informed the vicar?' she asked.

'Certainly. . . . He sent a curate.'

When one gives an evening-dress party and invites the governor, her mother's tone informed her, one does not expect to be fobbed off with an aide de camp.

'And the lawyers?'

'I shall leave all that to Francis,' said her mother. 'It was a pity you were not here at the end.'

'I'm sorry,' said Jane, 'but how could I possibly know?'

'I was here.'

'He must have been glad.'

'No,' her mother said. 'Not glad at all. He'd been upstairs all afternoon, fiddling with those – those *souvenirs* of his – then he came down to the drawing room. Hawkins finally informed me of the fact – a *most* unsatisfactory girl, but what can one do?

'Your father was reading *The Times* – or at least I assumed he was. When I came into the room he lowered it and looked at me. It was perfectly obvious that he resented my presence. . . . Then he lay back and I thought he was going to take a nap. In fact, he was dying, and his resentment was because I had impeded the process.'

Careful, now. Very, very careful, thought Jane.

'Why did you say that you *assumed* Papa was reading *The Times*?' she asked.

'Because he was holding it upside down. It would appear that he very much wished to die, and without interruption. Once he had arrived at that conclusion the whole faculty of doctors couldn't have saved him, let alone that dotard Somerville. You were drinking alcohol earlier today?'

'Yes, Mummy.'

'I could smell it on your breath. Not perhaps the most tasteful way of acknowledging your father's passing.'

Jane found that she was on her feet and yelling.

'I didn't know,' she shouted. 'How could I possibly have known?'

Her mother said, 'To look after us now we are reduced to a housemaid, a kitchen maid and a cook. Inadequate though they are, I consider them indispensable. You will refrain from conduct calculated to scare them away.'

'Indeed I will,' said Jane, 'if you will refrain from conduct calculated to enrage me.'

'Ah,' said her mother, and smiled: rather grimly, but she smiled.

'I have lost my husband in what I can only consider humiliating circumstances,' she said. 'Perhaps you are aware of them. I had thought they were forgotten, but quite recently your father revived his morbid interest in things past and best ignored.'

Then to Jane's relief she added: 'If you are aware of what I am referring to, you will oblige me by remaining silent.'

She waited, but Jane said nothing, and the grim smile returned.

'So this was a day of sadness – which I had anticipated – and of humiliation, which I most certainly had not. And on that day, refusing to live at home, living instead with a person she knows to be uncongenial to me, my daughter, indecorously clad, goes out with friends on a drunken spree. To say you couldn't have known is inadequate. Your place was here.'

'I had Papa's permission to go.'

'Naturally,' her mother said. 'He knew that it would annoy me.'

'He knew that Aunt Pen needed me too.'

'You are quite convinced that she is ill?'

'She's dying, Mummy.'

'So you and your brother are the only Whitcombs left.'

'Aren't you a Whitcomb then?'

'An honorary member only. You asked me to give your father a message.'

'Yes,' said Jane. 'Did you give it?'

'How could I?' said her mother. 'To do so would have meant interrupting his departure from life. He would not have thanked me for it.'

'I am sorry,' said Jane, 'that you were unhappy together.'

'I also,' said her mother. 'And I have no doubt that he was, too. I think we could have put up with each other had your brothers lived, but as it is – ' She paused, then deliberately changed the subject.

'You said you were well now, I believe?'

'It seems very likely.'

'That is good news, of course. Did I gather that your father was involved in the cure?'

'He gave me some advice,' said Jane.

'He was good at that,' her mother said.

It was a relief when Francis arrived, or rather it would have been had he not brought Cuthbert Pardoe with him. Mercifully she had changed from her Chanel suit to more appropriate mourning wear before his arrival. That he was pleased to see her was evident, but the bereavement prevented him from expanding on the subject, which irked him.

For a while he sulked, but at last Francis's inability to cope with the more practical aspects of death moved him to action, and even Jane found that he proved useful. It was he who interviewed the undertaker, and telephoned the vicar to make arrangements for the funeral – to such effect that the vicar, Dr Dodd, promised to call on Lady Whitcomb after dinner. He made lists, too, of people to be informed, such as *The Times*, and the India Office, and probable mourners, friends, colleagues, relatives – and reminded Francis that he must lock up his father's desks and files until his solicitors had called on him. But it was

Jane who remembered the heat of summer, and the need for ice in the room where the dead man lay, and told the undertaker to arrange it. Even Pardoe was slightly taken aback by that.

'It is necessary not to yield to grief, *of course*,' he said, 'but I really think – '

'An Indian background alerts one to such things,' Lady Whitcomb said. 'The dead could never be left for long. As for grief, I am in agreement with you that one should not yield to it, and so is Jane. She feels it, and suffers because of it, but she is aware that life must continue even so. I am quite sure that Francis feels the same way.'

'Yes, of course, Mummy,' Francis said.

'You feel that you will miss your Papa?'

'Anyone would,' said Francis. 'He had a first-rate mind.'

He'd had a body too, thought Jane, that had embraced his children – and Posy Sanderson and Mummy too come to that, or there'd have been no children to embrace: a body that knew precisely how to sit a horse, handle a gun, or a cricket bat; a body that had enjoyed champagne and claret and plovers' eggs and côtelettes Reform. But better not to mention that.

They went into dinner: Windsor soup, fillets of sole, roast mutton, summer pudding. No cheese – there had been no time. And no wine either, except that at the end of the meal Hawkins brought in port, on her mother's instructions, and Jane and she left the gentlemen to it.

'I expect they are used to it as they live in Cambridge,' her mother said. 'Your father seemed to think a sound knowledge of port essential to a university education.'

'I don't think Francis is much of a drinker,' said Jane.

'Probably not,' her mother said. 'Perhaps his friend Pardoe will teach him – though I doubt it.'

And indeed, Jane noticed, the port-drinking ritual did not take long, which was perhaps as well, as almost immediately after the gentlemen joined the ladies the vicar called. Dr Dodd was profuse in apologies for his earlier absence, fluent in references to a charity meeting in aid of the unemployed, a confirmation class, a visiting missionary lecturer, but his voice faltered when his eye met Lady Whitcomb's. She said nothing, except to introduce him to their visitor.

'Dr Pardoe – Dr Dodd,' she said, and waited.

Dr Dodd was small, plump, precise, and incurably inquisitive. He looked at Pardoe's flaming red tie.

'Your friend's field is not divinity, I take it?' he asked.

'Physics,' Pardoe said. 'I'm a PhD.'

Lady Whitcomb said, 'You must excuse us, Dr Dodd. My son and Dr Pardoe have just arrived from Cambridge. Under the circumstances I did not think it necessary to request that they change for dinner. I trust my conduct will not be considered disrespectful – or theirs either?'

'Of course not,' said Dr Dodd. 'At such a time – ' He looked again at Pardoe's tie, red as arterial blood, and then away.

'No indeed,' he said, and began to talk of funeral arrangements.

Lady Whitcomb had very clear ideas on the subject. Her husband would be buried not as he would have wished to be, but in his peers' eyes, how he ought to be. Pomp and circumstance, and all the old India hands that Jane's mother could winkle out of their Eastbourne or Cheltenham retirements. Hymns and an organ and floral tributes and notices in the newspapers. Francis, as head of the house, had little more to do than say 'Yes, Mummy', and Jane was not called upon to do even that. But she made no attempt to intervene: her father was beyond all pretension. . . . At last Dr Dodd said, 'Then everything is settled, I take it?' and Lady Whitcomb agreed.

'Then perhaps we can go upstairs to pray,' said Dr Dodd. Pardoe looked up, astounded. Really, thought Jane, he couldn't have shown more surprise if we'd all peed on the carpet. But she made sure he went, even so, by taking his arm on the way to the stairs. There might be pomp and circumstance at her father's death, but there would be respect, too.

They knelt around the bed, and the vicar launched into extempore prayer. 'Oh mighty and most merciful Father, trusting in Thy infinite love and mercy', and 'Thy servant Guy now departed', and on and on and on, while Jane thought of her father and knew that she was ready to weep, but would not while Pardoe could see her, and thought instead of Bollinger in the Hyde Park Hotel when the toast was confusion to Cuthbert.

At last the vicar paused for breath and her mother said 'Amen', very firmly, and clambered to her feet. Jane went to help her, and the others rose too, the vicar rather bewildered and not at all sure that he had finished. Lady Whitcomb advanced on him before he could make up his mind.

'I am very tired, as I'm sure you will understand,' she said. 'There is a spare bed in my husband's dressing room where I shall spend the night.' She offered her hand. 'Good night vicar,' she said. 'It was good of you to find the time to call on me. Come, Jane.'

They went together to the dressing room, where Hawkins had already laid out her mother's night clothes. Her mother looked about her.

'How nice it would be to get away from this place.'

'Are you going to move, then?' Jane asked.

'Certainly not,' her mother said. 'This is our home – yours and mine – *and* Francis's.'

'Francis will live in Cambridge.'

'He will need to visit London – and there are vacations,' said her mother. 'Then he will be married quite soon, and there will be children. A family needs a big house.'

'Has Francis told you he'll marry soon?' Jane asked.

'No,' said her mother. 'But it's what most people do, after all.'

'I must remember that,' said Jane, and her mother looked at her.

'You really are better,' she said, and added: 'Your aunt must of course be invited to attend the funeral. Will she do so?'

'If she's well enough,' said Jane. 'I doubt if she is.'

'Perhaps tomorrow you can make it your business to enquire. Good night, child.'

'Good night, Mummy.'

Once more the two women kissed, dry-eyed, then Jane went down to the drawing room where Pardoe waited for her alone.

'I sent Francis to take a look around your father's study,' he said. 'Very possibly there will be papers.'

'There's very little else.'

Pardoe beamed approvingly down on her, as if she were a beguilingly precocious child.

'Quite right,' he said. 'It's what studies are for, after all. You are bearing up rather well if I may say so.'

'Do smoke if you want to,' said Jane.

'I never do,' said Pardoe. 'I am convinced that nicotine would impede my form of exercise, which as I believe I mentioned to you tends to be violent.'

Jane took from her bag a cigarette case and lighter, selected a cigarette, and lit up, then ejected the smoke through her nostrils, a trick painfully acquired and rarely used. Pardoe watched her, censorious.

'I take no form of exercise whatsoever,' said Jane. 'Unless you count horse-riding at very infrequent intervals.'

'You should,' said Pardoe. 'In fact I'm going to insist that you must.'

Scrum-half? Jane wondered. Lightweight boxer?

'But not of course until the time of your grief is over,' Pardoe added more kindly. 'Talking of which I was sorry that you were subjected to that unfortunate piece of mumbo-jumbo upstairs.'

'Mumbo-jumbo?'

'The Tory Party at prayer,' said Pardoe. 'That ludicrous clerical placeman invoking his tribal God.'

'Oh the *prayers*,' said Jane. 'I rather enjoyed them. I usually do as a matter of fact. It gives one a chance to think one's own thoughts for a while.'

'And what did you think about this time?'

'God,' said Jane. 'And the fact that my father is dead.'

Even Pardoe took a little time to recover from that one, as if she'd clipped him a good un, she thought, not quite hard enough to knock him out, but sufficient to make him stagger for the ropes.

At last he said, 'I have not forgotten our last conversation.'

'Nor I,' she said. Nor had she.

'I'm delighted to hear it. It was conducted of course under much more agreeable circumstances than our present encounter, when custom demands a certain formality, even coolness, in our exchanges.'

It was clear that Dr Pardoe thought poorly of custom.

'That you should show a kind of coyness at this time is perfectly understandable,' he said, 'but when your gloom has lifted I shall come at once to discuss with you what sort of future we may expect together, wherever I may be. For the moment, naturally, I must say no more on *that* subject.'

And then Francis came down to interrupt them, which was perhaps as well, full of complaints about the fact that the study contained nothing but useless junk. Of the fact that it also contained much of their life, Jane thought, he seemed quite unaware.

13

Next day her aunt telephoned. Her voice seemed as firm as ever, but she took her time in phrasing her words, as if conversation were an art she had not quite mastered. Penelope Nettles, once described as the most brilliant chatterer of her generation. That will be the drugs, Jane thought, and the pain.

'I was coming to see you,' she said.

'Not today,' said Aunt Pen. 'Not possibly. I want to ask about the funeral.'

'It's tomorrow,' said Jane. 'There's a notice in *The Times*. All that sort of stuff.'

'I shan't be there,' Aunt Pen said. 'I might disgrace myself. Not up to it, my lovely.'

'I understand.'

'Besides,' said Aunt Pen, 'your mother has enough sorrows to endure at the moment without the sight of me.'

One more knight's move, thought Jane. Perhaps the last.

'Will I see you before you leave?'

'You *must*,' said her aunt, with something like panic in her voice. 'Come and tell me about the funeral – but come alone, darling. Nobody else will be admitted. Tell them I mean that.'

She hung up then, and Jane went to visit the dressmaker who was altering the black coat she had last worn at Uncle Walter's funeral. She took Foch with her, which her mother considered indicated a lack of respect.

'Though why that should be,' she told Foch as they walked

down Offley Villas, 'I've no idea. Papa liked you very much, and anyway you're in black from nose to tail.'

Old Mrs Blythe-Tarkington stopped her then, to tell her how wise she was to confide her grief to her canine friend. They had their own way of giving comfort, and it was one of the blessings of God. Jane was surprised to discover how warmly she agreed with old Mrs Blythe-Tarkington.

The funeral was a kind of formalised horror that seemed at one point as if it would go on for ever. No mourners – except Miss Gwatkin – were invited to the house, not even to see the body, and Jane was glad of it; not that many mourners would have come. Mummy had managed to quarrel with most of Papa's friends, and all of his surviving relatives, but even so the cemetery was thronged and the church was packed.

It was the pomp that was hardest to bear, thought Jane. Papa had been the least pompous of men, and yet here it all was: the elaborate hearse, silver and glass and black wooden panels all gleaming in the sunshine: superb, perfectly matched black horses, coachman and footman in black livery with silver buttons – like a photographic negative of Cinderella's coach, she thought, except that it was Papa who rode in solitary splendour, flowers heaped around him, from those same relatives and friends, (Aunt Pen's great mound of roses, and the words 'Much loved, much mourned', shakily and laboriously written in her own hand); flowers from colleagues and clubs and societies; from the school where Papa had been a governor, and the examining board for which he had set questions in Hindi, from groups and individuals she had never even heard of, including one from R.J. Chatterjee LLB (Lond) inscribed simply 'To the man who helped me above all others'. So many flowers indeed that they'd had to bring in a second carriage, a landau, just to take the overflow, and then Lady Whitcomb and Francis and Jane in a black Rolls-Royce, and Miss Gwatkin and Dr Pardoe, attendant lady and lord, in another.

Then there was the church, crammed full with figures mostly male, elderly, distinguished, with here and there a female of the same generation. Many of them were obviously soldiers, thought Jane, some vaguely familiar, and the rest mostly ICS, the Indian Civil Service which had absorbed most of Papa's adult life. She could sense the stir of interest as the three surviving Whitcombs,

Jane and Francis on either side of their mother, walked down the centre aisle of the neo-Gothic church, Miss Gwatkin and Dr Pardoe behind them, and took their place front centre stage, to be assessed for their performance as mourners: marks out of ten for their portrayal of grief, bereavement, despair. But it seemed that they were not, after all, the stars of the show, far from it: that rôle was reserved for Dr Dodd.

The reason, Jane discovered, was that he had all the best lines. A parson reciting the burial service is a Hamlet: all the splendid soliloquies are his. Dr Dodd knew it, and did his best to be worthy of the lines he had been given. In the stark black and white of his robes relieved by an MA hood, somehow he managed to look taller, more spiritual. Even his voice had deepened.

'I am the resurrection and the life, saith the Lord.' 'I know that my Redeemer liveth, and that He shall stand at the latter day upon the earth.' 'Before the mountains were brought forth, or even the earth and the world were made, Thou art God from everlasting.' 'O spare me a little, that I may recover my strength before I go hence and be no more seen.' . . . Are you listening Aunt Pen?

The words worked their own magic, distancing Papa from the world he had known, – Oxford, India, Offley Villas, – into that existence beyond time and space that the Elizabethan prelates had evoked so superbly, that Dr Dodd invoked so well. Of the magic she had no doubt at all; she had lived too long in India: rhythmical invocation of superlative verse, and Papa fading, fading, as it continued. Neatly and without fuss, Jane began to cry.

Outside, the burra sahibs clustered, and the occasional mem sahib also, curious no doubt, thought Jane, to see how well Honoria Whitcomb had worn. Some, a few, remembered Jane, and one had even met her in France when she'd driven the ambulance. He had just been promoted to brigadier general, Jane remembered, and was not best pleased to meet a young lady he knew socially engaged in changing a tyre.

It was the Hammersmith cemetery after that, and Dr Dodd still dominating his stage, as well-drilled Yoricks lowered Papa's coffin into its grave: 'Man that is born of a woman hath but a short time to live, and is full of misery. He cometh up, and is cut down, like a flower; he fleeth as it were a shadow, and never continueth in one stay.

'In the midst of life we are in death: of whom may we seek succour but of Thee, O Lord, who for our sins art justly displeased.'

Until at last the incredible words for the moment ceased, and first Lady Whitcomb, then Francis, then Jane picked up earth to throw down on to the coffin, and Dr Dodd resumed.

'Forasmuch as it hath pleased Almighty God of His great mercy to take unto Himself the soul of our dear brother Guy here departed, we therefore commit his body to the ground; earth to earth, ashes to ashes, dust to dust.' And as he spoke the words the earth fell, clod after clod upon the coffin, and Dr Dodd continued: ' – in sure and certain hope of the Resurrection to eternal life, through Our Lord Jesus Christ.'

And that was the splendid thing about Dr Dodd, thought Jane: intellectual snob he might be, social snob he undoubtedly was, but his hope of the Resurrection was both sure and certain. Papa had a powerful advocate when we needed one.

And then, suddenly, it was all over, and more people came to shake hands and mouth the ritual words: 'so sorry', and 'fine man', and 'I hope it was peaceful', and so on: and even when it was kindly meant it didn't have the magic of those Elizabethan prelates, three hundred years or so ago. But she didn't want to cry any more: the magic of the words had put a stop to that. Papa had left her, and there was an end.

Miss Gwatkin and Dr Pardoe came back to Offley Villas for sandwiches and sherry. Bollinger would have been far more appropriate, thought Jane, especially with Cuthbert Pardoe sitting there. Papa would have enjoyed the idea of Bollinger, of Pardoe drinking to his own perdition. . . . But perhaps not.

Before she had finished her first sandwich Mr Binns arrived: 'young Mr Binns', who must have been fifty at least, of Binns, Barbour, Crofton and Binns, her father's solicitors. He wore a frockcoat and black satin stock without any visible signs of embarrassment, and Jane assumed that he attended a great many funerals. He was delayed, he told them, because he had been obliged to see to the remuneration of the gravediggers. The undertaker's services had also it seemed needed adjustment. But now he was entirely at their disposal. Which meant, Jane gathered, that he was ready to read the will. Rather hard on Miss Gwatkin and Pardoe, who were not invited, and who appeared to have absolutely no interests in common. Unless Pardoe attempted to – what was that splendid word? – debauch, that was it; unless he attempted to debauch Miss Gwatkin, but it didn't seem very much of a possibility.

The Whitcombs and Mr Binns moved into the dining room, and sat round the table as if about to conduct a séance, then Mr Binns opened his briefcase, coughed once and began.

'I do not know if you are familiar with the terms of this will, Lady Whitcomb?' he asked, in a voice at once plummy and precise, and very appropriate to the frockcoat and stock.

'Not in the least,' said Lady Whitcomb. 'My husband was always reticent about money matters.'

'I see.' Mr Binns looked from Francis to Jane. 'And you Miss Whitcomb? Mr Whitcomb?'

They shook their heads.

'It is a very recent will,' said Mr Binns. 'Made in fact on the twenty-third of last month.'

Jane said involuntarily, 'Two Thursdays ago,' and her mother winced.

'Precisely,' said Mr Binns. 'I attended Sir Guy here. We took sherry together.' He looked at the empty table, sighed and asked: 'Do you wish me to read the entire will, or would you prefer it in more general terms?'

'General terms, please,' said Lady Whitcomb. 'I am too tired for jargon.'

'The principal asset is this house,' said Mr Binns. 'Its lease has some ninety-two years to run. You, Lady Whitcomb, are to enjoy its occupancy for life, after which it reverts unencumbered to your son, Francis.

'In investments, money on deposit in the bank and other holdings, Sir Guy had some twenty-three thousand pounds – '

'*Twenty-three thousand?*'

For once, Jane noticed, her mother's voice was completely out of control: the incredulity and rage totally apparent.

Mr Binns consulted his papers. 'Twenty-three thousand four hundred and eighty-eight pounds seven shillings and fourpence to my nearest computation, taking the shares at their market value on Friday last.'

'But that's impossible,' Jane's mother said. '*I* brought that – '
She broke off, her face once more became that horribly unpleasing mauve colour, but at least her voice was calmer when she continued.

'What sort of income would such a sum yield?'

Mr Binns pursed his lips. 'A thousand a year, perhaps,' he said. 'Sir Guy instructed me that he had a pension consequent on his services – '

'Two thousand a year,' Lady Whitcomb said. 'It died with him.'

'You receive some lesser sum, so I was informed.'

'Five hundred a year.'

'And there are insurances. Your income should be by my calculation somewhere in the region of two thousand five hundred pounds a year.'

'Fifty a week,' said her mother contemptuously.

A few months ago this to Jane would have been wealth untold, but since Aunt Pen's régime it seemed poverty indeed.

'Some people have to make fifty pounds support them for six months,' said Francis.

'I do not intend to be one of them,' his mother said, and then: 'Continue, please, Mr Binns.'

'You are to enjoy the interest on that sum for life – '

'*Enjoy*!' said Lady Whitcomb. 'Is that irony intentional?'

'Merely my instructions,' said Mr Binns. 'After which the principle reverts to Mr Francis Whitcomb.'

'The *entire* principle?'

'That was your husband's wish.'

'There is nothing for my unfortunate daughter?'

'His collection of Indian memorabilia,' said Mr Binns, 'and his pair of sapphire cuff-links, which he suggests should be turned into ear-rings. He does not however insist on that.'

'Dear Guy was always so thoughtful,' Lady Whitcomb said, then added: 'I think perhaps we should hear the will in its entirety after all.'

Mr Binns cleared his throat once more and began to read, and Lady Whitcomb sat upright, rigid with concentration, but when Mr Binns finished she was no richer than when he began. She turned to Francis.

'At least you have your fellowship,' she said.

'I'm quite comfortably off, Mummy. Really,' Francis said.

'Nonsense,' said his mother. 'You are not comfortable at all. You should have been. But you aren't. It won't take you very long to discover just how *un*comfortable you are. Even at Cambridge.' She turned to Jane. 'And you, my poor child, are quite, quite destitute,' she said, then added: 'For the moment.'

Jane said, 'I think we should offer Mr Binns a glass of sherry.'

'Yes, of course,' said Francis. 'I'll fetch it, shall I?'

He left the room a little faster than was necessary, and Lady Whitcomb advanced on Mr Binns.

'Sherry is something that you will no doubt always associate with the Whitcombs,' she said. 'I hope this will be a good one. It isn't something I shall be able to afford very often now.' Her face, Jane noticed, was severe again, the skin colour pale and clear.

'I lost control for a little while,' she said. 'I apologise for that.'

'Not at all, Lady Whitcomb,' said Mr Binns. 'Such experiences are always upsetting. I thought you conducted yourself very well. By the by, do feel free to call upon me if ever you need my services.'

'You are very good,' said Lady Whitcomb, 'but I fear that my means will preclude any prospect of litigation.' Then Francis appeared with the decanter. 'Come, Jane,' said her mother. 'We will leave the gentlemen to their drink.'

But of course there was still a gentleman in the drawing room. Pardoe sat on an upright and savagely uncomfortable chair, staring in horror at Miss Gwatkin, at ease on a sofa, prattling happily at an audience quite powerless to interrupt.

'Gloucester as I recall,' she was saying. 'Or had the dear canon moved on to Winchester at that point? Amelia had had a son – their third child. Such a *relief* after two daughters – he was destined for the church too, but went into the army. – The war you know. But one of the daughters married a missionary so that in the end there was a kind of fulfilment.'

Lady Whitcomb briskly turned off the unremitting flow.

'Francis and Mr Binns are taking sherry in the drawing room,' she said. 'Perhaps you would care to join them, Dr Pardoe?'

It was a kindly act, and Pardoe took advantage of it, leaving the drawing room with the air of a dog turned out for a run.

Miss Gwatkin turned to Lady Whitcomb. She was a short woman with iron-grey hair and a long, pointed nose which Jane considered she richly deserved. She was also, Jane noticed with satisfaction, rather plumper than the last time they had met, a fact all the more evident when she stood beside her stately and still elegant mother.

'I do hope it all went well, Honoria,' she said.

'Well enough,' said her mother, then turned to Jane. 'Wouldn't you say it went well enough?'

'Decidedly, Mummy.'

'Then you have no further plans?' Miss Gwatkin asked.

'None.' Miss Gwatkin pouted. There were to be no shared intimacies, at least not yet. Not when that very strange daughter of hers was present.

'I shall leave you now,' she said. 'You must rest.'

'Must I?' Lady Whitcomb said. 'Yes, I suppose I must. There'll be lots of time to do so now.'

'Rest is a great healer of sorrows,' said Miss Gwatkin.

'Then I shall rest a great deal,' said Lady Whitcomb. 'As an occupation it has the virtue of economy too.'

Miss Gwatkin turned to Jane. 'You must look after your mother. She's upset. Now please don't ring for your maid. I'll let myself out.'

But Jane showed her to the door, and on the doorstep Miss Gwatkin said: 'I take it everything really is all right? I mean your mother has always lived with a great deal of what she calls style.'

'I've no doubt she will continue to do so,' said Jane.

'She's not well you know,' Miss Gwatkin said. 'It's the strain of course. That's why she talks in that peculiar way.'

'Peculiar?'

'Rest has the virtue of economy,' Miss Gwatkin quoted. 'It doesn't make sense. Quite a lot of the things she said don't make sense.' She patted Jane on the shoulder. 'Try not to let it worry you,' she said, and was gone.

Jane went back to the drawing room, and her mother gestured to a chair. Jane sat.

'I've no doubt you find it strange that I should have made a friend of someone so utterly devoid of intelligence?' she said.

'Friendship has a great deal to do with habit, or so it seems to me,' Jane said. 'By observing others, I mean. I haven't made many of my own recently.'

'Would you put your Aunt Penelope in that category?'

'I wasn't counting relatives,' said Jane, 'but I should have done.'

'Let us hope so,' her mother said. 'Otherwise there is a problem. You may have gathered as much.' She waited, but Jane made no answer.

'You are an observant person,' her mother said. 'No doubt you heard me say "But I brought that much – "'

'Yes, Mummy.'

'I was referring to the fact that your father left twenty-three thousand pounds.'

'So I had supposed.'

'What I said was not precisely true. In fact when we married I had twenty-two and a half thousand pounds. Simple arithmetic informs us that I have inherited this house – and five hundred pounds in cash. After forty-two years of marriage. Say twelve pounds per year – a pound a month.

'And yet your father was fair, according to his lights. He gave me back what was mine – and squandered what was his. On what, you are at liberty to conjecture, but not in my presence.'

Posy Sanderson must have been as expensive as she was beautiful, thought Jane, and wished that she could love her mother more. To love her father less she rather thought would be impossible.

'I'm very sorry, Mummy,' she said.

'I believe you,' her mother said, 'but it doesn't heal the hurt. *Will* you turn those cuff-links into ear-rings? But of course you will. Your father decreed it.'

'They would make rather pretty ear-rings.'

'Charm,' said her mother. 'He had a great deal of charm. You must be careful. You may have inherited it. Heaven knows poor Francis hasn't. Yet perhaps not so poor after all. You see, charm must be paid for, child. If not with your money, then with someone else's. . . . Do you have any thought of marrying Pardoe?'

'No,' said Jane.

'He would marry you, I'm quite sure. Oh, Francis has explained to me that junior fellows have their way to make – though how he can equate that with being comfortably off is beyond my comprehension. . . . Where was I, child? I'm quite exhausted.'

'Pardoe,' said Jane. 'And me.'

'Out of the question,' said her mother. 'He is quite the most charmless person I ever met, and in no position to finance whatever charm you may have.'

'I have no intention of marrying Dr Pardoe.'

'I'm relieved to hear it,' said her mother. 'You feel trapped of course, and wish to escape. But Pardoe would prove an infinitely worse gaoler than I shall be.'

'I'll bear it in mind,' said Jane.

'Please do,' said her mother. 'Now your father was a most delightful gaoler.' Jane made no answer.

'He would dance with the prisoner, and serve champagne – which the prisoner helped to pay for. – And always the finest and softest silks wrapped round the chains and manacles so that they would not break the skin – though of course the chains and manacles were always there. That is what a woman is for. To be locked up, imprisoned, circumscribed, and occasionally stretched on the rack of what men are pleased to call love.' She looked once more at her daughter. 'You may not be so unfortunate as you may think,' she said, and rose. 'I shall follow Gwendoline's advice, and rest.'

'Gwendoline?'

'Miss Gwatkin,' said her mother.

'*Gwendoline* Gwatkin?'

Her mother smiled, very briefly, as if smiles were rationed, thought Jane, and must be used sparingly.

'Didn't you know?' she asked.

'No,' said Jane, 'but it was decent of you to preserve the secret for so long.'

'Poor Gwendoline,' her mother said. '*Her* life has not been precisely carefree either. . . . What will you do? Dine with the gentlemen?'

'Visit Aunt Pen,' said Jane.

'To be sure,' her mother said.

'She wants to hear about the funeral. I think I should go, Mummy. If you're sure you'll be all right.'

'Of course I will,' said her mother. 'And if I'm bored I can always get Dr Pardoe to teach me how to box. Tell Penelope that I send my best wishes. She won't believe it, but it will be true for once.'

14

MOUNT STREET WAS charming, as it always was, but there was an awareness in the house, an expectancy, that seemed to Jane rather more than servants anticipating death. Indeed, Marchmont, as he ushered her upstairs, seemed every bit as sure of eternity as Dr Dodd.

'Mrs Nettles is resting, miss,' he said, 'but she left word that you were to be shown up at once.'

Jane went into the bedroom, Foch at her side, and Marchmont left. Aunt Pen's Airedale, Bob, lay in his basket by the bed, and stood up at once when he saw Foch, the gesture of a host, no more, which Foch acknowledged by slumping down on the carpet as Jane went to the bed where her aunt slept.

This time she knew that her aunt was dying. Always slender, now she was emaciated, and her face had the yellow smoothness of ancient ivory. She breathed slowly and evenly, and lay quite motionless until Jane stretched out a hand to touch hers. At once her eyes opened.

'I've been with Walter,' she said. 'So naughty –'

And there you had it, thought Jane. The difference between the two women.

'I'm sorry I woke you,' she said.

'I wanted to be woken,' said her aunt, and then: 'Did I say something just now?'

'You said you'd been dreaming of Uncle Walter.'

'What a prude you are,' said Aunt Pen. Knight's moves to the end, it seemed.

'I have a nurse now,' Aunt Pen continued. 'She's downstairs having something called high tea. So far as I can gather, that's nursery tea for grown ups.'

'It sounds rather a good idea,' said Jane.

'If I'd got better I thought you and I might try it,' said Aunt Pen, 'but now it looks as if you'll have to eat it on your own. Tell me about the funeral.' And then she smiled; an enormous, genuine grin. Where Mummy hoarded, Aunt Pen squandered.

'Oh dear,' she said. 'What a morbid speech that was. All the same I should like to know.'

And so Jane told her about Dr Dodd and the burra sahibs – all of whom had to be described so that Aunt Pen could name them – and Pardoe and Miss Gwatkin and the words that had helped her to bear it all. But when she had finished her aunt said: 'There's something else.'

'I don't think so.'

'Binns, Barbour, Crofton and Binns,' said her aunt. 'Which one did they send?'

'Young Mr Binns.'

'The frockcoat and stock one? He's done very well out of the burra sahibs, but he knows his job. . . . Go on, my dear.'

'Papa left it all to Mummy for life – and then to Francis.'

'And how much is all?' Jane hesitated. 'Come on, my lovely,' said her aunt. 'It may sound like morbid curiosity to you, but then everything about me is morbid now. But I'm not a Nosey Parker. I want to know.'

'The house,' said Jane, 'and about twenty-three thousand pounds.'

'How much will she have to live on?'

'About fifty a week.'

'Crikey,' said her aunt, and then: 'A lot of people would think that was a fortune.'

'That's what Francis said.'

'But to your mother it'll be what they used to call genteel poverty. Did she cut up rough?'

'A bit.'

'One can hardly blame her. It meant that Guy spent every penny of his own.'

'So she told me.'

'And Posy Sanderson? Did she mention her?'

'Not by name.'

'It was a kind of madness,' said Aunt Pen. 'Some women can do it at will. They seem to be born with it – like having perfect pitch. I had it with Walter.'

'And others too, no doubt,' said Jane.

'Nosey Parker yourself,' said her aunt. 'And anyway, it all stopped with Walter. *He* saw to that. Where was I?'

'Posy Sanderson.'

'He used to think she loved him – and maybe she did. Certainly she wanted him to leave Honoria and set up house with her. He couldn't of course, and she knew he couldn't. – It was just a way to make him feel rotten.'

'Were we alive? My brothers and I?'

'You were two, I should think. But it wasn't for the sake of the children.'

'What then?'

'It just wasn't done,' said her aunt. She was perfectly serious. 'Not even with another white woman. With a halfcaste it would have been unthinkable. So he gave her money instead. All he had, it appears. It turned out to be an inadequate substitute. He embezzled a bit, too.'

'*Papa?*'

'I told you it was a kind of madness. He came to me and told me about it.'

'But why you?'

'Why do you think, you goose? So that I could turn it on and drive poor old Walter mad, and get him to lend Guy the money, which he did. Guy's wicked deed was never discovered, thank God.'

'Papa,' said Jane. 'Of all people.'

'You never met Posy Sanderson,' said her aunt.

'Did she have his child?'

'Guy thought she did,' her aunt said. 'Certainly she had somebody's child. It killed her.'

'Does Mummy know?'

'About the embezzling? It's possible. Honoria's very clever, but on the other hand so was Guy. He covered it all up very discreetly. You know what those native clerks were like for prying.' Then, as if it were all part of the same chain of thought she added: 'I'm going away tomorrow.'

'So soon?'

'I can't take much more of this beastly pain,' said her aunt. 'Time I was off to the opium den. We shan't see each other again.'

'I suppose not.'

'It'll be marvellous if I catch up with old Walter. I've such a lot to tell him.'

'Tell him that driving the ambulance was one of the high points of my life.'

'You'll be able to tell him yourself when the time comes. I'm not being beastly, my dear. It's just that I'm going to miss you. . . . Or maybe there's only oblivion after all, and maybe it's just as well.'

'I used to think that too,' said Jane, 'but it was you more than anybody who persuaded me I was wrong.'

Her aunt said, 'Open the bedside table drawer,' and Jane did so. In it was a brown manilla envelope.

'One more present for you,' said her aunt. 'Just to tide you over.' Jane hesitated. 'And please don't be misguided enough to have what they call qualms. Not with me.'

Jane put the envelope in her bag.

'Will you take Bob with you?' she asked.

'All taken care of,' said her aunt, then her face changed, her jaw clenched as though she were biting on something hard to prevent herself from screaming. 'It's time for you to go, my lovely,' she said. 'I do so wish it wasn't. Kiss me good-bye.'

She couldn't go home. Even the *thought* of Pardoe was unbearable, so she went to the cinema instead, and drove the Riley to the Alhambra, Fulham, and Miss Georgina Payne. The place was two-thirds full, even though it was early, but this owed more to the fact that Lillian Gish was due to appear in the main feature, rather than Georgina Payne who appeared all the time, and thumped her way determinedly through the *Keystone Cops* and the *Perils of Pauline*, who finished the episode, as she so often did, being strapped to the railway line by the villain as the express chuffed closer and closer.

At the interval she stood up and turned in profile to stretch like a cat. It was done, Jane had no doubt, to ease her back after all that 'Hearts and Flowers' and 'William Tell', but it was a gesture at once so graceful and so lascivious that Jane found herself remembering what her aunt had said about Papa's little spot of bother. Whatever Posy Sanderson had had, Georgina Payne had, too. She looked at her watch. Seven thirty. Pardoe and Francis would be at dinner. Plenty of time for her to go to an ABC for a sandwich and a cup of coffee, which suddenly seemed far more important than Lillian Gish.

When she got back, Hawkins let her in, and she asked about her mother. 'Still in bed,' said Hawkins. 'Cook made me go up and ask if she fancied a bowl of soup, but she said no. Soup's vegetables, she says, and herbs. And you only get a dish of herbs where love is. She's not delirious is she, miss?'

'No,' said Jane. 'She was quoting the Bible.'

'Oh the *Bible*,' said Hawkins, as if that explained everything. 'Well she would, wouldn't she? I mean this day of all days.'

'Exactly,' said Jane, and hoped that would suffice. Apparently it did. 'Where are the gentlemen?' she asked.

'Gone out,' said Hawkins. 'They had a meeting.'

'They often do,' said Jane. 'It doesn't mean they aren't upset.'

'Maybe,' said Hawkins, 'but if you don't mind my saying so, miss – '

'We'll see,' said Jane.

'That Dr Pardoe could stand a bit of watching,' said Hawkins. 'Doctor or no doctor.'

'Oh dear,' said Jane. 'I hope he didn't – '

'Not likely,' said Hawkins. 'Only I just thought I better mention it.'

'I'm obliged to you,' said Jane, and turned away.

'Just one more thing, miss,' Hawkins said, and Jane began to panic. My God what now?

'Yes?' she asked.

'Can you spell parsimonious?'

'I *think* so,' said Jane cautiously.

'I mean will you, miss?'

'Will I what? Oh. – P-A-R-S-I-M-O-N-I-O-U-S.'

'Thank you, miss,' said Hawkins. 'It's for these classes I go to, you see. On my night off.'

'What classes?'

'Self-improvement classes,' said Hawkins. 'I wanted

"parsimonious" for next week's competition. It'll look a lot better than "mean".'

She left, leaving Jane to wonder who was parsimonious: cook, her mother, or herself.

Next morning she decided that the tea and biscuits Hawkins brought should serve as breakfast. It was not that she had gone back to starving herself, but Aunt Pen's boat train would leave at breakfast time and the thought of poached haddock revolted her. She lay in bed instead, and drowsed, then looked once more at Aunt Pen's present. It was a hundred five-pound notes – 'just to tide you over'. Ten weeks of Mummy's genteel poverty. . . . Tide her over till what? To think about that might be to wish Aunt Pen dead, so she thought instead how five hundred quid meant she wouldn't have to give up the Riley just yet, but that too was a shame-making thought. She sat up and lit a cigarette, and considered instead what to do that day. First there was Pardoe – at one time she had begun to think that there might always be Pardoe, but death and sorrow had reduced him to his correct proportions. Pardoe was a minor problem, and one that she could solve. Mummy was another matter.

She needed someone to talk to. That was obvious. And it couldn't be Francis. That was equally obvious. Francis would either be outraged, which was bad, or indifferent because the affair lacked social significance, which was worse. Or did it? Posy Sanderson had been Eurasian after all. That would make her an object of pity: of comparison even, and Jane wasn't having that. In any case Posy Sanderson was dead, and so was Papa. There was only Mummy, here in Kensington, and Francis was anxious to get back to Cambridge.

It couldn't be Lockhart either. She could only discuss this business with a man if he were her lover, as John had been, and for her and Lockhart to be lovers was impossible. They both knew that. They had been more and less than lovers, but without the bed there could be no confiding. So it couldn't be a man. But of course she knew who it was. Harriet Ryland as was. Dr Harriet Watson as is. She'd been invited. Any time. . . . There was a tap at her door. Jane stubbed out the cigarette in her soap dish as Hawkins came in for her tea things, and thought I must get an ash tray. Hawkins's eyes went at once to the money on the bed. It was indeed an interesting sight, thought Jane, and belonged in a bank, for Hawkins's sake as well as her own.

'We got a problem below stairs, miss,' said Hawkins.

'What problem?'

'Your mother, miss. Cook went up to get her instructions as usual, and all your mother did was give her that bit about the dish of herbs, miss. Same as she gave me. Only this time she threw in a stalled ox as well.'

'I'll go and speak to her.'

'I should miss,' said Hawkins. 'First chance you get. There'll be ructions if you don't.'

No time to get dressed, then. Clean the teeth and put on a dressing gown and put the filthy lucre in her dressing-gown pocket. For Hawkins's sake, and for her own. She went to her mother's room and tapped on the door, called out, 'It's Jane, Mummy' and went in before Lady Whitcomb could tell her to go away. Her mother was still in bed. She looked, and obviously was, exhausted, which was not surprising, thought Jane.

'I'm resting,' her mother said.

'Good morning, Mummy,' Jane said firmly, and kissed her.

'Good morning. Please go away. I'm resting.'

'As Miss Gwatkin advised.'

'Precisely.'

'First you must see the cook,' said Jane. 'Then you can rest. Perhaps you would like tea and toast first.'

'Ah,' said her mother, as if Jane had just confirmed a theory. 'You're taking over, is that it? Arranging my day? My life perhaps? No doubt you will give cook her instructions too.'

'Certainly not,' said Jane. 'There can only be one queen to a hive.'

Her mother smiled that same fleeting smile.

'And what are you? Worker or drone?'

'A bit of both, perhaps,' said Jane. 'But the cook's a worker if ever there was one, and she can't take instructions from biblical quotations, however apt.'

'You considered it apt?'

'Certainly,' said Jane.

'But you still love your father? He dishonoured his family,

stole from his wife, risked your very life to prove a theory – but you still love him?'

'I can't help it, Mummy,' said Jane.

Her mother turned her back to her. 'Tell cook I'll see her,' she said.

Jane dressed then, and went downstairs. She wore a suit that Captain Molyneux had designed: blue and white stripes, the blue as close to the colour of her eyes as the captain's fabric designer could get. Foch, fussing beside her, checked at the entrance to the drawing room. Pardoe was there, alone, reading a copy of the *Daily Herald*. Jane went into the room and Foch followed warily.

'Good morning,' said Jane. 'Where is my brother?'

'Gone out,' said Pardoe. 'Fascinating newspaper, this. Of course you don't take it. Not in this house.'

'I don't believe so. Can you tell – '

'Bet you a hundred you don't. Five hundred if you like. Any odds you want. And I'm not a betting man.'

I have five hundred in my handbag this very moment, but I'm not going to risk it.

Aloud she said, 'Can you tell – '

'It's a Socialist paper, you see,' said Pardoe. 'Designed *for* the workers, *by* the workers. Not always all that sound on theory – Marx, Engels, Lenin's plans for collectivisation – but very good indeed on union affairs. Wage claims. Hourly rates. All that. Fascinating stuff. Literary, too. They've even got a literary *page*. Not run by a worker, unfortunately, but a jolly good chap. Ex-army officer. Won an MC and chucked it away because he didn't agree with the slaughter.'

'None of us agreed with the slaughter,' said Jane, but Pardoe was not there to listen.

'Chap called Siegfried Sassoon,' he said. 'Perhaps you've heard of him?'

'I've met him once,' said Jane. 'He seemed rather a nice man, but somewhat bewildered, like the rest of us.'

That at least got through.

'Of course,' said Pardoe. 'I keep forgetting. You were in it.'

'And you weren't?'

'Too young,' said Pardoe. 'Missed it by a year. Too bad, really. It would have given me a chance to prove myself.'

– 149 –

'You would have fought?'

'Of course not.' Pardoe sounded outraged. 'I would have *refused* to fight. Gone to prison. For my principles.'

Another form of martyrdom, she thought, but not as permanent as John's. She took the gold Cartier cigarette case from her bag, lit a cigarette with the gold Dunhill lighter. A paper spill torn from the *Daily Herald* would have been even better, but the fire wasn't lit.

'I wish you wouldn't do that,' Pardoe said, and then: 'I say. . . .'

'Can you tell me where my brother is, Dr Pardoe?'

'Gone off to see that lawyer of yours in Gray's Inn. Shouldn't think he'll be back for ages. Rather convenient really. I've been longing to have a chat with you.'

'But yesterday you said that now was not the time.'

'No more it was,' said Pardoe. 'But that was yesterday. Your time of mourning. As you know I disapprove most heartily of the ritualistic way in which it was expressed, but for the moment I shall say no more on that subject.'

'Thank you.'

Pardoe ploughed on. Like a tank, thought Jane again. A huge, unstoppable tank, trailing barbed wire, straddling trenches, on and on for ever, spouting words instead of bullets, while one's own words smashed impotently on his armour-plated sides.

'After a – sadness such as yours, a bereavement as the jargon is – one needs reassurance. Comfort if you will – for the body as well as the mind. Now I know what you are going to say – '

As if I'm to be allowed to say anything, thought Jane bitterly.

'You are about to tell me that I am younger than you. And so, in terms of mathematical computation of age, I am,' Pardoe continued. 'But I hope you will agree that in terms of what we may call worldly experience I am infinitely more mature? It was, after all, inevitable,' he told her kindly, 'given the different milieux we were destined to inhabit.'

Jane blew smoke towards him, which made him stop so that he might wave it away.

'You are, I take it, inviting me to enter your milieu?'

'I am indeed.'

'Today?'

'This very moment – if you will only put out that beastly thing.'

'You are aware that my mother is in her bedroom, mourning, and that her bedroom is close to mine?'

'I am not, I hope, altogether lacking in tact,' said Pardoe reproachfully. 'We will not, as you so delightfully put it, share our milieu here. No worker would consider such a thing for a moment, and where the worker leads, the intellectual must follow. I have a small flat in Bloomsbury, and you, Francis informs me, are the owner of a motor vehicle. It will not take you long to drive us there. How delightful that you should own a motor vehicle. It will be very useful indeed – for political purposes every bit as much as the shared milieu.'

Jane then achieved the most successful theatrical feat of her life by bursting into tears.

'My mother warned me about men like you,' she sobbed.

The tank stuck fast, engulfed in tears.

'What can you possibly mean?' he said at last.

'All that talk of comfort, of sharing,' Jane cried. 'And all the time you belonged to another. *Lots* of others. A whole harem of others. You've been unfaithful to me before we've even begun.'

'That's preposterous.'

'I knew you would say that,' Jane cried. 'I'd have bet five hundred pounds you would say that. – Any odds you want,' – and sobbed louder than ever.

Pardoe glanced furtively – the only possible word – at the door, and then, as Jane's sobs grew even louder, he rose to his feet.

'I assume,' he said, 'that I am the victim of some despicable form of joke.'

Jane covered her face in her hands. For him to see her laugh might lead to violence, and he knew how to hit, and so, her face hidden, shoulders shaking, she made sounds that could be mistaken for grief.

'I'm not a fool, you know,' said Pardoe, and for some reason that did it. Her laughter died and she dropped her hands.

'And neither am I,' she said.

'Then why embark on this charade?'

'It was the only way to shut you up.'

But already the tank was mobile again: the armour absorbing all words but his own.

'If you are referring to Marigold Ledbetter I admit to a certain intimacy. As I recall I already *have* admitted it. We are adults, and being human she has certain needs and aspirations that I can help her to fulfil: not all of them physical, I may add. Your assumption that monogamy is essential to a relationship, while understandable, is erroneous. If you were to glance through the works of Sir George James Frazer for example – '

'If you don't shut up I'll yell again,' said Jane. The tank grew still.

'It wasn't Titania,' Jane continued. 'It was Peggy Hawkins.'

'I know no woman of that name,' said Pardoe. 'Is she at Cambridge?'

'She's here,' said Jane. 'In this house.'

'Then I can assure you,' said Pardoe, then paused for a moment. 'Oh,' he said.

'Oh is right,' said Jane.

'The housemaid?'

'The housemaid.'

'You consider it degrading that I should consider her in that light?'

'For her I do,' said Jane. 'She's not quite ready for your game yet.'

'Game? What game?'

'Doctors and Housemaids is it? Or Workers and Intellectuals?'

'The intellectual can always learn from the worker.'

'Not this worker,' said Jane. 'You try it again and I'll scream the place down.'

It was at this point that Francis returned, and for once his entry was opportune.

'Nice to see you two getting along so nicely,' he said.

'We are not getting along nicely,' said Pardoe. 'We are not getting along at all,' and left the room.

'What on earth have you been saying to him?' Francis asked.

'That he must stop making advances to Hawkins,' said Jane, and then, anticipating the next question: 'Hawkins is our housemaid.'

'He'd treat her the same as he treats everyone else,' said Francis.

'Me for instance? But that isn't the point,' said Jane.

'What is the point then, if it isn't snobbery?'

'Hawkins would leave, and that would upset Mummy.'

'It's time we went back to Cambridge anyway,' said her brother. It was a kind of victory.

He took from his pocket a pipe and tobacco pouch, a new departure. Probably something to do with his newly acquired status as a don, but any enquiry, however innocent, would be taken as sarcasm. She lit a cigarette instead.

'I've been to see my lawyer,' he said.

My goodness, thought Jane. That didn't take long.

'Mummy's lawyer too,' she said.

'Of course. And yours – should you ever need one.'

'Too kind,' said Jane.

'No need to be touchy. After all – why should you need a lawyer?'

'Destitute as I am?'

'I didn't make the will,' said Francis. 'And anyway, you'll be all right. Mummy will take care of you.'

'I'm to be her companion then?'

'Bound to be – since you'll live in the same house.'

'But what an enchanting prospect,' said Jane.

'Had you made other plans?' Francis asked.

'Dr Pardoe's the one who makes plans for me,' said Jane. 'Or rather he used to be.'

'You've really got your knife into Cuthbert, haven't you?'

'Not yet,' said Jane. 'But don't let's quarrel. I'm glad everything went so well at Cambridge. It meant a lot to you, didn't it?'

'It meant everything,' said Francis.

'Then you've no more worlds to conquer?'

'On the contrary,' said Francis. 'My wars are just beginning.' And then: 'I say – you'll be all right with Mummy, won't you? I mean it won't be exactly destitution, will it? I mean Aunt Pen must have given you a pound or two for you to dress like that.'

'I'll be all right,' said Jane.

She left him trying to light his pipe. He needed a lot of practice.

Before she set off for the bank she looked in her father's study. It was meticulously neat, far more so than when Papa had used it, but of Posy Sanderson and her beauty there was no sign. No sign at all. The bank was delighted to see her and her five hundred pounds, and suggested a deposit account, but Jane insisted that it be a current one, and left the bank shaking its head over the wilful irresponsibility of young women these days.

15

HARRIET WATSON'S SURGERY was in Baron's Court, in a maze of dreary Victorian villas, each one surrounded by its neatly clipped wall of sooty privet. The privet outside Harriet's surgery soared to the skies, but the bell-pull gleamed. She tugged, and was answered by a furious clatter that died away at last as a bored maid opened the door, yawning, took in the glory of the Molyneux suit, the Paris hat, and more or less snapped to attention.

'It's free day, miss,' she said.

'I'm Jane Whitcomb.'

'Oh yes, Miss Whitcomb,' said the maid. 'The doctor did say you was coming. This way, miss.'

She led Jane down a passage covered in dark-green linoleum, the kind that's made to last, passing on the way a waiting room filled with ancient chairs made cheerful with cushions. There were pictures on the walls and a stack of magazines and children's comic papers. Two women sat there, with children, and a man whose head was bandaged. They all looked poor beyond belief.

Jane was shown into another room, smaller, smartly furnished, with rows of books on shelves, and a collection of photographs on a table.

'The doctor shouldn't be too long, miss,' said the maid. 'But you never know what might happen on free day. Shall I get you a cup of coffee, miss?'

But Jane was wary of coffee in such places as this, and asked for tea, looked at the photographs, then searched among the books, and took down a copy of *Pickwick Papers*. She was half way through Christmas at Dingley Dell when Harriet came in, dark and fiercely clever, as always, and kissed her.

'Darling,' she said. 'I'm so sorry. But I've had rather a rush.'

'I know,' said Jane. 'Anything can happen on free day.'

'Ah,' said Harriet. 'You've been talking to Minnie.'

'Bit of a snob, isn't she?'

'Appalling. But nobody can polish brass like she does. Pity she can't cut privet as well.'

'What is a free day?'

'What it says. The day when I treat people for nothing.'

'Anybody? You mean they just walk in off the streets?'

'Hardly,' said Harriet. 'The place would be crammed full. To qualify you have to be recommended – by a person or a health visitor or a councillor or something. I get quite a lot from Sally Ann officers.'

'Sally Ann?'

'The Salvation Army. Don't you know anything?'

'Not much.'

'They send too many actually,' said Harriet. 'More than I can cope with. I've told them I'll have to ration them if they don't ease up. I won't of course, but they don't seem able to get it into their heads that people who can afford to pay can be sick too. Will you stay to lunch?'

'Love to,' said Jane.

'Lunch is rather a grand name for it,' said Harriet. 'Actually it's poached eggs on toast, but I can offer gin to go with it.' She went in search of a bottle. 'Did you look at my photographs?'

'Yes indeed.'

'Recognise yourself?'

'It was the others I looked at.'

Harriet picked up a leather-framed photograph and passed it to Jane.

'Look at yourself this time.'

It was behind the lines of the Somme in winter; the snow in great ridges on top of the frozen mud, and all about the detritus of war: barbed wire, a pile of duckboards, a shattered gun limber; and in the foreground a motor ambulance, a converted Renault lorry, and in front of it five girls in knitted hats, mitts, and fur coats: two sables, a silver fox, a chinchilla, and a leopardskin. All five girls were laughing.

Jane looked at herself as she had been nearly ten years before. She was one of the girls in sables, a present from Uncle Walter and Aunt Pen. ('The most practical thing I ever gave you,' Aunt Pen had written. 'How can you drive our poor Tommies if you're laid up with pneumonia?') Grinning like an idiot, but dear God how *young* she looked. The photograph had been taken just three weeks after she'd met John.

'There we all are,' said Harriet. 'The Five Charioteers.'

It had been an RAMC colonel who had first called them that, when they'd ferried back the wounded to his field hospital.

'That's you in the silver fox,' said Jane.

'It was my grandmother's. She loaned it to me after I had 'flu and got home leave. She called it her war work.'

'Louise had the other sable,' said Jane. 'But she never liked it. I can't think why.'

'Because yours was better,' Harriet said, and poured two gins, then added Italian vermouth and passed one to Jane.

'I'm told it tastes better with ice,' she said. 'But it's the effect that counts. Cheers.'

Jane lifted her glass, and watched as Harriet sipped, then sighed in content.

'My God I'm whacked,' she said, and Jane stared.

'You used to say that in France,' she said. 'In just that way.'

'And I used to mean it. I still do.'

'You must be glad your work's over.'

'It isn't,' Harriet said. 'I've got the panel patients at six. They're the ones who *can* pay – but not a hell of a lot. And I've rounds to do before then.' She pointed to the photograph. 'That's Sarah in the chinchilla.'

'That was just about the time she got engaged to Billy Timms.'

'Of course it was,' said Harriet. 'Otherwise she'd have been the only one without a fur coat. . . . And there's old Fred in the leopardskin.'

'It was terribly her,' said Jane.

'Indeed it was,' Harriet said. 'It used to make me think of Tarzan. It's a terrible thing to say, considering what we were there for – but they were good days.'

'We were useful,' said Jane. 'That's always a good thing.'

'And you're not useful any more?'

'*Useless*,' said Jane, then Minnie brought in the poached eggs on a tray, and they sat down to eat.

Suddenly Harriet said, 'Daddy Howlett. Do you remember him?'

Jane giggled. 'Of course I do,' she said. 'He was battalion commander of the – Cumberlands was it?'

'It was,' said Harriet.

'That day they were marching back to the rest camp after that push at the Ypres salient.'

'Three hundred and sixty-something men,' said Harriet. 'Two weeks before they'd been eight hundred.'

'But we saved some of them,' said Jane. 'The Five Charioteers. We saved quite a few actually. And the ones that survived. . . . They were so happy. They just couldn't believe they were alive. They sang. My God how they sang.'

'They were on the road on the brow of the hill,' Harriet said. 'We were down below having a picnic. And they marched past us singing, and didn't even know we were there. It was a hot day – do you remember? – and Daddy Howlett had taken off his tin hat and knotted the ends of a handkerchief together like a tripper at the seaside to protect his bald spot.'

'And then the great man himself trotted past,' said Jane. 'Field Marshal Haig. Followed by his staff. And all of them mounted on the sort of horses they must give you to ride in Heaven.'

'And he looked down and saw us and we all stood up and he saluted and broke into a canter,' Harriet said. 'Because the Cumberlands were still singing. Do you remember what they sang?'

'Can I ever forget?' said Jane, and began in a husky contralto:

> Do your balls hang low?
> Do they dangle to and fro?
> Can you tie them in a knot?
> Can you tie them in a bow?
> Do they itch when it is hot?
> Do you rest them in a pot?
> Do you get them in a tangle?
> Do you catch them in a mangle?

Harriet joined in, her voice a small, true soprano. The two sang sweetly but softly together, because of Minnie.

Do they swing in stormy weather?
Do they tickle with a feather?
Do they rattle when you walk?
Do they jingle when you talk?
Can you sling them on your shoulder
Like a lousy fucking soldier?
Do your balls – hang – low?

They finished together then collapsed into helpless laughter, peal after peal. At last Jane gasped, 'And then Haig said, "I take it you are unaware that there are ladies present?"' – And the two women moaned again, until at last they could speak, and Harriet said, 'And now perhaps you can tell me why you came here? I don't want to rush you, but it's almost time for my rounds.'

Jane told her, and only once did Harriet interrupt, when she talked about Pardoe. 'Alistair knows him,' she said. (Alistair was her husband.) 'His work overlapped with some stuff Alistair was doing about X-rays. He may be a fool, but according to Alistair he's a learned fool. He's a physicist. The atom's his big interest. You've got to be insane to tackle the atom, according to Alistair, but you've got to be brilliant, too.'

'It's just that I can't stand him,' said Jane.

'Who could?' asked Harriet.

'Marigold Ledbetter for one.' Jane continued her recital.

When she had finished Harriet said, 'You've had your share – and maybe a little more.'

'I hope that's over now.'

'I hope so too. The horse-riding could have gone badly wrong. In a sense you risked your sanity to get better.'

'No,' said Jane. 'Papa did that.'

'I expect he had his reasons.'

'Mummy says it was all arrogance.'

'And he would have said it was all love. No doubt it was a bit of both, as usual. But at least you're here, and talking. Have you seen Dr Lockhart yet?'

'No,' said Jane.

'I should. You owe him that much.'

'I owe him everything.'

'What about your father?'

'Nothing would have worked without Jabber. I'll go to see him. Honestly I will. But not before I've heard about Aunt Pen. I couldn't somehow.'

'You'll just sit at home with your mother?'

'It won't be for long,' said Jane.

Harriet Watson nodded as if a valuable point had been scored. 'Then what?'

'Something useful,' said Jane. 'I can't do what you're doing, but I can be of some use, surely?'

'Find the right niche and you could be invaluable,' Harriet said. 'You're a very able woman after all. But be careful.'

'Of what?'

'You're looking for love, I think. And why not? But don't grab at the first offer that isn't Dr Pardoe. You're worth better than that. After all – you had it once, didn't you? That absolutely charming young captain in the Northumbrians.'

'You knew about us?'

'We all did,' said Harriet. 'You're not particularly good at hiding your feelings, you know.'

'But you never said – '

'We didn't think you'd want us to say,' said Harriet. 'Not then. Not the way things were.'

'We didn't have a day to spare,' said Jane. 'It was all used up so quickly. All the same, it was nice of you to stay quiet.'

'It was probably the hardest thing we ever did,' Harriet said. 'But we were fond of you, you see. We envied you too.'

'John was killed. The day before it ended.'

'And you were home on leave. We couldn't reach you, not then. There were still too many things to do. And by the time we could, it was too late. You'd shut yourself away. But you're back now.' She kissed Jane's cheek. 'Don't lose touch.'

After that she waited, because there was nothing else she could do. Books from the library at Boots, and furtive visits to the cinema, or theatre matinées; furtive because Mummy did not believe the cinema and theatre were either good for her nervous disposition, or appropriate to a time of mourning. Mummy practised her piano instead: mournful pieces by Chopin and Brahms, the more difficult passages played over and over, until

Jane would signal Foch to go for a walk, or bribe Hawkins to keep an eye on him while she watched a flickering screen or a West End stage, and tried to think of nothing at all. In the end she found that silent comedies were best: Charlie Chaplin, Buster Keaton, Mack Sennett's frenetic policemen. The furious car chases, fires, explosions, the frantic gyrations of pursuer and pursued, were like a mantra endlessly repeated, invoking oblivion. And if occasionally she cried, there was no one to see her in the dark, and if when the lights went up someone did, they would assume that they were tears of laughter.

The news came two weeks after Papa's death, while Jane was in the study, sorting out papers and photographs (still no evidence that Posy Sanderson had ever existed) for no good reason that she could see.

'A Mr Medlicott on the phone, miss. From Medlicott and Rubens. Says he's a lawyer,' Hawkins told her, while Mummy wrestled with the opening bars of a nocturne forever beyond her reach. Jane went to stand between the draughts in the hall, and listen.

At last, Medlicott said, 'I can come to you or you can come here, as you wish.'

'I'll come to you.'

'When will it be convenient?'

'Now,' said Jane.

'I shall look forward to meeting you.'

Jane went into the drawing room, where Mummy wrestled with Chopin. Never, never would Mummy give up, but Chopin was winning.

'Not now, child,' her mother said. 'Can't you see how busy I am?'

And so the hateful words could be left unsaid for a little while longer. She whistled for Foch, who deplored her whistling because it was unladylike, and took him to the Riley, which made him feel better. He adored being driven. Jane touched his head, where he sat perched, expectant, beside her in the two-seater.

'Bad news, I'm afraid,' she said. 'For your friend Bob and me – and maybe for you too. She was fond of you. She gave you bits of cake sometimes.'

Foch barked, softly. It was time to go.

Mrs Blythe-Tarkington watched the car pull out and nodded in approval. That nice young woman from Number 17 still talked to her dog, even if her clothes were rather too dashing for someone in mourning. But the poor child looked quite unwell, so she must be suffering inside. Mrs Blythe-Tarkington said a prayer.

Medlicott and Rubens had offices in Knightsbridge, not far from Harrods, which Aunt Pen had always considered very convenient. 'Whenever I have to visit my lawyers to see how much money I have, I can go round the corner and spend some of it.' These were lawyers who specialised in looking after the Aunt Pens of this world, thought Jane. Their offices reeked of money the way a pub reeks of beer. But that was unkind, she thought. At least Medlicott and Rubens were subtle about it. The only law offices she had ever seen before were those of Binns, Barbour, Crofton and Binns, and they had the sort of décor that matched young Mr Binns's frockcoat and stock. Deed boxes and leather-bound law books and sealing wax. Only Sidney Carton was missing.

Medlicott and Rubens would have none of this. Their offices were in one of the new office blocks, and their reception room was like the set of one of those plays she had stared at uncomprehending; all steel and leather, with an art nouveau carpet of multi-coloured squares, and the sort of sculpture, in welded metal, that could be anything. Foch looked about him. Apart from the sculpture he was impressed. The receptionist, pretty, with short skirts and shingled hair, said that Mr Medlicott would see Jane at once. She sounded surprised.

Mr Medlicott's office was rather as Papa had once described a gentlemen's club, thought Jane. Mahogany desk, worn leather chairs, a Turkey carpet and a parquet floor polished till it gleamed. Just the setting for Mr Medlicott, who wore tweeds and brogues, a shirt of fine check and a Balliol tie. He was tall and clean-shaven, ruddy-cheeked, silver-haired, and looked much more like a wealthy squire than a solicitor. Jane decided that he was probably both.

'Sherry, Miss Whitcomb?' he asked.

'Please.'

He gestured to one of the club armchairs, and poured them both a glass of amontillado, then sat on an armchair facing her.

No notes, no files, no deed box, only an envelope which he handed to her at once.

'I am instructed to ask you to read this before we begin our talk,' he said.

It was from Aunt Pen, of course, and written, obviously with great labour, in her own hand.

My dear, [Jane read]

By the time you read this I shall have left you. It's a very hard thing to do, leaving you. Remember how we both cried when I had to go to Glasgow with Walter for a sales conference and left you with Vinney and missed your birthday?

On the other hand I've kept poor old Walter waiting long enough. He's a darling darling man, but very impatient. . . .

I'm leaving you well off. I expect you knew it was going to happen, but I could see the thought of my money upset you, so I didn't mention it, though why you should be upset I can't imagine. It is *splendid* to be well off. There's a bit for Vinney and her good works, and a tiny bit for your brother, whom I scarcely knew, so that you won't let him come cadging. – He can't anyway. Medlicott's fixed that. Bit of a snob, Medlicott, and Rubens is much too fond of chorus girls, but they're both as clever as monkeys. I should stay with them.

The pain is becoming beastly again and I must finish now and go back to being a drug fiend. I shan't miss the pain, but wherever I'm going I shall miss you, my lovely.

Your very loving,
Aunt Pen.

For Aunt Pen, thought Jane, oblivion was out of the question. She folded up the sheets of paper, and put the letter in her handbag. It was not for Medlicott's eyes.

'My aunt says I'm a rich woman,' she said.

'There's a bequest of ten thousand pounds to a Miss Vincent, and five thousand to your brother Francis. The rest is for you.'

'And how much is the rest?'

Aunt Pen was right, as usual. It was silly to let money upset you.

'Approximately five hundred thousand pounds.'

She was not upset, she realised. She was astounded.

'Half a *million*?'

'Plus the jewellery, and the house in Mayfair. You're a rich woman, Miss Whitcomb.'

'Now? This minute?'

'There is the matter of probate,' said Medlicott, 'but I should be happy to advance whatever sums you may require in the interim.'

'I was thinking of her servants,' said Jane.

'Very proper,' said Medlicott. 'But that matter was attended to before Mrs Nettles left England. She financed their hotel venture.'

'And Bob? . . . Her dog?'

'He is now my dog,' said Medlicott. 'Your aunt asked if she might let me have a keepsake, and I asked for Bob. He lives in Berkshire now. He's become very fond of country life.'

'I'm delighted to hear it,' said Jane, and realised by that fact alone how much Aunt Pen had trusted Mr Medlicott.

Her mother, always unpredictable, provided none of the reactions Jane had expected. To begin with she expressed no surprise, except at the sheer size of the legacy, and the fact that Francis was now the richer by five thousand pounds.

'Thoughtful of her,' said her mother. Jane considered it unnecessary to explain precisely why Francis had inherited such a sum.

'You would not consider – er – augmenting it at all?' her mother asked.

'Aunt Pen has arranged things so that I can't.'

Her mother nodded. She might have been acknowledging a shrewd move in a chess game. 'You will move to Mount Street?'

'I shall sell it,' said Jane. 'It contains too many memories. . . . But I shall move out, if you have no objection.'

'I understand you, I believe,' her mother said. 'This house too is filled with memories of the dead.'

'Mummy, I didn't mean – '

'You will move away,' said her mother. 'Of course you will. You now have the means to do so – and as for: "If I have no objection" – I thank you for the form of words, because I'm quite sure that that is all it is.' Jane waited. There had to be more.

'I *have* no objection,' her mother said. 'None at all,' and had the satisfaction of seeing her daughter nonplussed.

'Use your brains, child. You do *have* brains, you know. How would you and I get on together here?'

'Badly,' said Jane.

'Of course. You are your father's daughter, after all, and your father was a man so accustomed to having his own way that on the few occasions when it was denied him he was not angry, not at first: he was amazed. And I too have been used to command the household at least. Impoverished, I might have been able to hold you at bay, but wealthy you would be invincible. Go with my blessing.'

Jane said, 'I should like to give you some of my wealth, if you will let me.'

'No,' said her mother. 'You are magnanimous – kind, even. But no. For some reason I consider that money not yours, but Penelope's. If she had wished me to have any part of it, she would have willed it to me. Will you be purchasing a motor car?'

'I have one,' said Jane.

'That ridiculous little box on wheels. I was thinking of something more spacious.'

'Like a Daimler perhaps? Or a Rolls-Royce? Too much trouble for me to drive.'

'One does not have to drive in order to enjoy comfort,' her mother said, and Jane knew then precisely what her mother would accept – in time. But for the moment there was only one thing she could offer.

'I know it's too early to go to a concert,' she said, 'but at least let me take you out to dinner.'

'We're still in mourning,' Lady Whitcomb said.

'We'd find somewhere quiet. No one need know.'

'God would know.'

'I don't think He'd mind,' said Jane.

'My God would,' said her mother. She paused for a moment, then hurried on: 'There is one thing you could do for me, if you would.'

'Of course,' said Jane. 'What is it?'

'I must warn you that it will cost rather more than a dinner – even a dinner at the Savoy.'

'Mummy, what is it?'

Lady Whitcomb said, 'There are these things called cruises. No doubt you've heard of them?' Jane nodded.

'Gwendoline Gwatkin has discovered one that goes to India and Ceylon. Bombay, Colombo, Madras. Gwendoline has planned to take this cruise for some little time now – was anxious indeed that I should go with her.'

'She is a woman of means?'

'Oddly enough, yes. She suggested that we go first class.'

'Well of course,' said Jane. 'How else would you go?'

'You will pay for it then?'

'Of course,' Jane said again.

'There is a boat leaving quite soon. In two weeks, I believe.'

Then God won't mind, thought Jane. The mourning will be over.

'I shall make sure you're on it,' she said.

'In a sense my absence will be useful,' her mother said. 'You will be able to engage in house hunting without my interference.' Then she flushed once more that unpleasing mauve colour.

'Please believe me,' she said, 'when I tell you that that remark was not intended to be malicious.'

And oddly enough, Jane did believe it.

16

SHE WENT TO call on Lockhart. Harriet Watson had suggested it, and Harriet had been right. Harriet so very often was right, Jane remembered. Strange how little her friends and acquaintance resented that fact. Jane knew that she too had something of the same pernicious habit, but achieved forgiveness far less often.

She had telephoned for an appointment and been given a time, but was asked to wait, even so. This was unusual. Jabber of all men knew how unwise it was to keep his patients waiting, to give them time to brood, and remember. Even more remarkably, someone else was waiting too in the small, ugly room with its faded carpets, insipid décor, cut steel fireplace and grey marble mantelpiece. Jabber did his best to ensure that his patients did not meet, especially his war patients. To meet might be to remember precisely where on the Ypres salient the German shell had landed; the spot where one had been buried alive. And yet there the man sat, immersed, so it would seem, in an *Illustrated London News* of four months ago. Foch's paws clicked on the linoleum and he looked up at once.

'Good morning,' he said.

Then, athletic-looking, of medium height, perhaps her age, perhaps a little older, with a scar that ran down his face from forehead to chin.

'Good morning,' said Jane.

'Nice morning.'

'Very,' said Jane.

'Rather a wonderful morning, really,' the scarred man said. 'Would you like a cigarette?' He produced a cigarette case. 'Only gaspers, I'm afraid.'

'Gaspers are fine,' said Jane. The young man proffered the cigarette case as if it were the keys of a city, struck a match as though to do so were a conjuring trick of incredible ingenuity.

Mad, quite mad, Jane thought. But content to be so.

'The reason I say it's a wonderful morning is that I've been declared sane,' said the scarred man.

'How wonderful,' said Jane. There didn't seem anything else *to* say. Then she thought: And there was I worrying about being right all the time.

'You're probably wondering why I'm sitting *here* if I'm sane,' said the scarred man, and flushed. Not mauve, like Mummy, she noticed, but a very bright red; almost crimson.

'Oh I say,' he said. 'I didn't mean you of course. You're obviously here on a social call. . . .'

'Coffee,' said Jane firmly. 'The poor man works much too hard. I interrupt him from time to time and make him give me coffee.'

'Jolly good,' said the scarred man. 'Interrupting him, I mean. Good for him. Chaps like me – we're jolly hard work. Or I was.'

'Shell shock?'

'Well . . . yes. Plus a few other odds and ends. I joined in 1915 straight from Cambridge. Infantry.'

'Which regiment?'

'Kicked off in the Gloucesters, then I was seconded to the Manchesters.'

Seconded meant he'd either been brilliant or terrible.

'What rank were you, may I ask?'

'Finished as major,' the scarred man said. 'I was commanding the battalion actually.'

He'd been brilliant: a battalion commander at twenty-four or -five.

'Jolly good,' she said.

'Yes,' he said. 'It was. It was jolly *marvellous*. I'd been reading law at Cambridge. God knows why – I'd have been a rotten lawyer – but I was a good soldier. Honestly I was. And one enjoys what one's good at, wouldn't you say?'

'Certainly I would.'

He smiled, and blew out smoke. 'You know you're a remarkable woman,' he said, then the smile died. 'I say – do you mind my saying that?'

'No woman minds being called remarkable.'

'But you *are*,' he said. 'You didn't ask me about the dead. Every other woman I know asks me about the dead. A lot of parsons, too. Do I repent? All that.'

'Why should you repent?' said Jane. 'You weren't committing a sin, you were doing a job.'

The scarred man stood up then, and so did Foch.

'It isn't like that,' the scarred man told the dog. 'This is homage.'

Gravely he bowed to Jane, and gravely she inclined her head in reply. 'I take it that killing was not what you enjoyed.'

'Killing,' he said, 'was the necessary means. The only way to get to the eleventh of November, 1918, if you like. To a soldier it was like killing sheep to a butcher, – it was what you had to do. But what I enjoyed was leading and tactics and looking out for men who needed me. Doing my best for them, and my best was what my don would have called alpha plus. Only of course three years in France was just too much. I should have been dead anyway. Only I went to pieces instead.'

'And now?'

'I decided I'd had enough of it. Being barmy I mean. So I sat down and tried to work out what I could do, and it wasn't all that much. Cambridge wouldn't look at me, and who could blame them? I'd tried going back in 1918. I lasted three days – and anyway as I say I'd have been a hopeless lawyer. All I knew about was madness and soldiering – and I'd given up madness; so soldiering it had to be.'

'You've rejoined the army?'

'Dear old thing,' said the scarred man, 'do you imagine for one moment that they'd have me? . . . I'm off to China.'

'China?'

'There are upteen war lords in China, each one fighting the next. They're only bandits, really. But there's a chap called Chiang Kai-Shek who's trying to put an army together to stop them. He needs foreign advisers and that's what I am. A foreign adviser. Signed up last week. Do you think they'll mind the scar?'

'The mark of a warrior, surely?'

'Not to boast,' the scarred man said. 'But you're absolutely right. They take you more seriously when you've got one of these.' He touched his cheek.

'When are you off?' asked Jane.

'Any minute, actually. Soon as I get a chit from old Jabber saying I'm sound in wind and limb I pick up my kit and get off to Liverpool. . . . I have enjoyed talking to you.'

'I too.'

'You make a chap feel awfully good.'

He said it, thought Jane, without the slightest hint of sexuality: as if I had been his governess, and he six years old. Then the manservant came in with an envelope on a silver tray, and told her reproachfully that Dr Lockhart was waiting.

'As if it were my fault,' said Jane, and Lockhart grinned.

'No doubt you appeared to be enjoying yourselves,' he said. 'Geekie could not possibly approve of that. He belongs to a very strict sect of some sort.'

'He had that look,' said Jane. 'Poor man.'

Lockhart glanced up sharply.

'*You* seem happy today,' he said.

'I am happy. Just like your splendid major. Tell me about him.'

'You know I can't.'

'Nothing about his illness, of course not,' said Jane. 'But did he do well?'

'DSO and bar.'

'Well enough,' said Jane. 'Wounded I see?'

'Four times. The last time was March, 1918. That's when I got him.'

'And cured him?'

'He cured himself.'

'That's what he told me. "I decided I'd had enough of being barmy." As if madness were something one gave up – like cigarettes for Lent. *You* did it.'

'Did he say so?'

'He didn't have to. It was enough to hear him say your name. . . . Jabber. . . . He loves you. I expect we all do.'

Geekie came in with coffee and biscuits, and Foch looked hopeful. Jane decided he'd been too indulged recently, but

Lockhart gave him a pink-iced horror after Geekie had gone.

Lockhart said, 'I rather think you've decided that you're cured, too.'

'The damnedest thing,' said Jane, then: 'Oh. . . . I *beg* your pardon.'

'Geekie is the one who deplores strong language,' said Lockhart. 'You can say what you like to me.'

'I always did,' said Jane. 'You knew my father died?'

'I read it in *The Times*,' Lockhart said. 'I'm very sorry.'

'It was very – peaceful. That's what people always say. "At Peace".'

'Or "At Rest",' said Lockhart. 'Sometimes clichés aren't just useful. They're essential. Tell me about the damnedest thing.'

She told him about riding Taff, and a suitably edited version of her dream encounter with John near Darjeeling.

'The dream was erotic, I take it?' Lockhart asked.

'Well yes it was,' said Jane, 'if you must know.'

'Of course I must know,' Lockhart said mildly. 'I may not want to, but I have to.'

'Yes of course you do,' said Jane. 'I'm sorry. It was just – a bit odd that's all. We were both so young and so happy in a place John had never even seen.'

'*You* were happy there. Perhaps you wanted to share it.'

'Yes, of course. It must be that.' She laughed. 'When I woke up – after the dream – my first thought was I could never possibly tell you, and now here I am –'

'Perfectly all right,' said Lockhart. 'Now tell me about the horse.' And she told him about Bridget O'Dowd.

When she'd finished, he said, 'That's all true, isn't it? The mare was handed on – like an inheritance?'

'All true,' she said.

'You lost a remarkable man,' said Lockhart. 'Once I thought the loss must be irreparable – but now –'

'I can go to fight the war lords in China?'

'You have a chance,' he said. 'A very good chance.'

'What did you think of my father's – experiment?'

'I think it worked,' Lockhart said.

'No more than that?'

'It was dangerous – it was a gamble, but it paid off. He must have been very sure of himself.'

'Well of course he was,' said Jane, then remembered her mother. 'He was always sure of himself. You would have liked him.' Lockhart was silent. 'Oh yes you would,' said Jane. 'You might not have wanted to, but you wouldn't have been able to help yourself.' She paused for a moment. 'Did I tell you about my chat with Foch?' she asked at last, and did so.

When she had done he said, 'And so I have a rival?' He bent to look at the dog. 'And a formidable one.'

'Do you think he got it right?'

'I've told you what I think.' The words were gently said. 'You're ready to face the world – more than ready. But you must stay on your guard – and you must find something to occupy your mind.'

'What kind of something?'

'Something useful,' Lockhart said. 'You'll never be content with frivolity, however elegant.'

Harriet Watson right again, thought Jane. Aloud she asked, 'Good works?'

'Why not? You don't have to be rich for good works. Just useful.'

'But I am rich,' said Jane. 'Enormously rich.' And told him about Aunt Pen's legacy.

He listened, delighted. 'But how marvellous for you,' he said, ' – unless you were very fond of your aunt.'

'She had cancer – the most dreadful pain.'

'Then it would be hypocrisy to wish her alive. Have you celebrated yet?'

'No,' she said. 'My mother thinks it would be inappropriate.'

'Do you?'

'No,' she said. 'Nor would my father.'

'Then perhaps you would like to accompany me to a party tonight.'

She looked at him. He was quite serious.

'I do *go* to parties, you know.'

'Part of the treatment?'

'If you like. But I do need a partner for this affair, and you're the only one I know who's free.'

She put her tongue out at him. 'What time?' she asked.

'We're asked for nine. I thought we might dine first. Say seven?'

'Seven,' she said, and thought: Now Mummy really will have something to grouse about.

But once again her mother surprised her, merely remarking that cook would be pleased if she had no dinner to prepare.

'Mummy,' said Jane, 'I want no more nonsense about dishes of herbs and stalled oxen.'

Her mother looked delighted. 'I told you that wealth would make you assertive and it has,' she said. 'All I meant to convey was that as I am alone I shall have a sandwich, no more than that. I really must get to grips with that Chopin nocturne. Will it be necessary to invite your friend in for a drink of some sort? He is not one of the "cocktail set", I trust?'

'Not if you don't wish it.'

'I do not,' said her mother. 'For me conviviality was always a problem. At the moment it is a virtual impossibility.'

She and her daughter ate lunch together, a perfunctory affair served by Hawkins at great speed. (She had the afternoon off.) When it was done her mother went to the drawing room to read the brochure of the P and O cruise which Miss Gwatkin had sent her, and Jane, bored, drove to Fulham and the Alhambra cinema. It was a hot and humid day and the place was more than half empty. And no wonder, thought Jane. The inside of the cinema was even hotter and stickier than the rest of London in high summer. But it was somewhere to sit and the darkness was soothing, the murmur of voices unobtrusive. Felix the Cat and Fatty Arbuckle and Mary Pickford in *Daddy Longlegs*, and the chance to yawn unobserved, and listen to Georgina Payne play the piano so much better than Mummy.

It occurred to her that it was because of Georgina Payne that she was sitting there. Not that she was going to set up as a rival to dear old Fred. Nothing like that. It was just that the woman fascinated her. And the reason was that she always looked beautiful. Even then, at that moment, thumping out 'In a Monastery Garden', adding more trills to coax more tears for the heroine's travail, even then she was beautiful; in last year's dress and too much lipstick and an audience that scarcely knew she existed. Beautiful. And what did it do for her? Jane wondered. Did that beauty give her power? Influence? Wealth? Obviously not, since she worked as she did. And did she regret it – the impotence of her beauty? Did she care about anything – apart from the fact of her existence? The question seemed to her important enough to keep her in her seat until the lights went up, but then she left at once, nervous that the blonde girl might see her.

Sitting in the Riley she thought the whole thing through again: the fascination of Georgie, the need to watch, and worry at a problem, like a much younger Foch with the corner of a carpet in his mouth. What was it the other girl had that she wanted so? Not her beauty – she was almost certain that that was so, though if she had possessed it it would have been no burden. But it wasn't that. Nor was it the way in which Georgina Payne wore clothes. Thanks to Aunt Pen she had no cause for envy there. And she was infinitely richer, though perhaps less free. And there was the answer. Georgina Payne's life was her own, to be lived as she wanted to live it, and nobody, nobody at all, would be allowed to get in her way. It was something to think about, perhaps even worry about: it was what she, Jane, wanted also.

The party was in Mayfair, but her host and hostess were interested in the ballet. Having been told as much, Jane dressed with a little more panache than Mayfair usually merited. (Stodge for Mayfair, Aunt Pen had said. 'All your most expensive stodge. Glitter for Chelsea, and just a *little* naughtiness.') So for Mayfair *and* the ballet a studied lack of ostentation, but rather a lot of décolletage, and some quite flawless diamonds. A dress by Patou and a cloak of white silk to cover all this glory until they got to the restaurant.

When Jane came out to his cab, ready to leave at once, Lockhart was much too good-mannered to look relieved, but she was quite sure he was. Evening dress suited him, she thought, emphasising his tall, lean physique. But in the restaurant she noticed that his sandy, thinning hair was unruly, his tie needed straightening. But to straighten it was a privilege she had neither earned nor wished for.

He ate with good appetite: potage Solferino, whitebait, poulet au diable, and as he shovelled down the chicken he looked at her and grinned.

'I never have more than toast for breakfast and I forgot to eat lunch,' he said, 'and Foch bagged my biscuit.'

And that was Jabber Lockhart, she thought. Too busy and too kind to eat.

'Tell me about my host and hostess.'

'They live in Berkeley Square,' said Lockhart, and Jane reminded herself that she need not be too impressed. She had a house in Mount Street.

'Sir Hugh and Lady Lessing. Isobel. What can I tell you about them? We were at Trinity together, Hugh and I. He read modern languages and hunted and wrote bad verse, in the manner, so he dared to hope, of Baudelaire. His family were bankers. *Are* bankers.'

'Lessing's Bank,' said Jane.

'Precisely,' said Lockhart. 'Small in number, vast in resources. Hugh was determined not to be part of it. Instead he was going to go to Paris and drunk absinthe and write verses and be decadent.'

'And did he?'

'He went to France all right, but not to Paris.'

'The war again,' said Jane. 'Guardee?'

'Artists' Rifles,' said Lockhart. 'I told you he was a poet.'

'And afterwards?'

Lockhart smiled. 'The family business, what else? After second Ypres he rather lost his taste for decadence.'

'But he likes the ballet?' Lockhart nodded.

'He's allowed to,' he said. 'He's a first-rate shot.'

'And Lady Lessing?'

'Isobel? She likes the ballet too. Adores it, in fact. My guess is she'd have been a dancer if she hadn't been born a lady.'

'That *is* a handicap,' said Jane.

'Insuperable barrier,' said Lockhart. 'Her father's a duke. What a damn silly world we live in. – Oh I beg your pardon.' He smiled.

'Granted as soon as asked,' she said. 'It *is* a damn silly world.'

'Damned unfair, too.'

'I've thought so in my time,' she said, 'and it seems I'm right. It *is* unfair. Even to dukes' daughters.'

Lockhart signalled for coffee.

'Have you thought of something useful to do yet?'

'I'm not sure,' she said.

'Because before you do, I think there's something else you should attend to.'

She stirred her coffee. 'Yes?' she said.

'That young man of yours. I think you should find out if he left any family – and if he did, whether they are in want.'

'Oh,' she said. 'I hadn't thought – '

'From what you told me, he wasn't born rich.'

'On the contrary,' she said: 'He was born poor. Really poor.' She thought, then realised that she had absolutely no idea what amount a workman might earn. 'Like a servant, I suppose. In the army all he ever had was his pay – but we managed between us.'

'Do you dislike the idea?'

'Of course not,' she said. 'But I know nothing about his family. We never talked about them. Or mine either. There wasn't time, you see. I don't even know where they live.'

'You're a resourceful woman,' he said. 'You could find out.'

It was one way to begin to live her own life.

'Yes,' she said. 'I could.'

'Come to me if you need any help,' he said, 'but I bet you a shilling you won't.'

She nodded, her mind busy with ideas for finding John's family, and for once Lockhart misread her mind.

'You look thoughtful,' he said. 'You're not worried about this little jaunt of ours, I hope?'

'Of course not,' she said. 'Is there any reason why I should be?'

'None at all,' he said. 'Believe me. No reason at all.'

'You approve of my dress then?'

'I do indeed.'

'I'm glad to hear it,' she said. 'It shows what good taste you have.'

17

S IR HUGH LESSING looked like a man who shot grouse and things, if by that was meant red-faced and moustached, with very sharp blue eyes, and the beginnings of a pot belly. When she was introduced to him and he saw her diamonds, he looked like a banker, too. He had not in the least the appearance of a ballet enthusiast, but when the subject arose it seemed to her that he was knowledgeable, and his French accent excellent.

Lady Lessing on the other hand looked so much a part of the ballet world that Jane would not have been surprised if she had worn a tu-tu. What she did wear was a dress that might have been, perhaps was, designed by Bakst, great splashes of colour on a soft, silken drape, with rubies round her neck and wrist. Aunt Pen might not have approved, because it didn't quite succeed, but never mind, thought Jane, she likes it. And that is precisely the point.

For a moment, after Lockhart introduced them, they talked, and almost at once the talk was of the ballet: not just *Scheherazade*, but *Spectre de la Rose*, and *The Rite of Spring*, and *Les Biches*. Jane had seen several of them in London (score six, she thought) and almost all of them in Paris (score ten and claim a prize. Any prize you like).

A footman brought champagne.

'Bollinger?' Jane asked.

'No. Krug I'm afraid. Does it matter?'

'Not in the least,' said Jane. This was one party that Dr Pardoe would not be attending. Lockhart led her away. There were more people to see.

So many. In a morning room, a drawing room, a music room where a man played a waltz on a grand piano, and already people were dancing.

'Do you dance?' Jane asked.

'When I must,' said Lockhart.

'You must now,' said Jane, 'before he plays a Charleston,' and turned to him, her arms lifted. For a moment he hesitated, and then he embraced her, firmly but carefully, as a man might grapple with a delicate piece of furniture.

It's gratifying, very gratifying, thought Jane, to know that I'm what he's after, but rather a relief to know he can't have me – and we both know it. I might not be his patient just at the moment but he knows too much about me, and he knows that, too. And understands.

When they had done Lockhart was instantly claimed by a girl in green, a tiny, vital girl who was obviously a dancer, just as another man came up to them, watched Lockhart take the floor, and spoke to Jane instead.

'One admires his courage,' he said.

'Does one?'

He turned to face her, and she saw a man even taller and leaner than Lockhart, fair-skinned and languid. Palely loitering, she thought. Not in the least like Jabber. Besides his hair was neatly brushed, and his tie immaculately tied.

'Indeed one does,' he said. 'That's Mirova.'

'Mirova?'

'Oh thank God,' said the languid man. 'Do I gather from that confession of ignorance that you can talk about things other than the dance, or are you just being a tease?'

The look he bent down upon her was one of earnest enquiry, and she found herself smiling.

'I shouldn't dream of teasing you on so short an acquaintance,' she said.

'Then that makes you unique,' said the languid man. 'But let me explain about Mirova. She belongs to the Ballet Russe of *course*, but quite recently she had the grippe or measles or something – anyway something quite *lowering*, and she's staying with the Lessings to recuperate. Rather a smart way to recuperate, wouldn't you say? – My name is Lionel Warley, by the way.'

'Jane Whitcomb.'

'Delighted to meet you, dear Jane. . . . Whitcomb? Now *where* have I heard that name before?'

Jane said stiffly, 'In *The Times* perhaps? My father died quite recently. *The Times* published his obituary.'

'My dear I must own up at once to the fact that I never read *The Times*,' Warley said. 'All those dependent clauses. Too exhausting at breakfast.'

'I have a brother at Cambridge,' said Jane, wary still.

'Who doesn't?' said Warley. 'At some time or other. No it wasn't that. . . . Yes, of course. At Lady Hexham's. She was telling me all about the Five Charioteers.'

'You know Louise, Mr Warley?'

'My dear I don't like to boast but I know *every*body. And do please call me Lionel. Mr Warley sounds far too pompous.'

'Then you must know everybody here?'

'All that are worth knowing – now that I've met you.'

'Then come and dance and tell me who I should speak to.'

'Delighted, my dear,' he said. 'Enchanted in fact. Why is it we have never met before?'

'I've been rather out of the world just recently.'

Lionel glanced briefly at Lockhart, now being led very firmly by Mirova.

'Always a mistake to become too reclusive,' he said.

'So I have discovered,' said Jane. 'Now bring me up to date.' He offered his arm, but she hesitated.

'What's wrong?' Lionel asked.

'It's a Charleston,' she said. 'I can't do it.'

'That hardly makes you unique,' he said. 'Just look at all the galumphing clodhoppers about you and do something different.'

Firmly he grasped her, and she did her best, which was, she knew, barely adequate. Not till the next waltz could she listen while he reeled off a list of notable guests: the kind of actors, actresses, peers and musicians – even a couple of lawyers and a junior minister – who might be found in the gossip columns.

'Too many,' said Jane. 'I should have brought a note book.'

'And spoiled that lovely piece of nonsense you're wearing? Paton by the look of it.'

'Paton it is. How knowledgeable you are.'

'One must work jolly hard to be as frivolous as I am. But it's the only way I can be noticed. Now you achieve that blessed state with no exertion at all.'

'Do I indeed?' Jane said, laughing.

'You do, you do. Believe me you do.'

'The charm of novelty, perhaps?'

'Just the charm, my dear,' said Lionel. 'Though I can see you still don't believe me. But here comes Bower to prove my point.'

'Bower?' said Jane. 'You didn't tell me about anyone called Bower.'

'That's because he doesn't appear in the newspapers: he *owns* them. One, anyway. The *Daily World*.'

'Good heavens,' said Jane. 'He really *is* a tycoon.'

'He's worse than that,' Lionel said. 'He's an *American* tycoon. Not that he chews tobacco or anything. But – worth watching, my dear. Inordinately fond of his own way, Mr Bower.'

Oh my God another one, thought Jane, as the music stopped and they moved to where a man waited for them, older than she, but not old: shorter, more heavily built than Lionel or Jabber. Not that he was fat, she thought. His body looked hard and muscular, and restless, and his face reflected that same restless, perhaps masterful quality. Hard grey eyes, hard chin, enquiring nose. And yet not unattractive. Not at all unattractive.

'Lionel,' he said. 'You're neglecting your duty.'

A pleasant voice, baritone: the American accent intriguing, no more.

'If I but knew what it *was* – ' Lionel said.

'But aren't you the one, the only one, who knows everybody? And don't you realise that my paper gets to know everybody also?'

'Your gossip column does its best, but – '

'Certainly it does. We have our rivals of course, and they do their best too, but we're first more often than they are. And not just with gossip, let me tell you. But gossip is my business tonight.'

'You are here as a reporter?' Lionel asked.

'I'm here as the *Daily World*, because that's what I am.'

He means it, thought Jane. And he loves meaning it. Bower added: 'That being the case you should have introduced me before now.'

'Oh dear,' said Lionel. 'Have I been remiss? Jane my dear, this terrifying if pushy person is Jay Bower, owner of the *Daily World*.' – He turned to Bower. ' – And this is Miss Jane Whitcomb.'

They shook hands and she looked just a little upwards at eyes that were telling her to be interesting immediately, or expect no space in his newspaper.

'I'm pleased to meet you, Mr Bower,' she said.

'The pleasure is mine,' said Bower.

' – But I must disappoint you, I'm afraid. I'm not newsworthy.'

'How can you *say* that?' said Lionel. 'A friend of Lady Hexham, *and* Sarah Unwin. Childhood in India while your father served the Raj, drove an ambulance during the war – '

'Did you indeed?' said Bower. 'Then I must disagree with you, Miss Whitcomb. You are most definitely newsworthy.'

He bowed to her and moved away to where a red-headed girl waited, a very pretty girl indeed.

'That's the new musical comedy star, Suzanne de Lys,' said Lionel. 'She's about as French as I am but she can oo-la-la when she has to and sings in broken English rather well. . . . Bower liked you.'

'He hid it well.'

'Yes,' said Lionel. 'He did. It's his way.'

Lockhart joined them and watched as Bower moved through the crowd, the girl on his arm. Quite a lot of people spoke to him, all of them moved out of his way. It's a progress, she thought. A triumphal progress.

Lockhart too watched him go.

'You've been mixing with the mighty,' he said.

'Singled out,' said Lionel. 'Positively singled out.'

'You want to become a celebrity?' Lockhart asked her.

'It seems I have no choice,' she said, then turned to Lionel. 'Or do I?'

'Oh, none,' he said. 'Le roi le veult and all that sort of thing.'

'Then a celebrity I shall be,' she said, and Lockhart nodded his approval. Another hurdle sailed over, she thought. If I go on like this tonight will be a clear round.

'Talking of celebrities,' she said, 'you didn't do too badly yourself just now.'

'The Mirova? She is a good dancer, isn't she?'

'She leads awfully well,' said Lionel.

'Bitch,' said Lockhart, entirely without rancour, and took Jane into supper: lobster and chicken so frothed and swirled they seemed to evaporate rather than be chewed, but deadly for the waistline: and champagne; always champagne.

'Celebrities do live well, don't they?' she said.

'The good ones also do things.'

'Now that I've given up being barmy, are you going to be my conscience instead?'

'You'll do that yourself,' said Lockhart.

'How well you know me. – But of course you do.' She ate a vol-au-vent, then: 'I'm going to find John's relatives.'

'John?. . . Oh yes. . . . And do something for them?'

'If there's something I can do.'

Mirova came in amid a swarm of young men. Lockhart watched her. 'Terpsichore with attendant lords,' he said.

'More like attendant ladies,' said Jane, and Lockhart snorted. 'Did you enjoy dancing with her?'

'Lionel was right,' Lockhart said. 'She does lead awfully well.'

'How did you meet her?'

'She's staying with Hugh,' he said.

'And Sir Hugh is a friend of yours?'

'I've known him since Cambridge,' said Lockhart. 'I told you.'

Patient, thought Jane. I bet he was a patient and you're not telling. You'd never tell.

'As a matter of fact,' said Lockhart, 'he lends a hand with a charity I'm interested in, too.'

'What charity?'

'Helping ex-servicemen. The ones who were – disturbed.'

'Like me,' she said.

'Like you exactly. Except that they're poor too, and very often the only kind of doctor they can reach hasn't the foggiest idea what's wrong with them.'

'Pull yourself together man,' said Jane. 'All you need is a tonic and a spot of exercise.'

'Exactly,' said Lockhart.

'I'll send a cheque,' said Jane, 'as soon as my will's been through probate.'

'I wasn't hinting,' said Lockhart, then, 'That's not true. Of course I was hinting. There are so many. . . . As a matter of fact there's a chap I ought to speak to now –'

'Then go,' said Jane.

'But I don't like to leave you on your own.'

'We celebrities are never alone for long,' said Jane.

And in no time someone joined her, not the hopeful young man she had half expected, but Georgina Payne.

White satin, not in its first season, Jane thought, but I do like the ear-rings, and the necklace is charming.

'Do you mind if I join you?' she asked.

'Delighted.' Georgina Payne set down her plate and champagne glass, and sat. Every movement could have been rehearsed, they flowed so.

'But why are you on your own?' asked Jane. 'Are all the men here blind?'

'My own particular man is busy talking at the moment,' the blonde girl said. 'He won't be long. But don't let me mislead you. He's only my own particular man for the evening.'

'On approval perhaps?'

'Perhaps,' Georgina said. 'It won't be easy. It never is. But then I suppose you know that.'

'Why should you suppose anything of the kind?'

'Well you've done it, haven't you? Paid up in full, I mean. One never gets one's deposit back, but I suppose you know that too.'

She wasn't drunk, Jane decided at last, only in the condition that Miss Gwatkin described as overwrought; even so Jane was glad to see her begin on her food. She ate quite greedily, Jane noticed, and with an enjoyment that for a moment showed through the tension.

'I saw you today,' said Jane.

'You must have seen me six times at least since I came to your house. Are you fond of the cinema?'

'It's the solitude I enjoy most,' said Jane.

'We get a lot like that. Sit like statues some of them. No tears. No laughter. Not like you.'

'In what way?'

'You always watched. You were part of it.' She put her napkin to her lips. 'This – this friend of mine – I told him about the day I called on you. . . . That oaf Pardoe. . . . My friend reads *The Times*. He told me that your father had died. I was so sorry.'

'You liked him then?'

'Of course.' It sounded as if no pretty young woman could fail to like Papa. And then, 'How did your mother take it?'

To describe how Mummy had taken it was out of the question. 'She's over the worst now,' said Jane.

'She's tough all right,' said Georgina Payne. 'But sometimes one has to be. . . . You never came to speak to me at the cinema. It's allowed, you know, during the intervals.'

'I didn't know,' said Jane. 'And anyway – our acquaintance was so short – I didn't want to bore you, Miss Payne.'

'You could never bore me. And please call me Georgie. Please.'

'I'd be delighted to. My Christian name is Jane, by the way.'

'Thank you, Jane. But it wasn't just not knowing whether you could speak or not, was it? There was something else.'

'It was a time of great sadness for me,' said Jane, 'and worry, too. Hence my need to be alone. And just watching you – you were so alive – you did me a great deal of good.'

'I'm delighted,' said Georgie. 'Really I am. And I'd love to hear more.'

'I too,' said Jane. 'I'm – obliged to go away for a while – it's something I can't avoid, but as soon as I'm back in London – I promise – Where can I reach you?'

'I may soon be able to manage without the Alhambra,' said Georgie, 'that is unless they decide to manage without me first. I've had rather a lot of time off just lately.' She opened her handbag of silver mesh.

Cartier, Jane thought, or perhaps Boucheron, and very pretty. But its glimmer was uneasy against that gleaming white. She'd never have worn it if she'd possessed another.

'Here,' Georgie said, and gave her a card. 'Georgina Payne', it said, and beneath that, 'Piano Accompanist'; then in the left-hand corner in smaller letters: 'Recitals'. Top right contained a Chelsea telephone number and address.

'A bit of an eyrie,' Georgie said, 'but the stairs are good for the figure and it's near the King's Road, which is rather important – at least I think so. Oh my God.' She gulped at her champagne.

Jane followed her gaze. A man had just come into the room. He was pleasant to look at, smiling, by no means tall, and yet he looked strong: not with Bower's incipient burliness, but with a kind of whip-cord strength that was at the same time graceful, even when he was drunk, as he was at that moment. The evening clothes he wore were so old as to gleam in the electric light, the coat cuffs frayed. He moved towards Georgie with a massive concentration.

'Oh *hell*!' Georgie said, and stuck the last lobster patty into her mouth, reminded Jane, rather thickly, to call as soon as possible, then rose to her feet and grabbed the man's arm and turned him towards the door. He rotated easily, like some part of an engine designed to revolve, and allowed himself to be turned agreeably enough. He seemed quite happy to follow wherever Georgie led.

Once more Lockhart joined Jane.

'Did you get lots of money?' she asked.

'Eventually,' Lockhart said. 'You were watching Browne?'

'Was that who it was?'

'Michael Browne,' said Lockhart. 'He's an artist. Painter. Pretty girl he had to look after him.'

'She's a pianist,' said Jane. 'Works in a cinema.'

'You celebrities meet the most fascinating people,' said Lockhart.

'Is he any good?'

'When sober – first rate they tell me. He's here because he was in the Artists' Rifles like his host. His company commander as a matter of fact.'

'*He* was Sir *Hugh's* company commander?'

'Hugh rose to the full rank of private and stayed there,' said Lockhart. 'He reckoned poets as officers went out with Sir Philip Sidney – and look what happened to him.'

Jane nodded, warily. She had no idea what had happened to Sir Philip Sidney. 'But why is Browne so drunk?'

'No doubt he's borrowed money from Hugh. I gather he's ashamed to borrow.'

'Then why does he do it? He can work surely?'

'He's a painter, as I say. He reckons it's the hardest work there is, but it doesn't pay.'

On approval indeed, thought Jane, but then Georgie too led a buccaneering life. The point was that she lived it, which might also be the point of Michael Browne. 'Let's dance again,' she said. 'I promise I won't lead.'

Next morning she telephoned Medlicott. Her request surprised him.

'A private detective?' he asked.

'Don't you know one?' Jane asked. 'I thought all solicitors did.'

'Certainly I know one. He's endeavouring to trace Miss Vincent for me.'

'He should do very well,' said Jane. 'If you'll give me his address.'

'Perhaps I can be of assistance?'

'No no,' said Jane. 'Just a personal matter. More of a whim, really.'

Mr Medlicott sighed, but gave her a telephone number, and promised to arrange an appointment.

18

SHE CALLED ON him the next day. He had offices in a place called Falcon Court, which, Medlicott assured her, was quite close to the Strand. It was even closer to the Middle Temple, a fact she found pleasing. The Temple was dedicated to the Law, after all, and so, she supposed, was Mr Pinner. Moreover Fleet Street was quite close, and Fleet Street meant mighty presses, and creatures called Press Barons, and Mr Bower, who couldn't be a baron because he was an American, and who in any case behaved more like an emperor. . . . But the point was that Mr Pinner belonged with Fleet Street too, and unidentified corpses and Horror In Kensal Rise Sensation. Though perhaps that had more to do with Sherlock Holmes and the *Strand Magazine*, she thought, and hoped that Mr Pinner wouldn't turn out to be like that. No opium, thank you very much, no violin. . . . She reached Falcon Court and parked at last.

It was a neat little quadrangle of old and pleasing brick, rendered dingy with soot. Inside it were an equally dingy lawn and some roses that clung on grimly. Dickensian, she thought, and hoped that Mr Pinner didn't blend with his environment too perfectly. She found her way to Staircase Three, and consulted the information board. 'G. Pinner', she read. 'Confidential Investigations'. Room Two. Floor Two. She climbed up stairs surprisingly well polished and carpeted.

Mr Pinner had three rooms: a waiting room with a bell that rang as soon as she entered, his own sanctum beyond it, and behind him again another room where a typewriter clattered and rattled as they talked. Mr Pinner took her into his own room at once, and sat her down in a leather chair as comfortable as it was elegant, while he himself sat at a mahogany desk. Neat and compact was Mr Pinner, much too small to be a policeman, in a discreet suit of blue serge, white shirt with a hard white collar, dark-blue tie in a tight little knot. A bowler hat and an umbrella hung on a hat stand, and the gold watch and chain across his waistcoat looked both substantial and real. A prosperous city gent was what Mr Pinner looked like, and Jane realised that he would indeed be prosperous if Medlicott and Rubens employed him. He had a round and curiously anonymous face, and grey receding hair. His only memorable features were his eyes: shrewd and brilliant and very dark, and a bushy Old Bill moustache of the kind that sergeants had favoured. In his left lapel he wore the lion-face badge, surrounded by blue enamel, of the British Legion, so the sergeant theory was likely enough.

'How can I help you, Miss Whitcomb?' Mr Pinner asked.

'It's a – sort of a missing person,' said Jane.

'Oh yes?' His voice was pleasing: deep, melodious and unhurried, the voice of a man who knew the importance of patience in his work. It made the stupidity of that 'sort of' even harder to bear.

'I say "sort of" because I want you to find out whether a friend of mine, now dead, has any surviving relatives, and if so where they can be found.'

'I see,' said Mr Pinner. 'May I have your dead friend's name?'

It was the most obvious question of the lot, and yet she found she didn't want to answer it. To do so would be to go back in time seven years; to dig up what she had so deeply buried. And yet she had to do it, if only to honour her dead.

'Patterson,' she said at last. 'Captain John Patterson.'

Mr Pinner made a note. 'Please smoke if you want to, Miss Whitcomb,' he said. She lit up at once.

'Where did Captain Patterson die?'

'La Bassée Canal,' she said. 'On the 10th November, 1918.'

Mr Pinner started, then at once apologised.

'Please don't,' she said. 'Everyone's surprised when they first hear. I'm quite used to it.'

'Nasty one, La Bassée,' Mr Pinner said. 'Piece of pie nine times out of ten, but the tenth one – ' He broke off. 'Sniper was it?'

'Machine gun,' said Jane.

'Then at least it was quick,' said Mr Pinner.

'Instantaneous,' said Jane, 'but then they always said that.'

'With a machine gun they had no need to lie,' Mr Pinner said. 'Honestly, miss. Infantry, was he?'

'Yes,' said Jane, and gave out the details.

'Second Battalion the Northumbrian Regiment,' Mr Pinner wrote. 'You wouldn't have his serial number by any chance, Miss Whitcomb?'

Miss Whitcomb had it by heart. It emphasised even more how besotted she was, but it didn't matter. Inside the few minutes that they had spent together, she had decided that she could trust Mr Pinner implicitly. She gave him the number.

'And where did he live, miss?'

'Just before the war he had lodgings in Bradford – he was a wool cloth salesman – but his family lived in the North East.'

'Did he tell you where?'

'Just the North East.'

Mr Pinner was looking surprised, and no wonder, she thought.

'I knew him for less than a year,' she said. 'Mostly we talked about ourselves. I told him I came from London and India – and he told me he came from Bradford and the North East. He may have mentioned a town, but if he did I've forgotten.'

'Did you talk about relatives?'

'Oh yes . . . of course, how silly of me. His mother and father – he called them Mam and Dad, and a sister – and I *think* two brothers. He mentioned a grandmother too, but I should imagine she'll be dead by now.'

Mr Pinner made more notes, then the door behind him opened, and the typist brought in tea, then left at once and closed the door.

'She can't hear us,' Mr Pinner said.

'I don't think that matters,' said Jane.

'If it ever does,' said Mr Pinner, 'she hasn't heard a thing – and these notes' – he gestured at his writing pad, 'I burn them once the investigation's over. You can ask Mr Medlicott, miss. Confidential means what it says.'

'In that case,' said Jane, 'I should like to offer you another job.'

'To do what, miss?'

'To find a missing horse.'

He took it without a blink. Jane decided that she liked Mr Pinner very much.

As she left Mr Pinner's office, Jane found herself confronting Miss Gwatkin, making her way along the corridor. She opened her mouth to speak, but Miss Gwatkin, staring glassily in front of her, moved on. Jane watched her retreating back with satisfaction. Really, Miss Gwatkin was becoming positively fat. If she persisted in her indulgence, the word obese might not be inadmissible. . . . She went to Harriet for gin and a poached egg, and a heart-to-heart about John.

When she returned Hawkins was waiting by the door, despite the fact that Jane used her latch key.

'Your mother's in the music room, miss,' she said, and made a curious sideways motion with her neck, thrusting her head up, and at the same time to one side. The only thing it seemed to signify was someone being hanged (at the end of the sideways motion, Hawkins's head suddenly drooped) and why should Hawkins be marked for death? She went towards the music room, and Foch emerged from the cloakroom and followed her. He had no more taste for badly played Beethoven (the E fantasy-sonata and well beyond Lady Whitcomb's range) than Jane herself, but he knew his duty.

Lady Whitcomb finished – for the moment – the passage that defied her, then rose to her feet, turned and faced her daughter.

'I should like to know,' she said, 'the reason why you found it necessary to visit a private detective.'

'Should you, Mummy?' said Jane.

'I should.'

'I suggest we sit down then,' said Jane. 'It may take you rather a long time.'

'You do not deny that you *did* visit a private detective?'

'What would be the point?' said Jane. 'You have a witness.'

Her mother flinched, a very little.

'It is true that Gwendoline Gwatkin saw you,' she said, 'and that she thought it her duty to acquaint me of the fact.'

'Why?' Jane asked.

'Ladies do not visit such creatures without a very good reason,' said her mother. 'An unmarried lady should have no reason at all.'

Suddenly, Jane understood. For most people, private detectives had but one function.

'*Divorce*,' she said. 'Oh goodness how priceless. Did Miss Gwatkin think that I was the other woman?'

'Heaven knows what she thought,' said her mother. 'But she saw you.'

'Of course she saw me,' said Jane. 'She walked right past me. How tubby she's getting.'

'Her over-indulgence is beside the point,' said her mother. 'Why did you go?'

'Why did she go, come to that?'

'She was visiting her nephew. He has an office there too. He works on behalf of the Christian Mission to the East Indies. *Why did you go?*'

'You know this is interesting,' said Jane, and then: 'I'm thirty-two years old.'

'I am aware of that,' her mother said.

'Old enough to attend to my own affairs.'

'No,' said her mother. 'Not if they involve private detectives.'

'If *you* went to see one, would you be answerable to me?'

'I can conceive of no circumstances that would impel me to see one.'

As if poor Mr Pinner were some sort of kept man. A – what was the word – gigolo.

'I am not the other woman in a divorce case,' she said.

'I'm delighted to hear it.'

'I give you my word on that.'

'No need,' said her mother. 'The courts would make it known soon enough. But there are other kinds of stigma.'

'Mummy,' said Jane, half amused, half exasperated. 'I hardly ever leave the house.'

'Not true,' said her mother. 'You spent weeks and weeks with Penelope Nettles, and even now that you live here – for however little time – you are rarely at home.'

'You think Aunt Pen corrupted me?'

'I consider it a possibility.'

She should have been on her feet then, yelling and screaming as once she had done. But what would have been the point? Aunt Pen had taught her that life was to be enjoyed rather than endured, but to protest that she had never played the rôle of amateur pimp would serve no purpose, and so all she said was: 'You're wrong.'

Her mother said, 'You rarely lie, but – '

'And never when there's no point,' said Jane. 'I hired the detective to find a horse for me.'

'Jokes are alien to me at the best of times,' said her mother. 'At the moment I find them unpardonable.'

'There's a horse I rather liked years ago and now I want to buy her, but first I must know where she is,' said Jane.

'But why in such an odd way?' her mother asked.

'Because I'm rich and I can afford to.'

'Are you reminding me that my cruise depends on your bounty?' Lady Whitcomb asked.

'Of course not,' said Jane. 'I went to Thomas Cook on my way home. Here.' She opened her bag, and handed over a P and O ticket. Her mother looked at it.

'At least you will have your revenge,' she said at last.

'Revenge?'

'I shall be sharing a state room with Gwendoline Gwatkin for eight solid weeks,' said her mother, and then: 'You have not lied to me? This person really is seeking a horse on your behalf?'

'A mare,' said Jane. 'A bay. Fifteen hands or thereabouts. Reared in Ireland.' The truth, but not the whole truth.

'I do so hope,' her mother said, 'that you will not become wayward.'

'I promise I'll do my best,' said Jane. 'Have you enough clothes? – For your cruise, I mean.'

'Perhaps not,' her mother said.

'Then we must go and buy some. Harrods, I think, since there's so little time.' For a moment, Jane thought her mother would cry, then the moment passed.

'I told you I would not accept Penelope Nettles's money,' she said at last.

'This isn't money. It's fripperies. I can't have you sharing a cabin with Miss Gwatkin and looking like a dowd.'

'You are vehement again,' said her mother.

'I'm sorry.'

'Please don't be,' said her mother, and smiled as she had not smiled in years. 'You have overborne me. May we go tomorrow?'

'Of course,' said Jane, and Hawkins came in.

'There's a Mr Warley on the phone, miss,' she said. 'Asking for you.'

'Tell him I'm coming,' said Jane, and when Hawkins had left: 'Mummy I promise you this has nothing to do with private detectives.'

Lionel said, 'So my dear, you *are* a celebrity?'

'Am I?' said Jane.

'The *Daily World* thinks you are. Or haven't you read it?'

'I'm afraid not.'

'My dear you must,' said Lionel. 'Not a dependent clause from first page to last. Are you free?'

'At this moment?'

'It really is rather important.'

'What is?' Jane asked.

'I must teach you to dance. Don't tell me it's a bore – I *know* it's a bore, but it's what one does. There's no escape, I'm afraid.'

'I would like to be able to dance – ' Jane said cautiously.

'Splendid. Then it's agreed. Take a cab.'

'But why should I?' said Jane. 'Why should you for that matter? We've only just met after all.'

'Tell that to Jay Bower,' Lionel said.

'But what on earth has it got to do with him?'

'Buy a copy of the *Daily World* and find out. Do say you'll come. It's the sweetest little mews just off Cadogan Gardens.'

She went back to the music room to tell her mother she was going out.

'Mr Warley?' her mother asked.

'He's quite safe, Mummy.'

'How reassuring,' her mother said. 'What does he do?'

'Amongst other things,' said Jane, 'he appears to be a dancing master.'

'How very odd,' said her mother. 'Is it all because of that appalling war you were involved in?'

Jane found herself wishing, in the cab, that Mummy and Dr Pardoe could have a long, long chat about the after-effects of that appalling war, and that she might be permitted to eavesdrop unobserved. And then, as it seemed most unlikely to happen, she stopped the cab by a news-stand, bought a *Daily World*, and turned to the gossip column, 'This Wicked World', to learn that of all the rich and famous at the Lessing party for Mirova, she,

Jane Whitcomb, was the only one who had made the evening memorable. Grace, beauty, a singular wit, and so on. All very great nonsense of course, but a powerful weapon in the hands of her mother.

Lionel's house was all that she had expected. A neat little gem all in stone, with window boxes full of geraniums on every available ledge. And inside a décor quite ruthlessly white. 'So virginal and improbable,' said Lionel. 'You've read the *World*?'

'Oh my,' said Jane.

'He did go on a bit, didn't he? All that *stuff* about grace and wit and not a word about charm.'

'I have charm then?'

'Obviously you must have,' said Lionel, 'or Jay wouldn't have gone on so, and I would not be about to teach you how to Charleston.' And he wound up the gramophone with grim determination.

They stopped briefly for tea and cucumber sandwiches, served by a parlourmaid of rigidly conservative bearing, whom Lionel addressed as Pott.

'Hasn't she a first name?' Jane asked.

'My dear I don't know,' said Lionel. 'I'm much too afraid of her to ask. And she deplores my friends. Deplores and despises. She thinks of them as quite unsuitable, which of course they *are*.'

Then they practised some more until friends dropped in and Lionel mixed cocktails and Jane was able to put into practice what she had been taught, as she danced with the friends. Unsuitable didn't do them justice.

But at last she had to go home. There would be other visits, other lessons, but her mother's moment could be postponed no longer, Jane thought. She must go back and face the opening salvoes of the long-sustained bombardment that would precede an annihilating charge.

As she removed her coat in the hall she thought how gloomy the house was, after all that glittering white, white wood and glass and chromium, she remembered, a heavy white rug rolled back from floorboards polished to sherry-gold so that they could dance. Even the gramophone had been white. She went into the drawing room.

'Why Francis,' she said. 'How nice to see you.' The *Daily World* lay on a table between Francis and her mother.

'I had no idea,' said her mother, 'how famous you were, until Francis brought it to my attention.'

'It is called "being a celebrity", Mummy,' said Jane.

'Is it indeed? I thought celebrities appeared only in the pages of journals read by housemaids. But perhaps that *is* the sort of journal read by housemaids.'

'Oh I shouldn't have thought so,' said Francis. 'They do a sound financial page – very sound. Well worth a look while capitalism lasts.'

'And its views of celebrities?' Lady Whitcomb asked.

Francis shrugged.

'I really know very little about such things,' he said.

'Nor I. I could wish to know less,' said her mother. 'Really Jane. How you could consent to give an interview to a journalist – '

'But I didn't,' said Jane. 'Of course I didn't.'

'You cannot possibly mean that they invented this rubbish without consulting you?'

'Rubbish' really was a bit hard, Jane thought. What about all that beauty, grace and singular wit?

'All I did was talk with Mr Bower,' she said. 'I'd no idea – '

'Bower?' said Francis. 'J.W. Bower?'

'I expect so,' said Jane. 'Everybody called him Jay.'

'He owns the *Daily World*?'

'So they tell me.'

'That's him,' Francis said. 'J.W. Bower.' Then to their mother: 'He's the most ghastly reactionary, but extraordinarily able.'

'If somewhat fulsome,' Lady Whitcomb said. 'Can you explain to me why he should choose to write such stuff, then print heaven knows how many million copies?'

Jane took her time thinking about it. At last she said: 'I rather think it's because he *can* print it. What I mean is he has the power to engage a perfectly ordinary female in conversation then make millions of people read about it next day and believe it's important.'

'He sounds most disagreeable,' said her mother.

'I am quite sure he could be.'

'And Gwendoline Gwatkin has already telephoned me about it. Try not to appear in the public print again before I am on shipboard.' She got up and left them. Soon there came the sound of the piano: Beethoven matched against Lady Whitcomb, no quarter given. Jane knew at once that the field was left clear for her brother, and was glad.

Francis took out his pipe and filled it, a slow and slightly uneasy ritual still. When it was drawing comfortably he said, 'You were right about Richard Poynter. He's gone down from King's. It seems he prefers the Life Guards.'

'He'll look very well in all that scarlet and horse-hair and burnished steel.'

'Yes,' said Francis. 'He will. I shall miss him.'

'I can understand why,' said Jane, then, as her brother jerked upright, 'That is merely a statement of fact. Sympathetic, if anything.'

Francis sat back again.

'Mummy's off on a cruise, she says.'

'India,' said Jane. 'With Miss Gwatkin. She'll enjoy it.'

'She says you're paying.'

'I can afford to. I'm a rich woman – as I've no doubt Mummy told you. Have you heard from Medlicott?'

'The solicitor? He said five thousand.'

'Congratulations.'

'You got rather more.'

'Just a bit,' said Jane.

'Don't you think I'm entitled to some of it?'

'No,' said Jane. 'Neither did Aunt Pen. She said I mustn't share with you. That's why you got five thousand. And anyway, why are you so worried about money? When Papa died, you said you had all you needed.'

'I was wrong,' said Francis.

Jane waited, but all that her brother added was, 'I need money now. And I've got to wait for this blasted probate.'

'How much do you need?'

Francis shrugged. 'I want to go to Germany with a friend of mine.'

'Dr Pardoe?'

For a moment he looked incredulous. 'No,' he said at last. 'Not Cuthbert.'

'A holiday?' she asked.

'You might call it that. Two or three hundred should do it. I could pay it back as soon as I got my whack.'

'I'll speak to Medlicott. He'll arrange an advance.'

'That's very nice of you,' said Francis, then smiled. 'At least we'll both be out of your way – Mummy and I. It won't matter what Bower puts in his paper.'

'How long will you be in Germany?'

'Five or six weeks. Till just before term starts.'

'Berlin?'

'I expect so,' he said, and was suddenly angry. 'I don't see why I have to be cross-examined. After all it's only an advance on my own money.'

'I didn't think I was cross-examining you.'

'What then?'

'Friendly interest. Obviously I was wrong. Let's drop it, shall we?'

'But you'll speak to that lawyer?'

'Of course,' she said.

19

H<small>ARRODS AND DANCING</small> took up much of her time. There was
more to it than the Charleston, she discovered. The foxtrot,
blues, Black Bottom, one-step and tango had also to be mastered.
But the Charleston was always the Charleston. 'Controlled dementia', Lionel called it, but she didn't fear the dementia because
the control was hers too. And there was never a shortage of places
to practise: from the Embassy or the Savoy, to the conscientious
wickedness of clubs like the Cave of Harmony or Ma Meyrick's
43. Or else you could simply give a party and roll back the carpet.
Not in her own house, of course. 17, Offley Villas belonged to
her mother, and Lady Whitcomb, who made no great objection
to her going out to dance, merely smiling grimly and inspecting
what Harrods had just delivered, could never, Jane admitted
fairmindedly, have countenanced such cavortings in her own
home.

That they *were* cavortings Jane did not doubt for an instant.
Frenetic, energy-consuming, angular and loud for the most part.
And difficult, that was the odd thing. For a long time one had
to concentrate very hard to perform these graceless antics, until
at last it became as simple and natural as breathing. But how
good one felt, whether concentrating or not. Always it was fun.
And not just at the time, but when it was over too. One sat – or
flopped to be more honest – and grinned at one's partner in
triumph as if together the two of you had just constructed a work
of art, and 'Goodness that was fun' one said.

And it was. That was the point. Fun in the music, fun in the movement of the dance, the cocktails, the antics of the band. Fun that had been deserved and earned. A right. Rows of young men in stiff white shirts and evening-dress coats, and oneself in diamonds and chiffon. A gardenia corsage, and the King of Roumania at the next table, and the Somme had happened on another planet.

She became popular and was not surprised. Half a million is a big secret to keep, and Lionel must have known because he knew everything, and Miss Gwatkin, who did not dance but had relatives, almost certainly knew too. So she was wary, and when a couple of her new male friends became rather too urgent in taxis – a strange mixture of correct behaviour physically and urgent passion vocally – she rang Mr Medlicott.

He said, 'Can you hold on a minute? I think I know but I'd better ask Rubens.' Divorce courts, chorus girls and an uncle in a commercial bank had all trained Rubens well.

'Your lord's about to go bankrupt,' Medlicott said after his consultation. 'As a matter of fact you're rather out of his class. All he needs is a hundred thousand quid.'

'How disappointing,' said Jane. 'Should I feel insulted?'

'Oh I don't know,' Medlicott said. 'He was reckoned to be rather a catch before he set up the racing stable. The other one –'

'The vicomte,' said Jane.

'That's as maybe. He's after your – ah – virtue.'

'But he can't be,' said Jane.

'Why can't he?'

'He's so frightfully well-behaved.'

'That's because he hasn't got it yet,' said Medlicott.

'What a gentleman you are,' said Jane. 'What would happen if he did get it?'

'Exposure,' said Medlicott. 'Or else a payment in cash – a large one.'

'Suppose I wouldn't pay?'

'He'd produce his wife,' Medlicott said, 'and start divorce proceedings.'

'What odd ways people choose to make a living.'

'Don't they though?' said Medlicott. 'You'll be careful, won't you?'

'No need to worry. I don't think either of them will be able to afford me much longer,' said Jane. 'But thank you for your concern, Mr Medlicott.'

'Not at all,' said Medlicott. 'Glad to help. And by the way I've arranged three hundred for your brother.'

'You're very kind.'

'How easy that is with other people's money. Going to Germany, you said?'

'I did.'

'Sensible feller.'

'Why sensible, Mr Medlicott?'

'Cheapest place in Europe just at the moment. Cheaper even than France.'

'So he should be able to live there for some time?'

'With three hundred pounds he could live like a rajah for six months.'

I do hope not, thought Jane, but she kept the thought to herself. It would take too long to explain.

Next day she received a letter from Mr Pinner. In the top right-hand corner were the words Confidential Investigations and his address. Below in precise typescript was written:

Dear Miss Whitcomb,
    I shall be glad if you will find it convenient to call at my office at any time between nine and five thirty on Thursday of this week.
    With best wishes,
    Respectfully yours,
    G. Pinner.

The signature was written in a clear, almost copy-book hand. Jane was quite sure that the 'G' stood for George.

'I hope he has found your horse,' said her mother, who had seen the letter first.

'He intends to surprise me if he has,' said Jane easily. 'But then he does describe himself as "Confidential", doesn't he? Where's Francis?'

'At work in the study,' Lady Whitcomb said. 'He claimed not to want breakfast. Most unwise.'

'Then he'll have to get out of the study,' said Jane. 'I still haven't finished doing that stuff of Papa's. I told him so.'

'Jane dear,' said her mother. 'This is my house – or had you forgotten? One day it will be Francis's house, but it will never be yours.'

'I'm aware of that, Mummy.'

'Then how can you order your brother out of a room I choose to allot to him?'

'I can't,' said Jane. 'Obviously.'

'And yet you do. Will you apply pressure of some kind?'

'Pressure? On whom?'

'On me,' said her mother. 'I am very much in your debt at the moment.'

'You owe me nothing,' said Jane. 'Presents aren't debts. But Francis knows about the request in Papa's will. He was there when it was read out – and I told him I was almost finished. I can finish today.'

'Not if he chooses not to move,' said her mother.

'Then I shall go and ask him,' Jane said, 'if you'll excuse me.'

'Certainly,' her mother said. 'But there's no great rush. You'll find nothing unsavoury among your father's papers, I assure you.'

'Thank you,' said Jane, 'but I want to finish this job now.'

'Very well,' her mother said. 'I think however that you should tell your brother that whether he leaves or stays is entirely up to him.'

As she climbed the stairs Jane pondered the fact that she didn't mind in the least that Mummy had opened Mr Pinner's letter – she had assumed she would, and arranged matters accordingly – but that the thought of Francis among her father's papers was unendurable. She flung open the study door, and Francis put down the pipe he was cleaning.

'Come to do a little work?' he said. 'Mummy said you wouldn't need this room today.'

'Mummy was wrong,' said Jane.

Francis shrugged. 'I'll leave you to it then.'

He picked up a couple of texts and a notebook, and prepared to leave.

'Where will you work?' Jane asked.

'My bedroom. The table there's just right to work on.'

'Thank you,' said Jane.

'Not at all,' Francis said. 'I expect you'll be glad to finish with all this stuff?'

'I expect I will,' said Jane.

'Is it any good?'

'It was his life,' said Jane, 'but I doubt if it has any commercial value.'

'I was thinking of it as history. You know, socio-political stuff.'

'Not unless you want to know who played Tum Tum in *The Mikado* at Amritsar in 1897.'

'I'll be off,' said Francis.

'Have a good morning's work,' said Jane. 'You should. I didn't have a chance to tell you yesterday, but Mr Medlicott's arranged the advance you wanted.'

'Two hundred?' Francis asked.

'Three.'

'That's absolutely marvellous,' said Francis. 'Thank you,' and rushed out and forgot his pipe.

Jane looked at the neatly docketed piles of photographs, letters, invitation cards. She knew her mother was right. They contained nothing unsavoury. No bills for jewellery, no letters of love, no photographs of Posy Sanderson. Nothing unsavoury at all. She set to work on the last unsorted pile. One big tea chest should do it, she thought. Store it all away, and when she moved house she would take it with her. After lunch, (mulligatawny soup, poached haddock, stewed pears) she returned Francis's pipe to him and their mother watched as if they were children still, and Jane giving back a much-valued toy.

'I hope you haven't been quarrelling?' she said.

'Not at all,' said Jane. 'The information you gave Francis about the study was wrong, that's all – and he left without his pipe.'

'Oh dear,' said her mother. 'Bear with me, children. I'm growing old, you see, and quite unreliable.'

But the smile she gave her daughter was brilliant. Just because you're rich, the smile said, doesn't mean I can't still give you a game.

Mr Pinner had asked permission to smoke a pipe, something he did much better than Francis. Jane had the feeling that he needed to smoke, that he had bad news to deliver.

'I've found your family,' he said at last.

'But that's marvellous,' said Jane.

Mr Pinner didn't look as if anything was marvellous.

'They live in a town called Felston in County Durham. They're at – ' he looked at his notebook, – 'Number 36, John Bright Street. The father's a widower now. There's two sons and a daughter and a grandmother.'

'The mother?'

'She died in 1919,' said Mr Pinner. 'Spanish 'flu. About four months after your friend.'

'How did you do it?'

'Army list,' said Mr Pinner. 'I took what I could from that. I could have asked his regiment for a look at their records – they'd have listed his next of kin and so on – but I knew you wanted this done discreetly so I went up there instead and got on to a local man. He'll cost you ten pounds but he was worth it – *and* he'll keep his mouth shut.'

'That's all right,' said Jane.

'Then we got on to the electoral rolls, but there's an awful lot of Pattersons in Tyneside, and so I went to the British Legion.'

'But John died before it was even thought of.'

'War memorials,' said Mr Pinner. 'The Legion knows all about War Memorials – and we found the right one at last. With his name and rank and regiment. That's where they are, miss. Number 36, John Bright Street, Felston. But if I were you I wouldn't go there.'

'Whyever not?' asked Jane.

'It's the most terrible place I've ever seen,' Mr Pinner said.

'But – but that's not possible,' said Jane. 'The war – '

'Well of course I saw a bit there,' Mr Pinner said. 'Arras and Nueve Chapelle and Wipers – all of that. But that was the *war*, miss. In Felston – ' He hesitated. It seemed as if the words were just not there. At last he said: 'It was like they'd just had a war of their own, miss. And they'd lost it.'

'And the Pattersons?'

Mr Pinner didn't shrug because he was too polite to shrug.

'No worse than any of the others I saw,' he said.

'But no better, either?'

'No, miss. . . . Of course I didn't get in too close – seeing you didn't want anybody to know about it. But they didn't look good, miss. They didn't look good at all. None of them did.'

'But in God's name what's wrong?' Jane asked.

'No work,' said Mr Pinner. 'And no prospect of work. Not this year – not next year, not never. My colleague in Newcastle he put it a bit different. Blasphemy you might call it, but not if you'd been there: not if you'd seen it. "As it was in the beginning, is now and ever shall be, world without end, Amen." He was talking about no hope, miss. – And no jobs either.'

'You're saying the whole town's like that?'

'The whole area's like that,' said Mr Pinner. 'And it's not the only one. You should try taking a look down the East End. But I reckon Felston's worse. You see it's *all* East End there, miss. They wouldn't know what the West End was.'

'I must go there,' said Jane.

And show them what the West End is? Mr Pinner wondered. A fat lot that's going to do for them – or you.

'You want me to go with you, miss?'

'No thank you,' said Jane. 'I once drove an ambulance through Ypres. I don't think I'll need a bodyguard in Felston. Any news of my horse?'

'I've got a couple of leads,' Mr Pinner said, 'but it's a funny thing – horses is a lot harder to find than people.'

'But you won't give up?' said Jane.

'Course not,' Mr Pinner said. 'I've never had to look for a horse before. It's what you might call a challenge.'

Jane rose and offered her hand. 'Thank you for your help,' she said.

Mr Pinner took it. 'Been a pleasure,' he said. 'Mind you take care of yourself, miss.'

But before she could set off, first her brother, then her mother, packed their bags and left. Francis, hopeless at packing, called on her for assistance, and she helped him arrange in his suitcase a great many books, which did not surprise her in the least, and a dinner jacket and full evening dress, which surprised her a great deal. After that he left, with sixty five-pound notes in his pocket, to meet his friend on the boat-train platform at Waterloo. He told neither Jane nor their mother who the friend was.

Her mother's packing took rather longer. There was a vast cabin trunk from her Indian days, there were valises and a Gladstone bag which had belonged to Papa, and a sort of vanity case that contained everything from curling tongs to a packet of pins, and functioned as a sort of portable safe as well, for her mother took with her every piece of jewellery she possessed, since dining at the captain's table, which might well happen, Gwendoline Gwatkin or no Gwendoline Gwatkin, was a serious business. To transport this vast mass of stuff to the train for Southampton something roomier than the Riley would be needed. A taxi would be considered banal, a van ironic. Jane hired a chauffeured Rolls-Royce for the day, and her mother was enchanted.

The enchantment survived even the bundle of newspapers she sent the chauffeur to buy for her mother to read on the train, for among them was the *Daily World*, and once more the name of Whitcomb appeared in the column called 'This Wicked World'. Not that to have avoided it would have made the slightest difference, Jane saw. For as her mother sat in her first-class carriage, reading and snorting, Miss Gwatkin arrived, brandishing her copy, thought Jane bitterly, like a Turk with a scimitar.

For this time Lady Whitcomb was mentioned too. She was the gallant and gracious widow, recently bereaved, off to visit India, scene of her former social and artistic triumphs. 'Artistic' thought Jane, must refer surely to her mother's unremitting attacks on the piano. Not that she escaped completely. She, the witty, elegant daughter, most unlikely of war veterans, continued to be seen in all the smartest places, the ones patronised by aristocracy both native and foreign.

'What can they mean?' Miss Gwatkin asked.

'I expect it's the Embassy nightclub,' said Jane. 'The Prince of Wales goes there once a week, so the rest of them feel they have to go.'

Miss Gwatkin was delighted. Here she was sitting in a railway carriage with someone who had actually been on the same dance floor as the Prince of Wales, *and at the same time*. Miss Gwatkin was a great disappointment to Mummy, for, as she said, if the dear prince was there, how could she disapprove? And when Mummy ventured to suggest that aristocrats, whether native or foreign, were often notorious fortune hunters, Miss Gwatkin once again invoked the sacred name.

'But not those who sit near the Prince of Wales, surely?' she said.

Mummy looked at Miss Gwatkin, then at Jane, and smiled, rather ruefully, Jane thought; the carriage doors began to slam, and she kissed first Miss Gwatkin then her mother, stood on the gritty platform as the guard's green flag waved, his whistle shrilled, and the cream and chocolate train slid out towards the west.

Jane looked in her purse and found two pennies. The first thing, she thought, was to ring darling Lionel and ask him what the hell he was playing at, for that it had been darling Lionel she had no doubt. But she stopped short of the phone booth. What had the poor man done anyway, apart from say apparently very nice things to be quoted or misquoted by whichever *Daily World* hack Bower passed them on to? Nothing offensive about Mummy, and who could object to being witty and elegant in the *Daily World*'s estimation? True, Mummy had been on to the aristocrats like a knife, but she could hardly explain the implications to Miss Gwatkin, and in eight weeks' time no doubt there would be other things to fight about. Like a visit to Felston, perhaps. And anyway, she was seeing Lionel at lunch.

Instead, she went in the Rolls to a jeweller's shop in New Bond Street, and showed him Papa's cuff-links. Ear-rings, she learned, *beautiful* ear-rings would present no problems. That *would* be a change, she thought, and was driven to Lionel's house in the mews.

- 205 -

20

H E WAS ALONE except for Pott, and the treasure in the kitchen and her satellites, which surprised Jane. Lionel liked an audience at lunch as much as any other time. But he explained it all to her as soon as Pott had gone from the room.

'I knew you'd be wanting a row with me,' he said. 'So much easier to have it without witnesses.'

'Well I must say – ' Jane began.

'Of course you must,' said Lionel, and picked up the cocktail shaker. 'White Ladies all right?'

'White Ladies are fine,' said Jane. 'Lionel, how could you?'

'Oh *easily*,' said Lionel. 'I ran into Jay at a party some maharani or other was giving – we all tried on saris. Such fun. Have you ever tried on a sari?'

'Only my own,' said Jane. 'Get on with it.'

'Well he was *asking* about you,' said Lionel, 'and I'd had rather a lot of champagne and crème de menthe – '

'A lot of *what*?'

'Champagne and crème de menthe. Really much too much.'

'But you can't have done,' said Jane.

'But I *did*,' said Lionel. 'Stop interrupting. Jay kept asking me what you were up to and what your mother was like, and what with the drinks and the saris I'm afraid I told him.'

'You don't mean to say that he tried on a sari as well?'

'The day he does,' said Lionel, 'I shall progress down Piccadilly in a tu-tu. Did you find it awful – all that gossip?'

'Not awful, exactly,' said Jane. 'I mean I do go to smart places and Mummy is off to India.'

'Well then?' said Lionel.

'The trouble is,' said Jane, 'that Mummy and I don't always get on all that well – and any stick's good enough to beat a dog with and if it's a bitch so much the better.'

'Do you mean me?' Lionel asked.

'I mean me,' said Jane, and looked at her glass. 'These White Ladies are lethal. . . . What I mean is, Mummy's awfully good at pained rebuke, and getting a mention in "This Wicked World" because of *me* gives her rather a lot of scope. If it hadn't been for – ' She broke off and giggled.

'Laugh your girlish laughter then,' said Lionel. 'Don't mind me.'

'Mummy's friend,' said Jane. 'She's called Gwendoline Gwatkin.' Lionel snorted. 'But that's not for publication,' she added.

Lionel winced. 'Touché,' he said, and then: 'Am I forgiven?'

'How can you be?' said Jane. 'You've committed no crime. You've convinced me of that – you and all that Cointreau and lemon juice and gin. You're lily-white, as usual. It's just – '

'Mummy?'

'Not only Mummy. Me too. The well-known Jane Whitcomb – observed at the Embassy, spotted at the Café de Paris, seen at the Savoy. I mean what am I well-known *for*? If I don't watch out I'll be well-known for being well-known, and where's the sense in that?' She looked again at her glass.

'Would you like another?' Lionel asked.

'Good God no.'

'Very wise,' said Lionel, and helped himself from the shaker. 'What you're saying is that you're not a completely frivolous person like me?'

'I don't know about you,' said Jane, 'but sometimes I have this urge to be very serious indeed, if only I could find something to be serious about.'

'Good works?'

'Jabber suggested that,' said Jane, 'and it may come to that, yet if – ' She broke off. 'I used to be a patient of Jabber's,' she said. 'Did you know?'

'I guessed,' said Lionel.

'Of course you did,' said Jane. 'You're as cute as a box of monkeys.'

'I'm what?'

'It's what a friend of mine used to say. It's sort of a Tyneside expression, one gathers.'

'Does one indeed? And why have you decided to tell me?'

'Because you're my friend,' she said. 'Such a bore, trying to hide things from one's friends.'

'What a devious person you are,' said Lionel. 'Nice, of *course*. But devious without a doubt. As a matter of fact I'm devious, too. I've invited someone for coffee.'

'Bower?'

'Who else?' said Lionel. 'Shall we eat?'

'I doubt if I could swallow a mouthful,' said Jane.

In fact she ate rather well, partly because Lionel's treasure could have been weighed in rubies, and partly because she had to do something about that lethal cocktail. As they ate, they discussed her other – problem. Could she call it that? Her need to get away; to find a house before her mother returned from India.

'You want me to help?' Lionel asked.

'Oh please – if it wouldn't be too much of a bore.'

'Not in the least,' Lionel said. 'I was born nosey. Few things give me more joy than poking about in other people's houses and knowing they can't do a thing to stop me. . . . Expense no object, as they say?'

'I don't want grandeur,' said Jane. 'Comfort yes, but not grandeur.'

'Mayfair is out of the question, then?'

'Completely,' said Jane. 'I'm selling up in Mayfair.'

'How grand you are,' said Lionel. 'All the same I'm delighted. I know far too many people in Mayfair as it is.'

They were still discussing possible areas when Pott announced Jay Bower.

The weather was still hot, but he was dressed with a more than British correctness. White shirt; discreet tie; blue suit. And yet he looked cool, easy and relaxed, even though, according to Lionel, he already would have done six hours' work at least, and have six more to go.

'Sorry I couldn't make lunch,' he said.

'Perfectly all right,' said Lionel. 'There were compensations.'

Bower looked at Jane with an eye that missed nothing.

'Yeah,' he said. 'I could see there would be. How are you, Miss Whitcomb?'

'Well, thank you.'

'That's it?' said Bower. 'Just well?'

'In my own estimation, yes,' said Jane. 'To say that I am witty and elegant would be extremely rude.'

'Even though you are,' said Bower.

'Even then.'

Lionel chuckled, and after a while Bower did so, too. 'OK,' he said, and then, 'At least you read the right newspaper.'

'Why do you say it's the right one?' Lionel asked.

'Because it's the only one that mentions me, of course,' said Jane.

'It won't be for long,' said Bower. 'You'll see.'

Jane smiled. To do anything else would only make her more vulnerable.

'What makes you so sure the others will take Jane up too?' Lionel asked.

'You tell him, Miss Whitcomb,' Bower said.

'I'll do my best.' She took a cigarette from the box beside her, lit it and said, 'My guess it's like covering a bet. Mr Bower has singled me out for attention, which may just be his particular form of naughtiness, or it may be because he has some sort of premonition that I may do something interesting at some point.'

'That's kind of a puny word, that interesting,' said Bower. 'You were going great till then, but cut out puny. Try exciting – maybe even sensational. And there you've got it.'

'And that's why Mr Bower's doing this,' said Jane to Lionel. 'You and I know it's all nonsense, but the *Mail* and the *Express* don't.'

'It may not be nonsense at all,' said Bower.

'People like me simply aren't "sensational",' said Jane.

'Driving an ambulance was.'

'That won't happen again.'

'Why not?' Bower asked.

'There won't be any more wars.'

'Then I'll be out of business,' said Bower.

'What nonsense,' said Lionel. 'You out of business indeed. How could you be? You fulfil an indispensable function.'

'I do?' said Bower. 'Tell me about it. I thought all I did was sell wood pulp for money.'

Lionel put down his coffee cup. 'You do rather more than that,' he said. 'You've taken the place of the Roman Colosseum. Wild beasts and gladiators and sacrificial virgins, scantily clad, throng your pages.'

'I grant you the sacrificial virgins,' said Bower, 'though they're not so scantily clad as all that – but gladiators?'

'Footballers,' said Lionel. 'Boxers. What else would one call them? In fact if I had your sort of money I'd start two newspapers. The *Daily Bread* and the *Daily Circus*. Perhaps the *Daily Bread* would have a little popular religion, too. Why don't you try it?'

'One daily's enough,' said Bower. 'Believe me. And if you'll excuse me I'd better go back to mine. Can I give you a lift, Miss Whitcomb?'

It was a challenge she could not refuse, but she would not make it easy for him. 'I have my own car with me,' she said.

'Send it away,' he said. 'I'd be glad of the chance to talk with you.'

'Very well.' She rose and kissed Lionel's cheek. 'I'll telephone you,' she said, and Lionel knew that he must hold his tongue, and did so.

Together they walked out on to the road that seemed hotter than ever.

'Aren't you going to get away out of this?' Bower asked.

'I intend to quite soon,' she said.

'Now that your mother has gone? At least we'll be cooler in my car. It's really very comfortable.'

They turned a corner to where Jane's car and chauffeur stood waiting. Behind them Bower's car was parked. It too was a Rolls-Royce.

'Never mind,' said Jane kindly. 'Yours looks bigger than mine.' Then, when they moved off she added, 'And mine's only hired after all. I drive a Riley.'

'I heard you were rich,' Bower said.

'Well of course you did. You hear everything. But I like to drive myself.'

'You reckon that's because of the ambulance in the war?'

'It's because I like driving,' she said. 'I always have.'

'Most women of your class stick to horses,' said Bower.

'Oh I like them too,' said Jane. 'But in London a car makes more sense. And how about you, Mr Bower?'

'Not cars,' said Bower. 'Mostly I prefer being driven, but horses sure. My father's got a ranch in Wyoming. I'd like to show it to you some time.'

'Oh how divine,' said Jane. 'Have you ever met Tom Mix?'

'Not in Wyoming,' said Bower. 'In Hollywood.'

'Does your father own a studio, too?'

'No,' said Bower. 'I do. A piece of one anyway.'

Game and set to Mr Bower, thought Jane. But not match. . . . Not yet. . . .

'How long have you known Lionel Warley?' he asked.

Jane thought: he asks questions like the reporter he is. The only thing important to him is one's answer. Good manners and hurt feelings don't come into it at all.

'Not long,' she said.

'You're kind of making your début, aren't you?' he said. 'I mean there doesn't seem to be anybody you have known for a long time.'

'I'm hardly making my come-out, however.'

'That's true in a way, but not in another way. I mean you're not a flapper exactly, but so far as I can gather – this is your first season.'

'I came out in 1914,' she said. 'But soon after that I had more important things to think about.'

'For eleven years?'

Not just a reporter, but a persistent one.

'I lost two brothers,' she said. 'My mother was quite ill because of that fact.'

'And your father?'

'Reclusive,' she said. 'We all were.'

'And yet you go to the Embassy. And the Bag O' Nails. That's a noisy ambience for a recluse.'

'My father died. My mother decided to travel, and I became rich. Shutting myself away no longer appealed to me.'

'Became rich, huh?'

'You know I did. You said so just a little while ago.'

'And I was right?'

'Of course you were,' said Jane. 'You know you were. My aunt's will was recorded. One of your staff must have shown it to you. That's how you know.'

This he ignored. It was not relevant to the line he was taking. 'And going to the Embassy's what you like doing?'

'Sometimes.'

He said, 'You don't much like talking about yourself, do you?'

'Not much.'

'That's OK.' He waved his hand as if she had just received his permission to stay silent. 'What I mean is – you're interesting because of what you are, now, this minute. Not because of what you used to be. Only going to nightclubs isn't going to sell my paper much longer. It's time you moved on to something else, Miss Whitcomb.'

'I must remember that.'

'You don't have to remember it,' said Bower. 'Either you'll do it or you won't. My guess is you will, which is why we're talking. And when you do it, whatever it is, I want you to let me know about it first. Not Beaverbrook. Not Rothermere. Me.'

'That wouldn't be exactly reclusive,' she said.

'No . . . but it could be useful.'

'For you?'

'For both of us.'

'You think that what I do will be newsworthy then?'

'Oh sure.' Another wave of the hand, but this time dismissive, as if she'd said something banal.

'You have been a reporter, I take it. As well as a newspaper proprietor?' she asked.

He looked at her in mild reproach, as if for her to ask questions were a breach of etiquette.

'Los Angeles Post,' he said. 'Chicago Messenger. Then I was a sub on the New York World. . . . Then I was a war correspondent for the Bowers Group.'

'You own a – group?'

'My father does,' said Bower. 'Among other things it's the Los Angeles Post and the Chicago Messenger and the New York World. I never had too much trouble getting a job on a newspaper, but I had to be good at it or my old man would fire me. Except being a war correspondent.'

'Your father didn't approve?'

'My mother. She didn't approve of the fact I might get shot.'

'My aunt and uncle had exactly the same prejudice when they bought me an ambulance.'

'And yet you drove it in France.'

'And you went out as a war correspondent.'

'You got shot, too. Well – not shot, I guess. But blown up anyway.'

'Who told you that?'

'Never ask a newspaper man to reveal his sources,' Bower said. 'He'd just as soon show you his entrails. It's what I heard. I haven't printed it.'

'Please don't,' she said.

'OK. . . . There's a fellow I want you to meet. In Paris. Would you like to go to Paris?'

'Not immediately,' she said. 'I have something rather important to do.'

'After you've done it?'

'We'll see,' she said, and he said, 'OK,' once more, as unperturbed as if he'd asked for change for a pound and she hadn't got it, then looked out of the window. They were on Kensington High Street.

'Soon be home,' he said, and reached out to touch the little jewelled leopard she wore pinned to her blouse.

'He's pretty,' he said.

'The person who gave it to me said that it's a leopardess,' said Jane, trying her best to make her voice sound matter-of-fact.

He hadn't touched her breast. Perhaps it was the exercise of scrupulous care, perhaps it was just that he was a rotten shot, but the point was that he shouldn't have done it, yet seemed totally unaware of the fact. He was not, she thought, the kind of man to force his attentions on an innocent maiden – well woman then – in a taxi at night, let alone in his own car with a chauffeur driving and the sun beating down for all of Kensington to see. He had simply wanted to draw her attention to the leopard, so he'd touched. If she'd complained he'd have looked bewildered and serve her right.

'Any idea where it came from?'

'No,' said Jane. She had no wish to see its twin sister embellishing Suzanne de Lys. Anyway, he'd get to Cartier's soon enough: Miss de Lys would see to that.

'You look good in pretty things,' he said.

'Thank you.'

'My pleasure. But it happens to be true. You're one of the ones who make money look good. You choose what's right and you wear it with style. And so of course you look rich. Which means that now and again somebody may get ideas above his financial station, if you follow me.'

'I'm listening,' she said.

'Birth and breeding, and a very pressing need of money.'

'Oh, those two,' said Jane, and at once Bower smiled. It was a grin of pure delight, and so unlike any other expression he'd used that she smiled back. I knew you wouldn't let me down, the smile said, and you haven't, and it's great.

'There'll be others,' he said.

'I'll keep you posted,' said Jane.

'You'll let me publish?'

'Maybe. Not the most flattering light for a young female, the cold glare of greed.'

The car pulled up. Her own hired car was already there waiting.

'It's ridiculous,' she said. 'Travelling in two Rolls-Royces.'

'It would make a nice piece.'

'Print it then,' she said.

'How can I?' he said. 'I'd have to say you were with me.'

'I don't mind,' said Jane.

'I do,' said Bower. 'Or rather my father does. News-paper proprietors should be read and not seen. What do you think?'

'Up to you,' said Jane. 'It's your newspaper.'

The grin came again. 'When can you go to Paris?' he asked.

'I'll telephone you,' she said.

'I'll look forward to that,' said Bower, and offered a hand. His grip was every bit as strong as she'd expected.

'May I have a word, miss?' said Hawkins.

Jane looked up from the bed. On it were an evening dress of a soft and subtle pink, fresh underwear and, reprehensibly, evening shoes of a deeper pink. Hawkins looked in her turn, and gasped.

'Oh it's lovely, miss,' she said. 'Paris?'

Jane nodded. 'Balenciaga,' she said, and reached for the shoes. 'Sorry about that. I wanted to see how they looked together.'

'They look lovely, miss,' said Mr Hawkins.

'Yes, they do rather. What can I do for you, Hawkins?'

Hawkins said, 'That's rather up to you, miss. If you take my meaning.'

'I'm afraid I don't,' said Jane. 'Not yet, anyway.'

You asked for that one, Hawkins, the maid told herself. Go ahead and explain, you silly cow. She won't eat you.

'I wouldn't want you to think I was eavesdropping, miss,' she said at last.

'Why on earth should I think that?'

'Because I've been hearing things,' said Hawkins. 'But when you're in service you're always hearing things.'

'And what have you been hearing?'

'That you'll be leaving, miss. Setting up on your own.'

Jane went to her bedside chair and sat. 'Yes,' she said. 'It's true.'

'And what with your mother being away we thought – me and cook – it'll be board wages for us once you move. Till your mother comes back.'

Left to their own devices, thought Jane, with their own food to find. 'No,' she said. 'I wasn't considering that. I mean I haven't even found a place for myself yet – haven't even *looked* – and by the time I've found one and it's ready it'll be almost time for Lady Whitcomb to come back.'

'And it'll all be just like before, miss? Except you won't be here?'

'This is my mother's house, after all,' said Jane. 'She'll be here as usual, and my brother will look in from time to time.'

'In that case, miss,' said Hawkins, 'I should like to give two weeks' notice.'

'Hawkins!' said Jane, and rose to her feet.

'I've thought it over very careful – carefully I should say,' said Hawkins, 'and while I don't mind admitting I need the money, I can't see my future here. It isn't congenial, miss.'

'Isn't what?'

'Congenial, miss,' said Hawkins. 'Isn't that the right word?'

'Well yes,' said Jane. 'That is to say – yes. But what will you do?'

'Find another place, miss,' said Hawkins. 'That is unless you would care to take me with you.'

'I?'

'In your new place, miss. You'll be needing a housemaid. Maybe a parlourmaid even. I could do that. I've been doing parlourmaid's work ever since Moreton left. And I've given satisfaction, haven't I, miss?'

'Of course you have, but – '

'And – you'll excuse my mentioning it, but I do know how to be discreet, miss.'

'You do indeed,' said Jane. To herself she wondered: 'congenial', 'discreet', 'carefully'. How much self-improvement did Hawkins feel she needed? How much did any parlourmaid need?

'Well, miss?'

'How does cook feel?' Jane asked.

'She quite likes it here, miss,' said Hawkins. 'Being used to it, she'll stay here.'

'In that case,' said Jane, 'I'll take you with me – since you're determined you won't stay here.'

'Thank you, miss,' said Hawkins. 'Would you like me to help you to dress?'

'I'll manage,' said Jane.

She needed time to think about how to say goodbye to a couple of blue-blooded optimists at the Café de Paris, and what to wear on a visit to Felston.

21

T HE NORTH EAST meant the Great North Road: Watford and
Grantham and Doncaster and York. It also meant easing her
way through parts of London of which till then she'd been
scarcely aware. Hampstead was all right – she'd been to dancing
classes there, with a girl who came from Highgate – but Hornsey?
Muswell Hill? Edmonton? The Riley chugged on, past rows and
rows of identical houses with identical chapels, past soot-
blackened terraces with no gardens at all: past small shops and
big shops, laundries and public baths, schools and cinemas and
tiny chapels and mock-Gothic churches so huge as to hint at
dementia.

And people. Not too many children: she'd set off late so
the children were in school for the most part. But there were
policemen and postmen and tram drivers and railwaymen – and
nursemaids and housemaids too, where the money was: odd
how the uniforms persisted, seven years after the war was over.
But for the most part it was men and women in civvies (though
that was uniform too, depending on which regiment you belonged to), bowler hats and smart suits if you were wealthy,
caps and blue serge if you were poor. And, this being England,
there were all sorts of subtle gradations in between. Uniforms
for officers, for sergeant majors, for NCOs and, down at the
bottom of the ladder, for other ranks. Upper class, middle class,
lower-middle class, and working class, each had a way of telling
you where they belonged as soon as they put on their clothes.
They didn't even have to open their mouths and speak.

And it was the same with the women, she thought. Their uniforms might be more subtle – hadn't she herself worn a sable coat to drive an ambulance? – but they were there if you knew where to look, especially if you were another woman. . . . She drove on to a sort of scrubland that was neither London nor anything else. Long roads of semi-detached houses with newly planted saplings in front of them, then more waste land, refuse dumps, and then another long, neat road. London pushing out, feeling its way towards more land, more space, until at last even London gave up, and she was in the countryside.

Fields and hedges, and very nice too, she thought, when one's idea of unlimited open country had been restricted to Kensington Gardens. Here were pasture, and corn land already golden, and cows and sheep and occasional horses. There were hay waggons too, with massive Clydesdales easing them along like ships through a brown-gold sea, and if she stopped the Riley and got out there would be the sight and smell of hedge flowers, bird-song, a glimpse of rabbits, or even a fox. The England she'd read about in India, she thought, and seen and learned about with Vinney in her uncle's rented mansion.

But she couldn't stop. She had to get on. This journey of hers was using up all her courage; if she dawdled and wavered she would never see it through, and she knew it. Yet still the countryside was beautiful. It was hard to put her foot down and keep on going. And still there were the villages, too: houses and people sleepy in the heat, where to hurry seemed a profanation as the Riley chugged grimly on. When she did stop at last it was at the top of a hill, with common land beside her. She got out and stretched, and spread a motor rug beneath a chestnut tree, took out her sandwiches and a vacuum flask.

Beneath her the common land gave way to a park, and in it the local great house, not huge, but big enough: grey stone, dark slate that sparkled in the sunshine. Money. And nearby, just far enough for a Sunday stroll, a church of the same grey and sparkling stone; no spire, but a most elegant bell tower. And beyond the spiritual and temporal power, the village, pictur-esque and straggling; duck pond and smithy and pubs; and the wrong sort of diet and chilblains in winter and rheumaticky cottagers, she had no doubt, but oh how beautiful it looked that day.

She poured out coffee and began on her sandwiches, and wished she had brought Foch with her. She knew it was impossible – she was going among strangers who might not like dogs, and Foch disliked strangers, besides being an unabashed snob, but all the same it would have been pleasant to watch him roam the scrubby grass, worrying about what he would do if he encountered a rabbit. It was just as well that he had Hawkins to wait on him hand and foot, she thought, and Foch would certainly see that she did wait on him. After all, she had nothing else to do.

Jane heard the soft thud of a horse's hoofs only just in time. She had begun to doze, but looked up at once. Coming towards her was a man on a mouth-watering roan gelding: a man quite old, with a white moustache, who wore, despite the heat, a buff-coloured riding coat, dogskin gloves, white breeches and boots. As he came up to Jane his sharp blue eyes took in the Riley, the motoring rug, the young woman at her picnic in one glance, touched the rim of his hat with his riding whip and cantered on, and Jane knew that despite the fact that she had with her neither chauffeur nor companion she had been accepted, she belonged.

Time to move on, more than time, but the heat made her lazy, and besides there were the aristocrats to think about. Cramming them both into the one night might have been clumsy, even tactless, she thought, but she really had had to get rid of them and get on with her life. The English one had really been quite grateful, she remembered, glad of the tip off that gave him the chance to look for somebody else before the pheasant season. But the vicomte had been more difficult and demanded a loan of five hundred for time and money wasted. For all the world as if I owed him a week's wages in lieu of notice, she thought. She had had to be quite sharp with him. It was the mention of Medlicott and Rubens that had done it. When she invoked them, he had gone like a lamb. Aunt Pen was right. It would be madness to go elsewhere.

She went back to the Riley and set off once more, through more enchanting country, pretty villages, neat and handsome little towns, through Huntingdonshire and Lincolnshire and into South Yorkshire, and at last the landscape began to change. Suddenly there were more railways, and factories, the first winding engine wheel of a coalmine, then another and another as she moved further into Yorkshire. No more cows at grass, but the narrow rows of pit cottages and soot-smeared waste land beyond, where children raced and shrieked, or else played grimly at a kind of cricket with rules of their own devising. The easy rolling hills too were gone, and in their place great jagged ones of slag and pit waste. And yet the sun still shone.

She reached York at last, looking down at its great cathedral – Minster, they called it – from a landscape grown kind once more. 'The Vale of York', the guide book said, where they grew fruit and raised cattle, and tended cows for the milk that they made into chocolate, a gentle, kindly sort of industry compared with the battlefields she had come through. She would stay there for the night, she decided. No point in arriving at Felston exhausted.

There were plenty of hotels, and she chose the best she could find, old and comfortable, and not far from the cathedral. The landlord seemed surprised that she was on her own, and looked at once at her left hand. No rings, at least not on the relevant finger.

'Come far, miss?' he asked her.

'London,' she said. 'Have you a room with a bath?'

'Not a room, miss,' said the landlord. 'Private baths is only with a suite.'

'I'll have a suite, then,' said Jane.

'On your own, miss?'

'I certainly don't intend to share it.'

'No, miss, of course not,' the landlord said. 'It's only that suites is expensive.'

'How much is expensive?'

'Three to five guineas a night, miss. Including breakfast.'

He made it sound like a lakh of rupees, she thought. A hundred thousand glittering coins poured out of great leather sacks at the feet of a maharajah. She took out a five pound note from her note case, and added two half crowns. 'I'll have five guineas' worth,' she said.

When she was taken up to see it, she understood his reluctance. It was the bridal suite. Rather more gloomy than one would wish on one's honeymoon, but the furniture was comfortable, and the bath huge, with loads of hot water. She wallowed happily, and soaked the stiffness from her bones. Really it would have been better to have someone to share it with, she thought. He could have dried my back, too.

As it was all she could do was be a tourist, and walk round the old city walls, squeeze her way up the narrow medieval streets and stand at last in the cathedral itself. Evensong was just finishing, and the clear sweetness of boys' voices, the richness of men's, blended in the great space of the nave, and she dropped on her knees and stared at the incredible stained-glass window that faced her. 'The Seven Sisters', so the hotel's guide book told her. 'A masterpiece of medieval craftsmanship.' The guide book didn't tell her that it was also a creation of a quite overwhelming beauty, the declining sun turning the coloured glass into the shining richness of jewels: rubies, sapphires, emeralds heaped up into the shapes of prophets and saints. But John had told her that, she remembered, one day as they looked at the stained glass in Nôtre Dame, told her then boasted, because he was a chauvinist, that the great Rose Window in Durham Cathedral was even better. . . . She went back to the hotel, and had dinner. The dining room seemed packed with clerics of one kind and another, all doing themselves well, and taking peeps from time to time at the young female bold enough to be dining alone. Jane wondered how many sermons she would appear in the following Sunday. It was obvious that neither they nor her waiter approved of her.

But next morning she found a garage with a young mechanic who approved of her very much, and even more of the Riley. He checked it for her carefully, filled it up with petrol, then asked where she was going, and when she told him he wished her luck for all the world, she thought, as if I'd said Passchendaele.

At first it was pleasant – up into the North Riding, and what was called the Dale Country, wild and open, with sheep wherever one looked, and the remains of ancient abbeys that had once existed because of wool. 'Bare, ruined choirs', Vinney would have called them, and as for John, they would have reminded him of the cathedral at Ypres that was just as impressive a ruin when he had last seen it. The sheep would have made him think of his civilian job in Bradford, and his prospects, and the career he was going to make for her and the bairns. If he'd lived he'd have been a rich man by now, she thought – if Aunt

Pen had liked him, and of course Aunt Pen would have liked him. There would have been no need for her to frighten off impoverished young aristocrats, either; then she vigorously repressed the thought that she'd rather enjoyed frightening off impoverished young aristocrats.

The Dale Country ended. As she crossed the border at Darlington more slag heaps appeared, the great steel mills stood strong as fortresses, then the landscape grew bleak indeed, the little iron towns and pit villages blending into their grimness. Only once more did that kinder England show itself, at Durham. She looked down at it from above, massive, enduring, beautiful, and remembered what John had told her and drove into the town for sandwiches at a teashop, then on to the cathedral; another glory of Gothic. And John hadn't been all that chauvinistic. The Rose Window too, glowing as if its light were all within, proclaimed its utter certainty in God's glory. Jane knelt and prayed. She had no doubt that there was a lot to pray for.

If Durham was the city of God, she thought, the country between it and Newcastle had long gone over to the Devil: pit heaps instead of downland – colliery wheels for spires. And so it was all the way to Newcastle, which was like an island of cheerfulness: trams and shops, and people who looked as if they were going somewhere, doing something, before at last she fumbled her way to a sign that said 'Felston', and left the city, and went back into the nightmare.

Dismal streets yielded to more pit heads, narrow-gauge railways held row upon row of waggons that looked as if they hadn't moved in months. Now and again the tall, gaunt shape of a factory appeared, a factory where no one worked, and then she was beside the river, – the Tyne it must be, – dark and filthy, crusted with rubbish, and lined with shipyards that were just like the factories, because no one worked there either. There were cranes and engines, the great stages where ships' hulls were assembled, the machine shops where engines were made, the whole intricate life of a steamship constructed, and all were empty. The only living things were the planing seagulls, and even for them the river held no hope of life.

The men who should have been in the shipyards and factories, down the pits, she saw in the streets of Felston. Because the weather was fine they lounged out of doors, most of them with their backs to a wall or seated on a doorstep: the miners – so she learned later – squatting down, easy as Cossacks, the way they squatted at their work in the narrow seams deep down below. None of them moved very much. When she had last seen a group of men like that, they had been in khaki, behind the lines, and they'd been skylarking, scuffling, playing impromptu football. But these men had learned that exercise makes you hungry, and it's foolish to make yourself hungry when there's nothing to eat.

Every one of them, she noticed, wore the uniform of the working class: the cloth cap, heavy blue-serge suit, white scarf and boots, even in the sunshine. There weren't so many women as men, but the ones there were wore a uniform of their own: old dresses with a pinafore over them, scarves or shawls round their heads, cotton stockings, enduring, clumsy shoes. Jane remembered the old gentleman in the buff-coloured riding coat she had seen the day before. He could have belonged to another country – even another planet. The thought that nagged her was that she belonged with the old gentleman (he'd known at once that she belonged) and not with Felston at all. Even so she had to find John Bright Street.

She pulled up beside a group of men at a crossroads, and they looked towards her at once. A woman, smartly dressed, driving her own car in a town where practically nobody owned a car apart from the more successful doctors, that was a sight to be savoured. Jane wound down her window and called out 'Excuse me.' At last a man came up to her.

'Yes, miss?'

'I'm looking for John Bright Street,' she said. 'Can you direct me?'

He began to speak in his turn, but apart from his pointing finger she understood nothing. His dialect was so thick as to seem like a foreign language, but how could she say so?

A voice from behind the first man said, 'Are you lost?'

She twisted in her seat. Looking at her was a small man with a bicycle. He seemed Jewish and, unlike every other man she'd seen, was bare-headed and wore a coat of some light material that could even have been silk.

'I'm looking for John Bright Street,' she said.

'Straight on till you get to the town hall,' said the bare-headed man. 'Left there and up Norman Purvis Street past the Labour Hall and second right.'

The other man beside her made noises that appeared to mean 'That's what I told her.'

'I'm obliged to you both,' she said.

The bare-headed man said, 'May I ask what number you're looking for?' He spoke with what Jane took to be a Lancashire accent, but not exaggeratedly so. He was also asking a question that was no business of his, but he was pleasant about it, and he'd helped her.

'Number 36,' she said.

'I hope the Pattersons aren't in any trouble,' said the bare-headed man.

'So do I,' said Jane, and drove off and left him. The invitation to gossip was a little too much.

22

JOHN BRIGHT STREET was where the bare-headed man said it was, and she drove carefully along it, easing her way past children newly out of school, who played games involving skipping ropes and lamp-posts, and a great deal of chalking of pavements, and who were liable without warning to run out on to the cobbled road that rarely saw anything more lethal than a horse-drawn milk cart.

Number 36 was exactly like the others: sooty brick and fading paint, but in common with the others too its windows were washed, its door handle gleamed, its front step holystoned. She got out of the car, went to the door and knocked, and the children flocked like sparrows as the door opened, and she found herself looking at John. The right age, the right expression, the right sort of cockiness, even in shirt sleeves, and no shoes.

'What is it?' The voice was brusque, harsh even, yet there was no hint of cruelty. It was a voice familiar to her, and yet quite new. For a moment she found it impossible to answer, for this was John looking at her and John was dead.

'Mr Patterson?' she said at last.

'Bob Patterson. . . . Aye. . . . What is it?'

Bob. The younger brother. 'Our kid.' She wished that John had warned her how much alike they were. Perhaps it wouldn't have hurt quite so much.

'I'm awfully sorry to bother you,' she said, 'but I once knew your brother you see and as I was passing this way – '

Behind her she could hear one of the children mimicking her

– 'awfully sorry' – 'as I was passing this way' – No wonder they mocked her, she thought. Her excuses were pathetic.

'You know our Andy?' Bob asked.

'Not Andy. . . . No. . . . Your brother John. . . .'

'Oh,' said Bob. 'I see.'

And maybe he did see, she thought, for he had John's quickness too.

'Not Andy. . . . No. . . .' the child mimic said, drawling out the vowels in a way that sent his fellows into ecstasies.

'Excuse me, miss,' said Bob, and went outside, stockinged feet and all, and roared once. The children scattered.

'Is that your car, miss?' he asked, and she nodded. 'It's a bonny un. You'd best come in.' He pushed the front door wider.

'Sorry I was a bit sharp,' he said. 'When you get a caller this time of day it's usually somebody selling something. Though where they think we can get the money to buy – this way, miss.'

He led the way up a steep flight of stairs. Their carpet was threadbare, Jane noticed, but the brass rods gleamed. At the head of the stairs was a tiny landing. Bob opened the door on the right.

'In here, miss,' he said. 'I'll just go and get Grandma – if you'll give us your name, please.'

'Jane Whitcomb,' she said. That it meant nothing to Bob was obvious.

'Right, miss,' he said. 'If you'll just take a seat. . . .'

He left her, and she sat down on a black, horse-hair sofa. It was flanked by horse-hair armchairs. Four indentations in a worn carpet marked the place where a table had once stood. The fireplace was filled with crinkled red paper, and in front of it was a wooden screen papered with scraps, then varnished over. On the mantelpiece there was one photograph, John in the uniform of a lieutenant, the ribbon of his DSO looking very new against the whipcord cloth. It could have been Bob dressing up. She got up and picked up the photograph, looked at it more closely. 'My but you are a bonny lass.' She remembered the words, and how and where he had said them, and the tears were very close.

Behind her a voice said, 'Aye, that's him all right,' and she turned to the door, and the old woman framed inside it. Quite small, the old woman, and stooped, but ablaze with vitality.

Formidable too, with a strong little chin and a nose like the beak of a predatory bird. Luxurious white hair, thick and gleaming, coiled in a bun. Only the dark eyes that should have gleamed with the power she had, did not belong, but looked milky, languid even. Going blind, thought Jane, but she's not giving in to it.

'Mrs Patterson?' she said.

'John's grandma. . . . He used to call me Gran.'

'I'm Jane Whitcomb. I used to know John.'

'So Bob tells me,' the old woman said. 'You've got him gawping like an idiot. Anyone would have thought there was a giraffe on the doorstep. Mind you I can't say I blame him now I've seen you.'

'Giraffe?' said Jane.

'How many young women do you think come knocking on our door – dressed the way you're dressed and driving their own cars?'

And she was wearing her oldest, plainest suit.

'As I told you,' Jane said, 'I used to know John, so I thought I'd look you up.'

'You took your time,' the old woman said. 'He's been dead seven years.'

Gently, Jane admonished herself. Gently. . . . She wouldn't talk like this if she hadn't loved him, too.

'Not quite,' she said. 'There's rather more than two months to go first.'

The old woman's face thrust forward towards her, then her fists clenched. She wants to see my face because I said that, Jane thought, but she can't.

'You know the date then,' she said at last.

'Tenth of November, 1918,' said Jane. 'At La Bassée Canal.'

The old woman's head bowed, but came up again almost at once.

'And where did you meet him?'

'In France. . . . Autumn. 1917.'

'Nurse, were you?'

'I drove an ambulance.'

The old woman seemed not to have heard. 'Our John was wounded the year before. 1916 it was. Just a scratch, he said. Some scratch. He was in the hospital six weeks.'

Some scratch indeed, thought Jane. A great curving scar from his collar bone to his ribs. A shell splinter that had hit him just right. A little more of an angle and it would have killed him. She used to stroke it. It was hard, ugly, compared with the smoothness of the rest of him, but it was a part of him and so she loved that too.

'You drove an ambulance, you say?'

'That's right. I met John at a dance.'

The ruins of a little château with one wooden floor surviving and a wind-up gramophone. . . .

'John was fond of a dance.'

'I too.'

The old woman said, 'Come over here a minute, will you? My eyes aren't what they were.'

There was a stool with a cushion by the old woman's feet. Jane went to sit on it. Now, she thought, you can look down on me.

Grandma Patterson said, 'Driving an ambulance – you'd be near the battlefield. The what-did-they-call-it?'

'The Front,' said Jane. 'Yes. I was.'

'And weren't you frightened?'

'Of course,' said Jane. The old woman waited. 'But somebody had to do it,' Jane added at last.

'It must have been nasty sometimes, chaps knocked about like they were.'

'Ghastly,' said Jane, but this time she added nothing.

'You didn't pick up our John when he was killed?'

'No,' said Jane. 'I was at home. On leave. But I did make enquiries. He was hit by a machine-gun burst. It was a clean death. Quick too.'

'It was still a death,' the old woman said. 'His colonel wrote and told us the same and we were grateful, but it won't bring John back.'

The old woman sat for a long time among memories more real than the sounds of the children outside, thought Jane, and she could understand that, but even so it had been a mistake to come. Better if she left and found a place to spend the night then drive back to London and go dancing with Lionel.

'I think I'd better go,' she said. 'I'm sorry to have bothered you like this.'

'You haven't bothered me,' the old woman said. 'It's just come as a bit of a shock after all these years. Our John. An officer. Dancing with a lady.'

'With an ambulance driver,' said Jane. 'And I'm sorry it's been so long, Mrs Patterson, but I've been rather ill for a long time – too ill to get about much, I'm afraid.'

'But you're all right now?'

'Oh yes. I'm fine.'

'And you came from a long way, likely?'

'From London.'

'You drove yourself all that way just to come and see us? His family?'

'To see whether you were all right.'

'You must have been fond of him.'

It was like being out to hounds, Jane thought. Either you went for the fence no matter how high it was, or you pulled up and turned away and went home.

'Fond isn't quite the word,' she said.

'I was hoping you would say that.' The old woman folded her hands in her lap. 'Would you mind telling me what the word is then?' she asked.

'I loved him,' said Jane.

'I was hoping you would say that, too.'

'We were engaged,' Jane said, and she opened her hand-bag, took out the little box and opened it too. 'When the war was over we were going to marry.' She took the ring from the box and gave it to the old woman, who held it close to her face.

'By it's a bonny un,' she said. 'Why don't you wear it?'

'Would you mind?'

'Our John gave it to you,' she said. 'And you chose to take it. Why should I mind?'

Jane slipped the ring on to her finger. It still fitted.

'That's better,' said Grandma Patterson, and added: 'So now you've come to see how the Pattersons are getting on.'

There was irony in her voice, but Jane thought she heard sympathy too.

'It's bad?'

'There's plenty worse. We've no bairns here, you see. – What you would call children. – Bairns eat money. Always hungry: always wearing out their clothes. And then we had the bit cash

John left – him having put Minnie down on his next of kin. – Minnie was his mam.'

She waited for a moment, but all that Jane said was, 'Of course.'

'But it didn't last for ever – and one by one they were out of a job – first Andy – that's the other brother. Then Stan, the father – then Bob. So there was nowt coming in and only John's money and the dole going out. And now it's only the dole.' She looked at Jane. 'Unemployment Benefit you'd call it, though where the benefit is in under three pound a week to feed three grown men and two grown women I'm blest if I know.'

'Two women?'

'There's his sister. Bet.'

'Oh yes of course. John used to talk about his little sister.'

'She's not little any more. She helps me look after the place. . . . No. . . . That's a lie. I help her when she'll let me. . . . I'm gettin' past it.' She looked up, at once puzzled, and irritated. 'Where was I?'

'The dole,' said Jane. 'Trying to manage.'

'Well you can't,' said the old woman. 'Not on two pounds twelve and six a week you can't. Not even if you were that financial genius our Andy's always on about. . . . What's his name? German would he be?. . . . Oh aye.' She looked at Jane in triumph. 'Karl Marx himself couldn't do it.'

'I believe you,' said Jane. 'So how *do* you manage?'

'Go on a diet,' the old woman said. '*That's* how we manage. The Wednesday and Thursday diet.'

'Why then?'

'Because the men's dole's paid on a Friday, and by Wednesday teatime there's nowt left. . . . Oh aye. And we simplify our lives an' all. Leastways that's what Bob calls it.'

'And how do you do that?'

'Get rid of stuff we don't need.'

'Like the parlour table?'

The old woman looked at once at the carpet, to the place where the four indentations were.

'You've a sharp pair of eyes on you. So did I, once upon a time. . . . Aye. Like the table. Solid mahogany that was. A proper good un. I could have cried when it went.'

'Why didn't you?'

'Where's the sense?' the old woman asked. 'You can't eat a table.'

'Very true,' said Jane, and Grandma Patterson made again that peering lunge. 'Are you mocking me?' she asked.

'Of course not,' said Jane. 'I want to know, that's all. But I just don't know what words to use.'

Surprisingly, the old woman accepted this. 'Bit of a novelty,' she said. 'Meeting with folks that are hungry.'

'Well not exactly,' said Jane. 'I was brought up in India – but of course only the natives were hungry there.'

'Your father in the army?'

'Indian Civil Service actually. He died earlier this year.'

'And your mother?'

'She's gone back to India on a visit.' How could I possibly use a word like 'cruise' after what she's told me? Jane thought.

'Mr Whitcomb would be a high-up, likely?'

Jane answered without hesitation. 'Very high. He was knighted for it.'

'You mean – ?'

'Sir Guy Whitcomb,' said Jane.

'And your mother?'

'Lady Whitcomb.'

'Sir Guy and Lady Whitcomb,' the old woman said. 'And you'd have a big house and servants and all that?'

'Our house in India was very big,' said Jane. 'Almost a palace – and as for servants – we must have had twenty at least. In Kensington not nearly so many. Never more than four. But of course the house is smaller.'

'Well I'll go to France,' the old woman said. That she was amazed there could be no question, but she was also lapping it up.

'And our John,' she said, 'you and our John – '

'He gave me this ring,' said Jane. 'We considered ourselves as good as married, and we acted accordingly.'

The old woman sat silent for a moment, then: 'I'm obliged to you,' she said.

'For what?'

'For being honest. There's a lot between us, but we'd get nowhere if we aren't honest. You've no bairn?'

'No,' said Jane. 'Perhaps it's as well.'

'Perhaps. . . . John was my favourite. I've never denied it and God knows I've been punished for it. But there wasn't many like John.'

'I know that,' said Jane.

'Well of course you do. Man and wife you were and I'm glad of it. The minister might not be, but I am. . . . For John's sake. Yours an' all. You had a good man while it lasted. Not that I'll be telling anybody else about it. You've my word on that. They're a prim and proper lot round here. Chapel mostly. – Though mind you the Catholics is just as bad. . . . Where was I?'

'Being glad for us,' said Jane.

'Well so I am,' the old woman snapped. 'And glad you've told me an' all. Our John and a proper lady. . . . But what took you so long, lass? I know you said you were poorly, but at my age – I might have died not knowing.' The thought was so appalling that for the only time her voice faltered. Her John had been happy and she could have died in ignorance of it.

I can tell only the truth, thought Jane, and if it's too much for her I can still drive back three hundred miles, and dance tomorrow with Lionel at the Savoy.

'I wasn't just poorly,' she said. 'I was mad. What they call shell shock. Maybe you've heard of it?'

'Heard of it?' said the old woman. 'I only have to walk out of that door to see it. . . . Sarah Barlow's lad. Back home for seven years and he thinks he's still in France. . . . Bad for you, was it?'

'Bad enough,' said Jane. 'I saw a lot of things I still don't believe – I was hungry and exhausted and blown up by a shell – but it wasn't that.'

'What then?'

'It was John,' said Jane. 'It was losing John.' Her hands came up to her face, and she sobbed, not yelling, the way she used to do when things were bad, but quietly, containedly almost, emptying out grief like water from a basin. The old woman's hand came out to touch her hair, and gently, softly stroked.

'Whisht, me bairn. Whisht now,' she said, over and over, and even as she wept Jane was aware of the power in that old and work-hardened hand, the grim strength still remaining in the worn-out body. When at last she had done, she looked up.

'I bet I look a mess,' she said.

– 232 –

'You looked better when you came in,' said the old woman, and smiled.

Jane took the mirror from her handbag, and examined her face that was blotched and tear-stained and smeared with make-up.

'Oh dear,' she said, and began to clean herself up with a handkerchief soaked in the cologne she carried.

'That's a good lass,' the old woman said, then watched in silence as Jane produced powder compact and lipstick and got to work, and showed to Grandma Patterson at last a face that might never once have wept.

'Well I'm blessed,' the old woman said.

'You've seen a woman make up before,' Jane said.

'No,' the old woman said. 'That's just it. I haven't. Like a conjuring trick. You look just like when you came in. And to think the minister's always going on about painted harlots.'

Jane said defensively, 'John liked me to look pretty.'

'I'll bet he did,' the old woman said, and then: 'What time is it?'

No clock on the mantelshelf either. Jane looked at her watch. 'Nearly five o'clock,' she said.

'They'll be wanting their teas,' said the old woman. 'There's fresh herring and potatoes. You're welcome to stay.'

'You'll have to excuse me,' said Jane. 'I had a huge lunch in Durham.' This was a lie, but she knew beyond doubt that the herring would have been allocated already. 'Besides – I'll have to think about finding a place to stay.'

'The Eldon Arms,' said the old woman at once. 'It's the only place that's fit. But if you don't mind my asking, pet – what are you going to do after that?'

'Pet' Jane thought, meant a concession, and not a small one either.

'I'd like to stay for a while,' she said. 'This was John's birth-place. He lived most of his life here. I'd like to look around. See what I can do to help.'

'You?' the old woman said. But it wasn't anger, merely amazement.

'I'm quite young – and healthy nowadays, and I'm not poor exactly. There must be something – '

'We'll talk about it tomorrow,' said the old woman. 'Now you better come and meet the family before they start chewing the oil-cloth.'

She got up and led the way into what was the centre of the household: kitchen, dining room and workshop, too. The room was dominated by a fireplace with an oven beside it, and even on that hot day the fire burned. The only source of power they had, thought Jane, for on a bar across the fire a kettle simmered, and on a ring beside it a pot of potatoes steamed.

Facing the fire was a deal table, its top covered with some kind of artificial material: what Grandma Patterson had called the 'oil-cloth', well worn and shiny, and decorated with unlikely flowers. There was a mat on the floor, and another, half finished on a frame. For the rest there were a set of kitchen chairs, a rocker, a wooden Windsor chair, a couple of stools, and a sideboard that looked homemade. A man and a woman sat at the frame, working on the mat. They had a supply of strips of cloth, cut from old clothes by the look of them, which they knotted with the aid of steel hooks into a canvas backing. The two were obviously father and daughter, and both looked like John and like Grandma Patterson. Only then did Jane realise that John too had resembled his grandmother, but he had inherited her combative self-reliance, too. The man and woman before her both bore the marks of defeat.

At the table another man sat, mending a boot on a boot last, banging in the nails with a sort of monitored aggression. He too had the family look, but in him the fierceness was apparent at once. This must be Andy, the reader of Karl Marx. Red Andy, John had called him. In a corner Bob, the only one she knew, fiddled with the earphones of what she assumed must be a crystal set.

Grandma Patterson said, 'Now then. Stan, Bet, Andy. You can stop your fidgeting. I want you to meet our John's fiancée.'

23

B OB HAD OFFERED to show her the way to the Eldon Arms, provided nobody pinched his share of the herring. He wants a ride in a car, thought Jane, and a chance to see and be seen beside a smartly dressed woman, and to talk about a place, *any place*, that wasn't Felston. He was in a fever to leave it, as John had been, but John had acquired skills, shorthand, bookkeeping, that gave him a start in a booming industry. Bob had trained as a printer, and been fired the day after he'd finished his apprenticeship, because skilled men cost money, and apprentices soon got the hang of things.

They drove, at Bob's suggestion, by the sea coast, a roundabout way to get there but at least she could see the gleaming yellow sands, the lazy-rolling waves, green as wine bottles, roaring softly in. Jane pulled up to watch.

'So there's something beautiful in Felston,' she said.

'I come here every chance I get,' said Bob.

'May one ask why?'

'It's the way out,' he said. 'It's escape, the sea is.'

'Escape to where?'

'Anywhere,' said Bob. 'There's the colliers for a start. They take coal to London. There's one. Look.' He pointed at a stubby, weathered little ship.

'I thought the pits were closed?'

'There's too much coal, that's why,' said Bob. 'When the stocks is low they'll let them back in – if they've a mind to go. Pitmen is gluttons for punishment. But that ship's off to London and I

– 235 –

can get a place on her for ten bob – cheaper than the railway.'

'Won't it take a long time?'

'Three or four days,' said Bob. 'Too far to walk.' He hesitated. 'Don't let Andy upset you. He gets a bit sharp sometimes – but he doesn't mean it.'

'Doesn't he?'

Bob smiled. 'He's going to change the world, you see. God knows it needs changing. But it's a bit hard on the temper.'

'He didn't spare you, I notice.'

'That's because of me crystal set. Most of it's second hand – or ninth hand or tenth hand mebbes. But batteries is only for cash.'

'He thinks you should spend it on food?'

'He thinks I should spend it on pamphlets,' Bob said. 'He's got a pal with a printing press and I set it for them – "Workers of the World Unite" and all that. But now and again he runs out of paper and ink, and he expects me to give a contribution. Me.' He shook his head, miming amazement at such idiocy.

'Two nights ago I heard Ambrose's band at the Café de Paris,' he said. 'That was before the earphones went.'

'Then you heard me,' said Jane. 'I was there that night.'

'You never,' he said, and turned towards her, as delighted as if he'd been at the next table. 'Was it marvellous?'

How could she tell him she'd gone there to get rid of a couple of millstones?

'Wonderful,' she said. 'They played "Mean To Me" three times.' She took one last look at the waves. 'Shouldn't we get on to this pub now? They might eat all your herrings.'

Andy Patterson said, 'She has no business here.'

'Well of course she has,' said Bob. 'Don't talk daft.'

'How has she?' Andy asked. Bob went on eating herring. The walk from the Eldon Arms had made him hungry. It was true that Jane had given him threepence for a tram ride that cost a penny, but that would go for a pint.

'You can't, can you?' Andy said.

Stan Patterson leaned forward. 'What Bob means,' he said slowly, 'is that that young lady was our John's intended.'

'That's what she says,' said Andy.

Bob speared his last potato and looked up. 'For God's sake man,' he said, 'why on earth would she lie about it?'

Stan Patterson said, 'No language Bob,' but his eyes were on Andy.

'What I mean,' said Andy at last, 'is that it's all wrong. Them clothes. That car. . . . They don't belong here. There's nothing about her belongs here. What did she come for?'

'To help,' his grandmother said. 'I asked her straight and she told me. She wants to help.'

'To help us starve?' said Andy. 'We can do that on our own.'

'She's got money,' the old woman said. 'Anyone can see that.'

'We don't want charity.'

'Don't we? We don't seem able to get anything else. But I wasn't thinking of her on her own. She couldn't keep the whole town.'

'She's got money all right,' said Bob. 'She was in the Café de Paris two nights back.'

'And what that might be?' his father asked.

'Nightclub,' said Bob. 'I heard it on the wireless.'

'You would,' said Andy.

'From what I hear nightclubs is sinful,' said his father. 'We don't want any of that.'

'We couldn't afford it,' said Bob, 'and anyway, she didn't look like a sinner, now did she?'

'She looked like a nice young woman,' said his grandmother, 'which is what she is. If she wasn't she'd still be in London going off to a dance.'

'I still don't see what use she'd be to us – or Felston,' Andy said.

'Then you need glasses like me,' said his grandmother. 'Look. She wants to stay here and look around for a bit. What's wrong with that? She's got a car. She can make herself useful taking folks to the clinic – and that way she'll get an idea what housing conditions is like.

'And when she's seen for herself – if she still wants to help – we can set her on going round her rich friends with the collecting box.'

'Collecting for what?' Stan Patterson asked.

His mother sighed. 'For what Felston needs,' she said. 'Free

– 237 –

milk for bairns, and medicine and specs and winter coats for poor old bodies like me.'

'Charity,' said Andy. 'I've told you before – we don't want charity.'

'You might not,' said Bob. 'I'll take whatever's going.'

Andy jumped to his feet then, angry, ready to hurt, but Bob sat tight. No sense in him having a barney with Andy, not when he had the price of a pint.

'You're forgetting something else, Andy,' Grandma Patterson said.

'*What?*'

'Sit down and I might tell you,' said his grandmother, and Andy sat. 'That's better. She was going to marry our John. No sense in making a mystery out of it – there's his ring on her finger, and like Bob said, why should she lie?'

'I still don't see – ' said Andy.

'You wouldn't,' said Bob. 'But I do. It means she's got a right to come here.'

'It means more than that,' his grandmother said. 'It means she loved him and he loved her. It means they would have been married and had bairns by now.'

'Posh bairns in a posh school,' said Andy.

'Your nephew – or your niece mebbes,' said his grandmother. 'Wouldn't you have wanted to see them given a better start than you had?'

Stan Patterson said, 'You make charity sound like a sin, Andy. But you're wrong. Charity's a wonderful thing. Remember St Paul.'

Bob watched, and chuckled inwardly as Andy bit off his reply. Nobody could tell his father what St Paul could do, least of all in Da's own house.

'"Though I speak with the tongues of men and of angels, and have not charity, I am become as sounding brass, or a tinkling cymbal." First Book of Corinthians that is. And then a bit later on: "And now abideth faith, hope, charity, these three; but the greatest of these is charity." The *greatest*, Andy.'

His mother had sat listening as he quoted, her hands folded in her lap. 'Very nice, Stan,' she said. 'Words of comfort, which is no more than you would expect from the Bible. And being the Bible it also makes sense. The best sense yet.'

Bet said, 'We can't turn her away. We just can't.'

These were the first words she had spoken, and the whole family turned to her. She blushed, but went on: 'She was very nearly one of us. How can we tell her we don't want her?'

'That's all very well,' said Andy. 'But we're forgetting one thing.' They waited. 'How is it it took nigh on seven years for her to come and find us? And how did she know where to look?'

'She's got a tongue in her head,' said Bob. 'There's ways.'

'All right,' said Andy. 'She found us – or had us found. But why did it take so long?'

'She was ill,' his grandmother said.

'For seven years? What on earth was wrong with her?'

'Never you mind,' his grandmother said repressively, and this time it was Andy who blushed. Women's ailments were a taboo subject in the Patterson household.

'The important thing is she's all right now,' Grandma Patterson said. 'Fit and well and ready to have a look round. I've asked her to call in on us here tomorrow morning, unless anybody objects?'

She looked about her and waited, but nobody objected.

Jane was taking stock of her room. It was the best room in the house and comfortable enough, with a view of the deserted market place and the river beyond. Faintly she could hear the clang of tramcars, the rumble of an occasional horse-drawn cart. Not many motor cars. Hers was the only one in the yard of the hotel, a yard cobbled and deserted, that had once been busy with horses when the Eldon Arms had been a coaching inn, and people had posted there to make money from iron and shipping and coal. But now nobody and nothing came to Felston, money least of all. Her treatment at the reception desk had made that all too clear. The Highlanders at Lucknow could not have been made more welcome.

She had dined well enough on lobster caught that day and a chicken that had died, she thought sadly, only because of her arrival. But it was quite delicious. The coffee however was not. The hotel waiter, and the manager, who brought the brandy she asked for, tried and failed to hide their surprise at such an extraordinary guest. If it hadn't been for the money. . . . But the money, they had no doubt, was there, and perhaps for some time to come.

The telephone was housed in a sort of cupboard by the stairs, and the manager acted as telephonist. Lionel was out, which didn't surprise her, and although she longed for conversation, it wasn't yet time to talk with Sarah Watson. There was too much to explain and it was far too soon, always supposing that she would be allowed to stay. She telephoned Offley Villas instead, and Hawkins answered almost at once.

'Lady Whitcomb's residence.'

'Hawkins? This is Jane Whitcomb.'

'Yes, Miss Jane?'

'I'm just telephoning to find out if everything's all right.'

'Everything's fine, miss.'

'Cook's all right?'

'Oh yes, miss.'

'And Foch?'

'I took him out for a walk like you said, miss. And he finished off the stew we had for supper.'

Foch was all right. He was very fond of stew.

'That's good. Take care of yourself, Hawkins. And give cook my best wishes.'

'Very good, miss. Thank you. I hope you're enjoying yourself, miss.'

'Well enough,' said Jane, though 'enjoy' was not the word.

'Only it's very quiet without you, miss. The house is like a graveyard.'

'Perhaps my brother will look in on his way to Cambridge,' said Jane. 'His term must start soon.'

'Yes, miss.' Hawkins didn't sound exactly elated. 'Will you be away long, miss?'

'Not long, I hope,' said Jane, and what else could she say? For all she knew Hawkins could be packed and ready to leave. 'I'll telephone, soon. Goodbye, Hawkins.'

'À bientôt, miss.'

À bientôt? What the *hell* was Hawkins up to? She hung up, and looked at her watch. It was only just nine o'clock. As she looked the town hall clock began its slow and utterly certain chime. She would need Lionel's help to work out what to make of that town hall, she thought. It had the frontage of a palazzo, and a clock tower like a campanile. It – and the Eldon Arms – were the only evidence she had seen so far that Felston had ever known wealth. But that was not exactly true. The shipyards, the factories, the mines said it also.

She thought of the Pattersons. Grandma was the inspiration and the source of all that energy, so much was obvious. It had skipped a generation, for Stan, her son, was of a different mould. Stubborn and enduring, but slow, so slow. Not like the three grandsons, all of whom had that same restless energy, that combative quickness. John. Andy. Bob. John had wanted to improve himself, she remembered, and Andy wanted to improve the whole world – provided the world saw eye to eye with him about what constituted improvement. But who or what did Bob want to improve? Not the world. . . . Not even Felston. He wanted to leave the place. And not himself either, not in the way John had done it: night school and competitive examinations, and the ladder of progress climbed rung by rung. His *lot*, that was what Bob wanted to improve. He wanted to dance at the Café de Paris.

She looked out of the window again. Below her a lamp-lighter moved from one lamp to the next, and as he moved the gas lamps glowed. There were still people about, and from the market place she could hear a steady thumping sound that might be music.

The people on the street – Queen Street it was called, (and who could the queen be but Victoria?) – were for the most part better dressed than the ones she had seen so far, but even so they stared at her, especially the women. She would have to do something about that, but for the moment she walked along the street of uneven flagstones while the trams swayed past, and passersby stopped to stare into the windows of shops long since locked and bolted – some of them for good, she thought. On across more tramlines to a great cobbled square, with a church on one side of it, and for the rest, pubs, stacked together like the stones of a wall, for this market was near the old harbour, so the manager had told her, and a harbour meant sailors and sailors meant pubs, pubs for the kind of sailor that would never be allowed in the Eldon Arms.

By the door of one pub, the biggest, with a great flaring gas lantern of its own high above, stood the source of the music: the

Salvation Army. Two cornets, two trombones, a tuba and a drum: in a raging glory of blue and scarlet and gold. And beside them three women, equally splendid, with tambourines and poke bonnets that Lionel would have adored, and a standard bearer with the army banner. A crowd stood in front of them in two concentric semi-circles, the poor at the front, the better off further back. There could have been a fence between them she thought, and went to stand with the well-to-do because it was where she belonged. She knew her place. The standard bearer had just finished his sermon, it seemed.

'We'll have a bit of a hymn now,' he said equably. 'I know very well that's what you've come for most of you and it'll do your souls good anyway, so let's be hearing you.' And he nodded to the cornet player who seemed to be acting as leader. The music was the first sound of joy she'd heard, clear and sweet, and with the rich power that only brass can give; then suddenly the tambourines were shaken, struck, and the singing began:

> Shall we gather at the River
> Where the angel-feet have stood?
> Shall we gather at the River
> That flows by the Throne of God?

Three sopranos, the standard bearer's tenor, the drummer's bass to begin with, but soon the whole crowd was singing:

> Yes we will gather at the River,
> The beautiful, the beautiful, the River.
> Yes we will gather at the River
> That flows by the Throne of God.

They sang it quite seriously in the main, each one enjoying the opportunity to be part of such a splendid noise. Here and there she could hear a hint of exaggeration, rather too much gusto, as she had during the war near the railway stations when the soldiers waited for the time to board the train that would take them back, and the Sally Ann offered hymns and tea – and a prayer if anyone was interested. John had told her it was usually the mockers who gave most when the collecting plate came round. And there was superstition if you like: buying off a sin with silver. The hymn ended, and the crowd waited for another, but first, the standard bearer announced there would be a collec-

– 242 –

tion 'from those who had the money to give'. A woman with a tambourine moved among the poor, a trombonist with a cloth bag headed purposefully towards the well-to-do, and quite a few of them left – absentmindedly for the most part, though some strode off purposefully as if they'd just remembered an appointment. Those who stayed, paid up: Jane dropped a half crown into the bag, then wandered across the square as the music followed:

> Yes Jesus loves me, Yes Jesus loves me,
> Yes Jesus loves me, the Bible tells me so.

Across the cobbles she went, God at her back, and facing her, not Mammon – these men had no faith in wealth – but Reason, Justice, the Egalitarian Society. No brass bands, no military ladies with tambourines, just three men in the shabby uniform of poverty she already knew so well, grouped around a speaker. One of them was holding a banner, and holding it all wrong. It was Andy Patterson, and she knew at once that he had seen her. It was too late to move away.

She joined the crowd confronting them – if you could call it a crowd, she thought. Not much more than a handful, and nearly all of them poor. No concentric circles. The speaker was the Jewish-looking man who had directed her to John Bright Street, still bare-headed, and this time he wore no jacket, but the shirt he displayed also looked like silk. He seemed to be quoting statistics.

'The way we live is not only evil but senseless,' he was shouting. 'This world of ours is a bounteous place. There's enough for everybody – more than enough – and yet in this country alone ninety per cent of the wealth is owned by five per cent of the population. People like you die ten, fifteen years earlier than people in Mayfair – '

Except in the war, Jane thought. Then we all died together.

'Fifty times more tuberculosis, a hundred times more rickets, and a million times more malnutrition – because the rich never starve. They'd take the bread out of your mouths first – or send their servants to do it.'

The crowd stirred, but without enthusiasm. It was an old theme, and no help to them. How could the rich take the bread out of their mouths? Their mouths were empty.

From across the square the little brass band exploded into 'Onward Christian Soldiers', jaunty, triumphant, and at once a couple of spectators slipped away. The man in the silk shirt acknowledged defeat.

'Now I want you to think about what I've told you,' he said. 'That's all I ask. Just think about it. And in the meantime I'll pass you on to Comrade Patterson.'

Andy came forward at once, body thrusting towards his audience, fists clenched, like a man running to a fight. For a moment he glowered at them in silence, then his voice sounded in an effortless roar.

'You don't look as if you've got any fight left in you,' he said. 'Well I'm not surprised. You've had more than your share these last few years. Lock-outs. Strikes. Dole money. Starvation. – And none of it your fault. . . . *Well of course it wasn't*. But that doesn't make it any better. Now does it?

'And there's nowt you can do about it, I hear you say. Nowt. Not a thing – except go across the road and join the army of God over there, and promise Him you'll give up the sins of the flesh, like eating four-course meals and drinking champagne and dancing all night at the Café de Paris.'

And that's one for me, thought Jane. But she couldn't move away because to do so wouldn't be a retreat, it would be a rout.

'The remedy's in front of your eyes, but you won't see it,' said Andy. 'It's within your grasp but you won't take it.'

'Tell us then,' said a voice from the front.

'I'll be glad to. Join us. . . . Is that so difficult? Be one of us. Help us grow to a majority, an overwhelming majority, a majority so great that we take back what is ours by right. Not just a bit here and a bit there. – Everything. The whole country. The entire means of production, distribution and exchange. The lot!'

His voice grew gentle.

'Comrades I tell you,' he said, 'there's a part of that religion over there that we are proud to copy – and that is the part that the boss Christians – the ones in fancy clothes and fancy cars – have forgotten. Well they would. Of course they would. Because there's nowt in it for them. – And that's their way of life when they first started. Share and share alike, and no man, no woman, holding back. Everything for everybody. You know what we call that? From each according to his ability: to each according to his need.

'Isn't that simple? Isn't it honest? Isn't it right? No private fortunes, no grand houses and flocks of servants. None of that. All done away with. Finished. And in its place – enough for everybody – aye and more than enough – when men work out of a need to serve, and not fear of the sack. Can't you see? – When that day dawns – there'll be more for everybody: for every one of us that works and makes his contribution to the community of the workers – but none at all for the boss exploiter with his selfishness and greed – and none for his women neither with their silks and their jewels and their idle, useless lives.'

Now it really was time to go, she thought: now she knew precisely where Andy stood.

24

NEXT MORNING AFTER breakfast she went shopping. There was one store, the breakfast waitress told her, that might have the things she wanted. Otherwise it would have to be Newcastle. But the store contrived to supply her needs. She bought a suit, a dress, blouses, gloves, hats: but not stockings or shoes or underwear. She was doing this for Felston, she told herself, but not even for Felston would she give up the feel of silk against her skin, the comfort of handlasted shoes.

When she had changed she went back to John Bright Street, and this time it was Bet who opened the door for her. Her eyes went at once to her clothes, and she seemed disappointed, but conducted her to the kitchen even so. Grandma looked up from the potatoes she was peeling.

'Come a bit closer, lass,' she said, and Jane did so. Grandma smiled. 'Bought yourself new clothes, have you?'

'This morning,' said Jane.

'I liked the old ones better,' said Bet.

Jane turned to her. Bet was blushing, and looked the prettier for it. With less hardship and better food, thought Jane, she would be pretty all the time.

'I'm sorry,' Bet said. 'That was rude.'

'Not really,' said Jane. 'The other ones were nicer – but if I'm going to look round Felston these make more sense.'

'You mean – ' Bet sounded incredulous, ' – you just went into a shop and bought all that? It must have cost pounds.'

'Well – yes.'

Bet looked at her, saucer-eyed. 'Andy's right,' she said. 'You *are* rich.'

'Well what of it?' her grandmother asked.

'Nothing,' said Bet. 'Only I've never met anybody who was rich before. None of us have.'

'Well now you've had a good look at her you can help me with the potatoes,' said her grandmother. 'She's not a wild beast from the circus.'

That raised a point of etiquette. She ought to offer to help, but she'd never peeled a potato in her life. Grandma vetoed the idea at once. There was, she said, no time to teach her just then. So she watched instead as the peel came away tissue-paper thin on to the newspaper spread on the table: a trick as far beyond her reach as pulling rabbits from a hat.

'Where are the others?' she asked.

'Andy's at the library,' the old woman said, 'reading books about setting the world to rights. Stan's at the allotment.'

'Allotment?'

'Bit of ground,' said Grandma. 'Sort of a garden. He grows potatoes, onions, cabbages. Keeps him happy and keeps us fed.'

'And Bob?'

'Loafing somewhere.' The old woman sat up straight for a moment. 'He misses the printing – he was a good un at his trade they tell me. He loved it and now it's gone. We can't all be potty about putting the world to rights or growing cauliflowers, but I wish he could find something. He's ripe for mischief, that lad.'

Jane stopped for lunch, or what the Pattersons called dinner, because Grandma insisted that to do anything else would be insulting. And so she sat and waited, until one by one the men came in: first Stan, with leeks and beans and potatoes, and marigolds and sweetpeas brought, Jane was sure, because his mother had demanded them; then Bob, empty-handed and yawning, but cheered at the sight of Jane; and last of all Andy, books under his arm, head up, body forward, because he knew at once that the fight wasn't over.

'It's broth,' said Grandma. 'And don't waste your breath telling us it's too hot for broth, because that's all there is.'

It was a good broth, too. Onions and vegetables and bones and scrag, and the potatoes she had seen peeled that morning. But Grandma was right. She had been generous with the pepper, and served it piping hot. When she had finished Jane wondered if she would ever feel hungry again. The others pushed away their empty plates, and looked towards her – in gratitude, or so she thought: as if she were the reason why they had eaten so well.

Andy said, 'You'll have to excuse us, Miss Whitcomb. We realise it's not what you're used to, but we do our poor best.'

'*We?*' said Jane. 'I thought your grandmother and your sister cooked a delicious meal.'

'Now look here – ' Andy began.

'Now you be quiet,' said his grandmother. 'I've made a jelly – and we'll have a bit of peace till it's finished.' She glared at Andy, who opened his mouth. 'Now mind, I mean it,' she said, and her grandson shrugged and was silent.

From the street there came an odd, wailing sound that somehow seemed to promise delight rather than pain.

'What on earth – ' Jane said.

'Ice cream that'll be,' said Bob. 'Crespo's Neapolitan Ices. They're good an' all.'

'Couldn't we have some?' said Jane. 'They'd be nice with jelly.' The silence seemed to reach out to punish her.

'What I mean,' she said, 'was that you've been so kind. If I buy the ice cream it gives me a chance to say thank you.'

'No,' said Andy.

'But whyever not?'

'You wouldn't behave like that in London.'

'In London I'd send flowers,' said Jane. 'It just seemed that ice cream might be more sensible. And anyway your father's just brought the most marvellous marigolds and sweetpeas.'

'And nobody can eat *them*,' grandma said. 'Take the basin, Bet. Fetch some ice cream – if Jane'll give you the money.'

'How much?' Jane asked.

'A tanner.'

'Sixpence?' Jane opened her bag and offered the coin, careful not to offer more. Bet took it and was gone.

'Is he in the street?' Jane asked. 'The ice-cream seller?'

'Back lane,' said Bob. 'Look out the window and you'll see him.'

She looked, and saw a little, two-wheeled cart that held a white-painted tub with a brass lid. The cart was pulled by a piebald pony, and driven by a fat, sallow man with a flopping moustache who from time to time called out that weird, encouraging cry.

'Fascinating,' she said.

'You mean you've never seen that before?'

It was Bob who spoke.

'Of course she hasn't,' Andy said. 'Miss Whitcomb's a lady. She's never seen a back lane in her life.'

'She hasn't missed all that much,' said Bob.

Grandma said, 'It's time she did see a back lane or two.'

'Where's the sense?' said Andy.

'We went into that yesterday,' said his grandmother. 'If she doesn't see for herself she'll never believe what *I* tell her.'

'No reason why she should,' said Andy. 'It's none of her business.'

His grandmother sighed. 'I was thinking you might show her round,' she said. 'There's no one knows this place like you do.'

'You thought wrong.'

'Then it'll have to be Bob,' said their grandmother, and Bet came in with the ice cream.

'Bob?' said Andy. 'What does he know?'

'He knows where the hardship is,' said his grandmother.

'He couldn't know much else; not in Felston,' Andy said. 'But does he know how to cure it?'

'You think you're the only one knows that? You and Manny Mendel?'

'We *do* know,' said Andy. 'And if the rest of you would learn we could *do* something.'

'Manny Mendel,' said Jane. 'Is he the one who was with you last night? The one who directed me here?'

'That's him.'

'You had a good go at me last night,' she said.

'Did you?' Grandma Patterson turned on Andy, ready to let fly.

'Not her personally,' said Andy. 'She was just a representative of her class.'

'Idle and useless,' Jane quoted.

'Aye. I said that.' Andy was still unperturbed.

'You had no right,' said Stan. 'She's our guest here.'

'No bourgeois is *my* guest,' said Andy.

'Idle and useless.' Jane stuck to her point. 'Well sometimes I am and sometimes I'm not. I don't think I was useless when I drove an ambulance.'

'I wouldn't know,' said Andy. 'I wasn't in the war.'

'Why not?'

'I was on me holidays,' said Andy. 'In Durham Gaol.'

'Conchy,' said Bob.

'And was Mr Mendel a conscientious objector too?'

'No, he was in France,' said Andy. 'He hated it.'

'Not many of us didn't. Is he *very* rich?'

'Manny? He's secretary of Felston Labour Party. He'd do better on the dole.'

'He dresses rather well, wouldn't you say? For a poor man? Silk jackets. Silk shirts. And those shoes he wore last night – they could do with a cleaning but they were made by hand – by some poor exploited worker, no doubt.'

Andy said nothing, and the others watched in silence.

'And his cuff-links,' Jane continued. 'Real gold were they? Paid for by exploitation to satisfy selfishness and greed? Those *were* your words. A typical bourgeois, Mr Mendel. Surely. And has *he* ever come to this house at your invitation?'

'He has,' said Andy. 'Though why I should answer your questions I'm damned if I know.'

'I'll have no language,' said Stan, and when his son made no answer: 'I'm talking to you, Andy.'

'All right. I'm sorry,' said Andy. 'But she's got no call to talk about Manny – '

'She?' said his grandmother. 'She? And who is "she" when she's at home? Where's your manners?'

'I left them at the shipyard gates last time they paid us off,' said Andy. 'Along with my illusions.'

Bob's head nodded. It was if if he were watching a fist fight, thought Jane, and acknowledging a good punch landing square.

'And where did Mr Mendel leave his?' she asked.

· Andy shrugged. 'It's true his parents have a bit of money,' he said.

'A bit?' Bob's voice was mocking. 'His da owns a wholesale tailoring factory – the only place round here that's open full-time – so he doesn't exactly have to pay union rates, does he?'

'That's his da,' said Andy. 'Manny isn't like that.'

'Left the fold, has he? Or been thrown out, perhaps?' asked Jane.

'No,' Andy said. 'Neither. You know what Jews are like when it comes to family.'

'And not just Jews,' said his father.

'Personally he admires them,' said Andy. 'But politically – he knows they're wrong. Knows they're bound to fail for that matter, the way the whole rotten system will fail.'

'So he's a worker?'

But Andy's dogged honesty would not accept that.

'He's never worked,' he said. 'Not like us. He's an intellectual.'

According to Cuthbert Pardoe, that made him a second-class revolutionary at best.

'University man?'

'Manchester. He studied history.'

'And his parents paid? Really Andy – he's no better than I am.' Bob chuckled.

'Oh yes he is,' said Andy. 'He believes in what we're doing.'

'But so might I – if you'd give me the chance to find out.' Andy said nothing. 'Is it because I'm a woman?'

'Of course not.' He looked and sounded outraged, but Jane thought that perhaps he might be lying, even if he were unaware of the fact.

So it was Bob who acted as her guide to Felston. Queen Street she knew, with its shops and cinemas and theatre, all somehow clinging on to life, and the town hall she knew, and the tram sheds, and the grim, well-scrubbed poverty of John Bright Street. Bob was to show her better – and worse. Better, far better, was Westburn Village, the suburb where the wealthy lived; neat, Georgian houses for the doctors and lawyers and works managers. Comfort marooned in poverty, she thought. Gentility shut in on itself, like some little station in an Indian state, where the sahibs entertained each other to dinner in strict rotation, and listened to gramophone records of shows long forgotten elsewhere.

'Do the Mendels live here?' Jane asked.

'That big one there,' Bob said, and nodded to a sturdy piece of Georgian brick: solid and enduring: set in a couple of acres or thereabouts: neat lawns and flower-beds, a tennis court with fading lines.

'Three of them,' said Bob. 'In *that*. . . . Not counting the servants, of course.' Then he disconcerted her by adding, 'Man it must be marvellous.'

Jane said severely, 'Now let's look at the worst,' and he smiled at her the way John used to smile, when she'd wanted to be serious and he'd needed her laughter.

The worst was very bad, as bad as anything she had seen in India. Courts and places and lanes that straggled up from the river in clumsy sweeps and inclines, and the older they were, the worse they were. At last they had to leave the car, and Bob struck a bargain with a man who lounged nearby to guard it. Bob settled for sixpence, and the man spoke quickly in the dialect that Jane found so hard to understand.

'For a tanner he'll watch it all day,' said Bob. 'He was wondering if you were from the council.'

'Why should I be?'

'Folks in cars that comes round here has to be from the council,' said Bob. 'They're the only ones who'd bother. He says if you're going to condemn any houses you can start with his.'

Jane walked down the steps and looked about her and could sense the despair all around. Dwellings in the last stages of dilapidation, broken windows patched with cardboard, no paint, no polish, no gleaming doorsteps; several of the houses leaned out of the vertical, slum towers of Pisa: one was even shored up by a baulk of timber that looked as if it were worth more than the house.

'You'd think it had been shelled,' she said.

'From what chaps that were in the war tell me, the Germans would have been more thorough,' said Bob.

All around the tenements, men and women, children too young – or too old – for school, were looking at them. They too wore the uniform of the poor, but this was a battalion that had been defeated once too often. They would never stand and fight again. Dirty, stinking, ragged. But what could you expect, Bob asked her, with one stand-pipe to a yard and an outside privy with no flush toilet? He looked at them with pity, but with interest too, as if they were some sort of a show, thought Jane. Near-human creatures that could never quite achieve humanity: chimpanzees in a cage waiting for food that never came. . . . A rat appeared from nowhere, snatched up a piece of cabbage stalk and disappeared down a gap in a crumbling wall.

'I bet it makes a change from Mayfair,' said Bob.

'Just a bit. I have to ask them some questions,' said Jane.

'They'll be a bit shy,' said Bob.

'But why on earth should they?'

'The only ones that comes asking questions is the Guardians. The Poor Law, you know. And they only come to see if they've got any money to stop out of their dole.'

'But how could they have money?'

'The man from the Guardians isn't paid to ask how, he's paid to look,' said Bob. 'Because if he didn't look he might get the sack and be like them. But you're too well-dressed for the Guardians. They'll think you've come to condemn their houses.'

'Surely they'd be glad if I were?'

'All right in the summer, mebbe. They could sleep on the beach. But what about the winter?'

'They wouldn't get somewhere else?'

'Not unless they can pay for it. And all this lot can afford is a slum.'

'Would they talk if you ask them?'

'Yes, of course,' said Bob. 'Might cost you half a dollar.' He saw her bewilderment. 'Half a crown.'

'All right.' She gave him one, then went back to the car. Its guardian still stood by. He was gaunt with undernourishment, she noticed, but shaven and clean, his boots were brushed. As he came towards her Jane saw that he limped as he walked.

'All present and correct, miss,' he said.

From a distance a group of children watched and waited.

'Thank you,' said Jane. 'I wouldn't want the paintwork damaged.'

'No miss,' said the man. 'She's a nice job.' He moved back to take in the Riley's splendour.

'You were in the army, weren't you?' Jane asked.

The man smiled. 'No prizes for guessing. It's my gammy leg, isn't it? Name of Laidlaw, miss. I was a corporal in the Royal Northumbrians.'

'I knew someone in that regiment,' said Jane.

'Half our street was in it,' the man said. 'The half that wasn't in the navy.'

'His name was Captain Patterson,' said Jane. 'He commanded B Company. Did you know him?'

'I was D Company,' Laidlaw said. 'Captain White. I don't

think – wait a minute. He was killed, wasn't he? Just before the Armistice?'

'That's right.'

'And he lived round here?'

'When he was younger. John Bright Street.'

'Bit better than this, John Bright Street.'

'Yes,' said Jane. 'It is. I'm – anxious to help the people round here.'

'Yes miss?'

I'm going too fast, she thought. The shutter's just dropped with a clang.

'There's a group of people in London,' she said, lying furiously – but at least there would be soon – 'Sort of a charitable trust. They want to help people in places like this. Only first we need to have the facts.'

'Facts, miss?'

'Housing conditions, health, diseases,' she said. 'Is there anywhere I can get any information? I suppose the town hall – '

'Them,' said Laidlaw. 'They wouldn't tell you the time of day. Stobbs and Messeter, miss.'

'I beg your pardon?'

'It's a report: *Felston* – by Stobbs and Messeter. You'll get it at the public library.'

He waved his hand and limped away as Bob came up. With him was a stunted man, a woman she took to be his mother and a cluster of children, one of whom looked ill indeed, too ill to walk.

'This is Mr Richardson,' said Bob, 'and his wife. He's Albert – she's Nan. The bairns are Frank and Les and Maude.'

If one judges by the age of the children, Mrs Richardson can be very little older than I am, thought Jane. She looks fifty at least. And her daughter seems very ill.

'You shouldn't have brought the girl,' she said aloud. 'She's exhausted.'

'She wouldn't be left,' said Bob. 'She wanted to see you close to.'

Maude could have been twelve, thought Jane. She looked up at Jane through blue eyes made big by the pinched and hungry face, her gaze devouring the make-up, the clothes, the neatly tended hair. Health and wealth together in one body.

'Ask your questions,' Bob said, and she did so, and at times Bob acted as interpreter as she fitted the pieces together. Man, woman and children shared one room, one bed. The room cost five shillings a week, on the occasions when they had five shillings. They lived mostly on bread and jam and weak tea – and fish if Albert managed to get a place in a boat, and broth when they could afford vegetables and bones. Albert hadn't worked in three years, and now he didn't even bother trying. The dole was starvation, but it was all there was. None of them had ever had a proper bath, or even seen one, except at the pictures, and Maude had pulmonary tuberculosis. Both parents were sure that she would die of it, and were equally sure that there was nothing they could do about it. The questions ended at last, and Bob handed over the half crown and they left.

'What will they do with it?' Jane asked.

'Eat if they've got sense; drink if they haven't.' As they watched the little girl was racked by a fit of coughing.

'There's a lot worse off than me,' said Bob. 'Wouldn't you say?'

'How on earth do you manage?' Jane asked.

'Blowed if I know,' said Bob. 'But I do.'

Mind your own business, Jane Whitcomb.

They drove to the public library, where 'Stobbs and Messeter', stencilled on cheap paper, was available price sixpence, Proceeds in Aid of the Shoeless Children's Fund. She took Bob back to John Bright Street, then returned to the Eldon Arms for tea.

Tea was in the lounge, which looked, thought Jane, like a room hired for a funeral where the corpse had only just been taken out to the hearse. Dark blue carpets, dark blue curtains more than half drawn, artificial flowers grey with dust. . . . She entered on tiptoe, and a waitress took her order for tea and biscuits. She gave it in a whisper.

It was a big room, not quite empty. In a far corner, beneath potted palms huddled like relatives waiting for the will, two men and a woman were taking tea, and doing it in style. Sandwiches, cream cakes, some kind of tart. One of the men wasn't eating much. It was Andy's friend Mendel, she noticed. The other two tucked in with good appetite. They had to be his parents. Their talk, which had been loud when she entered, had diminished to whispers, the hissing kind used when one had to conduct one's quarrels in public, but then her tea arrived and it was too late to leave.

Stobbs and Messeter believed in realism. Their prose was simple, their message plain, and there were graphs and charts to underline the message. Felston's casualty rate was the equivalent of a battalion in the Lines: at Loos say, or Ypres. If something didn't happen soon the battalion would be at the Somme. But here it was mostly the very young and the ageing (ageing meant fifty, sixty meant old), who suffered most, though tuberculosis attacked at any age, and childbirth too demanded its share. Malnutrition and rickets, scarlet fever and pneumonia, operations that succeeded and patients who died because they were too undernourished to heal, and the old ones who died just because they were cold and there was no way to make them warm. . . .

'You find it interesting?'

Jane looked up at Manny Mendel. Today a suit of light material, she noticed, and a tie.

'Horrifying,' she said.

He nodded. 'Stobbs and Messeter know how to diagnose,' he said. 'It's cures they find difficult. They just won't see it.'

'See what?'

'That there's only one way.'

'Your way? And Andy's? Oh – my name's Jane Whitcomb, by the by.'

'Mendel. Manny Mendel. My way and Andy's, that's right. . . . I sent you to him.'

'So you did. You saved me a lot of trouble.'

'You. . . . Yes. . . . Andy, I'm not so sure. You worry him, Miss Whitcomb.'

'He worries about many things, Mr Mendel. And with reason. He has absolutely no cause to worry about me.'

From the doorway the elder Mendel called out to his son.

'Excuse me,' Mendel said. 'I have to go.'

Over the pamphlet she watched him leave, mother and father moving in close to protect him. He'd been talking to a Gentile woman, which was bad, thought Jane, and what was worse – *she'd been smoking a cigarette.*

25

S HE WAS GOING through the pamphlet again when someone
else came in: a man in a grey suit, white shirt and a tie, the
complete uniform of the businessman in summer fatigues, but
ruddy-faced and heavy-shouldered as a farmer. He carried a
whisky and soda and came straight up to Jane.

'Do forgive me,' he said. 'But Nellie told me you were reading
our little effort and I hope you won't mind if I ask what you
make of it?'

'Nellie?' said Jane.

'The waitress. She helps in the bar as well.' He lifted his glass.

Clipped white moustache, Jane noticed. Very clever and rather
bloodshot grey eyes. He looked like a colleague of Papa's they
had met once in Nagpur, but the voice was different. This wasn't
a sahib's voice – or a servant's. If such a thing were possible, his
voice was classless.

'I'm Dr Stobbs. Frank Stobbs. I wrote that piece with Canon
Messeter. Do tell me what you make of it.'

'It's like the blueprint of a nightmare,' said Jane. 'I'd no
idea – '

'So many of us don't,' said Dr Stobbs. 'Up on a visit, are you?'

'Oh,' said Jane. 'Excuse me. My name is Jane Whitcomb.'

She offered her hand and Stobbs took it warily, as if he had
to think hard to remember how the trick was done.

'I suppose you could say I'm here on a visit,' she said, and
looked at the ring on the third finger of her left hand. There
could be no denying it, nor did she wish to do so.

'I was engaged to a man who once lived here,' she said. 'He was killed in the war. I suddenly had this urge to see what the place was like.'

'And now you know.'

'Dear God yes,' she said.

'May I ask – what was your fiancé's name?'

'John Patterson,' she said.

He thought for a moment. 'Don't know him,' he said at last. 'I know an Andrew Patterson – '

'His brother,' said Jane. 'But my John doesn't belong here.'

'Because he's dead you mean?'

'And so escaped from Felston? No. When you die, you escape from rather more than Felston. John had made his escape long before.'

'Like me,' said Dr Stobbs. 'But I came back.'

'But why – ?'

'My father was a ship's captain,' said Dr Stobbs. 'What they call a master mariner round here. He saw I had a few brains and sent me off to the grammar school at Newcastle, and from there to London because I wanted to be a doctor. My father thought that no man in his right mind would ever want to be anything but a sailor – but he'd decided I was a madman long before, so it didn't matter.'

'And your mother?'

'She was proud of me – and prouder still when I qualified, – and just about ready to burst when I set up in Harley Street.'

'You specialised?'

'Certainly. A lot of chaps seem to think you can only find gold in South Africa or the Yukon, but don't you believe it. The rest of London may not be paved with gold, but Harley Street is. Appendixes. . . . That's what made me. His late majesty King Edward VII had had his out not long before, and by the time I came along the queue was round the block. It was snip snip snip and fancy stitching right up to the war.'

'And then?'

'RAMC,' said Dr Stobbs. 'Advanced Field Dressing Station. It was just as well I'd kept my general surgery up to date as well.'

'You served for long?'

'Four years,' said Dr Stobbs, 'but I was lucky. Not a scratch. . . . Not like my dad. He'd retired, but he went back as soon as he was needed. Torpedoed in the Atlantic second voyage. But I came back.'

'Here?'

'Harley Street. Appendixes were still popular. And then my mother died. Cancer. I watched her but I couldn't help her.' The sharp grey eyes looked more closely at Jane. 'You've seen it too?'

'Yes.'

'Ghastly, isn't it? And yet Messeter still goes on about God. . . . But once my mother died – in her home in Westburn Village – you know – where you were earlier in your car – '

'How did you know that?' asked Jane.

'Felston's a shocking place for gossip – the biggest village in the world the locals call it – and there isn't much gossip escapes the doctor. Anyway, when my mother died I took a walk round the town – just as you did this afternoon round Crawford's Buildings – and I ran across Messeter trying to set a broken wrist for a child who had fallen off a coal cart – trying to steal coal, most likely. They can't help it, poor little devils – not in the winter. But there was Messeter with an old ruler and some rags and not an idea in his head – him being a parson – so I did it for him and one thing led to another and we've been here ever since. We run a clinic.'

'It must keep you busy.'

Dr Stobbs smiled. 'Full-time job. Trouble is, Messeter's away just now.'

'Oh,' said Jane. 'Why is that?'

'It's a damn nuisance, but his doctor says he's been overworking. He has to rest.'

Jane had the feeling that she was being gently but very efficiently backed into a corner.

'And does Mr Messeter – '

'Canon Messeter.'

'Does he have a good doctor?'

'Of course he does,' said Dr Stobbs. 'It's me.'

'Can't you get another parson?'

'He's more than that,' said Dr Stobbs. 'He's auxiliary nurse and cook when there's nobody else, and clerk and storeman and ambulance driver.'

'Oh,' said Jane. 'I see.' And then: 'Dr Stobbs – who told you that I had driven an ambulance?'

'You know how these things get about,' Dr Stobbs tried and failed to look guileless.

'No,' said Jane affably. 'I'm afraid I don't. Do tell me.'

Dr Stobbs finished his whisky, and tugged at a bell pull.

'Well as I understand it,' he said, 'one of the Patterson lads was in the Ring of Bells last night and somebody happened to ask him who the posh lady was that came calling. But please don't ask me who "somebody" was. I don't know and it isn't relevant.'

'Then I won't,' said Jane.

'But the barmaid at the Ring of Bells is Elsie Edwards, and her sister's eldest had tonsilitis – I took them out last week. She brought him in this morning for me to see how he was getting on and she just happened to mention – '

'I see,' said Jane. 'And I suppose it was ex-Corporal Laidlaw of the Royal Northumbrians who told you about my visit to Crawford's Buildings.'

'What makes you think so?'

'He told me about your pamphlet.'

'You're no fool, Miss Whitcomb,' said Dr Stobbs.

'No,' said Jane. 'I'm an ex-ambulance driver.'

Nellie came in, and Dr Stobbs ordered another whisky and soda, and sherry for Jane.

'Smart chap, Laidlaw,' he said when Nellie had gone. 'He just happened to say you'd been to Westburn Village, too.'

'I congratulate you on your intelligence service,' said Jane.

'It's efficient,' Dr Stobbs said, 'because it has to be. There are still far too many people who are afraid to come to me, so when I hear about them, I have to go to them.'

'Why won't they come to you?' Jane asked.

'Because the damn fools are afraid that I'll charge them money.'

'And you don't? Not ever?'

'What would be the point?' said Dr Stobbs. 'They haven't got any.'

'But how on earth do you manage?' asked Jane.

'We shame people into helping us.'

Nellie came back with the drinks, and Dr Stobbs paid, and was silent until she had gone, then: 'Now the point is this,' he said. 'We have an ambulance and you are an ambulance driver.'

'I *was* an ambulance driver,' said Jane.

'You can't expect me to believe that you've forgotten how to do it. And anyway it isn't precisely an ambulance. Not *specifically* an ambulance, I should say.'

'And what is it specifically?'

'A motor car. An Armstrong-Siddeley, as a matter of fact.'

'The large one?'

'The very largest, according to Messeter. Odd, really. He bought it when he rarely drove anybody but himself.'

'It seats five?'

'Good Lord no,' said Dr Stobbs. 'Eight at least.' He went into his old duffer act, which would have been so much more effective had his eyes not been so clever. 'It has to, you see.'

'And I am to drive it?'

'If you would be so kind. But only for a few days. I shall have a relief driver next week.'

'Does he know it yet?' said Jane, and Dr Stobbs chuckled.

Jane lifted her glass. 'I drink to you, Doctor,' she said. 'I do indeed. . . . And I'll start tomorrow.'

It *was* the biggest Armstrong-Siddeley, and a pig to drive, which was what she had expected. Nothing wrong with it precisely, just heavy and awkward. What it really needed was a man of Bob's size at least. But Dr Stobbs was right about one thing: it could hold eight people, if some were children and almost all were undernourished.

She drove about Felston and scooped up the people on the list that Dr Stobbs gave her, and discovered that Dr Stobbs was right. Most of them didn't want to come, but all of them did, because they were terrified of Dr Stobbs, and having seen him in a rage the fact did not surprise her. To help her find her way and lift the ones who couldn't walk she had Bob to help her. For money. She had insisted on that. Not that Bob had needed any persuasion. Ten bob a day and not a word to the man from the Guardians, he settled for. It was too much – but oh how he looked like John.

Dr Stobbs's clinic was in an old, decaying mansion by the riverside. Here he and Messeter lived and ate and worked together in rooms panelled with worm-eaten oak, plastered ceilings that seemed forever about to collapse, an elegant, fast-rotting staircase of carved mahogany. Jane asked him about it on the second day.

Dr Stobbs looked at the house as a king might look at his palace.

'There was money here once,' he said. 'All built out of coal this little lot.'

'I doubt if you'll have it much longer,' said Jane.

'You're wrong,' said Stobbs. 'I can make this place last as long as I need it. I've got plumbers and bricklayers and carpenters any time I want them.'

'Then why not rebuild the place?'

'Because then I'd have to pay rates,' said Stobbs, 'and where's the sense in that? No. This place is safe enough – just about. But it doesn't look safe.'

And it didn't.

'But if it looks unsafe shouldn't the corporation demolish it?'

'Of course they should,' said Dr Stobbs, 'but how can they? They'd have to turn me out, and my patients. Not to mention Messeter. Look good at election time, wouldn't it? Vote for the men who turned the sick and afflicted out on to the streets.' He turned to the nurse who waited beside them. 'I'll see the little lad with the earache now,' he said.

That was another thing, thought Jane. Dr Stobbs always had nurses, relays of them, all efficient, all highly trained. Most of them spoke better English, all were better nourished, than the people they treated. She supposed that it must be the doctor's favourite weapon – shame. He had other helpers too. Platoons of women who appeared like genies from bottles, women who brought buckets and brooms and scrubbing brushes; women in the uniform of the good poor, fanatic in their devotion to cleanliness. They scrubbed and polished the crumbling ruin till it gleamed.

'All the same,' Jane said to Bob, 'if he's got a house in Westburn Village I don't see why he doesn't use it. He'll have to pay rates on it anyway.'

Bob chuckled. 'One of the nurses was telling me about that,' he said. 'He rents his house out and gets money for the clinic, and also he goes round his posh neighbours with a collecting box. Lets them know what'll happen if they don't cough up.'

'And what will happen?'

'He'll get rid of his lodgers and put the clinic in there. Westburn Village invaded by scruffs and beggars, TB and body lice. And all of it catching. The toffs'd sooner pay up. Every time.'

Jane chuckled. 'What now?'

'Lord Nelson Street. A chap with some kind of a cough it says here.'

What the chap had got was the effects of a lifetime in the coal mines. He was a big chap too, with a body so exhausted that he couldn't even walk to the car. Bob had to go out to recruit another two men to help Jane and the man's wife and himself load him into the Armstrong-Siddeley.

At the end of it all, Jane found that she was trembling from the effects of sheer, physical effort, as she had not done since the war. Bob looked at her.

'You're not built for the job,' he said, 'and them blokes was very near useless. Not their fault, mind you. There's no strength left in them.'

Jane waited till the trembling ceased and drove to the clinic.

When they got there, they had to call in Dr Stobbs to help with the lifting, and the nurse on duty looked shocked. *Doctors do not help with the lifting.* But Stobbs had to, or leave the patient in the car. Somehow between them they got him out and stretched him on a bed in what had once been the house's dining room. The man wheezed and gasped as they lifted him, and strange bubbling noises came from his chest, like the sound of a vat in which cider was fermenting.

'It's George Habbershaw, isn't it?' Dr Stobbs asked.

The man gasped and made the strange, bubbling noise, and his wife had to answer for him.

'That's right, doctor.'

'Been seeing me off and on for three years now, haven't you George?'

Habbershaw settled for a nod of the head, and Stobbs turned to Jane.

'He's got a form of pneumoconiosis,' Stobbs said. 'Too much coal dust and not enough filtered air in the pit where he worked. Too much coal dust up here come to that. I spoke for him at his compensation case. How much did I get you?'

'Twenty-two shillings a week, doctor.' It was the wife who answered.

'Better than the dole – but not all that much – not when you need eggs and milk and a lot of expensive treatment and a holiday in Switzerland. And so three months ago you got worse. Right, George?'

Again Habbershaw nodded.

'So I went to court again and told a few truths and a lot of lies. Right?'

'Yes, Doctor,' Mrs Habbershaw said.

'And I got his money up to twenty-five bob and a lump sum of fifty pounds. *Fifty pounds*.'

He glared at Jane, who recognised her cue.

'That's a lot of money, Dr Stobbs,' she said.

'It is indeed, Miss Whitcomb. A hell of a lot for an idle, time-wasting, good-for-nothing I wouldn't trust with fifty pennies – not to mention the lies I told.'

The big man on the bed wheezed and gasped, his breath bubbled, until at last he said, 'No lies.'

'Don't you contradict me, you lying, conniving, useless lump of sub-humanity. You wretched, foolish, surplus-to-requirement Neanderthal – '

'No lies,' the big man wheezed again. 'I was poorly. Still am.'

'Certainly you are,' said Dr Stobbs. 'In fact you're worse than you were when you went to court. At least you could sit up then. Now why are you worse, George Habbershaw?'

After a struggle the big man managed the one word, 'Dust.'

'Dust be damned,' said Stobbs. 'There's no more dust in you now than there was three months ago. But a lot more fibrosis. Inflammation's up too, by the look of you.'

His hand moved, quickly and accurately to Habbershaw's coat pocket, and came out holding a packet of cigarettes and a box of matches.

'Wild Woodbinitis,' said Dr Stobbs. 'That's what's wrong with you. Cough cough cough. Tobacco smoke mixed in with the dust to give it a bit of help. And you Mrs Habbershaw – ' he turned on the woman. 'You went out and bought them for him.'

'I never,' said the woman. 'Honest, Doctor.'

'Who was it then?' Dr Stobbs asked. 'Santa Claus?'

'Marrer,' the big man gasped. 'Me marrer got us them.'

'Marrer means friend among miners,' Stobbs told Jane, then returned to Habbershaw. 'A fine friend you had to bring you the means of killing yourself. And I've no doubt you gave him a few coppers for his trouble? Why didn't you tell him to fetch you a cut-throat razor or a loaded revolver while you were at it?' He turned to the woman. 'Is he eating much?'

'He can't,' said the woman. 'Not with all that coughing. He manages a bit broth and a custard. Stuff he can drink.'

'Stuff he can drink,' Dr Stobbs echoed. 'Stuff you can get at the Ring of Bells and the Boilermakers' Arms and the Durham Ox – eh, George Habbershaw?' He waited for an answer, and waved the woman to silence.

'I might have had the odd one,' Habbershaw managed at last.

'The odd one? Man you were infesting the pubs the way rats infest sewers. When you couldn't walk you had yourself carried by those wonderful marrers of yours.'

'No!' This time it was a yell: a great cry of fear thought Jane: fear of what had been, and even more of what was still to come.

'It's "Yes" and I can prove it's "Yes",' said Dr Stobbs. 'Why do you think I had you brought here – to look at your shining, rosy face – the picture of health? To feast my eyes on your happy, smiling wife, singing away because she hasn't a care in the world? I'll take no more "Noes" from you, George Habbershaw.'

'Bit of company,' Habbershaw wheezed. 'A man needs a bit o' company.'

'A man?' said Dr Stobbs. 'Call yourself a man?' His voice slashed Habbershaw's self-esteem to shreds. 'Drinking the money I lied to get for you? Oh yes – you were every bit as ill as I said you were – no disputing that, but they asked me if you were doing everything you should to help yourself and I said "Yes". And if there's a God in heaven as Canon Messeter says, there goes my chance of salvation.

'You were smoking then and you were boozing then, and damn me if you're not smoking and boozing now – on the days when you've got strength enough to swallow. Do you imagine that's why I committed perjury? Do you?'

'No, Doctor,' Habbershaw gasped.

'That's one "No" I'll accept. I did it for that wife of yours and those children of yours so that they can have a little bit put by when the twenty-five shillings a week stops, and that won't be long now – will it George? Not at the rate you're going.'

'I'm bad then?'

'You're killing yourself,' said Dr Stobbs. 'With the help of your marrers of course.'

'What if I gave up the drink? And the smokes? Will I still die?'

'We all die,' said Dr Stobbs, 'but if you die teetotal you'll last a bit longer. I'll tell you how much longer after I've examined you.'

'All right,' Habbershaw wheezed, and then: 'Who shopped us, Doctor?'

'Shopped you?' Dr Stobbs roared. 'It was common knowledge, you cretinous hominid. Birds fly. Fish swim. George Habbershaw goes on the beer. Watching you carried home was a show for the whole street.' He turned to the woman. 'You'd better wait outside, you and the others while I take a look at him,' he said, then threw the cigarettes and matches to Bob, who fielded them neatly. 'Compliments of George Habbershaw,' said Dr Stobbs.

They went outside, to a cup of hot, sweet tea for Mrs Habbershaw, and a yawning wait for Jane. Bob offered her a Woodbine, but she declined. She could still hear Habbershaw's cough. Soon it would be time to take Habbershaw home, and then she would be finished for the day. A bath, she thought, after a nurse had checked her hair for nits. She herself would take care of the search for fleas. She looked at her hands that were grimy and beginning to blister. She really was back with the Ambulance Service.

When at last she had finished, Dr Stobbs was still writing up case notes. 'Same time tomorrow?' she asked him. Stobbs grunted and continued to write.

'Habbershaw wasn't any lighter going back,' she said, and Stobbs looked up.

'That's the beer,' he said. 'Beer and no exercise. What he eats wouldn't fatten a flea.'

'He's still heavy.' He sat still, waiting. 'I can't understand why you didn't go to him,' she said. 'I could have driven you.'

'He wouldn't have let me in,' said Stobbs.

'But he came here.'

'In a posh car,' said Stobbs. 'Carried on a stretcher. Making a lot of fuss. Driven by a lady. Of *course* he came here. There's not much in life he enjoys. He enjoyed that.'

'He enjoys beer.'

'Not any more,' said Stobbs. 'His life isn't much, but *he* thinks it is. I've frightened him off. Besides, his wife and children will need what's left more than the brewers. . . . Good night.'

'Not yet.' He sighed, and laid down the pen. 'I didn't mind lifting Habbershaw,' said Jane. 'It isn't that.'

'What then?'

'I'm not very good at it,' she said. 'I never will be. Any more than I was good at getting an eight-stone woman down three flights of stairs. You need stretcher bearers – ambulance men. Fellows with a bit of muscle.'

'Of course I do,' said Stobbs. 'I also need an operating theatre and an X-ray machine and a couple of Jersey cows. And there's only one reason why I haven't got them. There isn't the money. And anyway the fellers round here don't *have* muscles. Not any more. Not on their diet.'

'You've got a kitchen in here with water and electricity,' said Jane. 'It's got a kitchen range as well, but Bella tells me it's useless.'

'Bella?'

'The Queen of your Harem,' said Jane. 'The one who organises all the cleaners.'

'Oh. . . . Mrs Docherty.'

'That's the one. She used to be a cook in service. What that kitchen needs is a modern stove.'

'And what I need is a hundred thousand pounds,' said Stobbs. 'One's just about as likely as the other.'

'I'll buy the stove.'

Stobbs put down his pen. 'Why should you do that?'

'So that Mrs Docherty can cook meals for your coolies and keep their strength up.'

'They'd want paying.'

'Not if you fed them,' said Jane. 'They'd be queueing up.'

'There'd be food to pay for.'

'I'd pay for that, too. Bob Patterson's grandmother is the shrewdest person I've met round here. I'll arrange things with her. She and Bella will take care of things between them.'

'Under my direction?'

'Of course. I'll leave enough to feed the harem, too. We can't have the men eating while all the women do is watch. Not even in Felston.'

Dr Stobbs said genially, 'You know I'm glad you're not here

for long. Damn glad. It's not that I don't like your ideas, but if you were here a month I get the feeling I'd be working for you, and we'd neither of us like that.'

'I'll speak to Mrs Patterson,' said Jane.

'And Mrs Docherty?'

'I've already spoken to her. She says she can't wait to start.'

Dr Stobbs opened his mouth to yell, then burst out laughing instead.

26

GRANDMA PATTERSON LIKED the idea, but then Jane had been quite sure she would. It appealed to her every instinct: her quickness, her need to organise, her compassion – and her bossiness.

'Broth,' she said, as soon as Jane had finished. 'That's what we'll have for a start. It's cheap and filling – and it does you good an' all.'

'Have you met Mrs Docherty?' asked Jane.

'No,' said Grandma, 'but if you're happy with her she'll know what she's doing. We'll get on fine.'

Her son said, 'Docherty? She'll be a Catholic, likely.' He sounded uneasy.

'She'll be the cook,' said his mother firmly. 'Just like I'll be the supplier.' Then after a pause she added: 'Fish on a Friday?'

'Almost certainly,' said Jane. 'Is it cheap?'

'It will be where I'll go,' the old woman said. 'My – I'm really looking foward to this.'

It was Jane who formally introduced Grandma Patterson to Bella Docherty. There could have been nothing like it, she thought, since Queen Victoria met the Empress Eugénie, and Grandma Patterson was in no doubt which one of them was Queen Victoria. Even so, thought Jane, they got on surprisingly well, largely because they shared a contempt for the male sex that was almost total, including as it did men like Dr Stobbs, who did their best, which was no excuse. They settled down to a pleasurable and exhaustive discussion of the inadequacies of the male, and provided a list of dishes almost as a postcript:

broth, Irish stew, baked herrings, oven-bottom cake, and something called pan hagglety. Jane made a silent vow that she must, very soon, taste pan hagglety, if only to find out what it was.

Andy disapproved because it was charity, but then she had been sure he would.

'Don't you be so sure,' said Bob. 'Not till you've tried humping a twelve-and-a-half-stone man on a stretcher.'

'That isn't the point,' said Andy.

'It is when there's only two of you to lift him. Right, Miss Whitcomb?'

'We had to send out for help,' said Jane.

'No question,' said Bob. 'It wasn't all that easy even with four. A bowl of broth's not all that much for work like that.'

'It's still charity,' Andy said.

'It's commonsense,' said Jane. 'To do work like that you have to be properly fed – and the sick have to be healed, after all.'

'Do they?'

'But surely – ' said Jane.

'Healed for what, Miss Whitcomb? To get better again so they can go back on the dole in Felston?'

'But if there's no alternative – '

'Who says there isn't?' said Andy. 'They can protest, can't they? They can march and demonstrate.'

'The police and the special constables, and the mayor reading the riot act,' said Stan. 'That's where demonstrations get you. We saw it in the market place two years back, remember? That time the seamen were out and the ship owners brought in blacklegs.'

'Nowt wrong with demonstrating for your rights,' said Andy.

'Not even when you lose?' said Bob. 'The sailors lost that day, I remember. You could see the blood in the gutter.'

'That's enough,' Grandma Patterson said. 'Miss Whitcomb's only trying to do us a good turn, and if we're not grateful for that we should be.'

'Gran, I understand that,' said Andy. 'Honestly I do. But what *you* don't seem to understand – any of you – is that charity only makes you more dependent. Charity's never more than just enough to keep you alive – why should it be? – but as long as it's there folks accept it, and because they accept it they won't fight.'

'For a feller that was a conscientious objector you talk a lot about fighting,' said his father.

'That war was for the bosses,' said Andy. 'I wouldn't fight for them. But for my family, my friends, my union, my class – I'd fight for them all right. By God I would.'

'And what's more if you fought as well as you take the name of the Lord in vain you'd win,' said his father.

'I'm sorry, Da,' Andy said. 'But – '

'And so am I,' his father said. 'But it's the Lord you should apologise to.'

Andy walked out.

'Where's he off to this time?' said Bob.

'Off for a word with Manny Mendel,' said his father. 'Doing a bit of staff work for the Workers' Armageddon.'

'That's not very nice, our Stan,' said his mother.

'No Mam,' he said. 'I know it's not. But I've only one other cheek to turn.' He looked towards his younger son. 'Fancy a walk, Bob?'

'Suits me,' said Bob. 'Not too far, mind. I've a day's work to do tomorrow. How about taking a look at the Mafeking Hall? I hear the Colliery Band's rehearsing.'

'I'll put my boots on,' said his father. 'I've got nowt against music properly played. . . . Good night, Miss Whitcomb.'

'Oh please,' said Jane. 'I think it would be better if you called me Jane.'

'Would it?' said Stan. 'I'll have to think about that.' But his son had no such hesitations.

'Good night, Jane,' said Bob.

'Impudent thing,' said Grandma automatically, but without rancour. 'Still, you can see the sense in it.'

'What's the Mafeking Hall?' Jane asked.

Bet looked astounded that anyone should be ignorant of the Mafeking Hall. 'Why – there's everything there,' she said. 'Concerts, leek shows, pantomimes.'

'Sort of a Welfare Hall,' said her grandmother. 'Where folks can have a bit of a get-together. Though how they managed these days I'm blest if I know.'

'Short of money?'

'Like everything else in Felston.' She smiled, ruefully. 'Sorry, pet. Money's the only song I sing these days.'

Bet said, 'Now they're all out can I have a word with – Jane? You said I could.'

A grown woman, thought Jane. Long past her majority. But still Gran's word was law.

'There's nowt to stop you,' said Grandma. 'If she's a mind to.'

'Of course,' said Jane.

'In the bedroom,' said Bet. 'Please.'

Jane followed her into the bedroom. A double bed, and a vast wardrobe that seemed somehow uneasy in such a small room, the cheapest of dressing tables, neatly painted white, and a couple of small, hard chairs. Above one side of the bed was a page torn from a magazine and framed in passe-partout, a photograph of a mannequin in a gown that looked like Lanvin. Bet followed her gaze. 'That's my side,' she said.

'I beg your pardon?'

'My side,' Bet said again. 'Of the bed. I share with Grandma.'

'Oh,' said Jane. 'I see.'

'Sit down please,' said Bet. 'If you wouldn't mind.'

'Of course not.' Jane sat. 'What can I do for you?'

'It's about – about face cream and that. Make-up.'

'What about it?'

'I'm twenty-four,' said Bet. 'I reckon at my age I'm entitled to use it.'

Twenty-four. I'm eight years older than she, thought Jane – and I look eight years younger.

'Of course you are,' she said.

'Gran says she wouldn't object – not if there was money coming in. And I doubt if me dad would even notice. And as for Bob and Andy, it's none of their business.'

'Then why don't you do it?'

'I don't know how,' said Bet. 'I was hoping you could teach me. You always look so nice. I mean that suit you wore when you first came – '

'You liked it?'

'I loved it. Best clothes I ever saw.'

Nothing wrong with your taste, thought Jane, and said aloud, 'Would you like it? To keep, I mean?'

'Oh,' said Bet. 'Oh no, miss. I mean Jane. I couldn't.'

'Whyever not?'

'It doesn't belong,' said Bet. 'I'm not being silly. Honest . . . I don't mean I *shouldn't* have it. I mean I *can't*.'

'I still don't understand,' said Jane.

'How could I go about dressed like that when every other woman in the street dresses like this?'

She swept her hand down the front of her old and fading dress.

'You could say you bought it in a jumble sale.'

'Even if they believed me they wouldn't forgive me,' said Bet. 'It's – it's just too much, that suit. Like a bit of heaven.'

'Then take this one,' said Jane. 'I bought it in Queen Street. Don't tell me you couldn't have found that in a jumble sale?'

'I don't want you to give me things – ' said Bet.

'Not even if I want to give them?'

'Just tell me about make-up.'

'Very well,' said Jane, and opened her bag. 'Let's have a look at you. You've a lovely skin, thank heaven. That's half the battle won already.'

'That's as maybe,' said Bet, 'but when you're after a chap – claes like yours would be better.'

'Claes?' said Lionel.

'It means clothes,' said Jane. 'Sort of a dialect word.'

'Their dialect is very broad, I guess,' said Bower.

'Almost incomprehensible,' said Jane, and stirred her coffee.

Jay Bower dropping in like this was a nuisance in a way. Lionel had invited her to lunch because he was *almost* certain he'd found her a house, and at the end of lunch Bower had dropped in and demanded coffee and asked endless questions about Felston. Definitely a nuisance, except that she had found in herself this deep need, this compulsion even, to talk about Felston, and the horror and pity it awoke in her.

'Different landscape, different language,' said Bower. 'Creatures of another country?'

'It would be easier if one could believe it, but I can't,' said Jane.

'Was there nothing pleasant there?' Lionel asked.

She thought for a moment. 'There was a beach that was quite beautiful,' she said.

'A plage do you mean?' asked Lionel. 'Deauville? Cap d'Antibes? That sort of thing?'

She could see the beach quite clearly: the sand of palest gold, the high cliffs flecked with lichen, the bottle-green sea that even on the calmest day showed fast-darting whitecaps. And all so cold, even in summer.

'More beautiful,' she said.

'And no one goes there?' Bower asked.

He was wrong. The poor went there, as they went everywhere: to scavenge for driftwood, sea coal, coins if they were lucky. The poor were very seldom lucky.

'It's cold,' she said, 'even when the sun shines. And no one has the money for pleasure.'

'I have to know more about this,' said Bower. 'Come back to Fleet Street with me.'

'No.' Now was not the time. It was all too close, too real. 'I have an engagement – with Lionel.'

'Something important?'

'I think so.'

Near the Brompton Road. . . . A divine little terrace, just off Thurloe Square. Harrods virtually on your doorstep, my dear. Not cheap, of course. I should be very suspicious if it were cheap. But I shall not allow you to be robbed.

'It could be very important,' said Jane.

'This evening, then. Come and dine with me this evening.'

'You seem in rather a hurry,' Lionel said.

'I always am,' said Bower. 'It's the only way I can work. It's the only way a newspaper gets published, for that matter.' He turned to Jane. 'Café de Paris suit you?'

He got up then, and Lionel rang for Pott to show him to the door, then smiled at Jane.

'Too exhausting,' he said. 'Do you think you could stand a whole evening with him à deux? And what possible connection does he hope to make between you and the newspaper business?'

'I'll tell you tomorrow,' said Jane. 'Now I want to hear about the house.'

But they went to see it instead: the tall, narrow house on a corner, with a garden of lime trees and rose bushes, and inside enough room, more than enough, but never too much. Dining room and drawing room and book room, two bedrooms – (Quite sufficient, said Lionel. For once inside a house like this, no guest would ever want to leave). And a bathroom that he knew he could convert into something positively sybaritic. Heliogabalus himself would feel at home there.

The house was empty of course, and the floor boards creaked, the sun sought out the dust: but the rooms were light and gracefully proportioned, the house itself an elegant, up-ended box of Georgian brick. Aunt Pen's furniture would fit in awfully well, but she would have some modern pieces too. Lionel couldn't monopolise London's art-deco furniture completely.

'Certainly not,' said Lionel. 'And we must have a look at new fabrics too. Lady Lessing cannot be allowed to possess the monopoly of Bakst designs either.'

'Bakst? In a house?'

'Bakst.' Lionel was firm. 'Discreetly but inevitably. Now. . . . Is there anything else you would care to see?'

'I don't think so,' said Jane.

'The servants' quarters perhaps?'

'Oh my God.' Jane's hands went to her face. 'After all my fine talk of Felston. It was just – '

'The taste of freedom?'

'Exactly that,' said Jane. And so it had been, but it was a poor excuse.

The kitchen was roomy and well enough lit but the stove would have to go, said Lionel. The kind of cook he had in mind would never tolerate such an ageing monstrosity. Scullery and pantry as they should be, tradesmen's entrance in good repair. At the top of the house the servants' rooms, that seemed all right, so Jane supposed, but how was she to know? The only way was to show them to Hawkins and accept her judgement.

It couldn't be the Café de Paris she decided, not that night, and telephoned Bower to tell him so. She could stand up to an encounter with a discarded lordling – English or foreign – and even if she couldn't, Bower could. It wasn't that. What she couldn't stand was the thought of Bob listening in on his crystal set up there in Felston. It would have to be somewhere else. In fact the Café de Paris had been Bower's first choice.

'What's wrong with it?' he asked.

'Too loud. I thought we were going to talk.'

It was a reason that made sense to him.

'We can't go to the Embassy,' he said. 'Not on a Thursday. The Prince of Wales will be there and we don't want him to think the press is spying on him. I know it sounds banal, – but what about the Savoy? Pick you up at eight thirty?'

'I'll look forward to it,' she said, and was reasonably sure that she spoke the truth.

27

S HE HAD A fire lit in her bedroom – extra work, but Hawkins
was all in favour. And this time she allowed Hawkins to help
her dress: a gown by Paquin, of a warm, almost glowing pink and
cut loose. Too loose, she had thought, but Aunt Pen had been sure
she would grow into it, and she'd been right. Prescience, it must
have been. Was that the word? Foreknowledge. Just the sort of
thing Aunt Pen would be good at. Anyway the dress didn't hang
on her like a sack any more, but went out and in precisely where
it should. Soon it would be time to say 'no' to potatoes.

Hawkins loved the dress and said so, and Jane welcomed
her approval. More and more she was beginning to appreciate
Hawkins's intelligence. The maid began to brush her hair, and
Jane told her about the new house.

'South Kensington, miss?' said Hawkins. She sounded dubious.

'I honestly think we could call it Knightsbridge,' said Jane.

'And would you still want to take me with you?' Hawkins
asked.

'Of course,' said Jane. 'If you still want to come.' And then,
before Hawkins could speak: 'Best wait till you see it.'

Then she sat in the drawing room and waited for Bower. She
had no doubt that he would be prompt, and how right she was.
The clock was still chiming as his chauffeur knocked. Hawkins
helped her on with her cloak, then opened the door.

'Au revoir, miss,' said Hawkins.

'Hasta luego,' said Jane.

For once Hawkins looked puzzled, and not before time.

The chauffeur's presence meant that she was on parade, thought Jane, and was glad that she had chosen the Paquin dress (smart but not *too* revealing) and at the last moment pinned on the Cartier leopardess. It was unlikely that any other woman would be wearing such a thing, even at the Savoy.

She got in beside Bower, and the scent of Roger et Gallet cologne and Havana cigars. He made no move to come closer to her, nor had she expected it. Instead he at once began to talk politics: Gandhi and self-government in India – and why the British couldn't hope to prevent it (because they weren't tough enough): this guy Mussolini who everybody said would stop the Reds (but what was the point when he behaved just like them?): and why the Prince of Wales should get married (the popular press needed the story. The pictures alone . . .). They had got on to the subject of the Little Man's latest mistress and why they always had to be so goddam mature when the car pulled up and the doorman came scurrying. And two nights before this she had been eating fish and chips at Dr Stobbs's clinic.

When the champagne had been tested and approved, Bower said: 'Now I think *you* should talk for a while.'

'My innings? Is that what you mean?'

'Of course not.' He gestured impatiently: she had made a remark unworthy of her, it seemed. 'Tell me some more about Felston.'

'But why on earth should I?'

'Because I want to know.'

She gave him a kindly look, one modelled on that used by Vinney when she was about to correct a lack of manners.

'First you're supposed to ask me to dance, you know,' she said.

He glared at her, then threw back his head and laughed.

'May I have the pleasure of this dance, Miss Whitcomb?' he said.

'But of course,' said Jane.

He was no Lionel, but aeons ahead of Cuthbert Pardoe, and his presence on the dance floor set up a buzzing like bees.

When they had eaten and the coffee arrived, Jane said, 'Please smoke a cigar if you wish,' and this time he grinned at her, a grin of simple pleasure in her company. When the cigar was drawing easily she asked, 'What would you like to know about Felston? I don't have too many statistics. I did get hold of a pamphlet, but it's at home somewhere.'

'Not statistics,' Bower said. 'What I want is a story. An anecdote.'

She thought for a moment, then said, 'George Colley.'

'What about him?'

'He's a dustman now, but ten years ago he was Private Colley in the Tyneside Highlanders.'

'You mean he wore a kilt?'

'Just like all the others,' said Jane. 'He fought at Passchendaele.'

'Otherwise known as the third Battle of Ypres,' said Bower. 'I somehow get the idea this isn't going to be a very happy story.'

'I forgot,' said Jane. 'You were there too. I don't have to tell you what it was like.'

'It was hell,' said Bower.

'Private Colley thought so. He wasn't a very religious man, but he knew hell when he saw it. . . . He'd served eighteen months by then. Once promoted to lance-corporal, once reduced to the ranks for drunkenness. On the other hand he'd won himself a Military Medal for rescuing an officer under fire.'

'Not much of a story so far,' said Bower.

She looked at him. He was perfectly serious: a news editor rebuking a junior reporter.

'I think you'll find it gets better,' she said, ' – or at any rate more interesting.

'On 10th August, 1917, he and his platoon were in a communications trench moving up to attack, when the trench received a direct hit from a shell. Private Colley was buried alive, covered in mud and what was left of his comrades. He lay upon the body of his closest friend. The body was headless. On top of him was his corporal who was dying, and screaming as he did so. When they dug Colley out he was unmarked, so of course he was simply transferred to another platoon that was short of men. They gave him rum in his tea that night, and he slept well, moved up with the others, ready to attack. Another communications trench, another platoon, another shell: the mixture precisely as before, except that this time he was buried for rather longer. – His battalion had gone into the attack. There was no one to spare to hunt for Private Colley. This time when they brought him out he was quite mad.'

'You don't surprise me.'

'Only he didn't stay that way. He recovered in a month, returned to his battalion, finished his war and went back to his dustcart. When I asked him how he'd done it he said, "I had a wife and a bairn, miss – bairn means child – and another on the way."'

'A man of strong will,' said Bower.

'Perhaps even a fortunate man,' said Jane. 'But not entirely. The madness came back from time to time – mostly in nightmares. But he and his wife and children have learned to live with it. He has a job, you see.'

'A job is that important?'

'A job in Felston is life itself.'

'Even collecting other peoples' dust.' Bower examined the ash on his cigar, and decided to let it stay for a while. 'And how did you come to meet him?'

'I'd been having lunch with a friend.'

Baked herrings – again – and home-baked bread, and Dr Stobbs writing up case notes as he ate.

'When it was over I was going back to the car we used to bring patients to our clinic – '

'Sounds like another story,' said Bower.

'Perhaps. Let me finish this one first. I took a short cut to the car down a lane behind the house – what they call a back lane – and George Colley was going by with his dustcart.

'A child – a girl of about ten I suppose – had got one of those rattles, the kind that makes a noise like a corncrake. You swing them and they make a rattling sound very fast. You know.'

'I know,' said Bower. 'Swing it really hard and it could be a machine gun you're hearing.'

'Exactly,' said Jane. 'It was a machine gun that Private Colley heard. He was out of that dustcart and under it in about three seconds, and on the way down he'd collected a spade from the side of the cart and was there under cover, holding the spade like a rifle. It was – you may find this ridiculous – but it was rather beautiful to watch.'

'Not ridiculous at all,' said Bower. 'Extraordinary though. That you should see it – and remember.'

'Like an athlete,' she said. 'So quick. So elegant. So perfect. There in place, armed and ready – except that there was no enemy.'

'This cart?' Bower asked. 'What about the motor?'

'The motor was a Clydesdale mare called Mavis,' said Jane. 'Chestnut. Twenty-three hands at least. When Private Colley stopped, she stopped. We females have some sense.'

'So what did *you* do, being female and sensible?'

'I gave the little girl tuppence to fetch a man I know – an ex-corporal called Laidlaw who helps in the clinic – and told her there'd be another tuppence when she brought him. I even showed her the other two pennies. After all, she's a sensible female too. When I got under the cart beside Private Colley and said, "That was a close one." And he looked at me and said, "What in the name of God is a woman doing here?"'

'I said, "Driving an ambulance. What else would a woman be doing here? Now stay still. Our relief is coming."'

'And was it?' Bower asked.

'Of course,' said Jane. 'The little girl had come for her extra tuppence, and brought my friend Laidlaw, and a doctor called Stobbs. I told them both what had happened, and they talked him out in the language of Passchendaele because they'd both been there, and for a while it was 1917.'

'And then?'

'Suddenly George Colley said, "I'm being barmy, I know that. I'll be all right if I can have a bit of a lie-down but I have to take the horse and cart back – I've finished my shift. Trouble is I'm that tired." And he leaned against the wall of a yard and closed his eyes and slept.'

'So your friend Laidlaw took the dustcart back?'

'No,' said Jane. 'I did.'

'You?'

'Well of course me,' said Jane. 'Laidlaw had never handled a horse in his life – nor had Dr Stobbs. But Mavis and I got on very well. Two sensible females.'

'And George Colley?'

'Had a nap and a cup of tea at the clinic and went back to his wife and bairns. . . . Oh listen, they're playing a Charleston. I *adore* the Charleston.'

He got up and danced well enough to escape censure. When they sat down again he said, 'You told that well.'

'Thank you.'

'Do you think you could write it?'

'Write it?' said Jane. 'Why on earth should I? I'm not nearly old enough to be thinking of my memoirs. You're not very flattering.'

'I want you to write it as a feature for the *Daily World*,' said Bower. 'You won't get it right first time, – nobody does; but you'll soon get the hang of it.'

'But why should you want to print a story about Felston?'

'What I was looking for was a story about poverty.'

'Then I chose the right place.'

'Sure you did. But I also needed an angie. An attention grabber.'

'And you think you've got one?'

'Certainly I have,' said Bower. 'You. . . . You and Felston. A diamond among the coals.'

'I see,' said Jane. The idea revolted her, but she couldn't just abandon it. Not yet. 'And *why* do you want to print my story?'

'Because poverty's going to be fashionable,' said Bower. 'Not just poverty. The workers, the class war, Socialism. All that.'

'And you care about it?'

'Of course I care,' Bower said. 'It'll sell newspapers.'

'Oh I see,' said Jane, and indeed she did. 'And if I wrote this piece for you, would I be paid?'

'Certainly,' said Bower. 'Going rate. That's ten guineas for a thousand words – even if you are a beginner.'

'Then I'll do it,' said Jane, 'on one condition.'

'I better warn you,' said Bower. 'The editor's decision is final.'

'Well of course,' she said. 'All I want you to do is say in your newspaper that the ten guineas goes to the Felston Relief Fund.'

'I've never heard of it,' said Bower.

'That's because I've just opened it,' said Jane.

'And how are you going to organise it?'

'I'm not going to organise it,' said Jane. 'I'm simply going to ask people for money and pass it on to a man I know in Felston. A doctor.'

'Are you going to ask me for money?'

'Of course.'

'How much?'

'All you can spare. After all, you're the richest man I know.'

'I'll give you some,' said Bower. 'And some free advice. Plus your writing fee. Aren't I generous?'

'Depends how much you give. Let's have the advice.'

'Get yourself talked about. That way Felston will be talked about too.'

'And how do I do that?'

'You've a brother at Cambridge,' said Bower. 'Go and talk about it there. See if they can't discuss Felston in that debating society of theirs.'

'The Cambridge Union?'

'That's the one. If they do, the Oxford Union's bound to follow and then maybe some of the other newspapers will take it up. Then when you ask people for money they'll be bound to give because you're a celebrity. Would you like to dance again?'

'No thank you,' said Jane. 'But I must say you asked me very nicely. To the manner born, almost.'

Once more he gave her that friendly, almost conspiratorial grin.

'I think I may want you to go to Paris,' he said, 'if your article works out.'

'But why on earth should I?'

'Partly for Felston,' he said, 'but mostly for yourself. Save it for now, humh?'

She saved it, but she was curious. Any woman would have been.

Next morning there were letters: bills for the most part, and a postcard from Mummy: a picture of Bombay. 'Miss Gwatkin remains garrulous,' Mummy wrote, 'despite the heat, but the motion of the ship is soothing. I find that I think of Papa more often than I could wish.' There was a letter from Jabber's secretary too. Dr Lockhart would like to see her at her earliest convenience. Her ear-rings were ready, too. Jane telephoned Jabber's rooms and made an appointment, then rang for Hawkins.

'I think perhaps we should look at the house in South Terrace this morning, unless you've made other plans?' she said.

'None, miss.'

Jane was relieved, yet perhaps disappointed also, that Hawkins spoke in English.

'I want to call at Bond Street first,' she said, 'but it won't take long. We'll have to take Foch, I'm afraid.'

'Be a pleasure, miss,' said Hawkins. 'We get on very well, Foch and me. Foch and I, I should say.'

And it seemed that they did, though whether this was due to approval on Foch's part for self-improvement, or a sure source of extra stew, Jane was not sure. She and Foch had celebrated their reunion immediately on her return. Now he had reverted to his more formal manner, but consented to be squashed between two women with reasonable grace.

Hawkins accompanied them into the jeweller's shop. She had always wanted to see inside a shop like that, she said, but had never had the nerve. Once inside she stood deferentially by Jane and a little to one side, but her eyes, Jane was sure, took in everything. The assistant brought out the ear-rings. They were for evening wear, each of two stones, one beneath the other, and set in platinum.

'Very nice,' said Jane, and turned to Hawkins. 'What do you think?'

'They're lovely, miss,' said Hawkins. There could be no doubt that she meant it.

From the West End they drove to South Terrace, and this time they were met by a man from an estate agency. Somehow Lionel had managed to avoid his services, but Jane was not so fortunate. Round the garden they went, and then from room to room, from basement to attics, while the estate agent's man chanted his litany of praise; a remorseless flow that even Miss Gwatkin might have envied. When they had done, he asked if she had questions, and Jane turned to Hawkins.

'Have you?' she asked.

'I should just think I have, miss,' said Hawkins.

'Go ahead and ask them,' said Jane. 'Foch and I will wait in the garden. The sun is still quite warm.' Foch quite liked the house, she knew, but was even more pleased with the garden, not so much because of the sunlight, as because of the shade of the lime trees. A compromise, as usual. Jane thought that perhaps she was rather good at compromises, but that Hawkins was not: at least not with estate agents. At last Hawkins emerged to prove her right. The estate agent followed her, thoroughly cowed, and it was Hawkins who did the talking. The estate agent lifted his hat to Jane, then left, not quite running, but walking very briskly indeed when one considered the mildness of the weather.

'What *did* you say to the poor man?' Jane asked.

'Told him about the stove, miss.'

'Yes. Mr Warley spotted that.'

'Also the broken sash cords and the crack in the servants' washbasin and that bit of parquet near the garden window that needs renewing. And that loose moulding in the second bedroom and the light switch on the second landing and the radiator going rusty in the dining room.'

She didn't ask if Mr Warley had spotted them, too. She didn't have to.

'And what did the man say?'

'Said he'd report it, miss. I told him to look sharp about it. Not that he'll have it seen to, but it should bring the price down a bit.'

'You seem to have impressed him very much,' said Jane.

'I think he sort of got the idea that I was your adviser, miss,' said Hawkins.

'It's an idea I seem to have got, too.'

Hawkins said, 'Yes miss,' and left it at that.

'Shall I take it?' said Jane. 'I rather liked the central heating.'

'The last lot who had it were Americans, miss,' said Hawkins. 'Still, it'll come in handy in the winter.'

Jane took this for consent.

'What staff shall I need?' she asked.

'Well there's me,' said Hawkins, 'and I'll need a girl under me – a house that size. And we'll need a cook and a kitchenmaid and a jobbing gardener part-time and a couple of charwomen for the rough, and that's about it, miss. Always assuming we use the steam laundry.'

'Oh I'm sure we will,' said Jane. 'Poor part-time gardener and so many women. . . . There's no bath for the servants.'

'No miss,' said Hawkins.

'We'll have to have one fitted.'

'You mean a real bath – with taps and hot water?'

Jane thought of the zinc tubs in Felston that the miners used, laboriously filled with hot water boiled in pans on the fire.

'Of course,' she said.

'Golly, miss,' said Hawkins.

28

LUNCHTIME BROUGHT A note from Bower. He had a cheque for the Felston Fund as he called it, and looked forward to presenting it to her that evening over dinner at Ciro's. If it was convenient there was no need for her to reply. He would pick her up at eight thirty. He doesn't say how much, thought Jane, but it's bound to be pretty decent, then took Foch to call on Lockhart. He ought to be good for at least a guinea.

For once in his life Jabber acted as if he were angry with her. Well perhaps not that, exactly – Jane doubted if he could ever be really angry with anybody – but nervous and distressed. He sat her down, gave her a cigarette, then went to the window.

'You've been away,' he said.

'Certainly,' said Jane. 'You sent me. Don't you remember?'

'So I did,' he said. 'You're saying it's my fault, and of course you're very probably right – '

'Fault?' she said. 'You talk as if it had all gone wrong. But it didn't. Honestly. *Dear* Jabber – I had a wonderful time.'

'No more dreams?' She shook her head. 'No screaming?'

'Of course not. What on earth is this all about?'

'I had a letter from a colleague of mine. We both had consulting rooms in the same house years ago. He sent me some case notes. A man called Colley.'

'Dr Stobbs,' she said. 'You've heard from Dr Stobbs. But I thought he only took out appendixes in Harley Street.'

'So he did,' said Lockhart, 'but he was a damn good doctor and a very bright man, and what I was doing fascinated him. So when he treated Colley – you and he together I should say – he thought I might be interested, and wrote to tell me about it. Colley's an interesting case, of course – '

'Because of the way he can control it?'

'I doubt if it's control exactly. But yes. And he asked for my advice and of course I've given it, but that isn't the point.'

'What is then?'

'You,' said Lockhart.

'*Me?*'

'Stobbs doesn't know about our professional relationship of course – and he most certainly doesn't know, anyway from me – that you had been ill. But it seems the whole town knows it.'

'Knows that I was mad?'

'We had agreed you wouldn't say that – '

'I'm sorry,' said Jane.

'And anyway they have no idea of the exact nature of your illness. They think it was – '

'Was what?'

'Stobbs said the people he talked to got extraordinarily coy when he tried to pin them down. The best he could get was something they called women's problems.'

So Grandma had not betrayed her. But she must have said some thing to Bet and Bob and Andy and Stan. . . . It must have been Andy. She was sure of it.

Aloud she said, 'So that's all right then?'

'Is it? You've made yourself quite a reputation in Felston. Up to your old tricks. Driving an ambulance. Just like the war.'

'Making myself useful.'

'*Exactly* like the war. And getting mixed up in poverty and degradation. Trying to help a man who suffered as you suffered – '

'I didn't try. I succeeded. And anyway why shouldn't I?'

Lockhart said, 'I'll tell you. Because that man could drag you back into your nightmares. And not just him. *All* the things you're doing – '

'All I did was help Dr Stobbs.'

'And involve yourself in poverty and grief. Work too hard and worry too much and suffer because the people you help are suffering. It won't do, Jane.'

'Won't do?'

– 286 –

'I have to tell you this,' said Lockhart. 'What you are doing is as near as it's possible to get to what you did in the war – and in the end it almost destroyed you. It could do so again. And I sent you up there because I thought it might distract you, God help me.'

'There is one difference,' said Jane. 'John is dead.'

'He's all around you up there,' said Lockhart. 'Stobbs told me that, too. Just as he told me that you'll be going back there. Will you?'

'I must,' said Jane. 'Don't you see? It's *because* John's all around me there. I have no choice. . . .'

And not just John. Grandma and Dr Stobbs and Laidlaw and Bella Docherty. All of them. Waiting for her and needing her, and the money she could raise.

Lockhart sighed, 'All right,' he said. 'Stobbs said you were a marvellous help up there, and Stobbs didn't use words like "marvellous" for less than a fifty-guinea fee, not when I knew him. So he values your help. Of course he does. I know you. If you give at all you'll give the lot. But I really must warn you. If you go over again, you may not find it possible to come back.'

'Private Colley came back,' she said.

'And he's more important than you?'

'Not on his own,' she said. 'But put them all together – of course they're more important than me.'

'Then I wish you luck,' he said.

'But don't go crying to Jabber if things go wrong?'

'No!' He strode from the window and stood in front of her, glowering down into her face. Foch growled, disturbed, but her eyes still on Lockhart she touched the dog and he was silent. 'Of course come crying to Jabber,' he said. 'That's what I'm here for. I thought you knew that.'

The Erté dress again, she thought, because it really was her best and she was going to need all the money she could get – and looking her best would certainly help with *that*. Jabber had coughed up five guineas, which was really rather decent of him. He wasn't exactly rolling in riches and never would be – far too nice to drum his patients, so that really five pounds five shillings was awfully decent.

She examined the dress for marks and stains, found none, and began to ponder the fact that Jabber, Dr J.A.B. Lockhart, was very much in love with her. Never mind how, never mind why.

She just knew for a fact that he was, and that she didn't care for him at all, not in 'that way'. That's how one put it when one didn't want to be vulgar. Not in that way: i.e. she didn't want to go to bed with him. She didn't have to, either. Couldn't. What with the Hippocratic oath and all that. But sooner or later she'd want to go to bed with somebody, and what price Felston then? In the meantime she had to get her hands on a lot of money. Aunt Pen's wouldn't support Felston single-handed, and anyway that wasn't why Aunt Pen had left it to her. Other people would have to fork out too: and so she chose the Erté dress. It was nice to know that Lockhart was in love with her, but all she could do was feel sorry for him, and what was the use of that? The doorbell rang and it was Bower, punctual as always, but this time without his chauffeur.

The Erté dress was much admired, which was what it was for, that and arousing the envy of other women perhaps.

'But you aren't wearing your leopard,' said Bower.

'Leopardess – or so I'm told. No. She's having a night off.'

'You feel safe without her then?'

'The question doesn't arise,' said Jane. 'There just wasn't anywhere practical to pin her.'

'How on earth can you look and talk like that and spend time in Felston?' said Bower.

'That's simply asking how can I be Jane Whitcomb,' said Jane. 'But I manage it – and without undue difficulty most of the time.' Then the band played 'My Blue Heaven' and they danced.

They danced rather a lot, and there was rather a lot of champagne, and very little further talk of Felston, except for a brisk five minutes' cross-examination on the progress of her article. In fact there had been none, but she couldn't tell Bower that, not when she was after his money.

'I finished it,' she said, 'but the style was too florid so I tore it up. I didn't want to waste your time.'

'You were probably right,' he said, 'but I want to see something soon. Newspapers never wait. It's the one thing they can't do for you.' The band played 'Tea For Two'. They took to the floor again and Georgina Payne danced by her, in a blue dress so unsuitable Jane knew at once that it had belonged to someone else. The man holding her, and delighted to be doing so, was Michael Browne, sober this time, but still in his ancient dress-suit.

When they were seated once more, Georgina looked across to

Jane, a look that to a woman was as obvious as a firework display, but to a man non-existent. Obediently Jane followed the blonde girl to the powder-room, which was empty except for a fat girl sobbing in a corner while the attendant hovered with eau de cologne.

'What on earth – ' said Jane.

'Too many Manhattans probably.' Georgina sat at the mirror, took out powder compact and puff, and examined her complexion pitilessly. She could well afford to, thought Jane, as she joined her. Georgina's complexion was flawless.

'I love your dress,' said Georgina. 'Poiret?'

'You're close,' said Jane. 'It's Erté. . . . It would look wonderful on you.'

'Better than this, you mean?' said Georgina. 'It's borrowed. But of course you'll have guessed that anyway. I hadn't a thing to wear that I hadn't worn five hundred times already. It's different for men. Mike still goes around in that dreadful old ruin of a suit he bought before the war, and people merely think he's eccentric. Which is true enough, I suppose. He sold a drawing last week, which is why we're here. Celebrating.'

'I'm glad for you,' said Jane.

'Are you?' said Georgina. 'You never came to see me. After you *promised*.'

Jane decided that this time it was Miss Payne's turn to be not quite sober, and wondered how Michael Browne would cope.

'I've been away,' she said, 'for rather a long while. But I'll call on you soon. I promise.'

'Oh how gorgeous,' said Georgina. 'Now promise me again – you won't forget. Has Bower got his chauffeur with him?'

Jane separated the sentences.

'I won't forget,' she said. 'Bower drove me here himself.'

'I've never been one of Bower's girls,' said Georgina, 'apart from parties and things, but from what I hear – no chauffeur is a bad sign. Unless you think it's a good sign, of course.'

'I'm obliged to you,' said Jane, and rose to her feet. 'Ready?'

'You go back without me,' said Georgina. 'We don't want the chaps to think we've been talking. And in any case, a little pause for quiet reflection would do me no harm at all.'

Jane went back. The wine waiter had poured more champagne, but she wasn't with Cuthbert Pardoe after all: she didn't *have* to get sloshed. Instead, she sipped.

'Dessert?' Bower asked.

'Strawberries please, and lots of cream. I'll starve tomorrow.'

Bower gave the order. 'How's the fund doing?' he asked.

'It isn't,' said Jane, then remembered Lockhart. 'Well only just. I'm relying on you to really get things going.'

'Split infinitive,' said Bower.

'Which just goes to show how much I mean it,' said Jane. 'And in front of my publisher too.'

'Don't be too sure,' said Bower. 'I never buy until I've seen the goods.'

'Very wise,' said Jane. 'I'm rather that way myself.'

He looked at her; waited until the strawberries were gone. Her champagne glass was almost full, but she made no move to reach for it.

'Shall I take you home now?'

'Unless you would like to dance some more.'

'No more dancing.'

The flirting stage it seemed was over. 'Then home it must be.'

'Coffee,' he said. 'I forgot coffee.'

'I feel no need for it,' she said. 'And if you're feeling tired – '

'I am *not* tired.' He took a folded piece of paper from his wallet and passed it to her. It was a cheque for five hundred pounds.

'That's for Felston,' he said. 'No strings and no provisos.'

'You mean you'll still pay me for my article?'

'Well of course I will,' he said. 'If it's any good. But that isn't it. What I mean is that money's for your charity and I want you to have it because I believe it's a good thing and it sure won't hurt the paper – '

'Altruism like yours is so rare these days.'

'Now you just stop that,' said Bower amiably. 'And never let me catch you using that word when you're writing for me. Even the people who know what it means don't like to see it. They're afraid it might be catching. . . . That cheque's for your fund, OK? It's over and finished with, no matter what.'

'I understand,' said Jane, who understood not at all.

'Fine,' said Bower. 'Now when I said I was ready to take you home I meant that too, but I didn't necessarily mean your home.'

Now she understood. He looked at her closely. That he was a clever man she had never doubted, but that look told her he was a perceptive one too.

'I guess I'm rushing things,' he said.

Cuthbert Pardoe, Jabber Lockhart, and now Bower. Things were certainly looking up, even if she had turned down two lordlings.

'Just a bit,' she said.

'You're a very attractive woman,' said Bower. 'I don't believe for a minute you realise just how attractive you are – and that's part of it.' He signalled for his bill.

'You can sit in the back if you like,' said Bower.

'What nonsense,' said Jane, and got in beside him. On the way home Bower talked of Russia and the gold standard and whether Winston Churchill had a future, until Jane interrupted to say that it all sounded terribly worthy and informative, but she'd much sooner hear about Hollywood. So then he told her about Charlie Chaplin, and Douglas Fairbanks and Mary Pickford, and Clara Bow, all of whom he knew: talking about them as if they all lived just round the next corner, and to drop in on them for a drink would be the most natural thing in the world.

'How marvellous to know them like that,' she said.

'Marvellous? I never thought so, but maybe you're right. They're in the marvel business after all. The best thing is for you to meet them and judge for yourself.'

'You think I will?'

'Oh sure,' he said. 'It may take a little time, that's all.'

Then he pulled up at her door, and leaned across and kissed her, a smooth and easy flow of the body of a kind she'd seen a hundred times at the cinema, or what he would call the movies.

His lips were gentle, and there was no pawing. Really a most civilised embrace, she thought, and found her arms wanted to be around his neck as she thought it.

'I'll ask again,' Jay Bower said. 'Maybe not tomorrow, but I'll ask again,' then got out of the car and escorted her to her door, waited until she produced her key, and left her after an inclination of the torso that in anybody else would have been a bow. Jane realised that Pardoe was not the only amorous tank of her acquaintance; realised too that a certain kind of tank, if not watched very carefully, might gain its objective.

29

THE HOUSE WAS between the King's Road and the Fulham Road, not exactly the best part, but with big and airy attics with a north light, which was just as well, as Michael Browne appeared to have moved in there and used the place as a studio. It should have looked very artistic, thought Jane, or rather Artistic, with a capital 'A', easel and brushes and unshaded windows, and a battered upright piano and piles of sheet music. But it didn't look like that at all: merely easy and lived in, with its cheap and cheerful furniture, coffee mugs and bottles of wine. Both of them had been working when she arrived; both of them stopped at once.

'It was sweet of you to come so soon,' said Georgie. 'Michael darling, this is Jane Whitcomb.'

They shook hands. Jane could sense the contained power in the man: the first thing that she had noticed about him.

'How do you do?' he said. 'I'm told I should have seen you at Hugh Lessing's party – always assuming I could see anything. But I couldn't.'

'Go and put the kettle on,' said Georgina, 'while I show Jane around the place. It'll only take five minutes.'

'If that,' said Michael Browne.

Most of the flat was the studio: that was where they ate, lived, worked. The rest was simply a kitchen with a gas-ring, sink and stove, a cupboard of a bathroom, and a bedroom that showed the only signs of luxury in the place: elegant white furniture, a canopied bed. A lover's room, thought Jane, which was all very right if not proper, since lovers they were.

'Did you have problems last night?' Georgina asked.

'I might have done,' said Jane. 'But I didn't. It was sweet of you to warn me.'

'Forewarned is forearmed and all that,' said Georgina. 'I wouldn't want you to be embarrassed.'

'I wasn't. Not last night anyway. I like your Michael.'

'Isn't he scrumptious? But he isn't. Mine I mean. He's married.'

'It doesn't surprise me.'

'It was the war,' said Georgina. 'Everybody was getting married. Everybody.'

'I nearly did myself,' said Jane.

'Oh!' said Georgina and her hand went to her mouth: a gesture at once endearing and contrite. 'I didn't mean – '

'On the shelf,' said Jane. 'Spinster. Old maid.'

'You mustn't say that,' said Georgina fiercely. 'You mustn't think of yourself like that.'

'I don't,' said Jane, and after a second Georgina began to laugh. Even her laughter, thought Jane, was pretty.

'That's all right then,' she said. 'Let's go and see what hell brew Michael's making.'

But it was only tea the way the army made it, hot, strong and sweet. Browne poured her a cup and said, 'You were in it, Georgie says. The war I mean.'

'I drove an ambulance.'

'I rode in one once,' said Browne. 'But you weren't driving. I would have remembered.'

'A bad one?'

'First day of the Somme,' said Browne. 'Got me six weeks' sick leave. Probably saved my life, though.'

Georgina said, 'I don't want to talk about that.'

'No reason why we should,' said Browne. 'What do you do now, Miss Whitcomb?'

'Good works,' said Jane. 'The proper occupation for unmarried ladies of an uncertain age. But please call me Jane.'

'You never fancied becoming an art collector?'

'Never,' said Jane.

'Pity,' said Browne. 'There's a lot of art in this place going cheap.'

'But I might,' said Jane. 'I just bought a house in South Terrace.'

'Off the Brompton Road?' Browne asked, and she nodded.

'How dashing,' said Georgina.

'Pooh that's nothing,' said Jane. 'I used to have a house in Mount Street. Show me some of that art you've got.'

He had oils and drawings, and both were of two kinds: the war, and his celebration of the fact that he had survived it: a celebration that involved Georgina a good deal. The war was portraits of soldiers: mostly privates and NCOs and an occasional young officer to remind her of John. Together with the mad, smashed landscape of the trenches, guns and limbers, horses that were still alive and unhurt to remind her of Mavis and Bridget O'Dowd, and then a gun team that was dead: men and horses both.

Jane looked away at once to the postwar pictures and sketches, that were a kind of hymn to survival and more than survival: to life itself. Pictures of flowers and still lives of fruit and bread and wine that somehow throbbed with vitality, sketches and portraits of Georgie that praised her beauty like love sonnets. But always her glance went back to the dead horses, the dead men.

'It's all so morbid,' said Georgina. 'Don't you think it's morbid?'

Jane heard her voice say, 'No, my dear. That's pretty well the way it was.'

In her nightmares it had always been the horses: it was only now, when she was awake, that she was shown the image of dead men. Soon, she knew, she would begin to scream.

It was the noise from outside that saved her: feet stamping on the stairs and then the pounding of a fist on the door, and a voice made hoarse by anger shouting, 'Michael, Michael, I know you're in there so don't try to hide.'

Browne looked at Georgina Payne. 'Oh Lord,' he said.

'Lilian?' she asked.

'I'm afraid so.' The pounding intensified.

'I'm most awfully sorry,' said Georgina to Jane, 'but it's Michael's wife.'

'I'm afraid I'll have to let her in,' said Browne. 'We'll have the whole house here if we don't.'

The hoarse voice rose louder. 'Don't try to hide behind that bitch's skirts – if she's wearing any skirts that is.'

Browne got up and moved to the door, and Jane rose. This

was a private quarrel, and one that guaranteed the maximum quantity of embarrassment. Not her kind of thing at all. She handed the drawings and oils to Georgina.

'I should hide these somewhere,' she said, and Georgina did so, and Browne opened the door.

The woman exploded into the room, an entrance as dramatic as a demon king's at a pantomime, and perhaps she knew she was doing it, perhaps it gave her pleasure, but the overwhelming effect that she created was one of grief. Heartbreak. She stood just inside the door, kicked it shut with her foot, then posed with arms spread wide as if determined that no one should leave: an effect even more dramatic: even more heartbreaking, too.

'So there you are,' she said, and looked from Browne to Georgina. Jane might not have existed. 'Decent for once.'

'Lilian, for Christ's sake – ' said Browne.

'Go on,' said his wife. 'Blasphemy as well as fornication. Where is it?'

'Lilian!'

She ignored him. 'That tart's picture. . . . Where is it?'

Of medium height and with a good figure. Fair and not too badly dressed. She would have passed for a pretty enough woman if Georgina had not been there.

She darted away from the doorway, and Browne made a grab for her and missed. His wife headed straight for an easel covered with a cloth and swept the cloth aside. It was a nude of Georgina, and she had a magnificent body, or at least Browne had made it so, a body that proclaimed its joyful eroticism because it was alive, and to be alive was in itself a kind of miracle to be celebrated by love.

The most wonderful body she had ever seen, thought Jane. But Mrs Browne did not seem to agree with her.

'Bitch! Harlot! Whore!' she screamed, and grabbed a bread knife, swung back to lunge as if it were Georgina's body. Browne grabbed for her and swung her away from the picture. He needed all his strength. His wife struggled with a kind of hysterical force that he could only just contain, until at last he managed to grab the wrist of the hand that held the knife and forced it back, twisting as he levered until Mrs Browne screamed out loud.

'Oh please,' said Georgina. 'Please.' Then the knife dropped and Lilian Browne was still. Jane leaned forward and scooped it up, hid it under a cushion, but there was no need. The woman put her hands to her face and sobbed, then the sobs became moans, the moans great bellows of despair.

Almost apologetically Browne took her hands from her face, then struck her open-handed, hard enough to rock her on her heels.

'Stop that!' Georgina called, but he had no need to do it again. The noises ceased.

Lilian Browne said, 'I need a handkerchief' and Jane opened her bag and gave her hers, a scrap of linen with perfume by Worth. One of Jabber's bath towels would have been better, she thought, but Mrs Browne dried her eyes, then looked at the handkerchief.

'Very pretty,' she said, then her hand went to her cheek. She turned to her husband. 'You hurt me.'

'You wouldn't stop,' said Browne.

'I never will. You might as well come home, you know.' Browne shook his head, and she looked at the nude painting.

'Does she really look like that?' Lilian Browne asked, and then, 'Not that it matters. You'll come back to me. I'll make you.'

She went to the door and opened it. Outside, a group of spectators waited: some neighbours, mostly women, a milkman, and a grocer's delivery boy.

'Oh dear,' said Georgina.

A policeman came up to join them. 'Oh sod it,' Georgina said.

'Bit of trouble?' the policeman asked.

'I came to have a word with my husband,' said Lilian Browne. 'He's Michael Browne, the artist. At the moment he's cohabiting with this young lady. Miss Georgina Payne. That's P-A-Y-N-E.'

The policeman, who had produced a note book, put it back in his pocket. 'Matrimonial,' the policeman said. 'I see.' Then he saw the mark of the blow on Lilian Browne's face.

'Who hit you, Mrs Browne?' he asked.

'My husband.'

The policeman accepted this as very much part of the scheme of things, but turned to Browne even so, because the rules required it, thought Jane.

'Clocked her a bit hard, didn't you, sir?' The note book reappeared, and this time the policeman wrote in it.

'She was hysterical,' Browne said. 'Trying to destroy a picture of mine.'

'You got a witness, sir?'

'This lady,' said Browne, and Jane supplied her name and address. The policeman turned to Mrs Browne.

'Is it true what your husband says?'

'Of course it's true. It was a picture of his trollop with no clothes on.'

The spectators sighed. Their wait had been rewarded.

'Does either of you wish to charge the other?'

'No,' said Browne.

'I want him home,' said Mrs Browne. 'Not in one of your beastly prisons.'

'I'm assuming that means no,' said the policeman. 'Where do you live, Mrs Browne?'

'Acacia Avenue,' Lilian Browne said. 'Number 37.'

'And where's that?'

'Clapham,' she said.

'You take my advice and go there,' said the policeman. 'No sense in hanging about here.'

'*Sense*!' said Lilian Browne. 'There was no sense in coming here, no sense in marrying *him*.' Her head flicked like a hawk's towards her husband. 'Sense is for the lucky ones. All the same I *would* like to go home, but I don't think I can. Not on my own.'

The policeman, and the spectators, waited. Jane said at last, 'I have my car outside. I'll take you if you like.' The policeman looked relieved.

'That agreeable to you, Mrs Browne?'

'Certainly. Most kind,' said Lilian Browne, as if she were accepting a lift home from a bridge game.

'Then I'll ask you all to leave,' said the policeman, and waited with a massive yet threatening sort of patience until the spectators had gone, then asked, 'You're sure you'll be all right, Mrs Browne?'

'For the moment,' said Lilian Browne.

The policeman sighed. 'You'd best hop off then, miss,' he said to Jane, and then to Browne, 'I'd like a word with you inside, sir.'

He wants to see Georgina without any clothes on, thought Jane. But then what man wouldn't?

It didn't take long. Over Battersea Bridge and on to Clapham Common, and Acacia Avenue was just five minutes' walk away: near enough to take one's dog for a run, then return to the neat and shining little house that had a kind of gentility that would, Jane felt sure, have delighted Hawkins. All the way to it, Lilian Browne talked of Georgina Payne: the wicked soul in the beautiful body that had enticed away her wonderful man and left behind an emptiness that nothing could ever fill. On and on she went, until the Riley drew up at Number 37, and then the social manner returned.

'You have been most extremely kind,' she said, and then: 'Who did Mike say you were?'

'My name is Jane Whitcomb,' she said, and left it at that. No point in saying she was a friend of Georgie's. 'I came to buy a picture from Mr Browne.'

'You think he's good?'

'Very good,' said Jane.

'My father was a bank manager,' said Lilian Browne. 'He left me this house. He could never understand why I married Mike. He won't do anything else, you see. Except draw and paint I mean. My father could never understand how a grown man could go through life like that. I can't always understand it myself. All the same I tried. Honestly. I even built him a studio at the bottom of the garden.'

'You did?'

'Metcalf and Richards,' said Lilian Browne. 'The best builders for miles. Cost me three figures. But all he said was the light was wrong. No pleasing him. . . . It was the war.'

'I beg your pardon?'

'The reason I married him. You should have seen him in uniform.'

'You've no children?' Jane asked.

'No, thank God. Though we tried hard enough. – Oh I'm sorry.'

'Quite all right,' said Jane.

'But I heard Mike tell that policeman – you're *Miss* Whitcomb. He never – '

'Never what?' asked Jane.

'Tried it on with you?'

'I told you,' said Jane. 'I merely wanted to buy a picture.'

'That wouldn't stop him,' said Lilian Browne. 'A pretty woman like you. You're like pollen to the bees. Not that he can help himself any more than a monkey can. All the same it isn't easy when you're married to him.'

'You make it sound impossible,' said Jane.

'No!' Lilian Browne yelled aloud. 'It isn't impossible. How can it be? We're man and wife.' She fumbled for the car door. 'I've taken up too much of your time already. I'd better go. I'm sorry but under the circumstances you must excuse me if I don't ask you in.'

'Of course,' said Jane, and watched and waited until Lilian Browne closed the door behind her. It was inexcusable to have said that her marriage to Browne was impossible, though obviously it was. All that suburban gentility ranged against the painter's singlemindedness. But she should have kept her mouth shut, especially as Mrs Browne had just called her pretty – and done rather more than that. She'd helped her forget her husband's picture of the shattered gun team. Jane discovered that she could think about it without wanting to scream. All the same she didn't buy it when she went back to the Fulham flat to report Mrs Browne's safe return. She bought the pencil sketch of the infantry officer instead, paying cash there and then, which almost certainly meant that Georgie would dance at the Café de Paris that night.

'How was she?' Browne asked, when the notes were handed over.

'Calm,' said Jane. 'For the time being anyway.'

'It won't last,' said Browne. 'It never does.'

'You've left her before?'

'Not like this,' he said, and looked at Georgina. 'We were married during the war when I was an officer. I told her from the beginning that I was a painter in civilian life, but I don't think she really believed me. I mean she probably thought I went sketching on Sundays and worked in an office during the week.

'I don't think she believes that anybody could ever be a painter full-time. To her it just doesn't make sense. She wanted me to get a job in a bank. I went off and started painting instead – then she came to my digs and yelled and screamed till I went back to her and she had a studio built for me in the back garden. At least she called it a studio. It's more like a potting-shed.

'Then she got the idea I should be an art master at a school and I left her again.' Browne shook his head.

'It didn't make any *sense*,' he said. 'We'd made a mistake and she wouldn't admit it. Better for her if I'd been killed – she'd have made a marvellous widow – but I wasn't. God knows why.'

'So you could live with me, silly,' said Georgina.

'I meant it's not even as if we had any kids,' said Browne. 'She just won't let go.'

'There's no rush,' Georgina said. 'If she let go everyone would be telling us to get married – and I'm not sure it's such a good idea. Not yet.'

'I am,' said Browne, 'but we won't bore Jane with that one. And there's another thing.'

'What?' Jane asked.

'If Lilian doesn't let go she'll be back, shrieking about harlots and trying to slash my pictures.' He looked at the nude portrait, and Jane looked again, too. Really a quite extraordinary body, she thought.

'Bit of all right, aren't I?' Georgina said.

'We'd have to move,' said Browne. 'And she'd hire detectives to find us so that she could do the whole thing again.'

'Not today,' said Georgina. 'Today we'll be quite safe.'

She went up to him and put her arms about him as if he were her child.

30

Jane went to call on Lionel. He would enjoy the whole story enormously she thought, and she was right.

'I was always one for a bit of drama,' he said. 'Only do keep your voice down, my dear. I daren't for the life of me upset Pott.' Jane told it all.

'The gorgeous Miss Payne in the altogether?' he said.

'About as altogether as you can get,' said Jane.

'And really gorgeous?'

'Almost impossibly so – except that Michael Browne isn't that kind of painter. I've never seen a body quite like it, which isn't all that surprising really. The only naked women I've ever seen were at the Folies Bergères.'

'Will they stay together?'

'He will,' said Jane. 'I'm not too sure about her. Domesticity's the least of her wants. . . . Can we talk about my house?'

'You'll buy it then?'

'Yes, I think so. Hawkins approves – subject to certain modifications. Can you find me a good builder?'

'Easily.'

'Anybody except Metcalf and Richards,' said Jane. 'They build studios that look like potting sheds.'

'And an interior designer?'

'I was hoping you'd do that,' said Jane.

'I'd adore to,' said Lionel. 'How sweet you are.'

The telephone rang, and Lionel picked it up at once, 'to save Pott's poor feet'. It quacked ominously for a moment, and Lionel covered the mouthpiece. 'It's Bower,' he said. 'He wants to know if you're here. Are you?'

'Well of course,' said Jane.

'The thing is he seems to be in rather a tizz,' Lionel said.

In fact he was furious, and shouting so loud that at first Jane had no idea what she was supposed to have done. At last, Pott or no Pott, she began shouting back. Dear Lionel was in agonies, but it worked very quickly, especially when she swore.

'Oh,' said Bower, and then: 'Was I yelling?'

'Very loud,' said Jane, 'and quite incoherently.'

'All the same you shouldn't have done it.'

'For God's sake,' said Jane. 'Done what?'

'Gone to see Georgina Payne and that lover of hers. That Browne.'

'Why on earth not?' said Jane. 'She's a friend.'

'Because Mrs Browne came calling, that's why not. Tried to stick a bayonet into some nude painting or other.'

'It was a bread knife,' said Jane, 'and the nude was of Georgie.'

'That must have been something,' Bower said.

'Stick to the point,' said Jane.

'You shouldn't have been involved.'

'Who told you I was? And who said it was a bayonet?'

'The *Daily Express* got it first. Then my man got to hear of it. It was an eyewitness who said it was a bayonet. More exciting than a bread knife.' He sighed then, and his voice became reproachful. 'You're making trouble for me, Jane. You gave your full name – '

'I spoke to a policeman.'

To her fury, Jane realised that she sounded apologetic, but he continued unheeding.

'I had to phone Beaverbrook personally,' he said, 'and that is one guy I do not want to owe a favour to.'

'But why on earth should you? I mean what business is it of yours?'

'We have a deal, remember? You're doing an article for me, remember? All about the misfortunes of Felston and how we all have to help. And the *World* is building you up as some kind of Florence Nightingale who knows how to drive. Believe me that does not belong with artists and bayonets and pictures of naked ladies.'

'It was a bread knife.'

'I don't care if it was a meat axe,' said Bower. 'You keep your nose clean. And get that copy over here. I need it Friday.' He hung up on her then, and she turned to Lionel. She was spluttering with fury.

'Darling *please*,' he said. 'Think of Pott.'

She breathed in deeply once, then again, and realised that Bower was right. All the same, she thought, there were ways of being right, and Bower's way was awful.

'I have to leave you, darling,' she said. 'I have my composition to do, and my teacher's ratty enough as it is.'

But when she went home the first thing she did was write to Grandma, in John Bright Street, then she attacked the article the way Vinney had taught her: outline, then rough draft, then polish, and then, remembering her father's conversation with a friend in India which began with Kipling and ended with the iniquities of the gutter press, went through it all again and took out all the adverbs and adjectives she could find. He had asked for a thousand words and she had produced, at her final count, an irreducible twelve hundred and four. She rang Bower and got his secretary. She was expected, the secretary said, at precisely half past ten. Once again she felt the anger rise, and once again shrugged it away. He employed her after all.

Next day brought another communication from Mummy; a letter this time. Miss Gwatkin continued in good health, and continued to gain weight despite the heat. Indian sweets were so fascinating, and she had developed a passion for pistachio burfi. Her mother too continued in good health, and after the discovery of a small sum deposited by Papa at Cox and King's in Calcutta, had determined to accompany Gwendoline on a visit to Kalpur, the scene of that momentous cricket match. Gwendoline's cousin, it seemed, was now resident there. It would involve a change of ships, but the P and O people had been most helpful. She hoped that her daughter was in good health, and not exhausted by the demands of whatever passed for the season these days. In a PS she added that she had written to Francis, because Francis was one of those weaker vessels who required support. . . . Then I'd better go and support him, thought Jane, and take a few quid from his chums while I'm doing it, though she doubted whether Pardoe would be good for as much as even half a crown.

Bower was at his desk and talking hard on the telephone when she was shown in. A spokesman for the coal-mine owners had just issued a statement saying that the miners' wage demands were totally unacceptable, the world price of coal being what it was, and the miners' leaders had reacted with even more anger than had been assumed. A strike was more than possible, which meant more column inches, a leader, and at least one photograph. As he spoke he held out his hand to Jane, then scowled as she took it. It seemed he wanted her – what was it? – copy. She gave it to him, and he blinked, then covered the telephone.

'But this is hand-written,' he said.

'It's perfectly legible.'

He began to talk into the telephone about a man called A.J. Cook, a miners' leader apparently, then ran his eyes down her article as he talked, and reached for a pencil. Jane watched in horror as he butchered her careful prose, transposing, eliminating, deleting semi-colons, then he said goodbye to whoever it was, hung up the phone, and read her piece again.

'Not bad,' he said. 'For a beginner not bad at all.'

'I thought you hated it,' she said, 'the way you hacked it about.'

'Not at all,' he said. 'It happens all the time.' He took out a cheque book and began to write. 'Want to do me another?'

'I can't go to Paris just now.'

'Paris is for later. What I need now is Felston,' said Bower. 'And why can't you go to Paris now?'

'Because I'm going to Cambridge.'

'Best place for you,' said Bower. 'All that culture. Phone the "Wicked World" desk when you get there. They'll do a paragraph on you.' He handed her the cheque. 'There you are. Ten guineas.' She took it with an altogether disproportionate feeling of pride. Composition – eight out of ten.

'Now what's the next one going to be about?'

She and Bob had walked past a pub, she remembered. Inside, a group of men had been singing softly together, making the beer last longer:

If you want to find the sergeant, I know where he is,
I know where he is, I know where he is.
If you want to find the sergeant, I know where he is.
He's hanging on the old barbed wire.
I *saw* him, I *saw* him,
Hanging on the old barbed wire.
If you want to find the sergeant, I know where he is.
He's hanging on the old barbed wire.

On and on, over and over: the saddest, most defeatist song of
the whole war. She'd first heard it in 1917, and John and every
other officer had done their best to discourage it, but without
success. The men fought on, but they were telling John and the
rest that they'd had enough. The whole thing had better end
soon. 'Soon' meant another year. . . .

Then Corporal Laidlaw had come out of the pub – The Boilermakers' Arms was it? – and begun to talk about the riot of a
couple of years before when a group of the unemployed had
demonstrated in the market place, and a Tory JP had read the
Riot Act, the police had charged, and the crowd had retreated,
until, steadied by ex-NCOs like Laidlaw, they had counter-
attacked and were actually winning, until the police reinforce-
ments arrived. 'The Royal Northumbrians' Last Battle', Laidlaw
had called it: the only one the regiment had both won and lost,
because its members fought on both sides.

'That's great,' said Bower. 'You can have fifteen hundred
words.'

'Fifteen guineas?'

'If you make it quick,' said Bower. 'Spend some of your money
on a typewriter will you? Your handwriting's very nice but it
makes me feel silly.'

Then the phone rang and he began talking as soon as he picked
it up. This time it was about boxing and a man called Jack
Dempsey. She left him to it.

On the train to Cambridge next day, she checked that Bower
had mentioned Felston in the *Daily World*, then read her piece
and counted the words. There were nine hundred and eighty-
three, and all of them relevant.

Grandma held the letter about three inches from her eyes, and slowly and painstakingly read it with the aid of a magnifying glass. Her son and grand-daughter pegged away at the clippy mat that they were making, Andy struggled with a book by Sidney and Beatrice Webb, and Bob tinkered with his crystal set. All of them were impatient for Grandma's news.

'She writes a lovely fist,' the old woman said.

'But what does she say, Gran?' said Bet.

'She's missing us.'

'It took her three pages to tell you that?' said Bob.

'No it didn't, impiddence. But I thought it was nice of her so I told you that first. She says she's raised five hundred and fifteen pounds fifteen shillings for the Felston Relief Fund. . . . So far, she says.'

'But she can't have done,' said Andy.

'It's here in black and white,' said his grandmother.

'I mean she's only been gone a few days,' said Andy. 'Nobody can raise money that quick.'

'Of course she can,' said Bob. 'She's rich. All she knows is other rich people – and us.'

'Rich is right,' said Andy.

'You none of us say you're pleased, I notice,' said their grandmother. 'Or grateful.'

'I think it's wonderful,' said Bet.

'Well I don't,' said Andy. 'I think it's charity.'

'And we all know what you think of charity,' said his father. 'But I know what St Paul thought of it an' all, and I'll stick with him. She didn't have to do it, and I bet it won't be always easy for her – asking for money.'

'Begging,' said Andy. 'Begging for the poor unfortunates in the North East – so far away from Mayfair.' He tried and failed to mimic Jane's accent. 'Well we don't want begging. We want what's due to us. Our rights.'

'You speak for yourself,' said Bob. 'I'll take my share of five hundred and fifteen pounds fifteen shillings.'

'You'll take nowt,' said his father. 'That money's for the needy.'

'And just what do you think I am, Da?'

He smiled as he said it, but the old woman reacted to the bitterness in his voice, her almost sightless eyes searching for his face in vain.

Foch approved of Cambridge: its sedate and dignified masculinity held great appeal, Jane was certain. For herself she enjoyed the beauty of the Backs, the Cam still glowing in the autumn sun, the college buildings still not chilled by the wind off the fens: warm stone, rosy birch. She enjoyed the streets too, narrow for the most part, and leisurely, their most constant hazard the onrush of bicycles as she crossed. (Not yet at their worst, her hotel porter told her. Just you wait until the young gentlemen come back in a week or two.) Well, maybe she would, though she doubted it. But she did rent a bicycle, and coaxed Foch into travelling in the basket in front of the handlebars. He wasn't very gracious about it; he much preferred the Riley's padded leather.

Her first job, she supposed, was to seek out Francis and support him, though how she had no idea. As if he were a leaning tower, she thought. Or a political party. All the same Francis could be put to use: introduce her to the sort of people who might want to hear about Felston, and the sort who had money. She left a note at his college while she did her sightseeing, and he phoned her at her hotel at the time she had suggested. She was staying at the Baron of Beef, which was much more co-operative in the matter of telephones than the Eldon Arms.

'Jane?' He sounded incredulous, perhaps even appalled.

'Francis. . . . How *nice*.'

'But why didn't you tell me you were coming up?'

So that you could dream up all sorts of lovely excuses for avoiding me?

'It was very much a spur-of-the-moment thing,' she said.

'But why?'

'I've never seen Cambridge, which seemed rather remiss. What's wrong? Don't you like my being here?'

'Well of course,' he said, 'but – '

'Then let's meet,' she said. 'I have news of Mummy.'

'I can't come over this evening, I'm afraid,' Francis said. 'I'm giving a sherry party.'

'Then I'll come to you,' said Jane. 'Such fun to see your college.'

'There won't be any other women, I shouldn't think,' Francis said.

'Then I can hardly fail to be a success,' said Jane. 'And I promise you I can hold my sherry better than my champagne.'

- 307 -

Somewhere in that sentence a threat lay buried, and Francis knew it and surrendered.

'Six o'clock,' he said. 'My set is in the front quad. The porter will show you. And Jane – '

'Yes, Francis?'

'You will watch how you dress, won't you? I mean it won't be the Savoy.' He hung up.

And just who, Jane wondered, has been telling you that I went to the Savoy quite recently? A *Daily World* reader, no doubt, but certainly not Francis himself. Francis, she was sure, would never read the *Daily World*, was almost incapable of doing so. She went upstairs to change.

The Chanel suit, she thought. Neat and yet worldly, smart, and yet not too feminine. A chum's suit, perhaps even an equal's, though not in Cambridge, not yet. And over it for contrast a vast and swirling coat in red and green that seemed to have come out of the depths of central Asia, a hat with an osprey feather curled to its crown, and Foch on a scarlet lead. All very well for Francis to say that his college wasn't the Savoy, but what did Francis know about what clothes men wanted women to wear?

He was a fellow of Dorset College, which was neither as vast as Trinity nor as exquisite as King's, but charming enough, she thought. On her way across the quad she inserted a cigarette into a jade cigarette holder. The porter went ahead of her like an escort of cavalry, and a couple of ageing dons stopped to stare, though not in rebuke, and she followed the porter up one flight of stairs (and one was quite enough, given the shoes she was wearing: dyed kid and French, but ruthlessly tight, and Foch disliked stairs anyway), then stood as the porter tapped at Francis's door, and waited until he had observed her brother's reaction, then left with the air of a man for whom that day at least had achieved fulfilment, for Francis had taken one look and was appalled.

'Francis, my dear,' she said, 'how sweet of you to invite me,' and then, as he made no move: 'You *did* invite me, you know.'

'Oh yes,' he said. 'You'd better come in.'

Not exactly my house is yours, she thought, but at least he'd allowed her inside. And Foch. And why not? she thought. Foch's company manners were excellent.

Francis's set of rooms contained a study and a sitting room, both austere, and both book-lined. It was in the sitting room that his party was being held: a room, she thought, from which every hint of frivolity had been ruthlessly removed, a grey and brown room with only one picture, Courbet's 'Reapers', a painterly enough expression of peasants exploited by the capitalist system. Even the ranks of sherry bottles and glasses did little to dispel the gloom, though here and there a guest did his best: a pink tie, long hair languidly waved, a sapphire-blue waistcoat. And there *were* other ladies there, after all: three of them, in identical cloche hats and dresses which showed that they at least had obeyed her brother's instruction not to confuse his rooms with the Savoy. One of them was Marigold Ledbitter, and the man standing next to her was inevitably Pardoe.

Jane stepped across the threshold of the living room and all conversation ceased. It was an agreeable sensation, she discovered, to have eleven men and three women stare at her in precisely that way: a really quite delicious mixture of envy, admiration and carnality. Sarah Unwin must be used to it she thought, but for me it's the first time and I *love* it.

'Everyone, this is my sister Jane,' said Francis, and then to Jane: 'Best if you just mingle, I should think. There are far too many names for you to remember.'

'Yes, of course,' said Jane. 'If I might just be given the minutest glass of sherry. . . .'

Half the men in the room, including Pardoe, rushed to obey, but the winner was a squat and powerful man with the look of a games player.

'Fino or medium sweet?' he said, and she chose the amontillado. The squat man had brought both.

'My name's Robins,' he said. 'Tony Robins.' He sipped at the fino.

'Jane Whitcomb.'

'So I heard Francis say. He never told me he had a sister before. Pleased to meet you.'

He offered his hand, and she juggled with her cigarette holder, her glass and Foch's lead, and took it at last.

'I must say,' said Robins, 'that even if he had told me I wouldn't have been prepared for quite such a sister.'

'You don't approve?'

'Of course I approve,' said Robins. 'I wouldn't have believed it possible for one human being to light up this room the way you do. Believe me, we poor scholars are grateful.'

The man with the pink tie joined them. 'My very words,' he said, and Robins scowled. They had been his words after all.

'Do I detect the influence of Bakst on that *exquisite* coat?' the man in the pink tie asked.

'I expect so,' said Jane. 'He seems to have influenced everything else.'

'Flamboyant,' said Robins, 'and yet not in the least outré. How is it done, do you suppose?'

'By design of course,' said the man in the pink tie, and waited for applause. He didn't get it.

'What brings you here, Miss Whitcomb?' Robins asked.

She shrugged. 'The desire to see Francis in his native habitat,' she said.

The man in the pink tie giggled. 'How intrepid of you.'

'Wasn't it?' said Jane. 'But worth it. Such a lovely habitat.'

'It isn't fashionable to say so at the moment,' said Robins. 'The Backs and King's College Chapel are all very well in their way –'

'Their very much outmoded way,' said the man in the pink tie.

' – but we must be concerned only with what is real, functional, productive.'

'It all sounds rather bleak,' said Jane.

'It *is* bleak,' said Robins.

'And not in the least like my coat.'

'It could be argued – in fact it probably will be argued over Senior Common Room coffee for many days to come – that your coat is outmoded too,' said Pardoe. He had crept up on them, Jane noticed, and deserted Marigold Ledbitter.

'Then I'd better remove it,' said Jane. 'I simply cannot bear to seem outmoded.'

She left the three men and went to what she guessed was Francis's bedroom, took off the coat and hat. Foch snorted.

'I quite agree,' she said, 'but they've served their purpose. They got me noticed, which is why I brought them. Now let's see what the plucky little pal can do.' She straightened the Chanel suit – scarlet skirt, scarlet and white top – and went back to the party. In one corner the man with the languidly waved hair was listening to what Francis was saying. Suddenly he smiled, and Jane knew at once that he was the one who'd gone to Germany with her brother.

Pardoe the Tank crashed his way over to her, and Foch glowered. Pardoe bent to pat him and Foch was outraged.

'You are looking singularly well-clad this evening,' Pardoe said.

'I'm delighted that you noticed,' said Jane.

'I shall always notice you,' said Pardoe, 'despite your absurd misapprehension over that housemaid of yours. You did not dismiss her, I trust?'

'On the contrary,' said Jane. 'I promoted her.' Pardoe did not seem pleased.

'It has come to my notice,' he said, 'that you have been busy in a – how shall I describe it? – literary seems too beneficent, journalism too dismissive – in a socially aware kind of way, should I say?'

The man next to her joined them at that.

'So you're that Jane Whitcomb,' he said.

'Which Jane Whitcomb?' she asked.

'The one who wrote that piece in yesterday's *Daily World*.'

'That's the one I am,' she said.

'And presumably meant every word. . . . I'm Myers, by the way.'

And even I have heard of you, thought Jane. The Honourable Frederick Myers – Freddy: savant, mathematician, philosopher, atheist – and above all philanderer: which was why she had heard of him, she and every other reader of the *Daily World*, the *Mail*, the *Express* – any and all of them. Small, neat in build, with the most frankly disrobing eyes she had ever encountered.

'You're right. You must be right,' he said. 'You must allow me to make a contribution.' He pulled a cracked and ancient wallet from his pocket, and his fingers explored among tram tickets, laundry lists, a pageful of mathematical symbols, and emerged with a note that Jane thought could be twenty pounds. He offered it to Jane, but Pardoe stepped between them, pushed Myers's hand gently to one side.

'Freddy, I must beg you to think again,' he said.

'I never think again,' said Myers. 'Miss Whitcomb is right and there's an end on't.'

'Miss Whitcomb is not in the least right,' said Pardoe. 'Come. . . . Let us consider.'

'Consider away.' Myers put away the note, to Jane's dismay, but in his pocket rather than his wallet. There was still hope.

The other men in the party refilled their glasses and stood around Freddy Myers and Pardoe, rather like a circle of Regency bucks round a couple of prize-fighters, thought Jane, and at last even the three other women joined them.

'Consider the facts,' said Pardoe. 'The good people of Felstone – '

'Felston,' said Jane, and Pardoe winced. He was not used to being interrupted quite so early in the proceedings.

'Felston then,' he said. 'Let us try not to impede this discussion with unnecessary pedantry.'

'It isn't pedantry to them,' said Jane. 'It's the place where they live. It's important to them.'

Francis clicked his tongue at his sister's persistence, and some of the other men too seemed annoyed, but not Robins.

'She's right, you know,' he said. 'The place where we belong is almost as important as the name we bear – whether we like it or lump it.'

'Oh agreed, agreed,' said Myers, 'but do let Pardoe get on with it.'

He produced a large, curved pipe half filled with shag tobacco, which, when lit, smelled even nastier than it looked, but Jane noticed that Pardoe got most of it. Not that it put him off.

Pardoe's argument was simply Andy's after all, but with longer words. The 'good people' of Felston were ignorant of the fact that they were part of an inevitable historical process – and who could blame them for that? Starvation and despair were their destiny so long as the present system existed, and their only hope of betterment was to change the system, and the only way to do that was for them to overthrow the capitalist class. Charities and subscriptions and articles in the *Daily World* were at best an irrelevance, a way of postponing the inevitable.

Very violent the inevitable was going to be, according to Pardoe, thought Jane. And there seemed little doubt that Pardoe was looking forward to it. Words like 'smash' and 'crush' and 'overthrow' were in pretty frequent use. She looked at her brother, who was nodding in agreement each time they were uttered.

'Their position in life is awful,' said Pardoe, 'but it must be seen as a sacrifice: one that they must make for the unborn generations who will succeed them into a kind of world which to us would be a paradise – were we to believe in such places: a world where there is neither crime nor poverty, hatred nor hunger: a world where there is enough for all and superfluity for no man. We have to hurry towards that day, Freddy, not hold it at bay with bank notes.'

Not bad, thought Jane. In Felston market place he could always be sure of an audience, but his voice lacked the fury that Andy's had, that terrible intimation of the wrath to come.

Myers blew more smoke at Pardoe, who began at last to cough.

'Good stuff,' said Myers. 'Quite powerful stuff too – from time to time. But I deny your major.'

'Freddy, *please*,' said Pardoe, choking still.

'Eh? Oh, sorry.' Myers blew more smoke, slightly to Pardoe's right. This time it was the turn of Francis's friend.

'It's that word inevitable,' said Myers. 'Not an easy word for mathematicians. We tend to restrict its use – to mathematics. Anything living, anything that is born in fact, including homo sapiens, has only one claim to inevitability and that is the certainty that it will die. Now this being so – '

'I was talking of the theory itself: not its exponents,' said Pardoe.

'To be sure you were,' said Myers, 'and who created the theory but a finite being who was born, then died? All flesh is as grass you see, Pardoe. And I note that you used the word "theory" rather than "law". You fail, my dear fellow. Fail utterly. . . . To convince me that is.'

Once more it was Pardoe who received the tobacco smoke, rather as a much younger Pardoe might have received a stroke of the cane for failing to use π to three decimal places, thought Jane, and held out her hand to Myers.

'To be sure,' said Myers, 'I win, therefore I lose.'

His hand went to his pocket and came out with the bank note. It was for a hundred pounds. The way in which he pressed it into her palm seemed to cause him a certain amount of pleasure.

'We must talk some more about this,' he said. 'Over tea in my rooms, perhaps.'

'Perhaps,' she said, and thought: Not bloody likely. And then: I can do quotations, too.

'Tell you what,' said Myers. 'I'll pass the hat round. Do my own bit for Felston.'

He went to where Francis's academic square hung above his MA gown, and thrust it determinedly at one guest after another, refusing all offers he considered inadequate.

Pardoe said to Jane: 'I expect you took my intervention personally.'

'No more than you did,' said Jane. 'And anyway it doesn't matter. You lost.'

'I did not lose,' said Pardoe. 'It's just that I find tobacco smoke distracting. I shall not subscribe, of course.'

Jane said nothing, and in the silence that followed Marigold Ledbitter's voice rang out clear and shrill.

'More like a fashion show than a civilised party,' she said. 'Will she take off anything else, one wonders?'

Jane walked across to her and smiled. 'I will if you will,' she said, then looked once more towards Francis. The poor boy was sweating visibly.

31

J ANE AWOKE NEXT morning and found herself famous. More quotations, she thought, but after all, Lord Byron had been there too. There were notes and telephone calls, there were even flowers, and there was money to be counted yet again. Two hundred and four pounds seven shillings. Half a crown apiece from Marigold's companions, and two bob from the lady herself. All the men had given notes, except Pardoe of course; even Francis had managed a quid. He'd sort of hinted that he could do with it back when she took him out to dinner, but she'd been firm about that. Francis's well-being stood in need of such a sacrifice, and anyway the dinner had cost far more, what with his passion for Château Gruaud Larose when his rich sister was paying. Though maybe that was unfair. After all she *was* his rich sister.

She lay on the bed and took tea and biscuits, then saw she'd reached the last one and it was promised to Foch, and gave it to him.

'I hope you realise what a privilege it is sharing my bedroom,' she said, 'and I don't mean because you're a dog. That only took bribery. But when I think of the number of gentlemen eager to take your place. . . .' Freddy Myers of course, and quite a few of the others. When she'd offered to undress in competition with the Ledbitter, contributions had rocketed. And even Pardoe, when she left, had said that he still held himself in readiness for a certain delightful day. In some inexplicable way he'd acted as if she owed it to him because he'd lost an argument.

Francis had waited until the coffee before he'd begun to complain. Until then nothing must upset the texture and bouquet of the wine, and so she'd told him of their mother, and the decision to visit Kalpur.

'Kalpur?' Francis asked.

'Where Papa played cricket and the maharajah cheated.'

'I don't remember,' said Francis. 'Why has Mummy gone there?'

'Because the resident is a cousin of Miss Gwatkin's.'

'That ghastly old gammer who came to the funeral? The one who never stopped talking?'

'The very same.'

'Poor Mummy,' said Francis. Jane rather liked him for that.

Over coffee he said, 'I say.' Jane waited. 'You rather upset old Cuthbert.'

'Old Cuthbert must learn to get used to it,' said Jane. 'I have no intention of making him a present of my virtue.'

Not that I have it to bestow, she thought, but Francis is not one of those I can tell. Not like Harriet Watson.

'You mustn't say things like that,' said Francis. Jane looked up and saw that he was blushing.

'Why on earth not?' she said. 'Don't tell me you're a prude.'

'Oh dear,' said Francis, 'I'm afraid I must be. And me a you-know-what.'

'I like the look of your new friend,' said Jane.

'Dennis? He's an art historian. Doing research at the Fitzwilliam.'

'And rather sweet.'

'Well I think so,' said Francis, 'obviously.' And once again Jane liked him, but it didn't last. 'All the same – ' Francis began.

'Do go on.'

'I wish I knew what you're *doing* here.'

'Raising money,' she said. 'You saw me in action. I did rather well.'

'I'm sure you did,' said Francis. 'Where on earth did you learn how to do it? Papa?'

'It's mostly because I have to,' said Jane, 'but if there is any heredity involved I rather think it's Mummy.'

'You see,' said Francis, 'I happen to agree with Pardoe – about the charity thing. But then I think you knew that?'

'Suspected it, shall we say?'

'But that didn't prevent you from coming here and wrecking my party.'

'Like you,' said Jane, 'I can accept present suffering if it leads to future happiness. And besides – how can you think your party was wrecked? I thought it rather a success.'

'For you perhaps,' said her brother, 'but not for me. My parties are all earnestness and sherry. The instant you appeared one thought of champagne. Why on earth did you choose Cambridge? Surely you could raise far more money in Mayfair.'

'Oh I can,' said Jane. 'I do. But Cambridge has rather begun to take an interest in the Felstons of this world, wouldn't you say? Which means there'll be lots of useful talk. Cambridge can make Felston a cause for concern.'

'That's true enough, I suppose,' said Francis. The thought pleased him. 'But why on earth should you bother?'

'Because I was once engaged to a man from Felston.'

'*You?*' said Francis. '*Engaged?*' And then: 'Does Mummy know?'

'The way you said that was hardly flattering,' said Jane, 'and Mummy doesn't know – though you can tell her if you want to. The reason we're not married is that he was killed.'

'In the war you mean?'

'Of course in the war.' She pushed her left hand towards him. 'I'm wearing his ring.'

'And that's why you're doing all this?'

'That's why.'

'Sentimentality?'

'You could call it that. I went there to see how John had lived and didn't like what I saw and decided to do something about it. I'm sorry if you think I spoiled your party, but it's all in a good cause.'

'It's never occurred to you that Cuthbert may be right I suppose?' said her brother. 'Oh I realise that he may be a bit over-enthusiastic when it comes to sex and a lot of people find him funny, but he has a really first-rate brain. Alpha plus in fact. Have you *never* thought he might be right?'

'I couldn't be so cruel.'

Francis sighed. 'Cruelty doesn't come into it,' he said, 'just as love doesn't come into it. It's just what's going to be.'

'Let's wait,' said Jane, 'and see, and if you're right and it all comes to pass I'll apologise – if I'm not hanging from a lamp-post in Grosvenor Square.'

'You were always good at jokes,' said Francis. 'You and Guy and David. Not like me.'

You have only to add that Mummy never saw a joke in her life and you've split the Whitcomb family down the middle, thought Jane.

'Jokes can be useful in some ways, I suppose,' Francis continued, 'but I've never felt the need of them.'

'Does Dennis?'

'Well yes,' said Francis. 'He does – but then – ' He hesitated.

'But what?'

'He has other friends,' said Francis. 'Friends he can go to when he needs laughter.'

Not her most successful dinner party thought Jane, and looked down at the floor for crumbs, but Foch had left none at all, not even on his whiskers. The telephone rang. It was Freddy Myers, with offers of tea or lunch in Trinity, or even dinner in a discreet little place he knew of on the road to Ely. Jane pleaded pressure of work for the *Daily World* and indeed there were fifteen hundred words to be written. There were calls from other optimists at the party she could only just remember, then Robins whom she agreed to meet for cocktails, and then to her surprise, Dennis, Francis's Dennis, who wanted very much to take her out to lunch. Warily she accepted.

He arrived in a Daimler she was quite sure was hired, and took her to an hotel on the road to Ely. Jane hoped against hope that Freddy Myers always chose to dine there. The lunch was good, though expensive, far too expensive for a post-graduate student doing research at the Fitzwilliam, but Dennis was a good host, charming and relaxed. The lunch was good, too. The last of the season's asparagus, Dover sole, queen of puddings, and with it a hock that made even her relaxed and charming host blink when he saw the price. But he recovered almost at once, and Jane began to wonder whether it was her brother who was paying for the lunch, however unaware he might be, and if that were so how long it would take him to transfer the debt to her.

'Jolly nice of you to accept at such short notice,' Dennis was saying. Dennis Willis, she remembered. A most inappropriate surname.

'Sweet of you to ask me,' said Jane.

Dennis made a gesture at once graceful and deprecating.

'One could but hope, but I don't mind betting you've had all kinds of invitations.'

'One or two,' said Jane, and thought: And almost all of them improper, which yours most definitely is not.

'You see I've been longing to meet you for absolutely ages.'

'Good gracious,' said Jane. 'Where on earth did you hear about me?'

'From Lionel Warley,' said Dennis.

Of *course*, she thought. Where else would one go for jokes and laughter?

'I hope you'll treat that as confidential,' Dennis said. 'Your brother doesn't really approve of people like Lionel.'

'I expect a lot of people don't,' said Jane. 'But I do.'

'Well of course,' said Dennis. 'You're so like him in a way. And not like your brother at all.'

'I hope that's a compliment?'

'I hope so too,' Dennis said. 'It's meant to be. But the thing is I rather need your help. No. Not that exactly.'

And just as well, thought Jane. All the help I have belongs to Felston.

'What then?' she asked.

'I need to tell you something. I mean when I've told you I don't expect you to do anything about it, but I need to tell you. If you'll let me.'

'Go ahead.'

'Well. . . .' Dennis swigged at his hock, then leaned forward, lowered his voice: 'Your brother and I are lovers.'

'Obviously.'

'Oh Lord,' said Dennis. 'Is it as plain as that? Well we are, and I went to Germany with him. No problems there, thank God. Not about being queer, anyway. At least not in a general way.'

'What then?'

'Francis is – difficult. I mean he has these ideas. These Communist ideas.'

'And you don't share them?'

'No,' Dennis said. 'I don't. I'm not rich, but I like being with people who are. And I like eating in places like this and wearing nice clothes. All that.'

'So do I.'

'*You* do – but Francis doesn't. I mean in Germany he was weird

– always going into cheap cafés and workers' restaurants.'

'Did you go with him?' asked Jane.

'No fear.' Dennis realised that for once his carefully cultivated speech pattern had slipped, and added: 'Certainly not.'

'You don't like the workers?'

'My father's one,' said Dennis. 'In Wallasey. I can't stand them. I made Francis take me to nice places on the Kurfurstendamm and nightclubs with our sort of cabaret and real champagne, and in the end he always did, but there were the most tremendous rows. Still are, as a matter of fact. But I can't feel the way he does about the workers. I simply can't.' He divided the last of the hock between them. 'What I want to ask you is – do you think Francis will ever change?'

'I doubt it,' said Jane.

Dennis nodded. Suddenly he seemed much more mature, the languid hair an irrelevance.

'I was afraid you'd say that. Francis is awfully sweet you know – besides being rather good at making love – but he has this idée fixe. He simply won't let go, and he just can't believe that I won't change either. I shall have to leave him. I know it's what people always say – but it really is for both our sakes.'

'You want me to tell him so?' asked Jane.

'Good heavens no. That's my job,' said Dennis. 'I just wanted you to know. After all, he's bound to be upset.'

'I'll do what I can,' said Jane, 'but I doubt if it will do much good,' then added: 'Handling it yourself – it's the only way in the end. But it's never easy. I admire you for it.'

He paid the bill, and while they waited for change said, 'Thank you for coming. You certainly know how to put a poor bugger at his ease.' It was a bon mot carefully polished but badly delivered. Even so Jane smiled appropriately.

On the way out they passed Freddy Myers, taking an early tea in the hall. Marigold Ledbitter was with him, eating cucumber sandwiches. Dennis went ahead to speak to the Daimler's chauffeur, and Myers called out to her, then followed her to the doorway.

'Shouldn't think you'll do much good with your young friend,' he said.

'On the contrary,' said Jane. 'I think I have already.'

'You turned me down.'

'I said, "Perhaps".'

'Perhaps always means no. I learned that years ago. You turned me down after I gave you a hundred pounds.'

Bower had given her five hundred, yet he'd never made a remark like that. But then, she thought, Bower wasn't a philosopher, and anyway with Bower 'Perhaps' could turn out to mean almost anything. She went into the sunlight to join Dennis in the Daimler.

Back to the hotel in time to meet Robins for cocktails, but first she had to telephone the *Daily World*, ask for the 'Wicked World' desk and tell them what she'd been up to. They were delighted. Freddy Myers alone had made the call worthwhile. She changed then, into a little confection in black and silver by Paquin, which turned out to be not nearly so demure as it first seemed, then spent the time until Robins arrived blocking out the story of Corporal Laidlaw and the Royal Northumbrians' last battle. 'If You Want to Find the Sergeant', she called it.

Robins. Anthony Dempster Robins. Clever and quick, despite his bruiser's face, neat if not elegant in a dinner jacket. His appreciation of the Paquin dress included the girl inside it, she thought, and together they went out to his car, an ageing Jowett that needed cautious driving. It didn't get it. Robins was a terrible driver.

'We have to go out of Cambridge for cocktails,' he yelled, over the car engine's all too audible resentment of the treatment he gave it.

'So long as it isn't a little place on the road to Ely,' said Jane.

'Whyever not?'

'I just had lunch there. And I rather think Freddy Myers is there for dinner.' With Marigold Ledbitter for dessert, she thought.

Robins's car did an abrupt right turn, barely avoiding an oncoming van, and Jane decided that if she survived the night she would go back to London next day.

'There's only one other place,' said Robins. 'Roadhouse half way to London. Ghastly décor but the cocktails are good.' He put his foot down and the Jowett accelerated viciously. Jane contemplated closing her eyes but decided that she preferred the horrors she could see to those her imagination would create.

The roadhouse was a converted barn that had been whitewashed and spangled with gold paper stars. There was a bar, some tables for eating and a dance floor, and that was about it. When they arrived a band – piano, banjo, saxophone, drums – were doing their best with 'Varsity Rag', but Robins went at once to the bar, studied the cocktail list and suggested 'White Ladies'.

'It *is* ghastly, wouldn't you say?' he asked when the drinks arrived.

'Yes,' said Jane. 'But the drinks are good.'

'Mm,' said Robins. 'Do you like to dance?'

'Yes.'

'Me too,' he said. 'But I'll need at least one more of these before I have the nerve to ask you. Do you like this sort of place?'

'Sometimes,' she said. 'Do you?'

'Not often,' he said, 'but tonight I'm loving it. You see I've never held a dress by – 'he raised his eyebrows.

'Paquin,' she said.

' – by Paquin in my arms before. It will be something to warm my old age.'

'Where on earth,' she heard herself asking, 'did you meet my brother?' And then added, 'But that's silly. I suppose you work together.'

'Good heavens no,' said Robins. 'I'm not an economist.'

He said 'economist' as though it meant 'male prostitute', she thought.

'What then?'

'I'm an experimental physicist.'

'A colleague of Cuthbert Pardoe?'

'That's it.'

Jane found this even more extraordinary than the fact that he'd known her brother.

'Cuthbert's all right,' said Robins. 'If you can think of him solely as a scientific mind.'

Jane tried and failed to do so.

'You're working with him on this atom thing?'

'Now where on earth did you hear about that? Because that's exactly what we do. Cuthbert and the humble servant who stands here before you are the devoted slaves of Sir Ernest Rutherford and Peter Kapitza.'

'Of whom?'

'The New Zealander and the Russian who are really going to do the thing.'

– 322 –

'What thing? Blow up the world?'

'That's what the papers say, I agree. Your *Daily World*. All of them. But it won't be that.' He signalled for more drinks.

'What will it be then?'

'Power,' he said. 'The greatest power since Prometheus stole fire from heaven. More than all the big bad bangs in that big bad war.'

'You were in it?'

'Briefly and ingloriously,' he said. 'Not like you.'

'I think it's time you stopped remembering all the things you read in the *Daily World* and asked me to dance,' she said.

He danced rather as he drove, she thought: struggling with the concepts of rhythm, music, movement as though they were enemies, and yet he appeared to enjoy it. After a while they went back to the bar, and their drinks.

'You know I enjoy these things,' he said. 'Probably because I first came across them in America.'

'But aren't they illegal there?'

'That's probably why I enjoyed them,' he said. 'I was at MIT – the Massachusetts Institute of Technology. What a place. Everything I ever needed. Like Christmas. Every boy his own train set.'

'And yet you came back.'

'The atom bug hit me,' he said. 'For some reason the Yanks aren't ready for it yet. To them it's either crazy or the defiance of God.' He looked at his empty glass and signalled for more.

'I hope to God they're wrong,' he said.

Within another half an hour he was drunk. True he'd had five 'White Ladies' to her two, but even so he was much more drunk than he should have been.

Jane said, 'I'm rather hungry. It must be the country air.'

'No doubt, no doubt,' said Robins. 'I wrote to Rutherford you see, and there was a research fellowship going at Trinity and for once my face fitted and so here I am with the most beautiful girl in Cambridge. The one they all adore so. Just like Zulu what's it.'

'Zuleika Dobson,' said Jane. 'And anyway she was Oxford. And I wish you'd stick to the point.'

'Your point being?'

'*I want to eat.*'

She didn't in the least want to eat, not after the lunch she'd had, but it was the only course of action she could think of.

'Eat?' said Robins. 'Oh – eat. You know I rather think I want to eat, too. Of course I do. I haven't eaten all day. Come to think of it I don't think I ate anything yesterday either, apart from some cheese things at your brother's party, and I must say they were pretty ghastly.'

'You haven't eaten for two days?'

'Nothing of any significance. One can hardly count the cheese things.'

'But whyever not?' Jane asked.

'Busy,' said Robins. 'Busy busy busy. In the lab all day and up half the night writing the notes, doing the sums. I say. . . .'

'Yes?'

'I think we should have something to eat, don't you?'

The roadhouse could manage soup and a steak and crème caramel and cheese, and Robins ate the lot, and most of Jane's. She declined the wine list for both of them, but called for black coffee and watched as Robins drank it.

'How drunk was I?' he asked her at last.

'Well on,' she said. 'You really should eat from time to time.'

'That's one thing all the nutritionists agree on,' he said. 'I'm most awfully sorry.'

'Why?' she asked. 'I said you were drunk, but you were never nasty, so please don't apologise.'

'Will you marry me?' he asked.

Oh dear, thought Jane. It doesn't seem to have worked all that well.

'Are you sure you want to?'

'Of course I am,' he said. 'No other woman in the world would have let me off the hook the way you just did. I'd be all kinds of a fool if I didn't even *ask*.'

'Perhaps when I've had time to think about it,' she said.

'"Perhaps" is the word you used to Freddy Myers,' he said. 'I heard you. Not eavesdropping – word of honour. Just very sharp hearing. I deserve better than perhaps.'

'It's all you get at this time of night,' said Jane.

'The trouble is one works so hard,' said Robins. 'So hard one doesn't eat so that one can't drink and therefore disgraces oneself before a lovely lady. But it's so wonderful, you see.'

'What is?'

'The work. The things we do. Rutherford and Carr and Bell and Kapitza and Pardoe and me. It has a sort of pure beauty about it and yet it's so exciting, too. Do you suppose nuns feel like that?'

'Some might,' said Jane.

'Not the ones in Casanova,' said Robins. 'Have you ever read his memoirs?'

'Not yet,' said Jane.

'Not yet! Oh bliss,' said Robins. 'I do wish you'd marry me.'

Jane signalled for more coffee, and Robins appeared to go into a trance. When he emerged he said, 'I was considering something.'

'I'd love to hear it.'

'I was considering,' said Robins, 'that your brother is putting under the microscope of his mind the means whereby the world will be changed. Workers of the World Unite. Nationalisation. Everything in Common. A long and arduous process, preceded by a short and violent one. Overthrow Capitalism. Arm the Workers. The inevitable Upsurge of the Masses. Power to the People. It will take years for Francis Whitcomb MA to change the world. Years and years and years. And even then he's supposing that all his preconceptions are correct whereas I or rather Rutherford and Kapitza and Pardoe and all the others and I – could change the world in weeks. All we have to do is get one experiment right.'

'You're quite serious, aren't you?' asked Jane.

'Never more so. One successful experiment is all it would take.'

'About my brother, I mean. He wants to change the world?'

'We both do,' said Robins. 'I say I'm most awfully sleepy. I'd better drive you home before I nod off.'

Getting the right money to pay the bill then walking him to the car were major challenges: coaxing the car keys from him and putting him in the passenger's seat an achievement, but she did it at last and the Jowett fired first time, which was as well. Carefully she explored her way back to the Cambridge road.

'I've never been driven by a woman before,' said Robins.

'I've driven dozens of men. Hundreds,' said Jane.

'Ah yes,' said Robins. 'The war to be sure,' and promptly went to sleep.

The car knew how to move when it was handled properly, and Jane had no difficulty in finding her way back to Cambridge. She stopped the car at last near the great gate of his college, and gently shook him awake.

'Tony we're here,' she said, and he opened his eyes.

'Why did you call me that?'

'It's what you asked me to call me.'

'How sweet you are. . . . Did you like driving my car?'

'Very much.'

'You drive much better than I do,' he said. 'It's humiliating I suppose.'

'Why is it?'

'Male authority. All that.'

'Such nonsense.'

'You would naturally think so but then you haven't met my mother. My all-conquering mother.'

'Is she all-conquering?'

'She does it by giving in all the time and making one feel guilty.'

'Hardly the ideal mother-in-law,' said Jane.

'You said perhaps,' said Robins. 'Not very flattering – but I shall ask you again.'

'Can you get out of the car?' Jane asked.

Robins considered. 'I think very probably,' he said at last. 'But what about you?'

'I shall walk home,' she said. 'It isn't far. Will the car be all right?'

'Much safer than with me behind the wheel.'

He turned towards her and kissed her, a swifter, much clumsier kiss than Bower's.

'Forgive me for that,' he said. 'But these have been far and away the happiest hours of my life I ever spent outside a lab.'

'I forgive you,' said Jane. 'I had a happy time too. Shall I help you out of the car?'

'No,' he said. 'Please go. Watching me emerge will not bring back memories of Nijinsky.'

She left, and did not look back.

32

HARRIET WATSON SAID, 'Keith reckons he's good. In Pardoe's class even.'

'He's not in the least like Pardoe,' said Jane.

'I don't think that's strictly true,' said Harriet. 'They're both big and burly and first-rate scientists.'

'At least Tony Robins is human.'

It was lunchtime. They were eating poached eggs and drinking gin in the sitting room of Harriet's surgery.

'He asked me to marry him,' said Jane.

'Which is more than Cuthbert Pardoe ever did,' said Harriet.

'*Or* Freddy Myers,' said Jane, not without pride.

Harriet Watson goggled.

'Good Lord,' she said. 'You have been busy.'

'No I haven't,' said Jane. 'Not in that way. But what gets into these Cambridge fellows? Is it because they're shut off from us females so much?'

'Urges,' said Harriet. 'All men have them – you know that. Only at Cambridge they talk about it more because talking's what they do best. You didn't accept him, I suppose?'

'Tony?' Jane knew that she sounded surprised. It was unfair. 'No. But I liked him.'

'Then you haven't come to ask me to be your matron of honour?'

'Not yet.'

'Then what have you come for? Forgive me, that's rude, but I'll have to fly soon – '

'It's *mostly* about Felston,' said Jane.

'I thought it might be. How much have you got now?'

'With your ten bob I've passed two thousand three hundred quid.'

It was incredible, but it had happened. Already the cheques and postal orders had started coming into the *Daily World*, and often letters came with them. 'I was touched by your reference to the cart-horse, Mavis.' . . . 'I remember the Royal Northumbrians' gallantry at the Somme.'

'And how will you spend it?'

'Medicine mostly.'

'I can't advise you on that,' said Harriet. 'Your Dr Stobbs would skin me alive if I did, and quite right too.'

'I realise that. This is something more personal. John's grandmother.'

'The one you call Grandma?'

'She's going blind,' said Jane. 'At a guess it looks like cataract – I only say that because I saw a lot of it in India, and I wondered if anything could be done.'

'Who would pay?'

'Me.'

'Then the answer is probably yes. How old is she?'

'Mid seventies, I should say.'

'In good health?'

'Exhaustingly so.'

'There should be no major problem, if her heart's strong. Normally one would look to Harley Street – but there might be difficulties – '

'Naturally I would pay for a clinic,' said Jane.

'Of course you would, silly, but these old ladies who've got into the habit of ruling the family roost don't take kindly to moving away from it. It's the only pleasure they have in life. Better let me make enquiries. See if I can find you someone in Newcastle.'

'Will he be all right?'

'If I find him he will be,' said Harriet, and then: 'Good gracious. I never thought you'd turn into an intellectual snob. When will you come and dine with us?'

'As soon as you ask me.'

'The sooner the better. Now I simply have to go. Can I cadge a lift to Kensington?'

'Be a pleasure.'

Foch, Jane noticed, had no objection to squeezing up to make room for Dr Harriet Watson. He approved of her: considered her a serious person.

After she had dropped Harriet she moved on to Falcon Court, and Mr Pinner, neat and dapper and discreet as ever.

'It's about your horse, miss,' he said.

'You've found her?'

'I thought I had, miss – almost certain – but when I got there the description was wrong. Somebody had heard there was a bit of money in it, I reckon.'

'When it comes to horses somebody always does,' said Jane. 'I want you to keep looking.'

'The thing is, miss, it's going to cost you forty-eight pounds nine shillings and fourpence already, what with train fares and so on.'

'That doesn't matter,' said Jane.

'Nearly fifty pounds and nothing to show for it,' Mr Pinner said. 'That's a lot of money when there's nothing to show. I reckon you should try somebody else, miss.'

'Please go on looking, Mr Pinner,' said Jane.

'Very well,' Mr Pinner sighed. It was obvious that he now regarded Jane as a moral obligation rather than a source of income.

'There's one report I got,' he said, 'that just might get us somewhere. Oxfordshire. Did anybody who had anything to do with that mare have connections in Oxfordshire?'

Jane thought hard, and then remembered. . . . Goosey. . . . Captain Gander, the third officer to own Bridget. Hadn't John said something about being brought up by relatives who lived near Banbury? Pinner listened and made notes.

'That fits in pretty well with what I've got, miss,' he said. 'At least there's enough for one more try. But I shouldn't be in a hurry, miss. Oxfordshire's a big county.'

'I can wait,' said Jane.

She had waited for seven years, after all.

On to Fleet Street then, which Foch deplored as being irredeemably frivolous, though like Jane he took pride in the fact that he was the only dog allowed in the building.

Bower very much resented this. He took the view that during working hours Jane was a reporter and that reporters did not bring their pets to work. Jane's position was that if Foch wasn't welcome then she wasn't either. Since Felston was, in Bower's phrase, a bandwagon beginning to roll, they were both allowed in, for the moment. Felston, Jane realised, must be big news indeed, and Bower made no attempt to hide it.

'It's an angle,' he said. 'And a good one. Everybody knows the working class is in. Beaverbrook, Rothermere – everybody. Even *The Times* is beginning to admit they exist. But for them it's an abstraction. We've got a personal view, a place to identify with.'

'You've also got me,' said Jane. 'And I'm not exactly working class, now am I?'

'You're their guardian angel,' said Bower.

'I thought I was their Florence Nightingale.'

'You're anything that sells newspapers,' said Bower.

Jabber had once told her she might have something he called an identity crisis. It seemed that Bower had just solved it.

'And how do I sell newspapers today?'

'By helping Felston.'

'And how do I do that?'

'By being talked about. That needn't worry you. You've a natural flair for it. In Cambridge you knocked them out of the ball park.'

'The what?'

'It's what we Americans have to say because we don't play cricket. You were a hit. A smash. Like that girl at Oxford Max Beerbohm wrote about.'

'Zuleika Dobson,' said Jane, rather wearily this time. If comparisons had to be made she would have preferred someone rather more intelligent.

'I don't know how you do it,' he continued.

'Neither do I,' said Jane.

'It doesn't matter. You can't help doing it, and that's just fine. So you go about and do things and it helps sell my paper.'

'And what do I get out of it?'

'Money for Felston,' he said. 'Big money.' It was what she wanted after all.

'And what do I have to do today?'

'Two things,' said Bower. 'There are a lot of women who talk too much out in Hampstead. They run a thing called the Tea Club. Their speaker let them down today. You're going to take his place and talk about Felston.'

'I've never addressed a tea club in my life.'

'Now's a good time to start,' said Bower. 'Just tell them the way you told me. They'll eat it.'

Jane looked at him more closely. 'Whose place am I taking?' she asked.

'Mine,' he said, and grinned.

'I might have known,' said Jane.

'Sure you might,' said Bower. 'But whose is the greater need?'

Jane let it go. Talking at tea clubs could hardly be worse than dreams of the Somme.

'And the second thing?'

'There's a charity ball tonight,' said Bower.

'Disabled ex-servicemen,' said Jane. 'At the Piccadilly Hotel.'

'Are you going?'

'I'd thought about it,' said Jane, 'but I was too busy at Cambridge to arrange a partner.'

Coo hark at me, she thought. A year ago I'd no more have thought of going to a charity ball at the Piccadilly Hotel than of wearing an Erté dress. But it was true. . . .

'You'll go with me,' said Bower.

'Is it company orders, sir?'

'Look,' said Bower. 'This isn't fun, it's work, and when I'm working I talk like this because I don't have the time to be polite. You want to work tonight?'

'I'll be delighted.'

'Pick you up at seven. Wear something that'll photograph well. They're still describing the coat you wore at Cambridge. Oh and about the Tea Club. You can use all the stuff you put in those two articles. None of those women ever opened a *Daily World* in their lives.'

She found herself thanking him as if he'd been the soul of generosity, then Foch dragged her to the door. Bower was already flipping through copy, but he called out to her, 'Hey wait a minute.' She paused. 'Is it really true you offered to strip against some bluestocking girl?'

'Marigold Ledbitter,' said Jane. 'Certainly it's true.'

'Don't try it with the tea-club crowd,' said Bower. 'They'd call you.'

She had three hours to prepare a speech, change her clothes, and drive to Hampstead. The clothes took rather a long time, even with Hawkins to help her. In the end she settled for a severe Paquin suit, a silk blouse cut like a shirt, and Aunt Pen's Cartier leopardess. And a hat of course. Rather a nice hat from Paris.

The Hampstead Tea Club ladies were not at all like that. It was all either folk weave and sandals, or brogues and woollen stockings and tweeds like barbed wire. Writers and the wives of writers, professors and the wives of professors, architects and a doctor or two, teachers of the superior sort. They drank their terrible tea and talked about Virginia Woolf and a German called Spengler, then waited ominously as Madam Chairman told them that Miss Whitcomb would now address them. When Jane rose, they produced note books to a woman.

Jane looked about her wildly. I'm dressed all wrong, she thought. Silk suit in that incredible kingfisher blue, half a lifetime's wages of a working man pinned to my lapel. I should have worn the clothes I bought in Felston – but I gave them to Bet instead. . . . She had been silent too long. The big drawing room where the meeting was held rustled in unease, and somewhere a woman tittered. Definitely not on her side. Say something. Say *anything*.

'I'm afraid,' Jane began. Well God knows that was true. The trouble was she couldn't even begin to explain why she was afraid. The pause went on. And then suddenly Harriet Watson came into the room, sat at the back, and winked at Jane, and Jane heard herself saying: 'I'm afraid I must be a sad disappointment to you after your promised treat. All I can say is I know precisely how much Mr Bower regrets not being with you this afternoon.'

And that also is true, she thought. How much Mr Bower regrets is not at all. He only accepted in the first place so that he could cancel and offer me in his place as sacrificial victim.

'But since I have been so very kindly accepted here,' she said, and two other women at once turned to scowl at the titterer, 'I'd like to tell you about a place I know. A place called Felston.' And out it all came. The Pattersons, Dr Stobbs and George Habbershaw, Private Colley and the cart-horse Mavis, and then, because these were all women who thought a lot, thought in abstractions, Manny Mendel and Andy on one side of the market square and the Salvation Army on the other. Compare and contrast, as the exam papers say.

She was amazed at how quickly the half hour went by, and even more amazed that she should be applauded. Really, she thought, one could develop quite a taste for this sort of thing. No wonder Francis wanted to spend the rest of his life doing it. And then the questions began, and Jane discovered that tweeds or no tweeds, folk weave or no folk weave, these women knew their stuff. To begin with they had read all the books, because for the Hampstead Tea Club, to read all the books was mandatory, and Jane hadn't read one except for *Felston* – by Stobbs and Messeter. In fact she scored high marks for that, since no one else had read it, but her background reading was abysmal, non-existent in fact. *She hadn't even read Marx's* Capital. Eyewitness accounts, Jane gathered, were not to be compared in value with what one read in books. Then Harriet got up.

'Would the speaker tell us,' she asked, 'how she first became concerned with the town of Felston?'

Harriet was throwing her a lifebelt, letting human emotion back in if she chose to do it.

'Certainly,' said Jane. 'I served as an ambulance driver in the war.'

There was a purr of approval at this, for many of her audience had been suffragettes, and success in a man's job had to be taken seriously. 'As a matter of fact,' Jane continued, 'I was able to use the skills I'd learned at the Front when I drove an ambulance for Dr Stobbs in Felston.' The purr deepened to a contented growl of approval.

'When I was in the war,' Jane continued, 'I met a captain in the Royal Northumbrians. We were engaged to be married. Unfortunately he was killed. On the 10th of November, 1918.'

That got through to them, bang on target. There was not a woman there who had not lost a relative or friend, and the monstrous ill-fortune of the date of John's death was a disaster they could all share, and Jane continued her explanation. When she sat down there were no more questions, only a vote of thanks proposed and seconded, to more applause before Jane stood up for the last time. ('Don't forget to pass the hat,' Bower had warned her. 'If you don't nobody else will.') And so the hat was passed, and another seven pounds six shillings and sixpence, mostly in silver, raised for Felston, before Jane found herself shaking hands with Madam Chairman and assuring her what a pleasure it had been.

And so it was, Jane found herself thinking. You enjoyed all that showing off and spouting good works. You even enjoyed all that Hearts and Flowers stuff about poor old John – not that he would have minded, not if it had helped Felston, but it was the sort of sneaky newspaper's trick you learned from Bower, and John most certainly would have minded that.

All the same, when she met Harriet on the way out, she thanked her. 'Lord knows how I'd have managed if they'd continued to assess my reading,' she said.

'We're a hard lot to cut your teeth on,' said Harriet. 'Did you enjoy it?'

'I think rather too much,' said Jane. 'But I wish I could have you in the audience at all my meetings. . . . Just in case.'

'There will be more then?'

'I have a feeling Bower's set on it,' said Jane. 'As a matter of fact I think I am, too.'

Wear something that'll photograph well, Bower had said, but that was a man's remark. Everything she wore photographed well – inside the covers of *Vogue*. It was what the clothes would look like when they covered her that was important. She went through her wardrobe once, then again, and settled at last on a dress by Fortuny: charioteer dresses, as the fashion critics called them, modelled on the robe worn by the charioteer at Delphi. The one she owned was in white, heavy Chinese silk, pleated all around the skirt, each pleat weighted with a bead of Venetian glass to hold it in place. Not much on top, bare arms and shoulders, and so she chose a necklace of heavy gold, golden sandals, and Papa's ear-rings because she knew he would have enjoyed what he saw. . . . And the yellow silk evening coat, she decided; Hawkins agreed with her.

'I don't know how it is, miss,' said Hawkins, 'but it has the same à la Grecque touch as the dress.'

What on earth was Hawkins up to? Now was not the time to ask, not before a charity ball, but she really must find out, and soon.

For the moment she settled for a glass of cold milk (there'd be far too much champagne at the ball) and asked Hawkins if she intended to go to the pictures as she had the night off. Hawkins said severely that she had far too much reading to do to bother with Theda Bara. Tomorrow, Jane told herself. Tomorrow I shall ask her. Or the day after at the latest.

Bower was prompt, as he was always prompt. The politeness of princes, she thought, or at any rate newspaper tycoons. He looked at the coat and what he could see of the dress, and liked what he saw, then handed her into the car. He'd brought his chauffeur, she noticed.

'I hear you did well at the Tea Club,' he said.

'Like that man in the French Revolution, I survived,' she said, 'though you could say even that's doing well.'

'Not a dry eye in the auditorium, they tell me.'

'You had a spy there?'

'I like to think of her as a woman reporter,' said Bower.

'No doubt she's that too,' Jane said affably. 'Did she tell you how cerebral they all were – the books they'd all read? The only card I had was my womanly courage in the face of adversity.'

'You played it well.'

'If I did,' said Jane, 'it was because you taught me how. Who's giving this ball by the way?'

'The Countess of Twyford.'

'She does a lot of that sort of thing.'

'She has to,' said Bower. 'Twyford's just about broke. But she makes a living because she's good at it. As a matter of fact I thought she might organise your ball, too.'

'Mine?'

'The Felston Charity Ball,' said Bower. 'Around Christmas, I thought. To raise the money for toys for all the Tiny Tims. Beer and plum puddings. It'll have your name on it but Bella Twyford will do all the organising. You'll be far too busy.'

'Doing what?'

'You'll think of something,' said Bower.

They arrived at the Piccadilly, and the flash bulbs began to pop. ('Open your coat,' said Bower. 'Let them see the dress, too.' And open her coat she did.) Then off she went to the cloakroom, and came back without it. Bower looked at her and blinked, and she knew that she wore the right dress, then she joined the queue to shake hands with their hostess, the wife of a general Papa had once clean bowled for a duck, and Lady Twyford. The general's wife was the usual pouter pigeon, but Lady Twyford looked like an avaricious lawyer in an American film comedy who for some reason had decided to wear a dress in the wrong shade of green.

After that they went to their table: millionaires and their wives, a duke and his wife, a distinguished actor with his equally distinguished actress wife. Among the millionaires was Sir Hugh Lessing. His wife again wore a dress that looked as if it had been made from fragments of Bakst's scenery. Jane wondered if she had any other kind. The band struck up 'Get Out And Get Under', but there would be time enough for that. She accepted a glass of champagne instead.

Lessing said, 'We've met,' in a voice of absolute certainty, but he gave no indication that he remembered where.

'At a ball,' said Jane. 'Just like this – except that it was at your house. You and your wife gave it.'

'I remember,' said Lessing, though she doubted whether he did. 'But it wasn't a *ball* exactly. More a party with delusions of grandeur. We gave it for Mirova. Michael Browne was there.'

'And Georgina Payne.'

'Good Lord, yes. The poor chap's potty about her. Do you think he paints well?'

'Very well. I bought some of his stuff the other day.'

'Did you indeed? He was my company commander. All I ever managed was bad verse – rather in the manner of Baudelaire, I used to think – but bad. Quite ghastly, sometimes. Are you sure you wouldn't care to dance?'

'I think perhaps I will,' she said, and found that Sir Hugh danced rather well, as behoved a man who had had Mirova as a house-guest, but all he would talk about was Michael Browne. Browne, it seemed, had saved his life and wouldn't take a penny for it. When Lessing had asked to buy some pictures he'd given him one instead. And yet the poor fellow had to be helped.

'Endow an arts scholarship,' said Jane. 'Give it to him. He's good enough.'

Lessing wasn't sure.

'That wife of his would be after him,' he said.

'Make it a travelling scholarship.'

'Good Lord.' Lessing was so impressed he stopped dancing and couples swerved wildly round him as if he were a stray boulder on a roadway, thought Jane. At last Lessing apologised and led her back into the stream.

'But that's a marvellous idea,' he said.

'It'll get him away from his wife.'

'You don't think that's – well – an immoral thing to do?'

'I've met her,' said Jane.

'So you have,' said Lessing. 'You were in all the newspapers.'

Jane was glad to be led back to the table.

It was rather that sort of dance: predictable food, too much champagne, and foxtrots and tangoes with men who didn't know which was which; being presented to the inevitable royalty (a dumpy and very deaf old lady), and prizes for the raffle tickets. Bower spent fifty pounds and won a spray of gardenias, which he promptly gave to her. She detested gardenias – for some reason they made her look diseased – and promptly left them on an unoccupied seat. Lady Lessing returned and sat on them with her Bakst bottom and didn't even notice. Rather that sort of dance.

Just after midnight Bower said to her, 'Are you enjoying yourself?'

'Only if you are,' said Jane.

'No more than you. Want to get out of here?'

'Can we?'

'Sure,' said Bower. 'We're newspaper people. We have deadlines to meet.' Suddenly for Bower he looked furtive, shifty even. 'Just one thing,' he said. 'My chauffeur – '

'Has left?'

'He's had a long day,' said Bower, 'and his wife's not well. He asked if he could go early and I said OK. But I don't want you to worry. I can phone the newspaper and they'll send an automobile if you don't want a taxi – or else I could drive you somewhere if you're not too tired. I shan't – embarrass you or anything. You have my word on that.'

'I'm not in the least tired.'

'Then let's go,' said Bower. 'And remember to be nice to Lady Twyford on the way out – we're going to need her. And if there are any more photographers around be sure you give them your left profile.'

As if he were my manager, thought Jane, or even my husband.

33

S HE SAT BESIDE him in the Rolls-Royce, and absorbed again
the familiar scent of leather and eau de cologne and Havana
cigars. They drove through London and headed north, through
sleepy Hampstead, slumbering Highbury, and on at last into
Berkshire, and the sort of country where Uncle Walter and Aunt
Pen liked to hire a house for the summer: rich and lush and
sheltered and discreet. As they drove, Bower talked: Bower could
no more help talking, thought Jane, than a bird could help
singing. This time it was all about strikes, miners for the most
part, but railwaymen and engineers too, then on to the royal
family, and what possible use they were in a country that might
soon be following Russia. And yet they seemed to escape resentment, mused Bower. People actually liked them. So how could
a foreigner hope to understand a country where the people
didn't even understand each other?

Deeper and deeper into Berkshire, from a main road to a
by-road, and at last to a track that the big car waddled along
comfortably enough, until they rounded one last corner and
Bower stopped, put on the brake, and Jane looked in front of
her and gasped.

Ahead of her was a stretch of water and a stone bridge with a
single span, beautiful at any time, but now with a magical quality
because of the light of a half moon filtered through clouds like a
lamp through gauze. And beyond the bridge a water meadow,
and beyond that, formal gardens, and beyond the gardens a
house – William and Mary? Jane wondered, or as late as Queen

Anne? Slender and elegant and exquisitely proportioned as the Mirova herself. And surrounding the house, woodland like a frame for a picture. Bower switched off the car's engine, and the night was filled with birdsong.

'I suppose you arranged that, too,' she said.

'Arranged what?'

'The nightingales. They won't sing for much longer, you know. Not even for Jay Bower.'

'You like it?' Bower asked.

'Like it? It's the most beautiful place I ever saw in my life. Whose is it?'

'Mine,' said Bower. Somehow she had been sure that that would be his answer. He put his arm around her, and she made no objection: it was a gesture of companionship, no more.

'I've had people in there working on it for six months,' Bower said, 'and now it's ready.'

'When do you move in?'

'Tonight,' said Bower, 'if you'll go with me.' His arm tightened round her, but she had made no move to leave him, and he relaxed.

'It's for my wife,' he said. 'That's no place for a bachelor.' He nodded at the exquisite house. 'So all I'm asking is that you jump the gun a little. That house can't wait any more than I can.'

Aunt Pen had given her clothes, a car, a Cartier leopardess, and at the end of the day a fortune, and now this man was doing it all again, telling her she could be the mistress of a house that was like a dream. But too far from Felston.

'I shan't say it's a compliment,' she said, 'although it is. But it's far, far more than that. It is absolutely the most wonderful thing – '

'But you're turning me down?'

'Not you,' said Jane. 'It.' For once. Bower looked puzzled, which pleased her.

'Put it this way,' she said. 'I won't go into your *house* – not on the terms you offer. But you did once suggest I visit your – apartment did you call it? – in Fleet Street, and I wouldn't mind doing that.'

'It's second best,' said Bower, 'and I meant that. But I'll take it.'

It had been by any standards a remarkable night, she thought. Not just the sex, though that *had* been remarkable – far, far beyond anything poor darling John had ever done: the upper sixth after the junior school. Her instincts had been right about that: Jay Bower had been not only good at it, he delighted in sharing, and in teaching, too. And thoughtful. Delicately sounding her out on what means they should employ to prevent parenthood. When she told him that she had been to see her friend, a lady doctor, in anticipation of this very event, he looked first shocked and then delighted.

'Are you sure you won't marry me?' he'd said, but she'd been quite sure, and so he'd undressed her instead, and shown her what their bodies could do for each other. She'd been very happy to learn. And goodness how long you could make it go on, when you knew what you were doing. But it finished at last and he told her he could do no more, not that night anyway, which was perhaps as well. She did have to go home. So she'd used his shower, the first one she'd had since India, and he'd used it with her. That almost started him off again despite what he'd said, and then he'd driven her home, grumbling a little, but she wouldn't take a taxi, not at that hour. It was almost dawn when she climbed the stairs, and the servants were still sleeping, but she heard the clop of hooves and the clatter of bottles. The milkman had missed her by minutes and how Hawkins would have enjoyed it if she'd been seen.

When she awoke it was nearly ten but she always slept late after a ball and anyway Hawkins would assume it was champagne. As usual. She felt just a little sore still, but Jay had said that more of the same would take care of that, having assumed from the beginning that there would be more of the same, which wasn't surprising really after the way she'd behaved. Talk about abandoned women. . . . What fun we have, she thought, we abandoned ones.

Hawkins tapped at the door, came in with the tea tray, then drew the curtains quite ruthlessly.

'Ten o'clock, miss,' she said. 'You did say you were to be called by ten.'

And so she had. There was another Felston article to be written, and she'd promised to lunch with Georgina. Foch came in and waited for his biscuit. Neither he nor Hawkins seemed to have noticed any evidence of her shame.

'And Mr Warley phoned, miss. From South Terrace. He wants you to phone him there.'

'After I've bathed,' said Jane. 'Run my bath now, will you?' She and Foch settled down to their Rich Teas.

'What took you so *long*?' said Lionel.

'I was out late,' said Jane. 'That ball at the Piccadilly. I was gallivanting there.' And elsewhere she thought, but I'd better not gloat too much. Lionel could be very astute, especially about sex, even on the telephone.

'So you were,' he said. 'My dear, what a divine dress. The *Daily World*'s full of it. Some of the others have it too. How's the Felston fund?'

'Growing,' said Jane. 'I make begging speeches now and pass the hat round afterwards.'

'The *World* has that one, too,' said Lionel. 'What strange power have you got over that *dour* tycoon?'

Not strange, Lionel dear. Not at all strange.

'He thinks poverty's newsworthy, just at the moment,' said Jane. 'And the fact that I'm sort of rich gives it human interest.'

'Well *I* need your human interest too,' said Lionel. 'About South Terrace. I've been pacing and measuring like a lunatic. When can you come here?'

'After lunch any good?'

'Couldn't be better. Now you're quite sure you've told me everything you want?'

'There is one more thing,' said Jane. 'I want a shower. En suite with my bedroom.'

She took Georgina to the Brompton Grill. Georgina, she knew, loved the food there, and Jane had worked very hard on her article, which was about Dr Stobbs's clinic. She felt that she'd earned a treat. Besides, Medlicott had written to say that the South Terrace lease was now hers, so that lunch was a treat *and* a celebration.

'You looked gorgeous last night,' said Georgina.

'Another *Daily World* reader?'

'White's never an easy colour, but you looked stunning.'

'You look stunning now.'

'I've looked worse,' said Georgina. 'We both have. What's the betting those two foreigners in the corner try to pick us up. . . Who did you go with?'

'Jay Bower.'

Georgina looked up from her plate. 'Again?'

'It's only the second time,' said Jane.

'But so soon after the first.'

'Contain your excitement,' said Jane. 'We get on well together, that's all. I was chauffeur-driven both ways.'

A whopper, but she didn't want to share her secret with Georgina, or even Harriet. Harriet knew of course that there was a man, but she didn't know who. Nor would she. She would guess of course, but she wouldn't know.

'Quite a catch, Jay Bower,' Georgina said.

'I'm not fishing. How's Michael?'

'Working hard as usual. Worrying as usual.'

'Worrying?'

'In case his wife comes calling again. He wants us to move, but what's the point? She'd only hire detectives to find the new place. Maybe he should move by himself.'

'Could you bear it?'

'He could pop round to see me when he was feeling randy,' said Georgina. 'Or I was.' She cut into her food, then swallowed. 'This chicken is delicious.'

'It wouldn't be the same though, would it?'

'It's all I need,' said Georgina. 'I mean I love him madly and all that but his paints really do clutter up the place. I found some c : he piano keyboard yesterday.'

J ne realised that it was all she needed, too, but that was because her feeling for Jay was nothing like her love for John.

'Do you really?' she asked. 'Love him madly, I mean.'

'As madly as I ever loved anybody. I've been offered a new job. At the BBC.'

'The what?'

'The British Broadcasting Company,' Georgina said. 'You know – the wireless.'

'You're going to be an announcer?'

'Of course not,' said Georgina. 'I'm going to play the piano and prattle merrily about how lovely it is to dedicate one's life to one's art.'

'Does it pay well?'

'Twenty guineas for the half hour. Mind you it's only for three half hours so far, but if it takes I can pay the rent indefinitely.'

'Does Michael like the idea?' asked Jane.

'What choice does he have? We need the mun.'

The head waiter came to them. 'The two Italian gentlemen in the corner would like you to join them for coffee and liqueurs, ladies,' he said.

Jane said, 'No, we won't do that. But give them an extra brandy each and put it on my bill. Tell them it's for having such good taste.'

Life rather fell into a rut after that: writing articles, making speeches, inspecting South Terrace, being under or over Jay Bower. No word from Mummy, and no word from Vinney either, though Medlicott swore that every effort was being made to trace her. Maybe she should send Mr Pinner to Bombay, Jane thought, and then one day Mr Pinner called her, most inappropriately, at a time when she was under Jay. Frantically busy though they were, Jane noticed, the telephone could not be ignored. Jay poised himself on his left elbow, reached out with his right hand, and scooped what Mummy called the instrument to him, juggling it so that he got the earpiece to his ear, and the mouthpiece was cushioned by her left breast.

'Bower,' he said.

Jane saw no reason why she should stop what she was doing, nor did she. Bower's next words achieved a certain urgency.

'Hold the wire,' he said. 'She's right here.'

He moved the mouthpiece to her left cheek and handed her the earpiece, then resumed what he had been doing.

'Yes?' said Jane. 'Who?. . . Mr Pinner?. . . Oh. . . .' And then again, 'Oh,' for Jay was showing no mercy. 'You've what?. . . Oh marvellous. . . . I said marvellous,' and Jay smirked. He would pay for that. 'And where is she?. . . Oh that's wonderful. . . . Thank you.' Jay smirking more than ever. 'Thank you so much, Mr Pinner. You're an absolute treasure.' Somehow she put the earpiece on its hook and got back to the matter in hand.

After the shower, she said, 'That was Mr Pinner.'

'What was?'

'The man who nearly interrupted our bliss. But he didn't did he?'

'Not mine, certainly. How did he know you were here?'

'I always tell Hawkins where I can be reached in emergencies. Another thing you taught me.' She put on her petticoat, then sat before the mirror and reached for a comb.

'Mr Pinner's an emergency?' Jay asked.

'Not really. Just good news. I have to go to Ireland.'

'Why, for God's sake?'

'He's found Bridget.'

'And who the hell is Bridget? A cook?'

'A horse,' said Jane. 'My horse if I'm lucky. She's in County Meath – just outside Dublin.' And she told him the story. Jay was entranced.

'Maybe we can use that,' he said.

'And maybe I'll let you. . . . I'm not sure about that yet.'

Perceptive as ever, Bower asked: 'Do I have a rival?'

'No,' said Jane. 'Only a yardstick to be measured by.'

'The one who was killed on 10th November, 1918?'

She had told the Hampstead tea swillers, and of course he'd spotted it at once.

'The very same,' she said. 'I really do mean to get that horse.'

'I wouldn't blame you,' said Jay. 'You're in a hurry, right?'

'I am indeed.'

'The week after next wouldn't do?'

'The week after next she could be sold,' said Jane.

'You wouldn't want to risk that.' She turned to look at him, but he was perfectly serious. 'The trouble is,' he continued, 'I want you in Paris next Thursday.'

'Want me?'

'Not that way,' he said. 'I want you that way every time I get my strength back. I want you to do a piece there.'

'About *Felston*? In *Paris*?'

'There are other places in the world than Felston,' said Bower. 'This is about a guy who drove an ambulance in the war. He's going to the Quart' Arts Ball. I thought maybe we should go too.'

'I'd love to,' said Jane, 'but I'll lose three whole days just travelling. And buying a horse isn't like buying a pound of carrots. One's expected to haggle.'

'You could fly there,' said Bower.

'So I could,' said Jane, 'but I don't happen to have an aeroplane.'

'I do,' said Bower.

'Of course you do,' said Jane. 'You have everything. And thank you. . . . I'd love to go to Paris with you – but you must let me pay for the plane.'

'On the house,' said Bower, 'if you'll let me print the story.'

She looked into the mirror, lipstick in hand, but what she saw was John on Bridget's back, learning to canter, and grinning his delight when he found that he could.

'Very well,' she said, 'but the editor's decision is final, and this time I'm the editor.'

'You've got a deal,' said Bower.

God alone knows what Jabber will say when he finds out, thought Jane, but I don't think John would mind. He was very proud of Bridget.

Bower had arranged everything. It would be all too easy to get used to the idea that Bower always arranged everything. Plane waiting at Croydon, landing field arranged in Meath, and a car to meet her and take her to Mangan Castle. For Bridget it seemed now belonged to an earl. But Bower took earls in his stride. He'd once told the Prince of Wales that he put too much vermouth in his martinis.

Jane hired the Rolls-Royce once more, said farewell to cook – who, Jane knew, would put her feet up the instant the front door closed – and sent Hawkins over to assist Lionel, a euphemism for resisting too much Bakst.

Bakst made her think of Hugh Lessing, who obviously didn't like Georgina, no doubt because he considered her a bad influence on Michael Browne. But Georgina wasn't a bad influence on anybody – or not deliberately. She couldn't help the way she looked. Even Mummy had admitted that she was a lady. Papa had been bowled over. . . . Mummy. . . . She searched in her handbag as the Rolls moved serenely on, and took out Mummy's letter. Mummy was writing at a furious rate, which was not in the least like her. And at length, too. Sheets and sheets. The latest was eight pages. And all about nothing, really. Except that Kalpur was lovely and the new maharajah had converted the cricket pitch into a polo lawn. And the people were delightful and she had been asked to play the piano everywhere. Stuff like that. Eight pages of it. And a PS to say that Miss Gwatkin was well though approaching obesity. Not like Mummy at all, except for the PS. Could she have gone out in the sun without a hat?

At Croydon the pilot came to meet her and led her to her plane, which was big indeed compared to the fighter her brother David had used that day he flew over to visit her. She even had a cabin all to herself. She still needed her fur coat of course – the heaviest one, the silver fox, and the travelling rug over her knees, but she was out of the wind. There was even a flask of tea.

The plane took off and climbed steadily, heading west. Jane looked down to see London sprawling in every direction, then thought of Jay once more. She had gone to bed with him, she supposed, because after Tony Robins had so disastrously taken her out she had realised that Jay had a sexual attraction for her that Tony lacked. And power. He had enormous power – aeroplanes and earls and aid for Felston, and she found that sexually attractive, too. He'd acquired another MP just recently. All newspaper owners had them, he'd told her; backbenchers who obliged with little 'think' pieces on 'The Modern Girl' and 'Can Socialism Work?' and 'The Greatness of Our Empire'. Until recently Bower considered three to be an adequate number, but then he'd got this bee in his bonnet about poverty, and that meant taking on a Socialist. They'd met in Jay's office where they were discussing the Paris trip. His secretary had announced that Mr Lambert was waiting.

'In a minute,' said Bower.

'Who's Mr Lambert?'

'An MP,' said Bower. 'One of mine as a matter of fact. Maybe you should meet him. He's a man of the Left. At least that's what he calls himself.' He flipped the intercom switch. 'I'll see Mr Lambert now.'

A colourless man, she thought, despite a suit of an unbelievable, almost an electric, blue, and a scarlet tie. Colourless and nervous. Or perhaps one was caused by the other. Bower made a lot of people nervous. . . . But a nice man, with a face more pleasant than handsome, and a surprisingly rich, deep voice, with a slight Yorkshire accent.

'Pleasure to meet you, Miss Whitcomb,' he said. 'Of course

I've read a lot about you.' He looked at Bower. 'In the *Daily World* of course. Hard to believe such an elegant lady could have done what you did in the war.'

'Felston,' said Bower. 'That's what we have to concentrate on now. What Miss Whitcomb's going to do for Felston. Or do you find that hard to believe too?'

'It'll take courage,' said Lambert, 'but as I say she's got that. And determination.'

'I'm very determined about this,' said Jane.

'I'm delighted to hear it. There's the charity stigma of course, and a lot of folk don't like that, but the way I look at it you're still a life saver, Miss Whitcomb, only this time it's in the class war.'

'Do you want to make a note of that one?' said Bower.

'I already have,' said Lambert.

Jay might call him 'one of mine', thought Jane, but he's his own man, nervous or not. She'd rather liked him.

The aeroplane was flying over fields now, pasture and stubble for the most part, with the occasional dark patch of wheat still waiting for the reaper – and then in the distance, she could see another town. Liverpool, would it be? Or that place where the packets left for what used to be called Kingston and was now called Dunleary. Nice not to have to take the packet, not to risk being seasick. Cunning, powerful, *lustful* Mr Bower.

The earl, it seemed, had a wife, and a family, a son and heir, and two other children, twins, a boy and a girl. He also had a mother, Bower had told her, who was very much a power in the land. Whatever happened, mother must be placated. . . . The sea appeared, and she looked down into a dark and angry green, ominously heaving. Definitely a good idea to avoid the packet.

She had two nights to negotiate for Bridget O'Dowd. The Irish loved horse trading and were rarely in a hurry, but surely two nights would do. Probably all it would take was too much money. Irish peers were famous for their poverty. But she must get Bridget back. There was no proper reason for it but it was more than a rich woman's whim, the imperious demand of wealth that insists all gratification be immediate. It wasn't like that at all. Bridget O'Dowd was her last link with the John who had died at La Bassée, the John who had belonged to her before she knew that his family were any more than names rarely spoken.

She wanted Bridget almost as a keepsake, a reminder of a time long past, but with a special quality that would never be repeated. If the earl declined to sell it would not be the end of the world, but she longed to persuade him; had packed two of her most persuasive dresses.

Another dark smudge on the horizon, that slowly turned into ships and a harbour, then streets and more streets: Dunleary, and then Dublin. They flew on until the houses dwindled then ceased, and the special greenness of Irish grass gleamed below them, a green far more friendly than that of the sea. They passed a small town, and the plane dropped lower, headed out towards a village where they were flying so low she could see the children running. Then in the distance a great house with formal parkland, and before it a scatter of fields in which horses grazed. One field was empty, and in one corner of it a flag flew, a great spread of blue with some heraldic beast or other embroidered in gold. The pilot circled the field once, and appeared to approve what he saw, for he put the plane's nose down, let it drift slowly in for an immaculate three-point landing.

The plane stopped at last and the pilot clambered down, produced a portable ladder to assist her out of the cabin, then reached inside to bring out her suitcase. Jane set out to walk to where two figures were seated on a fence, watching her trudge. Both of them wore macintoshes. This was Ireland, after all, and it was raining. A young man and a young woman, so alike that they had to be twins. The young man swung down from the fence.

'Miss Whitcomb?' he said.

'Yes.'

'I'm Piers Hilyard. This is my sister Catherine.' He offered his hand and she took it. A good-looking young man, quite arrestingly good-looking, more beautiful than handsome, and his sister another of the same. Black and waving hair, brown eyes, aristocratic little beak of a nose, firm mouth that held a hint of sensuality too.

'We thought,' said Catherine, 'that it might be fun if we drove you home ourselves.'

'To the castle?'

'It won't be exactly a giddy round of pleasure,' said Catherine. 'Daddy's had to go to see a man about an entail in London and taken Mummy and Desmond with him.'

'Desmond's our elder brother,' said Piers. 'Viscount Hilyard. It's all a bit complicated and Daddy hates to think – '

'I expect the lawyers just shake him till he wakes and show him where to sign,' said Catherine.

'That's probably the way they work it. Desmond, too,' said Piers. They began to walk down the road to where a Bentley waited. Thank God, thought Jane, that the hood was up, then turned to thank the pilot and confirm the time of the return flight.

'Do you do a lot of this?' Catherine asked as he left.

'A lot of what?'

'Oh – you know. Riding in aeroplanes and driving ambulances and helping chaps with shell shock?'

'You read the *Daily World* I gather.'

'Granny does. She laps it up. So do we, rather.'

'And what do you do?'

'Oxford,' said Catherine. 'We should be there now as a matter of fact but we much preferred to stay here and meet you.'

'Won't there be trouble for you?'

'We'll be fined,' said Piers. 'We quite often are.'

'Piers reckons it keeps the dons in port. His. . . . Not mine. He's at the House. I'm at Lady Margaret Hall. The House is Christ Church, by the way.'

'I know,' said Jane. 'My father and two of my brothers went to Oxford. I nearly went myself.'

'Only you went to war instead,' said Catherine.

'I do wish I wasn't. At Oxford, I mean,' said Piers. 'Oxford was a mistake.'

'What should you have done?'

'Army. Only I rather promised Granny and there we are. Still, this term isn't so bad. I've managed to get three days hunting a week.'

'Me too,' said Catherine.

They were still standing outside the car, and the silver fox was rapidly becoming sodden.

'Do you think perhaps we should get inside?' said Jane.

'Yes of course,' said Piers, who had been brooding so intensely that the rain held no meaning. Oxford and hunting. Hell and heaven, if she read his face aright. He opened the door.

– 349 –

'Shall I drive – or would you prefer to?' he asked.

'You, please.' She ached to drive that car, but she had no doubt that he did too, and Bridget O'Dowd was as yet unsold.

34

H E DROVE FAST and well, but took the most appalling risks, at blind corners, 'S' bends, and overtaking carts, or donkeys, or other cars. Jane willed herself to listen as Catherine prattled on, apparently unaware that there was any other way to drive, and at last the gates of Mangan Castle appeared, and Piers waited impatiently for the lodge keeper, and shot off again down the gravelled drive. Then the final stop, precisely in front of the main doors of the castle. Not that it was a castle. What was left of the original fortress was a couple of miles northwards, close to the village. This house was eighteenth century in every classical line. A butler appeared, followed by a footman who headed for the suitcases, and the twins walked in with her, into a massive hallway that was graced with the most elegant double staircase Jane had ever seen. All the furniture she could see was Chippendale or Heppelwhite, or contemporary Irish copies, the pictures looked at once beautiful and expensive – one surely was a Rubens? Even the carpet she trod on was a washed-silk masterpiece from China. There was no thread of possibility that this was the home of the poverty-stricken. Charm was all she had left. The Earl of Mangan was far, far richer than she.

'Granny says you'll probably want a rest and a bath and things,' said Catherine. 'I'll take you up.'

'Sherry down here at seven,' said Piers. 'We dine quite early. Granny doesn't like to be up late.'

What Granny liked was obviously what everyone else had to like, too, thought Jane. Strange that two such forceful youngsters should allow themselves to be dominated. She followed Catherine up the left-hand staircase.

'We've put you in the Blue Room,' Catherine said. 'It's rather your colour, I think you'll agree.'

A pretty room, really exquisitely pretty, padded furniture, deep-pile carpet, and a fire burning in the grate. One picture only, but the one was a Canaletto view of the Thames. And Catherine had been right about the blue. It was exactly the kind she liked; neither coy nor strident.

'It's heavenly,' she said.

'Granny and I think it's our best, though not for brunettes of course. Mucky little blighters like me. You are lucky being fair.'

And I was envying her that dark beauty she has in such abundance, thought Jane.

'Have we given you everything you need? Books? Cigarettes? Matches? I *think* so. Yes. All here.'

She looked at Jane's suitcases, brought ahead of them.

'Shall I send a maid to unpack?'

'Yes please,' said Jane. 'She can do it while I bathe.'

'Bathroom's just here.'

Catherine opened a door to reveal a vast and elegant bathroom. Not even the need to walk in one's dressing gown down a corridor whistling with draughts. Here were riches indeed.

'I'll let you rest,' Catherine said, then; 'Granny's dying to meet you. And I must say I'm glad we stayed on. Those dons need their port after all.'

She left then, and Jane took off her coat, then lit a cigarette and went to the window. From it she could see the grass and flowers of a formal garden, glittering in the rain, and beyond, a lake that gleamed, more silver than grey, then, as she watched, a flock of wild swans flew across it. Like a poem by Yeats, she thought, and all done by money.

At exactly seven o'clock she went downstairs to meet Granny, the Dowager Countess of Mangan. She wore yet another Paris gown, from Poiret. When she'd packed in London she'd worried because it had looked so grand, but now she needed it as a Crusader needed armour when he rode against the Saracens. Cream silk with an abstract pattern of blue, the same blue as her room. She walked down the sweep of the staircase, as elegant as a debutante's curtsey, and at the foot Piers was waiting for her. Black tie, she noticed, and the claret-coloured jacket of some Oxford dining club or other.

'Charming,' he said. 'Absolutely charming.' And then, 'Come and meet Granny.' There was no doubt about it, thought Jane. Here they were all horses, and Granny the only jockey.

Piers took her by the arm and led her into a small drawing room, – Aubusson carpet, Louis Quinze furniture, – where Catherine sat with an old and dumpy woman in grey, who looked, Jane thought, as Queen Victoria must have looked, if ever she had felt cheerful.

'Granny,' said Piers, 'this is Jane Whitcomb. Miss Whitcomb – my grandmother, the Dowager Countess of Mangan.'

'How do you do?' said Jane. 'I'm awfully grateful to you for asking me here.'

'It's us that are glad you came,' said the dowager countess. 'We don't often get the chance to entertain exciting folk like you. Aeroplanes indeed.' And she giggled.

This was something of which she'd had no warning. The dowager countess had not been born an aristocrat. Her accent reminded Jane very much of her Uncle Walter, but yet was not quite the same. A little further south perhaps? But she was every bit as sure of herself as Uncle Walter had been.

'Do you like sherry?' the dowager countess asked.

Jane had decided that honesty was the only chance she had. 'Not much, I'm afraid.'

'Get her one of your cocktails,' the dowager countess told Piers. 'I'll have one as well.' And then to Jane: 'I can't abide sherry.'

Piers poured, and the dowager countess said: 'You have a lovely life.' It was a statement rather than a question.

'More often than not,' said Jane, 'but I lost my father just recently – and an aunt I was very fond of.'

'She married Walter Nettles,' said the dowager countess.

'Why, yes, she did,' said Jane.

'Then I've no doubt she had her share of a lovely life too,' said the dowager countess, then stopped.

'Oh – do go on,' said Catherine.

'Not for you,' said her grandmother. 'But he was a lovely man.'

'Yes, he was,' said Jane. There could be no doubt that the older woman meant it. 'And he was a man who made things happen.'

'What things?' It was Piers this time, putting a glass into her hand.

Renting a stately home as if it were a weekend cottage, she thought, being bowled by Vinney because he couldn't read her off-break.

'He bought an ambulance and insisted I had to drive it.'

'He *made* you?' Catherine asked.

'Not me,' said Jane. 'The War Office.'

'That Walter,' said the dowager countess. 'His family and mine – we were in the same line of business. Light engineering. Only he went off to India.'

And married Aunt Pen, thought Jane. And you married an earl.

'I'd like it if you'd call me Emily,' said the dowager countess. 'Being a titled lady's all very well and I've never regretted it – but I was born Emily Parkin.'

'Parkin's Car Components,' said Jane at once. So that was where the money came from.

The dowager countess smiled. 'You would know, wouldn't you? Being a driver yourself.'

Catherine said, 'I should call her Emily at once before she changes her mind.'

'And that's enough sauce from you,' said the dowager countess, and then to Jane: 'Well girl? Not holding back on me are you?'

'We have business to discuss,' said Jane.

'We have not. That horse is yours.'

'Granny,' said Piers. 'She's Daddy's horse.'

'Do you think your father would deny me the chance to do a bit of good in the world? And anyway I told – asked him before he went to London. He was more than glad.'

'Of course I'll pay for him,' said Jane.

'You'll do no such thing.'

'But I must,' said Jane.

'All right,' the dowager countess said, and turned to the twins. 'How much? The truth mind.'

Piers said, 'She's in foal you know. And she had a filly with her when Daddy bought her at that auction in Abingdon, and he bought her too. Do you want them both?'

'If I may.'

Brother and sister looked at each other. Jane had no doubt she was witnessing that telepathic quality that twins were said to possess.

'A hundred and twenty the two,' said Catherine at last, and Piers nodded his agreement.

'Bridget's a bit long in the tooth now but she's a damn good brood mare,' he said, 'and Bridie – that's her filly – could do very well indeed. A shade light, but she can go.'

'I'll write a cheque now if you like.'

'Sit down, girl,' said the dowager countess. 'You young people are always in a rush. Even watching you tires me.'

'Yes, Emily,' said Jane demurely.

'Oh super,' said Catherine, and Piers laughed aloud.

The dowager countess snorted. 'Because you're a celebrity you think you can say what you like, I suppose.'

'Indeed no,' said Jane. 'I'm trying to say what you like.'

This time the dowager countess smiled.

It was a pleasant evening, of a kind she didn't have all that often. Time spent with people older – and younger – than herself. Two who could hardly remember the war, and one who could remember long, long before it. And yet it was obvious that Catherine and Piers not only loved their grandmother but were perfectly at ease with her, as she was with all three of them. She had got what she wanted with no effort at all, but that wasn't it. The pleasure was in the people themselves.

The old woman's main preoccupation was power, but she was good at it, and handled it well, as she cajoled the twins into talking about themselves. They ate in the breakfast parlour, to the butler's rigid indignation. There was a guest present after all. But Granny was unyielding. 'There's twenty yards of mahogany across the way,' she said, 'and tomorrow I'll call a few neighbours in and you can show off another one of your frocks, but tonight we'll eat in comfort.' And indeed they did, thought Jane. Asparagus from their own garden, salmon from their own river. Even the most rigid patriots were drinking hock again, and Emily was not that. She enjoyed her hock too much.

'Are you enjoying Oxford?' Jane asked.

'It's all right,' said Catherine. Piers said nothing.

'What I mean is I'm reading history,' said Catherine, 'and I do read it – quite often, actually. Though not as much in the hunting season.'

'Naturally,' said Jane, and the younger woman gurgled her appreciation.

'What I mean,' Catherine said, 'is that it's frightfully interesting – all that stuff about Napoleon and Oliver Cromwell and Frederick the Great, but it won't ever get me anywhere. I mean it can't.'

All three men of action, Jane thought. Men of power. It seemed as if Catherine had acquired her grandmother's preoccupation.

'And do you read history too?' she asked Piers.

'When I must,' he said, then asked her how often she hunted. It was the only time that her friend Emily appeared less than content.

After dinner the twins declined coffee and went to sort through gramophone records. Jane and the dowager countess sat on.

'You seem to like my grandchildren,' the older woman said.

'How could I not?'

'There's a lot don't. They frighten some.'

'Frighten?'

'You should see them on horseback,' said the dowager countess – and she *had* seen Piers drive a car.

'The girl's all right,' the older woman continued. 'She'll marry some MP or other, and steer him to the top – but Piers,' she paused, then sighed. 'Piers is a problem.'

'You mean because he's a younger son?'

'Desmond's a good boy with a few more brains than his father. He'll manage the estate well enough – if our new masters leave us an estate to manage. And Piers won't interfere. It isn't that. He doesn't like Oxford.'

'I gathered that. What does he like?'

'The army.' The older woman sighed. 'He's always wanted the army. I asked him to try Oxford first and he agreed because he loves me. I hoped it might just be a passing fancy but there's no hope of that. The army will get him.'

'But whyever not?'

'The army got my husband too,' said the older woman. 'Or rather some bloody Boer farmer did. And I knew enough that died in the last one. And you must have known even more.'

'Two brothers – and my fiancé,' said Jane. 'But that was the war and it's over. Surely you can't think it will happen again? We're at peace.'

'Piers doesn't want to join the army to be at peace,' said the older woman. 'He'll find a war somewhere.'

Jane remembered the ex-officer in Jabber's waiting room, off to China to fight the war lords. It seemed as though men could always find a war if they needed one badly enough.

'Oxford will help him,' said Jane. 'He's bright anyway, but Oxford will make him think, and it's the thinking soldier who gets on.'

'I've just told you,' the older woman rasped. 'I don't want him to get on.'

'I was with the army for more than two years,' said Jane. 'I never once met a general who was shot at.'

Emily snorted. 'Good girl,' she said. 'And who taught *you* to think?'

'My father,' said Jane. 'He was an Oxford man.'

The older woman snorted again, as Piers and Catherine returned with a gramophone and records.

'We thought we might dance for a while,' said Catherine.

'What's the joke?' asked Piers.

'No joke taking care of the future,' said his grandmother, and Catherine put on a foxtrot. Piers went at once to Jane.

'May I?' he asked.

His dancing was as strong and skilful as his driving – unless one were in love with him, she thought, but I'm not. Any more than I'm in love with Bob.

Piers had an exhausting night of it, dancing with both ladies in turn, and even Lady Mangan insisted on a last waltz, dancing with intense concentration and counting audibly. One two three – one two three – *one* two three, and then looked at her watch pendant and announced that it was bedtime.

Piers said, 'I'll just take a look outside.'

'Well don't be all night about it,' said his grandmother.

He went off at once, and Catherine went to the window.

'Do come and look,' she said.

Jane joined her, and shortly she could see Piers, elegant in his dining-club jacket, and carrying a double-barrelled shotgun.

'What on earth – ?' said Jane. 'Poachers?'

'The IRA,' said Catherine.

'But I thought De Valera and Michael Collins had settled all that,' Jane said.

'The IRA won't be settled till it wants to,' said the old woman, 'and God knows when that will be.'

'Will they be armed?'

'If they come – of course they'll be armed,' said Catherine. 'They know Piers.' The thought seemed to please her.

'The local ones don't bother me,' said her grandmother. 'It's those loonies in Dublin I worry about.'

Then Piers came back in, the gun already put away.

'Nothing,' he said.

'How dreadful for you,' said his sister. 'Didn't you kill *any-body*?'

'I never said I'd kill them,' said Piers. 'I said I'd shoot them. And so I will.'

'Oh go to bed you bloodthirsty young devils,' said their grand-mother, and they obeyed her, but they kissed her before they went.

'I hope he doesn't spend too much time here,' said Jane.

'No more than I can help,' said Lady Mangan, 'but it is his home – and he loves it.'

'You really think he's safe from the local whatever it is – Chapter? Branch?'

'Battalion,' said her grandmother. She rose and took Jane's arm, moved to the door.

'Pretending to be soldiers?' said Jane.

'But their bullets are real. Still, they won't bother Piers.'

'Whyever not?'

'Parkin's Car Components,' said Lady Mangan. 'I've found jobs for half Mangan village there. They'd lose them quick if anything happened to Piers.'

Next day Piers and Catherine took her to the field where Bridget and her filly were out at pasture. They went in the Bentley, and this time Jane drove. A brute of a car, thought Jane, that needed all her strength: arrogant and assertive, frantic to excel. It reminded her of Jay Bower, and the way she had to use female cunning instead of male strength to achieve any kind of control reminded her of him too.

When they arrived, Catherine said, 'You really are good.'

'Better than me,' said Piers, but already his eyes were on the horses. She followed his gaze, and recognised Bridget at once.

A little longer in the tooth, she thought, a little more portly, but still so much the horse she knew that the field might have been in France. And beside her her filly, Bridie, a little lighter, as Piers had said, but with almost the same markings. Suddenly Jane amazed her host and hostess, and herself, by bursting into tears. But there was no thudding of guns, no vision of dismembered gun teams. Piers handed her a handkerchief large enough to satisfy even Jabber, and she dabbed at her eyes.

'It brought it all back, you see,' she said.

Piers produced a cigarette case and offered it round.

'Want to talk about it?' he asked. 'Because if you do we'd rather like to hear.'

'Oh yes please,' said Catherine.

And out it all came. Trooper O'Dowd and the Royal Northumbrians' first adjutant, and Goosey Gander and all the others, until it was John's turn, and John was the last, and he died.

'What a heartrending story,' said Catherine. 'No wonder you cried.'

'Rather wonderful though,' said Piers.

Oh dear, thought Jane. If my friend Emily hears it I'll never get Bridget. Or Bridie.

'I do wish I could ride her,' she said.

'You could ride Bridie,' said Catherine.

'I'd love to,' said Jane, 'but I haven't any gear.'

'Mummy's would fit you,' said Catherine. 'I'm sure she wouldn't mind.'

Nor did the dowager, and Jane found herself kitted out in very smart jodhpurs and handmade boots. Catherine and Piers rode with her and, like her, they took their fences straight and true. Bridie proved every bit as clever over the jumps as her mother, which was as well. Both Catherine and Piers were superb in the saddle, and with mounts that matched their skill.

'You ride well,' said Catherine, as they rode back to the stables.

'Very well,' said Piers.

'I had to, to keep up with you two.'

'Where did you learn?'

'India,' said Jane. 'There are wonderful places to ride.'

'Don't you miss it?' asked Catherine.

'I used to,' said Jane, 'but now I have so much to do I've no time to miss anything.'

'Those poor people?' He says it as one might say 'Those marmosets' or 'Those aardvarks', she thought. Creatures heard of, read about in books, but never encountered.

'What do you hope to do about them? Make them less poor?'

'Eventually,' said Jane. 'For the moment there isn't enough money for that. All I can do is help to make life a little better for the very worst off.'

'A lot of them were soldiers,' said Piers.

'Like my John. . . . Or sailors. But half of them are women.'

Catherine laughed. 'There's men for you,' she said, and turned to Jane. 'It must be worse for the women. Having babies. . . . Bringing up children.'

'Perhaps it is,' said Jane. 'But they bear it better. Maybe it's just our nature, or maybe it's because they have things to do, homes to run.'

'Poor devils,' said Piers. 'Why don't they start a revolution or something? I know I would.'

'Some of them are all for it,' said Jane. 'Perhaps there'll be more if things don't get better.'

The formal dinner that night was as dull and undemanding as such things usually are, except that on her left Jane found that she had an actor from the Abbey Theatre, and on her right an old Indian Civil Servant who had known Kalpur well. The dowager had gone to great lengths to see that she wouldn't be too bored. She'd been given by far the two most interesting men in the room. . . . As she undressed before the fire she thought: It's strange John is so close to me I feel as if he could walk in at any moment: as if we'd been married for years. And yet he'd never been in a house like this in his life.

That night she dreamed that the two of them were out riding together, in the maidan at Kalpur, but when the time came to turn back, only she rode off to the stables. John headed for the village, and the countryside beyond.

Next morning the twins asked if her aeroplane would be big enough for them, too, and she couldn't lie. How could she? They'd both seen it. At first the dowager was opposed to the idea, but in the end she gave in. At least it was a way of getting Piers out of Ireland. She hugged Jane warmly before she left.

'Catherine told me the story of Bridget,' she said. 'All those sad, brave young men.'

'I hope you didn't mind?'

'I don't suppose you had much choice in that matter,' the dowager said. 'Did Piers say how he'd get the horses to England?'

'He said your agent would handle it and send me the bill.'

'By far the best way,' said the dowager. 'Though I wish you'd come and fetch them yourself. I'd like to see you again. Will you come back?'

'As soon as I can,' said Jane.

'Good lass,' the dowager said. 'I'd like to hear some more about Walter Nettles.'

35

THE PILOT ACCEPTED two extra passengers and luggage without a blink and took the aeroplane from a field in Meath to Croydon the way a bus driver might go from Marble Arch to Kensington High Street, but the twins didn't see it that way. Their eyes blazed with excitement throughout the flight.

Please God let them stick to horses, thought Jane, and when they got down at last, and found that the Rolls was waiting, she asked where she could drop them.

'Paddington,' said Catherine. 'If we get the first train to Oxford we can be back in our cells before they can lock us out.'

The car moved off. Jane offered cigarettes, and as Piers lit hers, she asked him cautiously, 'Have you decided on the RAF instead?'

'No,' said Piers, 'but they're fascinating things, aren't they? They can move you around so quickly, and they're bound to get bigger, wouldn't you say?'

'Oh don't be serious,' his sister said. 'There's a meet near Woodstock on Saturday.'

Foch was pleased to see her back, in a formal sort of way. Hawkins was more effusive. The house had been like a tomb, she said, though Jane rather got the impression that she'd spent most of her time at South Terrace, consulting with Lionel and bossing workmen, an impression confirmed by Lionel when she telephoned him.

'A tartar,' he said, 'a positive fiend. Though sound on plumbing.'

'I hope she didn't try to interfere with *your* ideas.'

'Well she did,' said Lionel, 'but she failed, because I'm even more of a fiend than she is when roused, and much, much more of a bitch. Come and see the work in progress tomorrow.'

'I can't,' she said. 'Not tomorrow. I have to go to Paris.'

'*Have* to? You're only just back from Ireland. You journalists do see the world.'

'It's the Quart' Arts Ball.'

'Is it indeed? You just watch what you're up to, Jane Whitcomb. We don't want you turning into a gadabout.'

Little chance of that, thought Jane. Gadabouts are supposed to enjoy their gadding. She slept late and was woken by a call from Bower.

'It's urgent, miss,' said Hawkins.

The ones from Bower were always urgent – for Bower. She yawned her way to the hall and the precise intersection of its two draughts.

'Yes?' she said.

'What a greeting. Ireland OK?' Then without a pause, 'It must have been since you didn't call me. You can tell me all about it on the plane.'

'Which plane?'

'The one that's going to Paris. I may not have time to stay long. You've got a costume fitting at Mutrie's. Eleven thirty.'

'Costume?'

'Certainly costume,' said Bower. 'The Quart' Arts is fancy dress.'

'And who am I to be?'

'Cleopatra,' said Bower.

'And you, I presume, will be Mark Antony?'

'Do I look that stupid? Julius Caesar, that's who I am. Wait till you see me in a toga.'

'He was bald,' said Jane. 'That's why he had to wear all those laurel wreaths.'

But Bower was already talking. 'Don't forget,' he said. 'Mutrie's at eleven thirty, Croydon at three. Or shall I collect you?'

'Collect me,' said Jane. 'I adore being collected.'

She hung up. As if I were a stamp or a cigarette card or something, she thought.

Cleopatra didn't exactly overburden herself with clothes, a fact she took up immediately she joined him in the car.

'I'd hate to take one of your photograph calls in that costume,' she said.

'You never told me you were a prude,' he said.

'The way you go on how can I be?' she said. 'But there'll be publicity photographs, I suppose? And in your paper? They read it a lot in Felston. Not many actually buy it,' she added nastily, 'but they go to the public library and read it. And in Felston they're prudes to a man – *and* woman, which is more to the point.'

'We'll get you a cloak,' said Bower. 'I'd hate to lose my big order in Felston public library.'

They moved on towards Croydon and she told him about Ireland.

'A good horse, you say?'

'She and her filly.'

'You think you could write me a piece about it?'

'I could,' she said, 'but it wouldn't be a very sad piece. And I'd still have to mention Felston of course.'

'Of course.'

'I can hardly mention Felston when I do my piece on the Quart' Arts Ball.'

'It'll be on your by-line,' said Bower. 'Now let me tell you about the guy you're going to meet.'

'Go ahead.'

'His name is Billy Powell,' said Bower. 'His wife's a relative of my sister's husband. The two of them live in Paris. He's sort of strange.'

'They live in Paris by choice?'

'Oh sure. I'm not saying my sister's husband's heartbroken, but they're in Paris because they like it there.'

'What does he do?'

'Writer,' said Bower. Of course every second American in Paris is a writer. The rest are either painters or musicians. But Billy at least works at it when he isn't getting drunk or smoking hashish or firing his revolver. . . . Or chasing women,' he added.

'Will he chase me?'

'Bound to,' said Bower. 'I'll be upset if he doesn't.'

'He sounds wild.'

'Wild enough.'

'Was he in the war?' said Jane. 'Was it that kind of wildness?'

'You catch on quick,' said Bower, as if she had just reinforced his faith in his taste in women. 'I guess you know all about that.'

'No more than you,' she said.

'God knows that's enough. Billy was like you. He drove an ambulance.'

'And was he blown up like me too?'

'Yes,' said Bower. 'He was.'

'I don't think I'm going to like this job very much,' said Jane.

'That's journalism for you,' said Bower. 'Half the time you hate what you're doing but you go right on doing it because that's what gets you your pay cheque and your name in the paper – or Felston's.'

He was right, and she knew he was right, and she couldn't tell him about the nightmares. She couldn't tell anyone. John and Bridget O'Dowd and the happy times, yes, but not the nightmares.

'I don't mean I won't do it,' she said. 'Of course I will, but don't expect me to enjoy it. Unless – is he good-looking?'

'A lot of women think so.'

'In that case I might enjoy the chasing bit,' she said.

They were staying at the Ritz in adjacent suites, which did not surprise her. Indeed it had a kind of inevitability about it. In so many ways Jay Bower *was* the Ritz. The American bar alone seemed designed as a setting for him. They bathed and changed, and went to dine with the Powells. When Jane said she assumed that they had been invited Jay said of course, and if the Powells had remembered they had a very good chance of being fed.

At that time they lived in the XVth Arrondissement, in the rue Scribe, in a tall, narrow house with a small, elegant garden and courtyard. Jay paid off the taxi and said, 'Billy's wife's called Florence. She has a claim to fame too.'

'She paints?'

'She invented the brassière,' said Jay. 'Or a lot of people say she did.'

'Then I shall be nice to her at least,' said Jane.

The Powells had remembered their coming, or somebody had; perhaps the admirable manservant who admitted them; lean, clean and elegant, and nothing at all to do with the vie de bohème. Both Florence and Billy were in the salon to meet them, Florence sober, Billy reasonably so. Florence still had the remains of what Jane would later realise was a typically American prettiness, fresh-faced, and with just a hint of athleticism. There was a suggestion of weariness too, as well there might be, thought Jane, if what she had heard of her husband was true.

Powell was very tall and very thin, and dressed, as he always was, in black and white, though not in a dinner jacket, as Bower was. Black jacket of what looked like doeskin and trousers of the same material, white shirt of heavy silk, and the sort of black tie one wore at funerals. Three carnations in his lapel; two white, the one in the middle dyed black. Black hair, too, much, much too black to be natural. Black like soot. He opened a bottle of champagne. Veuve Clicquot, Jane noticed. Well, widows had their own blackness.

'Champagne for the Philistines,' said Powell. 'They don't deserve it, but at least they're family.' He poured four glasses and the bottle was empty. The manservant passed them round and was told to go.

'Here's to the lady Philistine,' said Powell, and gulped down half a glassful.

'She's not a Philistine,' said Bower. 'She's a philanthropist.'

'She's the one you wrote about? The one who wants to prop up the existing social system?'

'That's the one.'

'Then she's an idiot.'

Jane put down her glass. 'What a fool you are,' she said easily. 'If you go on like this I shall slap your face very hard, and then either you will assault me or your wife will feel obliged to do so, and poor Jay, who is much stronger than you by the look of you, will be obliged to join in and knock you down.'

'I've got a revolver,' said Powell.

'I don't think anyone even as stupid as you appear to be would use it to shoot a female philanthropist.' Jane picked up her glass and sipped.

'Now wait a minute – ' Powell's wife said.

'No,' said Powell. 'That's OK.' He turned to Jane. 'You know you interest me.'

He says it as if it were a compliment, thought Jane, as though nobody had interested him in years. 'I'd like to write about you,' Powell continued.

'Snap,' said Bower, and then as Powell turned to him. 'I told you.'

'Hey, that's right,' said Powell.

'I think I've changed my mind,' said Jane. 'I can meet all the Communist champagne swiggers I want in Cambridge.'

'Who are you calling a Communist?' said Powell. 'Just because I spoke about the existing social system, I suppose?'

'Then what is going to take its place?'

'Nothing,' said Powell. 'It's all over; the whole stupid mess. Over and finished. Only it didn't end with that big bang we all expected; it's just winding down like a gramophone. Kind of friendly of God to leave us a little time to enjoy ourselves, but when the record's finished – we're finished too.'

'And how long do you reckon we have?' Bower said.

Powell shrugged, gulped down what was left of his glass, and took another bottle of champagne from the cooler.

'Who knows?' he said. 'Who could possibly know except God, and why should he tell? But my guess is soon, very soon. Maybe tonight.' He twisted the cork and it popped discreetly, as well-chilled champagne should, refilled his glass and turned to Jane. 'Let's you and I go somewhere and write about each other,' he said.

'Are you quite sure you'll be strong enough to write?' she asked.

'I've got pills you can take for that,' he said. 'I'll be OK. You too.'

'Aren't they dangerous?'

'What difference does it make?' he said. 'I already told you. It's all over. Why don't you listen?'

'Perhaps she doesn't share your simple faith,' said Bower.

Jane said, 'I've had enough danger for one lifetime. I prefer to go on propping up the existing social system.'

'Danger?' said Powell. 'You? *You* are going to tell *me* about danger? You sit there in your Paquin dress – '

– 367 –

'Worth,' said his wife. Taciturn she may be, thought Jane, but she believes in accuracy.

'She drove an ambulance,' said Bower. 'Like you.'

'Yeah. . . . You told me in your letter. But I was blown up.'

'So was she,' said Bower.

At once Powell looked like a child who had been robbed of its best toy. And so he had, thought Jane. It was his uniqueness.

'Were you hurt?' he asked.

It too had been part of her sickness, Jabber had said, but she would not tell him so, or the others, either.

'No,' she said.

'Nor me. Except – it's funny, and it certainly can't be defined as a hurt or any kind of wound for that matter – it was only after it had happened to me that I needed to write at least one good thing before the world ended. Are you sure you don't want to go somewhere and talk about it?'

'Quite sure,' said Jane.

'But whyever not? Florence will have Jay here for company.'

'He'll have me for company too,' said Jane.

The implications of Powell's remark had startled her, but she had no need to reply. The manservant came in and announced dinner.

Soup à l'oseille, medaillons de boeuf, green salad, apple tart, and Château Montrose to drink, bottles and bottles of it. Powell didn't eat much, but Bower and Florence tucked in well, she noticed, and so did she. The food was delicious. If she ate much more the Cleopatra costume would have to be stuck on with glue. The manservant handled the plates, but Powell poured the wine so that no glass was ever empty, including his own.

'Did you ever carry one of my countrymen in your ambulance days?' Powell asked.

She said at once, 'No. I never did. I wasn't near your part of the Front. I carried just about everybody else, though.'

'Who, for example?'

'Oh – British, Canadians, Australians, French.'

'No Germans?'

That question again. 'Them too.'

'Why, Miss Whitcomb? Why carry them?'

'Because they couldn't walk,' said Jane.

'I carried mostly French – and then Americans, when we finally got here. But I don't think I could have carried Germans. What do you make of that, Jay?'

Bower looked up, slow, unhurried, but a blow had landed and had hurt. 'Why nothing, Billy,' he said. 'What is there to make of it, except that you and Miss Whitcomb are very different people.'

Florence Powell began to talk of the ball they were going to next evening. Everyone, but everyone, what the French called le tout Paris would be there. She tried to question Jane about her costume, but Powell forbade it. Fancy-dress costumes, he insisted, should be a surprise. Well hers could well be that, thought Jane.

After dinner the men stayed on at the table, while Florence took Jane back to the salon. No port was produced by Powell, but he was already pouring more claret as the two women left. Most unusual in France, thought Jane, and then: Money. It must be that. To live in this kind of style even in Paris must cost a great deal of money, and Powell didn't look as if he could hold on to the stuff for long. He certainly looked incapable of making it. . . . The manservant brought coffee, and Florence Powell poured.

'You work for Jay, Miss Whitcomb?'

'Sometimes. But I'm not on his staff.'

'You're a freelance?'

'Why, yes,' said Jane. 'I suppose I am.' For some reason the thought was pleasing. 'But most of my time is occupied with charity work.'

'And do you enjoy that?'

'Enormously.' It was perfectly true, and yet quite obviously Florence Powell didn't believe a word.

'And you,' said Jane. 'Jay tells me that you are a creative person, too.' She saw that Mrs Powell was on to the use of the name 'Jay' rather than 'Mr Bower' in a flash. It could only mean one, or possibly two things, to her. Either she was rich, or she was sleeping with Bower, or both.

'Inventive rather than creative,' said Mrs Powell at last. 'I assume you are referring to the brassière?'

'I am indeed. How did one manage without them? How clever you are.'

'It's in the family,' said Mrs Powell. 'My grandfather patented a new kind of printing press.'

And is that where your money meets with the Bowers'? Jane wondered.

They talked about dresses then, until at last the men reappeared. Powell was looking pleased with himself, and not appreciably drunker than he had been when she had seen him last. He immediately offered brandy, which Jane declined.

'Tell you what,' said Powell. 'Let's drive over to Montparnasse. There are some great cafés there. The Dôme or the Coupole or somewhere.'

Bower looked at her, and she nodded slightly.

'Who's going to drive?' Bower asked.

'That's kind of a nasty remark,' said Powell. 'But I guess we can put our lives in Miss Whitcomb's hands.'

'Sure you can,' said Bower, 'but we haven't signed those papers yet.'

'Then let's do it and get in the car,' said Powell. 'Let's enjoy ourselves.'

Pleasure at any cost, thought Jane, but whatever papers were being signed, Florence Powell knew all about it. She didn't move as the two men went out once more.

'Pleasure seems to be my husband's only aim, wouldn't you say?' she asked.

'An Epicurean, certainly.'

'I suppose it's mine, too. Even inventing things. It's a pleasure.'

'More cerebral than most,' said Jane.

'Oh sure,' said Mrs Powell. 'But when you believe the world will end soon – I mean really, deep-down believe it – '

'And do you really believe that too?'

Mrs Powell said wearily, 'What does it matter what I believe? It's what Billy believes. It's what makes him the special person he is.'

You say that as a priest who had lost his faith might say the creed, thought Jane, but all she said was, 'I see.'

Mrs Powell said, 'If you don't mind, Miss Whitcomb, perhaps we should get our coats. Billy doesn't like to be kept waiting.'

'Certainly,' said Jane, and wondered if the Powell car, whatever it was, would prove driveable by a lady wearing a Worth dress, Uncle Walter's sable coat and evening sandals that weighed about six ounces apiece.

It was a Voisin, if anything rather larger than the Hilyards' Bentley, but rather less powerful, and much more amenable to female driving. Bower's faith in her had been justified, but Billy Powell sulked rather when he found that she knew the way to Montparnasse without being told. He'd looked forward to playing the old Paris hand helping out a tourist.

Still, the Dôme was packed with writer, amateur, professional, real, and in certain cases, quite unreal, and Billy revived at once. He knew them all, from the burly American who drank wine by the bottle the way other people drank by the glass, to the slight, acid Irishman who accepted two very large Napoleon brandies as no more than his due. But it was the Americans who drank the hardest, almost with dedication, and suddenly Jane remembered why. In America they had this thing called Prohibition, and so they had come to Paris to catch up, or at least, according to Bower, to drink the sort of stuff that didn't taste of the bath tub it had been made in.

It was fun for a while, but then Florence Powell returned to what Jane guessed to be habitual taciturnity, and Powell wandered from table to table, drinking at every one, and occasionally bringing what he considered a particularly choice specimen to them for inspection. They included a very drunk yet strangely prim young American with a wife, who, Jane saw at once, was in dire need of Jabber Lockhart, and a couple of grim females who would have made Fred seem positively girlish. All of them invited Jane and Bower to visit them, but as Powell had omitted to introduce them the chances seemed remote.

When Bower said that they would leave, Powell was incredulous. There was still so much fun to be had. He was still declaiming pleasure's necessity when Bower went out and hailed a taxi.

'Goodness, how exhausting,' said Jane.

'His kind of fun always is,' said Bower, then to the taxi driver, 'Ritz Hotel.'

'Do you still want me to write about it?'

'Him, them, the Arts Ball tomorrow. The works.'

'But why?'

'There's Felston,' said Bower, 'and there's Billy Powell – the other side of the coin, living over here because he can get a bottle of champagne in Paris for the price of a Coca-Cola in New York for as long as the dollar stays strong.'

'He can also make his share of improper suggestions. More than his share.'

'He does his share of screwing I guess, and some of it may be fun. Most of it's more like necessity, because he's written his life like a novel, and that's the part he's going to play. You ever think about promiscuity?'

'Never,' said Jane firmly.

'The way I see it,' said Bower unheeding, 'it's more like ego than satisfaction. You take the girl for what she might be, without taking the trouble to find out what she is. It's like the Loterie Nationale. How can you be sure of winning unless you buy all the tickets?'

'And you only want one ticket? The winner? Is that what you're telling me?'

'Well maybe I've won a few smaller prizes too,' said Bower.

She nipped his wrist viciously and he yelled, and the taxi driver drove on stolidly. Americans. . . .

In the lift Jay Bower said, 'Now it's my turn to make an improper suggestion.'

'More than time,' said Jane, 'and I shall yield to your im-passioned pleadings – but in my room, not yours. I've no wish to scurry about the hotel corridor in my dressing gown, fetching though it is.'

'I like your nightgown,' he said, and began to remove it. 'Not much of it but what there is is pretty.'

'Not like that,' she said, and wriggled. 'You'll tear the lace. There.' His arms came round her.

When they had done he asked for one of her cigarettes, a rare thing for him who smoked only cigars – but not in her suite. She lit up for both of them, cautious of their nakedness, and he drew on the cigarette just once, dragging the smoke deep down, before he stubbed it out, pulled back the sheets and looked at her body.

'The nightgown was pretty all right,' he said, 'but you're a lot prettier. You're beautiful.'

'So that's why you took it off?'

'That's why.' He began to stroke her in a way she liked very much. 'You could still be my winning ticket,' he said. 'My first prize.'

'If this is a proposal of marriage,' she said, 'you should stop what you're doing, delightful though it is, and get down on one knee.'

He got out of bed and knelt on one knee.

'Please marry me,' he said.

But she would not. She liked him very well, but she liked her independence better, and was rich enough to afford it, but how could she tell him so? Instead she coaxed him back into bed beside her, coaxed him into doing once more what he did so delightfully.

At last he said, 'Billy Powell reckons he's laid more than three hundred girls – but I bet he's never had this in his life.'

'Not even from Mrs Powell?'

'I guess she'd give it to him if he'd let her,' said Jay. 'Hell. She's given him everything else.'

'Her money?'

'Some. . . . A lot of it's in trust. But he's not a money-grabber – just asks for it when he needs it. And he spends his own just as fast.'

'What then?'

'Her first husband,' said Jay. 'Her children by him that she has to keep out of sight.'

'But that's awful,' said Jane.

'Pleasure can be like that sometimes.'

'Not ours.'

'No, not ours,' he said, 'even if you do force me to live in sin.'

'Just for that you can go back to your own bed,' said Jane, 'and close the door quietly when you go.'

36

GRANDMA LOWERED THE magnifying glass and looked at her audience. Only Bet and Bob were there. Stan had heard of a job at Tyneside Engineering and thought that this time it might be true. Andy had taken one look at the letter in Jane's handwriting and gone off to the library.

'I can't make head nor tail of it,' said Grandma. 'My eyes are getting that bad.'

'Here, let me,' said Bob, and got up to take the letter, but the old woman clung to it. To let go would be to admit the onset of blindness, and she wasn't ready for that yet, not by a long chalk. She raised the glass again.

'People can be very generous in London,' she read slowly, 'provided that you harass them enough. And I've started addressing meetings now and passing the hat round afterwards – and looking scornful if people don't give enough. They very often add a little more, especially the men.'

She lowered the glass and cackled her old woman's laughter.

'By, I wish our John had been spared to enjoy it,' she said. 'It must be a sight worth seeing. Where was I?'

'Especially the men,' said Bet.

'Trust you to remember that,' said Bob.

'Oh give over,' said Bet, and blushed.

'Now that'll do,' said Grandma, and resumed. 'Especially the men. So far I've raised in the vicinity of five hundred pounds more.'

'Another five hundred,' said Bob. 'I wish I lived in that vicinity.'

The old woman said, 'You mean that, don't you? You can't wait to get away.'

'John got away,' said Bob.

'You were all in work then,' said his grandmother. 'We wanted for nowt. But now whoever gets a start'll have to keep the rest.'

Bob said nothing.

'Well?' the old woman snapped. 'Am I right?'

'Yes, Grandma,' he said at last. 'I know. But there's no harm in dreaming.'

'Oh but there is,' said Grandma. 'You keep your mind on Felston. No sense in hankering after the Savoy Hotel. Just be content to hear it on that wireless of yours.' She resumed her reading.

'Give my regards to Dr Stobbs and tell him that a cheque is on its way.' She looked at Bet. 'That reminds me,' she said. 'Friday tomorrow. We'll have to go to the fish quay, pet.'

'Go by tram, will you?' said Bob.

'Bob will you give over,' his sister said.

Grandma ploughed on. 'And that's about it, really. I'll have to post this in rather a hurry as I'm off to Paris tomorrow. Your affectionate friend, Jane Whitcomb.' Carefully she folded up the letter. 'A real caring girl, that one,' she said.

There could be no greater seal of approval.

'Paris?' said Bet. 'What in the world would she want to go to Paris for?'

But this time Bob didn't tease her, just doubled up in an agony of helpless laughter.

Jay looked at Jane in her costume.

'I see what you mean,' he said. 'Just as well you bought that cloak.'

Jane looked into the mirror and saw herself clad in a skirt that didn't begin to hide her legs and left her tummy (and navel) clearly visible, a skimpy example of Mrs Powell's intervention covered in gold lacquer, and a head-dress that had taken the combined efforts of herself and two maids half an hour to put in place.

'All the same,' said Jay, 'it's got its own kind of appeal.'

He reached for her, but she swayed out of his way, smoothly and easily. At least in a costume like that the clothes didn't hold you up.

'Not a chance, my friend,' she said. 'There may not be much but it takes for ever to put on. Try again after the ball.'

'You can bet on it,' said Jay, and opened champagne instead. She watched him as he poured. The toga suited him, and the laurel wreath that looked like gold. He looked every inch the emperor in all but name, but then he was. He handed her a glass.

'Last night we were talking about Billy Powell, but we got sort of sidetracked,' he said.

'Is that what you call it?'

'Make the most of it,' he said amiably. 'Nothing lasts for ever. Not even the Quart' Arts Ball. Did I tell you his wife's money was sort of mixed up with ours? My family's I mean.'

'I sort of gathered it.'

'And from time to time he needs some. Like now. And somebody has to give it to him. Like me. Last night. And get a receipt.'

'The document you referred to.'

He lifted his glass to her. 'O Queen, live for ever,' he said, 'and always be as smart as you are now. So now he's loaded. Ten thousand dollars' worth.'

'Will it last long?'

Jay shrugged. 'Depends what he buys. Three months maybe.'

Ten thousand dollars, two and a half thousand pounds, would keep the entire Patterson family for the rest of their lives.

'I thought you told me drink was cheap here.'

'Cocaine isn't. Or friends. Not his friends anyway. His wife is sort of a relative by marriage.'

'So you said.'

'So naturally Billy knows my family pretty well. Our background. Our name.' He paused.

'I'm listening,' said Jane.

'My name is Joachim Manfred Bauer. That's B-A-U-E-R.' He waited.

'So I should suppose,' said Jane.

'Why should you suppose?'

'Last night he asked me if I ever carried Germans and I said

– 376 –

yes, and he said he couldn't. There had to be a reason for it and you were the only reason there was.'

'Why me?'

'You'd just given him money – and asked for a receipt. '

'I said stay smart,' said Jay, 'but I didn't say too smart.'

'It's in the family,' Jane said smugly. 'My father was a scholar of his college; my brother is a fellow of his.' And then, as Jay looked worried: 'Jay, my darling. What's this all about?'

'You don't mind my being a German?'

'You're an American,' she said. 'You were on our side.'

His arms reached out for her, then dropped.

'Let's get this damn ball over with,' he said. 'I need to hold you.'

The ball was held in a vast hall at Luna Park in the Porte d'Auteuil, and to get in they had to fight their way through a mob that was mostly reporters and photographers. Jane's cloth of gold cloak, covered in what were supposed to be Egyptian hieroglyphics stitched on that afternoon, drew a crowd at once, but the cloak buttoned down the front and not too much leg was showing. When a sheikh and attendant belly-dancer arrived behind her, the photographers left at once.

'Good gracious,' said Jane. 'I feel positively demure.'

They went inside to find – because it was Paris after all – good food and good wine, and an orchestra that could match the Savoy's, but what caught attention at once, what it was for, were the set pieces ranged around its walls. Carefully, brilliantly built for one night and no more were miniature stages, each with its own mise en scène: Hell, Pompeii, a harem, Valhalla, and the rest, each with its own elaborate scenery, its elaborately costumed players. Jay marched firmly to the Roman Orgy stage, which at least explains our costumes, thought Jane.

'Who are we with?' she asked.

'This is the international press stand,' said Bower. 'The photographers won't bother us now.'

Most of the women around her wore even less than she did.

'I'd better take off my cloak then,' she said. 'I feel a positive dowd.'

And she did so, and was introduced to this one and that one: big in *Paris Soir* or the *Trib* or *La Stampa*. From time to time she danced with them or with Jay, but mostly she preferred to observe the merry throng as she reclined on her couch or whatever it was: it was draped in leopardskin which appeared to be real, and scratched rather. And then, bang on midnight, Billy Powell appeared. Billy and Florence, and one or two young men, and rather more young women.

What little the young men and women wore was designed to suggest the fairies of *A Midsummer Night's Dream*, Pease-Blossom and Mustardseed and the rest. The girl who played Puck was almost naked, and with an enviable body. Between them they pulled a sort of chariot that was designed like a lily, and in its cup sat Titania Florence, all in white, in translucent silk so fine it looked like moonbeams, and Billy Oberon, in black silk almost sheer and tight as a skin, and also silver boots and a wig of silver. They went to a bower of roses, forget-me-nots, moss and anemones, all real and already dying. By a rock pool a cascade played, glittering and frothing in the hall's relentless light; a cascade, she learned later, of champagne. But then what else could it be? At least, she thought, he has a sense of style. Not once did he look at her, let alone ask her to dance.

In the taxi Jay asked, 'Enjoy yourself?'

'Hardly,' she said. 'Got up like Theda Bara on an off-day and surrounded by men who could talk about nothing but their circulations.'

'Theda Bara was miles behind you on the best day she ever had.'

'I suppose you know her?' Jay nodded. 'Then mind I don't tell her so. And besides. . . . Quart' Arts. What Four Arts?'

'Music, Literature, Painting,' said Jay.

'And?'

He shrugged. 'Fornication maybe. Wasting Money.'

'Felston seems a long way away.'

'Four or five hundred miles,' he said. 'No more. That's the point I want you to make.'

'I'll be glad to.'

They drove on for a while in silence. 'Billy Powell was wasting money all right,' Bower said at last.

'He wasn't doing too badly at fornication either.'

In her bedroom Jane carefully removed the Cleopatra headdress then turned to where Jay lay waiting.

– 378 –

'Hail Caesar,' she said.

She slept late, not knowing when Jay had left her, and became aware of a persistent tapping.

Breakfast, she thought. Good, strong coffee and the most delicious croissants. Suddenly she didn't mind at all being wakened.

'Un moment,' she called, and reached for her dressing gown to cover her nakedness, but the waiter was already in the room before she had finished fastening it. Except that it wasn't the waiter, it was Billy Powell, still in his Oberon costume and carrying her breakfast tray. He looked drunk but by no means incapable. Deliberately Jane continued to fasten her dressing gown, and found that her fingers were shaking.

'Mr Powell, what on earth do you want?' she said. Her voice at least sounded calm, she thought. For the moment.

'I think that under the circumstances you might at least call me Billy,' he said, in a voice of such sweet reason she could have screamed.

'Who let you in here?'

'The floor waiter,' said Powell.

'He can't have done. It will cost him his job.'

'I gave him five thousand dollars. With that kind of money he can start his own café.' He put the tray down. 'Five thousand dollars was part of what Bower brought me last night,' he said. 'I gave it to be with you.'

'I'm not flattered.'

'Why should you be?' said Powell. 'It's only money. We have to be together.'

'We do not,' said Jane. 'Why should we?'

'We saw it all,' said Powell. 'The dying and the dead. We were both blown up. We nearly joined them. When we make love it will be a fantastic experience. It may even be our last one. It could all end – once we have done. Because after we have come together, what else is left?'

Not only drunk, but mad as a hatter, she thought – or was it drugs? – and talking like a Gothic novel. She was terrified.

'Come on,' said Powell, and stepped towards her. 'It'll be wonderful. You'll see.'

Like a swimmer shouting to the beach 'The water's fine. You'll love it,' she thought. But I won't love it at all. And I'm not *going* to love it.

'And you're all white,' he said. 'White robe. White skin. That's perfect.'

She backed away to her dressing table, felt behind her with her hand as he lurched towards her, almost out of control but still very strong. Her fingers felt for the hand mirror her parents had given her on her sixteenth birthday, a solid lump of Indian silver, and when his hands reached out for her she swung it hard with all her weight behind it, edge on, striking his temple. He went down flat the way she had seen rabbits fall when one of her brothers had shot them with a twelve-bore, suddenly and completely, and without a twitch, then looked at the hand mirror. Unbroken, she thought. No seven years' bad luck: then picked up the telephone and asked for Jay's room. Powell made no move to prevent her.

'I wish you'd stop drinking coffee,' said Jay. He sounded pettish.

'I want coffee,' she said. 'I *need* coffee. It's what the text books all say you should have after a shock.'

Jay continued to hold Powell's wrist. 'At least he's alive,' he said.

She was in a panic at once. 'Of course he's alive,' she said. 'I only hit him once.'

'Have you seen the side of his head?' Jay asked.

'No.'

'I shouldn't.' He straightened up. 'We'll have to move him. I don't know what the text books say about that, but it's what we're going to have to do.'

'Move him where?'

'My suite,' said Jay. 'If anybody sees him I can always say we were fooling around pretending to fight or something. Get some clothes on then go to the door. When we're in the clear open mine and I'll bring him in.'

She took off her dressing gown as she went for the clothes she needed, saw her naked reflection in the wardrobe mirror. Her body that the whole black farce had been about. Jay didn't even look. As she dressed he asked, 'How the hell did he get in here?'

'He bribed a waiter.' Jane fastened Mrs Powell's invention.

'He must have paid the earth.'

'Five thousand dollars.'

'Half of what I gave him last night. He probably owes the other half for costumes and chariots and champagne in woodland glades. Do you feel flattered?'

'Not at all.'

'I wouldn't blame you.'

Jane went to her door, and looked out, saw no one there, then opened Jay's door and called to him softly. Bower appeared at once, carrying her victim as if he were no more than a clumsy parcel he was anxious to put down before it burst. As he crossed the threshold Powell's wig fell off. Jane picked it up and followed them in.

'Go back to your own place,' said Jay. 'You're out of this now.'

'Can't I help you?'

'No,' he said. 'You've done enough.' She flinched at that and Jay went on, 'Forgive me. Maybe I'm in a state of shock, too. What I meant was you did what was right and I admire you for it, but now you're out of it. Now it's my turn. . . . OK?'

She went back to her suite and stripped again, bathed, dressed once more, and rang for more coffee, listening hard. For what? The clatter of an ambulance? The tramp of stretcher bearers? A gendarme's whistle? There was nothing. She was finishing her last cup when Jay came in once more, bathed and shaved and dressed.

'You sure do like coffee,' he said.

'Shall I get you some?'

'Brandy,' he said. 'I know it's early but I need it. God knows I've earned it.'

'It's all right to ring room service?'

'Sure,' he said, and then came over to her and kissed her lightly on the mouth. 'I guess I'm punchy. *Every*thing's all right. I should have told you as soon as I came in. I'm sorry.'

She smiled at him. 'Just let me get you your drink,' she said, 'then I want to hear it all.'

He had begun by telephoning the *Daily World*'s Paris office, and demanding a discreet doctor who could deal with head wounds. They had provided one almost at once, Jane gathered, which gave some idea of the kind of people we journalists are. While the doctor went to work Jay had telephoned Florence

Powell who had arrived almost as quickly as the doctor, and brought some of his clothes.

'Wasn't she asleep?'

'Billy had disappeared before the ball finished,' said Jay. 'She didn't know where he was or what he was up to. You bet she wasn't asleep. So when she arrived I made her wait while the doctor fixed Billy up with a bandage and helped me dress him, then gave him a snort of sal volatile or something and he came round, just sort of lay there while I paid off the doctor and took him to the door. When we got there the doctor said to me, "I did not have a chance to examine him properly, but it is my impression that if he does not change his way of life soon your friend will kill himself," and I said, "That's the whole idea." Then he left with five hundred bucks which I stop out of Billy's next allowance. Five hundred. Funny, wouldn't you say? A waiter making ten times as much as a doctor?'

'Then what happened?'

'I went back inside and I told her, and at first Florence was good and mad.'

'With Powell?'

'With you,' said Jay.

'With *me*?' The rage in her voice made Jay smile.

'No need to go reaching for your mirror,' he said. 'They're on their way home by now. Sure with you. When it comes to love – sex anyway – those two make their own arrangements, but even so Billy's the biggest child she's got – and so she wanted to do unto you as you'd done unto him.'

'How did you stop her?'

'I said you wouldn't press charges.'

'What charges?'

'The French are all for l'amour and all that – at least they keep saying they are, but they're just a much against rape as any other civilised country.'

'I never thought of it like that,' she said.

'But Florence did because that's what it was. So we stuck his hat on top of his bandage and I helped him to the elevator, then out to that vast car of his and their manservant drove them off. I doubt if anybody even noticed, and if they did he was just one more casualty of the Quart' Arts Ball. Now, what would you like to do before we fly home?'

She took his brandy glass and finished what was left.

'I don't know why it should be,' she said, 'but I want you to make love to me, even though it means undressing for the third time this morning.'

'Wear your Cleopatra costume and you've got yourself a deal,' said Jay.

'All of it except the head-dress,' she said.

They were lying in each other's arms, weary and yet exultant, when the telephone rang and she reached out lazily.

'A call from London,' said the operator, and then it came, hazy but audible. 'This is Hawkins, miss,' the voice said. 'You've got to come home, miss. Quick. It's awful.' There was a sound like a crash. China? Crystal? And then the line went dead. She hung up. 'The most extraordinary thing,' she said.

'What now?'

'Surely Hawkins can't be drunk, and even if she were, why should she phone me?' She turned to face him. 'I'm most awfully sorry, but I have to go home.'

37

HE FLEW HOME with her, bitterly regretting an opportunity missed to lunch at the Closerie des Lilas. And when they got to Croydon there were thin wisps of fog; the tattered remnants of what in London was an impenetrable curtain. 'A proper London particular,' Redman the chauffeur told them, not without relish. 'A real pea-souper.'

Jane went to a telephone, but there was no reply from Offley Villas: no connection even, and so Jay phoned the *Daily World* instead.

'Solid I'm afraid,' he told her. 'No visibility at all.'

'I don't mind giving it a try, sir,' said the chauffeur. He sounded like a hussar volunteering for the front rank of the light brigade. Jay ignored him.

'It might lift in a few hours they reckon,' he said. 'Let's go and get a drink somewhere.'

'It's quarter past three and it's England,' said Jane. 'We can't get a drink.'

'Tea then,' said Jay. 'God knows I couldn't face English coffee.'

It was nearly nine when the Rolls-Royce turned into Offley Villas and the chauffeur got out to take her suitcases.

'I'll take those,' said Jay, and walked with her to the door.

'Why not?' said Jane. 'I haven't any reputation left anyway.'

Jay ignored it. 'There could be things in there he shouldn't see,' he said.

'Oh dear God,' said Jane. 'The second time in one day. It just isn't bloody *fair*.' Then she inserted the key in the lock, turned it and went into the hall, with Jay close behind her.

It seemed all right, except for the absence of a large and very ugly vase from the telephone table, and a dark stain on the carpet nearby. Then she saw that the telephone, though neatly disposed, had had its wires wrenched from the skirting board.

She called out softly: 'Hawkins! Hawkins!'

A voice came from the kitchen. 'That you, miss?'

'Yes, of course it is. Hawkins, what's *happening*?'

Then came a sound which she later learned was Hawkins removing a chair from under a door knob, and then Hawkins appeared at last, straightening her cap.

'Oh, miss,' she said. 'I've been here ever so long on my own. It's been awful.'

'I came as soon as I could,' said Jane. 'There's a heavy fog. And what do you mean on your own? Isn't cook with you?'

'Cook did a bunk as soon as it started. There's only me and him.' Then she brightened. 'Unless he's scarpered.' And then the gloom returned. 'No. . . . I'd have heard him.'

'Heard *who*?'

Jane's sharpness got through to Hawkins, who made a massive effort to achieve coherence. 'A friend of Mr Francis came here this morning from Cambridge. He'd brought a note with him from Mr Francis saying he had permission to look through Sir Guy's papers.'

'He had no right – ' Jane began, and Jay pressed her arm, urging her to silence. 'But you weren't to know that, Hawkins,' she said at last. 'It wasn't your fault. Who was he? Not a Mr Willis?'

'Oh no, miss,' said Hawkins. 'Burrowes his name was.' A new one, thought Jane. 'He looked a bit untidy, not even clean, really, but I didn't think it was important. Some of those scholastic fellers tend to be like that.'

Scholastic. At a time like this.

'What was important,' Hawkins said, 'was he'd been drinking. Half past ten in the morning and he was half way home. Only he was in that quick – and he did have the letter, miss – and what could I do?'

'Nothing,' said Jane. 'Go on.'

'I showed him up to the study, miss, and he said that would

– 385 –

be all – and about an hour later he shouts down the stairs and tells me to bring him a bottle of whisky. So I took up the decanter, miss. And the siphon.'

'Yes, of course,' said Jane.

'Only he told me to take the siphon away again, miss. He said he didn't want no soda.' Then to Jane's astonishment, Hawkins began to weep.

'That's nothing to cry about,' said Jane.

'It isn't *that*, miss,' said Hawkins. 'It's the study.'

Jane began to feel the rage well up inside her. 'What about the study?'

'All that arranging and tidying you did,' said Hawkins. 'All them – those papers. He's chucked them about all over the place, miss. It's like a pig sty.'

Jane moved to the door, but again Jay's hand grasped her arm, holding her still. 'Finish it, girl,' he said.

'That was when I ran down to phone you, miss,' said Hawkins, 'only he came down after me and pulled the telephone like you see, only I clocked him one and he knocked the vase over and clocked me one. – "Tit for tat," he says. "Fair's fair. Clear up this mess," he says. "It's disgusting. And leave the phone the way it is. I don't like being disturbed when I'm working."'

Jane said, 'He didn't – he didn't – molest you?'

'Of course not, miss,' said Hawkins. 'I told you. He's a friend of Mr Francis. All he did was finish off the whisky.'

'How do you know?'

'I went upstairs and had a peep,' said Hawkins. 'Spark out, he was. Snoring his head off. Around teatime that would be.'

'And you stayed here by yourself all this time?'

'Yes, miss.'

'But why didn't you call the police?' asked Jane.

'I didn't think you'd want me to, miss.'

Here was devotion indeed. 'Well no, I don't,' said Jane. 'But even so – I'm very grateful to you, Hawkins.'

'You mean you'll still take me to South Terrace?'

'Indeed I will,' said Jane. 'One way and another I don't seem to be safe without you.' She turned to Jay. 'You'll come up with us?'

'Oh please, sir,' said Hawkins, suddenly aware how strong and aggressive Jay was.

'Well sure,' he said. 'Be a pleasure.'

Cautiously they all three climbed the stairs and Jane found herself remembering that piece of Gilbert and Sullivan, 'With catlike tread', and thinking how ridiculous they must seem. But no doubt she'd appeared ridiculous at the Ritz, running about in a flimsy dressing gown and using a hand mirror like a tennis racket. Twice in one day, she thought, and in two different capitals. . . . Then she looked round the study door, and realised that, ridiculous or not, it was serious too, just as Paris had been.

The study was a shambles. Papers, letters, photographs were thrown everywhere, some just crumpled, most of them torn in two, or in shreds. The tea chest that had held the stuff she had labelled miscellaneous had simply been stood on end and its contents strewn over the floor. There was cigarette ash everywhere, and there were cigarette stubs too, one even crushed out on the carpet, but mercifully there had been no fire. And in the midst of it all, flat on his back and gently snoring, Julian de Groot Burrowes, MA (Cantab) still clutching in his fist the empty decanter.

'Dear God,' said Jane, and put her hands to her face, and wept. Bower's arm came about her, supporting, comforting, until at last the tears eased and he gave her a handkerchief.

'No cops?' he said. 'Not even now?' She shook her head. 'What then?'

'Get him out of here.'

'Just throw him into the street? The state he's in that'll mean the cops anyway.'

'See if he's got an address we can take him to.'

Jay started forward, but it was Hawkins who bent over Burrowes and took out his wallet.

'There's his card, miss,' she said. '187, Gower Street. That's in Bloomsbury.'

'It would be,' said Jay. He looked down at Burrowes, and then to Jane. 'I guess I'm going to need some help this time,' he said.

'Your chauffeur?'

'He'll be OK,' Jay said, which meant he would keep his mouth shut, and sent Hawkins to fetch him.

'Tough for you,' he said, when Hawkins had gone. 'I remember you telling me how hard it was, collating all this.'

'Why?' said Jane. 'In God's name – why would he do it?'

'You won't find out tonight,' said Jay, 'but I sure would want some answers tomorrow if I were in your shoes. Still, by the state he's in, if you screech loud enough in the morning he'll tell you anything – just to give his head a rest.'

'I'll need to telephone my brother in the morning,' she said. 'Is it all right if I use the telephone in the *World* office? I don't want anyone else to hear.'

'I'll give you a note,' said Jay, and took out a note book. 'And that reminds me – I'm having a press card made out for you – and you'll be getting an application form for the NUJ.'

'For the what?'

'The National Union of Journalists,' he said. 'Don't you know anything? You're a woman of the Left. It's high time you belonged to a union.' He leaned forward and kissed her, a friend's kiss.

'It's tough on you,' he said, 'but you *are* tough. You'll make it. You'll see.' And then Redman arrived.

Together they picked up Burrowes, and he stirred at last and muttered something that Jay told her later was a quotation in Greek from Thucydides, and with hazy memories of his time at Harvard meant 'To famous men all the earth is a sepulchre'. Then he and the chauffeur carried him out, for all the world, thought Jane, like a couple of Tommies bringing in a wounded comrade.

'Do you want to do anything about this tonight, miss?' Hawkins asked.

'Not a thing,' said Jane, and looked again at the appalling mess, and reached a decision. 'Tomorrow we'll pack it all up in bags, and when Guy Fawkes night comes, we'll add it to the nearest bonfire.' Posy Sanderson was no more, after all, so why should the rest survive?

'Are you allowed to do that, miss?'

'It's mine,' said Jane. 'My father left it to me in his will.'

'But if it was left to you how could your brother – ?' Hawkins bit off the question. 'Beg pardon, miss.'

'Not at all,' said Jane. 'It's a fair question. But I don't suppose my brother ever expected anything like this. Are you hungry?'

'Starving, miss. I haven't eaten a thing since breakfast. I daren't. Not with him here.'

And I, thought Jane, have had nothing except coffee and

croissants in Paris and a cup of tea at Croydon aerodrome.

'Nor I,' she said.

'Shall I cook something, miss?' Hawkins asked.

'No.' There was a sort of brasserie in Dover Street that produced reasonably edible food until midnight. 'We'll go out.' And then she remembered something she should have thought of long before. 'Oh my God.'

'What's wrong, miss?'

'Foch. . . . I forgot all about him.'

'He's all right, miss. I had him with me in the kitchen. I even gave him a few dog biscuits. It's not what he's used to, but he's done better than us.'

'Hurry up and get ready then,' said Jane and went down the stairs. By the kitchen door she took out a cigarette, and found that her hands were shaking so much she dropped the lighter. She didn't cry, not then, but went into the kitchen instead and held Foch in her arms until it was time to go.

'I can't,' said the college porter. 'Honestly I can't. He'll still be asleep, miss.'

'You must wake him,' said Jane. 'There's been an accident. A very serious accident. His friend Mr Burrowes, and his sister. Go and tell him at once.'

'Yes, of course, miss,' the porter said. 'Will you hold on?'

'*Of course I'll hold on.*'

There was a silence, and Jane felt that she might begin to shake again, and picked up Foch instead, enjoying the comfort of his small, solid body and harsh, crisp-curling fur. Foch yawned – it wasn't yet seven o'clock – but snuggled to her, assuring her that she was loved before drifting back to sleep. Jane looked about her.

Not a bad little office, she thought. Leather swivel chair, generous desk, sporting prints between the filing cabinets. But the phone and the privacy were all that mattered. She yawned even more than Foch. Hawkins was still in bed. She'd told her to sleep late. The poor girl was as exhausted as she was, but she wouldn't be able to sleep, not until they had settled the thing. She'd enjoyed her meal, and looked pretty and smart in her best dress and the coat she'd lent her. Eaten nicely, too. A clever one,

Hawkins, one who watched and learned, but a nice one also. When she'd given her a tenner Hawkins had almost cried, and so had she. Loyalty and courage like Hawkins's were not things you could buy with money. The phone squawked and she picked up the earpiece.

'Yes?' she said.

'This is Francis Whitcomb,' said her brother. 'What's this about an accident?'

'This is Jane, Francis.'

'*Jane*? Hodges said you were hurt.'

'So I have been. And your friend, Burrowes.'

'Julian? Hurt?'

'He was unconscious when I last saw him,' said Jane. '*And* the house has been broken into.'

'I've got a lecture at eleven,' Francis said. 'I'll come as soon as it's over.'

Jane made her voice sound pleading and frightened. It wasn't all acting. 'You've got to come now,' she said. 'When I looked at Burrowes he could have been paralysed. *And* Hawkins was assaulted.'

'Hawkins?'

Neither he nor his friends ever seemed to know who Hawkins was.

'The housemaid, you bloody fool.'

And maybe that was what did it: the threat of violence in her voice.

'I'll come at once,' said Francis.

She had just finished lunch when Francis appeared: bacon and eggs that Hawkins had first fried, then served. She was taking coffee in the drawing room when Francis came in.

'Where's Julian?' he asked. And there's brotherly love for you, she thought. I'm supposed to be hurt, too.

'Have you eaten?'

'On the train,' he said. 'And look here – I thought you said Hawkins had been assaulted. Isn't she the one who let me in? And what's all this about a burglary?'

'Your friend Julian tricked his way in here yesterday, behaved like a vandal and assaulted Hawkins.'

'Jane – you can't be serious.'

Jane went to the bell. 'Let's ask her,' she said.

'No. . . . Wait. Tell me the lot. If getting me here was some sort of stupid joke – '

'I was away. In Paris as a matter of fact. Hawkins telephoned me in a panic. Thank God she got through to me before your friend Burrowes wrenched the telephone from the wall. I flew back to find he'd shown Hawkins some sort of letter – he claimed it was from you – '

'It *was* from me. I said he could have a look at those papers of Papa's. He's doing a piece about our administration of India. Or maladministration.'

'You had no right to do that. Those papers are mine.'

'Come on, Jane. Where's the harm? The letter I wrote was for you anyway. I had no idea you were jaunting off to Paris.'

'I was working,' said Jane, 'but even if I was jaunting, he had no right to go through those papers without my permission, and even less right to tear them up and crumple them and throw them all over the room.'

'Julian wouldn't do that.'

'Come and see,' she said, and they went to the study.

'Dear God,' said Francis, and then: 'Julian did this?'

'And the vase,' said Jane. 'I know it was a ghastly monstrosity and all that, but for some reason Mummy valued it.'

'Couldn't Hawkins have done that?'

'Why the devil should she? Hawkins was defending you property. It was your friend Burrowes who was trying to destroy it.'

'I wish you wouldn't keep calling him my friend like that,' said Francis. 'It sounds like – '

'Like what?'

'Like what it is,' he said, and again, fleetingly, she liked him.

'Whatever happened to Dennis?' she asked.

'He left me,' said Francis. 'I'm too serious, it seems. I suspect that I'm too poor, too.'

Unlike me, she thought.

'What do you want to do now?' he asked her.

'Go to see him.'

'But surely I'm the one to do that.'

'You can come too, if you wish,' said Jane, 'but I have to ask him why he did this.'

'He'll tell you he was drunk.'

'That's not an excuse,' said Jane. 'Not even a reason.'

'He can't help it, you see,' said Francis.

'You mean he's done this before, and you still sent him here?'

'Not this, of course not,' said Francis. 'But he's pretty wild, you see. I mean he tried for the navy but his health wasn't up to it, and even though he got a first there was no offer of a fellowship.'

'I expect his college prefers to keep its books inside their bindings,' said Jane, then before her brother could react: 'Have you heard from Mummy?'

'Not just lately.'

'I had a letter today. Masses. She's gone back to Bombay. Coming home, apparently. She and the Gwatkin aren't speaking.'

'Whyever not?'

'She wanted Mummy to accompany her at a concert when she sang one of those Amy Woodford Findon things. You know. . . . "The Indian Love Lyrics". "Pale Hands I Loved". All that. But Mummy refused.'

'Did she say why?'

'She considers Miss Gwatkin too fat to sing "The Indian Love Lyrics". "Like a haphazard collection of blancmanges wobbling in unison," she called her. But I rather think Mummy was too busy to practise. She's engaged, you see.'

'What?'

'Or as good as – whatever that means. Those are the words she used, but she didn't explain them. A Major Routledge. Late of the Puffers. He transferred in from the Gloucesters, she says.'

'What on earth are the Puffers?'

'The Punjab Frontier Force,' said Jane. 'A Puffer is considered quite a good thing to be.'

'I shall never understand India,' Francis said.

'In my day India wasn't there to be understood.'

'It was there to be enjoyed, I suppose,' said Francis.

'Yes, but enjoyment had to be earned.'

'And exploited.'

'In India the rich exploit the poor rather better than in most places. Part of Papa's job – the most important part – was to stop them. Let's call on Burrowes.'

'I don't want to see him.'

'I don't blame you. I'll go alone.'

'I mean I don't want to see him with you. But if I must – ' He turned to the door. At the foot of the stairs Hawkins waited.

'We're going to call on Mr Burrowes,' said Jane, 'to make sure this never happens again. My brother regrets it deeply. Don't you, Francis?'

'Oh yes,' said Francis. 'Deeply.'

'On the way home I have some other calls to make but I'll stop at an agency and find a cook. We can't eat eggs and bacon forever. Have you things to do?'

'Mr Warley telephoned when you were out, miss. About the drawing-room radiators.'

'You'd better go on over then,' said Jane. 'I'll join you if I can.'

She looked at Francis to see if the name 'Warley' had brought a reaction. There was none. His whole mind was devoted to the problem of Burrowes.

In the car she said, 'I'm moving into a new house.'

All he could manage was, 'I hope you'll be comfortable.'

She thought of Lionel, and radiators, and Bakst curtains and kitchen improvements and showers en suite.

'Sybaritic,' she said, and drove to Gower Street.

Handy for the British Museum, she thought, and for all the literary tea parties that Lionel spoke of with such horror, but not good for much else. Number 187 was a tall, narrow terrace house, its paint blistered, its bricks in need of painting almost as much as its windows needed cleaning. And yet it had once been an elegant house, before poverty and neglect had done their work. Not like Felston, she thought. In Felston there were no faded memories of grandeur, only poverty and neglect far worse than this.

Beside the door was a list of names: visiting cards, or scrawls on pieces cut from the backs of shoe boxes: everything from an ex-commander RN to a couple of obvious tarts. At least that's what Jay had said they were. Francis fidgeted about, looking for a bell, but Jane pushed at the door, which swung open to her touch, and went inside.

'Do you think we should?' said Francis, but he followed her even so.

Flat D, Burrowes's card had said. First floor. Up the stairs, treading on carpet worn thin as cotton, here and there a stair rod missing, past a lavatory and bathroom where the metal was beginning to show through the paint, and there was Flat D, with another of Burrowes's cards pinned to the door. Jane tried again, but this time the door stayed shut. She tugged at a bell pull, which by the feel of it was broken, then banged on the door with her fist.

'Jane, *please*,' her brother said, but the door opened at once and Burrowes faced them.

In a way, she thought, this was the first time she had seen him. Last night she had had eyes only for the havoc he had created. What she saw was a short man, shorter than Francis, and not so very much taller than herself, who was almost unbelievably beautiful, like some pre-Raphaelite vision of Lucifer before the fall. Black hair in curls that were not in the least effeminate, brown eyes at once loving and cruel, and a face that was perfect in its symmetry. He was clad in a dirty dressing gown, still unshaven, and stank like a polecat.

Oh Francis, my poor love, she thought. What have you let yourself in for this time?

Burrowes looked at her, uncomprehending, and then at Francis.

'Why sweety,' he said, 'how on earth did you escape from Cambridge? Do come in – you and your ladyfriend.'

Even his voice was deep and pleasant, without the least sign of homosexual affectation.

'This is my sister,' Francis said. 'Jane.'

'No matter,' said Burrowes. 'Bring her in. We're all men-of-the-world here. Except the ladies of course.'

Brother and sister followed him inside. The room stank rather less than Burrowes, but it still stank. And it too was a mess. Perhaps it's the only ambience he can live in, she thought, and looked from the divan bed still unmade to a table loaded with dirty dishes, books, letters and magazines. On the floor were more books, and a chair, once a rather splendid piece in buttoned leather, now scuffed and shabby and with one leg clumsily mended. The rest of the furniture looked as if it had been rejected by a junk shop, and competing with the feral smell of Burrowes and what she could only think of as his lair, was a strong and persistent odour of garlic. Empty bottles lay about everywhere, like booby traps.

'How do you like my little place?' said Burrowes, and then: 'What a question. I can see that you don't. But where do you live, one asks?'

'Where do I live?'

He looked at her. He seemed amused, yet slightly puzzled.

'It's a perfectly proper question,' he said.

'She lives at my mother's house,' said Francis. 'In Offley Villas.'

'Does she indeed? Kensington, I believe you said. The W8 bit. Not really my sort of place. All archdeacons and dowagers.'

'You enjoyed it well enough yesterday,' said Jane.

'I beg your pardon?' This time he merely looked puzzled.

'Or perhaps I'm wrong,' said Jane. 'Perhaps you didn't enjoy ruining my father's papers. Perhaps it's some new form of exercise.'

'My dear young lady,' said Burrowes, who must have been at least five years younger than she was, 'I've never been to your mother's house in my life.'

'I'm afraid that's not true, Julian,' said Francis.

'I'm absolutely bewildered,' said Burrowes. 'Is this a joke? Some new kind? Like your sister's concept of exercise?'

'Shut up and I'll tell you,' said Jane.

'By all means,' said Burrowes. 'But may I at least show some vestige of good manners and ask you to sit down?'

'No,' said Jane, and told him what he had done.

'But this is monstrous,' said Burrowes when she had finished. 'Do you have a witness?'

'I have three,' said Jane. 'Apart from myself.'

Burrowes turned to Francis. 'Your sister is not prone to hallucinations?'

Francis hesitated, and then said, 'No.'

'You paused there, sweety, before you answered,' said Burrowes. 'Definitely you paused. Are you sure your sister is quite as evenly balanced as a loving brother could wish?'

She hit him then, a round-armed, open-handed slap that caught him hard on the cheek and sent him sprawling into the leather chair.

'Jane – for God's sake,' said Francis, but all his sister could think was: Two in two days. But oh – how I enjoyed this one.

'Do you consider that an answer to my question?' Burrowes asked.

'Of course not,' said Jane. 'It was what you deserved and I gave it to you, as Francis seemed unwilling to do so.'

'I should like to stand up,' Burrowes said, 'but no more right hooks.'

'Then be careful what you say.'

Warily Burrowes got to his feet, then went to the only bottle in the room that still had drink in it. By the look of it it was gin and he drank it neat. He didn't offer it to either of the others.

'I must believe you,' he said, 'if only to avoid further assault, but I have no memory of it.'

'Oh, come on,' said Jane. 'Surely you can do better than that.'

'It's perfectly true,' said Burrowes. 'I take certain pills, you see – to alleviate the rather severe depressions that visit me from time to time.'

Jane turned to Francis. 'Are you sure,' she asked, 'that Mr Burrowes is quite as evenly balanced as a loving friend could wish?'

'Touché,' said Burrowes. 'Touché absolutely.' Then he continued: 'I also drink, dear lady. I drink far, far too much.' He gulped at his gin. 'The two combined do from time to time create a kind of amnesia, and so I accept your contention that I did the things you say.'

'Including your destruction of my father's papers?'

'Obviously I must, as I was seen doing it.'

'And the telephone and the vase and the assault on my maid?'

'All. All,' said Burrowes, with a kind of whimsical regret. 'Omnia mea maxima culpa.'

'And would you mind telling me why you did all this?'

'Ah, there you rather have me I'm afraid.' He thought for a moment. 'Your father was an Indian civil servant, I believe?'

'You must remember that at least,' said Jane. 'It was because Francis told you so that you talked your way in – to get material for an article. Or have you forgotten that, too?'

'My dear young lady, I can forget anything when I put my mind to it,' said Burrowes. 'But that I do remember, probably because they paid me for it. Five guineas advance, Francis dear – the cheque came this morning. We must dine soon. Definitely we must – before they find out I can't write it and stop the cheque.' To Jane he said: 'You should ask me why I can't write it.'

'It's of no interest to me,' said Jane.

'Oh but it is,' said Burrowes. 'I despise the British government's activities in India and the antics of their servants there disgust me so much I found I couldn't hold the pen. That may also be the reason why I treated your father's papers as I did, but I really can't remember.'

'I could take you to court for this,' said Jane.

'Oh, agreed. But you won't, surely? I mean think how upset your brother would be.'

'You have two choices,' said Jane. 'Either you pay for the damage you did or I'll take you to court.'

'I would gladly do so,' said Burrowes, 'but I'm broke, alas.'

'No, you're not,' said Jane. 'You have five pounds five shillings. You just told me so.'

'But it's all I have in the world.' Suddenly Burrowes's voice was a wail.

'It isn't nearly enough,' said Jane. 'But it will have to do. Make up your mind. I don't want to be late for my next appointment.'

Slowly, reluctantly, Burrowes produced a cheque and endorsed it over to her, then the resentment appeared to vanish and he handed it to her and bowed.

'I should treasure that if I were you,' he said. 'A cheque from Julian Burrowes is a rare edition indeed.'

Jane said to Francis, 'Can I drop you somewhere?'

'No,' said Francis. 'There are still a couple of things I have to settle with Julian.'

He wants to give him five pounds five shillings, she thought. Surely that must be it. He can't possibly want to make love to him amid all that stench.

38

BURROWES SAID, 'QUITE a card, your sister.'

'For God's sake,' said Francis. 'You upset her. What did you expect?'

'I had one of my amnesia attacks,' said Burrowes. 'Didn't you hear me say so?'

'I'm sorry,' said Francis. 'You never told me about them. Shouldn't you see a doctor?'

'Of course not,' Burrowes said. 'They don't exist – but they're a useful excuse, don't you think? I mean I don't suppose your sister believed it any more than I did – but it's not a thing you can disprove, now is it? I don't like your sister, by the way. Don't like her at *all*.'

'She was devoted to my father.'

'Of course she was,' said Burrowes. 'One rotten little bourgeois devoted to another. I read those papers before I tore them. Balls and tiger hunts and games of polo while an entire subcontinent starved. It was disgusting. It still is. . . . Don't tell me you admired your father?'

'I hardly knew him,' said Francis.

'Not a very brave answer, but effective.' He gulped more gin. 'One of these days you must tell me why you hesitated when I raised the question of your sister's state of mind. But not now. Now you slip the old tart the five guineas your sister stole from her, then she'll clean herself up and do her very best to earn it.'

Jane went first to the bank, and then to see Jabber. She hadn't
wanted to while her brother was with her, and it was just as well
he'd refused her offer of a lift, especially as that clever swine
Burrowes had spotted his hesitation when he'd questioned her
state of mind. But she'd made an appointment with Jabber and
was determined to keep it, and not to talk about Burrowes. It
was a suitably edited version of the Paris trip she discussed with
him, and on the whole he was pleased with the way she'd
handled it, but no more clouts on the head with hand mirrors,
he'd warned her. She'd tried her limpid look. Had he never
heard of death before dishonour? But in those cases it was the
maiden who was supposed to die, he'd told her, then kicked her
out. He might be in love with her, but he was a very busy doctor.

On to the agency then, and the promise of an adequate cook as
soon as one could be found. Mummy preferred her cooks adequate: they didn't cost so much, and even an adequate cook
would be better than eggs and bacon recurring over and over, or
getting Hawkins into the habit of eating in restaurants she couldn't
possibly afford. And then to Fleet Street to see Jay Bower by appointment – always by appointment, and say thank you and report.

'You're welcome,' he said. 'I guess it was pretty nasty for you.'

'I was very fond of my father,' she said. He nodded.

'Do you believe all that stuff about amnesia?'

'Of course not,' she said.

'But you didn't send for the police?'

'How could I?' she said. 'My brother was involved.'

'You did the right thing,' he said. 'That bastard will play every
card he's dealt.'

'You know something about him?'

'I've had a little work done.'

For the first time she found herself wondering how much work
he'd had done on her. 'And what did you find out?'

'Good family. Eton and Trinity. His father was in the navy –
killed in the war – but Burrowes still hates his memory. Highly
intelligent, an aggressive drunk, totally unreliable, and queer as
they make them.'

'No wonder his college didn't give him a fellowship.'

'He's a Communist too – at least he says he is every chance he
gets. Not too many people believe him.'

'Why not?'

'He buggers too many bourgeois. What are you going to do about your father's papers?'

'Get rid of them.'

'Good in bed,' he said, 'marvellous to be with, stunningly attractive, and smart, too. Why won't you marry me?' And then – 'Don't answer that. My ego couldn't stand it.' His desk telephone sounded, and his secretary's voice quacked.

'Three minutes,' said Bower, and motioned Jane to stay, then hung up and turned to her. 'I've got a couple of things for you.'

The first thing was her application for the NUJ, already filled in. All she had to do was sign it. The second was her press pass.

'One more thing,' he said. 'That office you were in this morning. It's yours whenever you want it.'

She looked at him warily. 'Do all your employees get offices like that?'

'You know they don't,' he said, 'but you're good for the *Daily World* right now.'

'And when I'm not you'll throw me out?'

'Sure.'

'Then I'll take it. But only for working in.'

'That's all offices are for.'

South Terrace then, and tea in the kitchen with Lionel and Hawkins. The rest of the house had reached that stage of heroic disorder that looked as if it could well be permanent, and was swarming with workmen. Together the three of them went over it, and she oohed and aahed gratefully as the two of them showed off the shower, the radiators, the kitchen already installed. Another cook, she thought, but rather better than adequate if the cook was to match the kitchen. Then Hawkins went off to rebuke a plumber because it was good for him.

Lionel said, 'She's good you know. Really awfully good.' And then, 'She told me about your visitor.'

'I told her she could.'

'He's a bad one. Vicious, cruel, unscrupulous. Did he try to get money from you?'

'I got some from him. For the damage he'd done.'

'But how marvellous,' said Lionel. 'That makes you unique – though of course you always were. Your brother is – emotionally involved, I take it?' Jane nodded. 'Such a pity,' said Lionel. 'Why couldn't he have stayed with dear little Dennis?'

'Dennis was rather too expensive – and altogether too frivolous.'

'The course of true love never did run smooth,' said Lionel. 'How right the Swan of Avon was. As usual. . . . Burrowes will hate you, you know.'

'For showing him up in front of Francis?'

'For besting him. He'll try his utmost to hurt you. You should be on your guard against that. He's awfully good at hurting people.'

'I met a man in Paris,' she said, 'who is utterly convinced that the world is going to end soon and that the only thing left for him is to have a good time, no matter who gets hurt. He doesn't set out to hurt people. It just doesn't bother him. But you're saying that Burrowes enjoys it.'

'He does,' said Lionel. 'It's what he does best. Believe me I know.'

You too, poor darling, she thought, though indeed Burrowes was extremely beautiful.

'Tell me,' she said, 'why does he smell so much of garlic? Is he afraid of vampires?'

'Hardly,' said Lionel. 'He's almost one himself. He just likes the stuff – as so many of us do. But Julian of course can like nothing in moderation.'

'But doesn't it put his chaps off?'

'Some,' said Lionel. 'Some have been known to be too fastidious to stand it. But there are those among us who have shall we say specialised tastes. And of course he will clean himself up if you offer him enough money. Julian has a very large circle of admirers. What are you doing this evening?'

'Georgina Payne has invited me to dinner at the Etoile.'

'In that case would you mind very much if I took Peggy to dinner?'

'Peggy?'

'Hawkins to you,' said Lionel.

'But are you sure you want to?' said Jane. 'I mean forgive the snobbery, but she is a parlourmaid.'

'Well of course she is,' said Lionel. 'But she's the only parlourmaid I ever met – possibly the only one who exists – who wishes to have the Romantic Movement explained to her. The urge to take her to dine was irresistible.'

'You intend to explain the Romantic Movement in one dinner?'

'The dinner was my idea. After such a request, how could I not? You don't mind?'

'Of course not,' said Jane. 'But not the Etoile. We'd both be embarrassed.'

'I thought the Savoy,' said Lionel. 'Or somewhere sombre like that. Oh – and she says she will go only if you'll lend her the same coat she wore when you took her to the brasserie.'

'Anything except Aunt Pen's leopardess,' said Jane.

Georgina Payne said, 'Lionel's taking your maid to the *Savoy*?'

'Why not?' said Jane. 'You've taken me here.'

'But she's your maid.'

This was pretty well what I said to Lionel, thought Jane. But Lionel's right. Hawkins is special.

'She's a very pretty girl.' And it was true, she thought. Suitably made up and dressed, Peggy Hawkins was very pretty.

'She's been a great help to us over South Terrace,' she said. 'And anyway they share an interest in what you might call cultural history. Lionel says it will be a treat for him.'

'I hope I don't sound like a snob,' said Georgina, 'because I'm not. Honestly. I mean la vie de bohème and all that. It's just that I'm astonished, that's all.'

'Talking of la vie de bohème,' said Jane, 'how is Michael?'

Their chicken Kiev arrived, and they waited while it was served.

'Michael is prospering,' said Georgina. 'But not in my humble abode. Not any more. Not in Lilian Browne's magnificent abode either, with its Metcalf and Richards studio.'

'Where is he?'

'Carcassonne, so I believe. Or is it Rimini? Taormina was mentioned, too. *And* Paris. Anyway it's somewhere really rather nice, wherever it is.'

'He must have sold a vast number of paintings.'

'He hasn't done too badly – including that rather lush one of me. It went for pounds and pounds, apparently.'

'Who bought it?'

'Some gallery. Acting for a client. Oh Mikey did make a bob or two, but not enough for Carcassonne, never mind Taormina.

He got a scholarship. A travelling scholarship – and so he's travelling.'

The idea had been, thought Jane, that he would take Georgina with him.

'He didn't want you with him?'

'Certainly he did. Rather went on about it as a matter of fact. I turned him down.'

'But Georgina. . . . Why?' Jane asked. 'I mean Paris. . . . Rimini. . . .'

'The BBC,' said Georgina, and then reproachfully: 'I told you. Only they've changed their minds.'

'Oh I'm sorry.'

'Not at all. After my audition they signed me up for six months. That's how I can afford to bring you here. They're going to make me into something called a celebrity, not the little woman trotting behind her great big talented man.' She smiled at Jane. 'We really are alike, you and I.'

It was what Jane had thought at the Brompton Grill after all, but she couldn't just leave it at that. 'Why do you say that?' she asked.

'Paris,' said Georgina. 'The Quart' Arts Ball. Jay Bower. That must have been fun.'

'Oh frantic,' said Jane. 'But it was work as well.'

'*Work?*'

'I'm doing a piece about it,' said Jane.

'Oh. . . . That's all right then,' said Georgina. She meant it, too. Then she signalled the sommelier to pour more burgundy.

It was time and more than time for her to go back to Felston. Not all the speeches and articles in the world – and she had done many – could compensate for being there. Not for Felston, but for her. She discovered, little by little, that she was beginning to need the place at least as much as it needed her, and so she took a taxi to King's Cross. Foch barked when she bent to pat him goodbye. He knew she was leaving him, and perhaps she should take Foch with her, she thought. But how could she take him to a place where a dog would eat better than the people who lived there?

An easy journey of it. Five hours to Newcastle. Much less than the Riley would take, and lunch on the way, then a hunt for the garage she had been told about, where she hired a Wolseley, a bigger car than her Riley, much bigger, but there was a strong possibility that she would have passengers if she knew Dr Stobbs. . . . The garage proprietor had not been all that keen until she had sat him in the passenger seat and driven him around for a while. When she left he had seemed almost cheerful, though the twenty pounds deposit might have helped.

She drove out of the city, and through the sad, ugly little towns that led to the sea. First Cambridge, then Ireland, then Paris, and now this, she thought. Ireland reminded her of Bridget and Bridie, and the fact that they were on their way to Oxfordshire, to a stable where Piers and Catherine would see them, exercise them, until she could decide what to do about them. It looks as if I am a spoiled, rich brat after all, she thought. I buy two living creatures and don't even think where I shall keep them. But I had to have them. I had to.

Before she could once more think about why, she was in Felston, and the car was at once conspicuous because it didn't belong. It was too big, even for a doctor. This was a toff's car, and toffs of that magnitude seldom visited Felston.

She reached John Bright Street and stopped at Number 36, and at once a swarm of children appeared, but fortunately Bob appeared too, and drove them off with a machine-gun burst of that guttural yet strangely sing-song dialect that she was only just beginning to understand. He looked at the car in admiration.

'Bought a new one, have you?' he said.

'Hired,' she said. 'It's good to see you, Bob.'

'And you,' he said.

'How are you? How's everybody.'

'Canny,' he said. 'Bet's courting. Andy and me's still out of work, but Da – he got a start at Tyneside Engineering.' He makes it sound as if poor old Stan had joined an expedition to the North Pole, she thought, so unlikely did it seem.

'And Grandma?'

'Her eyes is bad,' said Bob, 'but you'd better come in and see for yourself else there'll be ructions.'

They went inside and climbed the stairs.

Stan was still at work, and Andy was at a meeting – where else? – but both the women were at home and delighted to see her. Dr Stobbs's clinic was doing well and Canon Messeter was back driving the Armstrong-Siddeley that was even bigger than the Wolseley though he wasn't near as good a driver as Jane. And her idea of starting a kitchen was working a treat. They had all the stretcher bearers they needed, and all eating regular. And *they* were all eating regular too.

'On account of Stan getting a start, you see,' said Grandma. 'Rarer than rubies – jobs round here.'

'Mind you Andy doesn't think much of it,' said Bob.

'Whyever not?'

'Minimum wages,' said Bob. 'No piece work. No overtime. Da's not scabbing – he would never do that – but that's the best you can say.'

'It's still a job,' said Grandma.

'And that's more than the rest of us have got,' said Bob. 'I know.'

'Your turn will come,' Grandma said, but she'd said it so often that all conviction had gone, thought Jane.

Aloud she said, 'How are your eyes, Grandma?'

'Canny,' the old woman said. That useful non-commital word that could mean anything from not bad to splendid.

'Oh you fibber,' said Bet.

'You watch your tongue, me lady,' Grandma said.

'But Gran, this is Jane,' said Bet. 'She's one of us. You said so yourself.'

'All right,' Grandma said, and turned to peer at Jane. 'If you must know,' she said, 'I'm nearly blind and getting worse.'

'I've found a man who can cure you,' said Jane.

At once the old woman said, 'That's very thoughtful of you but I'm not going to London, not at my age. And where's the money to come from I'd like to know? Our Stan does his best but he couldn't manage that.'

'He wouldn't have to,' said Jane.

'Somebody would.'

'Well of course,' said Jane.

'And I won't have charity,' said Grandma. 'Any more than I'll leave here.'

'John would have paid – if he'd lived,' said Jane. 'But since he didn't, I'll pay instead. It's the same thing after all.'

'Don't talk so daft. How can it be?'

'Because if he'd lived I'd be Mrs Patterson,' said Jane and held out her left hand. 'And there's his ring to prove it. Besides, you wouldn't have to go all the way to London. There's a very good eye surgeon in Newcastle.'

'You've a tongue in your head all right,' said the old woman.

'And when you're in this mood I need it,' said Jane.

'Bella Docherty wil make a mess of things on her own,' said Grandma, fighting to the last.

'She won't be on her own,' said Bet. 'I'll be there. You've shown us how. And besides – you won't be any good looking at stuff till you can see again.'

'There, you see,' said Grandma to Jane. 'You've got our Bet at it an' all.'

'It's for your own good,' said Bob, but still the battle raged, until at last Grandma said she would think about it, which the whole room knew meant surrender, but with full military honours to the vanquished. Which was just as well, thought Jane, as I've already booked the surgeon.

Soon after that, Andy came in, and then at last Stan, back from the fettling shop at Tyneside Engineering, his boiler-suit scarcely marked, since fettling shop work demanded the kind of devoted and patient precision which was his whole nature. Nevertheless there was hot water ready for his wash before he would shake hands with Jane and pan hagglety to be fried for his tea, which he ate in solitary splendour, after he had said his grace, for he was the sole provider and king in this his kingdom.

And so at last she learned what pan hagglety was: bacon and sausage fried with potatoes and onions according to a formula knov once only to Grandma, and now entrusted to Bet. Stan offered her some to taste, amazed that anyone alive should be ignorant of what it was. Cautiously she swallowed, and found that it was delicious.

'Better than caviar?' asked Andy.

'No,' said Jane at once. 'But caviar is rather special.'

'You had your picture in the paper the other day,' said Andy. 'At some do or other. In Paris it was. More chance of caviar than pan hagglety there I reckon.'

'There was neither,' said Jane. 'Not if you mean that ball where I dressed up as Cleopatra.'

'What in the world did you do that for?' asked Grandma.

'It was fancy dress,' said Jane.

'Big gold cloak with picture writing on it and a head-dress like a heathen idol,' said Andy. Stan looked up from his food.

'Only she wasn't an idol,' said Jane. 'She was just a woman who happened to be a queen. Not that there were any Christians then. It was before Jesus was born.' Stan went on eating.

'She's in Shakespeare, too,' said Jane. 'As a matter of fact, Shakespeare was well represented. Titania and Oberon were there too – from *A Midsummer Night's Dream*, you know.' Mention of Shakespeare would invoke not merely respect, but the threat of boredom, too.

'Still, I bet you enjoyed yourself,' said Bob.

'Very well. The band was excellent. But I'd really gone there to get material for an article.'

'You've done with Felston then?'

'Not at all,' said Jane. 'Rich and poor is what the article's about. The Four Arts Ball and Dr Stobbs's clinic.'

'And do you condemn the rich?' Andy asked.

'No,' said Jane. 'I don't condemn the poor, either. It's up to the reader to decide.'

'I wish I'd been there,' said Bob. 'Shakespeare or no Shakespeare.'

Jane said, 'Are you still looking for a job, Andy?'

'Well of course I am,' Andy said.

'I think I know where I can get you one.'

'And where might that be?'

'Parkin's Car Components,' said Jane.

'Never heard of that one,' Stan said.

'But I have,' said Andy. 'It's in the Midlands somewhere, isn't it? Coventry would it be?' Jane nodded. 'And how could I ever go to Coventry? I'm needed here.'

'John went to Bradford,' said Grandma, 'and sent money home. We managed champion.'

'It's not just us here,' said Andy. 'It's the Party. I'm needed in Felston.' He looked at his family. 'You know I am.'

'Suit yourself,' said Bob. 'I wish it was me, but they don't need printers. Not in a machine shop.'

Bet got up to pour out tea for her father. Jane rose.

'I'd best be off,' she said. 'I want to leave my suitcase at the Eldon Arms and then go on to Dr Stobbs.'

'Can I come with you?' asked Bet. 'There's something I want

to ask you about.' She looked at once at Bob, but all he did was wink.

'Aye,' said Grandma. 'You go with her and have a bit crack. Since Jane's made up her mind she's one of us she'll have to be told sooner or later.'

Bet loved the car, the first she had ever travelled in, and indeed once it must have looked well enough, but now the leather was cracked, the bodywork needed polishing; but Bet sat in it as if it were the Coronation Coach.

Jane said, 'What is it you want to tell me?'

'It's sort of personal,' said Bet.

'Well I should imagine it would be,' said Jane, 'but I can keep a secret you know.'

'I suppose it started with you showing me about make-up,' said Bet. 'It does something for you, doesn't it?'

'For one's morale, you mean?'

'I'm sorry,' said Bet. 'I don't know that word.' And the shyness that always hovered close engulfed her, and she said no more.

Jane Whitcomb thought, what a snob I am. Thoughtless arrogant scribbler of an intellectual snob. Show-off, too.

Aloud she said, 'I mean it makes you feel better.'

'That's right,' said Bet, and then: 'Oh. . . . We're here. It goes so fast. Not like the trams.' And then for some reason she blushed.

Jane said, 'Come in with me. We can talk while I unpack,' as the porter came hurrying out. The manager was waiting with the register, and as she signed she asked Bet what she would like to drink, so that as she stowed away her clothes in the massive mahogany drawers and wardrobe, she drank sherry and Bet lemonade.

'All that silk,' said Bet in wonder, and then, 'You'd have thought they were expecting you here.'

'They were expecting me,' said Jane. 'I telephoned from London and booked.'

'I never knew you could do that,' said Bet.

Really she is too vulnerable, thought Jane, but she's looking prettier, *and* more positive. She even risked drawing Grandma's fire.

'Can you tell me now?' she asked.

Bet rose and handed the garments from the suitcase to Jane, and talked as she did so. 'Is it *all* silk?' she asked.

'Mostly,' said Jane. 'Now stop dodging the issue and tell me your secret.'

'It isn't a secret, exactly,' said Bet. 'It's just – I've got a chap.'

'I beg your pardon?'

'You know. A young man. Not that he's that young. He's thirty-three. And he's a widower. Da isn't too keen on that.'

'Whyever not?'

Bet shrugged. 'Da says one marriage is all that's needed.'

This could be religion, thought Jane, or it could be prudishness. Very possibly it was both, but whatever it was, it was best ignored.

'Has he any children?'

'There was one,' said Bet. 'A girl. She died of TB. And so did his wife, poor thing.'

'That's very sad,' said Jane.

Bet shrugged. 'It happens all the time round here.'

The poor have their own armour, Jane thought, and my God how they need it. 'What's his name?' she asked.

'Frank,' said Bet. 'Frank Metcalfe.'

'And has he got a job?' Really she thought, this is like pulling teeth.

'Yes,' said Bet. 'He has. He's a tram driver.' Unexpectedly she giggled. 'Bob says it was the glamour of the uniform. Bob's a terrible tease.'

'Tell me about him. What he's like,' said Jane.

'He was in the army during the war,' said Bet. 'Royal Artillery. And he can play the mouth organ. He doesn't drink – well not all that much – and he lives in Lord Collingwood Street. And he makes two pound five a week without overtime.'

'Tall? Short? Handsome? Fair? Dark?' asked Jane.

'Sort of fair,' said Bet. 'But his eyes are brown. Not as tall as Bob or Andy – but tall enough.'

'And he loves you?'

'He doesn't talk like that. – Like the pictures I mean. ''I love you.'' He couldn't say that – any more than I could. But he does.'

'And do you love him?'

'Oh yes,' said Bet. 'I can say it to you. I worship that man.'

'And when's the wedding?' Bet shrugged. 'But if he's got a job – '

'Oh he can afford us,' said Bet. 'I mean tram driving's a steady job. It isn't that.'

'What then?'

'It's Bob and Andy and Da and Grandma. Who's going to take care of the other Pattersons if I get wed and move away?'

'Couldn't Frank move in with you?'

'He wouldn't hear of it,' said Bet. 'He told us straight. He wants a wife. Not a share in a housekeeper.' The tears welled then. 'Oh Jane,' she said. 'What am I going to do?'

Jane took Bet in her arms and rocked her as Aunt Pen had once rocked a much younger Jane. 'There there,' she said. 'We'll think of something, you'll see,' and offered her a silk handkerchief which Bet resolutely refused to use. So Jane drenched it in perfume and gave it to her for her bottom drawer, as proof of her optimism, then drove her back home in style before going to the clinic.

39

D R STOBBS WAS busy as usual, so she went into the kitchen for a chat with Bella Docherty, a kitchen still redolent of stew, before she heard the characteristic thump of the Armstrong-Siddeley's gear change, and stood in the hall to watch as a couple of sturdy-looking men carried in a woman on a stretcher, a woman prematurely aged, her body wasted. Her idea to feed helpers seemed to be working, thought Jane, even though the burden they carried appeared beyond help. She watched as they lifted her into Stobbs's surgery, then a voice spoke behind her.

'Cancer of the breast, I fear,' said the voice, 'and quite incurable.'

Jane turned to face a man in a superbly cut, if ageing grey suit, and a dog collar.

'You must be Miss Whitcomb?' he said.

'Canon Messeter?' she asked, and offered her hand.

He was of medium height, but so lean as to look taller. In almost every way he looked the conventional upper-class Englishman: sprucely shaved, grey hair neatly cut as if he had been to Tramper's that morning, hand-lasted shoes. Nose the required aristocratic beak, she noticed, chin and mouth firm. Only the eyes departed from the norm. They were of the deepest, most shining blue she had ever seen, and with more than a hint of madness.

Messeter took her hand and bowed over it with a kind of studied nonchalance, and she knew at once that in his day the canon had had more than his share of success with the ladies.

'You drive my car much better than I do, so I'm told,' he said.

'It's not the easiest car in the world to drive.'

'Never was,' said Messeter. 'But then neither was a field ambulance.' He looked at her. 'You know it's a pleasure to meet you. I had my doubts about that, but it is.'

'Doubts?'

'We get them here from time to time. Mostly women. Ladies, I suppose one must call them. They come here oozing sympathy and beef tea, and sometimes a little money if we're lucky, but after their first encounter with someone like that poor soul in there – ' and his head bobbed towards the surgery, ' – they take the wings of the morning as the psalmist says, and away they fly. But you, I perceive, are back, just as Stobbs said you would be.'

One of Bella Docherty's helpers came in with tea and biscuits, and he took her to a room off the hall, a room that was all books and battered furniture, and a crucifix on the wall. Canon Messeter's room.

'A parson gets used to drinking tea,' he said. 'Occupational hazard. Before that I was a soldier. They drink tea at all hours, too.'

'Which regiment?' Jane asked.

'Rifle Brigade. . . . I enjoyed my time as a rifleman.'

'You must have been in France?'

'Lord yes. I was in India when it started, but they got me back to France in time for first Ypres, and I had the good fortune to be carried by colleagues of yours on a couple of occasions. Pity it wasn't you. It would have been more appropriate, somehow.'

'Did you say *good* fortune? To be wounded twice?'

'Oh good heavens yes,' said Messeter. 'I got better, you see. Or rather considerably better than I had been, but as a rifleman I was rather surplus to requirement then. I regretted it bitterly at the time – I was a major, you see, and next in line for the battalion. Vanity of vanities, you will say, but one is but human after all – though I do pray for forgiveness of course. The sin of pride is very terrible. I should warn you that I do pray rather a lot.'

'So I should suppose,' said Jane.

'On account of this?' Messeter touched his collar. 'Because prayer's my trade, so to speak?'

'Because of the kind of man you are.'

Messeter bowed once more, this time sitting down.

'Prayer is very necessary in Felston,' he said. 'The devil has such a strong hold. I cannot understand how a man can turn his back on God and live in this place – though Stobbs seems to have achieved it.'

'When did you go into the church?' Jane asked.

'In 1918. After I received the second one. . . . A shell burst. . . . I have rather a lot of German iron in me still. All the best authorities were agreed that I should be dead, and one day it occurred to me that as I wasn't – dead, I mean, – God must have had some further plans for me – and what they were seemed obvious. I took orders and did rather well – vanity again, you observe, although this time I speak no more than the truth. A curate in Mayfair, then rector in a quite delightful village in Hampshire, and then a canonry. The rank of major you see, and the battalion the next step up, by which of course I mean a bishopric.

'But God hadn't spared me to enact the same vainglorious foolishness a second time. Perhaps he gave me a reminder. Certainly it was His will, insofar as everything is His will.'

'What was?'

'I was ill again. A piece of shrapnel became dislodged after I fell when out hunting. Once again I nearly died. Once again I was spared, and obliged to ask myself why. . . . All the medicos were convinced that I would never work again, so I resigned my living and asked a politician I know what he considered would be the greatest contrast to a village in Hampshire, and he said Felston. So I sold up and came here and met Stobbs – and I haven't stopped working since, except for an occasional spell in hospital, which is why I missed you last time. You are a journalist, one gathers.'

'On the *Daily World*,' she said, not without pride. Almost she produced her press pass.

'Vanity, lust in a small and ineffectual way, belligerence, snobbery and occasional good works – mostly yours.'

'I covered the Four Arts Ball for the paper not long ago,' said

Jane. 'It was all the things you mention. And it will make money for Felston.'

'You accept money from such a source?'

'I'd take money from the devil himself,' said Jane, 'if it would help the poor people here.'

'Which is precisely why the devil won't give you any. You've raised rather a lot already, Stobbs tells me.'

'I seem to be good at it,' said Jane. 'I came out of a crisis of sorts not long ago. Nothing like yours, but important enough – to me at any rate. And after it was over I just sort of got involved. Largely because the man I was engaged to once lived here.'

'So Stobbs told me.'

'After I – felt better, I started to find out things about myself. And one was that I wasn't afraid to ask for money – not when the money was for Felston.'

'I thank God for it,' Messeter said; and he means precisely that, thought Jane. Then Stobbs came in.

'Miss Whitcomb,' he said. 'Nice of you to look in. Have you brought another cheque?' Then to Messeter: 'Mrs Elstob's dying. I've banged enough morphine into her to calm a platoon, but she's still conscious. She wants a prayer, she says.'

He says it as he would say she wants a corned-beef sandwich, thought Jane. Messeter left them at once.

'So now you've met,' Stobbs said. 'What do you make of him?'

'I like him.'

Stobbs looked at her. 'Not everybody does,' he said. 'He frightens people. Goodness often does.'

'I'd no idea he'd been so ill,' said Jane.

'Whalebone and leather that one,' said Stobbs. 'He should have died years ago. But he reckons God won't take him until he's outlived his usefulness. He gave me every penny he had the first day he came here. What a man.'

He began to go through his pockets, and produced a pipe at last. Jane lit a cigarette.

'Did you bring a cheque?' he asked.

'Have a heart,' she said. 'I've just about had time to cash the last one.'

'I know,' he said. 'But this place eats money.'

'I'll go back soon and raise some more.'

'The sooner the better,' said Stobbs.

'Just as soon as I see Mrs Patterson into hospital,' said Jane.

'Cataract?' Jane nodded. 'Who've you got?'

'A man called Hannay,' said Jane. 'At the Royal Victoria Infirmary.'

'Then you've got the best,' said Stobbs. 'That lad'll end up in Harley Street soon. But you don't have to stay here.'

'I want to be sure she's all right.'

'She's got a son. She's got grandchildren. She'll be all right. But I need the money you can raise now. This minute.'

'You can wait a week,' she said.

'The poor can't.'

You sound just like my very nearly brother-in-law Andy, she thought.

'Yes,' she said. 'They can. Because they'll understand why. I love that old woman and I think she's beginning to love me. Certainly for the moment she needs me, not just for the love, but for the way I can make her do things in a way her own family can't. If I go now she'll think I've deserted her, and what kind of love is that?'

Behind her Messeter said, 'She's right, you know. . . . Love first, and then good works. First Mary, then Martha, and perhaps this young lady is both. I think Mrs Elstob is dying, by the way. She would like me to take her home for more prayers before she goes.'

'We need your car,' said Stobbs. 'There are still patients to see.'

'I'll drive her,' said Jane. 'Just tell me where I have to go.'

There was uproar, of course, when Grandma found out that her operation was already arranged, and getting her to Newcastle a heroic labour, but she went in style in the Wolseley, with Bet and Andy and Bob in attendance, as well as Jane, and Stan swore to visit her as soon as he'd finished work and washed and changed.

The private room alarmed her: she had never felt so isolated in her life, but the others stayed on and there were flowers and fruit, and Bob had brought his crystal set. I should have thought of that. She won't be able to read for some time, thought Jane. And next day, when the operation was over and they all went back to see her, she took the latest and most expensive wireless she could find, and the old woman, eyes bandaged, body vulnerable still after the anaesthetic, listened enchanted to Peter Dawson singing 'Glorious Devon'.

'By, you certainly splash your money about,' she said.

'When it's in a good cause,' said Jane.

'So I'm a good cause, am I?' Grandma Patterson asked.

'The best.' Jane leaned over to kiss her.

'That means you'll be leaving us, I suppose?'

'I have to,' said Jane. 'I've had my marching orders. I've got a lot of money to raise.'

Mostly it was talks again, and mostly to women's groups. Middle-class women, she discovered, had a voracious appetite for being lectured and hectored, especially by another woman, provided she was rich and famous enough. And then there was the Quart' Arts Ball article. That went down very well. Disraeli's two worlds in a column and a half, Jay called it, and she told herself that she must ask Lionel what it meant. She thought of it as treacle, but the amount of correspondence – and even money – it generated was very gratifying.

'You can't beat righteous indignation,' said Jay, 'provided you cut it with Hearts and Flowers.' She'd done that, all right. Mary Pickford would have been proud of her, or even Charlie Chaplin.

Then there was the ball. Lady Twyford had been approached by Jay and her fee agreed. It was outrageous of course, but she would make sure she sold enough tickets to pay for it. The Berkeley to hold it, and the right band, the right caterers. Décor by whoever was fashionable at the moment and a dance programme that alternated pictures of the London season with pictures of Felston.

'But we've done that already with the Quart' Arts Ball piece,' Jane objected.

'Always repeat a success,' said Jay Bower. 'It's only with a failure that you pretend it never happened.'

There was a lot to do. Andy – or Francis for that matter – would have dismissed it as frivolous, but Jane treated it with the necessary importance. It was a means of making money, after all, and caterers and band leaders and entertainers – Bower had insisted on a cabaret; had even insisted that services be donated free for Felston's sake – were as important as medicines and drugs for Dr Stobbs's clinic. The one financed the other after all. At five guineas each the ticket price was astronomic, but Bower argued that all the snobbish rich and social climbers would clamour for tickets just because the price was astronomic, and he was right. On the other hand, she noticed, quite a lot of people wanted tickets because they thought that helping her – or Felston – was a good idea. All her fellow ambulance drivers, for instance. Bower promptly had an editorial written about it, and earmarked Sarah for the cabaret.

Suddenly South Terrace was finished. Lionel telephoned and she went over to 'ooh' and 'aaah' more than ever, while Lionel and Hawkins stood by and looked smug, and rightly so, she thought. The central heating worked so well that the fires were lit only as part of the décor; the Bakst curtains glowed in a drawing room that was white with touches of black, like shadows, the dining room was sumptuous and traditional. The shower worked.

'Would you like tea, miss?' Hawkins asked.

'Champagne,' said Jane. 'There should be champagne. But I forgot to buy some.'

'I didn't,' said Lionel. 'In the refrigerator, Peggy darling.' A refrigerator too!

Hawkins set off, and Jane called after her, 'Bring three glasses,' then turned to Lionel. 'I've had no time to ask,' she said, 'but how did the Romantic Movement go?'

'Very well,' Lionel said. 'She taught me quite a lot.'

'Lionel,' Jane said, 'darling. Please tell. What is Hawkins up to?'

'God knows,' said Lionel, 'but whatever it is she's working at it.' Then Hawkins came in with a bottle and three glasses, and they drank to a house brought to life, and Jane toasted the other two for having done it.

'I think I may have found a cook for you, miss,' said Hawkins. Jane noticed that she was handling her champagne glass far more elegantly than Pardoe had ever handled his.

'Mrs Barrow, miss. She used to be with Lord Carberry. You know – the one who owns all those ships.'

'Good gracious,' said Jane. 'He's incredibly rich. Whyever did she leave?'

'He didn't pay enough, miss.'

'And I will?'

'Enough isn't all that bad, miss,' said Hawkins.

'I'm delighted to hear it. Perhaps you'd better engage the rest of the staff as well – but make it a week's notice – just in case.'

'Very good, miss.' From the tone of her voice Jane gathered that Hawkins already had.

'It's this damn ball,' she said defensively. 'I'm frantically busy.'

'Of course,' said Lionel. He was maddeningly soothing.

'And when am I to be allowed to move in?' she asked.

'On Monday if you like, miss,' said Hawkins. 'All we have to do is pack your things and move the Mount Street stuff out of storage.'

'Then Monday it shall be,' said Jane.

Until then she spent most of her time in Fleet Street, where Foch lorded it over a following of devoted slaves and she harangued and cajoled to sell more tickets, raise more subscriptions. Sunday she spent mostly in Jay's bed, in the flat he called the penthouse. Living above the shop, she called it, and the expression was new to him. When she explained it he was delighted.

'It's the only place to be,' he said.

'Except Berkshire.'

'Not yet,' he said. 'Not while we're like this. If you won't marry me – above the shop will have to do.' His arms came round her, gentle yet pleasing. She knew that one. He was up to something.

'I have to go to New York,' he said. 'California too.'

'Before the ball?'

'No. But soon after.'

'How soon?'

'As soon as you're ready.' She stiffened against his coaxing hands.

'You want me to meet your family? Is that it?'

'That's not it at all,' he said. 'You'll meet them, sure – but I think you'll like New York. *And* California. And I want to be there when you do. That's *all*. Honestly.'

She believed him and relaxed, and let his hands resume their pleasing.

On Monday evening she ate a solitary and adequate meal prepared by the agency's adequate cook. Next day an equally new parlourmaid would begin work at Offley Villas. Mummy couldn't possibly take much longer to return home, and she wanted the place to be comfortable for her.

Jane went into the drawing room and tried the new cook's coffee. It was less than adequate. While she sipped it cautiously and read the *Morning Post*, Hawkins appeared.

'There's a taxi at the door, miss,' she said.

'Anyone we know?'

Hawkins looked puzzled. 'It looks like her ladyship, miss.'

'Good God,' said Jane.

'And with a gentleman.'

'Go and let them in,' said Jane, 'then warn cook that we may need extra dinner.' She put down her coffee cup and went into the hall.

There could be no doubt that it was Mummy. A little thinner, but still with a magnificent carriage, and scarcely darker than when she left England for India. Shady hats and parasols, thought Jane, and how attractive both can be when handled adroitly, which could well explain the attendant gentleman.

'Mummy, darling,' she said, and went forward to embrace her.

Lady Whitcomb looked long and hard at her daughter, and then, 'Well!' she said, and that one word said it all. That she had changed very much and not necessarily for the better, that she was much, much too self-sufficient, and far too well-dressed for a Monday in Kensington. Even so she returned Jane's embrace. Her arms about me are still familiar, thought Jane, and she smells as always of lavender, and when I move I shall miss her, but I shall be content.

'My daughter Jane,' said Lady Whitcomb. 'This is Major Routledge.'

'How do you do?' said Jane, and offered her hand to a man as tall, slender, spruce as Canon Messeter, but with none of the madness in his eyes. 'Are you staying for dinner?' she asked. 'I've warned cook – '

'We ate on the train,' said her mother. 'Really the prospect of sitting down to a meal while not in motion has all the charm of novelty.'

Major Routledge chuckled appreciatively.

– 419 –

'Kind thought on your part, but I must be off,' he said. 'I wired ahead and booked a room at my club. Digging in there for a while.'

'Major Routledge is a member of the Travellers,' said her mother. 'Not wholly inappropriate for one who has been to India and back seven times.'

Again the chuckle. It seemed the major had had a lot of practice.

'Hope I don't get lost on the way there,' he said, and this time it was her mother's turn to laugh. It was like being at a concert party behind the lines, thought Jane.

'Taxi's waiting so I'll say au revoir,' said Routledge. 'Just come along to see your mother's kit got in safely.' He turned to Lady Whitcomb. 'I'll telephone you tomorrow if I may, Honoria.'

'Certainly you may, George,' said her mother, then waited, implacably the only word, as Routledge bent to kiss her mother's cheek, and shake her hand, and go.

'Let us go into the drawing room,' her mother said.

'Shall we see to your luggage first?'

'The heavy baggage will be delivered tomorrow by van,' said her mother. 'Doubtless there will be men to help carry it upstairs. I see Hawkins is still about the place. No doubt she can take my overnight case upstairs and unpack it – if she's careful, of course.'

They went into the drawing room.

'Would you like anything?' Jane asked. 'Coffee? Sherry?'

'Nothing at all,' said her mother. 'And if I did I am perfectly capable of requesting it.'

'Of course you are, Mummy,' said Jane. 'I merely thought that the journey might have tired you.' She said it easily and without strain, and her mother was satisfied.

'That was kind,' she said. If only she didn't sound so surprised, thought Jane. 'You will have observed that little scene in the hall,' said her mother. 'George and Honoria, the shared jokes, the kiss on the cheek.'

'Yes of course, Mummy,' said Jane.

'The conclusion, need I say it, is obvious.'

'That you're now engaged?'

'Not quite that. I have been invited to become so, not once but on numerous occasions.'

Like daughter, like mother, thought Jane.

'At my age it is flattering, to be sure,' said her mother, 'but one does not accept such an invitation lightly, and technically it could be argued that I should still mourn your father.'

'That is entirely your own business,' said Jane firmly.

'A just and friendly observation,' said her mother, 'and I thank you for it. You have been busy while I've been away?'

'Yes, Mummy.'

'With that newspaper, no doubt. Tell me about it. You may smoke a cigarette if you wish.'

Jane lit up at once. The *Daily World* business was all right, and so were suitably edited versions of Ireland and Paris, but Felston, and her reasons for being involved with it, were high hurdles indeed. She had no glib story prepared: there was nothing she could offer but the truth.

'The Royal Northumbrians,' her mother said when she had finished. 'I attended a ball they gave once, in Simla, in the year I married your father. George was in the Gloucesters before he transferred to the Puffers, but I believe I informed you of that in my letter.'

'Yes, Mummy.'

'And so your captain was killed?'

'On the 10th November, 1918.'

'And decorated, you say?'

'DSO. Military Cross.'

'And it never occurred to you that I might be interested in hearing of all this?'

'It occurred to me very often,' said Jane. 'But I couldn't. I couldn't tell anybody.'

'Whyever not?'

'Because I was mad.'

'You were, my poor child, and I'm beginning to understand why. If you'd told me – '

'I wouldn't have been mad,' said Jane.

'You didn't tell your father?'

'Of course not.' The vehemence of the answer pleased her mother.

'But you're telling me now,' she said. 'Do I take it that means that you are cured?'

'According to Dr Lockhart I'll never be cured,' said Jane. 'But for the moment at least I seem to be able to control myself.'

'Very much so,' said her mother. 'How is your house hunting?'

'Finished,' said Jane. 'I bought one in South Terrace. I was supposed to move in tomorrow.'

'Then I beg that you will do so,' her mother said.

'Don't you want me to stay till you're settled in?'

'You told me before I left that there could only be one queen to a hive,' her mother said. 'You haven't changed your opinion, I'm sure. Please go. I have been settled in here as you call it for fifteen years.'

'I promised to take Hawkins with me,' said Jane.

'Really there is no end to your kindness,' her mother said.

'I have a replacement for her. She starts tomorrow. With your approval. And you have a new cook, too.'

'You have appropriated the old one?'

'She ran away,' said Jane.

'I suspect the beginning of a saga,' said her mother, 'and I am rather too tired for narrative at the moment. Let us save it for breakfast. How is your brother?'

'Well,' said Jane, 'but he's part of the saga too.'

'Then I shall bid you good night,' said her mother, and kissed her and left. Jane found it necessary to have a little brandy before she went to bed.

Next morning she told her mother about Francis's friend. She made no reference to the sexual nature of the friendship because she found it impossible to do so.

'He sounds a most unsatisfactory young man,' her mother said when she had done.

'He is, Mummy.'

'And what do you intend to do with your father's papers?'

'They will form part of a Guy Fawkes bonfire.'

'I congratulate you on your decision. It cannot have been an easy one,' said her mother, and added: 'He broke that vase in the hall, you say?'

'I'm afraid so.'

'It was a wedding present from a colleague of your father's,' Lady Whitcomb said. 'I always disliked it.'

'But I thought you adored the thing.'

Her mother smiled.

'I may have given you that impression,' she said, 'but that was merely to annoy your father, who detested it. At what time do you intend to leave me?'

'I'd like to be at South Terrace before lunch, if that's all right?' said Jane.

'Why not?' said her mother. 'It is your house after all. I am to be privileged to see it?'

'As soon as it's presentable,' said Jane.

'And in the meantime I shall remain here,' said her mother, and smiled. This time the smile seemed to be without malice. 'Unchaperoned.'

'You could always invite Miss Gwatkin to visit you,' said Jane. Her mother nodded as one acknowledging a hit.

'Did I not say that Gwendoline and I had quarrelled?' she asked.

'Something about her being fat, and her need to sing,' said Jane. 'It sounded the merest tiff.'

'It was nothing of the kind,' her mother said. 'Words were spoken. Unforgivable words.'

'And yet you shared a cabin on the way back?'

'We did not,' said her mother. 'We did not even share the same boat. I had a single state room.'

'Golly,' said Jane, and then: 'Forgive me, Mummy. But wasn't it expensive?'

'The money at Cox and King's took care of it,' her mother said. 'Really a most pleasant surprise. So like your father to forget about it.' She paused, and then, for her mother, became almost furtive. 'You remember Cox and King's office in Calcutta?'

'Quite well,' said Jane. 'In Chowringhi, wasn't it? Always a crowd of people.'

'A hotbed of gossip,' said her mother. 'A positive hotbed. Still, it enabled one to keep in touch, which is not always an easy matter in India.'

'You met someone there?'

'I had news of someone,' her mother said. 'An old acquaintance of yours. Perhaps rather more than an acquaintance. Miss Vincent. Vinney I believe you called her.'

'You saw her?' Jane asked.

'That was not possible,' her mother said, and then: 'I'm sorry, Jane, but there seems to be no way in which I can spare you this. Miss Vincent died. Two years ago. Of cholera.'

'Oh,' said Jane. 'Oh dear God how awful,' and she covered her face with her hands. Her mother got up from the table and came to her, patting her shoulder.

'It's as I thought,' she said. 'Miss Vincent was rather more than just your governess.'

'Yes,' said Jane. 'She was. . . . And her orphanage? Did that die with her?'

'No,' said her mother. 'It continues. A group of Eurasian women Miss Vincent recruited have stayed on. They are determined. Really quite determined. Able too, so I am informed. Though short of funds of course.'

'You have their address?' Jane asked.

'You wish to send money?'

'Aunt Pen left Vinney rather a lot for the orphanage,' said Jane. 'I'll add to it.'

'I've already done so,' said her mother, and this time her smile glittered with malice. 'That windfall from your father. Wherever he may be, he can hardly object to my helping a Eurasian woman or two. You have a telephone?'

'The number is in your book, Mummy.'

'Then be so good as to inform me on the instrument as soon as it is convenient to call on you. I should very much like to see your new home. And the major too, of course.'

Jane rose. Her mother embraced her and she returned the embrace.

'I think that I can understand your loss,' her mother said. 'I honestly think I can. From everything I heard, Miss Vincent was a remarkable woman. . . . I'm sorry.'

Jane left Offley Villas soon after. There was nothing to keep her there, apart from her mother's astonishing expression of affection, and that she thought had been shown simply *because* she was going away. She left her mother to her new parlourmaid, her adequate cook, and her major, talking on the instrument.

40

H ER OWN NEW staff were there to greet her, presented by
Hawkins: the cook, Mrs Barrow (why was it that all cooks,
whether married or single, were Mrs?), the kitchenmaid, and
the second parlourmaid, Brown, already, Jane noticed, firmly
under Hawkins's thumb. Such unimportant creatures as char-
woman and jobbing gardeners were not it seemed thought
worthy of presentation. What would Andy think, she wondered,
if he knew that it took four grown women working full time to
take care of me, and others working part time too? And even so
she didn't have a lady's maid to do her hair, manicure her nails,
look after her dresses. Ladies' maids were all very well when one
felt lazy, but they were great ones for prying, and gossips every
one. Impossible to have a lady's maid *and* Jay.

Lionel came over for cocktails soon afterwards, and to fuss
while Aunt Pen's cherished pieces and pictures were installed,
and when it was done they relaxed. The house was a delight
and she'd told him so, and Hawkins. Now it was time to test the
other creative artists in the establishment. From the first taste of
Mrs Barrow's vol-au-vents, Jane knew that she was enslaved.
The word 'artist' was by no means overdoing it. Lionel was
already using words like 'minor genius'. Over coffee which was
not like English coffee at all, he told her earnestly, 'You must
never lose her.'

'Lord Carberry did.'

'Carberry doesn't know a soufflé from a syllabub,' said Lionel.
'Of course she left him. Her cooking for Carberry would be like

– 425 –

setting Raphael to paint railings.' He turned to her. 'You look sad,' he said.

'I've just learned that a friend of mine has died,' she said. 'A friend I haven't seen for years. If you'll excuse me, I'll have to do something about it.'

She went to the little room Lionel had designed for her when she wanted to be alone to work, or think, or gossip on the phone with friends. The phone was there, already installed, an elegant affair of brass and ivory. She called Mr Medlicott. It seemed that he knew.

'Yes,' he said. 'That chap Pinner got on to it. I wrote to you just now to tell you so. He had the idea of writing to Cox and King's direct. Bright chap, your Mr Pinner. . . . You want me to go ahead with the legacy?'

'I want you to double it – if that's possible.'

'If you're sure. . . .'

'I have never been more certain of anything,' she said. 'As quickly as possible, please.'

'Yours to command, of course.'

He sounded puzzled, but she could not bring herself to tell him that she had lost a friend. She went back to Lionel.

'So now it's done,' she said.

'Now it's done. . . . You'll give a party to warm your little house?'

Georgina without Michael she thought, and the Lessings to see what they would make of it. Tony Robins if he would come, because he would tell Pardoe and that would annoy him extremely. Dennis because he was sweet and Francis because she must. All the girls from the ambulance corps, and then she could ensnare Sarah and tell her how important it was to do her bit for Felston. And darling Lionel of *course*. And Jay, if he would come. He wasn't very keen on parties that didn't sell his paper, especially if there weren't a lot of nobility present. And the only lady of title she knew was Louise (she could hardly count the Lessings, even suppose they accepted) and one by herself he would consider paltry. She knew no other nobility, except for Lady Twyford, who would probably want a fee for coming. But then she remembered that she did know some nobility. Well sort of. The Hilyard twins. Catherine was Lady Catherine after all, and Piers was the Honourable. She would ask them.

'I really must give a party,' she said. 'Drinks and canapés?'

'Caterers,' said Lionel firmly. 'We don't want Mrs Barrow prostrate. We'll hire a butler and footman, too. Add to your consequence. Shall I do it?'

'Would you, darling?'

'Well of course,' said Lionel. 'I adore parties. And you will give lovely ones, I'm sure.'

More talks, more and more talks, and more passing round of hats. She was now quite brazen about it, and of course she was in her way quite famous now, and that helped. More articles too, because Jay needed a stockpile. They would be off to America in the New Year, he told her, and he needed a supply of her work to appear while they were away. About the party he wasn't sure at all, until she mentioned Louise, and the Hilyard twins, and then he said he'd try.

Every evening she spoke to Grandma Patterson on the telephone, and heard the tired whisper of a voice after the operation grow stronger and stronger, until the bandages were removed: her right eye had regained its sight. 'And now they tell me I have to go through it all again with the other one,' the old woman said. 'By – you know how to make a body suffer, Jane Whitcomb.' And then: 'When am I going to see you? I *can* see you now, you know.'

'Soon,' said Jane. ' I promise.'

'Well mind you do,' the old woman said. 'I feel starved for the sight of you.'

It was time to invite her mother, and her major of course. Honoria and George. Impossible to explain to the minor genius in the kitchen that her mother's lack of interest in food was almost total: adequacy her only criterion. Instead she allowed Mrs Barrow full rein, because she would have to eat the stuff too, and Lionel. The chance of eating a meal cooked by Mrs Barrow more than overcame his dread of meeting Lady Whitcomb, so there was a menu of consommé and sole, partridges and soufflé, Riesling to drink, and burgundy, because there were gentlemen present.

They arrived punctually to time, but Lionel was already present, summoned early so that they could gulp a cocktail together before Lady Whitcomb arrived.

'Liquid courage,' said Lionel, and poured the last dregs of the shaker into his glass, then stiffened, listening hard. 'Oh my God,' he said.

There was the rattle of a taxi and Hawkins scurried in, scooped up the shaker and glasses, then scurried out again and was only just in time to open the door when the bell rang. Jane and Lionel rose as Lady Whitcomb entered with her major, already alert to the fact that his Honoria might make a joke at any moment.

Jane performed introductions, and her mother looked about her, an imposing presence in black with silver lace, and an emerald set that Jane had not seen for years, and which had been recently cleaned, too. Mummy was definitely courting. No doubt about it. And why not? Her father would never have wished her to do otherwise.

'Would you like me to show you round the place?' she asked.

'I would,' said her mother. 'It will be interesting to see the kind of environment you envisage as being appropriate to yourself.'

The two of them went out, and the major eyed Lionel warily. His evening suit was well enough, but Lionel wore his black and white like the plumes of a peacock.

'You and Miss Whitcomb friends?' he asked.

'I like to think so,' Lionel said.

'Known her long?'

'We met at the Lessings' party. The one they gave for the Mirova.'

'For the what?'

'The Mirova,' said Lionel. 'The Russian dancer. Lady Lessing wore a dress that was inspired by Bakst – if that's the word I'm looking for. Still – it gave me the idea for those curtains.' He nodded at the drawing-room window, ablaze with red and green and blue.

Major Routledge ceased looking wary, and looked appalled instead.

Come come, Lionel admonished himself. This really will not do. Talk about something manly, you silly old queen.

'Which regiment were you in?' he asked.

'The Gloucesters,' said Routledge. 'And you?'

'The Royal Flying Corps,' said Lionel, and Routledge looked relieved. No doubt he expected me to say the Women's Land

Army, Lionel thought, but he persevered, and poured out another glass of sherry which Routledge accepted, because, Lionel was quite sure, Lady Whitcomb was out of the room. When she and her daughter rejoined them the two men were discussing a château near Amiens where they had both, though at different times, attended performances of the same concert party. The fact that both performances had been dreadful rapidly became a bond between them.

Lady Whitcomb cut in ruthlessly. 'It is modern, of course,' she said. 'Extremely modern. But then Jane is modern, too.' Routledge looked severe, and Lady Whitcomb continued, 'I am however coming round to the opinion that Jane's kind of modernity has a rôle to play in society.' Routledge's frown vanished; a nod of approval replaced it. 'I refer to her charitable works, naturally. A distinctly modern approach. Publicity and so on. The newspapers. But their existence was known even in India, was it not, George?'

'Oh decidedly,' Routledge said.

'And even Gwendoline Gwatkin was impressed by what you had achieved.' She closed her eyes for a moment at the memory of a faithless friend. 'This house has a style all its own. Light, airy, fully of charm. I gather I am to congratulate you on that, Mr Warley?'

'One did one's poor best,' said Lionel.

'Well done, old chap,' said Major Routledge. It was rather a relief when Hawkins announced dinner.

Her mother ate sparingly, but made no adverse criticism, which was about as much as Jane had dared to hope for. She refused the burgundy, but had accepted the Riesling: again a sort of victory. Major Routledge made no effort to hide his delight at what was offered, and ate and drank almost as much as Lionel. When they had done, Hawkins brought in a decanter of port, Lionel opened the door, and the two ladies left for the drawing room.

'I am no judge on such matters, as I have no doubt you know,' Lady Whitcomb said, 'but I have eyes in my head, and I can see that you have hired an excellent cook.'

'I'm glad you think so, Mummy.'

'It's of no consequence to me,' her mother said, 'but a lot of people do set store by such things, I know, and it is thoughtful of you to indulge them, although of course money cannot be an object with you.'

'Precisely so, Mummy,' said Jane. 'May I offer you coffee?'

'I thank you. No.'

'It is very good coffee,' said Jane, and her mother smiled. In her own way, Jane knew, her mother was enjoying herself.

When the men joined them, they both accepted coffee, Routledge rather as if he needed it, thought Jane. Lionel took his and sipped and said, 'Delicious.'

'It is the best,' said Lady Whitcomb. 'It has to be. My daughter has such exacting standards.'

Game and set to you, Mummy dear, thought Jane. But not match. Not yet.

When at last a taxi was summoned for Lady Whitcomb and her major, Lionel was already wearing his coat and scarf, but he took them off again as soon as he heard the taxi's gears engage.

'I must,' he said, 'I simply must have some brandy.'

'Help yourself,' said Jane. 'I felt the same the night that Mummy came back to Offley Villas.'

'Every possible respect to you, my darling,' said Lionel, 'but what a tartar.'

'Do you suppose I don't know?' said Jane. 'But she does rather keep one up to scratch, wouldn't you say? And what about the major? What *did* you find to talk about?'

'Not the Russian Ballet,' Lionel said, 'and certainly not Bakst.'

'What then?'

'The war, what else? Who I was with. Where I served. All the usual trivia.'

'Who were you with?' Jane asked. 'How odd that I never asked you.'

'Not odd at all,' Lionel said. 'I go to great lengths to avoid such questions. I mean do I look as if I were ever in arms? I began in the Sussex Yeomanry, as a matter of fact, but transferred into the Royal Flying Crops as soon as I could. Very hearty, the yeomanry, but in the RFC I could at least be by myself from time to time.'

'You were a pilot?' Lionel nodded. 'Like my brother David.'

'Well hardly, my dear,' Lionel said. 'I survived.' He looked into his glass, swirled the golden liquid round. 'I can't think why.'

Lady Twyford was every bit as formidable as Jane had thought she would be, with a mind like a calculating machine, but at least that mind was being put to use for Felston, once a fee had been agreed. But even with Lady Twyford running the show, there were still things which needed her attention: points of protocol, sensitive egos. That was because a ball involved so many artists, said Lionel, all of whose egos were sensitive. This was largely because of the cabaret, of course. Bower's solution to finding performers for a cabaret was to tell them the date and time and make sure they did their best, or else incur the *Daily World*'s displeasure. It worked of course, but it meant that afterwards Jane had to take them out and soothe them: lunch after lunch at the Ivy, the Caprice, L'Apéritif. In the end she rebelled and told Bower at least to moderate his language. Or buy her a new wardrobe.

Mummy rang up to invite her to lunch, or dinner, and to bring her 'young man'. Jane assumed she meant Lionel, and begged off on the grounds that she was working every day, but accepted an invitation for tea. All the adequate cook would have to do, she was sure, would be to boil the water. The cakes would come from Fortnum's. And so Jane drove Lionel and Foch to Kensington in the Riley. Mummy had requested Foch's presence, as well as Lionel's, and for the life of her Jane could not think why, but the question was answered as soon as they came in.

'There,' said her mother to Major Routledge, 'doesn't he look exactly like that chaplain in the Cameronians we met in Delhi?'

Routledge laughed his distinctive laugh, at once hearty and dutiful, and agreed that Foch did, and they sipped their Earl Grey.

'My daughter,' said Lady Whitcomb to Major Routledge, 'is too busy to dine with her mother – or even to lunch. Even tea one must assume to be a kindness, the interruption of an all-too-demanding schedule. What are we to make of it, George?'

Major Routledge looked saddened but reproving.

'Young people, Honoria,' he said. 'Always obsessed with their own affairs.'

'This particular young person,' said Jane, 'is being modern –

in the most respectable way of course. I'm organising a charity ball – or rather Lady Twyford is, but I am expected to help.'

'In aid of Felston, perhaps?'

'Well – yes,' said Jane. 'We're rather hoping that you will come. And the major, of course. It should be really rather grand.'

'We're hoping for two good friends of Jane's,' said Lionel. 'The Countess of Hexham *and* Sarah Unwin. – The actress, you know.'

'Certainly I know,' said Lady Whitcomb, and it was obvious that the major knew too. 'They and my daughter spent a rather convivial afternoon together not so very long ago. But I fear it would not be appropriate for me to attend. My bereavement is rather too recent for quite such a public appearance.'

Jane said at once, 'Then you must come to my house-warming party instead.'

'House-warming?'

'A few friends to drink a little champagne and say nice things about my new house. Not exactly a public appearance, Mummy.'

'I hardly think – '

'Oh come, Honoria,' Major Routledge said. 'No one could possibly object to your taking a glass of fizz with your own daughter.'

And Mummy capitulated without even a skirmish, let alone a battle.

'Very well,' she said. 'A brief appearance would be permissible, I suppose. Thank you, Jane. We have lived rather sequestered lives lately, George and I.'

'Not like India,' said Routledge.

'Ah, India,' Lady Whitcomb said, and sighed.

'And just what do you suppoose they got up to in India?' Lionel asked as she drove him home.

'Church, a little bridge, theatricals, polo, musical evenings.'

'How can you be so sure?'

'Because that's what it always is. And balls of course. But she couldn't go to a ball so soon after Papa's death.'

'India sounds like one mad round of dissipation,' said Lionel. 'I don't think I could stand the pace.' And then: 'I say. . . .'

'What do you say, Lionel dear?'

'That major of hers. He seems rather smitten.'

'He proposes marriage from time to time.'

'Will your mother say yes, once she's out of her mourning?'

'She very well might,' said Jane. 'Why do you ask?'

'Blest if I know,' said Lionel. 'I mean he's a perfectly presentable chap. The Gloucesters, the Puffers, all that.' And then he said again, 'Blest if I know.'

She dropped him in Chelsea, then drove over to Fleet Street for a tête-à-tête with Jay Bower. He had some criticisms of her latest article, but she defended herself vigorously. They went to bed together, then resumed their argument over supper.

'I still think it's too long,' he said at last.

'Then cut it without altering the sense,' she said. 'I bet you can't.'

He grinned at her. 'You might win at that,' he said. 'You're a fast learner. Marry me?'

'No.'

'Then tell me about the ball.'

She told him and he approved. 'If it works out right we'll do a big spread,' he told her.

'I have an idea for a follow-up,' said Jane.

'Let's hear it.'

'Let's see if it works out right first,' said Jane.

'That's my girl,' he said. 'Nothing on approval, right?'

'Right.'

'Then tell me about your party. Who's coming?'

'Everybody,' said Jane.

'Including your countess friend?'

'*And* her husband. *And* the Hilyard twins.'

'Did I ask about them? Now did I?'

'I just thought you might be interested,' said Jane. 'And did I tell you my mother's coming? She's got a title, too. She's Lady Whitcomb.'

Suddenly Jay grabbed her, put her over his knee and slapped her, then turned her to face him and put his arms about her.

'I love you,' he said.

She rubbed her bottom solicitously. 'You have such an elegant way of showing it,' she said. The slap had been meant as a joke but it hadn't felt like one.

'I got mad,' he said. 'I'm sorry. It's just – there are times when I find that I can't reach you – and that never happened to me before.'

Francis didn't come, but even he telephoned at the last moment and apologised. A Fabian Society meeting, and he had been asked to take the chair. But all the others came. Louise with her husband whom she had picked up at the House of Lords, taking his dinner jacket with her, because otherwise, as she explained, he would certainly have forgotten to change and very probably forgotten to come: but he was a plump and cheerful peer, and full of information about the novels of Surtees, and India, where he had once been ADC to the viceroy. Harriet too came early, together with her husband Neil who looked more like a bank manager than the research scientist of fiction, and danced, as she later discovered, extremely well; Sarah Unwin arrived alone: Beddoes, her current husband, was being difficult. Fred arrived alone too, in a very daring black and white trouser suit of her own design that Lionel applauded instantly. 'I *must* have one just like it,' he assured her, and Fred blossomed. More and more people arrived, as the hired waiters served champagne and Hawkins carried round the canapés. The Hilyard twins came early too, despite the fact that Piers had been hunting all day and Catherine had hunted *and* attended a tutorial. At Oxford, she assured Jane darkly, four days hunting a week was not enough. She was expected to learn things as well. Just as well she had persuaded the dean to let her loose for the night so that she could see her dentist in the morning. Piers never had *any* difficulty in persuading his dean to let him loose for the night.

Until Catherine arrived, thought Jane, Louise and Sarah had been far and away the most beautiful women in the room, but now there were three, and all of them groomed with an unerring sense of their own beauty, Louise in silver, Sarah in scarlet, and Catherine in a simple, smooth-flowing white dress that only a young and very pretty girl could wear. And then Georgina arrived, in a new and very expensive blue dress, and that made four. Sir Hugh and Lady Lessing next, he uneasily aware of Georgina, and she once more gowned in what looked like remnants of ballet scenery, but this time all muted silver and pearly grey: a classical piece – *Coppelia* perhaps, or *Les Sylphides*.

Mummy and the major arrived, and Mummy was at once monopolised by Lord Hexham. They had never met, but he had heard a great deal about her, and demanded at once the true account of Sir Guy's exploits against the maharajah who cheated at cricket. Mummy was only too happy to oblige, and poor Major Routledge looked so sad that Jane took him over to Georgina and introduced him. That done, she looked about her. All safely gathered in, she thought; except Bower.

Lionel strolled over to her. 'Counting the house?' he asked.

'All here, I *think*,' she said. 'Except Jay.'

'Bower always likes to come last,' said Lionel, 'if he comes at all.'

And after that wallop he gave me perhaps he's too ashamed to come, she thought, but that was nonsense. Bower had never been ashamed in his life. Then the door opened, and Hawkins ushered in not one man, but two.

'Who on earth – ?' Lionel asked.

'The one who looks like a prize-fighter is a Cambridge don called Tony Robbins,' she said. 'The one who doesn't is Richard Lambert.'

'And what is he?'

'A Labour MP.'

'Not a gatecrasher then,' said Lionel.

'Of course not,' she said. 'Rather an afterthought, that's all,' and went forward to greet them.

'How kind of you both to come,' she said.

'I was delayed at the House,' said Lambert. 'There was a division.' His eyes were already searching the room. According to Bower he would be looking for other politicians, because that was what MPs always did at parties. Impossible to say whether he was relieved or disappointed to find that there were none.

'And did you drive down all the way from Cambridge?' she asked Tony.

'Without you to drive me back,' he said. 'Certainly not. I came by train.'

Jane eased them into the mob, and looked about her. Going well, she thought. Enough to eat and more than enough to drink. Soon they would be dancing, but not too soon, please God. Her mother came up to her.

'It is time that we left,' she said, 'although I find it hard to leave Lord Hexham. A most perceptive man. Will your party be in the newspapers, I wonder?'

'In the *Daily World*, certainly,' said Jane. 'If you would like your name excluded – '

'I think not,' said her mother. 'In fact I am quite sure not. Gwendoline Gwatkin is a voracious reader of the *Daily World*. Come George.'

She moved to the door and the major followed, calling out over his shoulder what a wonderful time he had had. Jane went with them, and Hawkins opened the door. There, facing them on the doorstep was Jay Bower. Jane hastened to introduce them.

'The *Daily World*,' her mother said. 'You work there with my daughter?'

'I'm her employer, Lady Whitcomb,' said Bower.

'I should not be too sure of that if I were you,' her mother said.

She was aglow with the attentions of Lord Hexham and Bollinger, but even so Jane could have kissed her. When they went back inside, Lionel was already rolling back the carpet while Piers dropped the needle on to a record. 'Get Out And Get Under' began and Jay's arms came round her.

'I would have come sooner,' he said, 'but I couldn't get away.'

'It doesn't matter,' she said.

'Doesn't it?'

'Oh so touchy,' she said. 'All I meant was I know how busy you are.'

'You've forgiven me then?'

'There's nothing to forgive.' He stiffened, but she pulled him to her, forced him to keep moving. 'By which I mean that it's over and done with, so stop looking like a wronged husband.'

'Stupid of me even to try,' he said, 'considering that I'm neither. Wrong adjective. Wrong noun. . . . You're very like your mother.'

This time it was she who nearly stopped, he who pushed her on.

'That's the first time anyone's told me that,' she said.

'All the same it's true,' he said. 'Tough as old boots, and with a cold eye for realities. Your employer indeed. She was dead right to question it. Employer suggests control. Ownership even. Who could own you? I might as well try to pick up a handful of mercury.' He danced for a while in silence. 'I wish we were in bed together.'

'It would certainly liven up the party.'

She danced with Dick Lambert then, who was competent, but rather lost concentration if one tried to speak, and then Piers, who wanted her to tell him about the war, and then, as a reward, with Sir Hugh who danced divinely, as usual.

'I took your advice,' he said. 'About Michael Browne.'

'So I heard.'

He looked to where Georgina danced with Lionel. He was making her giggle almost uncontrollably, yet she never missed a beat.

'I trust she's not too heartbroken?' he said.

'It seems unlikely.'

'You think perhaps I did the wrong thing?'

'If you did,' she said, 'it was because of my advice. But as it happens I don't think you did do the wrong thing. Michael has to paint no matter what. And you made it possible for him to do it. His private life is precisely that. Private. You never met his wife, I suppose?'

'I never did.'

'I did,' said Jane. 'If you're taking on Michael, you should prepare yourself for a little more action when he gets back from abroad.'

Neil Watson claimed her then, an even better dancer than Lessing, perhaps the best dancer in the room.

'Wonderful party,' he said at once. 'I don't go to nearly enough, according to Harriet.'

'Whyever not?'

'Busy,' he said. 'Always busy. Like your pal Robins over there. And Pardoe. Not that he's likely to be a pal.'

'Most unlikely.'

'He'd like to be, you know.'

'Indeed I do know,' said Jane.

'Ah,' said Watson. 'He seems obsessed with you if you don't mind my saying so. Always asking questions about you – because of Harriet, you see. I keep telling him I hadn't even met you but he wouldn't listen. Obsessive. But then he *is* an obsessive. Quite a lot of us are. It's the only way things get done. Do I have to come to this ball of yours?'

'That's rather up to you.'

'No,' said Watson. 'It's rather up to Harriet. Which means I'm coming. I shall enjoy the dancing – you'll save me one won't you? – but there's an experiment at the Cavendish that day and I have to be at Cambridge.'

Jane noted that the Cavendish, which sounded like a club, was in fact a laboratory.

'I shall have to leave early,' said Watson. He made it sound like quitting Paradise.

Tony Robins next, and last. He was still a terrible dancer, but he didn't let it interfere with his conversation.

'I'm glad I came,' he said.

'I too.'

'I didn't think I would be,' said Tony. 'After the way I behaved last time – and you turned me down, too. But I'm glad I came. Does me good to be in an environment other than Cambridge now and again.'

How these dons love to analyse each other, and themselves, Jane thought. Still, he was rather sweet about it.

'Besides I now know that there was a *reason* why you turned me down,' said Tony. 'So much better when there's a reason, as opposed to just a general distaste.'

'And what is my reason?'

'You're promised to another,' said Tony. 'I knew it as soon as I saw you dancing together.'

'My dear man,' said Jane. 'That's Neil Watson. He's married to one of my oldest friends.'

'Not him,' said Tony. 'I've known Neil for years. Of course it's not him. I mean the other chap when I first arrived. The one who affects an American accent.'

'The only one here with an American accent *is* an American. His name is Bower and I write for him sometimes. He owns the *Daily World*.'

'That's the one,' said Tony, and left it at that, to Jane's relief. But she couldn't help wondering how soon it would be all over Cambridge, and whether anyone there would believe it, especially Francis.

The party was ending. In ones and twos, people were leaving. 'Darling, how marvellous,' they all said, and 'Such a *lovely* house.' Jane looked at the little French clock on the mantelshelf, Aunt Pen's favourite clock. Lionel said it didn't belong, but she'd put it there anyway. Nine thirty-seven, the clock said. Not bad for a six to eight party. The hired men had cleared away the glasses, and the room looked rather less like a pub with pretensions. Too many cigarette stubs in too many ash trays, and much too much cigarette smoke, but it was a nice place to be, now there were only the Hilyard twins left, and Georgie, and Lionel, and Dennis, and Jay.

Jay said, 'Can your cook make Melba toast?'

'She can make anything that can be made,' said Lionel, who didn't seem quite sober.

'Can you get some?'

'You're not feeling well?' asked Jane.

'Never better,' said Jay. 'What I want is Melba toast for everybody.'

Jane rang for Hawkins. When she came back, Jay was dancing with Catherine, Lionel with Dennis, and Piers with Georgina: beauty to beauty, Jane thought. Innocence and experience, too. Piers kept looking at Lionel and Dennis: Georgie did not; probably was only vaguely aware that there was anything odd in the fact that they were dancing together. After all it was obvious that they liked each other.

Jane turned the record, and Piers took Georgina to her seat then came to Jane, and danced with her easily and yet respectfully, somehow. He hadn't danced with Georgie like that.

'How pretty your friend is,' he said.

'Yes, isn't she?'

'And talented too,' said Piers.

'Did she tell you so?'

'Of course not,' said Piers. 'But she's Georgina Payne.'

'Actually I do know that,' said Jane.

'Oh do stop ragging,' said Piers. 'What I mean is she's on the *wire*less. Surely you must have heard her?'

'As a matter of fact I haven't,' said Jane, trying not to sound too contrite. 'I've been rather busy lately – '

'Another talented lady,' said Piers. 'Sweet of you to find the time to give such a wonderful party. She's promisd to let me take her to tea some time. Then on to the studio where she broadcasts.'

'That should be fun,' said Jane.

'I should just about think it will,' said Piers.

The dance ended, and Hawkins came in with the Melba toast, then cleared the ash trays and opened one window, just a little.

A jewel, thought Jane, a positive jewel, and wondered when Lionel would have to lunch her at the Berkeley to discuss the Peloponnesian War. . . . Jay got up and left the room, then in a little while they heard his car-door slam, and he came back with the biggest pot of caviar Jane had ever seen. Goodness he must be feeling ashamed of himself, she thought. He knows how I adore caviar.

'I was going to suggest supper somewhere,' said Jay, 'and then I thought why not let's have some of this instead, if there's any champagne left? We can always go on somewhere afterwards if we feel like it.'

'Oh,' said Catherine, and clasped her hands, rolled her eyes heavenwards. 'There *is* a Santa Claus.' She looked about twelve years old.

The party began again, and the dancing. This time it was Jay's arms that embraced Georgina. When they had done Georgie came over to Jane, and spooned caviar on to a piece of toast.

'Numbered among the elect,' she said.

'I think I've had too much champers to cope with that,' said Jane.

'I had a Scots governess once,' said Georgie. 'Bit of a slave-driver, especially on the Sabbath. She was a Calvinist or something. She said that if you were numbered among the elect you were saved. At the top table. Up there with the cherubim and seraphim. That's the way I feel now. Among the chosen. It was sweet of you to let me stay.'

'No,' said Jane. 'Not sweet at all. I like having you here. Besides, I *may* want a favour from you soon.'

'If I can I will,' said Georgie. 'You know that.' And then: 'I say. That young friend of yours is sweet.'

'Piers?'

'Of course Catherine's sweet too,' said Georgie, 'and *so* pretty. But I do rather prefer the male, sweet old-fashioned thing that I am. He's of the noblesse, I believe?'

'Younger son,' said Jane. 'His father's the Earl of Mangan.'

'Irish,' said Georgina, 'but not impoverished, not if his sister's dress is anything to go by.'

'Not in the least impoverished,' said Jane, and then: 'Georgie. . . .'

'No no,' said Georgie, and laughed. 'Not marriage. Not me.

Not even for the chance to live in Ireland. I say – your friend Bower's making rather a hit with my boyfriend's sister.'

Jane looked to where Catherine smiled up at Jay.

'Santa Claus is always popular,' she said.

He danced with her next, and she thanked him at once for the treat.

'Not enough for everybody,' he said, 'which is why I hung on to it for so long.'

'But more than enough for the deserving,' she said. 'You are sweet.'

'I am when you say so. I want to phone for a photographer if that's OK. Of course we've got library shots of Hexham and his wife and Sarah Unwin – but I could do with a picture of those twins. They're really something.'

'I think so too,' she said.

'And I'd like a picture of your mother – if she wouldn't mind.'

'I think I can find one,' said Jane, 'and she won't mind at all.'

She found a photograph, and the *Daily World* photographer came, and the second party began to drift to a close. Lionel and Dennis knew of a place where they could practise the tango together, and Piers had offered Georgina a lift, which was really too bad of him since he'd arrived in a two-seater, thought Jane, though quite understandable. Jay suggested that they all go to a nightclub, but Jane was far too tired for nightclubs, and a day of hunting and tutorials and champagne was beginning to make Catherine yawn, so Jay offered to drive her home, instead, to the family house in Curzon Street. Jane went to the door with them to watch them go. Redman was at the wheel of the Rolls-Royce. Well of course he was, she told herself. Jay brought that caviar for *me*.

41

T HE PIECE IN the *Daily World* was gratifying enough: she was 'the popular and philanthropic girl about town', the 'well known', the 'eager supporter of those less fortunate', and, as always, the address to which the charitable should send their money was prominently featured. All of which was pleasing, if predictable: Jay Bower had spent a couple of hours there after all. What did astonish her was the length of the piece – almost the whole of 'This Wicked World' devoted to her party, and Mummy, and Sarah and Louise, and the twins, all of whom were described with an almost endearing disregard for the truth. Really this time Jay had gone too far, she thought, until she looked at the other papers: the *Express*, the *Mail*, the *Morning Post*, and there she was again: not in quite such detail, perhaps, but she was there. And so was Mummy, and her major, though sometimes described as Captain Rutledge, or even as Colonel Coolidge, but he was there every time: 'a gallant upholder of the Raj'. Nothing wrong with that, she told herself, after all he *was* an upholder of the Raj and presumably gallant enough since he'd been through the war; what baffled her was how the other papers had found out, and since they had found out, why they had bothered to pursue in such detail an enjoyable, but decidedly trivial evening. Even the caviar was mentioned in one column, but not that Bower had brought it. Bower himself must have passed on the story, she thought, but why she could not begin to comprehend – except that it would be to Bower's advantage, and perhaps to Felston's too.

Mummy telephoned. It was imperative that she see Jane, she said. There were things to be said that could not be discussed on the instrument. Jane went, but left Foch behind. Mummy had sounded upset, and Foch was never conciliatory.

Offley Villas was chilly that morning, its trees already stripped bare, and the new parlourmaid was a poor hand at building a fire. Jane reached for the coal tongs. Mummy was just back from India after all. By the time her mother joined her, the flames were already leaping, the coals beginning to glow. Jane kissed her mother, who looked at once at the fire.

'You must find it chilly indeed in a room without central heating,' Lady Whitcomb said.

'I cannot allow you to die of pneumonia because of a parlourmaid's carelessness,' said Jane. Her mother smiled.

'It would be a pity,' she said, 'now that we both enjoy such social triumphs.'

'You're pleased?'

'Delighted,' said her mother. 'A photograph too. And so many words. Most gratifying. Gwendoline Gwatkin has already telephoned.'

'*Miss Gwatkin?*'

'She has social aspirations too, it appears. She wishes me to – "use my influence" was the expression she used. I told her nothing was possible until she had lost at least two stones. George also telephoned. It would seem that he was not pleased with our success. On the contrary. He referred to it as notoriety.'

'I thought the *World* did him proud.'

'Friendly, but not fulsome,' her mother agreed, 'and yet George was not happy.'

'Whyever not?'

Her mother fidgeted. 'Would you care for coffee?' she asked. 'It is early for sherry.'

'No thank you, Mummy.'

'No indeed,' said her mother. 'Unpleasantness is always best tackled head on.'

So there was to be unpleasantness.

'George is a man very conscious of his family,' her mother said. 'They are apparently conscientious and hard-working. They are also dedicated to the ideal of service and disapprove of frivolity. They all, it would seem, share a pride in this.'

'The proud house of Routledge,' said Jane.

'I suspect a quotation,' said her mother. 'Some literary game you journalists play?'

'A misquotation,' said Jane. 'Lord Macaulay. *Lays of Ancient Rome*.'

'And apt,' said her mother. 'Macaulay is exactly the sort of poet the Routledges would approve. So worthy.' She paused, then hurried on, 'You may perhaps have noticed that George is – shall we say – malleable?'

Bullyable was more the word, thought Jane, but he seems to enjoy it.

'In the past he has been influenced by members of his family. Now of course he is more inclined to heed what I say.'

'Naturally.'

Her mother smiled her special smile: the one that signified enjoyment. 'It is good of you to say so. However this – what he considers to be frivolous notoriety – has alarmed him.'

'What are his family like, Mummy? Have you met them?'

'I have not. George has three brothers. A backbench MP – Liberal of course – an archdeacon and a county-court judge. Of modest achievement, I think you will agree, but eminently worthy, like George himself.'

'He doesn't sound much like Papa.'

'He is not in the least like your father.' Lady Whitcomb sounded appalled. 'Your father was a scholar of his college, a double first who declined a fellowship to take the ICS examinations which he passed with – what is that Balliol phrase? – effortless superiority. He administered a province bigger than the United Kingdom and advised a maharajah. He was a fine shot, a superb polo player, and as promiscuous as a monkey. George is none of these things.'

'Mummy!'

'You thought him faithful, no doubt, apart from one brief, romantic idyll with the Sanderson creature?'

'Well of course I did,' said Jane.

'Then you were wrong,' said her mother. 'Anything in skirts, provided it achieved his standards of prettiness, which I admit were severe. Colour he did not consider a handicap – but then you're aware of that.'

'Mummy,' said Jane, 'why are you telling me all this now?'

'You feel I should have spared you?'

'It isn't that at all,' said Jane. 'It's just – you've kept it bottled up inside you all these years.'

'As you did with your engagement,' her mother said. 'We are more alike than you might think.'

'Somebody else said that last night,' said Jane, 'and I accept it. But why now? That's all I'm asking. I assume it's the major but I don't understand why.'

'*Very* like me in your perceptiveness,' said her mother. 'It's *because* George is so different that I intend to marry him.'

'You are quite sure that he will be faithful to you?'

'Quite sure,' her mother said. 'I have observed him very closely – of course I have – and I'm sure.'

'But that's not a reason for matrimony.'

'I was as clever as your father,' her mother said, 'but being female I was never allowed to advertise the fact. George is not clever at all. Competent, but of moderate intellect. This time I shall do all the thinking that marriage requires – and George is quite happy to allow me to do it.'

'He is able to support you?' Jane asked. Really, she thought, I'm beginning to sound like a Victorian father, but this is my mother after all, and I'm beginning to realise how much love I have for her.

'Together we shall manage,' her mother said. 'I shall let this house which will supplement our income, and George has his pension. He has retired, of course.'

'Can he get a job?'

'He's skilled in the breeding of horses,' her mother said. 'He would make an excellent manager of a stud farm.'

'And will you enjoy being a stud-farm manager's wife?' Jane asked.

'I shall enjoy being George Routledge's wife,' said her mother, and sounded suddenly like a much younger woman, the woman who had taught her the future perfect tense of the verb venir.

'I wish you good fortune,' said Jane.

'I honestly believe you mean that,' said her mother. 'Will you forgive me if I say that I'm surprised?'

'But why on earth should you be?'

'I am aware how very much you loved your father.'

'I always will. He was that sort of a man,' said Jane, 'the sort of man one can't help loving, but every time you let me, I love you too.' Again her mother smiled that special smile. 'And it's your life, Mummy. You must live as you think best. Is there any way in which I can help? Financially, I mean.'

'I do not intend to become your pensioner,' said her mother.

'Of course not.'

'But the Indian trip proved rather more expensive than either of us had envisaged, despite the windfall at Cox and King's. If I might request a loan of fifty pounds – '

'Gladly,' said Jane. 'I'll write you a cheque now.'

'I should prefer cash if that's possible,' said her mother.

'Of course,' said Jane. 'I'll stop at the bank and have someone send it round. . . . Did Aunt Pen know? – About Papa, I mean?'

'She never said so,' said her mother, 'and she had her own preoccupations – but she must have known. Everyone else did. Perhaps that was another reason why she and Nettles were so willing to make a home for you.'

'What about Francis?' Jane asked. 'Will you tell him?'

'About your father – or my intention to remarry?'

'Both,' said Jane.

'I shall endeavour to do so,' said her mother. 'The difficulty will be to persuade him to listen to a word I say, particularly when he discovers that George is not an intellectual.'

Next day was the day of the Oxford telephone calls, first from Piers, then the principal of Catherine's college.

'She doesn't approve of hunting, you see,' said Piers, referring to Catherine's principal, 'and she's not all that keen on inherited wealth either, so you can see poor old Catherine's on a hiding to nothing.' (Catherine was the elder twin, Jane had been told, by twenty-seven minutes, and Piers liked it to be known.)

'But what on earth has it got to do with me?' said Jane.

'Your ball,' said Piers.

'What about it?'

'We want to be there,' said Piers, 'but it means coming down a day early. I've already told my chap – he's no trouble – but Catherine's dragon may be a bit sticky. She told Catherine so as a matter of fact so I said I'd phone you.'

'But why didn't *she*?'

'Gated,' said Piers. 'She went out to take a look at Bridget with me and forgot to ask permission. I must say women's colleges are a bit much. Might as well be chained to an oar in a galley. You'll tell the right lies for her, won't you? She's a deserving case really.'

'Do my best,' said Jane. 'How's Bridget?'

'Looks well,' said Piers. 'Could drop the colt any day. I took Bridie for a canter. Is that all right?'

'Most kind,' said Jane. 'I'll tell my best lies for both your sakes.' She went back to the cost of printing programmes, until once again the phone rang.

'Miss Whitcomb?' said the voice. 'Miss Jane Whitcomb?'

It was a voice Vinney had mimicked many times. Dry, precise, academic. The Oxford female don's voice. Jane replied in kind.

'This is she.'

'This is Dr Caswell. I think you know a pupil of mine. Lady Catherine Hilyard.'

'Certainly.'

'Is there any possibility that you will be in Oxford in the immediate future?'

'None,' said Jane.

'What a pity.' The voice continued to be precise, but now with a hint of condescension, too. After all, Dr Caswell was already *at* Oxford. 'Perhaps we may discuss the matter by telephone.'

'Matter? Catherine is not unwell I trust?'

'Catherine is never unwell,' Dr Caswell said, a little regretfully, Jane thought. 'She tells me that you have invited her to a ball on the eleventh of December. To do this she needs my permission to go down a day early.'

'A charity ball,' said Jane. 'For a project which is important to me.'

'Charity?'

Not a good word to Dr Caswell either, it would appear. Jane crossed her fingers.

'In the present state of society there is no other way to achieve my aim,' she said. 'This is regrettable – to me at any rate.'

'May I enquire the nature of this – charity?' A little more warmth in the voice this time. Lie away, Whitcomb. It's in a good cause.

'A town called Felston in the North East of England,' said Jane. 'It's poor and neglected and abandoned, and neither our present government nor anybody else seems prepared to do anything about it. There is a clinic there that should be the responsibility of the state. It is the responsibility of no one, and will be obliged to close if my ball is not a success. Frivolity to the rescue of necessity, you will say – but there is no other solution, not in our present state of society. And so I'm giving a ball, just as I lecture and write articles for the *Daily World*.'

It rolled off her tongue without giving her the slightest cause to think. Old stuff, most of it, bits and pieces of articles and talks.

'And Catherine can assist you in this?'

'As an aide de camp she would be invaluable.'

'Aide de camp? Do I take it that she will be working?'

'Flat out,' said Jane.

'Then of course she must assist you. I'll send her to you on the tenth, if you wish.'

'Too kind,' said Jane.

'You said lecture?' Oxford's most sacred, most talismanic word.

'On the present state of Felston,' said Jane. 'Its suffering and needs.'

'I am chairman of a small society interested in such matters,' said Dr Caswell. 'We call ourselves the Two Worlds Group. – The overtones of Disraeli will be obvious to you, of course.'

'Of course,' said Jane.

'We would be delighted if you could find the time to address us.'

'I too,' said Jane, 'though I must warn you that it is my invariable rule to pass the hat round afterwards.'

There was a pause, then, 'Quite so,' said Dr Caswell. 'Quite so.'

This time Jane did phone Lionel to find out why Disraeli should be obvious, before she returned to programme costing.

As a treat, when the programmes were finished, she made time to work on the piece she had promised to write for Sarah Unwin. Sarah had agreed at once to take part in the cabaret, and her agent had been delighted, even though there was no fee. The publicity, he was sure, would be greater than even Bower had promised. The problem was the material. Sarah had wanted to do something about Felston, and nobody had ever written anything about Felston except Jane, so Jane it would have to be.

The trouble was it would have to be a monologue, not a piece for Bower's paper: dramatic, simple, short. And all she could remember was John's story about Private Walker, so Private Walker it would have to be.

Catherine came down on the tenth, determined to convert Jane's lies to truth and work as aide de camp. Dogsbody was more like it, thought Jane, but there was no doubt about it; Catherine worked: answered the telephone, ran errands, collected packages, and told lies about Jane's unavailability with an astonishing and somehow worrying fluency.

The day of the ball dawned cold and clear and crisp, which was perfect. Furs always felt better on a cold, crisp day, and taking them off in a warm room would add a sense of gratification that every woman in the place would enjoy, and so be just a little better disposed to giving. Bower had promised to escort her, but at the last moment had been delayed, which did not surprise her, and sent Dick Lambert instead, and the *Daily World* editor, Don Cook, a harassed and nervous man who became even more harassed and nervous when confronted by Jane in the Fortuny gown. ('It must be wonderful to be old,' Catherine had said, 'and allowed to wear dresses like that.') With it she had worn sapphires left to her by Aunt Pen, and the sapphire ear-rings that had once been Papa's cuff-links. The trouble was that Jay had sent her a present that afternoon, and with it a message.

'I don't know why I'm sending you these,' he had written. 'A thank you for so many things, the thought that they are right for you, the fact that Christmas is near. I think it's just that I felt an overwhelming need to give you something, and these are the best I could find to give. I look forward to seeing you again above the shop. Oh boy, do I. Jay.'

Very nice. Gratifying even. But 'these' were a pair of diamond ear-rings that were splendid indeed, so splendid that she had no diamonds to match them.

The editor came to collect her and was confronted not only by Jane, but by Catherine, slender and elegant in rose-pink, wearing the pearls lent to her for the evening by Lady Mangan, and standing behind Jane in a sort of lady-in-waiting pose. ('Pearls,' Catherine had said. 'It would be. And I came out two years ago.' 'What's wrong with pearls?' Jane had asked. 'So virtuous,'

Catherine had said. 'So inadequate.' They were three feet long at least. . . .)

Don Cook took one look at the two of them and added incoherence to his nervousness, and envied the lot of an MP, even a Labour MP, who could claim parliamentary business as an excuse. Still Lambert arrived at the Berkeley in time, and took his place by the ballroom door to help shake hands as the major domo bawled out names, sometimes correctly, sometimes not. Next to him stood Lady Twyford in a gown of unrelenting mauve and a garnet set that clashed with it so violently Jane assumed that she had done it on purpose. And yet people had come at her bidding; masses of people. If a crowd was a sign of success, then the Felston ball would be a triumph.

Her arm was limp when eventually she went to her table, and was able to look about her. The Lessings had booked a table and filled it, and so had Louise and Lord Hexham. Georgina, she noticed, was sitting with the Lessings: a plea for forgiveness on Sir Hugh's part, and Piers was already hovering beside her when he should have been sitting next to his sister. The moth and the flame may be the greatest cliché of the lot, thought Jane, but that's because there's no other way to describe it. Then the band struck up 'After You've Gone', and Dick Lambert asked her to dance, no doubt because Jay had told her that he was supposed to do so.

On to the floor they went, and Jane forced herself to prattle merrily because after all they were supposed to be enjoying themselves and people were watching, photographers hovering, and poor Lambert was quite incapable of talking and dancing at the same time. On the way back to their table he said: 'Well at least your ordeal's over quickly.'

'Ordeal?'

'Your duty dance with the amateur Trappist. I'm sorry, Miss Whitcomb, honestly I am. But I have to concentrate or else I go wrong.'

And that would never do for Dick Lambert, she thought.

Aloud she said, 'I think Jane would be more appropriate, don't you?'

'I don't know about appropriate,' he said, 'but I'd like it. Thank you.'

'Do you find these affairs a strain?'

He grinned. 'Give me a political meeting every time. You won't find me tongue-tied then.'

'I'll look forward to it,' said Jane, 'but if it's such a strain – why do you do it?'

'Felston,' he said, promptly. 'Never mind this talk about charity not being the answer. We all know that, but it's all there is, and if there's money going then Felston must have its share.'

'No matter how many Charlestons it takes?'

'For Felston I'd even make it a tango,' said Lambert, 'even if it does mean looking like a Tory.'

Her next partner was Lionel, and that of course meant only dancing and laughter. Lionel was enjoying himself, which meant he talked even faster than she had talked with Lambert. Only at the very end did he ask: 'Is my chum the major still courting your mama?'

'To the best of my knowledge,' said Jane.

'It's none of my business,' Lionel said, 'of course it isn't, and yet – better from me than anyone else.'

'Better *what*, Lionel darling?'

'Cheltenham races,' said Lionel. 'He was there, so I am told, keeping the bookies in champagne and accompanied by a lady. Quite an elegant lady. Your mother's not a gambler, I take it?'

'Not in the least.'

'The Cheltenham lady was. . . . Sorry to tell you now, but I was afraid that somebody else might.'

'Not at all,' said Jane. 'I'm grateful to you.' And so she was, but not just at that moment. She needed all her mind for Felston.

Piers next, and the course of true love. It was true that he was just turned twenty-one, he told her, but he was a very mature twenty-one, and after all Georgina couldn't be *that* much older, surely? And so sweet and feminine and *young*. All of which meant that Georgie too would have to be thought about. But not *then*. And still Jay hadn't appeared. Really it was quite a relief to dance with Sir Hugh, and Neil Watson, neither of whom was interested in anything but the dance.

Supper, and then the cabaret. Singers and dancers, and Sarah last of all. Sarah the star, in the sketch that Jane had written. The improvised stage in the centre of the ballroom went black, and Jane realised that she was terrified. Every word of what was to come had been written by her. The lights went up to reveal Sarah in the uniform of a VAD nurse – the kind worn at the front in 1917. The band's drummer thumped his bass, softly and insistently, and here and there the lights of the ballroom flickered: a crude enough imitation of shell fire, but real enough to create a kind of tension in every second man there.

'I want to tell you,' Sarah said, 'about Private Walker of the Royal Northumbrians. He was married and had two sons – and he was very shy, and like a lot of shy men he made jokes, sheltering his shyness behind a barrage of laughter.

'In 1917, at Passchendaele, he won the Distinguished Conduct Medal, for rescuing a comrade under fire, and sustaining severe wounds. He should have been dead, of course, quite a lot of those who won the DCM *were* dead – and the rest were lucky. That time Private Walker was lucky.

'His friends congratulated him, and bought him beer, smuggled into the hospital behind the Line, but all Private Walker said was, "I should have rescued an officer, and then I'd have got the Victoria Cross." And his friends all laughed and thought "Good old Walker. Always ready with a joke." But for once Private Walker had been serious. With the VC you got a pension, and he could have put the money by for his wife.'

Sarah's voice went on, calm, precise, the voice of a nurse remembering the words she had heard on night duty: Walker sane and Walker raving, remembering the days of peace and his work as a riveter in the shipyards, until at last he had gone home on sick-leave, home to his wife and sons.

'The wound was a bad one,' Sarah said, 'a Blighty one we used to call it. Bad enough to send him back to England – to Blighty – for weeks and weeks. Private Walker had three months, and arrived back with his wound stripe and his medal ribbon just in time for the next big push. A shell burst got him before he'd gone ten yards, and that was how I had the pleasure of Private Walker's company a second time.'

'Because it *was* a pleasure. He was so patient, even cheerful, and so concerned about me, even then, because of the humiliating and degrading things I had to do for him, the things he could no longer do for himself. He was dying of course, and we both knew it, though it was never mentioned. But once a day he would ask me to look at a photograph in his wallet: his wife and his sons: his "bairns" as he called them.

'One day his Company Commander came to see him. Captain Patterson. Like Private Walker he was a Felston man, and together they talked about their town, their home, how busy it was and thriving, and what a future Private Walker would have there. But both of them knew that they were lying. Private Walker had no future at all. When the captain had gone I went to him and he said, "You heard all that?"

'"Yes," I told him. "I heard it."

'"Sounded a bit of all right, didn't it?" he said. "But it's what I wanted, you see. What I was hoping for. It isn't what I'm going to get."

'"Now now," I said.

'"Oh give over," said Private Walker. "Don't you start looking on the bright side. There isn't time." He settled back in his pillows and looked, for the first time, relaxed, and I knew that he was ready for death.

'"Felston was all very well in its way, " he said. "Playing football on the sands when I was a lad. A pint with your pals before Sunday dinner. But I can't say I'll miss getting up at half past six on a February morning to be in time for the half-past seven hooter, and the wind cutting up the river like a butcher's cleaver. I've had my share of that – and the others can have the rest.

'"But I'll miss the wife – lying warm and snug beside us at a quarter past six and me waiting for the alarm to go off and my arms around her. Aye . . . I'll miss that – wherever I'm going. I hope I'm not speaking out of turn, sister."

'"Of course not," I said.

'"Aye well," said Private Walker. "It takes a bit of thinking about. . . . I'll just close my eyes for a few minutes. I mustn't keep you, sister."

'And so I left him, because he wanted me to leave. But I hadn't reached the end of the ward before he spoke again, and this time the voice was strong and young, the voice of the man who had rescued a comrade under fire and had the Distinguished Conduct Medal to prove it.

'"I won't leave them," he said. "I won't. How can I? I'm all they've got." But by the time I got back to Private Walker he was dead.'

The applause was deafening. First the men rose, the ones who had been there, and then the others, and the women too, and Sarah curtseyed and became no longer a VAD but an actress in costume. At last she held up her hand for silence, and when it came, said: 'You're very kind. But remember all your kindness tonight is for Felston. And just one more thing. I'm delighted to see how much you were moved by what I've just done – I know I was, when I first read it. So I'd like to let you into a secret. It was written by a good friend of mine, a fellow ambulance driver who carried many a Private Walker in her day. – Our hostess for this evening. Jane Whitcomb.'

Her arm reached out, pointing into the darkness to where Jane sat, and a spotlight obeyed the gesture, then swung across the dance floor to pick her out at last. More applause, prolonged, ecstatic, for this was not just a piece of entertainment: this was an experience shared. She got to her feet and bowed, over and over, until at last the lights of the ballroom came on and the band played 'Dardanella'.

Jane looked about her. Her entire table was staring at her as if she'd just turned lead into gold, but it was all Sarah's doing, and John's. All she'd had to do was remember. She looked away, towards the door. Bower was standing there, and as she watched he began threading his way among the dancers to the vacant chair beside her. For once nobody seemed to have noticed him.

'Mr Bower,' she said. 'How good of you to come.'

'I promised I would,' said Bower. 'I hope you got my present.'

'Very nice,' said Jane. 'Extremely nice in fact. But not with sapphires.'

If he did not mind being overheard, then neither would she. The band began to play 'Ramona', and he rose.

'I should very much like to dance with you,' he said. She rose too.

'Just as well,' she said. 'You are one of the hosts after all.'

'I hope Don Cook did his best,' said Bower.

'It's hard to tell,' she said. 'The poor man's so nervous.'

'That's because I pay him three thousand a year on a day's notice.'

'Good gracious,' said Jane. 'Is he worth it?'

'He must be,' said Bower. 'He hasn't had the day's notice yet.'

They began to dance. 'You really liked the ear-rings?' he asked.

'I really did.'

'Will you take them with you to America?'

'And tell everyone that you gave them to me?'

'No. . . . Not unless you want to,' said Bower. 'Just take them.'

They were beginning to like each other again, she thought.

'What made you so late for your own ball?'

'Politics,' he said. 'There's a strike brewing. A big strike.'

'There's always a strike brewing.'

'Not like this one,' said Bower. 'This one's going to be *big*. If it happens – but maybe it won't. Still if it does – I want the *World* to be there first. You too.'

'In Felston they don't have to strike,' said Jane. 'There's no work anyway.'

'Maybe it's time you moved on from Felston,' said Bower. She stiffened.

'I don't mean get rid of it. You couldn't do that. And anyway it would be bad for the paper. I mean cover other things as well. This could be just what you need.'

He wasn't going to tell her, she knew that: and so she wouldn't ask.

'Does it mean postponing New York?'

He shook his head. 'We'll be back before the balloon goes up. If it does. . . .' He danced on then said, 'Hey, that reminds me – why were you taking a bow when I came in?'

'I thought you'd never ask,' she sasid. 'A little piece of mine has been most kindly received by the public.' She told him about Sarah – and Private Walker.

'You should have saved it for the paper,' said Bower.

But he was pleased for her, she knew.

The ball was a success, inasmuch as it made even more money than she had dared hope for, even after Lady Twyford had been paid. Bower stayed till the end, and did his duty nobly: that is to say he danced with a great many women who were rich and plain as well as Louise and Georgina and Sarah and Catherine. Jane knew her duty and accepted invitations from wherever they came – every man there had contributed after all – but found time for another dance with Dick Lambert, though she avoided Mr Cook.

As they left the floor Lambert achieved speech at last. 'I'm glad Mr Bower managed to get here,' he said.

'It was his ball as much as anybody's said Jane. 'He *had* to get here.'

'Hamlet without the prince otherwise,' said Lambert, and smiled. 'Did he say why he was so late?'

'He had a meeting,' said Jane. 'You'll find when you've worked for the *World* a little longer that he very often does.'

He blushed a mottled, unpleasing red that reminded her of her mother.

'I wasn't trying to be rude,' he said.

'Of course not,' said Jane. 'Just inquisitive. But it won't do, you know. Not with Jay Bower.' Sarah came up to her then. She had changed back into her ball gown, fresh powder, new lipstick. She looked as if she had just arrived and the time was half past nine instead of ten to two.

'Darling,' she said, 'I must have a word.' And then to Lambert, 'Do you mind, darling?' Lambert fled. 'Who was that?' Sarah asked.

'Don't you know?' said Jane.

'Should I?'

'You called him darling.'

'I call everybody darling,' said Sarah. 'It saves having to remember names. That piece of yours went well, I must say.'

'Because you did it well.'

'That was part of it,' said Sarah, and sounded quite objective, for this was work. 'But a lot of it was the writing. There's a new revue coming up shortly and I've been asked to be in it. I want to do "Private Walker". May I?'

'I might want something in return,' said Jane.

'Well, of course.' The famous smile appeared: happy and eager, and yet intimate – a smile only for one person, the one who looked at her. And she doesn't even know she's doing it, thought Jane.

'Darling, I must fly,' said Sarah. 'I have to get home and be nice to poor old Beddoes. I just remembered he's putting money into the review. Now remember, *you promised*.'

It was time to go. Jay offered a lift, so she sent Catherine home in her car, and left Piers among the group offering to escort Georgina home. She really must talk to Georgina, she thought. And Mr Pinner. That was not a nice thought, but it had to be faced. Major Routledge had been seen with another lady, and

Mummy needed fifty pounds in cash and she would have to find out why, because Francis would be hopeless, even if he could be made to see the necessity. . . . She found that she was yawning, and apologised.

'A tough day,' said Jay.

'Adequately so.'

'I wish I could share your bed,' said Jay. 'Just to sleep.'

'So do I,' said Jane. 'But you can't. Sorry.'

'At least you didn't make a joke about it.'

'Well of course not.'

'Last time you did. Last time you said, "It would certainly liven up the party."'

'Well so it would,' said Jane, 'and anyway last time, a: there was a room full of people, b: you weren't talking about sleeping –'

'And c: I'd just smacked you far too hard,' said Jay.

Her hand covered his. 'Tonight's different,' she said.

'You're right,' said Jay. 'Everybody's crazy about that piece of yours.'

'Sarah wants to do it in her new revue,' said Jane. 'I told her she can – only I want her to do it in Felston first.'

'*Felston?* Sarah *Unwin?*'

'And Georgina Payne,' said Jane. 'And anyone else who'll go. So far all Felston's been given is medical aid and nourishing soup. I think they deserve rather more than that. They deserve a party, too.'

'Toys for the kids,' said Jay. 'Beer for the men. Scent for the women.'

'Golly,' said Jane. 'That'll cost a bit.'

'The paper will launch an appeal,' said Jay. 'If we do it right it won't cost a cent. You sure you don't want Don Cook's job?'

'Not even for three thousand a year would I want to be as worried as Mr Cook,' said Jane, and then remembered her other host.

'Dick Lambert coped quite well,' she said.

'I'm glad,' said Jay. 'He wasn't too keen at first and I don't blame him. A Tory charity ball won't do his reputation any good with his Party – unless he sells them the idea he was keeping an eye on what the capitalists were up to.'

Perhaps he had been, thought Jane. Aloud she said, 'Was it Tory? The ball I mean.'

'The guests certainly were. I had to lean on Lambert to make him go. I told him it sort of went with the job.'

'Will he know about this strike you were talking of?'

'He'll know,' said Jay. 'He's a union-sponsored MP. But he doesn't know that I know.'

Clever Mr Lambert, thought Jane, and Jay echoed her words.

'He's a very smart guy,' he said.

'Likeable, too,' said Jane. She meant it.

'Oh sure,' said Jay. 'But he's a guy to watch.'

42

MR PINNER DIDN'T like it, and said so. In fact for Mr Pinner he was quite vehement about it. It never did any good, he told her, for other people to get involved in what he called 'matrimonials'. Jane remembered the policeman, and Mr and Mrs Michael Browne, and was inclined to agree with him, but pointed out in the interests of accuracy that the major was unmarried. Mr Pinner said darkly that that remained to be seen.

'Oh dear,' said Jane, 'I do hope you're wrong.' The truth, she thought. There's nothing else for it. 'It's my mother, you see, Mr Pinner. She considers herself engaged to him. In fact I rather think she'll marry him as soon as she's out of mourning.'

'Lady Whitcomb?' said Mr Pinner. 'Well now that's different, miss. You'd better tell me all about it.' He smiled. 'You know our motto: Discretion Guaranteed.'

And so she told him. About the courtship in India, and the need for cash, and the furtive visit to Cheltenham races with a lady most definitely not her mother.

'I know it doesn't sound like much,' said Jane, 'and yet I have a feeling. I most certainly don't want her deceived or made a fool of. I'm very fond of my mother.'

'Yes, of course, miss,' said Mr Pinner, 'and that makes it different, I must say. I'll get on to it straightaway. If I may ask – how's your horse coming along?'

'She should foal any day,' said Jane. 'I'll be off to see her soon.'

'And your other business?' said Mr Pinner. 'That went off all right?'

'Splendidly, thank you,' said Jane.

Getting the Christmas treat together involved the kind of staff work they should have had at the Somme, she thought. Availability of artists, cash for Christmas puddings, toys by the gross, paper hats, mistletoe, beer. And most difficult of all, who should go to the treat, and hence who should be excluded. That was a terrible choice, and one that she didn't feel in the least qualified to make. In the end, after furious arguments by telephone, she left it to a committee composed of Grandma, Corporal Laidlaw and Canon Messeter. Between them they could assess the wealth – and poverty – of every family in Felston. There was a hall to book, too, the Mafeking Hall, the only one big enough to hold the crowd – and the entertainers, for Jane had found no difficulty in obtaining offers of help. Jay's free publicity had seen to that. It was only getting them all there on the same day that was the problem. Once again she called in Catherine Hilyard to run errands and smile sweetly and tell lies, and once again Catherine was invaluable.

At last they fixed the day, the twenty-eighth of December, and Jane and Bower between them booked the entire cast of a Newcastle pantomime as well as Sarah and Georgina, and a dance band complete with male and female singers. Not even a London variety theatre could top that, Bower's professional adviser told them, even supposing they could find one that could afford it.

But before that there was Christmas. Its eve she spent with Jay. They dined at the Ritz, and danced, and went back to his flat for midnight and an exchange of gifts: for him a box of cigars and a Longines wrist-watch; for her a pot of caviar and a diamond necklace.

'Now you can wear those ear-rings,' he said, then added, 'I wanted to buy you a steamer ticket as well, but I guessed maybe you'd prefer to buy your own.'

Again that sudden and quite surprising sensitivity. Bower was quite right. Diamond necklaces were one thing, keys to state rooms quite another. She put hers on, despite the fact that she was wearing nothing else.

'I like your outfit,' said Jay. 'It suits you,' and put on his watch. 'But don't expect me to light a cigar. There are some risks I just won't take.' She was still giggling when his arms came round her, easing her to him.

Christmas Day, rested and demure, she took lunch with her mother and the major and Francis. Foch was in attendance, wearing a new collar of black and white, which Mummy insisted made him look more like the Cameronians' chaplain than ever. They dined on pheasant, which the adequate cook had cooked adequately, and a Christmas pudding bought at Fortnum and Mason. Jane had brought champagne, and Francis a couple of bottles of his college claret, and afterwards there were gifts: a bracelet for Mummy, cigars for the major, a pair of briar pipes for Francis: and Jane became in her turn the owner of a phial of the sort of perfume she detested, from the major, a riding crop from Mummy, (what convoluted ironies did that involve, she wondered?) and a copy of R. H. Tawney's *Religion and the Rise of Capitalism* ('Pretty basic, most of it,' said Francis, 'but after all you have to start somewhere, and it may help you to get your work in Felston into perspective').

'Far above my head, that sort of stuff,' said the major. 'Ruff's *Guide to the Turf* is about all I can manage these days.'

Lady Whitcomb smiled at him indulgently. 'You have other qualities George,' she said. 'Even Francis would not expect us all to be intellectuals.'

'Good Lord, no,' said Francis. 'The workers come first, you know. Always.'

'Surely darling,' said Lady Whitcomb, and turned her smile on Francis, the *other* smile, 'you can find room for one grasshopper among all those ants?'

The major said he would like to hear Lady Whitcomb play the piano, something jolly and perhaps seasonal, and they went to turn over the sheet music together.

'I'm most grateful for the pipes,' said Francis. 'They're absolutely first-rate.'

'You're very welcome,' said Jane.

Francis said, 'There's something I should tell you.' Jane sipped at her coffee, and waited.

'I've broken with Burrowes,' Francis said at last. 'After what he did to you – I just couldn't go on any more.'

'I'm delighted to hear it,' said Jane.

'That's all I want to say about it really,' said Francis.

'That's all I want to hear.'

'So now we're friends again?' he asked her.

'Yes please,' said Jane.

'Tell me what you're up to in Felston.'

It was a question deliberately designed to please, and she was touched by it, and told him at length, until at last the major came to call them. He had prevailed upon Lady Whitcomb to play a little Chopin, and afterwards he had allowed himself to be persuaded to sing a couple of songs: 'Goodbye Dolly Grey' and 'God Rest You Merry, Gentlemen'.

'But it must have been too exhausting,' said Lionel.

He had come to South Terrace that evening to deliver her present: a set of records by a new American band leader called Paul Whiteman, and to be persuaded to accept a little more of Jay's caviar, though this time she didn't tell him that Jay was the donor.

'It was a *little* trying,' she said, 'though he did hit the note more often than not. But he expected us to join in the chorus of "God Rest You Merry, Gentlemen".'

'Probably because it was seasonal,' said Lionel. 'Dear dear. The times we live in. All that *and* R. H. Tawney. Nothing was mentioned about Cheltenham, I suppose?'

Jane said firmly, 'Not a thing.' Cheltenham must wait on Mr Pinner.

Lionel rose to his feet. 'I must away to Santa's Grotto where all the other fairies await me,' he said. 'Thank you so much for the present, *and* the caviar.' His present was a Charvet scarf he had put on immediately.

'I'll drop you off if you like,' said Jane. 'Louise and her husband are giving a party in Eaton Square.'

'How grand you have become,' said Lionel. 'Positively magnificent.'

They went by train. She had arranged for the Wolseley to meet them at Newcastle, but Don Cook had gone further than that. He'd had toys and gifts and food sent up by goods train, and loaded on to lorries to await Jane's arrival, and waiting at the station were Bob and Bet with Grandma, soon to be the subject of a *Daily World* article. (Stan had had to go to work; Andy had refused to come.) But Grandma was there, and Jane had rushed down the platform to embrace her, while the flash bulbs popped. Bob stood transfixed, staring at the three young women who walked down the platform to follow Jane. He was still staring when Jane turned to embrace Bet, then shake his hand.

He had never in his life, Jane was sure, seen anything like Georgie, Sarah and Catherine walking towards him. Separately each one would have passed for a very pretty girl, but together all three achieved a kind of magic that transformed them into a picture: a modern Three Graces perhaps. And they were dressed and made-up as no women in Felston had ever been dressed and made-up. Bob, who prided himself on a kind of imperturbable sophistication, was gawking like the veriest yokel.

One of Cook's minions appeared and began to marshal the procession: Jane and Grandma and her three friends crammed into the Wolseley, and Bet and Bob riding in a bus with the musicians: another wonder; riding with a band that had played on the wireless. There were more cars to bring up the rear: loaded with reporters, mostly from the *Daily World* and the agencies, but there were stringers from the other papers too. Like an army convoy, thought Jane, as they assembled outside the Central Station: an army whose sole objective was the distribution of happiness; a rare thing in the life of any town, and probably unique in Felston's, and all because Jay had had the idea that it would sell newspapers.

It was clear and fine when they moved off, Jane leading, driving the Wolseley, then the four loaded lorries, and the bus, and last of all the shoal of reporters' cars. Even in Newcastle heads were turning, but it was outside Felston that Cook's man had organised his master stroke. Another lorry was waiting, but this one was decorated like a float at carnival time, all bunting and streamers and balloons. The band climbed on to it, and began to play, and on each side of the bus a painted message appeared: 'The Daily World Wishes Felston A Merry Christmas.'

The sound of the band brought the children running before the convoy had even crossed the borough boundary, then in ones, in twos, in groups, their elders appeared, lining the pavements, silent at first, then roaring their approval as their children taught them how to shout aloud for happiness. Round and about and through the town they went, and finished at last outside the town hall where a mayor in a cocked hat and chain, and a fur-lined robe designed for a man six inches taller, read out a painstaking message of welcome, Jane told them how happy they were to be there, and the band played 'Jingle Bells'.

The lorries went to the Mafeking Hall then, to be unloaded under the careful eyes of Grandma and Bella Docherty and their helpers. Every item would be counted twice, Jane knew, and nothing would be missing, not with those two watching. The others went off to the Eldon Arms to change for the concert. The hotel was crowded with bandsmen, and Jane, Catherine, Georgie and Sarah had the four best rooms in the place. If the rest of the town thought of her as a benefactor, to the manager of the Eldon Arms she was Santa Claus incarnate. He even produced champagne when Canon Messeter and Dr Stobbs came to call. Stobbs still did not believe that money spent on Christmas pudding would not have been better spent on medicine, but the priest would have none of it.

'To the poor people here, Christmas pudding is a medicine,' he said.

'And a lot of them won't get it,' said Stobbs.

'Then we must pray to God to guide Miss Whitcomb's endeavours so that it will,' Messeter said, and his blue eyes looked from one to the other of the women about him.

'God has been good to you today, Stobbs,' he said. 'And to me. Stop grousing, for goodness sake, and enjoy your company.'

They finished the champagne, and Jane drove them to Dr Stobbs's clinic, so that the three young women could see for themselves the misery that Felston endured. She sat, waiting, as Messeter showed the others what she had seen so often, and Bob came up and sat beside her.

'Are they all like that in London?' he asked.

'Like what?' said Jane.

'Those three.' He gestured to where the three heads, two dark, one fair, nodded obediently to the point that Messeter was making.

'Not all,' she said. 'No,' and remembered the work that Harriet did. 'Quite a lot of them are like the people here.'

'But where you live,' said Bob, 'the people you meet. I'm not asking if they're all like you – because you're unique. But are they all like them?'

Jane thought, first the flattery, then the demand for knowledge. Even Jay would have been pleased with that one, but even so Bob was almost frantic with the need to know.

'Some of them are men, you know,' she said, 'the people I know. But most of the ladies dress and talk like that. Not all of them look like that of course. But then they are far and away the prettiest girls I know.'

'Aye,' said Bob. 'They would be. The tall one in the yellow's Sarah Unwin. I've seen her picture in the paper many's the time.'

'And the fair one is Georgina Payne,' Jane said. 'You must have heard her on that crystal set of yours.'

'On the one you gave Gran,' said Bob. 'Gran thinks she's lovely. . . . She's right an' all. And the other dark one?'

'Her name is Catherine Hilyard,' said Jane. 'She's the daughter of an earl.'

'She's never.' Bob was by now in a world that transcended even the cinema.

'She studies at Oxford and spends most of the rest of her time in Ireland,' said Jane, 'and she's helped me organise this little jaunt rather well. *And* the ball at the Berkeley.'

Bob said, 'You could do us a favour.'

'If I can.'

'Introduce us,' said Bob, 'so I can shake hands with them. That's all. Just shake hands.'

'That's easy,' said Jane. 'They want to meet all the family, and I've promised they will. But not here. Not now.'

Bob looked at the crowded surgery waiting room, so many of them women, so many with sick children. They too were staring at her friends, like a flock of half-starved sparrows, she thought, visited by a flight of kingfishers.

'Aye,' said Bob. 'I see what you mean.'

He left her then, and soon after Bet took his place.

'Like a kid in a sweet shop,' she said, and Jane looked puzzled.

'Our Bob,' said Bet. 'I had to go to the kitchen to see the meat was ready for tomorrow's dinner for the helpers, and when I came back, there he is. Goggle-eyed.' She was clearly enjoying the fact: a small revenge for the teasing she had endured.

'Don't tell me Frank Metcalfe doesn't goggle at you like that,' said Jane.

Bet said, 'That's different.' And indeed it was.

'How's it going?' Jane asked.

'The same,' said Bet. 'Nothing's changed. Frank says we'll just have to wait – but you sharp get sick of waiting,' she sighed. 'But what else can we do?'

Obviously not what Jay and I do, thought Jane, and even to suggest it would be lunacy.

'I'm sorry,' she said, and Bet turned to her.

'Oh no,' she said. 'You mustn't say that. It isn't your fault. And anyway – you've done wonders for us here.'

It all seemed so damned unfair that Jane wanted to cry, which wouldn't achieve a damn thing. Two damns in one sentence, she thought, and even inside my own mind that's one damn too many. High time I took a long sea voyage, with or without Jay Bower.

The concert was a blend of familiar classics and music-hall entertainment that the band had done a hundred times, and Georgie said wasn't all that different to playing in the cinema. But her gown was blue and silver, designed by Molyneux, and someone had found her a hairdresser who could set her hair just right, and the applause was deafening. A little Chopin, Brahms's 'Lullaby', Sinding's 'Rustle of Spring'. Not quite Pachmann, but the best that Felston had heard for many a long day. The applause was deafening: as it was for the dance music – 'Running Wild', 'Lady Be Good', 'Yes We Have No Bananas'. And then Georgie came back again, in black, with pearls, and played with the band this time, the songs that they loved best of all, even though they reminded each singer of a time of nightmare – except that they didn't, thought Jane. They were reminders of leave, and rest camp, and comfortable route marches. 'Tipperary', 'There's A Long Long Trail A-Winding', and last of all, 'Pack Up Your Troubles'. Georgie coaxed them into song like the pub pianist she once had been, and the band, towards the end, stopped being a dance band and became as military as the band of the Coldstream Guards. Trumpets blared, side drums rattled and swaggered and, as Jane looked around her, the women's hands touched the sleeves of their menfolk, the men's shoulders straightened. All that was missing was the rhythmic crunching sound of a battalion marching at ease.

> What's the use of worrying
> It never was worth while – so!
> Pack up your troubles in your old kit bag
> And smile – *smile* – *smile*!

Then the applause, tumultuous, deafening, Georgie making curtsey after curtsey, and the band leader bowing, then gesturing to where Jane sat, beckoning to her. Once more she rose in her seat and faced a crowd, and the applause grew louder still, then one by one men rose to applaud, and women too, until at last the entire audience was on its feet, clapping and cheering till they could do no more.

Messeter leaned over to Dr Stobbs. 'Don't tell me that's not medicine,' he said, but Stobbs made no answer. He was too busy yelling.

Grandma put her hand on Jane's arm. 'Eh, me bairn,' she said. 'I'm proud of you.'

There was a reception of course, in a sort of ante-room behind the stage. Always there were receptions afterwards, because how else could triumphs be relived? But Don Cook's representative had done his work well. There were sherry and whisky and beer and lemonade instead of champagne, and the sandwiches were substantial. Jane kept her promise and introduced the Pattersons to everyone in sight. Georgie looked elegant and bewitching even when drinking pale ale, and Sarah was all smiles and congratulations because she knew her turn would come next day. Catherine divided her time between checking notes and urging Jane to eat (she'll be telling me to sit down and put my feet up next, thought Jane), but all the time she could have said which woman Bob was watching. Bob was a very good-looking man, but then so had his brother been.

The mayor was there, being gracious, for even though his politics were as Red as the robe he'd worn that afternoon, he knew a contented voter when he saw one, and that evening he'd seen a hall full of them. So he thanked Jane and the *Daily World* and the band leader and Georgina. It took him rather a long time to thank Georgina, Jane noticed, and wondered if she'd *ever* failed.

The presence of the mayor had not surprised her – after all he needed votes the way a horse needs hay – nor did Andy's absence.

Bet sounded indignant about it, but for Jane it was a blessing.

'All those songs from the war,' she said. 'How could Andy have endured it after what he went through in prison?'

Frank Metcalfe said, 'Miss Whitcomb's right, you know, pet. Andy would have hated it. Better for him to keep away.'

Jane had decided from the start that she liked Frank Metcalfe, shrewd and solid and reliable, though maybe with a touch of the Puritan about him. But then Bet could be puritanical, too. They really ought to be married, she thought. They'll never be happy until they are.

Manny Mendel was there, which did surprise her. He had a girl with him, slender and pretty and Jewish, and much more expensively dressed than any other woman in Felston. This was not a night for shrinking violets. She went up to him.

'How are you, Mr Mendel?' she asked.

'Miss Whitcomb,' Mendel said, but did not answer her question. 'May I introduce my fiancée – Miss Perlman – Bernice – this is Jane Whitcomb.'

'Oh Miss Whitcomb,' Bernice said. 'I've been absolutely dying to meet you.'

'No. Really?' said Jane.

'Bernice is very interested in women who do things,' said Mendel.

'One of these days I'm going to write a book about them,' said Bernice Perlman, 'and if you don't mind, I intend to put you in it. At the moment I write bits and pieces for women's mags. Bottling Fruit, Removing Stains from Tablecloths, Does Love Really Conquer All? You know. But we have to start somewhere.'

'Yes indeed,' said Jane. 'I started here in Felston.'

'And now Manny's leaving it,' said Bernice.

'Are you?'

'I've got a job,' said Manny. 'Based on a new idea from America. It's called doing market research. For a pharmaceutical company in Slough. Rather a good job. – We're getting married, you see.'

He smiled down at Bernice, and Jane knew exactly how Manny Mendel was. He was wonderfully, deliriously happy.

'Of course,' he said. 'I shall still support the Labour Party.'

'Of course,' said Jane, and thought: Poor Andy. Another reason why he didn't come.

That night she dreamed of John. They had been making love, and now they had done, and he wanted to hold her in his arms and talk and make jokes, and look at her lying there, naked, because although he was shy about it, much shyer than she, he enjoyed her nakedness. Sooner or later he would always say the same thing. 'By – you are a bonny lass.' But this night she couldn't stay. There was an alarm. A strafe, or a big raid perhaps, or the Germans were attacking. Whatever it was she had to get up and dress and John couldn't understand why. She tried to explain, but he couldn't understand.

'You're always in a hurry,' he said. He looked so young.

Jane woke up thinking: But then he was young. He was only twenty-six when he died.

Next morning at breakfast her three friends could talk of nothing but the clinic and the horrors they had seen there, which was as well, thought Jane. They would work all the harder for Felston. And work they did, and all the other people that the *Daily World* had hired. There was a potted version of *Cinderella* performed at break-neck speed by the company from the Theatre Royal so that they could be back in time for the evening perform-ance, but including, even so, a splendid comedian dame whose jokes were in dialect and well-nigh unintelligible, and a trans-formation scene that included a carriage and Shetland ponies, which had taken a score of skilled craftsmen all day to arrange. Afterwards there was a high tea, the first Jane had seen, and a very high tea indeed according to Grandma; tinned salmon and tongue and boiled ham, *and* potted meat. Tomatoes even, in late December. And cream cakes and Christmas cake and biscuits to take home. And balloons. And presents. Toys and scent and beer. And after that there was Georgie to play for them, the songs they liked so much to sing, and when they had sung themselves hoarse, there was Sarah to tell them the story of Private Walker and make them weep. 'Not a dry eye in the house,' she told Jane in triumph. 'It went even better than at the Berkeley.' Even Catherine dabbed at her eyes.

'And I never snivel,' she said, 'but it was all so sad. Yc⹁ ᷿̌ jolly clever, the pair of you.'

Georgina was in floods, Jane noticed, yet still looked beautiful.
Last of all there was dancing: after the children left, each
one presented with an orange and a boiled egg. (Vitamins *and*
nutrition, Harriet had told her, and Dr Stobbs agreed.) The band
was far better than the floor of the Mafeking Hall, but the
caretaker had done his best with French chalk, and even the
heaviest boots could slide a little. It was not just the modern
dances either. There were old-fashioned waltzes too, and the
Bradford Barn Dance and the Military Two Step. Canon Messeter
led out Jane for the first dance to thunderous applause, and for
a complete turn of the room they danced alone, while the rest
of the dancers watched and clapped.

'And all for you,' Canon Messeter said. 'They know what you
have done, and they bless you for it.' He smiled. 'If you asked
them to invade France they'd form fours and march off this very
minute, so long as you marched in front.'

'Then I shan't ask them,' said Jane. 'I shall remember what the
slave told the conquering Roman general instead.'

'Remember that you are but mortal,' said the canon. 'It's a good
thing to remember.'

He danced on, and gradually others joined them, Bob among
the first, leading out Georgina, and so already a hero.

Canon Messeter danced well, surprisingly well for a man who
had such a quantity of what he described as 'German iron' inside
him, but others took his place: Stan, nimble and inventive in the
Military Two-Step, Bob, whose Charleston matched anything in
London, and even the mayor, like Dick Lambert, waltzed in
silent concentration. Could it be something to do with their
politics? she wondered. The night sped by, and the whole room
danced, Grandma revolving cautiously in the arms of Dr Stobbs.
Bet, predictably, danced only with her Frank, but Bob danced
with everyone, and especially Georgina, Catherine and Sarah.
By now he had become the stuff of which legends are made.

But it ended at last, and the band played 'God Save The King'
and everyone sang; then Canon Messeter called for three cheers
for Jane, and the roof, according to Georgina, only just failed to
lift. The bus and a car came for the band and Georgie and Sarah,
who were catching the sleeper to London for appointments the
next day. *She still hadn't talked to Georgina about Piers.* But that
would have to wait for London. So many things would have to

wait for London. For now there were questions to be answered, people to talk to; Bella Docherty, Grandma, Dr Stobbs, reporters; all with the need to know, until at last Catherine dragged her off to the Eldon Arms, and a sleep with no remembered dreams.

43

O N THE TRAIN next day, Catherine said: 'I enjoyed our little outing. I thought it would be just good works, but it wasn't. It was fun as well. You are marvellous.'

'Don't you start,' said Jane. 'I saw something that needed to be done and I'm trying to do it, that's all. Just like you.'

'But you make it happen,' said Catherine. 'If it weren't for you I wouldn't even be here. You must be exhausted. Why don't you put your feet up? Nobody will see.'

Just as I predicted thought Jane, then said aloud, 'Certainly not.' She lit a cigarette. 'What did you think of the Patterson family?'

'The one they call Grandma's a devil to go,' said Catherine. 'She could even give my granny a game.'

'And Bob?'

'He's a very good-looking boy,' Catherine said, and added hastily: 'Don't you think?'

'Well of course I do,' said Jane. 'He looks exactly like my John.'

'*Does* he?' said Catherine. 'How marvellous.' She was silent for a moment. 'Forgive me,' she said. 'I was trying to imagine Bob in a captain's uniform, instead of that terrible suit.'

His best one, thought Jane, the trousers ironed by Bet specially for that evening, the tie bought that day with the money his father had given him for Christmas.

'Imagine two medal ribbons and a wound stripe too,' said Jane.

'He must have looked marvellous.'

'He did,' said Jane, but now it was becoming difficult to imagine exactly how John had looked. She could think of Bob of course. She hadn't been wrong: the resemblance was there. But it was Bob she saw in her mind and not John. John had been different, but now she couldn't remember the difference.

'If I may ask,' said Catherine, 'how old was your captain when he died?'

'Twenty-six,' said Jane.

'That's just Bob's age now,' said Catherine, then blushed, but prettily, the colour becoming.

'Is it indeed?' said Jane.

'We were talking about ages,' said Catherine. 'You know how one does. I'm twenty-one.'

'Did he ask?'

'Of course not. He's not gauche, you know. I just told him. He's a jolly good dancer.'

'Almost as good as Lionel.'

'Almost,' said Catherine, and giggled. 'But not in the least like him.'

'Not in the least,' said Jane.

'It's a pity he's poor,' Catherine said. 'With a proper haircut and a different accent and some decent clothes he could go simply anywhere.'

'Perhaps he will, one day,' said Jane.

Catherine shook her head. 'Not if he's poor. I know it's a perfectly ghastly thing to say but I could never not be rich. I just couldn't stand it.'

'Don't worry,' said Jane. 'It's hardly likely to happen.'

The train slowed down for Durham, and once again she saw the massive splendour of its cathedral.

'Are you sure you don't want to rest?' said Catherine.

'Thank you no,' said Jane. 'I was wondering – if you give me the support of your arm – whether I could totter as far as the dining car. I thought I might stand us both a gin and It before lunch.'

One more talk that year, to a group of women in St John's Wood who met once a month to assure each other that the world would be a better place if everyone was nice to everyone else, and they might well be right, thought Jane, and set out to convince them that a good way of being nice was to give a lot of money for Felston. Seventeen pounds seven shillings and sixpence. That made them really very nice: nothing less than half a crown. And afterwards a call on Mr Pinner, even if it was New Year's Eve. Mr Pinner didn't hold with New Year's Eve, which was all very well for Scotsmen, but this was London. There was work to be done.

The typist brought in tea, and Jane, who thought she must have drunk about half a gallon of the stuff in St John's Wood, nevertheless accepted it. Mr Pinner was embarrassed, and tea would at least help to get him started, tea and the pipe which he asked permission to light almost at once. Then came questions about her Felston concert, and she doubted whether he even heard the answers, for Mr Pinner could no more evade an unpleasant issue, than could her mother.

'About Major Routledge,' he said.

'Yes?' said Jane.

'He did go to Cheltenham Races with a woman,' said Mr Pinner. 'No doubt of it.'

'Oh dear,' said Jane. 'Woman' made it even more ominous.

'No,' Mr Pinner said. 'Nothing like that.' He sounded stern.

'Then what was it like, Mr Pinner?'

'I do a bit of racing myself, miss,' Mr Pinner said. 'So I know a few people. Otherwise it wouldn't have been easy.'

'I'm obliged to you,' said Jane. 'Of course. And I've no doubt some of the people you talked with wanted a thank you. It's only natural. I understand.'

'Thank you, miss,' said Mr Pinner. 'The woman's a Miss Dawson. Lives in Camden Town. Your major picked her up there. They went by train – came back soon after the race meeting.'

'But there was nothing – irregular?'

'Not a thing, miss,' said Mr Pinner. 'There couldn't be.' Jane watched, and knew that he was bracing himself for a storm to come. 'Miss Dawson's his half sister.'

'What?'

'Not legitimate, miss, unfortunately, and not all that bright, either. A bit tenpence in the shilling as they say. What the Aussies call "Not the full quid".'

'I remember,' said Jane, 'but do get on, Mr Pinner.'

'Sorry, miss.' Mr Pinner sought comfort in his pipe. 'The major's father was the squire – in a modest sort of way, but he was very clever with the horses, and the major's sort of inherited that.'

'Is this relevant, Mr Pinner?'

'You'll have to be the judge of that, miss,' Mr Pinner said.

Bitch, thought Jane. Arrogant, supercilious bitch.

'I'm sorry,' she said. 'Of course it is or you wouldn't have mentioned it. Do go on.'

'Yes, miss.' Mr Pinner blew out smoke. 'Miss Dawson's mother was a housemaid, miss. Lucy Dawson. Same as her daughter. Of course she left when – ' He waved his hand.

'Quite,' said Jane.

'But he paid up like a gentleman,' Mr Pinner said. 'Left a bit of money in trust. Miss Dawson's mum married again, had another daughter – and she's the one who looks after Miss Dawson now. You'll be thinking it's the money and it probably is, but from what I gather there's sisterly feelings too.'

'But why on earth did Major Routledge take her out?'

'She loves racing, miss. The crowds. The excitement. And the horses most of all. The major took her because it's a treat for her.'

'Oh,' said Jane. 'But why Cheltenham?'

Mr Pinner said, 'Major Routledge is not well off, miss.'

'Majors on half pay seldom are.'

'Major Routledge is skint,' said Mr Pinner, then added darkly, 'investments. Always a mistake for a military man.'

'Oh dear,' said Jane.

'Get rich quick,' said Mr Pinner. 'Double your income. . . . I don't think. He's got the price of a room at the Travellers and that's about all he has got,' said Mr Pinner, 'except the nags.'

'Are you telling me that Major Routledge is a professional gambler?'

Mr Pinner looked shocked. 'The major's a gentleman, miss, but from what I gather he can pick 'em. Fifty quid at Cheltenham is what I'm told.'

'And that's all?' said Jane.

'All I know, miss.'

Fifty pounds profit and fifty pounds in cash for stake money.

'Good gracious *what* a relief,' said Jane. 'The major emerges without a stain on his character.'

But Mr Pinner was a realist. 'He's hardly in a position to support Lady Whitcomb,' he said.

'Then I must think of something,' said Jane. 'I owe him that much at least.'

From Falcon Court below them there came the sound of singing. Mr Pinner went to the window, and Jane joined him, to look down on a group of ragged men, huddled beneath a gaslight, who sang to a mouth organ and banjo. All of them wore medals, and one of them carried a small placard that read: 'Ex-Servicemen. We Wish You A Happy New Year.'

Oh the moon shines bright on Charlie Chaplin, [they sang]
His boots are cracking for want of blacking
And his little baggy trousers they'll need mending,
Before we send him to the Dardanelles.

'Last time I heard that was outside Amiens,' said Mr Pinner. September 1918 that would be. Just before the last big push. . . . If you don't mind, miss?' He nodded at the window.

'Of course not,' said Jane, and Mr Pinner opened the window and whistled clear and shrill. At once the men below looked up, and Mr Pinner threw down a shilling, and Jane opened her bag and threw down another, before Mr Pinner closed the window and shivered.

'A bit cold for open-air concerts,' he said.

'Yes indeed,' said Jane, and held out her hand. 'Happy New Year, Mr Pinner.'

Dinner with the Watsons. That meant something simple, she thought, but by no means abject. A discreet little confection in blue and white silk by Vionnet, and Jay's diamond ear-rings, though not of course the necklace. Far too grand. As she hooked in the ear-rings she thought of Jay. Time, more than time, that they shared a bed together again. The sort of satisfaction that they could create for each other was rare – she was quite sure of it – and should not be neglected.

Hawkins came in and looked her over, critically the only word. 'Very nice, miss,' she said, and somehow Jane managed to suppress a sigh of relief. Really it was like being married, without the fun.

'Thank you,' she said.

'There's a car outside, miss,' Hawkins said. 'Driver says you ordered it.'

'So I did,' said Jane. 'Is it very grand?'

'Rolls-Royce, miss.'

'The thing is,' said Jane, 'there may be rather a lot of champagne. My host is a Scot.'

'I see, miss.' I might as well have said he's an Eskimo, thought Jane.

'Don't wait up,' she said. 'Or do if you feel like it. Its New Year's Eve after all.'

Harriet was delighted to see her, and yet contrite too. The Millingtons had let her down. 'Flu, both of them. Not that it wasn't raging . . . Still, they had only been six to dinner in the first place, and now there were four.'

'Like the ten little niggers,' said Jane.

'Good Lord I hope not. There were none of them at the end. But Keith's here, bathed and shaved, and how he tore himself out of his lab I'm blessed if I know.'

'Of course you know,' said Jane. 'You look gorgeous.' And indeed she did, in a dress of orange satin that set off to perfection her dark, clear skin.

Harriet giggled. The drinks must have started early and it's time I had one, thought Jane.

'Come and meet your dinner partner,' Harriet said. '*He* hasn't caught 'flu, thank God.'

She was introduced to a man called Lovell, Charles Lovell, who had that same neat and well-brushed air she had seen in Canon Messeter and Major Routledge, but his eyes, though dark, were more reminiscent of the canon's than the major's: not that they looked mad, but they glittered with intelligence which he did his best to hide, almost as if it were bad form. About thirty-eight, she thought. Jay's age. And then: Why on earth make such a comparison? Jay's as clever as they come and doesn't give a damn who knows it.

Watson was saying, 'Charles and I met in the war.'

'Just like Jane and me,' said Harriet. 'Really without the war we'd have had no social life at all.'

'Which regiment?' Jane asked.

'Rifle Brigade,' said Lovell.

'He saved my life,' said Watson, and offered Jane a glass of Bollinger.

'Nonsense,' said Lovell.

'Not nonsense at all,' said Harriet. 'You got a medal for it.' She turned to Jane. 'It wasn't Keith's turn to die, you see. I hadn't finished with him. Hadn't even started on him actually.'

Lots and lots of champagne before I got here, thought Jane. To Lovell she said: 'Did you by any chance know a Major Messeter?'

'Teddy Messeter?'

'No doubt. I always referred to him as the canon. He's a parson now, you know.'

'*Messeter?*'

She had surprised him, astounded him even, and for some reason she was glad of it.

'You hadn't heard?'

'I knew he'd been badly wounded – and discharged, I believe. But I never thought – Messeter? A *parson?*'

'He's sort of retired,' said Jane. 'He gets ill from time to time – but when he's well he works in a voluntary clinic in Felston. Why is it so surprising?'

'He was the most thorough-going ladies' man I ever met,' said Lovell.

'I can believe it,' said Jane. 'And the charm's still there, believe me. Though he uses it for good works now.'

'I've read about you and Felston,' said Lovell. Like everybody else, thought Jane, but at least you don't look at me as if I had two heads.

'Everybody should read about Felston,' she said. 'It's important.'

He smiled, but left it at that, which was a pity, she thought. If he'd been in the Rifle Brigade he was bound to have money.

The parlourmaid came in and announced dinner. Cockaleekie soup, but no haggis. Watson wasn't that sort of Scotsman, and even if he had been Harriet would have been firm. But there were grouse, and cheese, and a sorbet, and a burgundy that the men approached with a respect bordering on reverence.

Jane grinned at Harriet. 'Better than poached eggs on toast

washed down with gin,' she said, and Harriet grinned back.

After they had left the men to their port and Harriet had admonished them not to dawdle, she learned a little more about Charles Lovell.

'He really did save Keith's life,' Harriet told her. 'It was in an advanced dressing station. The Germans shelled it – more bad luck than malice, Keith reckons. He'd just finished plugging a damn great hole in Charles's side and gone on to the next case. The first shell knocked him flat. The second one didn't go off. Keith just lay there and looked at it sticking out of the ground, because now his leg was broken, and Charles sort of shambled over and picked him up and carried him out, and all Keith could do was nag him about what would happen if Charles's dressing slipped. Keith reckoned they must have made about twenty yards when the damn shell went off and knocked them both over. Charles got a Military Cross for that one.'

'I should hope so.'

'He got other things as well. A Croix de Guerre, even. Keith seems to think he's quite mad.'

'What does he do now?'

'Lives elegantly. Hunts. Shoots things.'

'Hardly a sign of madness.'

'Oh he's sane enough in peacetime,' Harriet said, and then: 'Damn that champagne. I didn't mean to be offensive.'

'You weren't,' said Jane. 'I'm sane enough in peacetime too. For the moment.'

And then the men came back in and they danced, Lovell remarkably well for a man with a hole in his side; but then Canon Messeter too had ignored German iron when he wished to dance. 'I Want To Be Happy' was the record they played, and happy they were in the movement of their bodies.

When skies are grey and you're lonesome and blue
You'll see the sun shining through Pom-Pom-*Pom*
I want to be happy still I can't be happy
Till I've made you happy too.

But it really doesn't apply, thought Jane. I haven't been lonesome since I went to Felston. Or blue either . . . Keith Watson went over to the gramophone and lifted the needle, and Jane glanced at the clock on the mantelshelf. One minute to midnight.

'If you don't mind, Charles,' said Watson.

'Of course,' Lovell said, and walked out of the room.

'You have everything?' Watson called after him.

'Of course,' said Lovell over his shoulder. 'My nurse came from Inverness.'

Jane turned to Harriet, eyebrows lifted.

'Barbarism,' said Harriet. 'Sheer barbarism. But he couldn't get through the year without it.'

The clock on the mantelshelf wheezed, then began to strike the hour. When it had done Jane could hear a distant church clock chime, and then a measured knocking at the front door. Watson went to it at once, and Jane and Harriet followed as Watson opened the door to a Lovell dappled white with the fall of the first snow of the year.

'Happy New Year,' he said, and gravely handed over a silver sixpence, a twist of salt and a piece of coal to his hostess, then kissed her on either cheek, before shaking hands with Watson and kissing Jane.

'Happy New Year,' he said.

'Happy New Year.'

It was like an incantation, a rite, and even though they might not be true believers, they observed the form.

Watson bustled them back into the drawing room, and champagne for the women, whisky for the men. For a man at this time, he said, a dram was the only possible drink.

'Barbarous,' Harriet said again.

'Not at all,' said Watson. 'We North Britons are a practical and scholarly lot on the whole. We get all our superstititions over in one go on the thirty-first of December, and a lot of our drinking, too.'

'Charles here is our first foot. No offence to the suffragettes, but the first foot over the threshold in the New Year has to be a man, and preferably a dark man like Charles – bringing money and fuel and the savour for our food that represents the food itself. The promise that we'll neither starve nor freeze nor fall into poverty.'

'I damn near froze on your doorstep,' said Lovell. 'Still, let me give you a toast.' And then to Watson, 'Oh don't worry. It's a Scottish toast. Scottish regiment. Argyll and Sutherland Highlanders would it be?' He lifted his glass and said in creditable

Glaswegian, 'Here's tae us. Whae's like us? Damn few.' And they drank.

Harriet said, 'Jane and I know one, too,' and turned to Jane. 'That château in Picardy, you remember? We had a leave there in 1917.'

Jane nodded and went to her.

'I looks towards you,' said Harriet.

'I catches your eye,' said Jane.

'I bows.'

'I likewise bows.'

And then together: 'We links and drinks according.' And they linked arms and sipped their champagne.

There had been snow in Picardy, Jane remembered, and champagne too, and later had been the first time that she had danced with John – and all so long ago that it might have happened to a completely different woman . . . Then Keith wound up the gramophone and asked her to dance, after which it was Lovell's turn and the record was 'Roses Of Picardy', and she thought she might cry, but only because she had drunk too much champagne.

Lovell said, 'I'd like to hear more about Felston. Perhaps we could lunch some time.'

'A donation would be better,' she said.

'Maybe I could manage both.'

And then it was two o'clock and the hire-car came, with the news that the snow was still falling, and beginning to lie in the sidestreets.

'Not a lot of taxis about I take it?' said Lovell.

'None, sir.' The thought seemed to cheer the driver enormously.

'I'll give you a lift,' said Jane. The driver looked reproachful.

In the end Lovell escorted Jane to South Terrace first, before going on to Eaton Square, where he was staying with friends.

'I really should get a flat in London,' he said. 'The trouble is I'm lazy and I've got lots of friends who can just about put up with me. And being on one's own can be ghastly – in London, I mean. But you don't find it so?'

'I scarcely ever am alone,' said Jane. 'Nor would you be – with all those friends.'

'Probably not,' said Lovell. 'I think perhaps the truth of the matter is that if I bought a place I should feel obliged to use it –

and I do so like the country.' They drove for a while in silence, the snow in the windless air drifting like blossom in the car's headlights.

'Harriet said you were engaged to a chap in the Royal Northumbrians,' he said at last. 'A chap called Patterson. Do you mind if I talk about him? I knew him, you see.'

'You did? How marvellous. Of course I don't mind.'

'Well I didn't exactly know him – but I met him. We took over the Northumbrians' section of the Line in 1916 – and he saved my life.' He chuckled. 'I know what you're thinking. It's a big night for life-saving. All the same it's true – without any hyperbole I mean. Captain Patterson gave me some advice. If I hadn't taken it I'm quite sure I'd be dead.'

'Please go on,' said Jane.

'I carried a revolver,' said Lovell. 'A damn great brute of a thing that would stop a charging rhino if you could get close enough to hit it. Almost all officers carried revolvers, come to that, so that when we went over the top the Germans, being a logical people, killed the chaps with revolvers first, and left the other ranks leaderless. As I say – logical.'

'So what did John advise you to do?'

'Carry a rifle, like everybody else. It seemed a bit infra dig at first, but when I thought about it it made sense. I mean I had no objection to running the same risks as my men, but there seemed no point in running more . . . So I did what he suggested. It caused a bit of a stir in the mess at first, but it was surprising how many of the survivors came round to my point of view. After all we were the Rifle Brigade, not the Revolver Brigade. He seemed an awfully nice chap, your fiancé.'

But he's still dead, and you're still living. Not that it was his fault – or yours.

'Yes,' said Jane. 'He was.'

Well of course he was, thought Lovell. How could he not be, since you accepted him.

The Rolls moved on into the swirling whiteness. In the side streets the snow was already lying.

'I meant what I said – about giving you lunch,' Lovell said at last.

'Then you must telephone me. I'm in the book,' said Jane, and again there was a silence, a silence that felt like anger. But how could it be anger against her?

The car pulled up in South Terrace, and Lovell got out, walked with her on the snow to her door, and offered his hand.

'Happy New Year,' he said again.

'And the same to you.' In the schoolroom her brothers had invariably added, 'With knobs on.'

'I'll call you soon then.'

'Please do,' she said, and thought, Really if I annoy him that much why all this frantic haste to buy me lunch?

She went inside quickly. Her shoes were of fine kid, and already wet.

There was a light on in the drawing room: a black mark for Hawkins. Dead against waste was Hawkins, as she'd told Jane herself. Lights burning in empty rooms were like burning pound notes. Wicked waste. Jane went into the room and was confronted by a tableau. Bob Patterson, wrapped in a travelling rug, sat in an armchair drawn up close to the fire, and hovering in attendance were Mrs Barrow with a bowl of soup, Brown with an extra cushion, and Hawkins with the whisky decanter, for all the world, Jane thought, as if Bob were already preparing to take over Teddy Messeter's vacant throne.

'What's this?' she said aloud. 'Charades?'

Bob began to stand up, remembered he was in his underwear, and sat down again.

'He says he knows you, miss,' said Hawkins. 'He's just come from Felston.'

That 'he' said it all. Hawkins at least remained unsmitten.

'Certainly Mr Patterson knows me,' said Jane, and then, turning to the pasha himself, 'I didn't know you were planning a visit, Bob. You might have warned me.'

'By sea, miss,' said Brown. 'He came by sea, the poor feller.'

'Half starved,' said Mrs Barrow. 'And soaked to the skin. We've got his clothes drying in the airing cupboard, Miss Whitcomb.'

'A jolly good idea,' said Jane. 'And I see you're feeding him, too. Which bedroom have you chosen for him?'

'The pink room, miss,' said Hawkins.

The smallest, darkest room in the house, and pink was *not* Bob's colour.

'No,' said Jane. 'The bed's too small. Move him to the blue room.'

'Yes, miss,' said Hawkins. She looked annoyed, but Mrs Barrow and Brown were smirking.

'And go to bed,' said Jane. 'Don't you know what time it is? I have a meeting tomorrow.'

They turned, and then she remembered her manners, and called out to them, 'No wait.' There was port in the decanter, a drink, according to Beau Brummell, fit only for the lower orders, so her father had told her, but she poured a glass for herself too, and lifted it in a toast.

'A Happy New Year,' she said.

'You certainly keep them in order,' said Bob.

'All those innocent females,' Jane said, 'and a man loose in the place. Somebody had to keep them in order.'

'And they all work for you?'

'When you let them. Bob – what on earth is all this stuff about a sea voyage?'

'I told you,' said Bob. 'Don't you remember? The cheapest way to get to London is on a collier.'

'Yes,' said Jane, 'I remember.' She quoted him. 'A ten-bob note and bring your own food.'

'That's what I did,' said Bob. 'Food for three days, but the weather turned nasty. It took us nigh on five. Not that it mattered. I was seasick most of the time.'

He was foxing. Trying to hide something. She was certain of it.

'And why did your harem tear your clothes off?' she asked. 'What happened to your overcoat?'

'I pawned it,' he said. 'The price of my ticket.'

'Bob,' she said. 'It's late. I've had rather a long day.'

'Me an' all,' he said. 'It's a fair step from Rotherhithe.'

'You *walked* here?'

'By the time we docked I had ninepence left. I squandered half of it on beer and bought a tram ticket. When they put us off I *had* to walk.'

'In the snow?'

'Uncle Tom's Cabin wasn't in it,' he said.

'But why, Bob?'

'I came to do you a favour.'

'You're very kind.' She said it without irony, and Bob knew it.

'It's Andy,' he said, and gulped at his whisky. 'God knows I don't want to shop him –'

'Is that what you're doing?'

He shrugged. 'What I'm telling you – it wouldn't put him in prison. Nothing like that.'

'If it did I wouldn't want to hear it,' she said, but he wasn't listening.

'Another spell in the clink – I doubt if even Andy could stand it . . . But it isn't that. He's just out to harm you. I don't like that.'

'How?' Jane asked.

Bob flushed, seemed almost embarrassed. 'You went to Paris,' he said.

'You know I did. The Four Arts Ball.'

'Aye,' said Bob. 'There was a chap came up from London to have a word with Andy. He never let on to the rest of us – but I saw the two of them going into the Boilermakers' Arms. Into the saloon. What you might call the posh end,' he explained.

'Now our Andy never goes into pubs,' said Bob, 'so I went into the Boilermakers' meself and bought a half – in the public bar. There's a hatch there between the bar and the saloon, and if you ease it forward a bit you can hear very nicely. So I –' he hesitated.

'Eased it forward a bit?'

'Aye. You might think I was just being nosey, but you'd be wrong.'

'You've no idea what I think.'

'No more I have. What I thought was our Andy was heading for trouble. One look at the toff he was with and I knew it was trouble.' He smiled. 'Poor Andy. Drinking his lemonade, and thinking he was putting the world to rights.'

'What were they talking about?' said Jane. 'Or don't you want to tell me?'

'I *have* to tell you,' said Bob. 'They were talking about you.'

'What about me?'

Bob hesitated, then said, 'I'm only telling you what that toff said.'

'Of course.'

Bob braced himself. 'You were a tart,' he said at last. 'A prostitute. And they had a picture to prove it. A picture from Paris.'

'But you saw that picture yourself,' said Jane. 'In the *Daily World*. I wore that Egyptian head-dress and cloak. That doesn't make me a tart.'

'In this one you weren't wearing the cloak,' said Bob, and waited.

At last Jane said, 'Go on.'

'Andy asked if the toff had the picture – and the toff showed him. I didn't see it,' Bob added hastily. 'Didn't want to. But Andy said it was very bad. Felston couldn't take the charity of a loose woman like that.'

'What will they do?'

'There'll be copies made,' said Bob. 'Sent out to different organisations . . . Churches. Women's groups.'

'Will it have any effect?'

'Bound to,' said Bob. 'They're a straightlaced lot in Felston. Da . . . Bet . . .'

'And Grandma?'

'Not her,' said Bob. 'But she's a bit whacked just now. She couldn't put up much of a fight, even for you. It's true then?'

'Of course it's true,' said Jane. 'But I wasn't indecent. At least I didn't think so. I went as Cleopatra.'

'Depends what you mean by indecent,' said Bob. 'In Felston that's showing your knees.'

'How long have I got?' Jane asked.

'A week, mebbe,' said Bob. 'All the toff had was a print. They have to wait for the negative.'

'This toff,' said Jane. 'What did he look like?'

Bob gave her an accurate description of Julian Burrowes.

'I see,' she said, and then: 'Does Andy know you're here?'

'I'm not that daft,' said Bob. 'I told them I was off after a job in Coventry.'

'All of them?'

'The whole family. Aye.'

'And what did Grandma say?'

'Nothing,' said Bob. 'But she didn't believe a word of it. I know she didn't. Just wished us luck and told us not to forget to write when I was settled. What are you going to do, Jane?'

'What do you suggest?'

'Well we're nothing to you, are we?' said Bob. 'I mean if there's scandal and name-calling – why should you put up with it? You've done your whack. More than your whack. I mean look at Christmas. If a lot of narrow-minded old biddies want to make your life a misery why should you bother? Like I say – you've done your whack. Take yourself off to Paris or somewhere.'

'Is that what you want me to do?'

'Of course not,' he said. 'But the folks up there – they're not like me. They'll hate you. They'll say you let them down.'

'You talk as if I were some kind of saint,' said Jane.

'Well you are to them,' said Bob, 'and saints don't go around with no clothes on.'

Jane said, 'I'm obliged to you. Now what can I do in return?'

'I thought –' said Bob. 'I mean it just crossed my mind – you must know this feller Bower.'

You know I do, Jane thought. You heard Burrowes say so.

'We've met,' she said.

'He must use a lot of printers,' said Bob.

'And now you want him to use one more?'

'They pay good money, the press,' said Bob. 'If he took me on I could get myself a room and still send money home.'

'I thought you'd told the family you'd gone to Coventry?'

'If I was sending money home,' Bob said, 'they wouldn't care if I was in Timbuktu.'

'I'll speak to Mr Bower,' she said, and rose. 'Finish your soup, then up the stairs, second door on the left. Don't forget to turn the lights off. Hawkins is very fussy about turning off lights.' For the last time that day she held her hand out.

'Happy New Year,' she said, 'and thank you.'

44

B Y NEXT MORNING the snow had blanketed the whole of mainland Britain. Only in Ireland were the horses running, and that was much too far for the major to travel. She phoned him at his club, and he was at once wary and evasive. Only the mention of Cheltenham brought him to heel. On the second her dear mother had an appointment with her dentist, he said, which would make it convenient, *most* convenient, for him to come to lunch. Jane wondered which was the greater incentive: the threat of Cheltenham or the lure of Mrs Barrow.

He ate well. Jane had told him that this lunch was a private matter, between the two of them, and so he drank well, too. Bob took his lunch in the kitchen: as he told her, he'd have eaten it in the coal-house so long as Mrs Barrow did the cooking. Throughout lunch the major talked of horses. He knew they were the reason he was invited, and so he talked about them, fluently and knowledgeably enough even to impress the Hilyard twins, she thought.

And so she let him talk, and was impressed herself, but even so, she thought, a man who could make fifty quid at one meeting at Cheltenham had more than knowledge. He had luck, too. She offered him coffee in her little sitting room, where they would not be disturbed, and permitted a cigar, lit a cigarette herself.

'Someone saw me at Cheltenham, I take it,' he said at once. 'Saw me with a lady not your mother.'

This was getting down to business indeed, but by far the best way.

'Saw you with your half sister,' said Jane.

He looked at her sharply, and for the first time, with dislike. 'How do you know that?'

'I hired a detective to make enquiries,' said Jane.

'That was a monstrous thing to do,' said Routledge. 'You had no right – '

She interrupted him. 'Monstrous, certainly. But as for no right – '

'You refer to your mother?'

'Of course,' said Jane.

'You intend to tell her?'

'I think you should do that.'

'I?' said Routledge. 'The knowledge would appal her, surely?'

'Why should it?'

'She has a particular horror of marital infidelity,' said Routledge. 'She told me so herself.'

Oh Mummy, Mummy, thought Jane. Am I not to have a secret either?

'My mother is a realist,' she said. 'She would understand perfectly well that it wasn't your fault. She also has a great respect for discretion. You seem to have shown that rather well – till now.'

'Lucy – Miss Dawson – needs her little outings,' Routledge said. 'They wake her up, you might say. I've taken her racing every leave I've had in England. I just can't abandon her.'

'Of course not,' said Jane. 'Just explain it all to Mummy.'

'I might lose her.'

'I don't think so,' said Jane. 'But if you don't tell her somebody else will.'

'Yourself?'

'Certainly not,' said Jane. 'But sooner or later you'll be spotted. Some of Mummy's friends are very well-informed.'

'That damn Gwatkin,' said the major. 'She was a one-woman intelligence unit even in India.' Jane waited. 'What do you know about me?' he asked at last.

'That you were a major in the Gloucesters,' she said.

'I was a captain in '14,' he said. 'A forty-eight-year-old captain. And I was about to retire when the war came. After Mons and Le Cateau and first Ypres they could find a use even for forty-eight-year-old captains. I even had the battalion for a while

– when they made me a major. Then I got pneumonia. My war ended in 1915. – Before yours had even started.'

'How did you know about that?' she asked.

'Your mother told me,' Routledge said. 'She's very proud of you.'

Jane willed herself not to look astonished.

'I was useless in France but I wangled my way into the Puffers,' Routledge said. 'A good life. Useful too. Left the younger men free for the Western Front. Kept things going. . . . Took my discharge in 1919 and came home and lost all my money.'

'How did you?'

'Backed a feller who knew how to find oil in the North Sea,' Routledge said. 'All he really knew was how to take the life savings of middle-aged fools like me. So I went back to India.'

'Why did you?' asked Jane.

'Pension goes further there. And I could make a bit – horse trading. That's how I met your mother. I'd got a couple of polo ponies the maharajah wanted to buy. And that was it.'

'I'm sorry?' said Jane.

'I fell in love,' said the major simply. 'For the first time in my life. Sixty years old and smitten like a subaltern. Only – '

'Yes?'

'I'm broke,' he said. 'And I gather that your mother's not all that well off either.'

'No,' said Jane. 'She's not. I'm the rich one in the family.' She waited.

'There you are then,' said the major, and Jane knew it would be all right.

'Mummy thinks you might make a living breeding horses,' said Jane. 'Suppose I bought a stud farm – could you manage it for me?'

'I could try, I suppose,' said Routledge. 'The trouble is you see – what I can do with horses is pick 'em. Breeding them's another matter. I'm not a dashed vet. And anyway – your mother doesn't like the country.'

'She'd do it for you, but I think it would be a mistake.'

'I must do something,' said the major. 'We can't live on my pension.'

'Of course not,' said Jane. 'What you should do is become a racing correspondent.'

All of which meant that she had to see Jay Bower very soon. Jane Whitcomb, the threefold suppliant: for Bob, for Major Routledge – and for herself. It didn't seem to her that there was a damn thing to be done about that *bloody* photograph, but if there were, it would be Bower who would know what to do. If not, he could certainly do something for Bob, and very possibly the major.

Surprise, so her military friends had never tired of telling her, was the essence of attack, and so she went to call on Bower one evening at the penthouse, without telling him so. She wore simple, easily removable garments, a lot of French perfume, and Uncle Walter's sables. It really was very cold, so cold that she left Foch behind with Hawkins; so cold that he didn't even sulk.

But the Riley started without too much nonsense, and the main roads were easy enough, all the way to Fleet Street. The doorman knew her at once, and she went to the lift, which was empty, and pressed the button that would take her to what for most people was the top of the building, but not for her. She had a key that opened a scarcely visible door to another lift: 'the elevator', Bower called it, a luxurious affair in black and ivory that went up one floor only, to another door that opened with a key, and beyond the door Bower's penthouse.

She went in, calling out his name, but there was no answer, which did not surprise her. Day or night Bower always was aware of someone who had information to give, at lunch, or dinner, or a party. Even at breakfast. She went into the drawing room, ugly and comfortable as it always was, except that against one wall a painting had been rested, a painting covered with a piece of sackcloth. She lifted it up, and found that she was looking at her friend Georgina Payne, whose body was every bit as scrumptious as the last time she'd looked at it. Sackcloth, she thought, was the last thing to cover Georgina with, then she left, locked the door, and went down to her own office, and sat at her desk. This was going to take a bit of thinking about, but not yet.

The thing was that she needed Bower, whatever that picture meant. If she were going to go on helping Felston, she really needed Bower, to get off the hook of that *bloody* photograph. Not to mention Bob, and the major. *They* were what she had to think about, she realised, before ever she could *begin* to speculate on that fruit salad upstairs; the delectable Georgina, all peaches and cream and a couple of cherries for garnish.

What Bower was after was obvious, even if he'd chosen a damn funny way to go about it. But the point was did it matter? – or rather, did it matter enough when compared with Felston and Bob and the major, or even Jane Whitcomb's continued social acceptability – for she was in no doubt that whatever first became known in Felston would spread, rippling out in ever-widening circles until even Knightsbridge and Chelsea were encompassed; even Miss Gwatkin would know. Poor Mummy. . . . And poor Jane, too, she thought. For her reputation wouldn't stand that kind of revelation. It would mean purdah for her: the Italian Lakes at least.

But it wouldn't be good news for Bower, either, she reflected. The *Daily World* had backed her, made her into the kind of shining heroine she neither could be nor wanted to be, were it not for Felston. The other newspapers would never forgo such a chance. It would be against their every principle. Jay Bower would have to fight for her, whether he wanted to or not.

She put paper into the typewriter, and pecked away with two fingers and a thumb for the space bar, putting down on paper Bob's account of his sea voyage south. Jay hadn't asked for it, might well reject it out of hand, but it was better than sitting in South Terrace wondering if that picture really meant that Jay and Georgina had done it while she was delivering a lecture.

When at last the telephone rang she heard it with a sense of relief. For her, action had always been better than brooding, no matter what the outcome – at least until they'd had to pack her off to Jabber Lockhart.

'What the hell are you doing down there?' said Jay.

'Working.'

'You've got something?'

'I think so,' she said.

'Great,' said Jay. 'Want to come up and talk about it when you've finished?'

'I'd love to.'

'When will that be?'

'Say another half hour,' she said.

'See you then.' He hung up first. He always hung up first.

She would have to go to bed with him, she thought, and it

would have to be good, whatever she knew or thought she knew about Jay and Georgina Payne, because he had to be grateful. Unless he was grateful she hadn't a hope.

It seemed that he was grateful. He even liked the piece about Bob's journey, which he insisted on reading as soon as he had done. She must have been good, she thought, though for her there had been little memory of pleasure: she had been far too busy concentrating on what one might call the job in hand.

'I like this,' he said at last. 'It's a good piece. I'll use it. We'll put it with the rest of the stuff for while we're away. Is he still here – this Patterson guy?'

'He's staying with me.'

Jay nodded, that feminine streak of his assuring him that Bob was no threat. 'Why did he come?'

She got up and walked naked across the bedroom. Jay liked to watch her do that, but that wasn't the only reason. She had to know if Georgina's portrait was there, and so she walked on across the hallway and into the drawing room. No Georgina. No sackcloth, either. Not on Georgina anyway. She picked up a table lighter, turned to go back, then paused. There was snow on all the roofs she could see below her, and yet naked as she was the room was warm. In his own way Jay knew all about pleasure.

He appeared beside her, a dressing gown belted about him.

'Now what are you up to?' he asked.

She took a cigarette from the box and lit it.

'Admiring the view,' she said.

'Me too.' His hand reached out, began to fondle. 'Why did young Patterson come here?'

'To warn me,' she said.

'Warn you of what?'

She told him.

'Oh boy,' he said. 'Somebody doesn't like you.'

'Julian Burrowes doesn't like me,' she said. 'He doesn't like either of us.' His hand moved away.

'Go on doing that, if you please sir,' she said. 'You know I enjoy it.'

She knew the request would please him, and besides it was true. What he did was soothing.

'I can't do this and think,' he said.

'Of course you can,' she said. 'You're Jay Bower.'

She turned to find an ash tray, and his hand moved with her.

At last he said, 'It'll be rough.'

'What will?'

'Getting you off the hook.'

'I expect every fish thinks that at the time. Tell me what I have to do.'

He told her, and first she smiled, and then she laughed, a full-throated chuckle that went on and on.

'You don't mind?'

'I love it,' she said, 'but will it work?'

His hand moved down and squeezed. 'Bet your ass,' he said.

She turned to face him then, loosed the knot on his dressing gown.

'Let's celebrate,' she said.

'Go back to bed?'

'I can't wait that long.' She lay down on the couch and Jay joined her. At least Georgina wasn't there to watch.

Bob had been no problem. Jay would send a chit to the printers' father of the chapel, who owed him a favour, and that would be that. But the major was another matter. Jay was all for racing tipsters, provided they gave a winner now and again. The trouble was so many of them didn't. But she'd been ready for that, and brought the major's profit and loss account over the jumping season. Even Jay was impressed.

'I'll give him three months' trial,' he said. 'Fifty a week.'

She'd been expecting six weeks at best.

'You must think he's good,' she said at last.

'He's good so long as he does this,' he said, and tapped the sheet of paper, and then: 'He'll need a name, I guess. I don't think he'll want to use his own. Any suggestions?'

'How about "The Major"?' she said.

'Hell why not?' said Jay. 'I like it. You hungry?'

'Ravenous,' she said.

'Then why don't we go out and eat?' said Jay. 'Unless there's somebody else you want me to find a job for.'

They went to the Embassy, so that they could dance as well.

Bob was delighted and grateful, and told her so many times. Indeed his delight was such that she opened champagne, and he was delighted and grateful all over again. No question of pretence, she knew: no hankering after Northern beer behind a feeble, unconvincing smile. This was Bob's first champagne ever and he adored it. The one thing needed to make his happiness complete was to thank Mr Bower in person, it seemed, and she could even do that for him, beneficent fairy godmother that she was. Bower had been asked to dine at the American Embassy and bring a lady, and she was the lady. He called for her in South Terrace, and she introduced him to Bob.

They got on well, which surprised her at first, until she realised that they both had the ability to project a seeming frankness that was in truth not frankness at all, but a mask for a deviousness more appropriate to Bengal, or Kerry perhaps. Each recognised it in the other, and responded to it. Then Hawkins called her to the telephone, which was irritating. She had enjoyed watching them: an immensely tortuous yet hugely enjoyable music-hall turn.

It was Lovell. They still hadn't had their lunch, and even if it sounded a little presumptuous, he would like to arrange a time and place. She hesitated for a moment: Jay's plan held all the excitement and wit imaginable, but there was no written guarantee of success. On the other hand Lovell had not seemed the sort of man to be bothered by either scandal or convention. It would be interesting to find out if she was right, and so they settled on the Ivy in two days' time. Just a week before they sailed, she realised. Her tickets for the *Mauretania* had arrived that morning.

When she got back Jay and Bob had settled whatever it was between them, and Bob was trying to explain the finer points of English soccer to Jay, who wanted to know why it was forbidden to tackle a guy just because he wasn't holding the ball. Each man was as devious as ever, and enjoying himself hugely.

Dinner with the ambassador was dull by comparison, though her diamonds – or rather Jay's – were much admired. When at last they left Grosvenor Square, Redman was still waiting to drive them; so she was to sleep alone, it seemed, and perhaps as well. She was lunching with Mummy the next day.

'You were a big success,' Jay said.

'Your diamonds were.'

'I'm glad,' said Jay. 'That night at the Felston Ball when you didn't wear them – it really bothered me. You know that? But it wasn't the diamonds, it was you.'

'I wonder if it will still be me when our story breaks?'

'Of course it will,' said Jay. He seemed utterly certain. 'It's every woman's dream. A chance to act like a courtesan without having to be one.'

'All those tiresome gymnastics,' she said.

'Is that what you do with me?'

His voice was light, but the vulnerability was there. She knew precisely how to hurt him if the need ever arose. But oh you bitch, she thought, you silly, silly bitch.

'Of course not,' she said. 'But that's for us – for affection. You were talking about courtesans, and what are they after all but very expensive tarts?'

If he didn't mention her diamonds, she was home and dry.

'Oh my God,' he said. 'I'm sorry. I didn't mean – '

She too could be devious, it seemed.

'Of course you didn't mean,' she said. 'Go on about me acting like a courtesan.'

'It'll be a sensation,' he said, then added: 'It'll sell one hell of a lot of newspapers.'

'So you are suggesting that George becomes a kind of tout,' said her mother.

'Exactly,' said Jane. 'But an anonymous tout.'

She took another spoonful of her only just adequate soup. Careful, she admonished herself. Don't muff your lines. The major had met her in Harrods, taken her to tea, discussed his talent for picking winners, and he had told his Honoria, but of course he knew nothing about Jane's plan to utilise his talent.

'Anonymity of course would be an advantage,' said her mother.

'It's absolutely vital,' said Jane. 'Otherwise you would be plagued by all sorts of persons.'

'Very true,' said her mother, and rang the little table bell for the parlourmaid.

After the lamb had been served she said, 'What kind of remuneration is contemplated?'

'Fifty a week,' said Jane, 'for a three-months' trial.'

Her mother looked startled: gratified too.

'Of course,' said Jane, 'if Major Routledge is a success – and I see no reason why he should not be – he could always ask for a little bit more, from time to time.'

'Like Oliver Twist, in fact,' said Lady Whitcomb.

'I hope not, Mummy,' said Jane. 'Oliver Twist was refused, you will recall.'

Over coffee Lady Whitcomb said, 'You seem on good terms with this Mr Bower.'

Careful, Jane told herself. Be very, very careful.

Aloud she said, 'Not really. Bower is a very shrewd and very successful newspaper publisher. His entire life is devoted to selling more newspapers. When it was discovered that I had a talent for journalism – '

'How did that come about?' her mother asked.

'Quite by chance,' said Jane. 'A sort of happy accident.'

'Serendipity,' said her mother, delighted. 'I have always enjoyed that word.'

'He devised this – plot, I suppose you would call it, in which my destiny and Felston's were interlinked. It helped him sell more newspapers, but it was also good for Felston, and so I agreed.'

'And was it good for Jane Whitcomb?'

'Indeed it was. I enjoy what I do, Mummy, and so long as I do it well he will continue to publish me. Because he believes that I have inherited at least some of my mother's intelligence he will also listen to me. When I told him of the major's ability he saw at once that it would help to sell newspapers – and so he made the offer.'

'Suppose George fails?' her mother asked.

'Then he will be got rid of. But I see no reason why he should fail.'

'Can't you? It has perhaps escaped your notice that George is a rather timid person?'

'Of course he is,' said Jane. 'But he has you, Mummy.'

'You are suggesting that I too should become a tout?'

'Not a tout, precisely. No,' said Jane. 'A tout's mate, perhaps.'

This time her mother did not smile. She threw back her head and laughed.

At last she said, 'Why did you do this?'

– 497 –

'Because I couldn't believe that you would be happy in the country, helping the major to breed horses.'

'You are perfectly right,' said her mother, 'but I should have tried. It would have been my duty to do so. Except that – ' she hesitated.

'Yes, Mummy?'

'George did not think he could have made a success of it either, once I had discussed it with him. But he will make an excellent tout, I'm sure of it.'

'The word is tipster, Mummy.'

'Whatever it is,' said Lady Whitcomb, 'we are both most grateful to you.'

Jane tried to say something modest, but her mother motioned her to silence. She was doing sums in her head.

'Fifty a week is two thousand five hundred a year,' she said, 'which is what your father left me. So we can double that and add in George's pension and the money we will get when we rent this place – and you say George can ask for more, later. I shouldn't be suprised if we were worth seven thousand a year quite soon.'

'You think the major will be a success then?' Jane asked.

'I'm quite sure of it,' said her mother.

Bower fired his first salvo in the 'Wicked World' column next day. Jane Whitcomb To Visit America? queried the headline, and the answer could only be yes. Jane Whitcomb was indeed going to visit America, and the good fortune was all America's, for the gracious Miss Whitcomb was taking with her not only her unrivalled beauty, grace, charm, writing talent and compassion for those less fortunate than herself (try as she might, Jane still found that she winced at that one) she was also to confer with certain heads of the entertainment industry not only in New York, but on the West Coast also, and the West Coast, as devotees of the 'Wicked World' column knew only too well, meant Hollywood.

She poured one last cup of coffee and lit a cigarette, waited for Hawkins to come and clear away. That Hawkins would have a comment she was quite sure. Hawkins might prefer *The Times* these days, but she always looked into the *Daily World*, especially the 'Wicked World' column. But when she appeared, it was Bob that she wanted to talk about.

'Had his breakfast early, miss,' she said. 'Eggs and bacon. Two eggs. Five rashers. *And* a sausage. I toasted half a loaf for him too.'

'Eating well is still a novelty to him. Let him enjoy it. Did he say where he was going?'

'To find a room, miss. He's getting a start next week.'

'So he is. Did he say where he would look?'

'High Holborn, miss.'

'Nice and handy for Fleet Street,' said Jane.

'Yes, miss. I got – I have a sister there, miss. She's a widow. Got a room to let. He's gone to have a look at it.'

'I see,' said Jane.

'She's a respectable woman, my sister,' said Hawkins.

'Well of course she is,' said Jane.

'Lost her husband two years ago,' said Hawkins. 'Lung trouble it was. On account of he was gassed in the war. She gets a pension of course but it isn't all that much. Renting that room'll be a Godsend if Mr Patterson takes it. Not that she can afford to serve him half a pig for his breakfast every morning.'

'Will you miss Mr Patterson?'

'He's good company. He can always make you laugh,' said Hawkins. 'Of course a lot of it's that funny accent of his, but he has his own kind of wit if you follow me, miss.'

'Indeed I do,' said Jane. 'He's very like his brother.'

'I didn't mean to be personal, miss,' said Hawkins.

'Oh we are touchy this morning,' said Jane. 'You read about Captain Patterson in the *Daily World* half a dozen times at least.'

'Yes, miss,' said Hawkins. 'But Bob – *this* Mr Patterson – he's not an officer, miss. He's got his way to make in the world. Just like me.'

'And do you think he will?'

'Oh yes, miss,' said Hawkins. 'I mean just look how he got here. Turning up on your doorstep more like a drowned rat than a human being – and inside a week he's got a thumping good job. I only hope my sister can cope, that's all.'

'I'm sure she will,' said Jane, smiling, 'if she's anything like you.'

Hawkins chuckled. 'She can look after herself all right,' she said. 'Well you have to if you're a widow renting a room in Holborn.'

There was a dress she very much wanted to wear for her lunch at the Ivy, a sequinned georgette dress by Chanel in the palest possible blue, with a top that tied to the dress in a bow, and a hat that wasn't for once the inevitable cloche, but a Gaby Moro masterpiece that was brave enough to sport a brim, and no jewellery at all except a thin gold necklace. No diamonds, and certainly no coloured stones. The trouble was the shoes. Satin with ankle straps was the only possible answer, and the snow outside was still thick and frozen hard. It would have to be Russian boots and change when she got to the restaurant, she thought. Only when she was inside the Rolls-Royce and huddled into her sables did it occur to her that this was going to a very great deal of trouble to take lunch with a man who might and only might be good for a twenty quid subscription for Felston. But by then it was too late to start examining motives.

At least he appreciated the dress, and very right that he should, she thought. Even in the Ivy that dress was really something special. He had read the piece in the 'Wicked World' column, and that too was gratifying, as was the fact that he didn't want her to go to America, though he did his best to hide it. He was also dying to know why she was going to Hollywood, and Jane found that she was dying to tell him, only she couldn't: not without ruining Jay's oh-so-carefully contrived effect. Not the best atmosphere for a companionable lunch. And yet it was companionable at first.

Perhaps she had Canon Messeter to thank for that. Lovell had said he wished to know about Felston, and the canon was his only link with the place. He shook his head in wonder as Jane told him about Messeter's work as hospital chaplain, ambulance driver, orderly.

'St Paul on the road to Damascus was nothing to this,' he said at last. 'And did you really drive that damn great Armstrong-Siddeley?'

'When I had to,' she said. 'Don't for heaven's sake think I enjoyed it.' And then: 'Tell me about yourself.'

'There isn't an awful lot to tell,' he said.

'Gentlemanly modesty? The reticence of the sahib? The Balliol cult of effortless superiority?'

'I was at Magdalen,' he said. 'In my day we were effortless –

in the literal sense – to the point of inertia, but I'm damned if we were superior.'

'You were in the army.'

'So was everybody else. The Lovells have only two talents – for being rich, and for staying out of the public eye. They made a lot of money in the eighteenth century, and have hung on to it ever since. It's mostly in banking now – and land. I have a place in Sussex – and I rent another in Northumberland – for the shooting, you know. And a little box of a place in Leicestershire.'

'For the hunting?'

'Precisely.' He was perfectly aware of the irony in her voice. 'And that is how I fill my days. Shooting game birds, chasing foxes, counting dividends. This last is not a gentleman's business, but it's what we Lovells do because we have a talent for it. Maybe that's why we have always refused a peerage.'

'Always?'

'You are right to rebuke pretension,' he said. 'We have declined a peerage on both the occasions when one was offered.'

'Do you know Sir Hugh Lessing?'

'Quite well,' said Lovell. 'We are friends for the most part. Rivals occasionally.'

'He was in the Artists' Rifles.'

'He's a much better banker than he was a soldier. Will you take dessert?'

'Apple tart,' she said.

'With Calvados if I may suggest it,' said Lovell. 'This kind of weather rather justifies it.' And when she had finished it he asked, 'Do you plan to stay in Hollywood for long?'

Oh clever you, she thought. First you ply a girl with spirits, *then* you ask her questions. Every barrister in England would jump at the chance.

'It depends on circumstances,' she said. 'Believe me I know how feeble that must sound, but this time it's true.'

'I've been invited to visit Los Angeles,' he said. 'We have investments there. What they call real estate. If you're there for any length of time then I shall go.'

'And if I'm there only briefly?'

'Then I shan't.'

'Goodness,' said Jane. 'You really are the head of the firm.'

'Yes.'

The monosyllable was pleasantly spoken, and utterly assured.

'There is always one,' said Lovell, 'in every generation. For the moment it's me – or is it I? I never remember.'

'"It is I" is correct,' said Jane, 'but rather pompous.' Suddenly and without warning, the Calvados struck. 'You should marry, you know. Think dynastically.'

'I am married,' said Lovell.

She suddenly felt very foolish. 'Nobody told me,' she said.

'Not many of my friends know,' he said. 'Keith Watson certainly doesn't. My family knows of course, but not my friends.'

'Whyever not?'

'She's mad, I'm afraid,' said Lovell. 'Has been since 1913. She's been in a place in Switzerland ever since. Not exactly what I wanted to tell you – but how could I not tell you?'

Oh no you don't, thought Jane. Not yet. Perhaps not ever, but certainly not yet.

'What's wrong with her?' she asked.

'They don't know,' said Lovell. 'Twelve solid years – and they don't know. She won't tell them, you see.'

'Tell them what's wrong?'

'Tell them anything,' said Lovell. 'She simply refuses to communicate. I've tried. The doctors have tried. It isn't any use. The specialists seem to think that life simply became too much for her – and so she left it as best she could without actually dying.'

'And this was before the war?'

'1913,' he said. 'I told you, and I know what you're thinking. So many of us went mad because we were in it – but even more of us didn't. Keith. . . . You. . . . Me. . . . But for Anthea it wasn't like that at all. She was doomed from birth, you see. Ypres Salient or a hunt ball; it wouldn't have made the least difference. She was doomed, it seems.'

'How awfully sad.'

'For her parents while they lived, certainly. For me, to this very day. For her – it's impossible to tell. She smiles a lot. She has a very beautiful smile.'

'I don't think you should tell me any more of this,' said Jane.

'I wish you would explain to me why.'

'You've known Keith and Harriet for years and they aren't even aware that you're married – and yet you tell me at our second meeting.'

'Surely the reason for that is obvious.'

'Not to me,' Jane said firmly. 'I think it's best to leave things as they are for the moment.'

No Rochesters and no Mrs Rochesters, she thought, and certainly no chance of me applying for the post of governess – even if I do happen to be sane for the moment.

'Very well.' He beckoned to the waiter and ordered coffee. 'All the same I had to tell you – in the sense that I had no choice.'

Chorus girls from West End shows, she thought. Poules de luxe at Deauville or Paris. But he wouldn't tell *them*, and she doubted if they would ask.

'Do you eat here often?' she asked him.

'My first time. But I was told it might be rather your sort of place.'

And indeed it had been, but her eyes were stormy.

'You think that perhaps I brought you here because nobody would recognise me?'

'It's possible.'

'Indeed it is,' he said, 'but the thought never crossed my mind. I give you my word. Don't you believe me?'

'Yes, of course,' she said. 'All the same, it's time I went home.'

45

G RANDMA SAID, 'I'm speaking from the Eldon Arms. We went there on Bet's chap's tram. The manager said it would be all right.'

'Of course it will,' said Jane.

'I suppose I should have written,' said Grandma, 'but I'm not much of a hand at writing. Never was.'

'You got my letter?'

'Certainly I did. A joy to read. And the money. . . . That's what's paying for this contraption. So our Bob's settled?'

'He's got a room and a job,' said Jane. 'That's settled enough for a young man of his age. He'll be sending money home, soon.'

'We could do with it,' said Grandma, then, voice lowered: 'He never did go to Coventry, did he?'

'No,' said Jane.

'Straight to you. . . . By sea, you said. All the way in a storm. You said there was a reason.'

'It's true.'

'But you never let on what it was.'

'I couldn't. Not then. Perhaps I can now. It may seem ridiculous to you – '

'I doubt that,' Grandma said. 'Not you and Bob.'

'Somebody appears to be trying to ruin my reputation,' said Jane, 'for reasons I find it hard to understand. It seems to be a combination of politics and spite.'

'Politics?'

'Ruthlessness,' said Jane. 'The utter certainty of the rightness of one's cause. It sounds more like religion than politics.'

'That isn't the way my Stan worships,' Grandma said.

'This has nothing to do with Stan.'

'Well of course not.' The old woman paused for a moment. 'It's begun already. . . . Gossip. Sniggering. Dirty talk. Only they call it "seeking after truth" and "no smoke without fire".'

'Who do?'

'The ones that's doing it. You've a good body on you, they tell me.'

'Not bad,' said Jane, 'considering how little exercise I take.'

The old woman chuckled. 'Good lass,' she said. 'You'll fight them?'

'Well of course,' said Jane. 'I'm told I'll beat them.'

'You must,' said Grandma. 'Only the folks that live here could think Felston can manage without you.'

'It's lies, you know,' said Jane.

'Well of course it is,' said Grandma. 'Anybody that spent ten minutes with you knows that. Anybody with any sense that is.' And then: 'We're a bit short of people with sense up here. Maybe sense is something you get when you eat properly.'

'Does Bet believe it?'

'Not to say believe,' Grandma said. 'More like interested. What's the word? Fascinated. She'd have more sense if she was married.'

In this, as in every other field, doing, for Grandma, was infinitely more important than talking.

'I'm going back into hospital soon,' the old woman said. 'They reckon the other eye's about ready. I'll be glad to get away from here. . . . Dear God.'

'Grandma,' said Jane, 'what's wrong?'

'To think the day would come when I'd be glad to go to hospital. . . . You sure you can get out of this?'

'I must,' said Jane. 'I have a piece of good news for you.'

'I could do with it.'

'I raised another hundred pounds for Felston yesterday. I wore my prettiest dress and flirted and smiled and said "thank you" ever so prettily while he wrote it out and signed. But that's all I did, Grandma. And it was for Felston. Not for me.'

'A lot of silly cats,' said Grandma. 'Just wait till I get my strength back.'

Somehow Jane knew that Bella Docherty was one of them.

'I'll be in America by then,' she said.

'So you will. But you'll come back to us, won't you?'

'Well of course,' said Jane.

'Word of honour?'

'Cross my heart,' said Jane, 'and hope to die.'

'That's all right then,' said Grandma, and hung up.

Jane looked at her watch. There was still time to phone Medlicott and tell him to take care of Grandma's hospital bills, and then go back to her brooding about Charles Lovell.

This time it had been she who had lost her temper, and for very much the same reason: because Lovell had a wife who somehow had managed to insinuate herself into the restaurant, silent and smiling beautifully. Now simply wasn't the time to go into all that. There was simply too much happening. That morning Bower had struck again. 'Cleopatra – the truth' – the 'Wicked World' column had trumpeted. 'Jane Whitcomb to consult with world-famous experts to learn the facts about Egypt's Queen of Beauty on the eve of her departure for Hollywood.' And so on and on and on and on.

The *Mauretania* was incredible. Every bit as vast as she had expected, and with a certain elegance despite its old-fashioned Edwardian solidity. Her state room – was it? in a hotel it would have been a suite – contained every possible comfort, including a writing desk, so that she embarked almost at once on a letter that was almost a journal – events, thoughts, imaginings all written down just as they occurred to her. But there was nothing intimate of course, or even personal. No mention of that well-groomed Rochester who had converted Switzerland into an attic for his wife to rave in. How could there be, when she avoided thinking about him? But there was nothing about her own problem either, at least not directly. Grandma's eyes might not be well enough to read by the time the letter reached her, and if someone else read it to her there would be no secret. Still, there were ways. Bower's success was living proof that there were always ways.

I had a very nice lunch with a gentleman from Oxford, a professor no less, who told me all about Cleopatra – or as much as he could during one lunch. It seems that she was much more than a mere beauty, if indeed any woman can be called mere, who lolled about in flimsy skirts. (Though as the professor said, why wouldn't her skirts be flimsy? Egypt is a *very* hot country and there is simply no demand for tweed.)

However, she was also a very clever woman, and a very patriotic one, not at all keen on seeing her countrymen exploited by the Romans, and determined to do her best for them. I won't go on about it now, but I hope to have more news about C. when I get to Hollywood.

She crossed out the word Hollywood, making sure that it was still legible, and inserted the words Los Angeles. Just the sort of thing Jay Bower enjoyed. She found that she enjoyed it too, and was quite sure that Grandma would.

The rest of the voyage appeared to be vast meals – incredible menus for lunch and dinner, and even breakfast, cocktail parties with canapés, and beef tea served on the sunny side of the deck where one reclined on a folding chair after being tucked up in a steamer rug. In between the feasts there were deck tennis and dancing and bridge and parties, official and unofficial. There was even a palm court where a trio played the kind of music Miss Gwatkin liked so much. Even Amy Woodford Findon.

She was lucky. The Atlantic Ocean, for January, was calm, far calmer than the North Sea had been for Bob. By avoiding every second course on the menu and not eating at all at parties, she managed well enough, despite the huge ship's hurtling speed. Jay of course was fine, circling the promenade deck lap after lap, winning at bridge, sweating in the Turkish bath: treating the ship like a huge toy specially chosen for him alone – and yet delighting in sharing it.

They slept apart. The stewards were far too zealous and Jane was by no means sure that her tummy would stand the strain of the gymnastics involved. There was also the problem of Georgina – and of Charles Lovell, come to that, neither of which she looked like resolving, and certainly not by discussing them with Jay. But they danced a lot, and drank a lot at parties and enjoyed it all, even the fancy dress ball, for which, forewarned by Jay, she wore her sari again, successfully enough to be awarded a prize. But then so many people were awarded prizes.

'The closer we get to New York,' she wrote to Grandma, 'the more the Americans drink. But it isn't because they think their country's awful – on the contrary. It's because they have this thing called Prohibition in America, which means that the sale of alcoholic drinks is forbidden from one end of the country to the other. Poor darlings, what do they do when they want to celebrate? . . .' Jay had told her that after Prohibition came in the American people had done nothing *but* celebrate. She decided to save that till she'd seen for herself, and told Grandma about the fancy dress ball and the sari – 'another flimsy skirt. Bare midriff too. But it can't be too naughty. Scores of millions of women wear them every day.' She considered telling how they dined, because of Jay's eminence, at the captain's table, if only because it would annoy Andy, but decided against it. They were fighting a war, not a vendetta.

At last Jay spotted what to him was a very familiar smudge on the skyline, and he dragged her up on to the deck, swathed in furs, to watch New York slowly, inevitably emerge. A cold day, much, much colder than London, and for the time being no snow, but a sun that looked small and clear and almost white, and coloured the city like no other city she had ever seen. And such a city. Towers that soared like arrows, that statue on the island that she was quite sure would be a cliché until at last she saw it, and everywhere people, working, talking, shouting, ants in an ant hill that soared to the sky. And the cars and lorries: automobiles and trucks, Jay said she must call them. And why not? It was his city after all.

Porters came aboard, some of them black men; the first negroes she had ever seen outside a circus, and not at all like Indians, not even Tamils, though Tamils were often far blacker than some of those she saw. And then it was time to tip her steward, and the stewardess who had acted as her maid, and venture into the enormous customs shed, and be confronted by some of the rudest men she had ever met in her life: customs and immigration officials. Prohibition would have no terrors for them, she thought. They were drunk with power from the moment they put on their uniforms.

Then Jay came to collect her, and two very Irish-seeming men with a trolley piled their suitcases on to it, and followed them out to where a line of cars stood waiting, and headed at once for the biggest one, a car that was quite enormous, far, far bigger than the Hilyards' Bentley. Outside it a waiting chauffeur, boots polished, every button gleaming, snapped to attention and saluted as soon as he saw Jay.

'Herr Joachim,' he said, and the rest made no sense at all. He spoke in German, and in German Jay replied, and called him Karl. The two Irish-seeming men looked on as if they were watching a movie that might turn out to be rather good.

'I never heard a chauffeur talk foreign before,' said one.

'He's never a chauffeur,' said the other. 'He's an admiral.' He thought for a moment then added, 'At least.' The chauffeur called them to him, and they began to load trunks and bags into the enormous boot.

'What a huge motor car,' said Jane.

'It's a Cadillac sedan de ville,' Jay said. 'Belongs to my father. I said he should get a Bugatti for a change, but he doesn't like Italians. Says they're all gangsters – even the accountants.'

'Do all your servants speak German?'

'Yes,' said Jay. He hesitated, then added: 'He doesn't even spell his name the same way I do. He and Mom are a little set in their ways.'

'But they do understand that you and I are just good friends?'

'They don't understand how good.'

'No jokes,' said Jane. 'Not now. I'm serious.'

'They know that you're a colleague,' said Jay, 'as well as the daughter of a distinguished man, and a distinguished person in your own right.'

'You're very good,' she said.

'No I'm not.' The words came quickly: almost angrily. 'I told them these things because I believed them to be true.'

Karl appeared once more, and spoke in German, and they got into the Cadillac. On impulse Jay picked up the speaking tube and gave instructions.

'I told him to drive us around for a while,' he said. 'Give you a chance to get used to the city.'

The Cadillac moved off: a softer, more yielding ride than a Rolls-Royce, but even so the power was there.

The city would certainly take some getting used to, even the cramped, restricted city which was the only one Jay thought important: the city of Manhattan. Cars everywhere, people everywhere: policemen bundled up like bears, women in fur coats. Men, too. Buildings that grew higher and higher, the more one drove. In Wall Street (where Jay told her that money was invested and reinvested, but never actually spent) the buildings pushed so high that from inside the car she could see no sky. But in Central Park the view seemed to stretch forever, the sky was limitless, and the skaters swirled on the lake in a cold that seemed unending. But not in the Cadillac. In the Cadillac she perspired with the heat, and loosened her furs. Jay spoke again into the tube, and the car set off into the city, down another long driveway, as straight as anything the Romans made, then turned and turned again into somewhere called 8th Avenue, and suddenly the light was dimmed from above. She looked up, and a train swooped above her in a great arc, swerving like a fairground switchback into somewhere called 53rd Street.

Jay chuckled. 'The El,' he said. 'The Elevated Railroad.'

'No Underground?'

'Oh sure,' he said. 'But we call it the subway.'

The car slowed, and from its window Jane could see an ugly box of a building: dirty red brick six storeys high, with a zig-zag fire escape down its centre. Jay followed her gaze.

'Tenement,' he told her. 'Walk-up. That's about as far down as you can get unless you sleep on the street, and if you try that at this time of year you die.'

'But it's so close – ' she said, and he knew what she meant. To Madison Avenue, and 5th, and Park, and the rich hotels and theatres and shops.

'We're different,' he said. 'You see that now. It's like our elevators compared with yours. With us up and down is a hell of a lot faster.'

The great car moved on, heading northwards, and at last even New York came to an end, and all she could see was farm land under snow.

'Where now?' she said.

'My parents' place. I told you.'

'Yes, but where?'

'Connecticut,' he said. 'Near New Haven.'

'Difficult to say and impossible to spell. Like Massachusetts. New Haven is a good place to live, I take it.'

'It's the best.' He sounded amused, she thought, but he also sounded surprised that she had asked.

'Tell me about it,' she said. 'Tell me about *them*.'

'Well,' he said. 'They're rich. You're probably thinking that's a banal thing to say – but just give me a minute. They've always been rich, that's the point. My grandfather was rich back in Düsseldorf, Germany, and the only reason he came to the United States was he wanted to be richer.'

'What did he do?'

'He was a banker. He came here in the Eighties and brought my father with him. He got in on the grain boom, then went on into oil along with Mellon and Rockefeller and a whole lot more. He was rich and he got very rich. And powerful.'

'Like a maharajah,' she said. 'If you're so rich you have power whether you want it or not.' And you always win your cricket matches, she thought.

'Like the king of a small country. Right. And maybe not all that small. . . . He liked me. Hell, he must have done.'

'Why is that?'

'When I was twenty-one I told him I wanted to be a journalist – and he let me – and made my father let me. In spite of the fact that I was supposed to be a banker, like everybody else.   Then when I made a success of it – ' he turned to her. 'I did, you know. Make a success of it. I was good.'

'Well of course,' she said. 'I've watched you. You taught me.'

'When I proved myself – when I was twenty-five, he bought a newspaper and made me editor in chief. And when I was twenty-eight – ' Again he hesitated. There were some things that were too much, even for Jay.

'Go on,' she said.

'I *made* that paper,' Jay said. 'Doubled its circulation – but I didn't *own* it. So on my twenty-eighth birthday he gave me a million dollars and told me to buy one of my own. Only the war came and I went off as a war correspondent instead. He loved the United States but it seemed he still loved Germany too, and when they went to war with each other – it killed him. Heart failure they called it. He had a heart like a lion. He died of grief.'

So much poetry from one so prosaic, she thought. And yet it hadn't sounded like a lament for a million-dollar donor.

It began to snow. . . . The house was called the Towers, and there were plenty of them, from attenuated pepper pots to a sullen great brute by the stables that would have heartened Sigmund Freud, if she had understood Lionel correctly. A damn great schloss of a place, as German as the Brothers Grimm, especially in the middle of a snow storm. And vast. Really quite enormous. It would take an army to run a place that size, but then the Germans were rather good at armies. . . . Now now, she admonished herself. At least wait till you've met them.

Jay took her by the arm and led her inside, into a vast hall two storeys high, and everywhere one looked, antlers and stags' heads and black oak furniture, and a vast open fire that seemed to be burning an entire orchard, so that the room smelt of apples. But it wasn't the fire that made the room so warm. Double windows, she thought, and steam radiators, then loosened her coat, and at once a maid-servant appeared to take it from her, as Jay was confronted by a – butler, would one call him? in frock coat and stiff collar and a cravat instead of a tie: like an ambassador in a musical comedy, she thought, all foreign accent and mispronunciation before the chorus tripped on in bathing suits to sing about the delights of Deauville; except that this one didn't speak with a foreign accent, he spoke German, and in German Jay replied, before taking Jane's arm and following the butler to a flight of stairs, and on into a drawing room where three women and two men drank coffee and ate cake. Jay's parents, she decided at once, and three others. Both his father and mother were stout – the cakes they were eating were oozing cream – but otherwise he resembled both of them. Perhaps they were related as well as married? Of the rest, both the women looked like Jay, and the young man looked vaguely and tantalisingly familiar. And then she remembered.

Jay was saying, 'Jane my dear, I should like you to meet my mother and father.'

She went forward at once, and held out her hand. There could be no compromise on this. 'How do you do?' she said to Mrs Bauer.

'So nice to meet you, my dear.' A voice at once pleasant,

cultured, and American. No hint of Teutonic overtones. She turned to the man.

'Mr Bauer?' she said, and offered her hand once more.

'How do you do?' said Bauer, in a voice very like his son's, then added: 'You don't speak German?'

'I'm afraid not,' said Jane. 'I can manage a little French.' Or Urdu, she thought, or Hindi. Gujarati at a pinch.

'No, no,' said the elder Bauer. 'We will continue in English. German is for the game we play. The nostalgia game.'

'Nostalgia?'

'We pretend we are there,' said Bauer. 'In the Black Forest maybe and it is all as it was. German servants, German food, German wine.'

'As it was?' Jane asked.

'In the game,' said Mrs Bauer, 'the year is always 1911, and nobody knows that the war will ever begin. Would you like some coffee?'

'Oh yes please,' said Jane, and the butler wheeled over a trolley. Jane took coffee only, but Jay allowed his plate to be filled. As he did so, his father said, 'May I present my daughters? This is Erika, who stays here with us to help her mama to run this place – and this is Louisa, who is married to Joe here. Joe Ballantyne.' More handshakes, and the chance at last to drink her coffee.

'We haven't met,' said Ballantyne, 'but I believe you're acquainted with my sister and brother-in-law, Florence and Billy Powell? In Paris?'

'We did bump into each other,' said Jane. 'Quite briefly.'

'That's what most people say,' said Ballantyne.

'Joe!' His wife sounded stern, but sympathetic too. 'It's not your fault, Joe. It could have happened to anyone.'

'Yeah,' said Joe. 'But it happened to me.' He turned to Jay Bower, and began to ask questions about the London stock market.

Erika said, 'You work for my brother, Miss Whitcomb?'

'I write articles for him from time to time,' said Jane, 'for which of course he pays me, but I doubt whether either of us would call that working for him.'

Jay interrupted to say 'Certainly not', then at once went back to discussing the impending British miners' strike and its probable effect on British steel shares.

'Just as well I should think,' said Erika. 'I don't think my brother would be all that great to work for.'

'Yes and no,' said Jane. 'He's a bully of course, but he does make things happen, and he turns out a wonderful paper, even if I do write for it myself.'

'You are a writer, Miss Whitcomb?' Louisa Ballantyne asked.

'A journalist, anyway.'

'And is that a rewarding thing to be?' Jay's mother asked.

'In money terms barely adequate – but it's exciting, and it has its own sense of achievement.'

'And these things are important to you?' Jay's father asked.

'I think so.'

'You don't sound very sure,' Jay's father said.

'She should be.' Ballantyne, bored with the future prospects of gilt-edged, plunged in with relish. 'Miss Whitcomb drove an ambulance in the war and got herself blown up, just like brother Billy.'

The elder Bauer acquired a sort of glazed look: the two sisters looked appalled. Joe Ballantyne had broken the first and great commandment: Thou shalt not talk about the war.

'Oh that was all ages ago,' Jane said. 'Ages and ages.' She looked about her. 'What an incredible room this is.'

And indeed it was, with its overwhelming furniture, and tapestries that looked and probably were medieval, and a chiming clock like a miniature fortress, that looked as if it could only be wound by direct assault.

'It is what we like,' said the elder Bauer.

'Of course,' said Jane.

'It is – conservative. I use the word in the sense of traditional. It is what my father liked, and so we keep it as it was, to honour his memory.'

'Your son has told me a little about him,' said Jane. 'He appears to have been a remarkable man.'

'Very remarkable,' said the elder Bauer. 'Everything he did was on the grandest scale. Even his mistakes were vast.' He did not look at his son, but Jane was in no doubt that it was Jay for whom the words were meant. He spoke in German, but his father said at once, and in English, 'No, no. You must not be impolite to our guest.'

This to the man who was impolite to everybody. But this time it was meant to wound, and did.

'Perhaps you would like Erika to show you over the house?' said Mrs Bauer. 'I don't know whether that is the English custom?'

'Sometimes,' said Jane. 'I should like it very much.'

Erika rose at once, to conduct her through what was like nothing so much as a very well-maintained series of museums: the library a museum of books, the music room a museum of instruments, the dining room a museum of furniture: each selection the very best, the most expensive of its kind. She was a good guide, the younger Miss Bauer, knowledgeable and fluent, if not particularly enthusiastic. And not particularly young, either, thought Jane. Pushing thirty rather hard. Soon she'll be middle-aged like me. She examined a wheel-lock musket, hung, for no reason that she could discover, in the morning room.

'Made for the Duke of Bavaria in 1618, the lock plate chiselled with a bear hunt.' Erika rattled it off. 'The stock inlaid with flowers and leaves in white stag horn.' She paused – for breath.

'What did your brother say to your father?' Jane asked.

'The stock is signed by Hieronymus Borstorffer,' said Erika, and then: 'I don't think you should ask me that.'

'Was it so very dreadful?'

'Heck no,' said Erika Bauer. 'It wasn't dreadful at all. One point three million is what he said. I guess they were talking about money. This family often does. You saw for yourself. Joe Ballantyne. He couldn't wait.'

'In a way they were talking about money,' said Jane. 'One point three million is the latest circulation figure of the *Daily World*.'

'Sounds a lot.'

'It is a lot.'

'My God,' said Erika. 'That means that everything you write is read by one million three hundred thousand people.'

'More like four million,' said Jane. 'They reckon that for every one who buys a newspaper, two more people read it.'

'My God,' said Erika again, and then: 'How I envy you.'

Suddenly the plain face became attractive; a transformation brought about by nothing more than animation.

'I've been lucky, I suppose,' said Jane.

'You certainly have,' said Erika. 'You wear pretty clothes, too.'

Well I'm damned if I'm going to apologise for it, thought Jane.

'Paris mostly,' she said at last. 'One has to be careful in one's choosing. That's the trick. Not to let the designer bully you.'

'I've never been to Paris.'

Oh God, thought Jane. Does she want me to apologise for that, too?

'It's much, much easier for me,' she said. 'Living in London.'

'Father still wouldn't let me go.'

There was nothing to be said, and so she said nothing.

'I know what you're thinking,' Erika said at last. 'I'm a grown woman. My life is my own. Well maybe it is – but my money isn't. It's all tied up with father's. I can't even get a couple of dollars for a book unless I ask.'

Still there was nothing to be said, and yet this time she had to say something.

'Couldn't you visit your brother?'

'I couldn't visit Joachim if he lived in the next house down the road,' said Erika.

'Whyever not?'

'Because my father hates him. You see that little Madonna next to the gun? It's from Augsburg. Father's experts say it dates to around 1519. It's probably by Hans Holbein the Younger and if it is it'll be worth a lot more money than if it isn't. But nobody can say for sure.' The last statement seemed to please her greatly.

'How much longer do you intend to keep me here?' Jane asked.

They were in the conservatory, the only place that Erika had not shown her, perhaps because it contained no tapestries or arquebuses or Meissen china, though the plants too looked expensive – and nasty too, quite often.

'It was a mistake,' said Jay, 'and I apologise for it, but my mother went on and on about it – and if I didn't bring you here, people might get the wrong idea.'

'Your people, you mean?'

'Not just them.' He took her arm and turned her to face him. 'Our relationship's important to me,' he said. 'I wish it was even more important. – But I don't want gossip about you. And if I was seen with you in New York without coming home first – oh boy would there be gossip.'

'I'm obliged to you,' she said. 'I mean that. After all I've seen your father in action. This can't have been easy for you.'

'It wasn't meant to be.' Jay stared moodily at an orchid, as well he might, she thought. It looked like decaying flesh.

'I'm not a banker,' he said at last. 'I make a hell of a lot of money, but I'm not a banker. When father goes there won't be a Bauer to take over.'

'What about Ballantyne? Couldn't he change his name?'

'He's in wood pulp,' said Jay. 'That's where his business mixes with mine – and Florence Powell's. He's OK I guess – but he'll never make a king. Not even a crown prince.'

'There's only Erika left,' said Jane. 'She'll have to marry.'

'She nearly did, once,' said Bower. 'Second gardener. Good-looking lad from Saxony. Very fair. Father fired him. I don't think he minded all that much – father also slipped him a thousand bucks. The price of a farm – but Erika did.'

'I want to go away from here,' said Jane.

'Two more days,' said Jay. 'That's the minimum sentence. In this place they never even heard of remission.'

46

Two days later she and Jay left in the Cadillac for New York. Bauer senior was attending a meeting in the library, and his wife had a migraine, but Louisa and Joe Ballantyne joined her for breakfast, and told her how very much they had enjoyed Jay's account of her rudeness to Billy Powell in Paris. Verbal rudeness only, she gathered. Assault with a deadly hand mirror was still a secret.

'It was a pleasure,' she told them, and they begged her to come and dine with them, any time, at least any time except the immediate present. There was trouble at a saw mill across the border in Canada, and Joe simply had to go up there and put it right.

She was going to an apartment instead of a hotel. It had been Jay's idea, and she thought it a good one. An apartment rented by the week for a two-week minimum: small and expensive, but on Park Avenue, and with a couple of servants included.

'And where will you be?'

'Near,' said Jay. 'But not too near.'

She waited for him to move closer at that, but instead he nodded towards the front of the car. Karl's duties, it seemed, included spying on the young master.

'Il parle français, le conducteur?' she asked.

'Pas de tout,' said Bower.

They talked in French all the way to New York.

Jay, it seemed, had meetings there: with banks, with investment companies, with brokers and finance houses; because whatever his father thought of the way that Jay chose to run his life, his grandfather had thought highly enough of him to make it difficult, maybe even impossible, for his father to administer the Bauer millions without his son's active participation. Jane was delighted to hear it, even though it meant that Jay would not be free to show her New York.

'Still you'll be comfortable,' Jay said. 'That apartment's really good, and the servants – ' He paused, suddenly.

'What's wrong with them?'

'Nothing,' said Jay. 'They're as good as our own. I really mean that. Only – '

'Only what?' said Jane.

'They're black,' said Jay. 'I forgot to ask you. Does it bother you?'

'My dear Jay,' she said, 'I never even knew white servants existed until I came to England. But who's going to show me New York?'

'All taken care of,' said Jay. 'I've talked to Barry Golding.'

'Who's Barry Golding?'

Jay chuckled. 'Don't ever let him know you said that,' he said. 'Barry Golding, my dear, is New York's answer to Lionel Warley.' He reached into an inside pocket, and pulled out a sheet of paper. 'I almost forgot,' he said. 'This came this morning.'

She found that she was holding by far the longest telegram she had ever seen, and that quite a lot of it was about her. The 'Wicked World' column once more. 'Will Jane Whitcomb accept the challenge?' it demanded. 'Will the glamorous and intrepid champion of the unfortunate succumb to Hollywood's pleadings and take on the rôle of CLEOPATRA, sultry temptress, serpent of Old Nile?' For it was no longer a secret that Miss Whitcomb had already tested for the part in Paris, where she had worn a costume perhaps a little startling in its brevity, but *absolutely correct* in historical detail.

'Was it?' she asked, intrigued.

'You'd better ask Mutrie's,' said Jay. She read on.

Cleopatra, Jane read, had been famed as much for her patriotic fervour and steely dedication to duty as her gorgeous looks, which was yet another reason why Jane Whitcomb . . . etc., etc. It went without saying that every penny she earned would be donated to her favourite charity, the people of Felston. But there was inevitably a price to pay. If Miss Whitcomb were to dedicate herself to this – and perhaps other – rôles for Felston's sake, then Hollywood would claim her for years and years. Perhaps for ever. She handed back the Western Union sheet.

'You're taking the devil of a risk,' she said.

'How so?'

'Suppose they – what's the word they use? – suppose they call me? Give me a test? Have you any idea how badly I can act?'

'What difference does it make?' he said. 'I own the studio. At least grandfather's trust owns a lot of the bank that owns fifty-one per cent of the studio's shares.'

The 'small apartment' had no more than five rooms, including a master bedroom with a shower en suite. Jay's memory really was remarkable. The two servants were a woman cook, and her husband who served as butler. They seemed clean and capable, and Jay left her with them after seeing her in. He would be back soon, he said, with Barry Golding, then went to check that the apartment's drawing room contained a piano before he left. Jane went to confront her entourage.

'Mr Bower was in such a hurry,' she said, 'that he forgot to tell me your names.'

'I'm George, Miss Whitcomb,' said the butler, 'and my wife is Martha.'

Jane blinked. 'You must forgive me,' she said. 'I'm English and perhaps not as well aware as I should be about your country's history, but George and Martha – surely there's a reference there.'

'The first president of the United States was George Washington,' said the butler.

'And his wife's name was Martha,' said his wife.

'Is this something that was forced upon you?' Jane asked.

'Oh no, miss,' said Martha. 'It just sort of happened.'

Serendipity, thought Jane. Mummy's favourite word.

'So you don't mind?'

'Not at all, Miss Whitcomb,' the butler said. 'For good or ill, most people tend to remember our names.'

'I should think they would,' said Jane. 'Now I must go and unpack. Mr Bower will be back soon.' She hesitated. 'I have a feeling that there ought to be cocktails.'

'Yes, miss?' George said this as if he were absolutely certain that there ought to be cocktails.

'What I mean,' said Jane desperately, 'is where do I go to buy the gin?'

'Some blue-jewelled individual in a white fedora with a dubious bottle wrapped in a New York *Daily Mirror*,' said Barry, who had turned out to be a smaller, younger version of Lionel Warley. Jay had told her that he played the piano rather well.

'What did George do?' Jay asked. 'Laugh?'

'Certainly not,' said Jane. 'George is a butler and a gentleman. But a man more obviously not laughing I never saw in my life.'

'What *did* he do?' Jay asked.

'Showed me the drinks cupboard,' said Jane. 'What he called the cellarette. Four kinds of whisky, three kinds of gin, cognac, Calvados, every liqueur I ever heard of.'

'What did you expect?' said Jay.

'She expected to be shown the bathroom,' said Barry Golding. 'Because that's the place where we're supposed to make the gin.'

'*What?*' said Jay. He not only sounded surprised: he sounded outraged, too.

'Well, of course,' said Jane. 'Isn't it all supposed to be illegal?'

George came in with a shakerful of martinis, and Jane discovered the importance of ice, and exact proportions in the blending.

'Delicious,' she said to George, and continued, 'But it's all illegal, surely? As illegal as morphine or cocaine? Of *course* I expected a blue-jewelled gangster.'

'Al Capone's in Chicago,' said Jay.

'And of course they do tend towards a certain lack of polish in Chicago,' said Barry. 'Though he did begin his career in New York, one must admit.'

'So you do use gangsters here?' said Jane.

'*We* don't,' said Barry, 'but a lot of people are obliged to, poor dears.'

'And go blind? And die of alcoholic poisoning?'

'It rather depends on one's supplier,' said Barry. 'The worst thing that most of them can do is give you the most ghastly hangover. Could I have another one of these before I play?'

So he not only expects to play, he insists on it, thought Jane.

All the same he is rather sweet. . . . George replenished his glass.

'Do you like your apartment?' Jay asked.

'Yes,' she said.

'You seem a little blue.'

'I'm missing Foch,' she said, and then to Barry: 'Foch is my dog. He's a Scots terrier.'

'With a prodigious appetite for the fleshpots,' said Jay. 'In his canting, Calvinistic way.'

'We Americans are often like that,' said Barry. 'Disapproving and desirous at the same time. Booze may be sinful, but we couldn't possibly be expected to do without it – so we make it squalid, and then it's all right.'

'You wouldn't care to do me a piece on that?' Jay asked.

'I'd much sooner play the piano.'

He took his glass and went over to it, picking out chords at first, selecting and choosing as a woman might select and choose a hat.

Jay said, 'I got your picture.'

'Which one?' She was listening to Barry play a tune at last, 'What'll I Do?' He played it very well.

'Cleopatra,' he said. 'Want to see it?'

'I suppose so.'

He took a photograph from an inside pocket and handed it to her, and there she was sprawled out on a scratchy tigerskin and leaving little to the imagination.

'I must say,' she said, 'I don't look too bad, considering my age and the amount I eat.'

'It doesn't bother you?'

'It'll bother some people I love,' she said. 'Mostly older ladies like my mother and possibly Grandma and Lady Mangan.' She thought of Bet. 'It may bother some young ones, too. But there's not a great deal I can do about it except to say that I did it all for art, just as you suggest. Burrowes really is a swine, isn't he? But one day I'll catch up with him. You'll see.'

The melody had changed to something she hadn't heard before. Very softly Barry was singing

I'm just a little boy who's lost in the wood
I wish I could always be good

to a melody as delicate as gossamer. Jay tried to speak and she motioned him to silence. Barry sang on.

> Won't you tell her please to put on some speed,
> Hear when I plead. Oh how I need
> Someone to watch over me.

The music died at last.

'Who wrote that?' she asked.

'Gershwin,' said Barry. 'Who else?'

She reached for her handkerchief. Gershwin and martinis were a lethal combination.

'He told me once,' said Barry, 'that he wrote his music for young girls sitting on fire escapes on hot summer nights in New York and dreaming of love.'

'He did,' said Jane. 'Oh dear God he did. Come and look at my naughty picture before I burst into tears.'

Barry came and looked. 'My,' he said. 'Are you going to work for Mr Ziegfeld?' and then, answering his own question: 'Well of course not. He couldn't afford you. You look good, Jane.'

'Thank you so much,' she said.

'Now,' said Barry, 'I guess we ought to get started. We have at least three parties to go to, and then dinner and Jack and Charlie's and the Stork Club.'

'Goodness,' said Jane. 'How many days will that take?'

Jay said, 'That's it?' Barry turned to him, eyebrows lifted. 'Jane's picture,' Jay explained. 'You look good, Jane. Let's go to five or six parties. . . . That's *it*!'

'Well,' said Barry, 'what else can I say? When it comes to what you might call a Baby Bunting sort of costume, some girls can get away with it and some can't, and Jane's obviously one of those who can. *And* it's for art's sake. I mean I know you're worried about what Jane's fellow countrymen will say, but goodness – that won't matter.'

'Won't it?' asked Jane.

'Well of course it won't,' said Barry. 'Because as soon as that photograph appears in the press you'll be denounced by some of *my* countrymen, and if there's one thing that's guaranteed to make your fellow citizens forgive you – cherish you even – it's the fact that you'll have been blackguarded by a bunch of Yanks. You'll be a national heroine, my dear. Baring all for Britain.'

'Well not quite all,' said Jane. 'But I do see what you mean.'

'So we go to some of these parties?' Jay asked.

'We go to all of them,' said Jane firmly.

Two more Manhattan apartments, and one small (so Jay said) but beautiful house near Central Park, with the most comprehensive collection of eighteenth-century French paintings Jane had ever seen: Fragonard, Watteau, Boucher, Chardin, de la Tour. And at each one Barry played Gershwin, or Kern, or Berlin, or that new young man called Richard Rogers, and Jane began to drink lemonade instead, because this was not the time for tears. Then on to Jack and Charlie's Luncheon Club on West 49th Street, a speakeasy where to Jane's delight the ritual was scrupulously followed: the elaborate knock on the door, the sliding panel that allowed two hard grey eyes to survey you, and then the spoken formula: 'Harry said it would be OK.' And then in to crowds of people and real champagne, and the kind of sandwiches that only Americans dare attempt.

Jane seemed to spend at least an hour there saying 'How do you do?' and accepting invitations to parties, tomorrow, next week, next month (this last to a party which had already been going on for several days). New York City, perhaps even the whole of the United States of America, had decided that it was time for a party, and only the Bauers had not been invited. Jay had, but then he wasn't a Bauer, after all, he was Bower, hard at work even at Jack and Charlie's bless him, showing off her picture and telling all and sundry it was art, while she at last was allowed to converse, rather than simply accept invitations, and found herself discoursing, apparently simultaneously, on Coco Chanel and the Prince of Wales, Braque and Joyce and the Russian ballet, but that was merely champagne on top of martinis, she thought, then regretted the 'merely'. It was a word she must learn to use sparingly.

On then to the Stork, with Barry and Jay, and a girl called Thelma who did nothing but lament the fact that she had never been to Venice and must do so at once, before she became old.

'How old is old?' Jane asked.

'Twenty-four,' Thelma said. 'That's what I'll be next year.'

Jay chuckled. 'You leave that photograph where it is,' said Jane.

The Stork Club was not disappointing exactly, but it was predictable. For this sort of thing she preferred the Embassy in London. But it was a speakeasy – no ritual to be recited, but a careful scrutiny of membership cards – and it did have music. ('Not Paul Whiteman,' Barry told her. 'Not this time. He's down in Florida selling real estate.' In other words, she gathered, Whiteman and his band were the sugar on the pill of a Florida land sale.)

They joined a group of theatre people who had already begun their supper. Was it so late already? And indeed it was, but all the same she had to dance – with Jay, with Barry, with the jeune premier among the actors, and the play's director who talked the whole time of Shakespeare and Dryden and Shaw, all of whom, she remembered, had written plays about Cleopatra. To dance was sobering, but it was also tiring. Jay's publicity machine had done its work already: wartime heroine, indefatigable charity worker, even her offer to strip with Marigold Ledbitter at her brother's college. But all of it wholesome. The good sport, the patriot, the pretty pal. Everything that filled out a Chanel suit.

'You're a success,' said Barry. 'Un succès fou.' They were sitting out for once.

'Are you surprised?'

'Not at all. But it's always gratifying to find one's prophecies fulfilled.'

The theatre director leaned across to them. 'I doubt if Cassandra found it so,' he said. Barry pouted. 'It's far too late at night to try to remember the stuff they used to tell me at Princeton,' he said.

'Do you remember the Serpent of Old Nile?' the director asked.

'If there are marks out of ten for that then I want some,' said Barry. 'That was Cleopatra.'

Jane said, 'I must have met about two hundred people tonight – and it's just too many names. If anybody told me yours I've forgotten it.'

'Tom Waring,' said the director, and offered his hand. 'Nobody introduced us.'

'How do you do?' said Jane. 'I should explain that when people are talking about me – however obliquely – I like to know their names.'

'You reckon I'm talking about you?'

'I think that's what Jay Bower hired you to do.' She looked across to where Bower danced with the ingénue of the play. He was talking. Of course he was.

'Am I right?' she asked.

'Quite right,' said Waring.

'Could we leave it till tomorrow?'

'Sure we could.'

'Because my feet have recovered you see, and Barry needs the exercise.'

The band played 'Ain't We Got Fun', and Barry danced it well, but not so well as Lionel.

He escorted her home too through air he described as being as cold and crisp as the frosting on a daiquiri.

'I like to scatter these little gems around,' he said, 'in the hope that somebody more energetic than me will steal them – and then I can claim co-authorship. Do steal that one.'

'Do my best,' said Jane, 'though they don't drink many daiquiris in Felston.'

'Speaking of the written word,' said Barry, 'shouldn't you be escorted home by Jay? I mean I'm charmed – utterly charmed – but all the same you were his date.'

'Jay,' she said, 'is watching the print of the bulldog edition of the New York *Herald*. Does that make sense to you?'

'No,' said Barry, 'except that it sounds exactly the sort of thing he would do. He doesn't own it, does he?'

'No,' said Jane, 'but it's a newspaper, and it's printing, and if he doesn't see a newspaper at work at least twice a week he has one of his turns.' The cab stopped by her apartment building.

'You like him, don't you?' Barry said.

'Enormously,' said Jane, and he kissed her cheek.

'An acquired taste, dear Jay,' he said. 'So glad you acquired it.'

An acquired taste is right, she thought as she lay in bed, and there's no doubt that I've acquired it, but do I still love him (or more precisely want him) as once I did, after all that hard labour to buy jobs for Bob and the major and a way out of trouble for me? In Felston they had a word for that sort of hard labour, and no doubt they were right, but life was never quite so simple as that. Take George, for instance. George had been waiting up for her when she came in, and was vaguely surprised, no more, at her anger that he should do so. Indian servants, as she remembered, would have fallen asleep and stayed asleep until somebody began to shout and swear.

She slept well: alcohol for a sleeping draught, good bed, warm room, and when she woke a shower en suite so that all she had to do was take off her nightdress and stagger under the deluge. But it reminded her of Jay, and his room above the shop. If his desires were carnal, and when were they not, how would they achieve fruition? Mercifully that was his problem. She telephoned George on the internal telephone (would Hawkins permit an internal telephone in South Terrace, she wondered?) and asked for breakfast. Fresh orange juice, George suggested, and ham and eggs. Fresh orange juice pressed from Florida oranges it seemed, where Paul Whiteman serenaded, and quite delicious. And Virginia Ham like no other ham she had ever eaten. Fed on peaches, George assured her, and George would know.

By eleven thirty she was dressed in a sweater and skirt and sitting by the window, watching the snow fall, which it did in a busy and determined kind of way that was somehow very American. Soon, Jay had told her, she would take a train to California, something called the 'Super Chief' and, when she got there after several days of cocktails and steak dinners, the sun would be shining. Which was very nice. She liked the sun. But what would she do? Jay had muttered something about a screen test, but they both knew that was nonsense. Or did they? If it was nonsense, why was she seeing Tom Waring?

George came in, with the dreaded tabloids that Jay had warned her about: McCormick's *Daily News*, Hearst's *Daily Mirror*, and McFadden's *Graphic*. All three of them, Jay had told her, were friends of his. They weren't friends of hers – or perhaps McFadden was. He certainly made a lot of fuss about the body beautiful, and included hers in that category. But gracious how he did go on. The other two were simply old-fashioned lechers disguised as moralists, but all three had printed the picture. If Barry's theory was correct, England would rise to her defence to the last man. . . . The telephone rang, and George came in to tell her it was Jay.

'You've seen the papers?' he asked her.

'I can't remember when I've had more fun,' she said. 'What have you in mind next? Tar and feathers?'

'I heard what Barry told you,' said Jay. 'He's right. This is the way to lick this thing. You believe me, don't you?'

'Well of course I do,' she said. 'You're the expert. This is what you're for.'

'OK then,' he said. 'Just go along with me and enjoy yourself.'

'Aren't I going to see you?'

'Not where you are,' he said. 'I haven't given out your address but they'll find you soon enough.'

'Where then?'

'I've got a suite at the Waldorf,' he said. 'If you would care to see it.'

'I should adore to see your suite at the Waldorf,' she said. 'Would four o'clock be convenient? I'm promised to Barry at seven.'

'Four is fine,' he said. 'Enjoy yourself till then.'

She spoke quickly, before he could hang up. 'Any message for Tom Waring?'

'Just listen to him,' he said.

'My pleasure,' she said, then for the first time since she had known him, she hung up first. It must be the air, she thought.

Tom Waring was prompt, and looked sober and rested, but just a little apprehensive. She offered him a drink, and he asked for a Manhattan – rye whiskey, Italian vermouth and bitters over cracked ice, plus a Maraschino cherry. She asked for a glass of Chablis for herself, and George produced both without a blink. Waring raised his glass.

'Your health,' he said.

'And yours.' Jane raised hers.

'You've heard from Mr Bower?' She nodded. 'What did he say?'

'That you were to talk and I was to listen.'

'Yes, of course,' said Waring. 'I understand. For him that has to be the simplest way.' He sipped his drink. 'You know I directed this play on Broadway?'

'*Summer's Lease*? Of course. I look forward to seeing it.'

'I also work in Hollywood from time to time. Most directors – once they go to Hollywood they stay there – but I like to come back East occasionally. It isn't just the theatre. It's things like the seasons. That.' He nodded at the window where the snow now gyrated like feathers from an exploding eiderdown. 'But when I am in Hollywood I usually work for Worldwide Films. Do you know about that?'

'I know that Mr Bower's family owns quite a lot of it.'

'Yeah,' said Waring. 'Quite a lot.' He finished his drink and Jane poured him another. There was no point in bothering George, not when he was helping Martha prepare their lunch.

'He wants us to make a film,' she said.

'Not a film,' said Waring. 'Not right off. Just a test. But if the test's good – '

'The idea's preposterous,' said Jane. 'I've never acted in my life.'

'Eighty per cent of Hollywood's never acted in its life,' said Waring. 'The camera acts for them.' He gulped again at his drink. 'Look, Miss Whitcomb – it isn't going to last because any year now there'll be talking pictures and then people will *really* have to act – but just for now a person who looks good and can project the way they're asked to feel. That's all it needs.'

'And you think I can do that?'

'Oh boy. Look, Miss Whitcomb – I've seen your picture.' He hesitated. 'I'm sorry. Maybe you – '

'My dear man,' she said. 'Half of New York has seen my picture. Tell me about this projection business. And do call me Jane.'

'Projection's just looking the way I ask you to look. I mean if I say look sad – could you do that?'

'How?'

'By thinking of something sad. And happy the same.'

'I'll try,' said Jane. 'Just give me a moment.'

Suddenly her sadness was there; wounded, heartrending.

'Great,' said Waring. 'Now happiness, please.' And she duly obliged. 'Fantastic,' said Waring. 'How on earth did you do it Miss – Jane?'

'For sadness I thought about my dog and how much I miss him,' she said. 'For happiness I imagined that I was present as an observer while a man named Burrowes was mercilessly thrashed by a man named Pardoe. They were both arrested for disturbing the peace. Mr Waring this is all a very great nonsense.'

'But it pays,' said Waring earnestly. 'I get twenty grand – that's twenty thousand dollars for every picture I make. That's the heck of a lot of money.'

'I've got the heck of a lot of money,' said Jane.

'For you it would be more. Maybe even fifty thousand. More than twelve thousand of your pounds for just ten weeks' work.'

'Ten weeks?' said Jane. 'Jay expects me to prance around in that ludicrous piece of peau de soie for ten whole weeks?'

'You could give the money to that town of yours,' said Waring.

As if I owned it, she thought. Felston. My town.

'Tell me why,' she said. 'I'm over thirty. I've never acted in my life – oh you say that's not important and I believe you – but I've never even wanted to act. So why pick on me?'

'First I must tell you that you're an unusual woman,' said Waring. 'Almost unbelievably so. America is full of people who want to be in pictures: to be stars. Especially young and pretty women.'

'Over thirty,' said Jane. 'And I didn't even tell you how far over.'

'It doesn't matter,' said Waring. 'It's all in the lighting. We could make you eighteen or even eighty-three if we wanted to. I could have a queue from here to Times Square if I said I was looking for a girl to play Cleopatra – in Hollywood it would be half way to San Francisco – and you tell me you don't want to do it.'

'I don't,' said Jane, 'but let's have lunch while you tell me about it.'

Lunch was lobster bisque and lamb chops and a soufflé, and all of a kind that Mrs Barrow would have approved. While they ate Waring told her about the movies in general, and his plans for Cleopatra in particular. To him Hollywood meant money: the kind of money that would subsidise the work in the theatre he loved but could by no means afford, what with an ex-wife and a fiancée, and a Packard coupé he liked so much that he had two of them, one in Los Angeles and the other in New York. But it wasn't only money. There was a kind of crazy ingenuity involved in what he did that he found immensely stimulating.

'Every picture I make I'm Pearl White tied to the railway track,' he said, 'and I never know till the last reel whether the express is going to hit me or not.'

'And the prospect doesn't terrify you?'

'Every time I think it might I come back here,' he said, 'and take anything that's going, even summer stock. But to do that I need Hollywood for half the year at least.'

'And Jay really wants us to do this?' Jane asked.

'Yes, mam.'

'Where Shakespeare and Dryden and Shaw have triumphed, you and I will triumph too?'

'What we'll do is a carnival really,' said Waring, 'although the critics will call it an epic. You know the kind of thing – Roman legions, chariots, toiling slaves. Mark Antony at war with Caesar Augustus, and you as sort of a warrior queen. Ben Hur, you know. D. W. Griffiths stuff.'

'It sounds quite wholesome,' she said, 'if rather violent.'

'Most of it will be.'

'Most?'

'She was the kind of woman who could break one of the world's great rulers and captivate another. A woman who used sex as Mark Antony used his sword.'

'You should approach Pola Negri,' said Jane.

'Mr Bower wants you,' said Waring.

And indeed he did, she thought, in that grand and rather pompous suite at the Waldorf. First he wanted me and then he had me, and it was still pleasant enough, and only afterwards did they talk.

'What's this about seeing Barry?' he asked.

'He wants to show me Harlem,' said Jane. She had showered, and was drying herself on the fluffiest, most luxurious towel she had ever used.

'You should see it all right,' said Jay, 'but you could have problems.'

'Why should I?'

'The gentlemen of the press. . . . They didn't bother you at the Stork Club last night?'

'No.' She reached for her comb, and the towel slipped.

'They will tonight,' said Jay. 'Even if you got to the YWCA.'

'Then I must remember to stay away,' said Jane. She wandered into the bathroom, leaving the door open, and found the box of talcum powder she had brought for the occasion, and the huge powder puff that went with it.

'Tell me about Waring,' she said.

'Don't do that,' said Jay.

'What nonsense,' she said. 'You know how much you enjoy it.' She began to powder her breasts.

'He's a good director,' said Jay. 'He likes money so he does what he's told. . . . Come here.'

'Without even a please? Tell me about this screen test.' The powder puff moved lower.

'It's a gag,' said Jay. 'A publicity gag. It gets you known. Good for Felston – and good for the *Daily World*.'

Her body wriggled as she applied more powder.

'He doesn't believe that,' she said.

'Tom Waring believes what I tell him,' said Jay. '*Please* come here.'

And so she went. It was nice to know that she could have such an effect on a man, she thought, but not nearly so fulfilling as their early days together. More like General Knowledge, really: the Principal Rivers of Europe, perhaps, or how to get a stone out of a horse's hoof. When they had done he said, 'You must be feeling pleased with yourself,' and it was true that he had performed prodigies. But all she did was smile. It was better than saying, 'Not really.'

47

'I THOUGHT WE'D start at the Hotsy-Totsy,' said Barry, 'and then lower the tone a little. The Sligo Slasher's or somewhere like that. And then supper somewhere and on to the Cotton Club.'

'Aren't I just a little overdressed for roughing it?' Jane asked. 'I mean a Paquin dress *and* sables?'

'If I'm being rebuked for not admiring that *exquisite* gown then so be it,' said Barry. 'My dear, such a blue. But for the rest – fear not. The proprietors of these dens of iniquity are all friends of mine. My God they should be – the money I spend there. You will notice that I'm wearing a tuxedo.'

'I have indeed.'

'Well let me tell you that I could go into Tony's on East 53rd Street clad in no more than a derby hat and an athletic support and be perfectly safe.'

'My poor love,' said Jane. 'Are they all blind?'

'Martinis will be the death of me,' said Barry. 'I don't even listen to what I say any more. Shall we go?'

'Play a little Gershwin first.' – What with one thing and another, it seemed a good time to be sad. As he played, she said, 'What makes Jay think that Cleopatra was a blonde?'

He was playing his own version of the 'Rhapsody in Blue', and almost missed a beat. 'Does he?' he asked.

'You *have* noticed the colour of my hair?'

'Oh that,' said Barry. 'Colour isn't the thing. Really it's not. Blonde and brunette. All that. A femme fatale, that's what Jay's after. That's what wigs are for, surely?'

'Let's go to a den of iniquity,' she said.

They went to many, starting at the Hotsy-Totsy, then Tony's, then the Sligo Slasher's, and then on a downward spiral to the sort of place where you either sat on a box or stood at the bar, and whatever you drank was served in a cup, and after one sip of her drink she marvelled at the resistance of New York china. Not that she drank much: she had come to watch, and there was a lot to see. A clientele mostly male, listening to music on a gramophone, a radio, or from a group of musicians, and at the same time telling each other which stocks had risen highest that day. Stockbrokers, bank clerks, cab drivers, barbers, it didn't matter. They all knew which stocks had done best. Even the bartenders knew it; in fact they knew it best of all.

They went to a supper club then, and on to Harlem, in north east Manhattan, which turned out to be a district inhabited largely by middle-class blacks, and so to the Cotton Club, which was every bit as much an institution as the Brigade of Guards, she thought, and with the same high standards of discipline and physical perfection. Except that these were chorus girls, tall, elegant, and with a colour never darker than milk chocolate; what Barry told her was called 'high yellow'. Slender and lovely and aloof, they danced to the music of a black orchestra to amuse an audience entirely white on whom black waiters attended. Like the Raj, she thought, but it wasn't like the Raj. Brown men waiting on her had never seemed a problem, but this did. And then the music reached her, and she forgot everything else. Strong, rhythmic, inventive; she heard brass and woodwind played as she'd never heard them before.

'Like it?' Barry asked.

'It's incredible,' she said. 'How do they do it?'

'I've asked them often enough,' said Barry, 'but they can never tell you. You just do it, they say. I expect Rachmaninov and Heifetz would give you the same answer.'

The girls danced again: every one of them a much more probable Cleopatra than she.

'Would you like to go to a party?' Barry asked.

'Now?'

'Why not now?'

'Isn't it rather late?'

'It's never too late for a party in New York,' Barry said. 'You should know that by now.'

But before they could leave they had to fight their way out. The press had caught up with them at last. Seven men and two women, not counting cameramen, whose flashlights blinded like flares, while the questions came at her like gun fire. 'Miss Whitcomb, have you a comment on yesterday's article?' 'Miss Whitcomb, do you approve of semi-nude pictures?' 'Do you regard yourself as a corrupter of morals?' 'If you were a mother, would you like your child to see you like that?' and even, 'Do you believe in God, Miss Whitcomb?'

And all the time she smiled like a maniac seeking an axe, and kept on repeating over and over, 'Such a happy place, New York, and the people so helpful and friendly', until Barry came up with a taxi-cab, and they rode off at last.

'Rough?' he said.

'I've seen worse,' said Jane. 'But not for eight years.'

The party was in a penthouse of an apartment in 64th Street, and she could hear the music from two floors below. When they left the elevator Barry led her at once to a door where two men stood like sentries, and gave his name, and hers. One of the men consulted a list, then nodded, and the other man opened the door. They went inside.

'Just like a speakeasy,' said Jane, and for some reason Barry smiled.

Inside, the apartment was more like Bedlam on a bad day, she thought, or perhaps like 'The Rake's Progress', Barry suggested, except that everyone was having such a good time. And indeed they were. They ate, drank, smoked, embraced, in a conglomeration of bodies; man with woman, man with man, woman with woman, black with white.

Jane blinked. 'Well well,' she said. 'Didn't I just tell the press that in New York the people are so helpful and friendly?'

'Come and meet our host,' said Barry. He led her up to a man who simply had to be a gangster, she thought. Blue jowls despite a close shave, draped tuxedo and diamond ring. With him with was a girl of maybe thirty, who was very beautiful and very black, and who might well be the reason for the racial mixture.

'Frank Cardona, this is Jane Whitcomb,' said Barry.

Jane offered her hand. 'How d'you do?' she said.

'Miss Whitcomb's from England,' Barry explained.

'Pleased to meet you.' His hand touched hers then let go very quickly. 'This is Maebelle Barton.'

The black girl smiled. 'Enjoying the music, Miss Whitcomb?'

'I've never heard anything like it,' said Jane.

'You never will,' said the black girl, 'not anywhere else in New York. Chicago maybe, but not New York.'

'Get my guests a drink,' said Cardona, and a young man near him took off like a greyhound out of a trap, and came back with a bottle and glasses. The bottle was Dom Perignon, and Jane and Barry toasted Cardona, then went to dance.

'I think I know why you smiled when I mentioned speakeasies,' she said.

'Doucement, petite,' said Barry, looking about him.

'Because a certain gentleman owns them,' said Jane. Barry winked.

On and on went the dancing, and the drinking and smoking and loving, until at last the black drummer left the others – white banjo player and clarinettist, black pianist and trombone player – and searched around the room until he found a neat, contained white man asleep in a chair, a ring of empty glasses around him. The drummer shook the white man gently but firmly until he awoke. He blinked at the drummer, then fumbled to his feet, picked up what she thought was a trumpet, and lurched with the black man over to the band. The banjo player at once provided a seat, and then, without any apparent signal, they began to play together.

'"Jazz Me Blues",' said Barry. 'Oh what bliss.'

And indeed it was. The neat contained man could conjure sounds out of a brass instrument she would not have believed possible, even though he was obviously very drunk.

'Who is that trumpeter?' she asked at last.

'Cornet player,' said Barry. 'When you go back to London you can tell them you heard Bix Beiderbecke.'

'Is he always so drunk?'

'Very often. He should be in Florida with Whiteman. He's been offered a job in his band.'

'Why isn't he?'

Barry shrugged. 'He probably forgot to go.'

'Poor lamb,' said Jane.

Maebelle Barton joined the band and began to sing in a rich yet husky contralto, and Beiderbecke's trumpet wove variations around it. It was like no other blending she had ever heard.

Another late morning. Did anyone *ever* go to bed and get up at the right time in New York? she wondered. But that was ridiculous. Everybody did except the rich parasites, but what a lot of them there seemed to be. How happy Andy would be here, she thought. So much scope for righteous indignation.

George said, 'Mr Bower telephoned, Miss Whitcomb. He says he'll call here at around noon.'

I ought to go out, she thought. How dare he *say* he'll call. He should ask. But Jay never asked. He didn't know how.

He looked angry, and she wondered why. She had done nothing after all except to go to parties and clubs and dance with Barry.

'You went to Cardona's,' he said.

'The most marvellous music,' she said. 'There was a dear drunken man called Bix – '

'Never mind,' he said. 'You shouldn't have gone.'

'Because he's a gangster?'

'How did you know that?'

'Because I looked at him,' said Jane. 'Of course he's a gangster. It couldn't be more obvious if he wore a label with "Gangster" on it. He served the best champagne I've had since I got here.'

'You could have been seen by the press,' said Jay. 'What would have happened to that wholesome image then?'

'I was seen,' said Jane, 'at the Cotton Club. They took enough bites out of me there for one night.'

'You played that quite well,' said Jay. He sounded grudging. 'Helpful, friendly New Yorkers. But Cardona. He's what they call the head of a family. Big-time crook. Booze, gambling, prostitution.'

'Like Al Capone?'

'Cardona despises Capone,' said Jay. 'He makes too much noise. Cardona likes things discreet. That way he makes more money. But you keep away from him.'

'We'll see,' she said. 'I liked his music and I liked his girl. If I'm invited again – '

'You won't be,' said Jay. 'Barry won't take you – '

'You seem very sure.'

'Of course I'm sure,' said Jay. 'He owes me money.'

'He's also very fond of you,' she said, but he didn't hear. He was talking.

'And anyway Cardona – ' he said, then hesitated.

'Owes you money too?'

'Not owes,' said Jay. 'And not me. . . . But he'll do me a favour even if you won't.'

'Not you?' she said. 'Your father perhaps. Does Mr Cardona get him all that lovely hock and Moselle he's so fond of?'

'You're still a smart one,' he said.

'When I can be bothered. . . . I see in my newspaper that your mother's giving a reception in that schloss of hers tomorrow. All New York is going, it says. Have you brought my invitation with you?'

'You're not going.'

'Why not? You are. The paper said that, too.'

'I didn't have my picture in the tabloids,' said Jay.

'You bastard,' she said.

'Not at all,' said Jay. 'We discussed the whole thing – remember? You knew what the *Graphic* and the rest of them would say. So you must have known how my mother would feel about inviting you.'

She chuckled. 'Touché,' she said. 'But tell me just one thing. Does your mother know she's living off Mr Cardona's immoral earnings?'

He was up on his feet at once, fist pulled back. She chuckled again.

'Mummy's boy,' she said. 'You know that's interesting. I'd never have suspected it.'

He said stiffly, 'You know how to hurt, but then you always did. I guess that's part of your charm.' He went through his pockets, and at last came up with a cigar.

'We've had letters,' he said. 'At the *Daily World*. About you going to Hollywood. At the moment they're running at twenty-three to one asking you to stay. When the great British public reads about what the New York tabloids have said about you it'll be fifty to one. At least.'

'And so?' she said.

'And so you have a choice,' he said. 'If for any crazy reason you want to know what I think, then I'll tell you. Whether you go or stay, at least go to Hollywood and do the test. Make it a cliff-hanger.'

'I told you I would go to Hollywood,' she said. 'I don't go back on my word.'

'OK then, we'll go,' said Jay. 'Thursday suit you? We'll be there on Monday of next week. Drawing room. Take all your warm clothes. Those trains are cold till long after Chicago.'

She understood very little of what he was saying, but she nodded. 'And where am I allowed to go until then?' she asked.

Jay winced. 'Theatres,' he said. 'The ones that show improving plays. Carnegie Hall. Art galleries. And stay way from speaks.' And then incredibly, 'Just one thing more. You still haven't changed your mind? You still won't marry me?'

'What an extraordinary man you are,' she said. 'Of course not.'

For three more days she shopped at Saks and Tiffany's and the little places Barry recommended, and went to see *Rose Marie* and *Showboat* and *What Price Glory?* Barry took her to all three, but never again mentioned Jay. And then at the appointed time the most enormous motor car arrived, to take her and her luggage to Grand Central Station, and to leave behind two servants whom she knew she would miss for a long, long time. The Century was only the Century as far as Chicago, after which for some reason it became the Super Chief, perhaps, she thought, because one had to change stations. But there really was a drawing room, and a place to wash, and a bed, and a flock of white-jacketed negroes who provided their own bootlegging service and made the beds as well.

Jay had the drawing room next to hers, but for most of the journey he stayed in it and worked his way through the pile of telegrams that seemed to be waiting for him every time the train stopped, or even slowed; though from time to time he did join her to drink martinis or eat an enormous steak called a tenderloin. While he ate and drank he told her all about the world's news.

When they got to Chicago there was another enormous car waiting to help them change stations, and more negroes in white jackets to bring them martinis. Chicago was even colder than Manhattan, and she felt very sorry for the negroes, because it was cold on the train, too. But at least there were letters, waiting for her in her drawing room, brought across from England in the liner *Aquitania*. A few, a very few, from lunatics who denounced her immodesty, shamelessness, lust: and a very large number from people who begged her to reconsider, stay out of America, come home to the rescue of those who needed her. There was a picture postcard from Lionel, a portrait of Britannia, and on the back he had written: 'Britons never never never. . . . Come back soon you idiot. Love. Lionel.' There was a letter from Mummy too, which said the same thing at much greater length.

The major was, of course, deeply upset, but with brothers like his what could one expect? The costume was perhaps a *little* exiguous, but one had been assured of its historical accuracy. On the other hand, while the lure of Hollywood was doubtless wildly exciting to impressionable minds (Gwendoline Gwatkin had placed Offley Villas under a state of siege since first she read of it) there were other and perhaps more cogent reasons why it should be rejected. Felston needed rather more than her money: it needed her presence.

Grandma wrote to say the same. The latest operation had worked, God be thanked, but eyesight was a blessing of God to allow us to look at the ones we loved – and not on a screen or in a newspaper either. Bet had been dubious at first, but now she thought the same. And she, Grandma, had had a big row with Dr Stobbs for saying that Jane could go where she liked so long as she sent money.

Jay came in. 'There's a bunch of entertainers in the club car,' he said. 'They'll be singing soon. Do you want to hear them?'

'Why not?' she said, and folded up her letters.

'Nice mail?' he asked.

'About what you told me. A little over twenty to one – not counting the lunatics.'

'There's one from your mother,' he said.

'My mother is sane,' Jane said, 'and, as far as I can gather, on my side.'

'I didn't mean to suggest she wasn't,' said Jay.

'Of course not. Let's go and listen to your entertainers.'

A ukulele and a mouth organ, a blonde who sang and a brunette who danced. But it was pleasant and relaxing: 'Show Me The Way To Go Home', 'Me and My Shadow' – without any suggestion of the emotional demands made by the music at Frank Cardona's.

'The weather will be better tomorrow,' said Jay.

'Oh really?'

'We're moving south all the time. Soon it'll be too warm for snow.'

'Very nice.'

Jay slammed his hand down on the bar counter.

'I'm trying to make conversation,' he said.

'You can usually do better than the weather,' she said.

And then at twelve o'clock [sang the blonde]
We climb the stairs. We never knock
'Cos nobody cares.
Just me and my sha-dow,
All alone and fee-ling blue.

'Do you own them?' Jane asked.

'Just the brunette,' said Jay. 'The others are under option for when we switch to sound.'

Touché, she thought, and went back to her drawing room to read her letters and drink a Sidecar (one third cointreau triple sec, one third brandy, one third lemon juice) prepared by one of the black bootleggers. Reading and drinking were about all one could do – the Middle West from her window seemed one vast, flat field in which nothing ever happened. And so she read. Not just her fan mail but books about Cleopatra that Waring had sent her: almost every book about Cleopatra that had ever been written, or so it seemed. She didn't much like what she read.

Then somewhere south of Kansas City, Missouri, the weather became warm, and for no other reason than that she need no longer spend all day in a fur coat, she began to feel more cheerful. She finished all her Cleopatra books too, and began on a novel called *The Great Gatsby* by someone called Scott Fitzgerald. There was a photograph of him on the back cover, and she discovered that she had met him in Paris. She enjoyed the book very much.

Jay she saw only at meal times. He made no further attempt to share her bed. There were others who had joined the Super-Chief in Chicago, bankers for the most part, and a newspaper owner. He spent a lot of time with them, but made no effort to persuade Jane to join them, and she was glad. She enjoyed her privacy and her reading, and if she needed conversation there were always the black bootleggers. But she didn't much. All the self-improvement, 'how-to-be-a-nicer-person' books would stress that this was a perfect time for what they liked to call 'a period of quiet reflection', 'a chance to think things through': but she found that she couldn't do that. She could *remember* effortlessly: Michael Browne's wife and Georgina Payne's picture, the feel of Burrowes's skin under her palm when she walloped him, Jay's house in the country, taking a fence on Bridie's back. And Felston, endlessly. The slums, the market place, and most of all the clinic. And even further back than that. With the girls in the Ambulance Unit; and her first dance with John; and beyond that even, to India and Mummy and French irregular verbs. It was all as clear and accurate as if it had been recorded on film: but quiet reflection must lead to decisions, and she wasn't yet ready to make decisions. Certain events had still to take place, but when they did she would know.

One morning she woke up to find that the scenery too had improved. The vast field had ended in the night, and in its place was one of the Americas that one saw in the cinema, the Wild West of Tom Mix and Hoot Gibson. Desert and grass land and distant mountains, but no stage coaches and no Indians, though once she was almost sure she saw some cowboys.

Jay joined her for lunch.

'We'll be in this evening,' he said.

'You say the nicest things,' she said.

He looked contrite for once. 'It must have been lonely for you,' he said. 'The thing is I was going to arrange some company but it didn't work out.'

'Please don't apologise,' she said. 'After New York I needed some peace and quiet.'

'A chance to think things over?'

'Exactly,' she lied, and then: 'I take it that there won't be much peace and quiet in Hollywood?'

'There'll be none at all,' he said.

And he was right. The first crowd of reporters was waiting for them at the station, and at first their questions were directed at Jay, and what they asked was not *if* he would make the picture, but when. And how much would the budget be, and who were the co-stars, and was it true that Tom Waring would direct? Jay was polite, anxious to help and extremely vague, but they wrote down every word. After all he owned one newspaper already, and one day he might own theirs. Then it was her turn, and she braced herself, but they were surprisingly gentle, after New York, even friendly in a weird sort of way. What were her impressions of California? Was she looking forward to working in Hollywood? Was she ever homesick at all? How did it feel to be a heroine?

She tackled them in turn. Your state is magnificent, she said, and the most delicious oranges. To work here is the fulfilment of my wildest dream, but I miss my dog. I'm not a heroine, merely a woman who was lucky enough to have the chance to serve.

Then an earnest and rather stout girl asked her: 'Is it true that you believe a beautiful body to be a gift of God?'

Jane flicked a glance at Jay. 'Indeed it is,' she said, 'and it must be treasured as such.'

The black bootleggers carried her luggage to another enormous car, and she gave them money, far too much, according to Jay, but she had been glad of their company.

'You might have warned me about that beautiful body nonsense,' she said as the car pulled away.

'We Americans are a religious-minded people,' he said. 'If we can plant the idea that to look like you is a burden then we'll all feel good about it.'

'Where am I staying?' she asked.

'You mean I forgot to tell you?' She nodded. 'And you didn't ask.'

'I was too busy thinking,' she said, 'and anyway I'm quite sure it'll be the best. It always is.'

'Why thank you,' said Jay. 'You're staying at the Garden of Allah.'

'You're usually wittier than that.'

'I'm perfectly serious. It's a hotel. Surely you know that?'

'The only hotel I know to stay in is the Eldon Arms at Felston.'

'You used to know the Ritz,' said Jay.

' – And the Ritz in Paris,' said Jane. 'Who could ever forget the Ritz?'

They arrived at this vast and quite extraordinary hotel which didn't look as if it had been designed at all: rather written by a screen writer adapting a novel by Ethel M. Dell. Jane looked about her, awestruck. 'Golly,' she said. But Hollywood was having one of its better December days, with hard, clear sunshine, and the palms and the orange trees looked green, the roses still bloomed. She and Jay walked into the foyer, and a flock of Mexicans came out for her luggage as reporters swooped. They were different reporters, but their questions were the same. There were more letters waiting for her too, brought over to New York in the liner *Berengaria*, then on by train. She was obviously an important person. When she signed the register there was almost a round of applause.

Jay went with her to her suite and inspected it personally: the living room, the dressing room, the bedroom with its quite heavenly bed after the joltings of the Super-Chief, and the bathroom that had everything, including a telephone, but no delicious shower close to the bed. A chapter, it seemed, was ending.

'Seems OK,' said Jay.

'Of course,' she said. 'Didn't I say you always choose the best? My mother tells me it's the only standard I'm used to.' And then she smiled. 'Thank you,' she said.

'You're welcome.' He hesitated. 'There is just one thing. I hired you a maid. Now don't get sore.'

'I'm not,' she said. 'Not yet, anyway. Please go on. Tell me why I need a maid.'

'Because this is Hollywood,' said Jay. 'Here everything depends on status. You start with the kind of car you have. Ford, Buick, then on up to Packard, Olds, Cadillac.'

'That's the summit? A Cadillac?'

'Hell no,' said Jay. 'After that you start on foreign cars. Rolls, Bugatti, Isotta-Fraschini.'

'I drove a Voisin once,' she said.

'Sure you did,' said Jay. 'I was there, remember? And tomorrow you'll drive a Hispano-Suiza. But for now you're beyond cars. You're a suite-at-the-Garden-of-Allah lady. That's almost the tops.'

'Only almost?'

'Your own maid is the clincher,' said Jay, 'and so I got you your own maid.'

'Is she nice?'

'Judge for yourself,' said Jay. 'If you don't like her you can always change her.'

She hated that, but in fact Amparo seemed fine; about her age, with a restful prettiness and a golden skin that seemed designed to be exactly the colour to set off her glittering dark eyes. Jane offered her hand at once, and Amparo took it warily, before Jay sent her to unpack.

'She's a Mexican,' he explained. 'They're never too easy with us gringos.'

'Why not?'

'Because we exploit them,' said Jay.

'You too?'

'I'm different,' said Jay. 'I exploit everybody. But remember this. I could have got you a French girl or a fraulein, but I chose Amparo – because she's the best there is. Would you like to rest for a while?'

'I would,' said Jane. She meant it.

'Why don't you nap for an hour then change and I'll pick you up around eight thirty? There's a party I want us to go to. A lot of important people I want you to meet.'

'Must I?' she asked.

'Sure you must,' said Jay. 'It's to impress the good people of Felton when they queue up at the public library to read about you in the *Daily World*.'

'I'll be ready,' she said.

48

SHE WAS AS good as Jay had promised she would be: evening
clothes laid out exactly as she would have done it herself.
She had even suggested a massage, and very refreshing Jane
had found it, the only possible thing to put enough life in her
body to get her through another party. She was the best, all
right. Jane wondered if she could also be Jay's spy.

He was prompt – he was always prompt – and she hurried
down to join him at once after telling Amparo not to wait up.

'Yes, Miss Whitcomb,' said Amparo. Even her voice was
pretty, with the distinctive 's' sound that makes the Spanish
language so pleasant to listen to.

'Whose party is it?'

'David Greenglass. He's a big producer these days. I knew
him before the war when he was just a writer.'

A writer, she gathered, was a very unimportant thing to be.

'I worked out here for a while,' he said.

'In the movies?' She felt rather proud that she had said movies
rather than films. Et in Arcadia ego, her father would have said.

'Hell no,' said Jay. 'On the Los Angeles Times. The only thing
to do in the movies is own a studio. The rest is just as boring as
any other salaried work.' He looked at her and grinned. 'Unless
you're an actress, of course.'

'Will there be actresses at this party?'

'Sure there will. And actors. And directors. Maybe even a few
writers – if they're foreign and over here on a visit.'

'And the press of course.'

'Of course. But only to see who came and who didn't.' He went through his pockets, seeking a cigar. 'Your dress is just great.'

'One does one's best. So does Amparo.'

A midnight-blue velvet dress that showed a lot of skin, and over it a beaded evening coat that deepened in colour from pale grey to black, and trimmed with midnight-blue velvet. Not that he would know, or even care, but he would and did know at a glance how good it was.

'Paris?' he asked.

'Yes.'

'If anybody asks, mind you tell them so,' he said.

'But almost every woman you introduce me to buys her clothes in Paris.'

'No,' he said. 'They buy clothes *made* in Paris, but mostly they buy them in New York or LA. You *buy* in Paris. That's the tops too.'

They turned into a driveway, and a road through a garden that was mostly hibiscus and oleanders and roses. There should have been bulbuls, she thought, until she saw the house, which was what Californians called Colonial. By that they meant Spanish Colonial, Jay explained, and indeed it did look vaguely Moorish, and rather like a film set, though once inside she could see that it was substantial enough. There were perhaps fifty people there already, and to judge by the number of glasses, at least as many more expected. A hired butler who looked precisely what he was, an actor out of work, enquired their names, and a hovering flock of reporters ticked them off against their lists.

'Miss Jane Whitcomb, Mr J.M. Bower,' he called, in a voice that could have cracked windows.

An eager, bustling little man scurried across to them, beckoning to a waitress as he came.

'Jay, good to *see* you,' he said. 'And Jane – how nice of you to drop by.'

To her certain knowledge they had never met, but this was Hollywood after all: to admit ignorance of her identity would be the deadliest of insults. She took a chance.

'David,' she said. 'It was sweet of you to invite me.'

The waitress offered yet more champagne. Jane wondered what Americans had drunk before prohibition.

'Let me introduce you to my fiancée,' said Greenglass, and beckoned once more, this time to a girl about half his age. She was a very pretty fiancée, just as the waitress was a very pretty waitress, but then every woman in the room was pretty, except for a very few who all had that air of being indissolubly wedded to wealth. The fiancée seemed oddly reluctant to join them, Jane thought, and looked at Jay, who for once seemed startled, and then she realised why.

'This is Thelma,' Greenglass said, and of course it was. When last seen she had been lamenting the fact that she had no hope of seeing Venice before she became old next year. That was Venice, Italy, she'd explained. Venice California she had seen too often already.

'How do you do?' said Thelma and offered her hand. There was a frantic look about her eyes that made instant sense.

'How do you do?' said Jane. 'So nice to meet you.' The frantic look faded a little.

'Thelma was in New York too, last week,' said Greenglass. 'Had to go to visit her poor old mother. Thelma's a real mother's girl.'

'Really?' said Jane.

'You didn't run into each other in the wicked city then?' The eager look was still there, but now it was a shrewd look too.

'How could we?' said Jay. 'I doubt if Thelma's mother belongs to the Stork Club.' He turned to Jane. 'Would you care to dance?'

They went to a drawing room where the furniture had been pushed back to leave the parquet clear. In an alcove a quintet led by a cornet player attacked 'Way Down Yonder In New Orleans'. The cornet player did his best, and he seemed sober, but he was not Bix Beiderbecke.

'Why are we lying?' Jane asked.

'About what?'

'About Thelma what's-it?'

'Tanagra,' said Jay. 'She's Thelma Tanagra.'

'Golly,' said Jane.

'Well she is now,' said Jay. 'Greenglass reckons he's going to make her a star and Thelma Schultz didn't have the right ring to it. Trouble is he wants to make her an innocent, sweet kind of star like Mary Pickford. None of this Pola Negri bad-girl stuff – so speakeasies and clubs are out.'

'And did she really go to New York to see her mother?' Jane asked.

'I guess so,' said Jay. 'When she could spare the time from the Sligo Slasher's.'

'And will Mr Greenglass succeed in making her a star?'

'Maybe,' said Jay. 'She moves well – and she even talks well. Come next year she'll be in with a chance – but she'll never be in your class, naturally.'

'I want to talk to you about that,' said Jane.

'Not now,' said Jay. 'Half the people here can lip read, and all the agents.'

From time to time the brass-hinged butler roared out more names: famous names most of them, the Hollywood royalty who never arrived early. 'Miss Theda Bara', 'Miss Mabel Normand', 'Mr Ramon Navarro', 'Mr Arbuckle', 'Mr Fairbanks', 'Miss Pickford'.

Like living inside a movie magazine, she thought, as Jay introduced her to this one and that one, not forgetting Tom Mix.

She sipped champagne and chatted and danced when asked, which was fairly often. Jay's influence, she supposed, and dutifully told the three men who mentioned it that she bought her dresses in Paris. None of the women mentioned it all. Waring was there and danced with her, and she told him at once that they were not to talk business on account of the lip readers. He looked puzzled and relieved at the same time. When the supper interval came she went out into the garden instead. No nightbirds sang, but the scent of roses persisted, the air seemed warm after New York, and there were lights in the trees by the pool – and nobody to ask her where she bought her clothes and offer to buy her some more. There had been two, so far. Not bad for an elderly person when it wasn't yet midnight. Then she caught a glimpse of movement by the oleanders and turned too late to go back in. She had been seen.

'Miss Whitcomb,' Thelma Tanagra called. 'Give me a minute, will you?'

Jane went over to her. There was a stone urn with a broad base near the shrubs: on it were a bottle of champagne half full and two glasses. Only one glass was being used.

'I needed some air,' said Thelma Tanagra, then added: 'Also

I needed a drink. Mr Greenglass doesn't like it when I need a drink.'

'So I gathered,' said Jane.

'Who told you? Jay Bower?'

'Why yes,' said Jane. 'But it wasn't gossip, you know. He was just explaining to me why we couldn't say we met at the Stork Club.'

'Was that what Jay says he was doing for me? Protecting me?'

'More or less,' said Jane. 'But it was nothing, really. A few tactful lies.'

'Jay's good at lies,' said Thelma, 'but I never heard him called tactful before.'

Jane thought, she must have gulped that champagne awfully quickly, and then remembered that one did sometimes, when one was miserable.

'Have a drink,' the younger woman said. 'I brought an extra glass. I guess I thought I might get lucky.'

She laughed then, shrill and mocking laughter at the suggestion of Thelma Tanagra of all people thinking she might get lucky. Jane allowed her to pour champagne into the other glass.

'Here's to us girls,' Thelma Tanagra said, then gulped down her drink and promptly poured another. 'Jay was crazy about you,' she said.

'Indeed?'

'Indeed,' said the other girl. 'Hey – maybe that's why.'

'I don't understand you,' said Jane.

'The way you talk. That English-rose voice . . . . Indeed . . . .' She tasted the word.

'We're colleagues, no more,' said Jane.

'It's not what he wants you to be,' said Thelma Tanagra. 'A partner's what he wants you to be. His partner in a double act.'

'Even if it were true,' said Jane, 'it's hardly your business.'

'If it were,' repeated Thelma Tanagra. 'You see? Not even "If it was". He gets the hots for a voice.' She paused then, her glass half way to her lips. 'My God yes,' she said at last. 'That's what it must be. The way you all talk.'

Jane said, 'I honestly think we ought to go back inside. You'll be missed.'

'Who would miss me?' asked Thelma Tanagra.

'Your fiancée surely?' said Jane.

'By now David will be in the library talking money,' said Thelma Tanagra. 'The library – that's a hot one. Twenty yards of phoney leather and a half a dozen scripts, and him on his knees to Jay Bower saying "Of course you keep Canada, Jay sweetheart. But maybe I could have Peru?"' She gulped once more.

'All the same,' said Jane, 'I made him promise to take me back to my hotel by twelve thirty and you know how prompt he is.'

'I used to,' said the other girl, and added: 'I've been drinking all day.'

'So I should suppose.'

'I'm that bad?'

'I'm afraid so,' said Jane.

'There's a pool hut here with a shower,' said the other girl. 'If I go in there for a while I'll be OK. I've done it before.'

'Do you want me to keep watch for you?' Jane asked.

'I don't think I could bear for you to do me another favour,' said Thelma Tanagra. 'I'm sorry about that but it's true.'

She turned, and lurched towards the pool hut, and Jane poured the champagne out on to the soil of the urn and hid the bottle and one glass beneath it, then took the other glass and walked back into the house. Neither David Greenglass nor Jay Bower was present, but this was neither the time nor the place for quiet reflection: the quintet had just begun on 'Japanese Sandman'. She allowed Gary Cooper to dance with her instead.

Jay emerged with Greenglass at exactly twelve thirty and held the beaded coat for her as if it were the pleasantest task he had performed all evening. Greenglass looked round the room and spotted his fiancée at once, sipping a glass of non-alcoholic fruit punch. He came back to Jane and Jay, his arm about Thelma Tanagra's waist.

'I wish you could have stayed longer,' he said.

'I promised Jane,' said Jay. 'It's a punishing trip all the way from New York.'

'You're telling me,' said Thelma Tanagra.

Greenglass laughed, and kissed her cheek. She stood as still as stone, but at least she seemed sober.

'You'll think over what I said?' Greenglass asked Jay.

'Oh sure,' said Jay. 'There could be a deal here once you cut your costs a little. I'll call you in a couple of days. Goodnight.'

'And the good Lord was right like always,' said Grandma. 'Now you take yourself off to your clinic and never mind about our Bet. She'll be all right once she's married and got a few bairns to worry about.'

It wasn't that Stobbs and Messeter weren't glad to see her. They made all the right noises and asked all the right questions, but they treated her as if she were someone who'd brought comforts to the Front Line just before a big push. They were kind and they made her welcome, but their minds were elsewhere. Both of them wondered if she had brought money this time, but Messeter was too polite to ask. Stobbs wasn't.

'I'm sorry,' he said. 'I know it's rude and uncouth. All that. But I can't help it. If you haven't brought money I'll have to close.'

'I've brought money.' Both men looked up at her. 'Twenty-five thousand American dollars and three thousand English pounds from the ball.'

'That's over eight thousand pounds,' said Messeter. 'We can survive for quite a while on that.'

'Two years,' said Stobbs, 'and into a third.' He turned to Jane. 'I'm obliged to you. It can't have been easy.'

'Some of it was fun,' she said. 'Like the ball – and the concert here. And some of it wasn't, but it had to be done.'

'Duty, stern daughter of the Voice of God,' said Messeter. 'How irritating of Wordsworth to be so often right. I'm grateful too, dear Jane.'

She smiled. 'I'm in the way, aren't I?'

'There'll be a clinic soon,' said Stobbs.

'I have the Wolseley – if you need another car.'

'Cars are no longer a difficulty,' said Messeter. 'There are certain businessmen who live in rather large houses in Northumberland and have social aspirations, as indeed do their wives. It occurred to me that if I could arrange for them to dine with a duke or a marquis they might feel grateful. . . . We now have a bus and an ambulance.'

'So much more convenient than an Armstrong-Siddeley,' said Jane, and rose, then said: 'Oh – I almost forgot. Do you remember a Charles Lovell?'

Then all the goodbyes were said, and Thelma Tanagra called out: 'Goodbye, Jane. It was just great to meet you.' They went out to the car.

'You and David's girl have a chat?' Jay asked.

'No.' A lie, a real whopper, but now was definitely not the time.

'Then why did she say it was great to meet you?'

'Maybe it was,' said Jane.

He laughed, and took her hand. 'I was crazy for you the first time I ever saw you,' he said. 'And I can't think of anybody who'd be surprised by that.'

'Except your parents.'

'Except, as you say, my parents. But then I never fail to surprise them. But don't interrupt me – not when I'm talking about you. . . . One of the million reasons why I feel this way about you – '

'Love me, you mean?'

'Love you then – is that you can always make me laugh.'

He had said he loved her, probably for the last time. Tomorrow he wouldn't even remember he'd said it, but it had been said.

'Do you like my voice?' she asked.

'Sure,' he said. 'It's a beautiful voice.'

'Is there something in English voices that you find specially attractive?'

'No,' he said. 'Just yours. Once the movies start to talk you'll be an even bigger star.'

'Will Miss Tanagra really be a star? That's what you and Mr Greenglass were discussing, I take it?'

'You wouldn't listen at a keyhole,' said Jay. 'You're British.'

'I also have eyes in my head,' said Jane. 'I saw the way he made a beeline for her the instant the two of you appeared.'

'I'll never try to hide anything from you,' he said. 'It can't be done. Yeah. . . . He needs money for a picture, and my father's bank can let him have it – if the price is right.'

'The price of money.'

'It always comes high,' said Jay. 'Still – as I say – the girl's not bad: I've seen her tests – and the script is good. His little Thelma could turn out to be a star this time next year.'

'If she does she'll leave him?' said Jane.

'What makes you say so?'

'I watched her when he kissed her.'

'Maybe you're right,' he said, in the voice of one who didn't care much either way. 'Still, if she gets to be a star she won't need him any more.'

Jane found herself willing the car to go faster. She wanted to be in her bed, alone. She wanted to cry.

Next morning she still felt rotten, so she wore the Cartier leopard pinned to the lapel of a white silk suit by Worth. 'Are all your clothes made of silk?' Bet had asked her, and the answer seemed to be, well almost. But there were the fur coats, of course. The suit was simple, with a pleated, unfussy skirt. Shoes were of white kid with an enamel buckle, and a cloche hat by Martine Callot. Much too good for Worldwide Studios, she thought, but only just good enough for Cleopatra. But the brooch made her feel better. As she pinned it to her lapel she heard Aunt Pen's voice. 'It'll be all right,' it said. 'You'll see. Only try not to fret too much, my lovely.' And then, it was gone. But it had been there – for as long as it takes to say fifteen words. It helped quite a bit.

She was going to the studios with Waring, but for once he wasn't driving his Packard: this time she would be driving, an enormous great beast like a scaled-down version of a clipper ship, according to Jay, a Hispano-Suiza that he had acquired by some intricate deal or other. Jay Bower, she had observed, rarely bought things: he acquired them. That way he could make a profit. Waring arrived, looking nervous, and with him yet another batch of post, which was awkward. There were far too many to take with her, and Waring was fretting. He'd borrowed his best lighting cameraman from a feature, and couldn't keep him for long. Jane flipped through them and found only two with handwriting she recognised. She locked them in a drawer, then called for Amparo, who came at once.

'Have you ever been to a studio?' she asked.

'Once I work as an extra. Two days,' Amparo said.

'Would you like to go to Worldwide?'

'Oh yes, miss.' There could be no doubt that she meant it.

'Then get your hat,' said Jane. 'And mine.' Amparo fled.

Nice to make someone happy, thought Jane. And if she's with

me at Worldwide she can't be going through my letters here. . . .
Garden of Allah, indeed.

'It's not really a big production,' Waring was saying. 'But we
can let you have a dresser too.'

'I like Amparo with me,' said Jane. 'I feel more comfortable.'

He didn't argue: he'd been coping with female stars for years:
ladies who insisted on having their hairdresser with them, or
their love-birds, or their pekinese. Once it had been a chimpanzee
in a dinner suit. A maid was nothing at all. A cloche hat, brisk
but not too businesslike, with a spray of feathers to one side,
and she was ready. They went out all three. Just like the movies,
she thought. The star, her director and her personal maid.

The Hispano-Suiza brooded in the sunlight, looking as if it
were about to set sail from Australia with a load of grain. Beside
her stood its chauffeur, dressed like a uhlan lancer who had
decided to exchange his helmet for a peaked cap. He waited
uneasily by the driveway of the hotel as Jane walked towards
him, pulling on a pair of white, gauntletted gloves as she did so.
I mean Mr Bower said she'll be OK, he thought, and she surely
looks OK, but this car is unique.

'Good morning,' said Jane. 'Perhaps you'd better tell me a few
things before we start.'

He began to do so, and around him camera flashes flared, a
movie cameraman cranked away. This time Cinderella was going
to drive the coach herself – or crash it. And either way, it was
news.

At last she interrupted the chauffeur's nervous gabble in
mid-sentence, and motioned Amparo and Waring into the back.
The Hispano-Suiza's body was curtained and flower bedecked
and far from visible, but the chauffeur's place was open and
uncovered and on display. No wonder that cunning so-and-so
had decreed that she should drive. The chauffeur swung the
handle and got in beside her, and she did what he had said and
the whole contraption took off, moving easily enough. Not as
friendly as the Voisin, but not nearly as antagonistic as the
Bentley. She patted the little leopard for luck and drove out
through the gates.

But she didn't need luck. Not really. The car was far too vast
an object for the transportation of four people, but not as big as
an ambulance, and a damn sight easier to drive. All the same the

chauffeur didn't begin to relax till they reached Sunset Boulevard, and even then he started twitching again when a truck appeared alongside them, with another movie camera aboard to take more pictures.

But at least they arrived at Worldwide Studios, and Waring flourished his pass and was waved on by the guard, so that Jane could drive beneath the arch surmounted by a globe on which a winged figure perched, rather uneasily she thought. A symbol for David Greenglass? She drove to the front office and parked, and the chauffeur smiled at last. His car was being returned to him. Jane went in to meet the president.

Her memory of such things was hazy, but for her presidents had names like Washington, Lincoln, Roosevelt. Murray Fisch was a surprise, and so was Waring's attitude towards him. Presidents, she thought, were there to be grovelled to, but Waring's attitude to Fisch was polite, yet firm, and Fisch took it without a blink. Another twinkler like Greenglass, but older and fatter, with more of a survivor's look, and not in the least resentful when Waring explained in detail exactly the back-up that he and Jane needed. And then she realised why. Of course. Waring was there as Jay's man, and Jay controlled the money. So of course he got everything he demanded – or rather requested. Waring was a very polite young man.

Fisch's attitude to her was puzzling, too. When it came to eager bustle he was every bit as good as David Greenglass: ash tray, coffee, turn down the air conditioning, anything you want just ask, anything at all; it was all there, and yet behind the pleasing there was something else, something she found it diffi-cult to define. Almost a sense of transience. He had a hard time masking his relief when at last they left him for the Hispano-Suiza.

This time the chauffeur drove them to a bungalow near the stage where they were to work. Amparo was already at work, blissfully bossing a couple of workmen she had commandeered. The shower dripped, and the dressing-table mirror had stuck.

The drawing room was prettily furnished, she thought, and all the furniture elegant, except for one large sofa that was sturdy indeed. The place where the stars relaxed, she thought. Singly or in groups. . . . Waring brought her a slim folder of yellow typescript.

'Your script,' he said. 'Look it over. Want a drink?'

'Will you?'

'Not when I'm working,' Waring said.

'Then I'll wait.' She began to read: Mid Shot Cleopatra, at ease in her palace, reclining on a divan. . . . A slavegirl enters.

2 Shot. Slavegirl and Cleopatra.

Another Angle. The slavegirl prostrates herself before the queen.

Close Shot. Cleopatra. Her lips move. 'Well?' She signals to the slavegirl to rise.

Mid Shot. Slavegirl rises, speaks. Caption: 'O great queen, Mark Antony approaches.'

Close Shot. Cleopatra. Her eyes blaze at the news, her bosom heaves. She is ecstatic.

'I think perhaps I will have that drink,' said Jane. 'Gin and Italian vermouth if they've got it.'

Waring opened a cupboard and she went on reading. It was all pretty much of a muchness. Mark Antony entered in Roman armour and they rolled about on the couch a bit – though first, she noticed with relief, she helped him out of his breastplate and things. Then he told her he had to return to Rome and live with his wife again for reasons of politics, and Cleopatra's bosom heaved even more. . . . Jane took the drink Waring offered.

'Will this really work?' she asked.

'If you and the slavegirl and Mark Antony do it right it will.'

'But it's all so simple,' she said. 'So – crude. Forgive me – '

'I've heard it before,' said Waring. 'But you're forgetting one thing. What you've got is words on a page, and that's not what we're after. What we're after is pictures on a screen. Do you want to try it?'

'I don't think I can,' she said.

'Of course you can,' said Waring. 'What's your problem? All this mid-shot and two-shot stuff? I'll take care of that.'

'It's not that,' she said. 'It's just – doing it. I know it sounds silly, but I'm shy.'

'We'll try it here first,' he said, 'and don't let it bother you. A lot of people get camera fright.'

'Even before they see the camera?'

'Miss Whitcomb,' he said, 'you know damn well we've got to do this, so finish your nice drink and let's get on with it.'

She finished her drink and imitated his gestures, and was so stiff and wooden that for once Waring looked worried.

'I don't get it,' he said. 'Back in New York you had no problem. Yet. . . . Wait a minute.'

'Oh God what now?' she said.

'Nothing. Relax. In New York you were thinking of your dog – and two guys you couldn't stand the sight of.'

'So?'

'So now you've got to think of Mark Antony. Don't tell me you haven't had one in your life, Miss Whitcomb. The way you look.'

So now it seemed she was going to have to act out her farewell to Jay Bower in his own studio, and record it all on film for posterity.

Amparo was waiting for her in her dressing room to help her out of the Worth suit and twentieth-century underwear, and into the minimum amount of material the front office thought they could get away with, then they wrapped her in a motor rug and drove her to the stage where the camera waited. It must have been all of a hundred yards. Thank God the head-dress thing isn't so heavy this time, she thought. But it did have a tendency to slip. Make-up next on face and body, and goodness what a nasty colour it was, and then on to the stage and this weird new brand of purgatory. There was the couch or whatever it was, and on it a tigerskin that scratched every bit as much as the one in Paris. Suddenly she was back there, Jay was making her laugh and that idiot Powell was prancing about as Oberon, and soon they would make love, and later she would clobber Powell, and Jay would come charging to the rescue. Really, Mark Antony wasn't all that far away. . . . Enter slavegirl.

She missed her marks a couple of times, and responded to the wrong cues, but at least Waring and his cameraman and crew treated the whole episode as a job, and not as some sort of comic treat. At last Waring said, 'That's the one. We'll print that one. Lunch break. – Thank you, Jane.'

To her amazement she discovered that they had been filming for over two hours.

Jane and Waring went back to the bungalow, where he telephoned for food, but he sent Amparo to the commissariat.

'She looks after you well,' he said. 'She deserves a treat,' then laughed at her bewilderment. 'Half the stars of Worldwide will be there,' he said. 'She'll be able to talk about it for weeks.'

They went over the remainder of her test, with him as Mark Antony. His grip was disappointingly tentative, she thought, and then she remembered whom he worked for.

'I've got Guy Fielding to play Mark Antony,' he said.

'I don't know him,' she said. 'Is he nice?'

'He's OK,' he said. 'Not quite at the top but better than most. He's a faggot. You don't mind, I hope?'

'I beg your pardon?'

'You know. A homosexual. Like your friend Barry.'

She looked down at her costume. 'I hope I don't put him off,' she said.

'He's an actor,' said Waring, 'so he'll act.'

He did, too. Very ardent and warlike, and with a splendid profile, even if it was only a test, and he knew how to take hold of a girl, or at least he acted as if he knew.

Then at last Waring said it was over and Guy kissed her cheek and went off not quite mincing, and telling everyone who would listen how lucky the Romans were to be able to wear skirts and not get arrested.

49

S**HE SHOWERED AWAY** the make-up, and Amparo helped her dress (really, it was like being back in the nursery), then drove back to the Garden of Allah and the two letters that she recognised: one from Charles Lovell, and one from Georgina Payne. Strange that she should recognise Lovell's so easily, she thought. She had only received one note from him before, and a very brief scrawl it had been, to tell her how much he regretted the way in which their lunch had ended.

He was not a good letter writer: or at least he was not good at writing a letter of this kind. Spelling and punctuation good, even VGI or Very Good Indeed, according to Vinney's system of marking. The letter had been carefully planned too: point followed point; argument evolved from argument. But it was never him speaking, reaching out to touch her. . . . Close Shot heaving bosom would have made far more of an impression – if men did have bosoms. But of course they did. Abraham had one, according to the Bible. But did it *heave*?

She said aloud, 'Now that's enough. Get on with your letter,' in a voice like Vinney's. Which wasn't surprising really. She had often tried frivolity as the way of dodging something unpleasant. It had never worked with Vinney.

'Essentially what I am trying to say is that I have never been more miserable in my life than since your departure. Perhaps you realise what an overwhelming effect you had on me when I was privileged to meet you at the Watsons': as a mere male I have no way of telling. What I do know is that I grossly mishandled our luncheon engagement, my only excuse being that from the beginning there would be no deception between us. I had deceived many people: for reasons of shame perhaps, or self-disgust, or mere secretiveness, but I could not deceive you. I admire you too much.'

And so on. At very great length indeed.

Admire. Not at all the word she'd wanted to read. Even Jay had admitted that he loved her, when she'd finally resorted to the forceps. Well either Charles did or he didn't, but he'd never put it in writing. She'd have to face him if she really wanted to know. But if he didn't love her, why write all this screed? All this admiration and need to see her, and 'my fondest hope is that we can meet again'? Suddenly she longed very much to be in South Terrace, where she could at least telephone him at Eaton Square. It was, she decided, time for decisions, then realised almost at once that hers had already been made.

Best tell Jay face to face, she thought. They were due at another party that night – when money came to town it seemed that Hollywood was always en fête – but a party was not the place. She went to the telephone, but before she could reach it the doorbell rang, and Amparo came in, then to the hallway. There was a murmur of voices, both female, which was a pity. She had hoped it would be Jay, and was in no mood for a lady reporter. Amparo came back in.

'A lady to see you,' Amparo said. 'I told her not without an appointment, but she says you know her.'

'Well of course you know me,' said Georgina Payne.

'Hello Georgina,' said Jane. 'Yes. . . . I rather think I do know you.'

'Darling I did write to you,' said Georgina. 'Don't tell me you didn't get it?'

Jane held up the letter. 'You were next on the list,' she said, then turned to Amparo. 'Can you make martinis?' she asked.

'Yes, Miss Whitcomb.'

'Make us a shaker then,' said Jane, 'and telephone room service for some canapés.'

'Yes, Miss Whitcomb.' Amparo left them.

'What splendour you live in,' said Georgina, 'but then I live in splendour too.'

'Where, may I ask?'

'The suite above yours.'

Suddenly Jane burst out laughing, and got up from her chair to embrace Georgina.

'That's better,' Georgina said. 'At first I detected a distinct nip of frost in this mild California air.'

'No darling,' said Jane. 'Just shock. A couple of days ago you'd have encountered frost, Antarctica in fact, but that was all my own foolishness. Or almost all.'

'Oh,' said Georgina. She wore a pink silk suit, and shoes of pink dyed glacé kid, and looked as edible as she always did.

'Am I on the carpet?' she said.

'Certainly not,' said Jane. 'You're one of my chums. Oh by the way, Amparo my maid is a spy of Bower's I think, so if you don't want anything to be reported you'd better give me some sort of signal.'

'Finger to lips sort of thing?'

'Something like that.'

'I'd much sooner have a girlish chat,' said Georgina, 'and if you should need written evidence there's always my letter.' Amparo came in with the shaker and poured two drinks, her face expressionless. Jane raised her glass, then drank as Amparo left them.

'I really needed that,' she said, then added smugly, 'I've been filming all day.'

'Never mind the glamour,' said Georgina. 'Tell me all.'

'It started with your picture,' said Jane.

'The one of me in the altogether?' Jane nodded. 'You saw it at that terrible house in Fulham, the day Mrs Browne popped in to borrow a bread knife, I remember.'

'I saw it again after that,' said Jane. 'In a rather grand penthouse in Fleet Street.'

'Oh,' said Georgina, and Jane waited. 'But I didn't know he belonged to you then, honestly I didn't. I mean I knew he'd fed you from time to time, and he was printing your collected works, but I didn't know that you – ' She hesitated. 'You know.'

'He bought me some ear-rings, and I wore some others instead,' said Jane. 'Nothing personal. It was just that his didn't go with my dress. But we quarrelled, rather foolishly, and it wasn't entirely his fault, and being the sort of man he is he felt he needed a little consolation.'

'It was more like revenge,' said Georgina. 'And only the once, I promise you.'

'Of course.'

'Made it up for a while, did you?' Georgina shook her head. 'Sorry. Not my business. But why did he buy my picture? I mean I didn't own the thing. Unless –'

'Go on.'

'He *said* it was so a lot of randy little bastards –'

'Randy?'

'Horny was the word he used, but he meant randy – he said he didn't want them gawping at me. This was nonsense and I told him so and he said that the picture would hurt my career at the BBC so he'd bought it as a favour to me.'

'My God yes,' said Jane. 'The British Broadcasting Company. What's happened to them?'

'Still there so far as I know,' Georgina said. 'I'm the one who upped and left.'

'To come here?' Georgina nodded, her martini on its way to her lips.

The canapés arrived, a whole trolley-load, and Jane gave its trundler a dollar, then turned to Amparo, who was serving the canapés. 'I think we'll have another batch of martinis,' she said.

'Yes miss,' said Amparo. 'Mr Bower said he'd stop by at eight, miss.'

'Just the martinis,' said Jane. 'For the moment.' Amparo took the shaker and left.

'Goodness you are stern,' said Georgina.

'Are you going to the Ogden party tonight?' Jane asked.

'A man called Waring was supposed to take me,' said Georgina. 'I hadn't even met him. It's weird. Then I bumped into Michael in New York and thought I might be delayed so I wired this Waring at the studio and told him not to bother – only I wasn't delayed after all. Michael's got this new girl he met in Rimini who says she's a contessa.' She smiled. 'What fun for him if she is. Only besides being a contessa she's an American widow with oodles of money so I arrived here on time anyway.'

'Have you got a maid yet?'

'A Swede,' said Georgina, 'but she starts tomorrow. You are lucky having a brunette.'

'Go and get your evening dress and bring it down here,' said

Jane. 'We'll talk while we change. Amparo will help you.'

'But if she's a spy – ' said Georgina.

'Then she'll tell it all to Jay and save us a lot of trouble.'

Georgina said, 'This is rather important to me.'

'I know,' said Jane. 'But it will be all right. You'll see. Just trust me.'

Georgina left, and Jane rang the bell for Amparo, who looked if anything even more impassive.

'I want you to telephone Mr Bower,' she said, 'and tell him I've been delayed – that I shan't be ready till nine o'clock. Then I want you to telephone Mr Waring – the studio will know where to reach him, and tell him to be here at nine, too. He's to collect Miss Georgina Payne. Will you do that?'

'Yes, Miss Whitcomb.' Bewilderment replaced the impassive look, but she went to make the calls in the bedroom, and Georgina came back with a small travelling bag.

'What now?' she said.

'Amparo makes a couple of telephone calls, then we bathe and change. . . . Jay told you half the truth about that picture. It was to avoid embarrassment, but it wasn't the BBC's, it was his. Or rather Worldwide's. He's offered you a contract, I suppose?'

'Well yes,' said Georgina, then dropped her voice. 'Has he got some kind of a weird thing about voices?'

'Talking pictures,' said Jane. 'In the future the likes of us will have to sound nice as well as look nice. Or rather the likes of you will. You knew I was being tested for Cleopatra?'

'My dear the whole country knows it. Especially the ones who read the *Daily World*. Will she, won't she? Too bad you weren't there to see it.'

'And did they show my picture?'

'Well yes,' said Georgina. 'Such a lot of fuss about nothing.'

'Nothing?'

'No no,' said Georgina laughing. 'You were more than adequately covered.' Jane gathered that a little discreet art work had been done. 'Not like me.'

Jane said, 'I tested for the Cleopatra part today, and I *think* it was adequate. Just about. The whole thing was a put-up job, anyway, to get me out of a nasty situation. Bower at his best. But at some point while it was happening he got the idea that there might be money in it – '

'Bower at his worst,' said Georgina.

'Maybe. But you're the one he wants to replace me, I'll bet. That's why he signed you up'

'Oh my God,' said Georgina. 'Me? Are you sure you won't mind?'

'Not in the least,' said Jane. 'Do you think you'll enjoy it?'

'At least I won't be playing the piano,' said Georgina, 'and it's far more money than the BBC.'

'Tell me,' said Jane, 'how did Bower get you out of their clutches?'

'Bower had nothing to do with it,' Georgina said. 'I handled that myself.' Somewhere in the British Broadcasting Company there worked a man in need of sympathy.

Amparo warned them that it was their last chance to change. Their gentlemen were impressed. The quality of her gown suggested that Georgina was receiving either a dress allowance or an advance on her salary, and it was the first time that Tom Waring had seen her and it was pretty to watch, Jane thought. She was wearing her Fortuny dress, as it was very possibly the last time that she would attend a party with Jay as her escort.

'You look beautiful,' he said, and she curtsied. He had brought her an orchid, and Waring had brought one for Georgina. The problem was where to pin them, but Amparo managed it.

'Tell me about Ogden,' Jane asked.

'Rick Ogden is the highest-paid star at Worldwide,' said Jay. 'He's also the meanest son of a bitch I ever met. In fact he's so damn mean we had to put it in his contract that he gives four parties a year, and somebody else does the catering. They tell me that when he got the bill for the first one he cried. Now are you going to tell me how you and Georgina met up?'

'Serendipity,' she said, and he nodded.

'What's that?' asked Waring.

'Discovery by happy accident,' said Jay, and she discovered that there were occasions when she still liked him very much, then told him how Georgina had walked in on her.

'Georgina was to have been my surprise companion on the Super-Chief, I take it?' she said.

'That's right,' said Jay. 'But she got delayed in London as well as New York.'

'The BBC were rather reluctant to let me go,' Georgina said.

'I don't blame them,' said Waring. 'Whoever they are.'

They went to the party.

Jay danced with Georgina first. There was a protocol in these matters, and the first girl that the representative of the owners of Worldwide danced with was thereby proclaimed the important girl, the one on the way up, the one to watch, just as the one he didn't dance with was the girl on the way down. So Jane danced with Rick Ogden instead. He was under contract after all, and had had his orders. As they danced he talked of nothing but the escalating price of grapefruit. Waring was scarcely better. When she danced with him she tried to talk about her test, but he was evasive. He hadn't finished cutting. Much too early to say. Obviously he wouldn't tell her a thing until Jay had told him what he was *allowed* to say.

The third dance was Jay's, and he said: 'I saw your test.'

'What about the lip readers?' she asked.

'They may as well know it now.'

'But Tom Waring said he hadn't finished cutting it.' For some reason, now that she could know, she didn't want to.

'It's not the fine cut but it'll do,' he said, and then, 'Relax. You were OK. Not sensational, but better than most.'

For some reason she felt enormously relieved. Adequacy for once was all she had wanted. The band began to play 'Horsey Keep Your Tail Up' and Jay stopped dead.

'If you don't mind,' he said, 'I'd rather talk.'

'Of course. Shall we take a walk by the pool?' She hadn't seen it, but there was always a pool.

'OK,' he said. 'We won't run into Thelma this time. She and Dave are at Mack Sennet's party.'

'I looked Tanagra up,' she said. 'It was a town in ancient Greece famous for its terra-cotta figurines, also called Tanagra. Why would anybody be called after a terra-cotta figurine?'

'Because it's better than Schultz,' said Jay. 'Where did you look it up?'

'In a dictionary.'

'Where in God's name did you get a dictionary at the Garden of Allah?'

'Room service,' said Jane. 'You can get anything at room service.' They were out in the garden, which Ogden had been forced to maintain under threat of suspension, and so it looked pretty. Other couples were strolling too, but as soon as they saw Jay they moved away.

'I'm sorry you missed Georgina,' he said.

'She's going to take my place, I gather?'

'Now wait a minute – '

She laughed, a low, gurgling sound, and he was surprised and relieved to note that it held nothing but amusement. 'As Cleopatra you ass.' He said nothing, and she added, 'That *is* the idea, isn't it?'

'Well yes,' he said. 'If you don't want it.'

'Oh come off it,' she said. 'I'm sure her test will be much better than mine. But I *don't* want it.'

'What do you want?'

'To go home,' she said. 'I gather the jury's in and I've been found Not Guilty and without a stain on my character. Well nothing visible anyway.'

'Back to Felston?'

'Sort of,' she said. 'Hollywood was fun and I adored New York, but the hols are over, my dear.'

'And I'm part of the hols?'

'Obviously,' she said.

'You going to tell me why?'

'On account of Miss Terra-Cotta Figurine.' He nodded. He had known it was coming after all.

'It started last year when I came out here,' he said. 'Then she met David Greenglass and I thought that it was over. Then I met her again in New York and found out it wasn't.'

'I was in New York,' she said.

'But you didn't want me, except that one time.'

'I was still there.' They walked on and strolled round the edge of the pool.

'Did you tell Georgina about Thelma?' he asked.

'Not her business.' A few more steps, and an amorous couple scurried into the shadows.

'I don't suppose I'll see you again,' she said.

He said at once, 'You mean you're quitting the paper?' He sounded amazed.

'Not if you don't want me to.'

'Of course I don't want you to.' He was impatient, which

meant that things were back to normal. 'Your stuff's good now. Your features are going over big. I want more.'

'Then I won't say goodbye.'

'I should say not. When are you planning to leave?'

'Three or four days. As soon as I decently can. It wouldn't look too good if I scuttled off back home tomorrow.'

'It would not. I thank you for that. Maybe I could arrange a trip or something?'

'Some other time,' she said. 'I have about five thousand letters to write. But I would like to see my test if I may.'

'Be a pleasure. Shall we go back inside?'

The agenda was completed: there was no point in wasting further time. 'Why not?' she said.

More dances, with Jay, with Tom Waring, with the men who had been told to dance with her, until it was time to go home in the Hispano-Suiza, which she let the chauffeur drive. It was if she'd tipped him a hundred dollars. On the way Georgina told her that her screen test was due in two days' time, and that Tom Waring would be working on it with her at the Garden of Allah the next day. Jane advised her to order plenty of Sidecars. She was so tired her whole body ached.

In her suite Amparo was still up, and as impassive as ever.

'You didn't tell me to go to bed, miss,' she said.

'Just as well,' said Jane. 'I'm dying for a massage – if you're not too tired.'

'Be glad to.'

Her hands were as strong and sure as the first time, and Jane wallowed in it.

At last Amparo said, 'What you said about my spying, it was all true.'

'Of course it was,' said Jane. 'I hope he paid you in advance?'

Amparo chuckled. 'Cash on the barrel,' she said. 'Two hundred dollars. It's the only way to do business.'

'Quite right,' said Jane. 'So we're both all right. I didn't tell you anything I didn't want anybody to know, and you've got two hundred dollars. What could be nicer? But – forgive me for prying – but why did you tell me?'

'I never did it before, Miss Whitcomb,' said Amparo. 'And the first time has to be a lady I find I like very much. And now I'll have to tell it in confession. Would you like a shower, miss?'

'No,' said Jane. 'I'll take a bath.'

There was thunder during the night, and sheet lightning, but no rain. Jane dreamed of Passchendaele. She was in the château, lying in John's arms. Together they listened to the guns.

Next morning while Amparo helped her to dress (really she must stop getting used to this nonsense) she thought about the dream and decided that Jabber would be as happy with it as she was, then ordered breakfast and looked at the papers. The *Hollywood Reporter* had discovered Georgina. 'Graceful yet glamorous English rose', 'Worldwide's latest beauty', 'centre of attraction at Rick Ogden's delightful party'. She was there too, at the end of paragraph three. 'Jane Whitcomb, talented and fashionable friend of the beautiful Miss Payne'. She had been demoted to the rank of friend. She was safe.

It was time to begin on the letters. She sorted out the obvious fan mail first, dividing it into two groups: adoration and abuse, and found herself wishing there had been more abuse, since she had no intention of replying to it. For the rest she devised one standard letter which replied to every possible point raised, and stated in three different forms of words how happy she was, and how she had no intention of abandoning her trust. Then she rang the desk and enquired if she could hire a typist and was asked how many she would need. Three would do, she said. They came up to collect her standard reply and she asked for three hundred and seventy-seven copies. No carbons. The girls treated it as part of a perfectly normal day's work.

Then she read Georgina's letter, which told her nothing Georgina had not already told her, and began on the others. One from Bob, congratulating her on the way folks was all on her side, and how a bloke in a pub off King's Cross had got a punch on the nose for saying she was no better than she should be, 'and not' (heavily underlined) by me either. Though I would have done if I'd been there.

A letter from Bet. She had seen the photograph of Jane in fancy dress and couldn't understand what they were all on about. (She simply must see what the *World* had done to it, she thought.) Everybody was fine but they all wished she was back except Andy and he kept going on about how nobody listened to Andy, not any more, even though times were bad and getting worse and Da had been paid off, so there didn't seem like much chance of wedding bells this year. There was a PS from Grandma. 'Bet's right, me bairn. Things are bad and getting worse, and the clinic's working full blast already. But there's trouble brewing. I can smell it. It's time you were back. Lucky for us Bob's in London and sending money back regular. There's lots of folks here don't have that luck. From your loving Grandma.' I must pass the hat before I leave Hollywood, thought Jane. Another picture postcard from Lionel. It depicted a Christian martyr (female) fearlessly confronting a Roman gladiator (male). 'If I had wanted to take an interest in the Perils of Pauline,' Lionel had written, 'I should have gone to the cinema. *Do* come home.' Acha, Lionel. I hear and I obey.

She went up to Georgina's suite then, to help with the rehearsal. This time she was the slavegirl. From star to bit player overnight – but what were best friends for? Georgina worked at it as a miner might search for gold, striving to give each gesture meaning, even reality. 'O great queen, Mark Antony approaches,' she said, and my God did that bosom heave. But then why not? It was why she was here. Georgina really did want to be a star.

She lunched with them, rang the desk again, and found that she could hire a car and took charge of something called a Buick Six which she'd come across in England too. In it she drove out into the California countryside, that was all canyons and mountains and orange groves, and down to the ocean to watch the great surf pounding, along a seemingly endless coast until she even reached a place called Venice, but not the one that Thelma yearned for.

Next day she called on Jay at the studio, and he promised her a copy of the photograph, and showed her the test. She knew at once that Georgina would be enormously better, and said so, and asked for the film test as a gift. It seemed that for a studio executive to give up film was a far more serious matter than to give up arterial blood, but in the end Jay yielded and it was hers. Her very own three-minute reel.

'Can you fix me up with a drawing room on the train?' she asked.

'Be a pleasure. When do you want to go?'

'The day after tomorrow.'

'I envy you,' he said. 'It's always a good idea to get out of this town.' Her eyebrows rose. 'Movies,' he said. 'Dreams on a production line to order. My God what a way to make money.'

'When are you going back to the paper?'

'Soon as I can,' he said. 'Week after next at the latest. Murray Fisch will be glad to get back to work. He likes it.'

He took her – and Georgina – to one more party, one last lunch, and at this he handed her an envelope, which contained train tickets and a ticket for a suite on the *Aquitania*, too. This time she let him pay. She was going back alone after all.

'You're very kind,' she said, 'but there is just one more thing. . . . A donation for Felston.'

'From the *Daily World*?' Bower sounded horrified.

'From Worldwide Studios.'

Bower grinned. 'I'll get Murray Fisch to send you a cheque.'

And that really was the end of it: a tearful farewell from Amparo, and her promise that next time she came to Hollywood she would send for her at once, a promise she was sure she would have no difficulty in keeping; then breakfast with Georgina who couldn't come to the station because she had a lesson with her movement coach, but who kissed her and wept a little, and said to be sure to give her love to that dear sweet youth at Oxford. She must mean Piers, thought Jane, and wondered how he would take it. She went down to pay her bill, but Worldwide had paid it all, including the Buick, and there was money for her: a cheque for twenty-five thousand dollars from Murray Fisch, and her photograph from Jay.

It was time to go to the station, and Worldwide had taken care of that, too. They had sent a Cadillac – the Hispano-Suiza was taking Miss Payne to her movement coach – but it was nice to see the black bootleggers again, and to be alone, because now, she thought, I really do need time for quiet reflection, all the way to Chicago. Just south of Kansas City she had to put on her fur coat again, and by Chicago the cold was brutal, but there was another Worldwide Cadillac waiting there to take her to the 'Century'. At the Grand Central Station Barry was waiting, and there was time for neither reflection nor quiet. They went to speakeasies instead, or stayed indoors while the snow fell so that he could play more Gershwin. When it was time to leave, Barry drove with her to Pier 13, where the *Aquitania* was berthed, and took her to her suite, the Gainsborough, that was filled with flowers – from Georgina, from Jay, from Tom Waring, and all those delightful people she'd met at Jack and Charlie's, and the Hotsy-Totsy and the Sligo Slasher's. Quite a lot of them came aboard to see her off, and it was really a very nice party until the stewards began beating gongs and shouting 'Visitors ashore, please'. After that she was alone again

But not for long. She had been placed at the captain's table. More Jay Bower manipulation, she wondered. But whether or not, she was a celebrity, she was known, the famous Jane Whitcomb who had turned down Hollywood and written about Felston and dressed up as Cleopatra. She had studied that photograph dozens of times, not for any reasons of narcissism but to try to work out how it differed from the one she'd first seen. It was the same photograph, and yet it wasn't. Elegant, feminine, even dashing: it was all of those, but it displayed and indeed promised far, far less than the original. The point was, as Jay had written on the note he sent with it, that everyone would believe that this one *had* been the original. After all it had been in a newspaper, hadn't it? Anything more revealing would be the one that had been tampered with, the work of malicious persons motivated by grudges unknown. And so far there had been no attempt to display the other photograph, which was why she was so often asked to dance and invited to passengers' parties, and applauded so heartily when she won a prize at the Fancy Dress Ball by wearing her sari yet again. So that in the end she had to give a party too, or her steward and stewardess would never have forgiven her. Not that the Gainsborough suite was such a bad place for a party: the vast drawing room like a section of a country house, with a copy of Gainsborough's portrait of the Duchess of Devonshire on the wall, heaps of room for dancing, and endless champagne.

And the dinners! Gargantuan to the point of caricature. One night perspiring stewards rolled in a vast chafing dish about the size of an Austin Seven, on which was a sort of herd of grilled antelope grouped round a hillock of foie gras and surmounted by peacock fans. Quiet reflection was impossible, the more so as she detested venison, but on the other hand, she thought, perhaps I've done enough. Action is much more my thing.

50

LONDON SEEMED MILD after New York, though the snow still
lay on the side streets. Even so she thought of the California
orange trees without regret. She picked up Foch and hugged
him as soon as she reached South Terrace (some divining mech-
anism of his own had brought him to the door as soon as the
hired Rolls drew up) and she continued to hold him as the Rolls's
driver unloaded her luggage while Hawkins supervised. Almost
she could have done the unthinkable and hugged Hawkins too,
but she wandered about from room to room instead, and said
hello to the other servants, who, if not exactly overjoyed at
having to work again, appeared less than appalled. Mrs Barrow
seemed positively glad, but then Mrs Barrow was a creative artist
who would shortly resume her creativity.

She telephoned her mother, and found her at home. Major
Routledge and she were dining the vicar, it appeared. They
wished to know when, with propriety, they might announce
their engagement, and the vicar struck them both as one who
would know.

She remembered the funeral, and Dr Dodd's voice saying, in
tones of utter certainty: 'I am the resurrection and the life, saith
the Lord.' And now he was to advise the widow on when she
might be married.

'How is the major?' she asked.

'In good health,' said her mother, 'but he has not as yet
embarked on his literary labours. The weather has not been
conducive to horse-racing. On the other hand – '

'Yes, Mummy?'

'We have worked together on the way in which he will conduct this – ah – enterprise, and I think he will do well. And I must say, child, that shared employment can be most gratifying.'

Was there a barb there? It was certainly not a request for corroboration.

'I'm delighted to hear it, Mummy,' said Jane.

She telephoned Lionel, who promised at once to come round and dine provided Mrs Barrow was still with her and said he'd be round in a jiffy, which meant in fact an hour and a half, and gave her ample time to bathe and change. Hawkins came in to help her dress.

'I've just about finished your unpacking, miss,' she said, 'and I must say somebody looked after you very nicely.'

'The maid on the ship, but the one at the hotel was better,' said Jane. No point in stirring up trouble.

'Do you mind telling me which hotel, miss?'

'The Garden of Allah.'

'Oh gorblimey,' said Hawkins, then instantly flushed scarlet. 'I'm sorry, miss – but did you really stay there? No that's daft. Of course you did. But what was it like?'

This was not a girl one could lie to, and Jane had no intention of trying.

'A year or so ago you would have thought it wonderful,' she said. 'Now I rather think you'd find it vulgar.'

Hawkins looked at her, the flush marks fading. 'Thank you, miss,' she said at last.

'Button me up will you?' said Jane, and as Hawkins did so, asked, 'Is Bob Patterson still at your sister's?'

'Yes, miss.'

'Could you get a message to him? Tell him I want to see him?'

'Certainly, miss. Any particular time?'

'Tomorrow. Soon as he can. I'm going North again.'

Lionel said, 'Always so restless. Now you're back can't you stay back, for heaven's sake?'

'Don't worry, darling,' said Jane. 'I'll invite you to dinner again as soon as I return.'

'Well I must say Mrs Barrow hasn't lost her touch,' said Lionel, and sipped at his brandy. 'That was the best meal I've had since you deserted us for the fleshpots.'

'That reminds me,' said Jane, and hunted about her, handed over a parcel labelled Saks Fifth Avenue. Lionel unwrapped it cautiously, then gave a soft trill of delight. It was the most splendid, most *American* cocktail shaker he'd ever seen.

'As used at Jack and Charlie's,' said Jane.

'Who or what are Jack and Charlie?'

'It's a speakeasy. I told you.'

'A speakeasy!' said Lionel. 'Oh what bliss.' He looked towards her drinks cabinet.

'Not now,' said Jane. 'You're drinking cognac.'

'Then as soon as you get back,' said Lionel. 'You must be the first. Until then I'll practise on my own.' He put the shaker down. 'You didn't say how dear Jay was.'

'No,' said Jane. 'I didn't, did I? The short answer is that he is well. He has also discovered a new star to add to his particular firmament.'

'The delectable Miss Payne?'

Jane nodded. 'You knew that Jay and I were lovers?'

'The thought had crossed my mind,' said Lionel.

'Of course it had. You and my mother are the two sharpest people I know, and I've no doubt it crossed her mind, too. Well now we're not. But not on account of Georgie.'

'Another girl?'

'Rather a pretty girl, quite young, who drinks just a little too much because otherwise thwarted ambition would choke her. He'd decided to give her up once he met me, I gather. But suddenly she was available when I wasn't.' She thought for a moment. 'I honestly think there are certain excuses I might accept for unfaithfulness,' she said, 'but availability isn't one of them.'

'Did you weep for him?' Lionel asked.

'No,' she said. 'I wept for Captain Patterson.'

On the train to Newcastle she thought a little longer about Lionel, postponing for a while the time when she must think about her mother, and Bob. Lionel had wanted to know all about her trip, and made her tell him about the Cardona party twice, and the screen test. She hadn't dared tell him that she had a copy of the test. He'd have dragged her off to a cinema then and there and bribed everyone in sight. About other things, about what was going on, he had absolutely no idea. All the seriousness, the interest in the world of affairs, had been burned out of him in his two years flying a Sopwith fighter.

Her mother was better informed, of course. Her mother read *The Times* right through every day, including the racing pages now. She had embraced her daughter with more warmth than Jane could remember for many years, then looked at her and said, 'Hm,' without further comment. It seemed that she was satisfied. They took coffee together, and Jane put her questions.

'Of course there will be trouble,' said her mother, 'and almost certainly it will begin with the miners. They sustained another wage cut while you were away. Doubtless you will see its effects when you visit Felston. You have money for them?'

'Yes, Mummy.'

'They will need it, I fear. Some of them are very close to starvation.'

'But how – ?'

'Incredible as it may seem,' her mother said, 'the Poles and Germans can produce coal even more cheaply. The miners are understandably – if irrationally – incensed.'

'They'll strike?'

'Of course,' said her mother. 'But not yet. There are some men of sense among them. They won't strike till the weather's warmer.'

'Will they win?'

'No,' said her mother. 'How can they? They may drag others into it with them – railwaymen and the like – but they cannot possibly win unless they drag in the army and the police also.'

'Revolution?'

'Precisely,' said her mother. 'But revolution in this country is never easy. Without an Oliver Cromwell it will be impossible.'

They began to talk of more personal affairs, and especially of her mother's engagement.

'Dr Dodd proved rather difficult to pin down,' her mother said, and smiled her smile of pleasurable malice. 'One understands why, of course. To set a date for me would be to create a precedent. Perhaps he feared a positive stampede of widows determined on *secondes noces*.'

'But he gave a date?'

'Ultimately. Late summer, he thought, would be in order. I – *we* decided that mid July was quite late enough, and we shall marry in the autumn. In the meantime we go racing, taking care of course to conceal the fact that George is employed.'

'That's where you come in,' said Jane. 'The major will be with you and you provide the camouflage. The right sort of clothes are essential, Mummy.'

'Then I hope and pray that you will advise me.'

'Tweeds,' Jane said at one. 'Tweeds all the way till the flat season starts. I should get the Donegal kind if I were you. Harris is far too heavy. In fact when I come back from Felston I should like to buy you some if I may – just till the major's in funds.'

To her amazement her mother had said 'You're very kind', and nothing more. But why be amazed? she wondered. She too had learned about the need for love and money.

Bob had been brisker. There was a hell of a row coming, no doubt about it. Once the summer came. . . . In 1914, she remembered, it had been a question of waiting till August when the harvest was in.

'You'll be in it?' she asked.

'Might be,' said Bob. 'If I'm still in this job. But it mightn't get as far as the print unions.'

'What mightn't? And why do you say *if* you still have a job? Are you likely to be sacked?'

'Sacked?' said Bob. 'No fear. I need to work to send the money home. You know that. I just might get a change of job, that's all. And as I say – there's talk of a big strike in the summer.' He shrugged. 'But it'll be the miners who start it. It always is.'

'But you'll be all right?' she asked him.

'I didn't come all this way to strike for the bloody miners.' He paused. 'Sorry for the language,' he said. 'But I didn't. . . . You'll be going up there?'

'I heard from Bet when I was in Hollywood,' she said.

'"When I was in Hollywood,"' he quoted. 'It's grand to hear you say that.'

'Your dad's out of work again.'

'Yes,' said Bob. 'Grandma wrote and told us. Poor old Da! My bit money's all they've got now barring the dole.' He smiled. 'Andy'll be in his element.' Suddenly he changed the subject.

'Do you happen to know if Mr Bower's still in America?' he asked.

'He'll be sailing back soon,' she said. 'He doesn't like Hollywood.'

'Well I'm blest,' said Bob. 'What does he like?'

'The *Daily World*.'

She should have spoken to Dick Lambert of course, but there simply wasn't time, not if things were as bad as that. There hadn't even been time to see Charles Lovell, though she had written to him, suggesting that they meet when he was next in London, then dashed off to King's Cross. Indecent haste, Lionel had called it, and he was just about right. Foch had watched her departure appalled. If a dog could be said to do such a thing, he washed his hands of her. But he, and Lionel, were wrong. Felston was all the excuse she needed.

'But didn't you read about it in the papers in America?' Grandma asked.

'In New York they're too busy making money to worry about what's happening in England,' said Jane. 'And in Los Angeles they don't even bother what's going on in San Francisco, unless it's an earthquake.'

'Well I'll tell you what's going on,' said Grandma. 'Starvation's going on. Not everywhere mind you. But it's started. For the miners anyway. Since them last wage cuts. The rest is mostly like us – jogging on the best way we can and lucky if they've got somebody working away and sending money home.'

'I was going to bring some stuff up with me but I hadn't the remotest idea how to shop for you so I brought this instead.' She opened Grandma's worn leather handbag and stuffed bank notes into it.

'Thanks, pet,' the old woman said. 'There was a time I'd have chucked it at you – but not now. We're going to need it.'

You and Mummy seeing sense at the same time, thought Jane, and was glad of it.

'How about the clinic?'

'That doesn't change,' said Grandma. 'More clients, that's all. But that money of yours still feeds the helpers, thank God.'

'How's Bob?' Stan asked.

'Working hard,' said Jane. 'He asked me to tell you how sorry he was that you'd lost your job.'

'Aye,' said Stan. 'Me an' all.' His mother clucked her disapproval.

'How's Andy?' Jane asked.

'At a meeting,' said Grandma. 'As usual.'

Jane wasn't surprised. Once Andy knew she was coming he'd have *called* a meeting, if one wasn't available. She turned to Bet, who sat busy and abstracted, knitting a scarf.

'And what does he think of what's happening?' Bet sat silent.

'Tell her girl,' said Grandma, and this time it was the voice that there was no denying.

'It's got him all excited,' Bet said reluctantly. 'You'd think it was Christmas. He says this is going to be our chance.' She rose to her feet. 'It's time I was off to the clinic,' she said.

'I hired the Wolseley again,' said Jane. 'I'm going there too. Let me give you a lift.'

'That's all right,' said Bet. 'You stay and finish your tea.'

'I almost have,' said Jane, but the younger woman had already put on the coat that had hung behind the door, and was adjusting her hat before the mirror.

'It's all right, honestly,' she said, and kissed her grandmother. 'Ta-ra,' she said, and hurried out.

'She's in a hurry,' said Stan.

'After a tram ride, likely,' said Grandma.

'There's more to it than that,' said Jane. 'Bet wrote to me in America and she was fine then. She isn't fine now.'

Grandma sighed. 'That Bella Docherty talks a lot about morality,' she said. 'There's times you'd think she'd invented it – and our Bet's a good listener. Then there's that fiancé of hers.'

'You don't tell me he disapproves?'

'She's worried he might,' said Grandma. 'Oh I know it's daft but when a girl has to wait too long she does get daft ideas.'

'I see,' said Jane, and turned to Stan. 'And what do you think, Mr Patterson?'

'I prayed for you,' Stan Patterson said. 'And then I listened. And it seemed the good Lord was telling me that you might not be over-modest but you understood compassion.'

'He has a house quite near, has he not?' said Messeter. 'But he was of no use to me. He's a commoner.'

Stobbs said, 'If you'll excuse me I have things to do. I'll leave you to your gossip,' and left.

He isn't even aware that he's been rude, thought Jane. How I wish he could meet Jay Bower.

'But do you remember Charles in the war?' she asked Messeter.

'Of course,' said Messeter. 'A very gallant officer.'

'He said the same of you,' said Jane. 'But since the war?'

'A little adrift, if you will excuse my saying so. No sense of purpose. Not like you – or me, thanks be to God.'

There was the rattle of a motor vehicle outside, and Messeter was on his feet at once. 'If you'll excuse me,' he said.

'Of course.'

They went outside together. The hall of the clinic was already beginning to fill up with the chronically sick, who sat or lay in dreadful contrast to the fit young men who helped them, the glittering clean nurses who were already beginning their business. It was like a casualty Clearing Station in the middle of a battle, except that this time the wounded were women and children, as well as men.

She left Messeter to his work, and made for the door, easing her way through the growing crowd, until she collided with a woman carrying a tray of empty cups. It was Bella Docherty. She looked at Jane angrily as Stobbs appeared at the door of his surgery.

'Oh it's you,' she said. 'What you're doing here getting in the way of decent folk I don't know. You've no business here. You're not wanted.'

'Then I won't stay,' said Jane, and went out of the door. Behind her she could hear Stobbs's furious roar. 'Mrs Docherty, you damn fool. What in *hell* do you think you're doing?'

It was the first time she had heard him swear, but she continued walking to where the Wolseley was parked. She could hear footsteps behind her, but she continued to stride out.

'Miss Whitcomb.' It was Messeter's voice. 'I wonder if I might ask you to stop? Or at least slow down.' She turned to face him. 'Thank you,' he said. 'I'm afraid all this German iron is rather a handicap when one wishes to walk off a rage as you are doing.'

Jane waited.

'For some reason,' Messeter said, 'I find it difficult to talk in the street. There is a church nearby. Could we go inside, do you think?'

'You're needed at the clinic,' said Jane.

'This will not take long,' said Messeter. 'Besides, it's possible that you may need me too.'

She walked with him past the Wolseley to the church of St Andrew. It was a small church of raw, red brick and quite the ugliest ecclesiastical building Jane had ever seen. Inside was no better: whitewashed walls, chipped and grimy chairs instead of pews, an even uglier table, partly covered by a purple velvet cloth, for an altar, that bore only a cross and two candlesticks, and two bunches of chrysanthemums begged no doubt from someone like Stan. Messeter knelt at once to pray, and she joined him. She had no words to say, but the act of kneeling helped to calm her, just as the angry walk had done.

Messeter said, 'Mrs Docherty insulted you, and Stobbs rebuked her.'

'Dr Stobbs,' said Jane, 'would swear at anyone who imperilled his goose that lays the golden eggs.'

'Can you blame him?' Messeter asked.

'No more than I blame you for doing something much the same – though rather more practical.'

'Stobbs would have run after you too, but he was needed where he was.'

She said nothing.

'Forgive me,' Messeter said. 'I must ask you this – '

'I'll go on asking for money,' said Jane. 'Of course I will. But don't expect twenty-five thousand dollars every time.'

Messeter brushed that aside. 'And you'll come back to us?'

'No,' said Jane. 'I shan't do that. I have it on the authority of two good women that I'm not wanted.'

'As if that mattered,' said Messeter.

'It matters to me,' said Jane.

He was looking at her deeply: the look of a man beyond sexual love, but who remembered well its demands and its rewards.

'I shall pray for you,' he said.

'Heaven knows I need your prayers,' said Jane, and rose. 'Good night.'

As she went back to the Wolseley she thought, at least when Stan prays, he tells me what God's answers are, then stopped. Andy was waiting by the car. She went up to him.

'Yes, Andy?'

'I've got to talk to you,' Andy said.

'Not here,' she said. 'It's far too cold to talk out here. Shall we go back to John Bright Street?'

'No,' he said. 'Da's there. And Grandma. This is private.'

'The Eldon Arms then?' He shook his head. 'Some pub? *Any* pub?'

'It'll have to be here,' he said. 'There's nowhere in this town you and me can be seen and not set tongues clashing.'

'Get in the car then,' she said.

'Where will we be going?' he asked.

'Nowhere,' she said. 'We'll just drive round until you've told me what you have to say.'

He got in, and listened as the engine fired, the car eased forward.

'Nice engine,' he said.

'It would be,' said Jane, 'if the plugs were cleaned. Did you come to talk about motoring?'

'I came to talk about you,' said Andy.

And why not? she thought. Everybody else is talking about me.

'Go on,' she said.

'I reckon I owe you an apology,' Andy said, and she almost lost control of the car. It was the one thing she had not been ready for.

'Indeed?'

'You know about that picture,' Andy said. 'I reckon Bob must have told you. He disappeared fast enough after I got it, *and* landed himself a good job.'

She said, 'It isn't Bob's peccadilloes we're discussing at the moment. It's yours.'

'Peccadilloes,' Andy said. 'That's little sins, isn't it?'

'It is.'

'Well I don't know about the size of Bob's sins,' said Andy. 'But I don't reckon mine was all that little.'

He was silent as she drove towards the coast road, dark and empty on that bitter cold night.

'Do get on with it, Andy,' she said. 'We can't drive round for ever.'

He said stiffly, 'I'm sorry. . . . It's about that photograph.'

'Of course.'

'Not the one the *Daily World* fixed up. The real one. The original. A chap brought it to me from London. A posh chap.'

'Did the posh chap have a name?'

'He didn't give one and I didn't ask. But he knew all about you and your charity.'

'And disapproved of me because my good works got in the way of the revolution?'

'That's right. And I agreed with him. I still agree with him. You have to be stopped. Only –'

'Only what?'

'Not like that. Not with indecency. Dirt. That's not the way.'

'What is the way, Andy?'

'To fight you,' said Andy. 'Head on. That's the way. It's the road you took. Flaunting yourself, off to Hollywood our English Cleopatra and will she never come back and keep the people in subjection with a Christmas concert and a cracker? I might hate what you're doing, but you did it fair.'

'And you didn't?' Her question was a torture deliberately applied.

'You know fine well I didn't. And I'm sorry. Honestly I am.'

'Tell me one thing, Andy?' said Jane.

'If I can.' His voice was wary. Loyalty, thought Jane. One of your favourite virtues.

'This posh chap,' she said. 'Did his breath smell of garlic?'

'Would that be like very strong onions? Aye, it did.' He thought for a moment. 'You know him?'

'He's a friend of my brother's.'

'Well I'll go to France,' said Andy. Jane drove him home.

She had gone back to London almost at once, stopping off only to say goodbye to Grandma, choosing a time when she thought that Bet might be at the clinic. She was lucky. Grandma was on her own, cosy by the kitchen fire with her shawl around her. She made tea at once.

'So you're off back, are you?' she said. 'Can't say I blame you. Tongues like Gillette blades, the folks round here.'

'I can't help with the driving any more,' said Jane, 'now that the canon's got his clutches on a bus *and* an ambulance. And I can't work indoors, not with Bella Docherty there.'

'Bella Docherty doesn't have to be there,' the old woman said.

'Be sensible, Grandma,' said Jane. 'Bella Docherty's indispensable. What use would I be in a kitchen? And it isn't only Bella Docherty.'

'Our Bet?'

'Her. . . . Perhaps others. The rest of the country think I'm innocent – but not the whole of Felston, it seems.'

'We owe you too much, said Grandma. 'That's never an easy thing to forgive. But you and me are still speaking, I hope?'

'How could we not be?' said Jane. 'You'll write to me sometimes?'

'If you'll promise to write back I will.' She brooded over her tea cup. 'I'm due at the clinic tonight,' she said. 'I'll be having a word with Bella Docherty.'

'Please Grandma,' said Jane. 'Not on my account.'

'Accounts,' said Grandma darkly. 'The Meat Account, the Fish Account, *and* the Vegetables.' Suddenly she cackled. 'If my Stan was here he'd give you a text,' she said. 'Let him that is without sin among you cast the first stone.'

London had begun to thaw, the dark grey snow turning into a squelching mess as the rain began. She telephoned Charles Lovell in Hampshire, and was told that he had gone to Switzerland. As February gave way to March, she spent a lot of time dancing in nightclubs with Lionel. Then one morning Hawkins came in and woke her. It was eight o'clock: she'd had five hours sleep.

'Hawkins, what on earth – ' she said.

'It's Mr Bower, madam. He says if I hang up he'll just go on ringing back. Best to call it force majeure, madam.'

Jane was too tired to argue. She got up and went to the telephone.

'I need an article,' Bower said

'I think I've rather had enough of Felston just for the moment,' she said.

'There are other places,' said Bower. 'Get yourself over here and we'll talk about them.' He hung up.

It seemed, she thought, that they were still speaking, or at least he was.

51

WHAT HE WANTED, it seemed, was more Two Worlds stuff. Elegance and Deprivation.

'It's a steady market, you see,' he told her. 'The rich seem to have discovered the working class the way they discovered appendicitis in Edward VII's time. And anyway, how can you enjoy being rich if you don't know about the poor?'

'Is that what I'm doing?' she asked. 'Helping the rich to enjoy themselves?'

'They don't need any help,' said Bower. 'What you're doing is helping the poor. Get yourself around the East End for a change, then tell us all about your snob friends.'

'I'll need someone to show me round the East End. A reporter perhaps.'

'Not a reporter. They'll think they know what I want, and maybe they do. But they won't know what you want. You can have Dick Lambert.'

'Does he know?'

'It's all arranged.' His hand reached out for a sheaf of type-script. She stood firm.

'How's Georgina?' she asked.

'Fine.' His hand moved again towards his papers.

'Don't be so bloody silly,' said Jane. 'Tell me how she *is*.'

He scowled. 'Her test was good. I'm leaving the Cleopatra picture written for her. Fisch thinks we ought to let her talk in the last scene, and I'm beginning to think it's a good idea.'

'And the terra-cotta figurine?'

'She's playing the slavegirl.'

Despite herself Jane was moved to comment. 'You bastard,' she said.

'Not at all,' said Bower. 'It's a nice little comedy cameo. She's got to start somewhere. Now will you kindly let me work?'

Dick Lambert invited her to lunch at the House of Commons 'to discuss the whole thing'. Discussing the whole thing largely meant getting a good table so that others could see Dick Lambert lunching with a pretty woman for once, instead of having sandwiches and a half of bitter in solitude. She was still noteworthy, it seemed. Several members made some excuse to come over and talk to them, including at least one junior minister. All of them knew who she was.

'Sorry about that,' said Lambert, who had enjoyed every minute of it. 'We'd better get on with it before any more come.'

Poplar, they decided, the Elephant and Castle and the Isle of Dogs. Lambert knew Labour Party workers in all three, and every one was a connoisseur of misery.

She took him in the Riley, and it irked him rather, being driven by a woman, and he said so.

'But you can drive if you want,' she said.

'That's just it,' he said. 'I can't drive.'

'Then you should learn,' she said, 'instead of grousing at those of us who can.'

'I'd learn if you'd teach me,' he said, and then: 'No. That's not true.'

'Why not?' she said. 'It would be a pleasure to teach you.'

'But I wouldn't learn how to drive,' he said.

'Whyever not?'

'I wouldn't want the lessons to end.'

Best to say nothing, she thought, and drove on down the Blackfriars Road.

'I'm a Yorkshireman, Miss Whitcomb,' he said, 'and we're rather proud of our direct way of speaking. Too proud, maybe. That last remark of mine –'

'You wish to withdraw it?'

'No I don't,' said Lambert. 'What I wish to do is rephrase it – some other time. If you'll let me.'

And what was she supposed to say? Oh I'd much rather you didn't? Once again it was best to say nothing.

'My party's the party of idealists,' Lambert said at last. 'There's times we go on about it a bit too much. Complacency you might say. Still, by and large it's true. Poverty, sickness, class distinction, the inferior status of women – we're determined to tackle them all – and we will, too. But I know which one will come last.'

'And which will it be, Mr Lambert?'

'The status of women,' said Lambert at once. 'If you ask me, that won't happen until there's enough women activists to vote it through.'

'I'd like to use that some time, if you've no objection,' said Jane.

'I'd be honoured,' said Lambert, and sighed. 'I'm as idealistic as the next man,' he said, 'but – '

'Not when it comes to sex equality?'

'That's just it,' said Lambert. 'Once you got that through – you wouldn't be our equals. You'd be our superiors. It may not have dawned on the chaps down here, but up in Yorkshire we've always known that.'

And in Felston too, she thought, because in Felston at its worst only a woman could strive to hold together a family, and far more often than seemed possible they succeeded.

She turned on to the London Road and the Elephant and Castle, and the sort of streets that could give even Felston a game when it came to the kind of poverty that stopped so tantalisingly short of death. It was time to go to work.

She got far more material than she could possibly use. Each Labour Party activist had his own particular horror to display, as if poverty were a sort of competition and a mention in the *Daily World* the prize. But then it was the prize. Those men and women knew precisely what Jane had done for Felston, and hoped that she would do it for them. Their attitude was different, Jane noticed. They were, every one, as dedicated and idealistic as Andy, but for them the revolution would have to wait until the troops had had at least one decent meal.

Sarah Watson, when she visited her for scrambled eggs and gin, could not quite agree. The poor she treated – though admittedly they had not reached the appalling poverty that Jane had just seen – still had one more fight left in them, and were indeed looking forward to it with a sort of grim relish. Jane asked for names, and the ones she talked to all bore out Sarah's theories. Jane wondered why Dick Lambert hadn't shown her them, too. But for Lambert, she realised, no amount of ardent love could imperil his idealism.

The rich, she thought. Now is the time to visit the rich, but where do I begin? It was Dr Caswell who solved her problem, calling to remind her that she had promised to address her little group when Jane had returned from more exotic climes. She wants to ask about Hollywood, thought Jane, and accepted at once. Gilded youth would be just the thing, and she reminded herself to look up Catherine and Piers.

She drove up in the Riley, and took Foch with her, telling Hawkins no more than that she would be away for a night, perhaps two. She had no wish to be badgered by Bower and his 'Wicked World' bloodhounds. This was serious stuff; and so she booked in at the Mitre and bribed enough people to keep Foch with her, then took him for a walk to look at the High before dinner. Together they approved the soaring beauty of St Mary the Virgin and Magdalene's manifold charms, but it was at the solid dignity of the Queen's College that Foch lingered. 'Puritan to the last drop of your blood,' she told him. 'But I can't take you to Cambridge every time.'

She dined alone with only Foch under her chair for company. Best leave reunion with the Hilyards until next day, when she would have the strength to cope with all that youthful energy. She went to bed early, and had an early call, then scribbled notes to Piers and Catherine before, dressed in riding boots and breeches, she set off for the farm where her horses were kept. Foch sneezed once, but he enjoyed the run. Oxford in the half dark of a March morning, brooding and damp, had lost a fair proportion of its frivolity. The countryside too seemed sunk in gloom: soggy fields, dripping hedgerows, but Hyde's Farm, where her horses were, seemed cheerful enough: grey stone unsullied by smoke, blue-grey tiles, a cobbled courtyard between farmhouse and stables. Its owner came out to greet her himself. Mr Benson had written often enough to Jane, even telephoned when Bridget had finally given birth – to a foal this time: not a filly.

He was a big and cheerful man, instantly crestfallen when she made her request. Mr Benson, she saw at once, hated to deliver bad news.

'If only you'd thought to write to us, Miss Whitcomb,' he said. 'We'd have known what to do then – of course we would. But the young lady came so bright and early the way she usually does – '

'Lady Catherine Hilyard?'

'Exactly so, miss. And with her having the gentleman with her, and Bridget and Bridie both needing the exercise – '

'Quite all right, Mr Benson,' said Jane. 'But I'll take a look at the foal if I may.'

'But of course, Miss Whitcomb,' said Benson, and led the way to the stables.

She liked what she saw. Three months old now, a chestnut with one white stocking and a white blaze on the forehead, already strong, yet elegant in his shape.

'Well *well*,' she said.

'You're right there,' said Benson, who approved of taciturnity in others. 'He'll be a real good un to go when he puts his weight on. Good hocks and shoulders, and just right for size. Fifteen hands or a bit over – and a real good goer, I'll bet.'

'He certainly looks it.' She put out her hand, and the foal nuzzled into her.

'Have you decided on a name for him yet, miss?'

She felt the push of the foal's head, already strong, determined.

'Bridget's Boy,' she said. 'What else?'

'Would you like a bit of refreshment, miss?' Benson asked. 'Though I doubt if my wife has coffee – '

'Tea,' said Jane firmly, 'will do very well. And a biscuit if possible.'

Benson brought them himself into a parlour that glowed with polished mahogany, and did his best to entertain with stories of his days in the yeomanry – out in South Africa that had been, a cruel place for horses – but left them at last. Foch snorted as the door closed.

'I quite agree,' said Jane. 'But at least he's keeping my new horse in good trim.'

Foch yawned. Horses bored him; always had.

'Then what shall we talk about?' said Jane. 'My lecture to the bluestockings this afternoon? You know that almost as well as I do. What about my piece for Mr Bower? We mustn't call him Jay any more, I'm afraid. That would show a lack of respect.'

He had been great fun when one lacked respect, she thought. Eager and inventive – if vaguely surprised that a female too could be having such a good time. She wondered if Charles Lovell – Now that's enough, she told herself, and gave the last biscuit to Foch. He's gone to Switzerland, remember, and he can only have gone to Switzerland because of his wife. And anyway, he's pompous. But she knew that wasn't true. His letter may have been pompous, but that had been because his emotions were too much for him. Emotions like that always were too much for an English gentleman. Except for Papa, of course.

She had been drowsing when the sound of hooves woke her, hooves that slithered on the cobbles outside. Foch sat up, and barked sharply. He too had been dozing.

'Oh be quiet,' said Jane. 'You've met Catherine before, and Piers is just like her.'

She got up and went outside, and reluctantly Foch followed. The fire's heat had been pleasant.

Jane looked at Catherine astride Bridie. She was slender and elegant, even in jodhpurs. Beside her, astride Bridget, was Jay Bower.

'Why Jane,' said Catherine. 'This is a surprise.'

'Yes, isn't it?' said Jane.

'But why didn't you tell us you were coming?'

'It was one of those spur of the moment impulses that one so often regrets afterwards,' said Jane. 'If you'll excuse me, I must get on.'

Catherine said, 'But we've only just seen you. Can't you stay?'

'No,' said Jane. 'I'm afraid not. I've an awful lot to do. Come along Foch.'

She walked to the Riley, then turned.

'Catherine darling,' she called. 'Are you quite sure that Bridget is up to Mr Bower's weight yet?'

Then she drove away.

She had told Catherine and Piers where she was staying, so that it was necessary to drive to the Mitre at once, change, and stay out of sight by driving around the Oxfordshire countryside with Foch beside her. The awful thing was that she didn't know how to react. Twice in as many months really was a bit much, she thought, but even so, *how did she feel* about it? Surely to God she should know. But she didn't. Should she laugh or cry? Give way to disgust, despair, righteous indignation? She simply didn't know and couldn't force herself to find out. All she did know was that she wished it hadn't happened.

She lunched on bread and cheese at a pub in Banbury, (Foch had a ham sandwich) then drove back to Dr Caswell's cottage and a collection of what Jane thought of as sort of Hampstead women assembled in her rooms, though they would have been outraged if they'd known it. An old campaigner now, she kept the text-book references to a minimum, and played up her rôle as an ambulance driver both on the Western Front and at Felston. It was because of her stint in the war, she told them, that she had missed her chance to come up to Oxford herself. My goodness that went over big. For good measure she threw in Private Walker at the end, and the reaction could only be described as ecstatic. The odd thing was that she really had enjoyed giving her performance, despite what had happened that morning, and enjoyed even more the fact that she'd gouged twenty-three pounds eleven shillings and sixpence out of them. Then came tea, which she swallowed affably – it was in fact rather good tea – and a further barrage of questions before she was free to go and wonder whether she should see Piers; not because of Bower's article, but because of Georgina. He had a right to know, after all. But it was Bower she found waiting for her, beside the Riley. For the first time since Foch had known Bower, he growled at him.

'Even your dog hates me,' he said.

'Whatever emotion he shows is the one he senses in me,' said Jane. 'And I don't hate you.'

'How do you feel?'

'I've no idea.' It was true enough. 'Please get out of my way.'

'If we could sit down and talk for a minute or two – '

'For God's sake will you get out of my way?' He saw he had no choice, and moved, and Jane unlocked the door: she and Foch drove off at last.

At the Mitre Piers was waiting, every bit as elegant as his sister.

'Sorry to be so late,' he said. 'There was a meet today. I've only just got back and your note was waiting, so here I am.'

'Would you like a drink?' Jane asked.

'Enormously,' said Piers, 'but I'm what is called in statu pupillari, little more than a microbe, less than the dust in fact, and so I can't drink strong waters in bars. But there's a club in Walton Street I belong to. We have sort of a guest bar that lets females in. We could have one there. We could have a dozen if we felt like it.'

'One,' said Jane. 'At a time, anyway.'

The guest bar had once been a breakfast parlour and they had it all to themselves, whether because of taste or shyness Jane had no idea. But the martinis were at least adequate, even by the Hotsy-Totsy's standards. Jane sipped and began to answer a barrage of questions about Hollywood. At last she could put it off no longer.

'I saw Georgina there,' she said.

'Oh yes?' At once Piers looked away.

'It seemed to me that she may be thinking of making her career there.'

'Not coming back you mean?'

'Not for a long time.' To her amazement he seemed relieved. 'You're not sorry?' she asked.

'Sorry? Well no. . . . Not really. I mean I liked her enormously –'

'You must have done,' said Jane. 'You wanted to marry her.'

'Oh do stop ragging. As I say I liked her enormously but I'd forgotten something really frightfully important. I mean it just goes to show what an effect you women can have on a man.'

'Ought I to apologise on behalf of us all?'

'This is serious,' he said severely. 'I'd quite forgotten that in any decent regiment subalterns aren't allowed to marry. I mean it isn't a rule or anything – but you just don't.'

'You had a lucky escape,' she said.

'Jane!' Was it the resilience of youth or its censoriousness she found hardest to endure? she wondered. The club steward came over to them, followed by Catherine.

'Your sister's here, sir,' he said.

'I should just about think I am,' said Catherine, and then to the steward: 'I think we'd better have another lot of these.' Piers nodded, and the steward took the shaker and left as Catherine turned to Jane.

'I've been looking all over for you,' she said. 'Just as well that I remembered Piers's pompous club.'

'They make jolly good martinis,' said her brother. 'But isn't it a bit late to be wandering about on your own? Shouldn't you be in purdah?'

'I told the dean Jane had asked me to dine,' said Catherine. 'I'm afraid you'll have to do it if only to lend verisimilitude or whatever it is.'

'Delighted.'

'I must say,' said Catherine, 'that the dean was no trouble. Positively worships at your shrine.'

'I think it's mostly Hollywood.'

'Very likely,' Catherine said. The martinis came, and she took one. 'But I didn't spend my time scouring Oxford just to talk about the dean. It's about Bridget and Bridie.'

Not Bower? Jane wondered. 'Nothing to talk about,' she said.

'What's wrong with them?' Piers asked.

'Nothing's *wrong*,' his sister said. 'It's just that Jay Bower was in Berkshire yesterday.'

Checking on that fairy-tale country house of his? Jane wondered.

'And he asked if he could see Jane's horses – I was going to ride this morning anyway – and he appeared in this vast Rolls, right outside the door of our nunnery.'

'Was he driving?' Jane asked.

'Chauffeur,' said Catherine. 'Anyway, he was wearing riding kit and when we got to Benson's farm he asked if he could see how Bridget went – just hacking about, you know. And I said yes.'

'*You did what?*' Her brother was furious. '*Without asking Jane?*'

'Oh dear,' said Catherine. 'I knew I'd done wrong.' She turned to Jane. 'You were furious, too.'

'Well yes,' said Jane. 'But not any more. And not at you. He had no business to ask you.'

'And you had no business to let him,' said Piers.

'Perhaps we'd better go and eat that dinner,' said Jane. She had no wish to endure a sibling quarrel to round off what had already been a very trying day. Besides, while feeding them she could ask them about the more gaudy aspects of Oxford life: the parties, the Common balls, the hunting. First of course she had to warn them why she was asking her questions. They couldn't wait to tell her.

They had eaten at the Mitre, and once they had gone she sat with Foch beside her, making notes on what the twins had told her. There was enough for two pieces at least, if Bower wanted them. Suddenly Foch grunted, and she looked up. Bower, wearing a dinner jacket, was standing by her chair.

'Hello,' she said, and went back to her notes.

'I've come to apologise,' he said.

'That's all right,' she said, 'but please don't do it again without asking.'

'I want to explain,' he said.

'There's no need,' she said. 'It happened and it's over. Let's leave it at that.'

'Damn it I have to explain,' he said.

'Then sit down and do so,' said Jane. 'But try not to shout.'

'I've been dining at Oriel,' he said. 'Hence the dinner jacket. There's a don there who works for me sometimes. I didn't have to dine at Oriel and I didn't want to dine at Oriel but I had to kill time while I found out where you were – so I did. You should have told me you were coming to Oxford, Jane.'

'You should have stayed off my horse,' she said.

'OK, maybe I should, but – '

'Not maybe.'

'All right then. I should.' His hands searched his pockets and found a cigar, and he prepared it for lighting. 'But I didn't. I asked Lady Catherine if it was OK to let me ride – only I asked her in such a way she couldn't refuse. You believe that?'

'You Americans have an expression for it,' she said. 'Taking candy from a baby.'

His hands shook for a moment, the match flame fluttered as he lit his cigar.

'It was a stupid thing to do,' he said. 'It was a crazy thing to do. She'd have told you – of course she would. There was no way of avoiding this little talk we're having – '

'And yet you did it anyway.'

'You and that horse,' he said, 'and the story of it. There's some kind of mystique about it.'

'There's John,' she said. 'There was no mystique about him. He rode that mare and a machine gun got him at La Bassée and we loved each other. That isn't mystique. That's just life and death.'

'To you, maybe,' Bower said. 'But not to those who know you. The way things happen with you – there's a sort of, I don't know – almost a magical quality. It's rare. Very rare.'

Indeed I hope so, she thought. It's called going mad then becoming sane, again. And perhaps being grateful for one's sanity.

'So I thought,' said Bower, 'that if I rode the horse – this isn't easy for me, Jane.'

'You thought you might find out what John was like?'

'It was the man on the horse you'd loved,' he said. 'For that brief while I was the man on the horse.'

'Oh dear,' she said.

'Well now you know,' said Bower. 'Is there anything you'd like to do about it?'

'No.'

'I'll leave you to it then. When can I see your copy?'

'Thursday,' she said.

'Thursday will be fine.' He got up and left with no other word.

As she undressed she thought about how simple her life had been in wartime. She'd met a man and loved him until he was killed, knowing with each day that passed that the odds against his survival increased, knowing, too, that there was no choice. He was there in the trenches and he stayed there till that last machine-gun burst, till the biography of John Patterson was no more than the inscription she had seen once on a headstone in a graveyard: a whole family mourned, recorded, tidily buried, and then, carved in the only space left vacant, the name of a twenty-year-old boy, Killed in Action, Ypres, 1917; and the words 'His country called. He answered with his life.'

That was war. Peace was Jay Bower, Jay Bower of all people, behaving in a stupidly romantic way – love and despair and the Horse As Sexual Symbol – it sounded like an article by Burrowes. And she still didn't know how she felt about Jay, except that she didn't want to share his bed, ever again. On the other hand it seemed as if he were still in love with her, Thelma Tanagra notwithstanding. And Catherine? Catherine had given no sign of wanting him, but that didn't necessarily mean that this year next year sometime, she might not have a place in Bower's plans. . . . Jane got into bed and fell asleep at once.

The article appeared, and was good enough for Bower to demand another, and she took Mummy to Harrods and bought her tweeds and hats and shoes. Mummy had suggested brogues, but Jane was firm. 'If you're seen in brogues everyone will know you're in disguise,' she said, and took her instead to a shop in New Bond Street that sold French silk scarves to soften the tweed's hard line. Lady Whitcomb was delighted and said so, and even more delighted when there was racing at Newton Abbot and a rear admiral tried to pick her up. 'George,' she told Jane on the telephone, 'is furious.' She sounded in ecstasies.

For the rest there was Lionel, and there were occasional men to take her to dances, to wrestle with in a taxi on the way home and the occasional lecture and hat-passing. She missed Felston. Sending off a cheque to Stobbs and Messeter, writing to Grandma, weren't the same. She missed the place. But there was nothing she could do about it. Grandma needed her presence: Felston didn't. She turned to the newspapers instead. The *Daily World* was utterly certain that some kind of confrontation between Capital and Labour was on the way, and so was Mummy, when she could be dragged away from thoughts of the Cheltenham Gold Cup, which wasn't often.

'Unavoidable,' her mother said. 'Some writers even talk of Armageddon. Though how they can do so after the Somme is beyond my comprehension. . . . I saw Gwendoline Gwatkin the other day, quite briefly. At Fortnum's. She was buying cream cakes, poor thing. She asked me why I travelled so much these days. I told her that widows are notoriously flighty.'

The major tipped an unlikely horse for the National and it won at 66 to 1. Not only that but he backed it himself and bought a motor car with the proceeds; a quite capacious Hillman. The *World*'s circulation improved considerably because of the tip, and he received a substantial fan mail which Mummy answered personally. He also received a bonus and a rise in salary. Small wonder that Mummy had little time for Armageddon.

Dick Lambert had, but then he had little time for anything else. She invited him to a dinner party with Harriet and Neil

Watson and Sarah – once again not speaking to her husband. Sarah she thought would be adequate bait for any man, but he telephoned in an agony of remorse on the day of the dinner, and said he had to go to a meeting in Wapping. She had to call in Lionel instead. Lambert called next day, still remorseful.

'My dear man,' said Jane, 'I've no doubt that what you had to do was far more important.'

'If it had been anybody but you,' said Lambert. One in the eye for Sarah, thought Jane, but how could I possibly tell her?

'It's coming then,' said Jane. He nodded. 'An all-out strike? What they're calling a General Strike?'

Lambert said, 'I love you. I think you know that. But I must ask you this. Will you keep secret what I tell you?'

'Of course.' She smiled. 'I'm a woman, and by your definition inferior – for the moment, but I don't chatter.'

'They'll all come out,' he said, 'and soon. It's like a bottle of champagne. You twist the wire off and let it get warm and give it a good shake – the cork'll come out like a bullet.'

'The miners?'

'The unlucky ones,' said Lambert. 'Again. They're never anything else. You've seen them.' She nodded. 'Down underground, deeper than a grave, and danger and hard labour and black when they come home.'

He must be quoting from a speech she thought, and a good speech at that.

'So they'll start, and the rest will follow.'

'Like sheep?' she asked.

'I didn't say that,' he said. 'Like Kitchener's Army. The Pals' Battalions. The miners'll go over the top and their friends'll follow: railwaymen and transport workers, shipyard men and steel men. . . . And then the others because they think it's right, or because their mates are doing it, or even because it's a bit of a lark – if they're young and unmarried. And none of them will want to scab.' And then, more softly, almost with regret: 'It'll be rough on scabs, this one.'

Jane said, 'And will it be only about money? The miners' pay cut?'

'That's where they're weakest,' said Lambert. 'They can't make up their minds what it's about. The extremists want to make it political, but – '

'But what?'

'They'd have to storm the House of Commons,' he said. 'And what chance would they have? It's not as if it were the Winter Palace in Leningrad.'

'More coffee?'

'It's the best I ever tasted, but I can't stay,' he said.

'Mrs Barrow made it,' said Jane. 'She cooked the dinner you missed.'

She smiled, but he'd been too busy to remember what one did about jokes.

'I told you I love you,' he said.

'Yes,' said Jane.

'But you said nothing.' He waited, but again she found there was nothing she could say.

'I'm probably the only man in London who'll be glad when this bloody strike starts,' he said. 'At least it'll keep me busy.' He hesitated. 'Bower wants you and me to cover this strike together,' he said. 'The places you wrote the articles about. Are you going to?'

'Yes, of course,' she said. 'Are you?'

'You'll have to drive again,' Lambert said.

52

T HE MINERS STRUCK on 26th April. All across the country they finished their shifts and refused to go back, and Jane's thoughts went at once to Felston and its five collieries, the wheels of their cages no longer spinning, the men in their allotments, or fishing from the pier, eking out the money they had put by; the handful of notes and silver that was all they had to keep them alive. And still they didn't want her.

Bob called, but this was Bob transformed: pin-striped suit, blue shirt and collar, blue and red striped tie.

'Good gracious,' she said, as Hawkins showed him in. 'How successful you look. Printing must pay well.' He waited till Hawkins closed the door behind her.

'I'm not working at the press any more,' he said. 'Mr Bower's given me an office job. Liaison he calls it. He sent you this.' He handed her a sheet of paper that bore no address, simply M.J. Bower across the top.

'I want you to cover this business with Dick Lambert,' it said. 'I gather he told you and he said it was OK. Bob'll go with you when Dick's too busy. Use your own office when you need it, but get out and about as much as you can. This thing will be happening everywhere. Every street corner a movie set. I want an epic. Bower.'

Jane said, 'Liaison?'

'That's what he calls it,' said Bob. 'More like being nosey. Finding out what's happening. I'm good at that.'

'My photograph,' she asked.

'Aye. You might say that was luck, but some of us have to make our own.' He paused, tried to think of something more to say. 'The money's canny.'

'Will you work with Mr Lambert, too?' she asked.

'Just with you,' said Bob. 'When Lambert's got you I work on my own.'

'And do you like what you're doing?'

'Chance of a lifetime,' said Bob.

There was now, everywhere, a sense of inevitability in what would happen, almost as if everyone wanted it to happen, thought Jane, despite the moderate voices that called for more talks, more bargaining: for in the main both sides had done with talks, and were demanding action instead.

'Just like 1914,' said her mother, and Jane had no doubt that she was right. A General Strike was announced for the third of May.

Lionel was sunk in gloom. His cook, it seemed, who was Extremely Red, had announced her intention of picketing Harrods throughout the strike. Jane told him that he could lunch or dine at her house whenever he wished, since Mrs Barrow held no discernible political convictions, and Lionel was himself again, then suddenly he grew bored with the high-camp posturing and came down to earth.

'Some of this will be nasty,' he said.

'Lionel,' said Jane, 'this is a strike for heaven's sake. People are bound to get angry.'

'Some of them will do more than that,' said Lionel. 'The country's split in two, chosen sides. . . . Usually when there's a strike they negotiate, don't they? I can't give you a shilling but I might manage sixpence. That sort of thing. Not this time. One lot's got to win. Or more significantly, the other lot's got to lose.' He sighed. 'Dear God. I thought we'd finished with all that eight years ago. Would you like to go to the Embassy?'

On the morning of the strike a *Daily World* car brought Lambert to South Terrace: not a bus, not a tram, not a tube was running. Lambert got out and the *Daily World* car sped off, and Jane was ready and waiting for him. Lambert was pale and on edge.

'Where do we start?' Jane asked, and then: 'Oh, I'm sorry. Would you like coffee first?'

'No thank you,' he said. 'I'd rather get on with it. Elephant and Castle?'

'Why not?' she said. 'Then on through to Poplar and the Isle of Dogs. . . . Shall we take a look at the West End first?'

'Still hankering after the Two Nations?' he asked her. But it was a good idea. 'All right.'

She was drawing on her gloves when the telephone rang, and she picked it up at once. If it was Bob doing his liaison tricks, she didn't want Hawkins announcing the fact to Lambert. He was nervous enough as it was. 'Hello?' she said.

'Miss Whitcomb?' said the voice. 'Jane?' And she knew at once who it was, that day of all days.

'This is Charles Lovell.'

'How kind of you to call.'

'I'm in Eaton Square,' said Lovell. 'When may I come to see you?'

'Not now,' she said. Oh God how could he choose such a time? 'I'm really frantically busy. This strike – '

'You're not involved in that, surely?'

'I'm writing about it. . . . May I call you when I'm free?'

'Yes of course. I have rather a lot to tell you. At least I hope I have.'

'The instant I'm free,' she said, and hung up. Lambert was looking at her. There could be no doubt he was aware of her feelings. 'Shall we go?' she asked.

Along Knightsbridge, past Hyde Park, now firmly closed to the public, its gates guarded by police. It was a good depôt, said Lambert, and nobody could come in without a pass. She pulled up as a lorry loaded with crates swerved suddenly across their path and chugged towards the park gates. It was driven by a young man wearing a Balliol tie.

'What on earth – ?' she said.

'A volunteer. There's hundreds of them. Came up at the weekend. Doing their bit, they call it.'

'I expect they'll enjoy themselves.'

'The workers won't.'

She drove on down Piccadilly to the Circus, then back to Belgravia, and Eaton Square, where there was no more exciting spectacle than housemaids polishing doorknobs, and over to Chelsea: Sloane Square and the Embankment. In the whole drive there was nothing to indicate a General Strike except the absence of buses. Shops were open, taxis plied for hire. There were perhaps more policemen than usual on their beat, but not *so* many more. And then she noticed something. The news-stands were deserted: the newsboys who usually worked the area by the tube stations were not there. She had begun her day too early to bother about her own newspapers, but apparently it was as well. There weren't any. Not even a *Daily World*.

She drove on, past the Oval to Kennington and on to the East End, past Southwark and the Borough to Kennington Causeway, and on to the Elephant and Castle, and at last she believed in the Revolution.

Heaven knew what she had expected in Mayfair and Belgravia: fat profiteers in top hats hanging from lamp-posts perhaps: anything other than that air of preternatural calm; but the Elephant and Castle provided everything a good journalist could wish. The great square was thronged with people on foot – here of all places, not a bus or a tram would be tolerated, although Lambert told her that volunteers were going to drive them too. But not in the Borough, not in Newington. She eased the car: pedestrians that day were using the road, as well as the pavement, and she could see that men and women alike were far more animated, more alert than the last time she'd been there. They were even smarter in their appearance: many of them wore their best clothes, as if they were on their way to attend a great occasion. All of them wore a look of savage expectancy. All that's missing is Madame Defarge, she thought, then grimaced in self-disgust. To them at least this was real and overwhelmingly important.

A policeman pushed his way through the crowd to them – the whole area was saturated with policemen. He was a vast man with a row of medal ribbons, and made his way through the crowd as if wading in pygmies.

'A bit far from home aren't you miss?'

She produced her press card.

'I see miss,' he said. 'Well you can stay if you like, but there won't be nothing happening here till the evening. No speeches till then. Nothing.'

'Then what on earth are they all doing here?'

'What else have they got to do miss?'

They went on to Poplar and the Isle of Dogs, taking in Limehouse on the way. And still there were no buses, trams, carts or delivery vans, in an area where only the doctors had cars – and not all of them. Instead, the people were there on foot, by the hundred, the thousand, and she heard the first jeers as she turned down the West India Dock Road into a scene of pure fantasy. In the dock a detachment of the Brigade of Guards was unloading bags of flour, and while they did so the Band of the Coldstream Guards was playing 'Poor Little Buttercup', from *H.M.S. Pinafore*. She found it very hard not to laugh. Lambert was almost incoherent with rage. A guards subaltern came over to them.

'Sightseeing?' Once again Jane produced her pass. The guardee read it carefully, and changed at once from a six-foot whiplash of inherited authority to a devoted admirer. '*The* Jane Whitcomb?' he said. 'Cleopatra? . . . Gosh.'

'May we get out for a little while?' she asked.

'Yes, of course,' said the subaltern, and turned to Lambert. 'Mr . . .'

'Richard Lambert. I'm the MP for Leeds West.'

'Help yourself, Mr Lambert,' the subaltern said, then turned once more to Jane. 'I'm glad you came back,' he said simply.

They went on to the dock side where the guardsmen grunted and heaved, and experimented with equipment rather more complex than a 303 Lee-Enfield. They were doing their best, but the work was new to them, they were slow. Even so a steady trickle found its way to where the lorries waited in a row, ringed round by pickets five, seven, ten deep. Slowly, irresistibly the lorries filled, and the band moved on to Ketelby's 'In A Monastery Garden', a tune, Jane thought, even more wildly inappropriate. She glanced at Lambert. The rage was returning.

'Not yet,' she said. 'Don't waste it. There'll be far more important things to be upset about before this is over.'

His face relaxed, but he didn't smile. 'Look at the lorry drivers,' he said.

There were three to a lorry: one equipped with a street map to find the way, one to drive, and a policeman for escort. Nearby another squad of policemen watched the crowded pickets. All big men, she noticed: at least a head taller than the men they watched. Even so they were twenty against what – five hundred?

a thousand? and yet they didn't seem in the least apprehensive, standing easy and relaxed in the hazy spring sunshine.

A guardsman dropped a bag of flour and it burst on the pavement, and the crowd cheered ironically. The guardsman looked at them, glaring his hate, then went back for another. Not the way to bring on the Revolution, she thought. The trick is to subvert the military not antagonise them. The lorries were almost ready to leave when a voice from inside the picket called out: 'Stop it, soldiers. Don't do no more. It's your mates you're hurting. Your comrades.'

The guardsmen laboured on with the mindless application of men on fatigue, but the inspector in charge of the police squad growled to his men, they stiffened to attention as the last bags were loaded, and the guards' band still thumped on.

The lorry crews in groups of three began to climb in to their lorries. One driver, she noticed without too much astonishment, was Piers. He had never looked happier.

One by one the engines fired, and the first lorry moved forward to the final gate where the picket waited. Deliberate, unhurried, moving like soldiers, the police squad marched past the lorries and lined up as the gates swung open. The inspector in charge moved in front of his men, one step, then another, then another. An insanely courageous thing to do unless one were utterly sure, she thought. But how *could* one be utterly sure?

'Stand clear of these gates,' he said.

The crowd made no move to obey. Instead there was a low and angry growl, like some large beast waking from sleep.

'I'll say it again. Stand clear.'

The growl grew louder. From the crowd came whistles, cat-calls, jeers.

Behind his back the inspector snapped his fingers and a sergeant caught the signal, rapped out an order. At once every policeman produced his baton. Jane glanced over to where the guards' fatigue men stood waiting. They stood at ease, but in that way of drilled relaxation that only guardsmen can achieve, and on their faces was a look of anticipation, enjoyment even. As if they were at the cinema, thought Jane. . . . The band stopped playing.

'Have you got a spokesman?' the inspector asked.

Beside her Lambert said, 'Not a leader, you notice. Pickets are mobs, and mobs don't have leaders.'

A grey-haired man came forward. He was small, wiry, bespectacled, and he wore his Sunday best. Like the inspector he took three steps forward, matching courage with courage.

'Tim Potter,' he said. 'I'm a shop steward here.'

'Tell me what you intend to do.'

'Peaceful picketing,' Potter said. 'That's all we intend to do. What the law says we can do.'

'Two men to each lorry,' said the inspector. 'And keep away from my constables.'

'The law doesn't say that,' Potter said.

'I'm saying it.'

He snapped his fingers again, and again a sergeant barked orders. The police squad moved in close to the inspector.

'I have my orders,' the inspector said, 'and you may be sure I'll obey them. And so will my men here.'

The voice that had called to the guardsmen shouted, 'Don't listen to him, lads.'

The inspector's voice went on, unheeding: 'These lorries are coming out,' he said. 'Now it's up to you, Mr Potter. You can let them through, or else I'll clear the way for them first. And believe me I'll do it.'

The shop steward stood impassive, but his face was sweating.

'You have no right,' he said.

'I have my orders, Mr Potter. That's all the rights I need.' His voice grew gentle, almost, Jane thought, compassionate.

'You can't win, man. Not with this lot.' His head gestured to the policemen behind him. 'Get out of our way. . . . Don't make us hurt you.'

Potter said, 'You're right. We can't win. Not this time. But there'll be others.' He turned to face the picket. 'Let them through,' he called.

The picket stood firm for a moment, then again there came a sound from them, one sound, the moan that said they had lost. Reluctantly the ranks parted, and the first lorry moved forward. As it did so the whistles and jeers began again. Jane looked for Piers. He was driving with such concentration that the lorry could have been his Bentley doing ninety, and he was still bursting with happiness.

'So we lost a skirmish,' said Lambert.

She watched the police put away their batons. Were they disappointed, she wondered, or was there relief that they hadn't had to club down men who were very like themselves after all?

'But you'll win the battle.'

'Not this battle. . . . Not this strike. And I'll tell you why not?' Under the stress of emotion his Yorkshire accent had grown more pronounced. 'Because the government were ready for it and we weren't. See for yourself. Troops to move food supplies, drivers to take care of distribution. And folks still getting to work.'

'Scabs?'

'Lower-middle-class folk,' he said. 'Office workers. You saw them. On bicycles. Sharing lifts. Walking. Miles and miles some of them. They'll keep business going till we wear ourselves out. You'll see.'

'Is that bound to happen?'

'Of course it is.' For the first time he was impatient with her. 'It's like I told you – we don't know what we're fighting for. But we will next time – and by God we'll win.'

The last of the lorries went through the gates, and the pickets moved away: slouching, disconsolate.

'Where now?' she asked.

'House of Commons,' he said. 'I've a meeting there. I hope it isn't out of your way?'

'Of course not,' she said.

She took him back to Westminster and left him by the House of Commons. Extra policemen on duty, she thought, but not so many more, and the customary flow of MPs and visitors. Business as usual, in fact. She drove on along Birdcage Walk, past St James's Park, to Constitution Hill and still the place seemed as if it had always been: gleaming motor cars, well-dressed pedestrians, many of them exercising superior kinds of dogs. On Knightsbridge she saw a small queue, and she parked the Riley and joined it. It was a news-stand with three newspapers for sale, *The Times*, a single sheet, the *Daily Mail*, proudly announcing that it had been flown in by air from Paris, and something called the *British Gazette*, which she had never heard of.

She turned to the paper seller, an ageing gentleman who wore a suit that a duke might envy.

'What is it?' she asked.

'Issued by the government,' the paper seller said. 'Edited by Winston Churchill.'

'No *Daily World*?'

'Sold out,' said the paper seller, and even at that stage of their relationship she was glad for Bower's sake. And for the *World*'s, she thought. The paper was beginning to demand her loyalty. After all it was almost a family affair.

She returned to South Terrace to find that it was only just lunchtime. Hawkins came into the hall at once.

'Mr Warley's here, miss,' she said.

'Yes,' said Jane. 'His cook is out supporting the strike.' Suddenly she remembered something. She had consulted Mrs Barrow about her feelings, thinking perhaps that all cooks might have leftist tendencies, but she had ignored Hawkins.

'I should have asked you before,' she said. 'Are you quite happy working while this goes on? I shan't hold it against you if you say no.'

'Perfectly happy for the moment, miss,' said Hawkins. 'I haven't got on to Politics yet.'

When she went to join Lionel he was looking at his watch.

'Don't worry,' said Jane. 'You'll be fed soon.'

'All this upset makes me nervous,' said Lionel. 'And when I'm nervous I feel hungry.'

'What upset?' said Jane. 'There wasn't a sign of trouble here – or in Chelsea. Make me a cocktail, there's a love.'

Lionel picked up the shaker and began mixing: handed her the results.

'A Bronx,' he said. 'But I warn you – my heart isn't in it.'

Jane sipped. 'Nonsense,' she said. 'It's delicious.' She sipped again. 'Do tell me why you're fretting so. If you want to, that is.'

'Of course I don't mind,' said Lionel. 'I'm a frivolous person, you see – and all I'm really good at is frivolity. All this stern purpose stuff gets me down. I suppose you think that's bad of me –'

'Well yes,' said Jane. 'I do rather.'

'And so do I,' said Lionel. 'But it's as I told you. I used up a lifetime's supply of seriousness in the two and half years I was in the Royal Flying Corps – I was thinking of going to Paris till it's over.'

'How would you get there?'

'Drive to Dover of course, then cross on the steamer. Oh . . . I suppose the Merchant Navy's on strike too?'

'Of course,' she said.

'Not a sailor to be had,' said Lionel. 'What a fate for a queen. . . . I'm losing face, aren't I?'

'What a question,' said Jane. But he was.

'In fact there's rather more to it than that,' said Lionel.

'Do tell,' she said. 'You know I'm good at keeping secrets.'

'The man I'm in love with's rather keen on all this class-war stuff.'

'Oh my God,' she said. 'Not another Burrowes.'

'Oh no no,' he said. 'As a matter of fact he's a plumber – and awfully sweet. But he wanted me to *do* something about it all.'

'Do what?'

'I've no idea,' said Lionel. 'I asked him if there was any sort of fund I could subscribe to and he got awfully angry and said he couldn't be bought and stormed out. And considering I'd just bought him dinner at the Ritz I thought that was a bit much.'

'Perhaps he did too,' said Jane. 'People don't like being bought. They don't mind being treated, but that's different.'

'Oh Lord,' Lionel said. 'How right you are. What on earth am I going to do?'

'You could try telling him that all sorts of people have been pestering you to volunteer to drive buses and lorries and be a special constable and you've refused.'

'A bit negative,' Lionel said.

' – And all your friends are furious with you.'

'He'd like that,' said Lionel. 'He's dead against us toffs. Bless you, my sweet. I didn't know you did the Advice to the Lovelorn bit as well.'

Hawkins came in to announce lunch, but she told her that there would be a short delay. Advice to the Lovelorn applied to her as well, and she suddenly wanted very much to hear Lovell's voice that instant instead of waiting until after lunch. She went to telephone.

The butler of his friends in Eaton Square told her that he was out on business, and would not be back till evening.

Lionel ate a good lunch, and set out to find his plumber, and she settled down to make her notes. It would be a strong piece;

very strong, she thought. Maybe too strong even for Bower. 'Labour's Last Big Push?' she wrote, then wrote down the facts haphazardly, as she remembered them. The pattern would emerge in time – after she had gone back to the East End, with or without Dick Lambert. At night perhaps Bob would be better. He wouldn't be inhibited by the thought of trouble. She left a message at the number she was told would get him, and telephone Charles Lovell again. He came to the telephone at once.

'May I see you now?' he asked.

'I have to go out,' she said. 'Work. . . . How about later?'

'I have a dinner engagement.'

'Oh damn,' she said. 'How about very late?'

'Of course,' he said. 'Where?'

'My parlourmaid's a bit of a prude,' she said. 'How about Eaton Square?'

'My friends are all away,' he said.

'If you're sure that's all right.' The doorbell rang.

'Eleven thirty,' she said.

It was Bob, in a sports jacket and grey slacks and a flannel shirt. He had the fit and confident look that only a very young man who is eating well can achieve, and his eyes showed some of that same excitement that she'd seen in the eyes of the guardsmen at the docks.

'Where are we going?' he asked.

'The Elephant and Castle to start with.'

He nodded. 'Lively there. Will you be taking the car?'

'Yes of course. How else – '

'I could phone the *World* and get one.'

'We'll take mine,' she said. 'We don't want anything too grand.'

There was the same stark contrast of West End and East End. The West End still living its elegant life: theatres, cinemas, restaurants, bars all open; even the occasional bus erractically driven by volunteers. Only the big electric signs were missing, switched off, Bob told her, to save electricity. But otherwise the West End was as it always was: except that perhaps the people there seemed to be enjoying themselves rather more than usual: as if pleasure were a form of defiance.

As they drove eastwards, Bob said, 'We got word the Honourable Piers Hilyard's driving a lorry.'

'Who's "we"?' she asked.

'The "Wicked World" lot, of course. I pass on things I hear to them.'

'As a matter of fact I saw him,' said Jane. 'At the West India Docks.'

'Doing his bit,' said Bob. The thought seemed to amuse him. 'There's a lot of them at it.'

'Bob,' she said. 'Doesn't it make you angry?'

'No,' said Bob. 'He's doing what he wants to do. Same as me.'

No time to ask what that was. They had reached Newington Butts and already the press of people was so strong that the car had to crawl. She turned off into a side street and parked beside a police van after Bob had got out and had a word with its driver, then they moved back into the crowd. There were policeman everywhere, but they weren't moving singly as they had been that morning: now it was like the docks, with small, compact groups stationed here and there, each one under the command of a sergeant or inspector.

'Trouble?' she asked.

'Not yet,' said Bob. They moved on further into the square. There was a sort of makeshift rostrum by the pub, with its sign of an elephant bearing a howdah, and round it a crowd stood grouped, packed in tight, staring up at the speaker. It was Dick Lambert.

'We can win,' he was saying. 'Only be patient. There are five million of us. A bigger army than ever Marshal Haig had. How can we not win?' The crowd listened, but what they heard was not what they'd come for, and Lambert knew it.

'What we're doing is right,' he said. 'The bosses are trying to cheat us, but our demands are just. A living wage – that's all we ask. Is that so unreasonable? Of course not. It's the very foundation of a free and just society – and we'll get it, comrades. This strike is our show of strength. Overwhelming strength. Five million of us united as one. Let the rich men in Mayfair think of that, and tremble. Brothers, comrades. I promise you. Only let us stand firm and we shall win.'

He left the rostrum, and there was a mutter of applause, no more. Among the crowd, the 'Red Flag' began to be sung, tossed backwards and forwards from one activist to another, until at last the whole great audience responded:

Let coward flush and tyrants cheer,
We'll keep the Red Flag flying here.

Jane looked at the squads of police. They still stood easy, relaxed. It seemed that Bob was right.

'Is it over?' she asked.

'For tonight it is.'

She looked at her watch. Almost nine thirty. Still a couple of hours to go.

'I wonder if we could go and get something to eat in that case?' she said.

'There's a sort of artists' caff in Chelsea,' said Bob. 'We could get a bite there.'

'Will they let you in like that?'

'They'll let anybody in,' said Bob.

And so it proved. Not a bad meal either. Onion soup and lamb chops with basil and cheese brought over from Normandy. There wouldn't be any more of that till the strike was over. She asked for wine, and so, to her surprise, did Bob: a rough and cheerful red that he seemed to enjoy.

'What do you do for Jay Bower?' she asked.

'Find things out,' he said. 'I told you. Mr Bower's the sort of chap that needs to know things.'

'So you spy for him? I'm sorry if that sounds rude, but – '

'Quite all right,' he said. 'What I do could upset a lot of people. It didn't do you any harm though.'

'Me?' she said, then: 'Oh. . . . Of course.'

'Of course,' he said. 'Cleopatra – Queen of the Sunday School. . . . It's best to be forewarned in this life.'

'And is that what you do? Forewarn Mr Bower?'

'That's it,' he said. 'It's better than printing. Pays better too.'

The bill came at last and she offered to pay it, but he settled it himself. 'All on expenses,' he said. His tip was generous, and she wondered if he had informers among the waiters.

The next day she would spend with Lambert, and Bob was relieved, if anything. Nothing would happen on the next day. It was the day after that when the excitement would begin. . . . She agreed at once to share it with him. She didn't want Lambert where there was excitement. He was strong enough, but he had too much to lose.

53

At Eaton Square, Lovell answered the doorbell himself.
'Where's the butler?' she asked.

'Night off.'

She moved at once into his arms. Later she thought that they might have rehearsed it, so inevitable was it. He tried to talk to her, to explain what had happend, but she kissed him into silence, made him take her up to his bedroom, where it was all most satisfactory. Not like Bower: neither better nor worse, only different – and just as worthwhile. Except that when they finished he had a tendency simply to lie there and keep his hands to himself. But it was early days, and he *did* have a lot to tell her.

'That dreadful letter I wrote,' he said.

'Awful.'

'I wanted to tell you everything.'

'And you ended up by telling me nothing,' she said. 'Certainly you never gave me any idea that you ever felt like this.'

She gestured across the bed and touched him. It really was time he began to learn.

'I couldn't marry you,' he said. 'Still can't.'

'Did I ask you to? Did it never occur to you that I like my freedom too? For the time being at least.'

'I went to Switzerland because I was told my wife might be dying. God help me I – '

'That's quite enough of that,' she said. 'This is here. This is now. Just enjoy it.'

Her hand moved again. 'What on earth are you doing?' he said.

'If you don't know,' said Jane, 'there's no hope for either of us.'

He was still laughing as he embraced her.

But she couldn't see him the next day. The omnipresent butler was back, and she needed an early night anyway. She hadn't got into her own bed till three, and Lambert called at nine. It was the day for attending committees in Lambeth. Strike committees, hardship committees, ways and means committees. And here Lambert was at his best; cajoling the waverers, restraining the hotheads, and always holding out to them that shining vision of the day when they would win. And in small groups at least it seemed to work.

'You did well today,' she said, when it was over.

'Oh yes,' he said. 'Give me a classroom full and I can reach them.' His voice was bitter. 'I used to be a schoolteacher, you know.'

'I didn't know,' she said. 'But what's wrong with that?'

'I'm trying to teach the grown-ups now,' he said. 'I didn't do so well last night at the Elephant and Castle.'

'Didn't you?'

It would have been an appalling cruelty to say that she had heard him.

'No I damn well didn't.'

'But surely you must have made speeches in Yorkshire – in your constituency?'

'Preaching to the converted,' said Lambert. 'Solid Labour my lot. Fifteen thousand majority. If a bulldog could make the right noises he'd walk it.'

'Didn't you make the right noises last night?'

'I thought I did,' said Lambert, 'but my audience didn't agree with me. I was preaching moderation. What they wanted to hear was revolution.'

They walked back to the car. On the way they passed a news-stand where a couple of young men were distributing copies of a newspaper called the *British Worker*. Working men in shabbily respectable clothes queued up to receive their copies.

'We seem to be fighting back,' said Lambert.

'We do indeed.' The two young men, Jane noticed, were

dressed exactly as Piers would have been dressed if he'd ever decided to distribute a Socialist broadsheet.

'That work "fight",' said Lambert. 'It's a tricky one. The Marxists keep saying we should arm the workers, but how the hell can we? I wouldn't know where to put my hands on a blunderbuss, never mind a rifle. We can't fight that way – though there's some that keep saying we must. On the other hand there are limits – and we've started going beyond them already.'

'What limits?'

'Over at a tram depot in London,' he said, 'they held a football match this morning. Police versus strikers. They've been out less than two days and they're playing football. . . . *And* they lost.' He saw her lips twitch. 'It isn't funny.'

'No indeed,' she said. 'But it's human. And it's better than handing out blunderbusses.'

'I keep trying to tell them how serious it is,' he said, 'but they just won't listen.'

'*And* you keep telling them they mustn't fight,' she said. 'But these are simple people. If you say it isn't a war, why shouldn't they play football?' As she drove home, a fog was beginning to form. It seemed the perfect comment on the day.

She slept long and late, and was awakened just in time to prepare for Bob. As she ate breakfast she put on the headphones and listened to the wireless news bulletin, which was remarkably impartial, she thought, considering that the government owned the BBC. But it might not stay like that if things began to go wrong from the government's point of view. The unions should have thought of that. The unions should have thought of so many things.

'I thought we'd have a look at the toffs this morning,' said Bob, 'then maybe we could go and have a look at a few diehards this afternoon.'

Really, she thought, he might have been an ornithologist showing off his rarer species.

So in the morning they went to *The Times*'s offices, to watch a row of debs led by Lady Diana Cooper folding the single, flimsy page of that day's issue, then on to the *Daily World* where Bob took off his jacket and helped Jay Bower and a couple of executives set that day's edition in type. Bower, she noticed, was covered in printer's ink to the eyebrows and sublimely happy, like a small boy at Christmas who had received the Meccano set he'd always wanted. They went on then to a Territorial Army drill hall in the city, special constables whose uniform consisted of an arm band, a whistle and a truncheon, were receiving instructions in crowd control, and finished up at Euston Station, where only one train waited, and a man in a bowler hat assured everyone who would listen that he was the engine driver, and he hoped to take them as far as Manchester. In fact, Jane learned later, the train was derailed at Harrow, a few minutes's ride away. Even so she was beginning to realise that the government was at least a match for the strikers in determination, and streets ahead in efficiency.

The next morning was Bob's. He arrived prompt to the minute, wearing the same grey flannel slacks and brogues, and another and very elegant sports jacket. He carried a bag like an army pack.

'Fancy a little excitement this afternoon?' he asked.

She eyed him warily. 'What kind of excitement?'

'What you lot in Hollywood call a hi-jack,' he said. 'Or a try at one anyway.'

'By all means. Where is it?'

'Bethnal Green. Just off the Whitechapel Road.'

'We can't possibly get there till eleven,' she said.

'Take your time,' he said. 'It isn't due to happen till eleven thirty.'

She looked at him. 'How the devil do you know?' she asked.

'I get about,' said Bob. 'I talk to people.'

'Have you told Jay Bower?'

'Not this time,' he said. 'I don't want to tell him all I know. You and me's going to find this one by accident.'

'Serendipity,' she said.

'How much?'

'Never mind,' she said. 'You silly ass. Bower would want a reporter there – *and* a cameraman.'

'You're a reporter,' said Bob. 'At least you've got a card that says so. And I've brought a camera. I can work it an' all.'

'Does he know you've got it?'

'It was his idea.' They set off for Aldgate.

'Guess who's come up to town?' he said.

'How can I possibly?'

'Andy,' he said.

For a moment her hands tightened on the steering wheel, then she relaxed. 'Andy? But why? Hasn't he enough to do in Felston?'

'Felston's chock-full of Andys,' said Bob. 'His lot decided he'd be more use down here.'

'His lot?'

'The garlic chewer's lot,' said Bob. 'I reckon that means the comrades, don't you? . . . He wants to see you.'

'When?'

'After the hi-jack. Pub I know. Will you come?'

'Certainly,' she said. 'But why did he come to you?'

'Blood's thicker than water,' said Bob. 'At least Andy reckons it is. Redder, too.'

They drove to Aldgate East, and on to the Whitechapel Road. The cars became fewer and fewer, until there was only theirs, but everywhere, as usual, men and women were walking, and here and there a cyclist skimmed past, or a horse and car grimly plodded.

'Turn left at Brady Street,' said Bob. 'There's a bit of waste ground there.'

She did as he bade her, and found herself a place to park in front of a couple of ruined houses that seemed to have collapsed from sheer exhaustion.

'How did you know about this?' she asked.

'I came over on my bike first thing this morning,' he said. 'To do a what d'you call it? Like the war.'

'To reconnoitre,' she said. Suddenly he looked very like John in the early days.

At eleven twenty he looked at his watch. 'Time to go,' he said. 'Just round the corner.'

'Aren't you perhaps a little worried?' she asked. 'Taking a mere female into possible danger?'

'You?' he said. 'Do me a favour.'

Which was flattering in a way, she thought, but only in a way. The danger remained. Nevertheless she had to follow him. He moved swiftly and easily ahead of her. He'd removed his brand-new jacket and was carrying the bag that must have held the camera, easing his way through the crowds. She wore her oldest clothes, but still she knew she must look conspicuous. Tomorrow she must borrow some from Hawkins. Fair's fair, she thought, and then her mind went back to Bob. For him the General Strike was his great opportunity and he was grabbing it with both hands. 'Do me a favour' . . . . Even his speech was changing. . . . The crowd grew thicker and he waited for her, helping her to a street corner where a flight of steps led up to a house.

'This'll do,' he said, and looked at his watch. 11.28. But it was ten minutes later before he heard the sound he had been waiting for, the clattering yet rhythmic beat of a motor engine in bottom gear, doing its best to move in a crowded street.

'What's supposed to happen?' she said.

'You'll see.' Bob had that same absorbed, excited look, as if he were in a cinema and the Apaches were preparing to attack.

A lorry came up to their corner. It was heaped with bags of what looked like vegetables, and as usual had a crew of three: a driver, a map reader and a policeman. The driver was Piers, cautiously edging the lorry forward. Suddenly from the houses round about men appeared, dozens of them, moving with the disciplined speed the army had taught them. One group stood unmoving in front of the lorry, the rest flowed round to the sides and back. Piers braked, and at once the men at the back of the lorry climbed on to it, cut at the ropes that held them and began throwing the bags of vegetables into the crowd. The men at the sides joined in, all except a few who stayed on as guards. One of them, she noticed incredulously, was Pardoe. Well at least he practised what he preached. Suddenly from Brady Street came the sound of police whistles, and the watching crowd began to heave like a sea as the men on the lorry jumped clear, and the men at its sides began to push at it.

'Heave – heave – heave,' cried the crowd, and at last the lorry began to tilt; the men in the cab had no choice but to jump clear. The policeman had already drawn his truncheon, the map reader held a starting handle, but Piers had nothing but his fists. He used them as well as he could, until he found himself matched against Pardoe, who at once began to beat him in a cold and scientific sort of way to which Piers could find no answer. Beside him Bob was frantically taking pictures. She tugged at his sleeve.

'Help him, can't you?' she said, but he looked at her bewildered. 'The driver,' she yelled. 'He's Piers Hilyard. He's a friend of Jay Bower's.'

'Oh my God,' said Bob, and handed her his camera, then leaped into the fight. Pardoe saw him coming and turned to meet him, fists up, right arm protecting his belly and chin, left arm extended, in the scientifically correct boxing stance. Bob, two stones lighter, three inches shorter, stopped just out of the left arm's range and kicked Pardoe in the testicles with his brogue-shod foot. Jane took the picture with Bob's camera and wound on as the crowd beside her split suddenly, like a paper bag, and a squad of police charged in.

Lady Mangan said, 'I don't know how to thank you.'

'It's Bob Patterson you should thank,' said Jane. They were in the drawing room of the Grosvenor Square house.

'I've done that,' said Lady Mangan. 'He's a useful lad, that one.'

'He is an' all,' said Jane, and Lady Mangan grinned.

'Cheeky,' she said. 'But I really am grateful. From what Piers said, the chap that was hitting him was a boxer. Knew what he was doing.' Jane nodded. 'Then how did that lad manage to beat him?'

Jane told her, and the old lady wheezed in delighted laughter.

'The only way he could win,' she said. 'Oh I do like that lad.'

'Where is he?' Jane asked.

'Using the telephone. Who does he work for?'

'Jay Bower.'

'Well of course,' Lady Mangan fidgeted. 'Are you and Mr Bower still friends?'

'Not as close as we were,' said Jane.

'I see. . . . He's been seeing quite a bit of Catherine off and on,' said Lady Mangan. 'Especially since you both came back from America. Is that a good idea, would you say?'

'He wouldn't try to seduce a virgin, if that's what you mean,' said Jane.

'I should hope he'd have more sense. What I do mean is why is he?'

'He wants to marry,' said Jane. 'It's not surprising. He's of an age for it.'

'He's too old for my Catherine,' said Lady Mangan. 'He's rich, of course. I know that. But how rich?'

Jane thought of the house in New England, the platoons and companies of servants, the bank and the studio.

'Enormously,' she said.

'Oh dear,' said Lady Mangan. 'Come and have a word with Piers before you go.'

He was lying on a bed, his face painted with arnica. Already one eye was darkening, and his face was heavily bruised.

'It looks as if I should learn to box,' he said.

'Much better ask Bob to give you kicking lessons.'

'Don't make me laugh,' he said. 'It hurts. . . . How did it end?'

'The lorry went over just before the police arrived,' she said. 'They cleared the crowd rather quickly.'

'With truncheons?' She nodded. 'The text-book way,' he said. 'If you must go in, go in hard. But – '

'But what, my sweet?'

'I've driven down those streets where those people lived,' he said. 'I never had, before. The "great unwashed", we called them at Oxford. How can they wash if there's ten of them to a tap? And horse dung all over the streets where the children play without shoes? They call it the class war, don't they? Well now I've seen the casualties.'

'Do you wish you hadn't driven that lorry?'

'Of course not,' he said. 'There has to be discipline. But when it's over there should be some compassion, too.'

She bent to kiss him, then left. Best not to tell him that the man who beat him was a Cambridge don, she thought. He had enough to think about without that.

Andy was waiting for them in a gloomy cavern of a pub near King's Cross Station. A typical Andy pub, she thought, totally without cheer. In front of him was a half-finished glass of lemonade, and he declined another. Bob went to fetch her a port and lemon, which was the only woman's drink she could think of. This was not the pub for cocktails.

'How's Grandma?' she asked.

'Fine,' he said. 'The eyes is no trouble. Da's fine too. They both send their regards.'

'Please give them mine. How's Bet? Still busy at the clinic?'

'That clinic of yours has never been busier,' said Andy. 'Bet's engaged.'

Bob came back with her port and lemon and a whisky for himself. Another change.

'Taking the plunge, is she?' he said.

'She's already done that,' said Andy.

'Oh aye?' said Bob.

'Aye.'

And that seemed to be it, because all Bob said was, 'What does Da say?'

'Da says once she started walking out with a widower we could expect nowt else. Blest if I know what he meant.'

'Got the habit,' Bob suggested.

'Watch your mouth,' said Andy primly. 'Frank Metcalfe's a decent chap. But he's human.'

'When's the wedding?' Jane asked.

'Soon,' said Andy. 'It has to be.'

'Will they accept a present from me?' Jane asked.

'They will if they've got any sense,' said Bob, and Andy agreed.

'That wouldn't be charity,' he agreed. 'It was her first said you were part of the family. Presents in a family – what could be more natural? But I didn't ask you here for that.'

'What then?'

'Bob said you're doing a lot of writing about the strike. For the *Daily World*.' She nodded. 'I asked to meet you because I wanted to ask you something. A favour you might say.'

'Ask and we'll see.'

'I asked if you'd give our side a fair look-in. No more, no less. . . . Now that wasn't my idea. The way I look at things you've very often been wrong, but you've always been fair. But others – chaps I'm working with – they said I had to ask. So I'm asking.'

'I'll be as fair as I can, Andy.'

'That's good enough for me.' He dashed off his glass of flat lemonade as if it were the wine before a battle, then Jane offered her hand and he took it.

'So that's it then,' he said. 'I'm making a speech next week. Bob'll give you the details when the time comes.' He hesitated. It was as hard as it always had been for Andy to ask a favour. 'I'd like you to come and write it up the way it is,' he said. 'If it isn't too much trouble.'

'It's my job,' she said. 'Of course I will.'

In the drawing room she rang for Hawkins, and asked to borrow some clothes.

'Be a pleasure, miss,' Hawkins said. 'At least it was when I borrowed yours.' She hesitated. 'There's something I have to say, miss.'

'Yes?'

'It's sort of a favour.' She hesitated. 'No, not really. It's hard to say what it is.'

'Take your time,' said Jane.

'I'll be giving notice in September, miss – and I want you to say it's all right. That's why I said it's a favour.'

'But it isn't all right,' said Jane. 'I shall miss you dreadfully. And I must say it's a bit much leaving me for somebody else. I thought we go on well together.'

'So we do, miss,' Hawkins said. 'I didn't think I could be so happy in service. I wouldn't leave you for anybody else, miss.'

'Why then?' said Jane. 'Oh my God! You're not ill, I hope?'

'Course not, miss,' said Hawkins. 'I'm going to London University.'

'What?'

'My gran died couple of years back,' said Hawkins. 'She had a corner shop. My share was five hundred quid. – Pounds, I should say. So I put it in the bank and went to night classes. They have a special exam for what the University call mature students and I took it while you was – were in Hollywood. Today they telephoned and told me I'd passed. They had to do that because there's no postmen working. I hope you don't mind, miss.'

'*Mind?*' Jane took Hawkins in her arms, and hugged her and hugged her. 'Hawkins I'm so proud of you.'

'Thank you, miss.' The two women parted at last. Both of them were crying.

'What will you study?' Jane asked at last.

'We don't specialise till the second year,' said Hawkins, 'but Mr Warley reckons I should have a shot at languages.'

'Oh Hawkins it's all too marvellous,' said Jane, and then: 'Will five hundred be enough?'

'If I'm careful, miss.'

'Don't be too careful,' said Jane. 'It never works. I'll tell you what – I'll pay the tuition fees and books and things, and you keep the five hundred to live on. Although how you can live on five hundred pounds over three years – '

'I'll manage, miss.'

'No you will not. I'd better double it and then we can all relax. I'll tell you what – I'll make it a scholarship. In memory of my father. You'll be the first Sir Guy Whitcomb Memorial Scholar.'

'But I couldn't, miss. It's too much.'

'Please don't say that.' Jane's hand reached out to touch her. 'You kept all my secrets in the dark days. One night when I was drunk – if you didn't save my life you most certainly saved my reputation. Please, Peggy.'

Somehow Hawkins achieved a smile. 'Thank you, miss,' she said, and would have wept again but for the fact that the telephone rang. She picked it up.

'Miss Whitcomb's residence,' she said, then covered the mouthpiece. 'Mr Lovell,' she said.

'Thank you, Hawkins.' Jane went to the telephone. 'I tell you what,' she said. 'Mr Warley's dining with us again tonight. His cook's still out picketing. Why don't you put some champagne in the fridge – something vintage – and we'll drink to our new scholar?'

Hawkins left then, and she picked up the telephone.

'Yes, Charles?'

'I've got a service flat,' said Lovell. 'In Bruton Street. It seems very nice except that I'm not too sure whether the bed's comfortable or not. I wondered if you'd come and advise me.'

'When?'

'I thought now might be a good time.'

'Not now,' she said. 'I mean not precisely now. I have a date to drink champagne with my maid which I'll tell you all about later. Would eight o'clock be too late for bed testing?'

'Eight o'clock would be splendid,' he said. 'And perhaps supper at the Berkeley afterwards for those of us who can stagger that far?'

She broke the news to Lionel before the champagne arrived.

'But I can't possibly,' he said. 'How can I dine here alone?'

'You won't be alone,' said Jane. 'You'll have Hawkins with you. You can mug up a few French irregular verbs together. She'll need all the irregular verbs you can teach her when she starts in October.'

Lionel jumped to his feet. 'You mean she passed?'

'Indeed she did,' said Jane. 'And what's more she's the first Sir Guy Whitcomb Memorial Scholar.'

'Dear Jane,' said Lionel. 'Thank you.'

And that, she thought, is Lionel. Abstractions bored him so much that he fled them, but give him a human being to worry about and he was marvellous.

'What a clever Pygmalion you are,' she said.

'No tutor could wish for a better Galatea. . . . *Why* are you going out?'

'Love,' she said.

'What better reason? You may rely on me to tell any necessary lies. Which reminds me – I took you advice about Fred.'

'Fred?'

'My plumber. I told him how staunch I was in my refusal to strike break or whatever one calls it. He's really quite proud of me.'

Let him stick with his irregular verbs, she thought. That way he'll come to no harm. Then Hawkins came in with the champagne.

The bed had proved adequate for its purpose, and now they rested on it.

'You never came to America,' she said. He grunted. 'You said you would.'

'Only if you stayed there a long time. You didn't. I'm awfully glad you didn't.'

'Me too.' She turned into his arms.

'Are you staying the night?' he asked. She nodded abstractedly: her fingers were busy trying out something that had just occurred to her.

'Bit tricky for you?'

'Not at all,' she said. 'All you do is tell the right lies. *This* is what's tricky.'

Later he said, 'Are we still going to the Berkeley?'

'Certainly,' she said. 'I'm ravenous.' She kissed him. 'Don't worry. If you're too exhausted I'll carry you. . . . Fireman's lift. They taught me in the Girl Guides. And then when you're refreshed and strong, we'll come back here and test the bed again for comfort.'

And that was the way the next week went. Bed testing and the General Strike. She'd told Hawkins she was visiting a sick friend. Hawkins didn't believe a word of it, but at least she'd be convincing if she had to talk to Mummy, thought Jane. But Mummy too was in love, and it was spring. She didn't call for a week, and then caught Jane just before she left to watch with Lambert another football match between strikers and policemen at Tower Hamlets. Poor Dick Lambert was in despair. 'They'll be organising a league table soon,' he said. Jane told her mother what he had said.

'I do not think so,' her mother replied. 'According to that ludicrous sheet of paper that calls itself *The Times* these days, Sir John Simon has declared that in his opinion a General Strike is illegal. He is a Liberal of course, but he is also a most able lawyer, – and the Liberals would err on the side of weakness on this issue, surely? It is their invariable rule.'

'But would the strikers worry about what Sir John Simon thinks?'

'Probably not. They are far too busy rioting and playing football. But their leaders might. I have yet to read of one cast in the heroic mould.'

That is because I haven't yet written about Andy, thought Jane. But it was true.

'But my reason for calling is quite other,' said Lady Whitcomb. 'I should like us to dine en famille.'

'I'd love to Mummy.'

'There are matters to be discussed. Family matters.' Lucy Dawson? Jane wondered. 'Could you bear to receive us at South Terrace? Dear George has never ceased to talk about your cook.'

'Delighted Mummy. I am rather busy at the moment. But if the twelfth isn't too late – '

'The twelfth will do admirably,' said her mother. 'Please do not apologise. I can imagine nothing more time-consuming than observing a General Strike.'

As so often after a telephone call from her mother, Jane had to resist the impulse to mop her brow.

On the 11th May Bob called her. Andy was due to make his speech that evening. It was time to borrow Hawkins's clothes. They were going back to the Elephant and Castle, it seemed, and the same makeshift rostrum next to the pub. On the way there what Bob told her made her sure that her mother was right.

'There's a lot of talk among the leaders about giving in,' said Bob. 'Respect for law and order! All that. Our Andy doesn't give a damn for law and order. Bloody revolution, that's what Andy wants. That's why they're putting him up there. Very Red around the Elephant and Castle. If you ask me, it's the last chance they've got.'

They left the car in a side street, then found a doorstep, as they had in Bethnal Green. The crowd moved in, tighter and tighter, so that Jane and Bob were imprisoned on their doorstep.

Exactly at four, two figures climbed the rostrum, Andy and his chairman, a small and earnest man whose voice was no match for the murmurs of the crowd. 'Fraternal delegate,' Jane heard. 'Down from the North East. . . . Workers' Rights. . . . Staunch Fighter.' Then he stepped back and Andy moved at once into the attack in a voice of effortless power, the voice that she had last heard in Felston market place.

'Comrades,' he roared, 'I come here to tell you that the miners and shipyard workers and steelmen of Tyneside send you their greetings. The miners especially say thank you for this display of solidarity, for no men have suffered more than the miners, comrades. And no women more than their wives. And yet they fight on. As you fight on. And for why?

'Because we see a vision. We see this country transformed into a fair and shining land where there is justice for all and fair shares for all, and an end to poverty and wage cuts and lock-outs, a country where a man can stand up and be free.'

He paused, and the crowd stirred and seethed like a giant flexing its muscles – 'No means tests,' Andy roared. 'No Guardians. No Charity. Never again. No yes sir no sir let me lie down in the mud so you won't have to reach too far when you kick me sir. That – is – over.'

The murmur grew louder.

'Take a look around you,' said Andy. 'Go on. . . . Take a look.' Half embarrassed, they did so. 'What do you see? The great army of workers, that's what you see. But not the whole army. Not a division. Not even a brigade. Just one regiment – but look at the numbers of it. The might of it. . . . The unions will tell you that unity is strength – and so it is – but numbers is strength too. Numbers is power. And it's high time we used that power!'

This time the giant lifted his fists above his head and roared, and then Andy raised his hands. The giant grew still.

'But not here,' he said. 'Power's not needed here. Here among the dirt and the poverty and the stink – that's where *we* are. Where our friends, our comrades are. And that's where the bosses want to keep us. Are we going to let them?'

'No!' the giant bellowed.

'Or are we going to go out there – ' and suddenly Andy's arm stabbed out, pointing to the west – ' to demand what should be ours by rights, and to take it if we have to?'

'Yes,' the giant bellowed.

'Now is the time for the haves to yield to the have-nots,' Andy thundered. 'Time and more than time, for I tell you this, comrades, if we don't show the bosses our strength and show it now, our leaders will betray us. We'll have suffered in vain.'

A man on the edge of the crowd, a big, red-shirted man, called out in a voice that rivalled Andy's. 'He's right, comrades. Let's go and get what's ours before somebody with more guts does it first.'

A plant of course, thought Jane, but none the less effective for that. The big man strode off down the London Road, and the crowd surged after him. Andy swarmed down from the rostrum to be with them.

'Well I'll say this for our Andy,' said Bob, and his voice was admiring, 'there's never any doubt whose side *he's* on.'

And still the crowd surged past, then suddenly it stuck, jammed fast like a cork in a bottle. From ahead there came the sound of screaming, then suddenly the crowd split, funnelling into side streets or racing back the way they'd come.

'Police,' said Bob. 'It must be.'

The crowd was running hard, breaking up. Now the roadway and the tramlines were visible once more. Andy stood in front of one group, roaring at them to stand firm, be brave, but they swept him aside, not even hearing, and the next wave knocked him off his feet.

'I'd better get him,' said Bob, but she had been listening hard, and now grabbed his arm.

'Leave him,' she said. 'He's safer where he is.'

The sound she had heard was like no other sound in the world: the sound of horses at a full gallop.

They came down the road like a cavalry charge, the heavy horses held well in, but moving strongly; their riders helmeted, silver buttons glittering against dark-blue tunics, and swinging in their hands the long baton of the mounted policeman. And suddenly Jane realised what it was that they looked like. She was back in India, watching Papa and his friends play polo, but this time with a human head for a ball.

One by one they galloped past where Andy lay, but the last horse reared and its rider paused to regain control, and as he did so Andy, dazed, bewildered, staggered to his feet. The policeman turned his horse to follow the others, kicked it into a gallop, then casually, almost lazily, struck Andy with his baton as he galloped by.

'Oh God!' said Bob, and ran to his brother, and Jane ran off to fetch the car. The police would be back soon enough searching for enemy wounded.

Between them they got Andy into the back seat of the car. His face was a mash of blood, more blood poured from a gash in his scalp, and he made the snoring noise that Jane knew meant concussion.

'What are we going to do?' said Andy. 'What the hell are we going to do?'

'Take him home,' said Jane.

'Home?'

In the state he was in, the only home Bob could think of was Felston.

'*South Terrace*,' said Jane.

'But he needs a doctor.'

'Of course he does,' said Jane. 'We'll get him one from there. Now hold on to him, Bob. I'll have to drive fast.'

She drove very fast indeed, on to the Embankment and heading west. Only once did a policeman stop her, and that was a special who turned out to be Mr Pinner, immaculate as always in bowler hat, dark suit and arm band. He took one look at her face and waved her through, holding up everyone else in sight. Somehow she and Bob and Andy between them got Andy upstairs and on to a bed and Hawkins found a towel to replace Bob's blood-sodden handkerchief as Jane telephoned Harriet Watson.

'She'll come at once,' she told Bob, and then, before he could speak: 'Don't worry. She's a friend of mine. She won't betray him.'

He was ill, of course, Harriet told them, but not nearly as ill as she had expected, and looked at Bob. 'Heads like mahogany where you come from,' she said. 'Or is it just in the family?'

'He'll be all right then?' Bob asked.

'Of course,' said Harriet. 'He'll need rest and nursing for a couple of days at least – '

'I'll do that,' said Bob.

'Nothing else?' asked Jane.

'Aspirin,' said Harriet. 'He'll ask for rather a lot of that. . . . I'll look in tomorrow.'

Jane took her downstairs.

'Is there a warrant out for him?' Harriet asked.

'I've no intention of asking,' said Jane.

'Very wise.' Harriet kissed her on the cheek. 'No rest for the wicked, is there?'

As Jane came in, the telephone was ringing. It was Bower.

'I'm told you were in the thick of it again,' he said. 'You and young Patterson.'

'I'm writing it up now,' she said.

'Good,' said Bower. 'I could use some copy.'

'In the middle of a strike?'

'We'll be printing next week – but that's only for your information. . . . How did Patterson find out about this one?'

'His brother told him.'

'The Red? Did you know he'd disappeared?'

'No,' said Jane. Nor did she.

'Keep away from him,' said Bower. 'Don't go looking. You've watched one victory and one defeat – fine. But we don't need any more. Not from you. It would look too much like inside information. No more serendipity. I've told Patterson the same. Still I'm grateful for what you've got.'

'There's masses more,' she said. 'Enough for a book.'

'Then write it,' said Bower. 'And if it's any good I'll serialise it. When am I going to see you?'

'When I bring my copy in.' He hung up.

Next day the strike was over, but Bower had been right, as usual. The dockers, transport workers and printers stayed out for another five days. (The miners stayed out for another six months and gained not a thing. But then a pitman only has three hobbies, Bob said. Whippets, leek shows and strikes.) He proved a remarkably good nurse for Andy, and Mrs Barrow found time to make him broth, despite her preparations for that night's dinner party. When Jane visited the brothers, Andy was already sitting up in bed. He demanded his clothes at once. He couldn't inflict himself on her, and in any case he had work to do.

Gently she said, 'I'm afraid you don't, Andy. . . . The strike's over.'

'I know that.' She looked at Bob.

'Not me,' he said. 'Well not really. We borrowed your wireless.'

'That doesn't mean there isn't work to do,' Andy said.

'Not by you,' said Jane. 'I don't think there's a warrant out for you yet, but there could be. You're said to have disappeared. Why not leave it at that?'

'But if they find me here – you'll be in trouble, too.'

'They won't find you here.' Andy looked at his brother.

'You bide where you are till you're better, kidda,' said Bob. 'We'll get you back to Felston then.'

And so she left them.

She and her mother and the major were drinking sherry when Harriet arrived, briskly apologetic for her lateness: a crossbirth, a broken leg and an outbreak of measles all in the same street. She had no time for sherry, but went at once to her patient, and scrawled a prescription for something she thought would be more effective than aspirin. She became even more brisk when Andy asked to get up, then hurried away. Jane went back to her guests.

'One of the servants is ill?' Lady Whitcomb asked.

'No, Mummy.' She told them what had happened. The major was appalled.

'But he's a Red,' he said. 'You can't harbour him.'

'I can't turn him out,' said Jane. 'He's ill. Anyone would be who was clubbed down like that.'

'He should have thought of that before he started inciting people to riot. Your good name's at stake here. And your mother's. You must – '

'George,' Lady Whitcomb said. Her voice was gentle, almost

caressing, and yet the major was silent at once. Like switching off a wireless, thought Jane.

'George dear,' Lady Whitcomb said again. 'This man is from Felston.'

'I don't see that –'

'*Felston*, George. . . . Because of my daughter's literary efforts, the *Daily World* takes a particular interest in Felston. Mr Bower takes a particular interest in Felston. Mr Bower is our employer, George. Why don't we simply accept the fact that this man's presence here is no business of ours, and leave it at that?'

Hawkins came in then to announce a dinner that did much to calm the major, and the port that Jane produced afterwards would intensify the treatment she was sure. None of it would be wasted. Harriet had suggested port, and Jane was determined that Andy should drink it, even if she had to use a funnel. . . . She and her mother left the major with his decanter.

'You will have observed that George's intellect is limited,' said her mother, 'and that it is tenacious besides, which is unfortunate.'

Here was frankness indeed. 'Yes, Mummy,' said Jane.

'However he is also morally admirable – far better than I am I fear – and affectionate, which is more than adequate compensation. It is also why his conscience has been troubling him, poor lamb.' Then she told Jane about Lucy Dawson.

'What will you do, Mummy?' Jane asked.

'Take her racing of course,' said her mother. 'What else can one do? Oh – you are referring to the moral aspect of the problem. I have decided that it does not exist. As I told George at the time, if there is one lesson that my daughter has taught me it is how to be broadminded.'

And make of that what you will, thought Jane.

'Which reminds me,' her mother continued, 'that we have decided to ignore Dr Dodd's advice. We intend to announce our engagement next week and marry as soon as possible after the Derby.'

'Congratulations, Mummy.' Jane rose and kissed Lady Whitcomb.

'I am tired of living alone,' said her mother, and then: 'You do not have that problem?'

Ambiguous to the last, thought Jane, who had no doubt what her mother was asking.

'No, Mummy.'

'I'm glad,' Lady Whitcomb said, and changed the subject at once. 'You have seen a great deal of this disturbance?'

'I have indeed.'

'And now you harbour one of its instigators, even though he is from Felston?'

'I saw what was done to him,' said Jane.

'And yet he is from Felston and, from things you have told me in the recent past, I rather gathered that you had washed your hands of Felston.'

'I thought that too,' said Jane. 'I was wrong.'

'You intend further involvement?' Jane nodded. 'You're very like me, you know. You cannot tolerate being directed. For us the need is always to direct. Consider dear George.' Lady Whitcomb put down her coffee cup. 'Perhaps the saddhu was right.'

'Saddhu, Mummy?'

'The one your ayah consulted all those years ago. Perhaps you will achieve greatness, as Shakespeare says. Or perhaps it will be thrust upon you.'

'Nonsense, Mummy,' said Jane.

'Not at all,' said Lady Whitcomb serenely. 'It would take a strength of purpose far beyond my capacity to put a town like Felston to rights.'

Nonsense yourself, thought Jane. Between the three of you, Lady Mangan, Grandma Patterson and you, you could square the circle. But she didn't say so aloud.

When her mother and the major had gone, Jane drove to the all-night chemist in the King's Road to have Andy's prescription made up, then went back into the car and sat. She was tired: far too tired for bed testing, but that was all right. She would see Charles next afternoon. Dear Charles who had been so conventional in his love-making, until they had started sleeping together, and now unhesitatingly followed wherever she led. . . . Oh my God, Mummy's right, she thought, and yawned.

She had a right to be tired. Football matches and victories and defeats, an aristocratic blackleg rescued, a wounded warrior in her house. Andy would fight on, of course. Andy would fight on till he died. He would fight and he would lose, she thought, because he wants everything now, this minute, and the only sure way is one piece at a time.

The pubs had emptied. Across the street a man was walking, not quite steady on his feet. Suddenly he began to sing in a true, pure tenor, and the war came back at once; almost she could feel John's hand touch hers.

> When this lousy war is over
> No more soldiering for me.
> When I get my civvy clothes on
> Oh how happy I will be. . . .

The drunken man turned the corner, and his voice faded. . . . The war I'm in now isn't over, she thought, whatever the wireless says. It's hardly begun. And no more have I. She started the car. It was time to go home.